PHARAOH

PHARAOH

Bolesław Prus

✝

Translated by
Christopher Kasparek

Hippocrene Books, Inc.
New York

For information, address:
HIPPOCRENE BOOKS, INC.
171 Madison Avenue
New York, NY 10016
www.hippocrenebooks.com

ISBN 13: 978-0-7818-1450-8

TRANSLATOR'S FOREWORD

Bolesław Prus was the favorite Polish novelist of the ten years younger Polish-English novelist Joseph Conrad. Conrad published his first novel, *Almayer's Folly*, the same year 1895 that Prus published his last major novel, *Pharaoh*. The two early-orphaned novelists shared a profound nexus: both had been traumatized by events associated with the Polish 1863 Uprising against the Russian Empire. In subsequent decades, further nexus would link their biographies.

Bolesław Prus ("Boh-*less*-wahf Prooss"; 20 August 1847 – 19 May 1912) was born Aleksander Głowacki ("Gwoh-*vaht*-ski") at Hrubieszów in the Russian partition of Poland. The town now lies next to Poland's southeastern border with Ukraine.

Alexander was the second son of Antoni Głowacki, an estate manager in the village of Żabcze, in Lublin Province; and Apolonia Głowacka, *née* Trembińska. Alexander would later adopt, as his pen surname, the appellation of his paternal coat-of-arms, *Prus*.

Alexander lost his mother in 1850, at age three, and was reared for four years in the historic town of Puławy by his maternal grandmother, Marcjanna Trembińska; then, following her death, in the nearby city of Lublin by his aunt Domicela Olszewska.

In 1856 Alexander was orphaned by the death of his father and, aged nine, began attending a Lublin primary school. Its principal, Józef Skłodowski—grandfather of the Polish future double Nobel laureate Maria Skłodowska Curie (Marie Curie)—administered canings, a common mode of disciplining, to wayward pupils, possibly including the spirited Alexander. The Skłodowski family will reappear in Alexander's life and will appear as well in Joseph Conrad's. Canings, too, will appear in *Pharaoh*.

In 1862 Alexander was taken by his schoolteacher brother, Leon Głowacki, to Siedlce, and later to Kielce.

Alexander's brother and Joseph Conrad's father, writer Apollo Korzeniowski, took part in clandestine political activities that eventuated in the 1863 Uprising. (About a year before its outbreak, in late 1861, Conrad's father was imprisoned by the Russian authorities, and in 1862 was exiled with his wife and four-year-old son Konrad to an insalubrious area of northwest Russia.) Politics will loom large in the writings of both Prus and Conrad: for example, respectively, in *Pharaoh* and *Nostromo*.

Soon after the outbreak of the Uprising, Alexander joined the insurgents. On 1 September 1863, twelve days after his sixteenth birthday, his unit fought Russian forces at the village of Białka, near Siedlce in Mazowsze Province. Alexander was knocked unconscious, taken prisoner, hospitalized at Siedlce, and kept in custody for a month. Four months later, in early February 1864, he was imprisoned for three months in Lublin Castle and was tried and sentenced to deportation; but on 7 May 1864 he was mercifully released by the Russian chief of the Lublin military district.

Alexander's experiences in the 1863 Uprising turned him against seeking Poland's independence through militant means, until his mind was changed by the Russian Revolution of 1905. Prus' Uprising experiences may also have predisposed him to his later agoraphobia.

Meanwhile his brother Leon, during a June 1863 mission to Wilno (now Vilnius) in Lithuania on behalf of the Polish insurgent government, had succumbed to a severe mental illness that would end only with his death in 1907. Themes of mental illness will feature in *Pharaoh.*

Alexander, released by the Russian authorities into the custody of relatives, resumed in Lublin his interrupted secondary education. He expressed a special affinity for mathematics and acquired a reputation among schoolmates as a "philosopher," in the original Greek sense of a "lover of learning"; as an adult, he would contribute to all three traditional branches of western philosophy—epistemology, ethics, and aesthetics.

In June 1866 Alexander graduated from secondary school and in October, aged 19, matriculated in the Warsaw University department of mathematics and physics. In 1868, however, poverty forced him to drop out of Warsaw University.

In 1869 he enrolled in the forestry department of the Agriculture and Forestry Institute in the town of Puławy, where he had spent part of his childhood. At Puławy, in 1801, Princess Izabela Czartoryska had erected a classicist Temple of the Sibyl—a museum (whose surviving collections are now in Kraków's Czartoryski Museum) commemorating the late, partitioned Polish-Lithuanian Commonwealth. Fifteen years after Alexander's enrollment at the Institute, the Temple grounds would become the setting for his brilliant 1884 microstory "Mold of the Earth," comparing human history with the mutual aggressions of molds which occupy a boulder representing planet Earth.

In January 1870, after just three months at the Institute, Alexander was expelled for insufficient deference to a martinet instructor of the Russian language. He now pursued a course of self-education, while supporting himself as a tutor and industrial worker. For his own edification, he drew up a condensed Polish translation of John Stuart Mill's *A System of Logic.*

In 1872 twenty-five-year-old *Bolesław Prus*—Alexander's new pen name, for his "less scholarly" writings—embarked on a forty-year career as a Warsaw newspaper columnist. His *Kroniki tygodniowe* (Weekly Chronicles) columns addressed developments in science, technology, education, economics, history, societal trends, and culture.

In 1873, a year after his journalistic debut, he delivered, under his birth name, two public lectures that illustrate the breadth of his scientific interests: "On the Structure of the Universe," and "On Discoveries and Inventions." The latter lecture (which this translator has rendered into English) brilliantly anticipated what half a century later, in 1923, would be proposed by Polish sociologist Florian Znaniecki as a new "science of knowledge," now known in Polish as *naukoznawstwo* ("the science of science," or logology)—the study of the scientific enterprise and its practitioners.

By 1875 Prus felt financially secure enough to marry a distant cousin, Oktawia

Trembińska, whom he had known since his early childhood in Puławy. In 1888 the child-less couple adopted Emil Trembiński, the two-year-old orphaned youngest son of Prus' brother-in-law. Six years later, Emil would serve as the model for six-year-old Rascal (*Psujak*) in Chapter 48 of *Pharaoh*. A decade after that, in 1904, then 17-year-old Emil fatally shot himself in the chest on the doorstep of a girlfriend who had resented his emotional possessiveness.

In an earlier traumatic incident, in 1878, Prus was confronted outside his home by several Warsaw University students who had demanded an apology for his newspaper-column criticism of their rowdiness at a public lecture; he had refused to apologize, and now one of them slapped him in the face. Another student in the group, Kazimierz Dłuski, would later marry Maria Skłodowska Curie's (Marie Curie's) physician sister Bronisława. Prus declined to press charges against the students; but in 1895, when he visited western Europe (his only travels outside Poland, soon after completing *Pharaoh*), memory of the assault still so rankled him that he may—accounts vary— have refused to meet with the Dłuskis, then living in Paris. (In Paris, too, his agoraphobia prevented his crossing a Seine River bridge to Paris' Left Bank.)

In a curiously linked incident, when Joseph Conrad in 1914, only days after the out-break of World War I, took refuge with his family in southern Poland's famous mountain resort of Zakopane, the same Bronisława Dłuska—she and her husband were now practic-ing medicine there—chided Conrad for writing novels in English, rather than in Polish for the glory of Polish letters. It was also in Zakopane that Conrad's niece and future Polish translator Aniela Zagórska introduced Conrad to the writings of Bolesław Prus, deceased two years earlier, who quickly became Conrad's favorite Polish author. (Prus, also, had visited Zakopane.)

The incidents involving the Dłuskis and the two novelists, Prus and Conrad, highlight some common Polish sensitivities and misunderstandings during Poland's 123 years of complete partition.[1] Such attitudes could lead to tragic mistakes, as illustrated in Prus' 1884 novella *Omyłka* (A Mistake), which ends in the execution, during the 1863 Uprising, of a civic-minded man mistakenly thought to have been a traitor to the Polish cause.

Prus' surviving private correspondence shows a circumspection that was doubtless motivated by awareness of mail censorship.

In 1882 Prus accepted the editorship of a Warsaw daily, *Nowiny* (The News), vowing, in the best Polish Positivist fashion, to turn it into "an observatory of societal facts." After less than a year, in 1883, *Nowiny* (financially shaky before Prus took it over) folded. He resumed writing columns and continued doing so to the end of his life, even after achiev-ing success with short stories and novels. *Nowiny*'s failure inspired Prus' evocative 1885 microstory *"Cienie"* ("Shades"), whose anonymous protagonist lamplighter "kindles light along his path, lives unknown ... then [dying] vanishes like a shade."

In 1909, three years before his own death, Prus published a review of H.G. Wells' 1901 book *Anticipations*, which predicted the world of the dawning 20th century. The English author's anticipations of technology, including flight, were very conservative; but he was prescient in writing that, by the year 2000, German imperialism "[would]

---

[1] A related patriotic sentiment prompted Maria Skłodowska Curie (Marie Curie) to name the first of the two chemical elements that she discovered, *polonium*, after her partitioned homeland.

be either shattered or weakened ... by a series of wars by land and sea" and that there would then come into being a European union, which would reach eastward to include the Poles and other western Slavs: in 2004 the western Slavic, and several other Central European, countries joined the European Union.

Prus died on 19 May 1912, aged 64, in his apartment at 12 *ulica Wilcza* (Wolf Street) near Warsaw's *Plac Trzech Krzyży* (Triple Cross Square). The epitaph on his monument in Warsaw's Powązki Cemetery, *"Serce Serc"* ("Heart of Hearts"), was borrowed from the Latin *"Cor Cordium"* on the Rome grave of the English Romantic poet Percy Bysshe Shelley.

Ten years earlier, the editor of the Warsaw *Kurier Codzienny* (Daily Courier) had opined that, if Prus' writings had been well known outside Poland, he ought to have received one of the recently created Nobel Prizes.

Prus' widow Oktawia, to whom he had dedicated *Pharaoh*, survived him by 24 years, dying on 25 October 1936.

A tablet in Warsaw's Holy Cross Church, adjacent to the column containing Frédéric Chopin's heart, memorializes Prus, "great writer and teacher of the [Polish] nation." Among his readers he has attained what was described, in an ancient Egyptian text from the transitional period between the 19th and 20th Dynasties, as "The Immortality of Writers."

‡

Prus' worldview was influenced by European and American thinkers including John Stuart Mill, John William Draper, Henry Thomas Buckle, Hippolyte Taine, and especially Herbert Spencer, whom Prus hailed as "the Aristotle of the 19th century." Prus featured Spencer's metaphor of society-as-organism ("the social organism") in his microstory "Mold of the Earth" and in his introduction to *Pharaoh*.

Spencer's metaphor had actually been coined in antiquity by Aristotle and had been elaborated in the 19th century by Auguste Comte, Herbert Spencer, and Émile Durkheim. Along with British Utilitarian philosophy, it influenced Prus' ethical and sociopolitical views. In 1897-99 he serialized, in a newspaper, his book *The Most General Life Ideals*, describing what he termed the "ideals" of *perfection, utility,* and *happiness*. As epitome to the book, he wrote: "*Perfect* the will, the mind, feeling, their bodily organs, and their material tools; be *useful* to yourselves, to your own ones, and to others; and *happiness*, insofar as it exists on this earth, will come of itself."

Early on, Prus deprecated fiction, particularly historical fiction, which he held must distort history. Eventually, however, he came to adopt the French Positivist critic Taine's concept of literature and the arts as additional means, alongside the sciences, for studying humankind.

Prus hoped to elaborate a theory of literary composition. His notes on the subject, set down beginning in 1886, were never turned into the planned book. They included the precept, "nouns, nouns, and more nouns"; and calculations of possible personality combinations, given a set number of potential traits. These ideas inform his novels, including *Pharaoh*.

One of his most evocative short stories is his first historically-themed story, "A Legend of Old Egypt" (1888). It was inspired by the fatal illnesses of Germany's warlike first emperor, Wilhelm I, and of his progressive son, Friedrich III, who inherited the German throne for only 99 days before himself dying. Six years later, "A Legend of Old Egypt" would serve as a preliminary sketch for Prus' only historical novel, *Pharaoh*, written in 1894-95.

"A Legend of Old Egypt" and *Pharaoh* show kinships in setting, theme, and denouement. Both play out in ancient Egypt: the "Legend," presumably during the 19th or 20th Dynasty; *Pharaoh*, at the fall of the 20th Dynasty, which marked as well the fall of the New Kingdom, dated to the early 11th century (variously in 1085, 1077, or 1069) BCE. In both the story and the novel, the protagonist plans societal reforms but perishes before he can implement them.

Prus the novelist was influenced by the prolific Polish novelist Józef Ignacy Kraszewski (author of over 200 novels) and by European and American novelists including Victor Hugo, Charles Dickens, Gustave Flaubert, Mark Twain, Émile Zola, and Alphonse Daudet.

‡

Prus' literary career strikingly paralleled that of his American contemporary, Ambrose Bierce (1842–1914). Each was born and reared in the countryside and had a "Polish" connection: Bierce grew up in Kosciusko County, Indiana, and attended secondary school at its county seat, Warsaw. Each sustained head trauma in combat: Prus in the Polish 1863 Uprising, Bierce (a bullet wound) in 1864 in the American Civil War. Each experienced false starts in other occupations before, at twenty-five, entering on a 40-year journalism career; failed as newspaper editor-in-chief (Prus, 1882-83; Bierce, 1881-85); won celebrity with his short stories; lost a son who had been disappointed in love (Prus, an adopted son; Bierce, as well his second son, to alcoholism-related pneumonia); mentored younger writers; attained humorous effects, portraying human egoism (Prus in *Pharaoh*, Bierce in *The Devil's Dictionary*); was dogged from early adulthood by illness (Prus, agoraphobia; Bierce, asthma); and died within two years of the other (Prus, in 1912; Bierce, probably in 1914).

Prus, however, unlike Bierce, went on to write novels. Over a decade's time, he completed three major novels on "great questions of the age"—*The Outpost* (1885-86), *The Doll* (1887-89), and *The New Woman* (1890-93)—and his only historical novel, *Pharaoh* (1894-95).

The three contemporary novels describe, respectively, Polish peasants' resistance to German *Drang nach Osten* efforts to replace them with German colonists; Polish societal weaknesses, observed by a self-made man who is smitten with a fatuous aristocratic woman (Czesław Miłosz regarded *The Doll* as the Great Polish Novel); and challenges faced by Polish feminists.

Prus' sole historical novel, *Pharaoh* (this translator's own choice for Great Polish Novel), presents a primer on power, while exploring the human condition and painting a compelling, painstakingly researched picture of life in ancient Egypt.

Prus' novels, in the manner of the time, were serialized in periodicals prior to issue in book form. *Pharaoh*, exceptionally, was written complete rather than in individual chapters just before the chapters' serial publication. Hence, of Prus' novels, *Pharaoh* shows the greatest unity of composition.

Even so, *Pharaoh* contains some incongruities. In Chapter 1, Herhor is introduced as "high priest of the greatest temple, that of Amon in Thebes"; while in Chapter 7 Queen Nikotris tells her son Prince Ramses that "Herhor will soon be high priest in Thebes ..."

Chapter 1 speaks of "a transport canal from Memphis to Lake Timsah"—in effect, an *east-west* "Suez Canal" linking the Mediterranean and Red Seas via the Nile River—that had in fact existed as early as Egypt's Middle Kingdom; while in Chapter 55 Prince Hiram *proposes building* "a canal that will connect the Mediterranean and Red Seas."

In Chapter 1 we are told that, when setting out for the Pi-Bailos maneuvers, Prince Ramses left his litters in Memphis; but later in the same chapter he calls for his litter to be brought to him!

When in Chapter 13 we first meet Kama (who gives her name as "Cuddles"), she is "a beautiful sixteen-year-old Phoenician dancing girl"—a very different figure from the worldly-wise priestess Kama who appears in Chapter 31.

The high priest of the Temple of Set appears under very different personas in Chapter 48—consulted about the illness of Ramses XII—and elsewhere, including Chapter 55, consulted by Ramses XIII about Hiram's canal proposal, and Chapter 62, in connection with the high priest's plan to seize control of the Labyrinth.

Finally, a vignette of a clown posing as a hero is associated first with Ramses XIII (Chapter 55), then with the priest Pentuer (in the Epilog).

Prus seems to have been inspired to write *Pharaoh* by public lectures on ancient Egypt delivered in 1893 by his Lublin secondary-school and Warsaw University schoolmate, the psychologist, inventor, and Spiritualism investigator Julian Ochorowicz ("Oh-hor-*oh*-veech").

Ochorowicz and Prus were both leading lights of the Polish Positivism movement. This version of Auguste Comte's philosophical system, Positivism, combined the pursuit of scientifically verifiable knowledge with advocacy of "organic work," which was intended to enable Poles to make progress despite their partition by three foreign empires (Russia, Prussia—later, Germany—and Austria). The Polish Positivist movement contributed to a remarkable efflorescence of Polish art and learning, including world-class mathematics following World War I (which enabled the Polish General Staff's Cipher Bureau to break German Enigma ciphers, beginning in late 1932, which subsequently in July 1939 kick-started the western Allies' World War II Ultra operation).

Julian Ochorowicz had earlier served as the model for a principal character, "Julian Ochocki" ("Oh-*hot*-ski"), in Prus' *The Doll*. During years spent in France, Ochorowicz had developed an interest in Egyptology; and on returning to Poland he had shared books on the subject with Prus.

Also in 1893, Ochorowicz introduced Prus to the Italian Spiritualist medium Eusapia Palladino, whom Ochorowicz had invited to Warsaw. (A dozen years later, Palladino's Paris séances would be attended by an intrigued Pierre Curie and a very dubious Maria Skłodowska Curie.) Palladino's 1893 Warsaw séances, attended by a skeptical Prus, inspired several striking scenes in *Pharaoh* (Chapters 20, 26, 31, 47).

Pharaoh imagines the final two years of Egypt's 20th Dynasty, as that country experiences economic decline, environmental degradation, external threats, and internal strife, culminating in the fall of its New Kingdom. The novel's depiction of Egypt's fall reflects the demise three millenia later, in 1795, of the Polish-Lithuanian Commonwealth, by then completely partitioned among the Russian, Prussian, and Austrian empires.

The book has been described by Czesław Miłosz as a "novel on ... mechanism[s] of state power and as such ... probably unique in world literature of the nineteenth century .... Prus, [in] selecting the reign of 'Pharaoh Ramses XIII' [the last Ramesside was actually Ramses XI] in the eleventh century [BCE], sought a perspective that was detached from ... pressures of [topicality] and censorship. Through his analysis of the dynamics of an ancient Egyptian society, he ... suggest[s] an archetype of the struggle for power that goes on within any state."

As Prus' primer on power unfolds, young Ramses learns that he who would challenge the powers that be, is vulnerable to their tactics of cooption, seduction, intimidation, deception, defamation, infiltration, subversion, and assassination. Following adumbrations—in chapters 14, 58, 60, 64—of the novel's denouement, the final lesson absorbed by Ramses concerns the power of science.

‡

Pharaoh's lessons were not lost on the Soviet Union's Joseph Stalin, who in late 1941 told Stanisław Kot, ambassador of the London-based Polish Government-in-Exile, that *Pharaoh* was his favorite novel. Prince Ramses' "[realization] that he must be cautious [and] not trust anyone excessively" (Chapter 37) must have resonated with Stalin's paranoid style of thinking. Sergei Eisenstein's film *Ivan the Terrible* (2 parts, 1944-45), produced under Stalin's ubiquitous artistic tutelage, plausibly shows influences of *Pharaoh*.

The Molotov-Ribbentrop Pact of 23 August 1939, paving the way for the September 1939 partition of Poland between the Soviet Union and Nazi Germany, could have been inspired by the Assyrian-Egyptian treaty, discussed in *Pharaoh*'s Chapters 20 and 51, to partition western Asia between the two ancient empires.

Stalin's murder of thousands of Polish military personnel and prominent civilians in the "Katyn Forest massacre" (which was actually part of a series of massacres which included several other murder sites) could have been inspired by the priest Mentesuphis' execution of Libyan prisoners of war in *Pharaoh*'s Chapter 45.

In a matter of strategic import, any doubts that Stalin might have had about a successful U.S. atomic-bomb project, and about the advisability of starting a similar Soviet project, may have been tempered by *Pharaoh*, Prus' cautionary tale about the power of science and technology.

A parallel American story involving the influence of a cultural reference upon the origins of the atomic bomb, is told in Robert Jungk's 1956 book, *Brighter than a Thousand Suns*. The 1939 letter by Leo Szilard and Albert Einstein, advising U.S. President Franklin Roosevelt of the possibility of an atomic bomb, was delivered by financier Alexander Sachs, who captured Roosevelt's attention by telling him of Napoleon's error in not adopting Robert Fulton's steamship for his planned invasion of Britain.

Two decades later, in 1961, *Pharaoh*'s denouement prompted the present translator to presciently wonder whether President John F. Kennedy—who, like Ramses, aspired to societal reforms while facing possible war with his country's arch-enemy—might not meet with a fate like Ramses'.

‡

Prus began writing *Pharaoh* around late May 1894 and completed it, as he noted, on "2 May 1895, at 3 p.m." Before composing it, for six months he immersed himself in Egyptology, including writings by Herodotus, Ignacy Żagiell, and Gaston Maspero and the Egyptological novels of Georg Ebers. He steeped himself in Egypt's geography, climate, history, architecture, husbandry, crafts, science, technology, customs, religion, art, and literature.

Prus incorporates into *Pharaoh*, like tesserae into a mosaic, historic Egyptian events and texts. Drawn from one Egyptian text (conventionally called "Do Not Be a Soldier"), and named for its ancient schoolboy copyist, is the character Ennana, who first appears in Chapter 1. Prus calls him *Eunana*, but Adolf Erman's *The Ancient Egyptians: A Sourcebook of Their Writings* more plausibly calls him *Ennana*. A scribe of the same name, Ennana, has been credited with having written another text, the "Tale of Two Brothers" (the D'Orbiney papyrus, which was acquired in 1857 by the British Museum), toward the end of the 19th Dynasty.

Pharaoh alludes to biblical Old Testament episodes involving Judith and Holofernes (Chapter 7), Moses (Chapters 7 and 10), and the plagues of Egypt (Chapters 10 and 64). Prus names several characters after Old Testament figures, including Sara, Gideon, Tamar, Taphath, Phut, Cush, and Isaac.

Pharaoh's Chapters 7, 10, and 16 anticipate by 42 years Sigmund Freud's thesis, in *Moses and Monotheism* (1937), that Moses and the Old Testament Jews adopted monotheism from ancient Egyptian prototypes. (Similarly, Prus' exact descriptions of Warsaw and Paris landmarks in *The Doll* anticipate, by 33 years, James Joyce's famously exact descriptions of Dublin landmarks in *Ulysses*, published in 1922.)

Pharaoh alludes to Homer's *Iliad* and to the wars at Troy, which had recently been excavated by Heinrich Schliemann; and Prus names two principal characters after the *Iliad*'s Patroklos (first seen in *Pharaoh*'s Chapter 1) and Lykon (introduced by name in Chapter 34).

Authenticity of characters' names is, however, not a *sine qua non* to Prus. He names an Egyptian female character (Chapter 61 ff.) after the extant Palestinian city of Hebron. Another name does triple service: Prus lends the name of Egypt's first pharaoh, Menes (Chapter 2), to both Sara's physician (Chapter 32) and the priest whose scientific discovery seals the outcome of the novel (Chapter 60 ff.).

Prus the journalist seems to observe, in *Pharaoh*, the journalistic practice of seeking at least two independent sources for a given fact. Thus his conception of Egyptian beliefs about the afterlife is confirmed by aspects of 19th-century Spiritualism, experienced at Eusapia Palladino's 1893 Warsaw séances featuring alleged communication with spirits of the dead.

Prince Hiram's proposal to dig a canal connecting the Mediterranean and Red Seas had a modern precedent in Ferdinand de Lesseps' Suez Canal, completed in 1869, a quarter century before Prus began *Pharaoh*; and an ancient precedent in a canal that, as early as Egypt's Middle Kingdom, connected the Nile River with the Red Sea, to the east.

Prus' description of ancient Egypt's Labyrinth, in Fayum Province, draws on Book II of Herodotus's *Histories*; and on vivid impressions that Prus took from an 1878 visit to the ancient labyrinthine salt mine at Wieliczka (now a UNESCO World Heritage Site) near Kraków in southern Poland.

Pharaoh's solar-eclipse scenes were inspired by a solar eclipse Prus had observed at Mława, northwest of Warsaw, on 19 August 1887; and probably by Christopher Columbus' prediction of a *lunar* eclipse for 29 February 1504 while marooned for a year on Jamaica—a prediction that Columbus exploited in order to extort provisions from the island's Arawak natives. In 1889, six years before Prus completed *Pharaoh*, Columbus' lunar-eclipse prediction may have inspired a solar-eclipse scene in Mark Twain's *A Connecticut Yankee in King Arthur's Court*—a novel which, like *Pharaoh*, highlights the power of science and technology.

Similarly, Prus' use of look-alikes (Berossus and his double; Ramses and Lykon; an allusion to doubles of Ramses the Great) had been anticipated by Alexandre Dumas, *père* (*The Man in the Iron Mask*, 1850), Charles Dickens (*A Tale of Two Cities*, 1859), Wilkie Collins (*The Woman in* White, 1859), and Mark Twain (*The Prince and the Pauper*, 1882).

‡

Prus favors authentic terminology. An example is the Polish term *paraszyt*, borrowed from the Greek *paraschistes* ("cutter"). At the start of the mummification process, a scribe marked a line on the corpse's left side, down which the *paraschistes* next made a single deep incision with a knife of Ethiopian stone, probably flint. The *paraschistes* was then pelted with rocks and chased away with curses. After that, through the incision, a *taricheutes* (Greek for "preparer") removed the corpse's entrails and lungs, while leaving in place the heart and kidneys. An embalming scene very similar to this appears in *Pharaoh*'s Chapter 53. In the absence of a commonly used English equivalent for *paraschistes*, I have replaced it with Prus' explanatory phrase, "opener of dead bodies," given in Chapters 5 and 18.

The 12 months of the Egyptian year were divided into 3 seasons:
- *Akhet* (Flood), roughly September-January: Thoth, Phaophi, Athyr, Choiak;
- *Peret* (Growth), roughly January-May: Tybi, Mechir, Phamenoth, Pharmouthi;
- *Shemu* (Low Water), roughly May-September: Pachon, Payni, Epiphi, Mesore.

The twelve months were initially numbered within each season; but as early as the Middle Kingdom they also came to be known (as in the above listing of the Greek-period versions of their names) by the names of their principal festivals.

For better and worse, Egypt no longer has a flood season since the construction (1960-70) of the Aswan High Dam.

Each Egyptian month comprised thirty days. The 365-day year was rounded out with a five-day "intercalary month" celebrating the birthdays of five gods. Each month was divided into three "decades" of ten days each. It has been suggested that during the 19th and 20th Dynasties, the last two days of each decade were usually treated as a kind of weekend, free from work, for royal craftsmen.

Prus generally uses Egyptian month names in their late Greek-period spellings. I have kept these because they are commonly used in Egyptological literature and because the Egyptian pronunciations of month names are uncertain due to the absence, in the Egyptian writing systems, of vowel representations. Scholarly transcriptions of other Egyptian words, including personal and place names, have also continually mutated. I generally use the most current transcriptions.

For over three millennia, beginning in Egypt's prehistoric period (before 3100 BCE), the country was divided into forty-two *nomes* (so termed, beginning in the Greek, Ptolemaic period, after the Ancient Greek word *nomos*, "district"): twenty nomes in Lower (northern) Egypt, extending from the Old Kingdom capital, Memphis, to the Mediterranean Sea; and twenty-two nomes in Upper (southern) Egypt, starting in the south at Elephantine, near Egypt's border with Nubia at the First Cataract.

The Upper Egyptian nomes were numbered sequentially, moving downriver. In Lower Egypt, the numbering was more or less orderly from south to north through the Nile Delta, first covering the territory on the west before continuing with the higher numbers to the east: thus Alexandria, in the west, was in the 3rd Nome of Lower Egypt; Bubastis, in the east—in the 18th Nome of Lower Egypt.

Prus sometimes uses the word "mile" (in Polish, *mila*). It may generally be understood as the German and Danish "geographical mile," equal to 4.6 U.K. and U.S. "international miles."

‡

The present English version of *Pharaoh* includes examples of what I term *convergent* and *divergent* translation. Thus I have often rendered a number of Polish expressions (such as "*biedak, biedny,*" "*nędznik, nędzny,*" "*nikczemnik, nikczemny,*" and "*podlec, podły*") convergently by the single English expression "wretch, wretched," which happens to offer all the pertinent meanings.

Conversely, I have rendered the Polish adjective "*mądry,*" which is used in a number of distinct senses, divergently, depending on context, as "wise," "sage," "sapient," "perceptive," "learned," "knowledgeable," "canny," "clever," "astute," "shrewd," "savvy," "smart," or "intelligent."

Another terminological ambiguity involves the Polish words *ręka* ("hand" or "arm"), *ramię* ("arm" or "shoulder"), and *noga* ("foot" or "leg"). (In Russian, an East Slavic language, the analogous *ruka* and *noga* show corresponding ambiguities.)

The Polish *majątek* can mean "wealth," "fortune" (in the sense of wealth), or "(landed) estate." How the expression is to be understood, again, depends on context.

Still another ambiguity occurring in *Pharaoh* involves the Polish *drzwi*, which can mean "door" (singular) or "doors" (plural). The respective Polish and English words *drzwi* and "door" share an identical ambiguity in that each, depending on context, can also mean "doorway."

Translation of more than very simple texts requires painstakingly close reading, in an effort to resolve ambiguities—which are ubiquitous in spoken as well as written language—and thereby to asymptotically approach the most accurate rendering of the source text. For example, when Prus writes in *Pharaoh* about a "mine" (*kopalnia*—an excavation for minerals), he often means a "stone quarry" (*kamieniołom*).

Prus shows a fondness for the Polish particle *nawet*, an expression often used to highlight the unusual, unexpected, or atypical nature of something in a given situation. *Nawet* can often, but by no means invariably, be rendered by the English expression "even," used as an adverb.

Techniques used in this translation, in the search for verbal equivalents between the

Polish and English languages, include back-translation and the consideration of word etymologies. Etymologies, because Polish and English, like other European languages, share
vast numbers of expressions borrowed from, or calqued on, the Latin. Curiously, it is some
Polish expressions derived from Proto-Slavic and Old Polish stem expressions—especially
those relating to emotional states—that can be difficult for a translator to comprehend
and to render accurately in the target language.

Every language employs a variety of *registers*—of styles employed in specific settings.
For example, when should formal, and when colloquial, language be used? Should ancient
Egyptians, when "speaking English," commonly use contractions such as "I'm," "don't,"
"aren't"?

Prus has been lauded for creating an ancient-Egyptian register—for stylizing his narrative and dialog with apt antiquated diction. The occasional absence, in the second or
"target" language, of equivalent antiquated expressions can sometimes be *compensated
for* by selective use, in other passages, of archaic or dated expressions that exist in the
second language. For example, the everyday Polish expressions *rad* ("glad"), *chyba* (an
expression of surmise), *kazać* ("to request" or "to order") and *patrzeć* ("to look" or "to
see") can sometimes be rendered, respectively, by the archaic or dated English expressions "fain," "daresay," "to bid," and "to behold."

Competent translation—analogously to the mathematical dicta of Kurt Gödel's incom-
pleteness theorems (1931) and Alfred Tarski's undefinability theorem (1933)—generally
requires more information about the subject matter than is present in the actual source
text. Consequently, in this foreword and in my notes, I have indicated some of the research
that Prus did, writing *Pharaoh*, and that I have done, translating it.

The translator's role, in relation to the original text, has been compared to the roles of
other interpretive artists, e.g., of a musician or actor who interprets a work of musical or
dramatic art. Translation, especially of a text of any complexity, involves *interpretation*:
choices of wording must be made, which implies interpretation. George Bernard Shaw,
aspiring to the most accurate interpretations of literary works, wrote in the preface to his
1901 volume, *Three Plays for Puritans*: "I would give half a dozen of Shakespeare's plays
for one of the prefaces he ought to have written."

It is due to the necessity of interpretation that—notwithstanding the story about the
seventy independent, identical 3rd-century BCE Septuagint translations of biblical Old
Testament books into Greek—no translations of a literary work by different hands, or by
the same hand at different times, are likely to be identical. Something similar can be said
about the *original writings* of authors, who have been known to produce more than one
version of the same work.

A picture-painter paints, using dabs of color; an original writer, and his copyist the
translator, paint using words. Each of these artists must "step back" from the composition
in order to properly see the overall effect of the dabs or words; and such a review may
inspire adjustments to the work, for a dab or a word gains its full resonance—its specific
meaning—from its context. Analogous comparisons can be drawn with other arts.

Readers might question this translation's use of the word "Negro," rather than
"Black," as equivalent to Prus' Polish term "*Murzyn.*" In fact "Negro," until the late 1960s,
was the correct English expression, and Prus wrote *Pharaoh* over seven decades before
"Negro" was supplanted in English by the word "Black," used as a noun. (Prus applies

"black" as an adjective, in chapter 9, to a "black slave," where the structure of the Polish language doesn't permit use of "Negro slave," with "Negro" used as an adjective.)

Prus, unlike some chauvinist Poles of his time and since, was not bigoted against racial or ethnic groups. Where such sentiments occur in *Pharaoh*, they should be attributed to the respective characters rather than to the author.

‡

Leonardo da Vinci—a perfectionist famous for abandoning works unfinished—and others have been credited with observing that "A work of art is never finished [that is, perfected], only abandoned." I began translating *Pharaoh*, at the suggestion of a family friend, in 1959, aged fourteen, and completed a first draft in 1962. In 1965, on first meeting my professor of Polish literature at the University of California, Berkeley, future (1980) Nobel laureate Czesław Miłosz, I startled him, venturing that *Pharaoh* was written in very simple language; I could not have been more mistaken. The present translation follows my versions published in 1991, 2001, and (an e-book) 2020 and an incompetent and incomplete[2] 1902 version by Jeremiah Curtin titled *The Pharaoh and the Priest*.[3]

Pharaoh has been translated into twenty European languages and into Armenian, Georgian, and Hebrew, and has been adapted as an idiosyncratic 1966 Polish feature film. It is the present translator's hope that his English version may become *Pharaoh*'s bridge to other lands and languages. This English translation has benefited greatly at Hippocrene Books from the editorial expertise of Priti Chitnis Gress; and from Barbara Keane-Pigeon's textual suggestions, formatting adjustments, and moderation of Prus' prodigal ellipses.

—*Christopher Kasparek*

[2] Curtin's rendering of *Pharaoh* lacks the novel's epilog, which did not appear in print in Prus' lifetime.

[3] The juxtaposition, in Curtin's title, of the pharaoh (Ramses XIII) and the priest (Pentuer)—at Prus' request— reflects two phases in Prus' life: that of the teenager who had fought in the 1863 Uprising in the hope of restoring Poland's independence; and that of the Polish-Positivist writer who worked to educate, and improve the lives of, his compatriots abiding for over a century under three foreign empires.

INTRODUCTION

I n the northeast corner of Africa lies Egypt, homeland of the oldest civilization in the world. Three, four, even five thousand years ago, when rawhide-clad barbarians were sheltering in Central European[1] caves, Egypt already possessed an advanced social structure, agriculture, crafts, and literature. Above all, she was carrying out gigantic works of engineering and rearing colossal structures whose remnants strike awe into modern engineers.

Egypt is a fertile valley between the Libyan and Arabian Deserts. It is several hundred meters deep, a thousand kilometers long, on average barely seven kilometers wide. On the west the gentle but barren Libyan hills, and on the east the fissured Arabian crags, are the walls of this corridor, down which flows a river—the Nile.

With the river's course northward, the valley walls descend and, a hundred fifty kilometers from the Mediterranean Sea, suddenly flare out, and the Nile, instead of flowing down a narrow corridor, spills through several branches across a spacious triangular plain. This triangle, called the Nile Delta, has for its base the shore of the Mediterranean Sea and at its vertex, at the river's outlet from the valley, the city of Cairo and the ruins of the ancient capital, Memphis.[2]

Could one ascend a hundred fifty kilometers and from there regard Egypt, he would see the curious shape of the country and the singular variations in its coloring. From this altitude, against the white and orange sands, Egypt would look like a snake that is writhing its way across the desert to the Mediterranean Sea, into which it has just dipped its triangular head adorned with two eyes: the left, Alexandria; the right, Damietta.

In October, when the Nile floods all of Egypt, the long snake would be the blue color of the water. In February, when the falling waters yield place to springtime vegetation, the snake would be green, with a blue stripe down its body and myriad blue venules on its

---

[1] Central Europe: *Pharaoh* was written in Polish, the language of Poland, which is a Central European country. *(Translator.)*

[2] Memphis: the ancient capital of Aneb-Hetch, the 1st Nome of Lower Egypt. Memphis was Egypt's capital during the Old Kingdom. Its ancient Egyptian name was *Ineb Hedj* ("White Walls"). At the beginning of the New Kingdom (ca. 1550 BCE) the city became known as *Men-nefer* ("Enduring and Beautiful"), which later in the Coptic (late-Egyptian) language became *Menfe*. *Memphis* was the Greek-language adaptation of *Menfe*. *(Translator.)*

head—the canals that traverse the Delta. In March the blue stripe would constrict, and the snake's body would take on a golden hue from the ripening grains. Finally in early June the Nile stripe would be very slender, and the snake's body, due to drought and dust, would turn gray as if shrouded in crepe.

A basic feature of the Egyptian climate is the heat: in January it is commonly ten degrees Celsius,[3] in August—twenty-seven;[4] sometimes the heat reaches forty-seven degrees,[5] the temperature of a Roman bath.[6] Moreover, in the vicinity of the Mediterranean Sea, at the Delta, it rains barely ten times a year; and in Upper Egypt, once in ten years.

Under these conditions Egypt, instead of becoming a cradle of civilization, would have been a desert ravine like many in the Sahara, were she not revived annually by the waters of the sacred river Nile. From late June to late September, the Nile rises and floods nearly all of Egypt; from late October to late May the following year it falls, gradually exposing ever lower stretches of soil. The river's waters are so saturated with mineral and organic particles that the river turns brown; and as the waters recede, a silt as good as the best fertilizers settles out onto the flooded lands. The silt and the hot climate enable the desert-locked Egyptian to enjoy three harvests a year and some three hundred grains of yield for each grain of seed!

However, Egypt is not an unvarying flatland but an undulant country; some of its soil imbibes the blessed waters for only two or three months, and other parts see none all year round; for the flood does not reach some points. Apart from that, there are years of scant flooding when part of Egypt does not receive the fertilizing silt. Finally, due to the heat, the earth quickly dries out and must be watered like a flowerpot.

All these circumstances determined that the people inhabiting the Nile valley had either to perish, if they were weak, or to regulate the waters, if they possessed genius. The ancient Egyptians had genius, and so created a civilization.

As early as six thousand years ago they noticed that the Nile begins flooding when the sun rises beneath the star Sirius,[7] and begins falling when the sun approaches the constellation Libra. This prompted them to make astronomical observations and to measure time.

In order to have water year-round, they dug a network of canals several thousand miles long. And to secure themselves from excessive flooding, they reared mighty dams and dug reservoirs, of which the artificial Lake Moeris covered three hundred square kilometers, to a depth of twelve stories. Finally, along the Nile and canals they built a mul-

---

[3] 10 degrees Celsius: 50 degrees Fahrenheit. *(Translator.)*

[4] 27 degrees Celsius: 81 degrees Fahrenheit. *(Translator.)*

[5] 47 degrees Celsius: 117 degrees Fahrenheit. *(Translator.)*

[6] Roman bath: The reference is to the *caldarium* ("hot room") in an ancient Roman bath complex: a room with a plunge bath of hot water, and sometimes with a *laconicum*—a hot, dry area for the induction of sweating. *(Translator.)*

[7] Sirius: The star's Egyptian name, *Sopdet*, was transcribed by the Greeks as *Sothis*. Sothis' "heliacal rising" took place within about a month of the start of the annual Nile flood. A "heliacal [from *helios*, Greek for *sun*] rising" occurs when a star or other heavenly body first becomes visible above the eastern horizon for a brief moment just before sunrise, having previously been made invisible by sunlight. *(Translator.)*

titude of simple but effective machines[8] with which to draw water and pour it into fields placed one or two stories higher. Moreover, each year the silted canals had to be cleared, the dams maintained, and causeways built for the army, which had to carry out marches during every season.

These vast works required—besides conversance with astronomy, surveying, mechanics, and engineering—also superb organization. Whether it be strengthening the dikes or clearing the canals, it had to be done—and done within a certain time, over a great area. Hence arose the necessity to create an army of laborers numbering in the tens of thousands, acting to a designated purpose and under a single command. An army that must have a host of captains small and great, a host of detachments carrying out diverse tasks, directed to a uniform result; an army that required great quantities of provisions, resources, and ancillary forces.

Egypt mustered such an army of workers and owes to it her historic works. That army seems to have been created and its plans next drawn up by Egypt's priests, or learned men; while the kings, or pharaohs,[9] commanded. Consequently the Egyptian people in its times of greatness formed, as it were, a single person in which the priesthood played the role of mind, the pharaoh was the will, the populace the body, and obedience the cement.[10]

Thus Egypt's very nature, demanding great, continual, orderly work, created the skeleton of the country's societal organization: the populace worked, the pharaoh directed, the priests laid the plans. And so long as these three agents strove harmoniously for the ends indicated by nature, so long the society was able to flourish and carry out its everlasting works.

The mild, cheerful, and not in the least warlike Egyptian populace fell into two classes: husbandmen (peasants, farmers) and craftsmen (or artisans). Among the husbandmen there must have been some small landholders, but mostly they were tenants of the pharaoh, priests, and aristocracy. The craftsmen who produced clothing, furniture, pottery, and tools were independent; those laboring at the great constructions formed, as it were, an army.

Each of these specialties, chiefly construction, required tractive power and engines: someone had to draw water all day from the canals or move stones from the quarries to where they were needed. The heaviest physical tasks, above all the quarrying, were carried out by convicts or by slaves taken in war.

The native Egyptians boasted their copper-colored skins and disdained the black

---

[8] machines: These manually operated machines for raising water from the Nile River, or from canals, into cultivated fields are known, from the Arabic language, as *shadoofs*. *(Translator.)*

[9] "Pharaoh" is a metonym meaning "Great House" (Egyptian for "royal palace") that is often used by modern authors for ancient Egypt's kings who ruled from the 1st Dynasty until Egypt's annexation by the Roman Empire in 30 BCE. The actual term for the monarch, whether male or female, used by the Egyptians themselves, was "king." The expression "pharaoh" was never used consistently by the Egyptians in reference to the king until the 25th Dynasty, about four centuries after the fall of the 20th Dynasty and New Kingdom portrayed in Prus' novel. *(Translator.)*

[10] Prus adopted this metaphor of society-as-organism ("the social organism") from English sociologist Herbert Spencer. *(Translator.)*

Ethiopians,[11] yellow Semites, and white Europeans.[12] The Egyptians' skin color, which distinguished their own from outsiders, promoted national unity more powerfully than religion, which can be adopted, or language, which can be learned.

With time, however, as the edifice of the state began breaking down, foreign elements streamed into the country in ever growing numbers. They sapped its cohesiveness, fragmented the society, and finally deluged and diluted the native inhabitants of the country.

The pharaoh ruled the kingdom with the help of a standing army and a police force as well as a host of officials who gradually came to form a hereditary aristocracy. In name he was the lawgiver, commander-in-chief, wealthiest landowner, supreme judge, a priest, even a son of the gods, and a god. Not only was he worshipped as a god by the populace and officials, but sometimes he erected altars to himself and burned incense before his own images.

Next to the pharaohs—very often, above them—stood the priests: an order of wise men who guided the destinies of the country.

Today it is nigh impossible to conceive of the extraordinary role that the priesthood played in Egypt. They were the teachers of the young, the soothsayers and thus advisers of the adults, and the judges of the dead, to whom their will and knowledge guaranteed immortality. They not only performed the exacting religious rites before the gods and pharaohs but tended the sick as physicians and influenced public works as engineers, and politics as astrologers—above all, as experts on their own country and its neighbors.

Of prime importance in Egypt's history were the relations that existed between the priesthood and the pharaohs. Usually the pharaoh deferred to the priests, made generous offerings to the gods, and erected temples. Then he lived long, and his name and images, engraved on monuments, passed from generation to generation covered in glory. But many pharaohs reigned only briefly, and not only the deeds but the very names of some disappeared. And on a couple of occasions a dynasty fell, and the serpent-encircled headdress of the pharaohs was donned by a priest.

Egypt developed so long as a homogeneous people, energetic kings, and wise priests worked together for the common good. But there came a period when the populace declined numerically as a result of wars and lost their vigor under oppression and exploitation, while the influx of foreign arrivals undermined their racial unity. And when additionally the energy of the pharaohs and the wisdom of the priests were drowned in a flood of Asiatic dissipation, and these two powers began fighting over a monopoly of fleecing the populace, Egypt fell into the power of foreigners, and the light of civilization that had burned for several thousand years at the Nile expired.

The following narrative relates to the eleventh century before Christ, when the Twentieth Dynasty fell[13] and when, on the demise of the Son of the Sun, the eternally living

---

[11] Ethiopia: name applied by some writers, at least since Herodotus in the 5th century BCE, to all lands lying south of Egypt, including Nubia, Sudan, and modern Ethiopia. *(Translator.)*

[12] A mural preserved at London's British Museum illustrates this ancient Egyptian view of skin color. *(Translator.)*

[13] The fall of the 20th Dynasty, and of Egypt's New Kingdom, has been variously dated to within a couple of decades after 1100 BCE. *(Translator.)*

Ramses XIII,[14] the throne was seized by, and the uraeus[15] came to adorn the brow of, the eternally living Son of the Sun, San-amen-Herhor,[16] High Priest of Amon.[17]

---

[14] Ramses XIII: The last pharaoh of the 20th Dynasty and New Kingdom—the last *Ramesside* pharaoh—was not Ramses XIII but Ramses XI. (There was no Ramses XII or Ramses XIII.) *(Translator.)*

[15] uraeus: the stylized upright form of an Egyptian cobra, used in ancient Egypt as a symbol of sovereignty, royalty, deity, and divine authority. *(Translator.)*

[16] Herhor (whose name is currently transcribed as *Herihor*, "[the god] Horus Is Raised"), an individual possibly of Libyan parentage, was an Egyptian Army officer and High Priest of Amon at Thebes (1080-1074 BCE) during the reign of Ramses XI, the last pharaoh of the 20th Dynasty and New Kingdom. The other parts of Herihor's name, as given by the author, differ from current transliterations. *(Translator.)*

[17] Amon: The god Amon had become Thebes' patron deity under the 11th Dynasty. After Thebes' rebellion against the Hyksos, ending in their expulsion ca. 1550 BCE, Amon had acquired national importance, expressed in his fusion with the Sun god Ra as Amon-Ra. Throughout the New Kingdom, except during the reign of Akhenaten, he remained the paramount deity—the transcendent, self-created creator deity. His position as King of the Gods developed to the point of virtual monotheism, with other gods becoming manifestations of him. As chief deity of the Egyptian Empire, Amon-Ra also came to be worshipped in Libya and Nubia, and in Greece as *Zeus Ammon*. More than 1,500 Egyptian gods and goddesses are known by name, and they appear in virtually every aspect of ancient Egyptian civilization. *(Translator.)*

CHAPTER 1

I n the thirty-third year of the happy reign of Ramses XII, Egypt celebrated two events that filled her loyal inhabitants with pride and joy.

In the month of Mechir, in December,[1] there returned to Thebes, showered with sumptuous gifts, the god Khonsu,[2] who had traveled three years and nine months in the land of Bukhten and had restored the health of the local king's daughter Bent-res and had expelled the evil spirit not only from the king's family but even from the fortress of Bukhten.[3]

And in the month of Pharmouthi, in February,[4] the Lord of Upper and Lower Egypt, the ruler of Phoenicia and the Nine Nations,[5] Mer-amen-Ramses XII, after consulting the gods, to whom he is equal, named as his *Iry-pat*,[6] or Successor to the Throne, his twenty-two-year-old son, Ham-sem-merer-amen-Ramses.

This choice delighted the pious priests, distinguished nomarchs,[7] valiant army, faithful

---

[1] Actually, the ancient Egyptian month of Mechir lay between February 8 and March 9 of the modern, Gregorian calendar. *(Translator.)*

[2] Khonsu was an Egyptian god associated with the moon. His name (Egyptian for "Traveler") may have related to the moon's nightly travel across the sky. He fostered the creation of new life in all creatures. At Thebes he was part of a family triad with Mut as his mother and Amon as his father. At Kom Ombo, Khonsu was worshipped as the son of the crocodile-headed god Sobek and the cow goddess Hathor. *(Translator.)*

[3] The god Khonsu had developed a reputation in Egypt and abroad as a healer. A stele records that an ailing princess of Bukhten, in Syria, was instantly cured upon the arrival there of an image of Khonsu. The incident is reported in Egyptian sources to have occurred under Ramses II (Ramses the Great) about a century and a half before *Pharaoh's* present time. *(Translator.)*

[4] Actually, the ancient Egyptian month of Pharmouthi lay between April 9 and May 8 of the modern, Gregorian calendar. *(Translator.)*

[5] Nine Nations is a reference to Egypt's enemies, who were traditionally reckoned as nine in number and were often represented in works of art. There was no definitive list of the nine peoples: it changed over time, as enemies changed. *(Translator.)*

[6] *Iry-pat* was actually a ranking title. As early as the 1st Dynasty, it was the highest ranking-title at Egypt's royal court, borne only by the most important officials. During the New Kingdom *(Pharaoh's* historical period), the title of *Iry-pat* was often held by the crown prince, or successor to the throne, and announced that its holder was the second ruler in the country; it is therefore sometimes translated as "Crown Prince." Prus uses a variant transliteration of the word: *"Erpatre." (Translator.)*

[7] nomarch: ruler of one of the forty-two nomes, or provinces (in the Egyptian language, singular, *sepat*), into which ancient Egypt was divided for three millennia. Lower (northern) Egypt comprised twenty numbered nomes; Upper (southern) Egypt, twenty-two. In each half of Egypt, the nomes were numbered

people, and all creatures living on Egyptian soil. For the Pharaoh's elder sons, born of the Hittite princess,[8] had due to inscrutable spells been visited by an evil spirit. One, twenty-seven years old, had been unable to walk from his majority; the second had cut his veins and died; and the third, after drinking tainted wine which he would not give up, had gone mad and, thinking himself an ape, spent days together in the trees.

Finally the fourth son, Ramses,[9] born of Queen Nikotris,[10] daughter of High Priest Amenhotep,[11] was strong as the Apis bull,[12] courageous as a lion, and wise as the priests. From childhood he had surrounded himself with soldiers and, while yet an ordinary prince, used to say:

"Had the gods made me pharaoh instead of a younger royal son, I would have conquered, like Ramses the Great,[13] nine nations never before heard of in Egypt, built a temple greater than all of Thebes,[14] and erected myself a pyramid beside which the tomb of Cheops[15] would look like a rosebush beside a full-grown palm."

Having received the longed-for title of *Iry-pat*, the young Prince asked his father to

---

serially in a northerly direction. Use of the Greek-derived terms "nome" (from *nemein*, "to divide") and "nomarch" ("ruler of a nome") began in the Ptolemaic (Greek) period of Egypt's history (323-30 BCE). *(Translator.)*

[8] Hittite princess: Over a century and a half earlier, Ramses II ("the Great"), having concluded with the Hittite Empire history's first known peace treaty, had married a Hittite princess. *(Translator.)*

[9] Ramses: name of 11 New Kingdom pharaohs. *Ramses* meant "Born of [the god] Ra." *(Translator.)*

[10] Nikotris: name borrowed from a putative 6th Dynasty Queen Nitokris, or from one of two so-named daughters of 26th Dynasty pharaohs. (In *Pharaoh*, the letters *t* and *k* in the name have been reversed.) *(Translator.)*

[11] High Priest Amenhotep: The historic Amenhotep (whose name meant "Amon is pleased") was high priest of Amon under pharaohs Ramses IX through Ramses XI and played a key role in the civil war that ended Egypt's 20th Dynasty and, with it, the New Kingdom. *(Translator.)*

[12] Apis bull: a sacred black bull that was worshipped in the Memphis region. It was identified as the son of the goddess Hathor, a primary Egyptian deity, and was initially assigned a role in Hathor's worship, being sacrificed and reborn. Later Apis also served as an intermediary between humans and other powerful deities. *(Translator.)*

[13] Ramses the Great: Ramses II (ca. 1303-1213 BCE), the third pharaoh of the 19th Dynasty, who lived to about age ninety and whose mummy is preserved in the Grand Egyptian Museum at Giza. He is often regarded as the greatest, most celebrated, most powerful pharaoh of the Egyptian Empire. He led several military expeditions north into the Levant and south into Nubia. After his death, new enemies attacked the Egyptian Empire, which also suffered from internal problems; in less than 150 years, the Egyptian Empire and New Kingdom came to an end. Their demise is the subject of Prus' *Pharaoh. (Translator.)*

[14] Thebes: the Greek name for *Waset*, an ancient Egyptian city located east of the Nile, 800 kilometers south of the Mediterranean Sea. Thebes was the eponymous capital city of Waset, the 4th Nome (the Scepter Nome) of Upper Egypt. Its ruins lie within the modern city of Luxor, which encompasses the Temples of Karnak and Luxor. Immediately across the Nile lie the monuments, temples, and tombs of the west-bank Theban Necropolis, which includes the Valley of the Kings and the Valley of the Queens. "Thebes" is the Latinized form of the ancient Greek *Thebai*, which is the hellenized form of the Demotic Egyptian *Ta-pe*. The latter was actually the local name for the Karnak temple complex on the northern east bank of the city. As early as Homer's *Iliad*, the Greeks referred to Egypt's Thebes as "Hundred-Gated Thebes" to distinguish it from Greece's own "Thebes of the Seven Gates." *(Translator.)*

[15] Tomb of Cheops: the Great Pyramid of Giza, near Cairo. It was the tomb of Pharaoh Khufu, known to the Greeks as Cheops. *(Translator.)*

graciously name him commander of the Menfi Corps.[16] His Holiness Ramses XII, after consulting the gods, to whom he is equal, answered that he would do so if the Crown Prince could give evidence of his ability to command a substantial body of combat troops.

To that end a council was called, presided over by Minister of War San-amen-Herhor, who was high priest of the greatest temple, that of Amon in Thebes.

The council determined that:

"The Crown Prince shall, in mid-Mesore (the beginning of June[17]), collect the ten regiments deployed along the line joining the city of Memphis with the city of Xois,[18] situated on the Bay of Sebennytos.[19]

"With this ten-thousand-strong corps, battle-ready, equipped with train and military engines, the Crown Prince shall proceed east to the highway that runs from Memphis to Khetem, on the border between the land of Goshen[20] and the Egyptian desert.

"In the meantime General Nitager,[21] commander-in-chief of the army that guards the gates of Egypt from invasion by the Asiatic peoples, shall set out against the Crown Prince from the Bitter Lakes.[22]

"The two armies, Asiatic and Western, shall make contact in the vicinity of the city of Pi-Bailos[23]—but in the desert, lest the industrious husbandman of the land of Goshen know hindrance to his labors.

"The Crown Prince shall be victorious if he does not let himself be surprised by Nitager—that is, if he gathers all his regiments and succeeds in drawing them up in battle array in time to meet the enemy.

"Personally present in Prince Ramses' camp shall be His Eminence Herhor, Minister of War, who will give a report on the course of events to the Pharaoh."

---

[16] Menfi Corps: an army corps possibly named after *Menfe*, the city commonly known as "Memphis." *(Translator.)*

[17] Actually, the ancient Egyptian month of Mesore lay between August 7 and September 5 of the modern, Gregorian calendar. *(Translator.)*

[18] Xois was the Greek name for the ancient Egyptian city of Khasu, which was located near the center of the Nile Delta on an island formed by the Nile's Phatnitic branch and the now nonexistant Sebennytic branch to its west. The city belonged to the Sebennytic Nome and later was the capital of the Xoite Nome, the 6th Nome of Lower Egypt. Prus calls Xois *Pi-Uto. (Translator.)*

[19] Bay of Sebennytos: a nonexistant bay, in the western Nile Delta, once formed by the nonexistant ancient Sebennytic branch of the Nile—the Nile's third branch, counting from the west. *(Translator.)*

[20] Land of Goshen: a fertile land in the eastern Nile Delta. It is named in the Bible *(Genesis 45:10)* as the land that Joseph's pharaoh gave to the Israelites. It was from there that the Israelites made their exodus from Egypt. *(Translator.)*

[21] Nitager: name possibly inspired by the epithet of one of Alexander the Great's generals and political successors, Seleukos I *Nicator* ("the Victorious" or "the Victor"), who established the Seleucid Empire, one of the major powers of the Hellenistic world. In chapter 51, Herhor will offer Ramses the same epithet, "the Victorious." *(Translator.)*

[22] Bitter Lakes: The Great Bitter Lake is a salt-water lake connecting the north and south parts of the Suez Canal, which mostly runs east of the Nile Delta. Before the Canal was built, the sites of the Great Bitter Lake and the adjacent Small Bitter Lake were occupied by dry salt valleys. From the Great Bitter Lake, the Suez Canal runs north through Lake Manzala and Lake Timsah. *(Translator.)*

[23] Pi-Bailos: a city in the eastern Nile Delta, in Lower Egypt's 20th Nome. *(Translator.)*

The border between the land of Goshen and the desert comprised two routes of communication. One was a transport canal from Memphis to Lake Timsah;[24] the other, a highway. The canal lay within the land of Goshen; the highway, in the desert, which was encompassed by the two routes in a semicircle. The canal was visible from nearly the entire length of the highway.

Apart from artificial borders, the adjoining lands differed in every respect. The land of Goshen, despite its undulant terrain, seemed a plain, while the desert consisted of limestone hills and sandy valleys. The land of Goshen looked like a gigantic chessboard whose green and yellow fields were set off by the colors of the grains and by palms growing on the balks; while, on the desert's russet sands and white hills, a patch of green or clump of trees and shrubs looked like a lost traveler.

In the fertile land of Goshen, every hill sprouted a dark grove of acacias, sycamores, and tamarinds, from a distance resembling our linden, hidden among which were villas with rows of squat columns, and the yellow mudbrick huts of peasants. Occasionally beside a grove there stood a town of white flat-roofed houses; or above the trees there rose ponderously the pyramidal towers of temple gates, like twin megaliths covered with peculiar characters.

In the desert, beyond an initial row of greenish hillocks, there loomed naked hills piled with boulders. It seemed as if the western land, surfeited with life, casts a regal bounty of verdure and blossoms across the canal; but the following year the ever-hungry desert devours them and converts them to ashes.

A little vegetation banished to the rocks and sands clung to lower places to which water could be conveyed from the canal via ditches cut through the roadbed. Thus among the bald hills near the highway, imbibing the celestial dew, were hidden oases where grew barley and wheat, grapevines, palms, and tamarinds.

In such places, too, lived individual families of people who, on meeting at the market in Pi-Bailos, might not even be aware that they were neighbors in the desert.

On the sixteenth of Mesore the concentration of troops was almost complete. The Successor's ten regiments which were to relieve Nitager's Asiatic force were already gathered on the highway above the city of Pi-Bailos with their train and part of the military engines.

Their movements were directed personally by the Successor. He organized two lines of reconnaissance: an outer one to surveil the enemy, and an inner to safeguard his own army from attack, possible in an area full of hills and ravines. Over a week's time Ramses made the rounds of the regiments marching by various routes, looking closely to see whether the soldiers had proper weapons and warm cloaks for the night, and whether the camps had enough biscuits, meat, and dried fish. Finally, he ordered that the wives, children, and slaves of the troops going to the eastern border be transported via the canal, thus reducing the sizes of the camps and facilitating the movements of the army proper.

The eldest generals admired the Successor's knowledge, zeal, and caution; above all, his diligence and simplicity. He had left his numerous court, princely tent, vehicles, and litters in Memphis; and, dressed as a simple officer, rode from regiment to regiment horseback, Assyrian-style, accompanied by two aides.

---

[24] Lake Timsah: a lake which in ancient times was the northern terminus of the Red Sea. As early as Egypt's Middle Kingdom, an *east-west* "Suez Canal," such as that mentioned above, had linked the Nile River with the Red Sea. *(Translator.)*

Thanks to this the concentration of the actual corps went very quickly, and the troops arrived at Pi-Bailos at the designated time.

It was otherwise with the Prince's staff, with the Greek regiment that accompanied it, and with several military engines.

The staff, assembled at Memphis, had the shortest way and so set out last, with a huge train in tow. Almost every officer—and they were young lords of great families—had a litter with four Negroes[25], a two-wheeled war chariot, a sumptuous tent, numerous chests of clothing and provisions, and many pitchers of beer and wine.

In addition, a large troupe of singing and dancing girls, with musicians, set out on the journey after the officers; and each girl, as a great lady, had to have a wagon harnessed to one or two pairs of oxen, and a litter.

When this throng issued out of Memphis, it took up more space on the highway than the Successor's army. And it marched so slowly that the military engines, which had been left at the rear, moved out fully a day later than ordered. To make matters worse, the singing and dancing girls at sight of the desert, which was not at all so terrible at that point, took fright and began crying. To calm them, it was necessary to hasten the night's bivouac, pitch tents, and stage a spectacle, followed by a feast.

The night's entertainment, in the coolness, under a starry sky, with a backdrop of untamed nature, so appealed to the dancing and singing girls that they declared that henceforth they would perform only in the desert. Meanwhile the Successor, learning about the state of affairs with his staff, sent an order for the women to be turned back to the city and for the march to be speeded up.

Present with the staff was His Eminence Herhor, Minister of War, but only in the character of an observer. He brought along no singing girls, but neither did he make any comments to the staff officers. He had his litter borne to the head of the column and, accommodating to its movements, rode on or rested in the shade of a great fan carried by an aide.

His Eminence Herhor was a forty-odd-year-old man, strongly built, reserved. He seldom spoke and equally seldom looked at people from beneath his lowered eyelids.

Like every Egyptian man, he had bare arms, legs, and chest, sandaled feet, a short skirt about his hips, and in front an apron in blue and white stripes. As a priest, he shaved his face and head and wore a leopard skin slung over his left shoulder. Finally, as a soldier he covered his head with a small guardsman's helmet from which a cloth, likewise in white and blue stripes, fell onto the back of his neck.

On his neck was a triple gold chain, and beneath his left arm, on his chest, a short sword in a costly scabbard.

His litter, borne by six black slaves, was constantly accompanied by three men: one carried the fan, the second the Minister's ax, and the third a box of papyri. The last was Pentuer,[26] a priest and the Minister's scribe, a thin ascetic who did not cover his shaven

---

[25] "Negro" was the correct English word for an African person of dark skin pigmentation until the late 1960s, when it was replaced by "Black," used as a noun. Prus wrote Pharaoh over seven decades before that terminological change. To have used "Black" as a noun in this translation would have been an anachronism. *(Translator.)*

[26] Pentuer: Pentawer, or Pentaur, was a copyist of a prose poem about the Battle of Kadesh, fought ca. 1274 BCE by Pharaoh Ramses II (Ramses the Great). A less likely namesake of the character in *Pharaoh* was a son of Ramses III and of a secondary wife, Tiye; this Pentawer was to have been the beneficiary of

head even in the worst heat. He came from the common people, but despite his lowly birth he held an important post in the Kingdom thanks to his exceptional abilities.

Though the Minister and his officials were installed at the head of the staff column and did not meddle in its movements, the Minister was not unaware of what was happening behind him. Every hour, sometimes every half hour, His Eminence's litter was approached now by a junior priest (an ordinary "servant of god"), now by a straggling soldier, now by a peddler or slave who, passing as it were casually by the Minister's silent retinue, tossed out some word. That word, Pentuer sometimes jotted down but most often committed to memory, for his was an extraordinary memory.

These little things went unremarked among the noisy crowd of staff officers. The great young lords were too busy running about, conversing loudly, or singing to watch who approached the Minister; the more so, as a great many people were constantly maundering along the highway.

On the fifteenth of Mesore the Successor's staff and His Eminence the Minister spent the night beneath the open heavens a mile from the regiments already taking up battle positions athwart the highway beyond Pi-Bailos.

Before the first hour of the morning—our six o'clock—the desert hills took on a violet color. From beyond them peeped out the sun. A rosiness flooded the land of Goshen, and towns, temples, magnates' palaces, and peasants' mudbrick huts looked like sparks and flames in a single instant ignited amid the greenery.

Presently a gold color suffused the western horizon. The green of the land of Goshen seemed to dissolve in gold, and the countless canals to run with molten silver instead of water. But the desert hills became still more violet, casting long shadows on the sands and blackness on the vegetation.

Lookouts posted along the highway had a perfect view of the palm-bordered fields across the canal. Some were green with flax, wheat, clover; in others ripened the second sowing of golden barley. Husbandmen were setting out for work from huts hidden among the trees—naked copper-colored men in only a short skirt about their hips and a cap on their heads.

Some turned to the canals to clear them of silt or to draw water and pour it into the fields, using machines resembling well poles.[27] Other husbandmen, scattering among the trees, picked the ripe figs and grapes. There were many naked children about, as well as women in white, yellow, or red sleeveless shifts.

And there was great activity in the area. In the sky, the desert birds of prey chased the doves and jackdaws of the land of Goshen. Along the canal swung creaking shadoofs with buckets of life-giving water, and fruit pickers appeared and disappeared amid the green of the trees like colorful butterflies. In the desert, the highway swarmed with the army and its attendants. A mounted detachment armed with lances swept by. After it marched bowmen in caps and short skirts; they carried bows in their grasps and quivers on their

---

Tiye's plot to assassinate Ramses III and replace him with Pentawer in lieu of the pharaoh's designated successor, Ramses IV. *(Translator.)*

[27] Well pole: this device is often called by the Arabic name *shadoof* or *shaduf*, and is also known as a "counterpoise lift" or "well sweep." It comprises a long pivoted pole with a bucket at one end and a counterweight at the other. The shadoof was used by the ancient Egyptians and Mesopotamians and continues in use in many parts of Africa, Asia, India, Europe, and America. *(Translator.)*

backs, and had broad short swords at their right sides. The bowmen were accompanied by slingers carrying sacks of projectiles, and armed with short swords.

A hundred paces behind them came two small infantry detachments: one armed with spears, the other with axes. Both carried rectangular shields and wore thick armor-like tunics and, on their heads, caps with cloths protecting their necks from the heat. Caps and tunics were striped blue-and-white or yellow-and-black, making the soldiers resemble great hornets.

After the advance guard, surrounded by a contingent of axmen, moved the Minister's litter; and after it, in copper helmets and armor, marched Greek companies whose measured tread recalled the blows of heavy hammers. In the rear there were sounds of creaking carts, lowing cattle, and shouting carters, and at the roadside a bearded Phoenician trader edged by in a litter suspended between two donkeys. Above all this there rose a cloud of golden dust and the heat.

Suddenly a mounted soldier galloped in from the advance guard and informed the Minister that the Crown Prince approached. His Eminence descended from his litter, and just then on the highway there appeared a handful of riders, who jumped off their horses. Then one of the riders and the Minister proceeded toward each other, every few paces stopping and bowing.

"Greetings, son of Pharaoh, may he live forever," said the Minister.

"Greetings, and live long, holy father," replied the Crown Prince, adding: "You move as slowly as if your legs had been sawn off, and Nitager will arrive before our corps in two hours at the latest."

"That is true. Your staff marches very slowly."

"Also, Ennana[28] tells me"—Ramses indicated an amulet-bedecked officer standing behind him—"that you haven't sent patrols out to the ravines. In actual war, the enemy could attack you from that side."

"I'm not the commander but the judge," answered the Minister calmly.

"What has Patroklos[29] been doing?"

"Patroklos and the Greek regiment are escorting the military engines."

"What about my relative and aide Thutmose?"[30]

"I gather still asleep."

Ramses impatiently stamped his foot and fell silent. He was a handsome youth with an almost feminine face made still more attractive by anger and a tan. He wore a tight-fitting tunic in blue and white stripes, a matching cloth beneath his helmet, a gold chain on his neck, and a costly sword under his left arm.

"I see, Ennana," said the Prince, "that you alone look out for my honor."

---

[28] Ennana: please see the last note in chapter 4. (Translator.)

[29] Patroklos: a Greek name, literally meaning "glory of the father," borrowed from a character in Homer's *Iliad*: Patroklos was the beloved brother-in-arms of Achilles. (Prus spells the name with an "e": *Patrokles*.) Several subsequent historic persons BCE bore the name *Patrocles*; due to the *Iliad*'s fame, the name *Patroclus* was used as a man's given name throughout the Hellenistic and Roman periods. (Translator.)

[30] Thutmose: the name of four 18th Dynasty pharaohs and of several other historic persons. The name meant "Born of [the god] Thoth." (Translator.)

The amulet-bedecked officer executed a deep bow.

"Thutmose is an idler," said the Successor. "Get back to your post, Ennana. The advance guard, at least, should have a commander."

Then, glancing at the retinue, which now surrounded him as though sprung from underground, he added: "Have them bring my litter. I'm as tired as a stonemason."

"Do gods tire?" whispered Ennana, still standing behind him.

"Get back to your place," said Ramses.

"O likeness of the moon, will you have me inspect the ravines?" asked the officer quietly. "I beg you, command me, for wherever I am, my heart chases after you to divine your will and carry it out."

"I know you are watchful," replied Ramses. "Go watch over everything."

"Holy father," Ennana turned to the Minister, "I commend to Your Eminence my most humble services."

Scarcely had Ennana ridden off when a still greater tumult arose at the rear of the marching column. The Successor's litter was being sought but could not be found. Instead there appeared, shoving his way through the Greek soldiery, a young man of peculiar aspect. He wore a muslin shirt, a richly embroidered apron, and a gold sash over his shoulder. Most notable, though, was his enormous wig comprising myriad little braids, and a small artificial beard resembling a cat's tail.

This was Thutmose, the premier dandy of Memphis, who decked himself up and doused himself in perfumes even during a march.

"Welcome, Ramses!" called the dandy, jostling the officers. "Imagine, your litter has gotten lost someplace; you must take a seat in mine which, though unworthy of you, isn't the worst."

"I'm angry with you," said the Prince. "You sleep instead of minding the army."

The astounded dandy stopped. "Me sleep?" he cried. "May the tongue wilt that utters such lies! Knowing you were coming, I've spent the past hour dressing, preparing a bath and perfumes for you ..."

"And meanwhile the detachment marches without a commander."

"Am I supposed to command a detachment which includes His Eminence the Minister of War and a commander like Patroklos?"

The Successor fell silent; Thutmose approached him and whispered:

"What a sight you are, son of Pharaoh! Wigless, hair and clothes full of dust, skin black and cracked like the earth in summer! The most worshipful Queen your mother would banish me from court at the sight of your wretchedness."

"I'm only tired."

"Have a seat in the litter. You'll find there fresh rose garlands, roast fowl, and a pitcher of Cyprus wine.[31] I've also," he added still more quietly, "hidden Senura in camp."

"Is she here?" asked the Prince. His eyes, glittering the moment before, grew misty.

"Let the troops go on," said Thutmose, "and let's wait for her here."

---

[31] Cyprus wine: Cyprus has been famous since antiquity for wine. Commandaria, an amber-colored sweet wine so named since the Crusades in the 12th century CE, is documented in Cyprus since 800 BCE and is the world's oldest named wine still in production. King Richard the Lionheart, at his wedding in Limassol, Cyprus, pronounced Commandaria "the wine of kings and the king of wines." *(Translator.)*

Ramses came to his senses. "Leave me alone! We face battle in two hours."

"Some battle!"

"At least it will settle the matter of my command."

"Laugh it off!" smiled the dandy. "I'd swear the Minister of War sent a report to His Holiness yesterday, asking that you be given the Menfi Corps."

"All the same. Today I couldn't think about anything besides the army."

"It's horrible, this penchant of yours for war, where a man goes months without washing, just to perish one day. Brr! If you did see Senura ... Only take a look at her."

"That's why I won't," said Ramses firmly.

Just when eight men had carried Thutmose's enormous litter out from in back of the Greek ranks for the Successor, a horseman galloped in from the advance guard. He slid off his mount and ran so fast that the images or nameplates of the gods rang on his chest. It was Ennana, all adither.

Everyone turned toward him, to his evident pleasure.

"Iry-pat, O highest lips!" cried Ennana, bowing to Ramses. "When, in accordance with your divine command, I was riding at the head of the detachment, closely watching everything, I espied two beautiful scarabs on the highway. Each of the sacred beetles was rolling a little clay sphere[32] across the road, toward the sand."

"So what?" interrupted the Successor.

"Naturally," continued Ennana, looking toward the Minister, "as piety requires, my men and I paid homage to the golden images of the sun and halted the march. It's such an important omen that, without the order, none of us would dare go on."

"I see you are a truly pious Egyptian, if your features are Hittite," answered His Eminence Herhor. Turning to several dignitaries standing nearest, he added:

"We'll go no farther down the highway, as we might trample the sacred beetles. Pentuer, can the highway be skirted by that ravine on the right?"

"Yes, it can," replied the Minister's scribe. "The ravine is a mile long and comes out onto the highway again almost opposite Pi-Bailos."

"A tremendous loss of time," broke in the Successor angrily.

"I'll swear they're not scarabs but the spirits of my Phoenician usurers," said the dandy Thutmose. "Being dead and unable to take back their money, in their malice they make me go through the desert!"

Since the Prince's suite anxiously awaited the decision, Ramses asked Herhor: "What do you think about this, holy father?"

"Look at the officers," replied the priest, "and you'll see we must go by way of the ravine."

The commander of the Greeks, General Patroklos, came forward and said to the Successor: "If the Prince permits, my regiment will continue down the highway. Our men don't fear scarabs."

---

[32] The scarab, a black dung beetle, actually rolls balls of *dung* to an underground chamber to feed its larval offspring. To the ancient Egyptians, the sacred scarab, *Scarabaeus sacer*, was a symbol of Khepri, the morning manifestation of the sun god Ra, from an analogy between the beetle rolling a dung ball over the ground and Khepri rolling the sun across the sky. The Egyptians also observed young beetles emerge from the dung ball and mistakenly assumed that the female beetle reproduced without need of a male; from this, they drew parallels with the eventide solar god Atum, who begat children alone. *(Translator.)*

"Your men don't fear even the royal tombs," answered the Minister. "Yet it mustn't be safe there, as none has returned."

The Greek withdrew in confusion to the suite.

"Admit it, holy father," whispered the Crown Prince in the utmost anger, "an obstacle like that wouldn't stop even a donkey."

"So a donkey will never be pharaoh," replied the Minister calmly.

"In that case, Minister, you will lead the detachment through the ravine!" cried Ramses. "I'm not versed in priestly tactics. Anyway, I need a rest. Come along, cousin," he told Thutmose, as he turned toward the bald hills.

CHAPTER 2

H is Eminence Herhor immediately directed his aide with the ax to take over command of the advance guard from Ennana. Then he sent an order for the catapults
to be wheeled off the highway into the ravine, and for the Greek soldiers to ease
their passage in difficult spots. All the chariots, wagons, and litters of the officers in the
retinue were to move at the rear.

As Herhor was issuing the orders, the aide with the fan approached the scribe Pentuer
and whispered: "I daresay it will never be possible to travel this highway again."

"Why not?" replied the priest. "But since two sacred beetles have crossed our path, it
wouldn't do to go on. It could bring misfortune."

"There already is misfortune. Didn't you see how Prince Ramses got angry at the Minister? And our lord is not one who forgets."

"It's not the Prince who's taken offense at our lord, but our lord at the Prince; and
our lord has chastened him," said Pentuer. "He did well, too, for the young Prince already
thinks he will be another Menes."[1]

"You mean a Ramses the Great?" said the aide.

"Ramses the Great heeded the gods and has creditable inscriptions in all the temples.
But Menes, Egypt's first pharaoh, was a disturber of the order and owes it only to the paternal mildness of the priests that his name is mentioned. Though I wouldn't bet a deben[2]
of copper that Menes' mummy exists."

"My Pentuer," said the aide, "you're a wise man, so you know it's all the same to us
whether we have ten masters or eleven."

"But it's not all the same to the populace whether they're to dig up a mountain of gold
each year for the priests, or two mountains of gold: for the priests, and for the pharaoh,"
answered Pentuer, his eyes flashing.

"You're thinking dangerous thoughts," whispered the aide.

"Haven't you complained at the excesses of the pharaoh's court and the nomarchs?"
asked the priest in surprise.

---

[1] Menes was a pharaoh of Egypt's Early Dynastic Period who is traditionally credited with having united
Upper and Lower Egypt and founded the 1st Dynasty. Menes is most commonly identified either with
Narmer (of the *Narmer palette*) or with the 1st Dynasty pharaoh Hor-Aha. *(Translator.)*

[2] Deben: an ancient Egyptian unit of weight. During the New Kingdom, it was often used to denote the
value of goods by comparing their worth to that of a weight of a reference metal, usually copper or silver.
Prus calls the deben an *uten*; by the 20th century, that common 19th-century mis-transliteration was
corrected to *deben*. *(Translator.)*

"Hush! ... Hush! ... We'll talk about these things again another time."

Despite the sand, the military engines, each harnessed to a pair of oxen, rolled faster in the desert than they had on the highway. Beside the first one walked Ennana, perplexed as to why the Minister had relieved him of the advance guard. Did the Minister mean to entrust him with a higher post?

Looking thus to a new career, or perhaps to quell the misgivings that shook his heart, he grabbed a rod and, where the sand was particularly deep, braced the ballista or shouted encouragement to the Greeks. They, however, paid little attention to him.

The retinue had been moving a good half-hour down the winding ravine of bare, steep walls when the advance guard again stopped. Here the ravine intersected another ravine, down which ran a fairly wide canal.

A messenger, sent to the Minister with word of the obstacle, brought back instructions to immediately fill in the canal.

About a hundred Greek soldiers set to work with pickaxes and shovels. Some knocked stones off the rockface; others threw them into the canal and heaped them over with sand.

Suddenly from the ravine there emerged a man with a hoe shaped like a stork's neck and beak. It was an Egyptian peasant, old, quite naked.[3] For a moment, in utmost astonishment, he watched the work of the soldiers, then suddenly jumped into their midst, crying:

"Pagans, what are you doing? That's a canal!"

"How dare you curse at warriors of His Holiness?" demanded Ennana, now present there.

"I see you must be great and an Egyptian," replied the peasant, "so I will answer you that this canal belongs to a powerful lord: he is steward to the scribe to the fan-bearer to His Eminence the Nomarch of Memphis. So beware lest you come to grief!"

"Carry on," said Ennana in a patronizing tone to the Greek soldiers, who had begun scrutinizing the peasant. They did not understand his speech but were intrigued by the tone.

"They keep on filling!" said the peasant in rising terror. "Woe to you bastards!" he cried, hurling himself at one of them with his hoe.

The Greek wrested it from the peasant and punched him in the teeth, bloodying his mouth. Then he resumed heaping sand.

Dazed by the blow, the peasant lost courage and pleaded:

"I myself dug this canal for ten years, by nights and on holidays! Our lord promised that if I managed to get water into this little valley, he would let me work it, would let me keep a fifth of the harvest, and would give me freedom! Do you hear? ... Freedom for me and my three children, O gods ..."

He lifted his hands and turned again to Ennana:

"They don't understand me, these bearded ones from across the sea, the progeny of

---

[3] "quite [or "completely"—*zupełnie*] naked": Here, as elsewhere in this novel, when Prus describes a character as "naked," it is not always clear the character is actually stark naked. In Chapter 1, Prus speaks of "naked copper-colored men in only a short skirt about their hips and a cap on their heads." In *Pharaoh*, "naked" seems generally to mean "*half*-naked." *(Translator.)*

dogs, the brothers of the Phoenicians and Jews. But you will hear me. For ten years, when others went to the fair or to dances or holy processions, I stole out to this inhospitable ravine. I didn't visit my mother's grave but dug; I forgot the dead in order to give my children and myself freedom and land, if only for a day before I died.

"Witness, O gods, how many times night overtook me here... how many times I heard here the mournful voices of hyenas and saw the green eyes of wolves. But I didn't flee, for where would I flee, wretch that I am, when some terror lurked on every path, and in this canal freedom held me by the legs? Once, around that bend, a lion, the pharaoh of all the beasts, came toward me. My hoe fell from my hand. So I knelt before him and said these words, as you see me: 'Lord, you wouldn't want to eat me... I'm only a slave!'

"The predatory lion pitied me; the wolf passed me by; even the treacherous bats spared my poor head; and you, an Egyptian..."

The peasant fell silent, having marked the approaching retinue of Minister Herhor. He could tell from the fan that it must be someone great; and from the leopard skin, a priest. He ran over, knelt, and struck the sand with his head.

"What do you want, man?" asked His Eminence.

"Light of the sun, hear me!" cried the peasant. "May there be no moans in your chamber, and may ill-fortune not follow you! May your deeds not founder, and may the current not sweep you away when you sail for the opposite bank of the Nile..."

"I ask, what do you want?" repeated the Minister.

"Good lord," said the peasant, "guide without guile who vanquishes falsehood and creates truth... who is father to the orphan, husband to the widow, apron to him who is motherless. Let me proclaim your name as the law in the land. Come to the word of my lips. Hear and do justice, O noblest of the noble."[4]

"He doesn't want the ditch filled in," said Ennana.

The Minister shrugged and moved on toward the canal, across which a plank had been thrown. The desperate peasant grabbed the Minister's legs.

"Away with *this!*" shouted His Eminence, recoiling as from a viper.

The scribe Pentuer averted his head, his lean face ashen. But Ennana grabbed the peasant by the scruff of the neck and, unable to detach him from the Minister's legs, called some soldiers. A moment later His Eminence, set free, crossed to the other side of the ditch, while soldiers carried the peasant nearly in the air to the rear of the marching detachment. They gave him several dozen punches; and noncommissioned officers, always armed with canes, counted off several dozen blows on him and finally dumped him at the entrance to the ravine.

The battered, bloodied, above all terrified wretch sat awhile in the sand, rubbed his eyes, then suddenly springing up, ran for the highway, moaning:

"Earth, swallow me up!... I curse the day I beheld light, and the night they said: 'a man is born.' In the cloak of justice there's not even a shred for slaves. And the very gods won't look on a creature with hands for work, a mouth only for weeping, and a back for canes...

---

[4] The peasant's prattle is authentic. *(Author.)* The peasant's last two paragraphs, beginning "Light of the sun, hear me!" are taken from a Middle Kingdom text, "The Complaints of the Peasant." *(Translator.)*

Death, reduce my body to ashes so that on the Fields of Osiris[5] I won't be born once more a slave."

---

[5] Fields of Osiris: The god Osiris was usually identified as the deity of the afterlife, of the underworld, and of the dead. In *The Book of the Dead*, the deceased were taken into the presence of Osiris, who was confined to the *Duat* (also known as the *Akert*, the *Amenti*, the *Neter-khertet*, etc.), the realm of Osiris and the region through which the sun god Ra traveled from west to east during the night and where he battled Apep, the deification of darkness and chaos. *The Book of the Dead* also depicted the deceased as living on in the "Field of Reeds," a lush paradisiac likeness of the Egypt of the living. *(Translator.)*

CHAPTER 3

Panting with anger, Prince Ramses tore up the hill, followed by Thutmose. The dandy's wig had twisted round; his artificial beard had dropped off, so he carried it in his hands. Despite fatigue, he would have been palefaced but for the layer of rouge.

At last the Prince stopped at the summit. They heard, below in the ravine, the hubbub of the soldiery and the clatter of rolling ballistas; before them stretched the land of Goshen, bathed in streams of sunlight. It seemed to be not earth but a golden cloud on which the fancy painted a landscape in emeralds, silver, rubies, pearls, and topazes.

The Crown Prince extended his hand. "Look," he called to Thutmose, "that is to be my land; and this, my army. There the highest buildings are the palaces of the priests; and here the highest commander of the armies is a priest! ... Isn't it insufferable?"

"It's always been that way," said Thutmose, looking about apprehensively.

"That's a lie! I know this country's history that is kept from all of you. The only army commanders, and masters of the officials, used to be the pharaohs, or at least the more energetic among them. Those rulers didn't pass their days praying and making offerings, but ruling the Kingdom."

"If that is His Holiness' will ..." said Thutmose.

"It's not my father's will that the nomarchs should rule as they please in their capitals, or that the Ethiopian[1] viceroy should practically consider himself the equal of the king of kings. And it can't be my father's will that his army should go around two golden beetles because the minister of war is a priest."

"He's a great warrior!" whispered the increasingly frightened Thutmose.

"Some warrior! ... Because he beat a handful of Libyan bandits who should have fled at just the sight of Egyptian soldiers' tunics? But look what our neighbors are doing. Israel delays her tribute and pays less and less. The wily Phoenician each year withdraws several ships from our fleet. We have to keep a great army in the east against the Hittites, while around Babylon and Nineveh a movement is brewing which you can smell throughout Mesopotamia.

---

[1] Ethiopia: Prus is referring to Nubia, part of which Egypt controlled and exploited for its gold. He uses the term *Ethiopia* after authors including the 5th century BCE Greek historian Herodotus, who applied it to all the lands south of Egypt, including modern Sudan (which encompassed southern Nubia) and modern Ethiopia. *(Translator.)*

"And what is the upshot of government by the priests? While my great-grandfather had a hundred thousand talents'[2] annual income and an army of a hundred sixty thousand men, my father has barely fifty thousand talents and an army of a hundred twenty thousand.

"And what an army it is! If it weren't for the Greek corps, which keeps them in order as a sheepdog keeps sheep in order, Egyptian soldiers would already be minding only the priests, and the pharaoh would drop to the status of a wretched nomarch."

"How do you know this? Where do you get these ideas?" asked Thutmose.

"Don't I come from a line of priests? They taught me before I became crown prince. Oh, when I become pharaoh after my father, may he live forever, I'll set my bronze-sandaled foot on their necks... First thing, I'll reach into their treasuries, which have always been glutted but began swelling under Ramses the Great and today are so bloated with gold that you can't see the pharaoh's treasury in back of them."[3]

"Alas!" sighed Thutmose. "Your plans would buckle this hill, if it could hear and understand. Where are your forces...helpers...soldiers?... The whole nation will stand against you, led by a powerful class. And who's behind you?"

The Prince mused. "The army ..."

"Much of it will go with the priests."

"The Greek corps ..."

"A barrel of water in the Nile."

"The officials ..."

"Half of them belong to the priesthood."

Ramses shook his head sadly and fell silent.

From the summit, by a bare rocky slope, they descended to the other side of the hill. Suddenly Thutmose, who had moved a little ahead, exclaimed:

"Is there a spell on my eyes? Look, Ramses! There's a second Egypt tucked away among these rocks."

"It must be some farm of the priests that pays no taxes," said the Prince bitterly.

At their feet, in the depths, lay a fertile fork-shaped valley whose prong ends were hidden among the rocks. Visible at one prong were several servants' huts and the handsome house of the owner or steward. Here grew palms, grapevines, olive trees, fig trees with aerial roots, cypresses, even young baobabs. Down the middle flowed a stream, and visible every few hundred paces on the hillsides were small ponds.

Descending into vineyards full of ripe grapes, they heard a woman's voice calling, or rather intoning wistfully:

"Where are you, my little chicken, speak up, where are you, dearest? You ran away from me, though I give you water and feed you pure grain, to the envy of the slaves... Where are you, speak up! Mind, night will overtake you and you won't find your way home, where everyone serves you; or a red hawk will fly in from the desert and rip out your heart. Then in vain will you call to your mistress, as I'm calling you ... Oh, speak up or I'll get angry and leave, and you'll have to return on foot."

---

[2] Talent: a Greek unit of weight, and later of currency. Prus' use of the term *talent* in *Pharaoh* is an anachronism. *(Translator.)*

[3] New Kingdom pharaohs made such great donations to the temples of the gods, especially Amon, that the priesthood became a powerful economic and political rival to the pharaohs and eventually supplanted them. *(Translator.)*

The singing was approaching the travelers. The singer was a few steps from them when Thutmose poked his head through the bushes and cried: "Look, Ramses, what a gorgeous girl!"

Instead of looking, the Prince leapt onto the path and blocked the singer's way. She was indeed a beautiful girl, with Greek facial features and an ivory complexion. Showing beneath the veil on her head was a great mass of black hair twisted into a knot. She wore a trailing white gown which she lifted on one side with her hand; visible beneath the diaphanous garment were maidenly breasts shaped like apples.[4]

"Who are you, girl?" cried Ramses. Gone was his frown; his eyes sparkled.

"Oh, Jehovah! ... Father!" she shouted, terrified, stopping motionless on the path. Slowly, however, she calmed, and her velvety eyes took on her wonted expression of mild sadness.

"How did you get here?" she asked Ramses in a slightly tremulous voice. "I see you're a soldier, and soldiers aren't allowed here."

"Why not?"

"Because this land belongs to the great Lord Sezofris."

"Oh, my!" smiled Ramses.

"Don't laugh, for you'll soon turn pale. Lord Sezofris is scribe to Lord Khaires, who is fan-bearer to His Eminence the Nomarch of Memphis. My father saw him and prostrated[5] himself on his face before him."

"Oh, my, my!" laughed Ramses.

"Your words are very audacious," frowned the girl. "If you didn't have a kindly face, I would take you for a Greek mercenary or a bandit."

"He's not one yet, but someday he may be the greatest bandit the earth has carried," said the elegant Thutmose, adjusting his wig.

"And you must be a dancer," replied the emboldened girl. "Oh! In fact, I'm sure I saw you at the fair in Pi-Bailos, charming snakes."

The two young men were now in excellent humor.

"And who are you?" Ramses asked the girl, taking her hand, which she withdrew.

"Don't be so bold. I'm Sara,[6] daughter of Gideon,[7] the steward of the farm."

"A Jewess?" said Ramses, a shadow passing over his face.

"What's it matter! What's it matter!" cried Thutmose. "Do you think Jewesses are less sweet than Egyptian girls? They're only more modest and more difficult, which lends their love an extraordinary charm."

"So you're pagans," said Sara with dignity. "Rest if you're tired, pluck yourselves some grapes, and go with God. Our servants don't take kindly to such guests."

---

[4] This apple simile will appear three decades later in Frank Harris' *My Life and Loves* (1922-27). *(Translator.)*

[5] Prostration is the placement of the body in a reverentially or submissively prone position. It is distinguished from bowing or kneeling by involving a part of the body above the knee touching the ground, especially the hands. Characters in *Pharaoh* prostrate themselves by touching the ground with their face, chest, or stomach (belly). *(Translator.)*

[6] Sara (also spelled *Sarah*): name borrowed from the biblical *Book of Genesis:* Sara was the wife of Abraham, and the mother of Isaac. Modern scholars doubt the historicity of the *Genesis* figures. *(Translator.)*

[7] Gideon (also written *Gedeon*, as Prus spells it): name borrowed from a biblical *Old Testament* Jewish prophet and military leader who defeated the Midianites. *(Translator.)*

She was about to leave, but Ramses detained her. "Wait... I like you, and you can't leave us like that."

"An evil spirit has possessed you. No one in this valley would dare speak to me like that," said Sara indignantly.

"You see," broke in Thutmose, "this youngster is an officer in the priestly regiment of Ptah[8] and is scribe to the scribe to the fan-bearer to the fan-bearer to the Nomarch of Am-Khent."[9]

"Certainly he must be an officer," said Sara, contemplating Ramses. "Maybe he is himself a great lord," she added, putting a finger to her lips.

"Whatever I am, your beauty surpasses my station," replied Ramses passionately. "Tell me," he said suddenly, "is it true you... eat pork?"[10]

Sara looked at him, offended, and Thutmose broke in: "How obvious you don't know Jewesses! Be informed, then, that a Jew would rather die than eat pigmeat, which I myself don't find so bad."

"But you kill cats?"[11] persisted Ramses, squeezing Sara's hands and gazing into her eyes.

"That, too, is a fable—a vile fable!" cried Thutmose. "You could have asked me about these things instead of talking nonsense. After all, I've had three Jewish mistresses."

"Before, you spoke the truth; but now you're lying," said Sara. "A Jewess won't be anyone's mistress!" she added proudly.

"Not even to the scribe to the fan-bearer to the Memphis nomarch?"[12] taunted Thutmose.

"No."

"Not even to the fan-bearer?"

Sara hesitated but replied: "No."

"Then she wouldn't be the Nomarch's mistress?"

The girl was lost for words. Bewildered, she looked by turns at the two young men; her lips trembled, and her eyes welled with tears.

"Who are you?" she asked, frightened. "You came down from the hills like travelers who want water and bread. But you speak to me like the greatest lords... Who are you? Your sword," she turned to Ramses, "is set with emeralds, and on your neck is a chain of such workmanship as our gracious Lord Sezofris doesn't have in his treasury."

"Listen, do you like me?" asked Ramses urgently, squeezing her hand and gazing tenderly into her eyes.

"You're handsome as the angel Gabriel, but I'm afraid of you because I don't know who you are."

Suddenly, beyond the hills, a trumpet sounded.

---

[8]Ptah was one of the triad of Memphis gods: he was the husband of Sekhmet, and the father of Nefertum. From the Middle Kingdom on, Ptah was one of the five major Egyptian gods, along with Ra, Isis, Osiris, and Amon. (Translator.)

[9]Am-Khent: the 18th Nome of Lower Egypt. Prus calls it *Habu*. (Translator.)

[10]Consumption of pork is prohibited by Jewish dietary law. (Translator.)

[11]Cats, for their hunting of destructive rodents, were among animals revered by Egyptians. (Translator.)

[12]Memphis nomarch: the nomarch of Aneb-Hetch, the 1st Nome of Lower Egypt, whose capital was Memphis. (Translator.)

"They're calling you," cried Thutmose.

"What if I were as great a lord as your Sezofris?" asked the Prince.

"You may be," whispered Sara.

"What if I were fan-bearer to the Nomarch of Memphis?"

"You may be even that great."

Somewhere on the hill, another trumpet sounded.

"Let's go, Ramses!" urged the terrified Thutmose.

"What if I were ... Crown Prince, would you come to me, girl?" asked the Prince.

"Oh, Jehovah!" shouted Sara, falling to her knees.

Now, at various points, trumpets were sounding a frantic tattoo.

"Let's go!" called Thutmose desperately. "Don't you hear the alarm in camp?"

The Prince quickly took the chain from round his neck and threw it on Sara's. "Give this to your father," he said, "I'm buying you from him. Be well."

He kissed her lips passionately, and she embraced his legs. He broke away, ran off a couple of steps, returned and again caressed her beautiful face and raven hair with kisses, deaf to the impatient calls of the army.

"In the name of His Holiness the Pharaoh I call on you, come with me!" shouted Thutmose, grabbing the Prince's arm.

They ran toward the trumpet sounds. At moments, Ramses staggered as if drunk and turned his head around. At last they began climbing the hill.

"And this man," thought Thutmose, "wants to fight the priests!"

CHAPTER 4

The Crown Prince and his companion ran a quarter-hour up the rocky crest of the hill, hearing ever closer the trumpets, which sounded the alarm more and more urgently. At last they reached a vantage that commanded the whole vicinity.

On the left stretched the highway, visible beyond which was Pi-Bailos, the Successor's regiments standing outside the city, and a huge cloud of dust rising above the opponent advancing from the east.

On the right gaped the wide ravine down which the Greek regiment had been drawing the military engines. Near the highway, the ravine merged with a second, wider one which came out of the desert.

At that spot, something remarkable was happening. The Greeks and engines stood idle near the junction of the ravines; at the junction itself, between the highway and the Successor's staff, stretched four dense ranks of another army, like four fences abristle with glittering spears.

Despite the steep way, the Prince dashed down to his detachment, where the Minister of War stood, surrounded by officers.

"What's going on?" he demanded. "Why do you sound alarm instead of marching?"

"We're cut off," said Herhor.

"Who? ... By whom? "

"Our detachment, by three regiments of Nitager's which have come out of the desert."

"That's the enemy, near the highway?"

"That is invincible Nitager himself."

The Successor seemed to go mad. His mouth twisted; his eyes bulged in their orbits. He drew his sword, ran to the Greeks, and shouted raspily: "Follow me against those who've blocked our way!"

"Live forever, Iry-pat!" cried Patroklos, likewise drawing his sword. He addressed his men: "Forward, descendants of Achilles! Let's show the Egyptian cowherds that we're not to be stopped!"

Trumpets sounded attack. Four short but erect ranks went forward, and there rose a cloud of dust and a cheer for Ramses.

In a couple of minutes, the Greeks found themselves before the Egyptian regiments— and wavered.

"Forward!" cried the Successor, running, sword in hand.

The Greeks levelled their spears. A commotion arose in the opposing ranks ... and their spears likewise levelled.

"Who are you madmen?" boomed a voice on the opposed side.

"The Crown Prince!" answered Patroklos.

A moment's silence.

"Open up!" said the same powerful voice as before.

The regiments of the Eastern Army slowly opened like heavy twin gates, and the Greek detachment passed through.

The Crown Prince was approached by a grizzled warrior in gold helmet and armor who bowed low and said: "You've won, Iry-pat. Only a great commander gets himself out of trouble that way."

"Nitager, the most valiant of the valiant!" cried the Prince.

Just then they were approached by the Minister of War, who had heard the exchange and said tartly:

"What if on your side there had been a commander as headstrong as the Iry-pat, how would we have ended the maneuvers then?"

"Oh, leave the young warrior alone!" replied Nitager. "Isn't it enough for you that he showed a lion's claws, as befits a scion of pharaohs?"

Hearing the turns the conversation was taking, Thutmose asked Nitager: "How came you to be here, General, when your main forces are in front of our army?"

"I knew how ineptly the staff was marching from Memphis while the Crown Prince was gathering his regiments at Pi-Bailos. So, for a lark, I wanted to surprise you lordlings. Alas, the Crown Prince turned up here and spoiled my plans. Always act like that, Ramses—with real enemies, of course."

"And if, as today, he happens on a force three times stronger than his own?" asked Herhor.

"Daring counts for more than strength," answered the old commander. "An elephant is fifty times stronger than man but submits to him or dies at his hand."

Herhor kept his peace.

The maneuvers were declared over. The Successor rode with the Minister and commanders to the troops outside Pi-Bailos, greeted Nitager's veterans, and took leave of his own regiments, ordering them east and wishing them godspeed. Next, surrounded by a great suite, he set out on the highway for Memphis through festively dressed crowds from the land of Goshen which greeted the victor with green branches.

When the highway turned into the desert, the crowd thinned; and when they approached the spot where the Successor's staff had entered the ravine because of the scarabs, there was no one on the highway.

Ramses beckoned to Thutmose, indicated a bald hill, and whispered: "You shall go to Sara's."

"Very good."

"And you'll tell her father I'm giving him a farm outside Memphis."

"Very good. You'll have her the day after tomorrow."

After this exchange, Thutmose fell back to the troops marching after the suite and disappeared.

Nearly opposite the ravine into which the military engines had rolled that morning, a dozen paces beyond the highway, grew a small but old tamarind tree. There the advance guard preceding the Prince's suite had halted.

"Are we meeting with more scarabs?" the Crown Prince laughingly asked the Minister.

"We shall see," replied Herhor.

See they did: from the frail tree hung a nearly naked man.

"What's this?" exclaimed the Crown Prince.

Aides ran up to the tree and found that the man was the old peasant whose canal the army had filled in.

"He did well to hang himself," shouted Ennana among the officers. "Would you believe it, that wretched slave dared grab His Eminence the Minister by the legs!"

Hearing this, Ramses stopped his horse, dismounted, and approached the baleful tree.

The peasant hung with his head drawn forward, mouth agape, palms turned to the viewers, horror in his eyes. He looked like a man who wants to say something but whose voice has failed.

"Poor man," sighed the Prince compassionately.

Returning to the suite, he asked to be told the peasant's story, then long rode in silence.

In his mind's eye he still saw the suicide, and in his heart he felt that a great wrong had been done to the despised slave. So immense a wrong that even he, the Pharaoh's son and Successor, might well ponder it.

The heat was unbearable; the dust dried the lips and stung the eyes of men and beasts. The detachment made a brief stop, and Nitager concluded his conversation with the Minister.

"My officers," said the old commander, "don't look down at their feet but in front of them. And maybe that's why no enemy has ever taken me by surprise."

"That reminds me, Eminence, I have some debts to discharge," replied Herhor, and he bade the officers and men at hand to assemble.

"And now," said the Minister, "call Ennana."

The amulet-bedecked officer appeared promptly, as if he had long awaited this call. His face was a picture of exultation barely checked by humility.

Seeing Ennana before him, Herhor began: "By the will of His Holiness, with the conclusion of the maneuvers, supreme military authority passes back into my hands."

Those present bowed their heads.

"This authority, it behooves me to use above all for the dispensing of justice."

The officers glanced at one another.

"Ennana," continued the Minister, "I know that you have always been one of the most diligent officers."

"Truth speaks with Your Eminence's lips," said Ennana. "As the palm awaits the dew, so I await the orders of my superiors. When I receive them not, I am like an orphan seeking his way in the desert."

Nitager's battle-scarred officers marveled at Ennana's smooth eloquence and thought: "He will be elevated above others!"

"Ennana," said the Minister, "you are not only diligent but pious; not only pious but vigilant as the ibis at the water. The gods have bestowed great blessings on you: they have given you the prudence of the serpent and the vision of the hawk."

"Pure truth flows from Your Eminence's lips," broke in Ennana. "But for my remarkable vision, I would not have spied the two sacred scarabs."

"Yes," interrupted the Minister, "and you would not have preserved our camp from sacrilege. For this deed, worthy of the most pious Egyptian, I give you ..."

The Minister took from his finger a gold ring.

"I give you this ring with the name of the goddess Mut,[1] whose grace and prudence, if you deserve it, will accompany you to the end of your earthly journey."

His Eminence handed the ring to Ennana, and those present raised a great cheer in honor of the Pharaoh and rattled their weapons.

Since the Minister did not move, Ennana likewise stood, looking him smartly in the eye like a faithful dog that, having received a morsel from its master's hand, still wags its tail and waits.

"And now, Ennana," resumed the Minister, "confess why you did not say where the Crown Prince went while the troops were marching toilsomely through the ravine. You committed a misdeed, for we had to trumpet alarm in the vicinity of the enemy."

"The gods are my witness that I knew nothing about His Eminence the Prince," said the surprised Ennana.

Herhor shook his head. "It can't be that a man endowed with vision such as yours, who spies sacred scarabs in the sand at several dozen paces, failed to notice so great a person as the Crown Prince."

"Truly I didn't see him!" said Ennana, beating his chest. "Anyway, no one told me to watch the Prince."

"Did I not relieve you of the advance guard? Did I give you another assignment?" asked the Minister. "You were perfectly free, precisely like a man called on to monitor important matters. And did you acquit yourself of this assignment? For a like mistake in wartime, you would have to die."

The hapless officer turned pale.

"But I have a father's heart for you, Ennana," said His Eminence, "and bearing in mind the great service you rendered the army in spying the symbols of the sacred sun, the scarabs, I am assigning you, not as a stern minister but as a mild priest, a very small penalty. You shall receive fifty strokes."

"Your Eminence ..."

"Ennana, you knew how to be happy; now be manly and accept this petty admonishment, as becomes an officer in the army of His Holiness."

Hardly had His Eminence Herhor finished, ranking officers laid Ennana in a convenient spot at the roadside. Then one of them straddled his neck, another his legs, and two others counted off fifty cane strokes on his bared flesh.

The intrepid warrior uttered nary a groan; indeed, he hummed a soldiers' song, and at the end of the proceeding he attempted to rise by himself. But his sore legs refused him obedience. He fell face down in the sand and had to be driven to Memphis in a two-wheeled cart, lying in which and smiling at the soldiers, he reflected that Lower Egypt's wind did not shift as quickly as did fortune in the life of a poor officer!

When after the brief stop the Successor's retinue set out again, His Eminence Herhor

---

[1] Mut was a mother goddess whose name meant "mother." She was a primal deity associated with the waters from which everything sprang and was depicted as a woman wearing the double crown of the kings of Egypt. The country's rulers fostered her worship in order, by association, to emphasize their own right to rule. Mut's many titles included "World-Mother," "Eye of Ra," "Queen of the Goddesses," "Lady of Heaven," "Mother of the Gods," and "She Who Gives Birth, but Was Herself Not Born of Any." (Translator.)

mounted a horse and, riding alongside His Eminence Nitager, conversed with him in an undertone about the Asiatic peoples, particularly about the awakening of Assyria.

The Minister's two servants, the aide with the fan and the scribe Pentuer, likewise struck up a conversation.

"What do you think of Ennana's experience?" asked the aide.

"What do you think of the peasant who hanged himself?" said the scribe.

"I daresay for the peasant this day is the best, and the rope around his neck the softest, that he's known in his life," said the aide. "I also think that from now on Ennana will be watching the Successor very closely."

"You're mistaken," said Pentuer. "Henceforth Ennana will never spot another scarab, were it as big as an ox. As for the peasant, don't you think he must have been badly off, very badly off ... very badly off in the holy land of Egypt?"

"You don't know peasants, that's why you say that."

"Who knows them better?" said the scribe glumly. "Didn't I grow up among them? Didn't I watch my father water the soil, clear the canals, sow, harvest—above all, pay taxes? Oh, you don't know the lot of the Egyptian peasant!"

"But I know the foreigner's," answered the aide. "A forbear of mine was a Hyksos[2] grandee but stayed on here because he'd grown attached to this land. And what will you say: Not only was his estate confiscated, but I still bear the stigma of my descent! You see what I sometimes endure from native Egyptians, though I have a considerable station. So how am I to pity the Egyptian peasant who sees my yellowish complexion and mutters under his breath: 'Pagan! Foreigner!' The peasant is neither pagan nor foreigner."

"Only slave," said the scribe. "A slave whom they marry, divorce, beat, sell, sometimes murder, and always require to work, promising that in the next world as well he will be a slave."

The aide shrugged. "You're strange, if so wise!" he said. "You know we all occupy some station, more or less lowly, where we must work. Does it bother you that you're not pharaoh and that your grave won't be a pyramid? You don't even think about it, because you know that's the order of the world. Everyone fulfills his duties: the ox plows, the donkey carries travelers, I fan His Eminence, you remember and think for him, and the peasant cultivates the soil and pays taxes. What's it to us if a certain bull is born Apis and is revered, and a certain man is born pharaoh or nomarch?"

"That peasant's work of ten years was destroyed," whispered Pentuer.

"Doesn't the Minister destroy your work?" asked the aide. "Who knows that it's you who rule the Kingdom, not His Eminence Herhor?"

"You're mistaken," said the scribe, "he rules. He has the power, the will ... I, only information. Anyway, they don't beat you or me as they did that peasant."

"But they did beat Ennana, and we too can get it. So we should be manly and happy in the stations allotted to us. Especially since, as you know, our spirit the immortal *ka*, in the course of its cleansing enters higher planes in order to dissolve, after thousands or millions of years, along with the souls of pharaohs and slaves, and even with gods, into the nameless, almighty Father of Life."

---

[2] Hyksos: The Hyksos ascendancy in Egypt had ended over four and a half centuries before *Pharaoh*'s present time. *(Translator.)*

"You talk like a priest," said Pentuer bitterly. "Rather I should have that peace! But instead I have a pain in my soul, for I feel the misery of millions."

"Who asks you to?"

"My eyes and heart. Like a valley between hills, my heart can't be still when it hears a cry but answers with an echo."

"I tell you, Pentuer, you think too much about dangerous things. You can't with impunity wander the cliffs of the Eastern Hills, where you'll fall at any moment; or wander the Western Desert, where hungry lions prowl and the furious khamsin[3] springs up."

Meanwhile valiant Ennana, riding in the cart, which only renewed his pain, called for food and drink in order to show his fortitude. When he had consumed a dry cake rubbed with garlic and imbibed sour beer from a slender jug, he asked the driver to whisk the flies from his injured flesh with a branch.

Lying prostrate on sacks and bundles in the creaking cart, poor Ennana sang a plaint on the hard lot of a junior officer:

"How can you say: better be an officer than a scribe? Come see my livid welts and broken flesh, and I'll tell you the story of a tormented officer.

"As a child I was brought to the barracks. For breakfast I got a fist in the belly to make my head swim; for midday meal, a fist to the eyes; and by evening my head was covered in wounds and all but split.

"Come, I'll tell you how I traveled to Syria. Bread and water I bore on my shoulder, burdened like a donkey. My neck was stiff as a donkey's, and my back was bowed. I drank stinking water, and in the face of the enemy I was like a trapped bird.

"I returned to Egypt, but here I'm as worm-eaten wood. For the least thing, they lay me on the ground and beat me like a book; I'm battered and bruised from the canes. I am ill, they must drive me in a cart, and meanwhile my servant makes off with my cloak ...

"Therefore, O scribe, change your opinion about the good fortune of an officer!"[4]

Thus sang brave Ennana,[5] and his tearful song has outlived the Egyptian Kingdom.

---

[3] The *khamsin* (named after the Arabic word for "fifty") is a hot, dry, dust- and sand-laden south wind that blows in Egypt intermittently, a few hours at a time, over a period of some fifty days from late March through early May. *(Translator.)*

[4] Authentic. *(Author.)* The text, available in Aylward M. Blackman's 1927 English translation of Adolf Erman's 1923 German version, urges schoolboys not to become soldiers. As here presented by Prus, several fragments are rearranged from their original order, and some passages appear in somewhat different interpretation. *(Translator.)*

[5] Ennana: name of the schoolboy who, when copying out the foregoing text, inserted his own name into the final paragraph: "Therefore, O scribe *Ennana* ..." Prus calls the schoolboy *Eunana*. *(Translator.)*

CHAPTER 5

As the Successor's retinue neared Memphis, the sun was sinking into the west and a wind saturated with cool moisture was springing up from the countless canals and the distant sea. The highway approached fertile areas again, and unbroken ranks of people could be seen working in the fields and thickets, though the peaks of the hills were already aflame and a rosy glow was upon the desert.

Ramses halted and turned his horse about. His retinue at once surrounded him, the higher commanders rode up, and the ranks of the marching regiments approached slowly with even step.

In the purple rays of the setting sun, the Prince looked like a god. The soldiers regarded him with pride and affection; the commanders, with admiration.

He lifted his hand, all became still, and he spoke:

"Distinguished commanders, gallant officers, obedient soldiers! Today the gods have given me the pleasure of commanding you. My princely heart overflows with joy. And since I would have you commanders, officers, and soldiers always share in my good fortune, I am allotting a drachma[1] for each soldier who has gone east and for each soldier who is returning with us from the eastern border. Additionally, a drachma apiece for the Greek soldiers who today, under my command, opened a way for us out of the ravine—and a drachma apiece for the soldiers of His Eminence Nitager's regiments who sought to cut us off from the highway!"

The troops were jubilant. "Bless you, our commander! Bless you, Successor of the Pharaoh, may he live forever!" called the soldiers, the Greeks loudest.

The Prince continued:

"For division among the junior officers of my army and His Eminence Nitager's, I am allotting five talents.[2] Finally, to be divided among His Eminence the Minister and the principal commanders, I am allotting ten talents."

"I decline my share in favor of the army," said Herhor.

"Bless you, Successor! Bless you, Minister!" called the officers and soldiers.

The red disk of the sun had touched the sands of the Western Desert. Ramses took leave of the army and galloped off for Memphis, while His Eminence Herhor, amid the jubilant cheers, climbed into his litter and likewise had himself carried ahead of the marching detachments.

---

[1] Drachma: a Greek coin. Its use in *Pharaoh* is an anatopism. *(Translator.)*

[2] Talent: a Greek unit of weight, and later of currency. Its use in *Pharaoh* is an anatopism. *(Translator.)*

When they had moved ahead so that the individual voices had merged into a single great murmur like that of a waterfall, the Minister leaned over to the scribe Pentuer and asked: "Do you remember everything?"

"Yes, Eminence."

"Your memory is like the granite on which we record history, and your learning is like the Nile, which floods and fertilizes everything," said the Minister. "In addition, the gods have endowed you with the greatest of all virtues—a prudent humility."

The scribe kept his peace.

"So you, better than others, can gauge the conduct and judgment of the Crown Prince, may he live forever."

The Minister paused. It was not his wont to speak this much.

"Tell me then, Pentuer, and make a note of this: Is it proper for the Crown Prince to pronounce his will before the army? Only the pharaoh may do so, or a traitor ... or a light-minded youth who commits rash deeds as readily as he utters impious words."

The sun set, and a moment later a starry night fell. Over the countless canals of Lower Egypt there began to thicken a silvery mist which the gentle wind carried even into the desert, cooling the weary soldiers and satiating the vegetation fairly perishing of thirst.

"Or tell me, Pentuer," continued the Minister, "and look into this: Where will the Successor get twenty talents to keep the promise he so improvidently made the army today? Though, wherever he gets the money, it seems to me—and doubtless also to you—a dangerous thing for the Successor to be making gifts to the army on the very day when His Holiness does not have pay for Nitager's regiments returning from the east. I do not ask your opinion on this, because I know it, as you know my most private thoughts. I only ask you to remember what you have seen in order to recount it to the Priestly College."

"Will it be convoked soon?" asked Pentuer.

"There's no reason to yet. I'll first try to settle the unruly youngster with the help of His Holiness' fatherly hand. It would be a shame to lose the boy, for he has great abilities and the energy of a south wind. But if, instead of blowing away Egypt's enemies, the wind starts flattening her wheat and uprooting her palms!"

The Minister fell silent, and his retinue was drowned in a dark avenue of trees leading to Memphis.

Meanwhile Ramses was arriving at the Pharaoh's palace.

The edifice stood on a hill outside the city, within a park. There grew here singular trees: baobabs from the south; cedars, pines, and oaks from the north. Thanks to the gardener's art, they lived several dozen years and attained considerable heights.

A shady avenue led from below to a gate the height of a three-story building. To either side of the gate rose a massive tower-like structure in the form of a truncated pyramid forty paces wide, five stories high. In the night, they looked like two huge tents of sandstone. These curious structures had small square windows on the ground floor and stories, and flat roofs. From the top of one pyramid, the watch was observing the earth; from the other, the priest on duty was observing the stars.

To right and left of the towers, called pylons,[3] stretched walls, or rather long one-story buildings with narrow windows and flat roofs, on which paced sentries. On either side of the main gate sat a statue whose head reached the first floor; at the statues' feet paced more sentries.

When the Prince neared the palace, accompanied by several riders, a sentry recognized him in spite of the dark. A moment later, a court official in a white skirt, dark cape, and hood-sized wig ran out of a pylon tower.

"Is the palace closed?" asked the Prince.

"Yes, Eminence," replied the official. "His Holiness is dressing the gods for sleep."

"What will he be doing afterward?"

"He is pleased to receive Minister of War Herhor."

"And then?"

"Later His Holiness will watch a ballet in the great hall, and next he will bathe and say evening prayers."

"I wasn't to be received?" asked the Crown Prince.

"Tomorrow after the council of war."

"What are the queens doing?"

"The first queen is praying in her late son's room, and Her Eminence your mother is receiving a Phoenician envoy who has brought her gifts from the women of Tyre."

"Are there also girls?"

"I understand there are several. Each wears ten talents' worth of valuables."

"Who is prowling around down there with torches?" said the Prince, pointing to the bottom of the park.

"They are taking Your Eminence's brother down from a tree where he's been sitting since noon."

"He won't come down?"

"He will now, because the first queen's fool went and promised to take him to a tavern where the openers of dead bodies[4] drink."

"Have you heard anything about today's maneuvers?"

"They said at the ministry that the staff got cut off from the main corps."

"What else?"

The official hesitated.

"Tell me what you heard."

"We also heard that, because of that, Your Eminence had a certain officer given five hundred cane strokes, and the guide hanged."

"All lies!" said one of the Successor's aides under his breath.

"The soldiers too say that these must be lies," said the official more boldly.

The Successor turned his horse about and rode down to the lower part of the park, to his villa. This was a one-story wooden pavilion in the form of a great cube with two verandas, a

---

[3] Prus models the gate to the Pharaoh's palace after the gates to Egyptian temples. A *pylon* (Greek for "gateway") was actually the *entire* monumental gateway to an Egyptian temple, comprising two tapering towers joined by a less elevated section enclosing the actual entrance. Prus mistakenly applies the term "pylon" to each flanking tower. *(Translator.)*

[4] Opener of dead bodies (in Greek, *paraschistes*, or "cutter"): this practitioner made the initial incision in the embalming process. Prus here calls him, in Polish, "*paraszyt*, or opener of dead bodies." *(Translator.)*

lower and an upper, which girded the building and rested on a multitude of posts. Inside burned torches, illuminating walls formed of boards carved like lacework and protected from the wind by curtains of many-colored cloths. The building's flat roof, enclosed by a balustrade, was topped by a couple of tents.[5]

Cordially greeted by half-naked servants, some of whom ran out with torches while others prostrated themselves on their faces before him, the Successor entered the house. In the ground-floor apartment he shed his dusty clothes, bathed in a stone tub, and donned a white toga, which he fastened at the neck and bound at the waist with a cord. On the first floor[6] he supped on a wheat cake, a handful of dates, and a cup of light beer. Then he went up to the roof terrace, lay down on a couch covered in lion skin, and dismissed the servants with instructions to send Thutmose up the moment he arrived.

About midnight a litter stopped before the house, and Thutmose alighted. When he stepped heavily onto the terrace, yawning, the Prince sprang up from the couch.

"You're here! Well?" cried Ramses.

"Aren't you asleep yet?" replied Thutmose. "Oh, gods, after so many days of travail! I'd hoped to nap at least till sunrise."

"What about Sara?"

"She'll be here the day after tomorrow, or you with her at the farm across the river."

"Only the day after tomorrow!"

"Only? Please, Ramses, get some sleep. Too much black blood has accumulated in your heart, and as a result fire rushes to your head."

"What about her father?"

"An honest and sensible man. His name is Gideon. When I told him you wanted to take his daughter, he fell to the floor and tore his hair. Naturally I waited through this outpouring of paternal anguish, had a bite to eat, drank some wine—and finally we got down to the negotiations. In tears Gideon at first swore he would rather see his daughter a corpse than anyone's mistress. I told him he would get a farm outside Memphis, on the Nile, which brings two talents' annual income and pays no taxes. He was indignant. I informed him he could also get a talent each year in gold and silver. He sighed and mentioned that his daughter had attended school for three years in Pi-Bailos. I advanced another talent. Gideon, still unconsoled, said he was losing a very good place as steward to Lord Sezofris. I told him he needn't give up this position and threw in ten milk cows from your barns. His forehead cleared a bit, and he confided to me in strictest secrecy that a certain terribly great Lord Khaires, fan-bearer to the Nomarch of Memphis, had evinced an interest in his Sara. But I promised to throw in a bullock, a small gold chain, and a large bracelet. Thus your Sara will cost you: a farm and two talents a year in cash; and, on a one-time basis, ten cows, a bullock, and a gold chain and bracelet. This you will give to her father, the worthy Gideon; and to herself—whatever you like."

"What did Sara say to that?" asked the Prince.

---

[5] The structure of Ramses' villa may have been suggested by the square, one-story 18th-century Little White House *(Biały Domek)* in Warsaw's historic Royal Baths Park *(Łazienki Królewskie, or Park Łazienkowski)*. Similarly, the descriptions of the park grounds may have been suggested by the gardens of the Royal Baths Park. *(Translator.)*

[6] Prus follows the European (including British) numbering of floors: a *ground* floor lies beneath the *first* floor. (In the United States and some other countries, the ground floor is the "first floor.") *(Translator.)*

"During the negotiations, she walked among the trees. And when we'd finished the business and toasted it with some good Jewish wine, she told her father ... you know what? That if he didn't give her to you, she'd climb a rock and throw herself from it head-first. Now I trust you'll sleep well," concluded Thutmose.

"I doubt it," said the Successor, leaning on the balustrade and peering into the emptiest part of the park. "You know, on our way we came upon a hanged peasant."

"Oh! That's worse than scarabs," hissed Thutmose.

"He hanged himself in despair because the army filled in a canal he'd spent ten years digging in the desert."

"Well, that man is sleeping hard. I guess it's time for us too."

"That man was wronged," said the Prince. "We must find his children, redeem them, and give them a leasehold of land."

"But it must be done in great secrecy," said Thutmose, "or all the peasants will start hanging themselves, and no Phoenician will lend us, their masters, a copper deben."

"Don't jest. If you'd seen that peasant's face, you couldn't sleep either."

Suddenly, down below in the thicket, a none too strong but distinct voice said:

"Ramses, may the one almighty God bless you, Who has no name in human speech nor statues in temples!"

The two young men leaned forward in astonishment.

"Who are you?" cried the Prince.

"I am the wronged Egyptian people," answered the voice slowly and calmly.

Then all was silence. No movement, no stirring of branches betrayed a human presence.

At the Prince's behest, servants ran out with torches, dogs were set loose, and all the thickets surrounding the Successor's house were searched. But no one was there.

"Who could it have been?" the moved Prince asked Thutmose. "The spirit of that peasant, do you think?"

"Spirit?" repeated the aide. "I've never heard spirits talk, though I've stood guard at temples and tombs. I'd sooner suppose that the person who spoke to us is some friend of yours."

"Why should he hide?"

"What does it matter?" said Thutmose. "Each of us has tens, if not hundreds, of invisible enemies. You should thank the gods that you have at least one invisible friend."

"I won't get to sleep tonight," whispered the agitated Prince.

"Oh, come on! Instead of running around the terrace, hear me and lie down. You see, Sleep is a dignified god, and it's not meet for him to chase after those who run at a stag's pace. But when you lie down on a comfortable couch, Sleep, who likes comfort, will sit down by you and cover you with his great mantle which cloaks people's eyes as well as their minds."

So saying, Thutmose seated Ramses on the couch, then fetched a crescent-shaped ivory headrest,[7] helped the Prince recline, and placed his head on the support.

Next he dropped the canvas walls of the tent and lay down on the floor—and in a few minutes both were asleep.

---

[7] crescent-shaped headrest: in their hot climate, to aid air circulation, Egyptians used, in lieu of a pillow, a headrest supported on a pedestal. *(Translator.)*

CHAPTER 6

The Pharaoh's palace outside Memphis was entered by a gate set between two five-story pylon towers. The outer walls of these sandstone structures were covered from top to bottom with low reliefs.

The lintel of the gate featured the emblem of the Kingdom: a winged sphere flanked by two serpents. Below sat a row of gods to whom pharaohs were making offerings. The jambs likewise had carved images of gods, in five tiers one above another, and at the bottom—hieroglyphic inscriptions.

On the walls of each pylon tower, the chief space was occupied by a low relief of Ramses the Great brandishing an ax in one hand, and with the other clutching by the hair a group of people bundled together like parsley. Above the king stood or sat two more tiers of gods; still higher was a row of people bearing offerings, and just below the tops of the pylon towers—images of winged serpents alternating with scarabs.

The five-story pylon towers with their tapering walls, the three-story gate that linked them, the low reliefs which mingled order with a somber fantasy, and piety with cruelty, made a depressing effect. It seemed as though it would be difficult to enter, impossible to leave, and hard to live here.[1]

The gate, before which stood troops and a crowd of minor officials, opened into a courtyard surrounded by porticos supported by one-story pillars. This was a small ornamental garden where aloes, small palms, orange trees, and cedars, of matched height, were cultivated in pots, all drawn out in rows. In the middle spurted a fountain; the paths were strewn with colored sand.

Here under the porticos sat and strolled higher government officials, whispering softly.

From the courtyard a tall portal led into a hall supported by twelve three-story columns. The hall was large, but due to the thickness of the columns seemed cramped. It was illuminated by diminutive windows in the walls and by a large rectangular opening in the ceiling. Here reigned coolness and near-twilight, which however did not prevent a view of yellow walls and pillars covered with tiers of paintings. At the top were leaves and blossoms, below that gods, still lower people carrying statues of them or making offerings, and between these groups, rows of hieroglyphics.

All this was painted in bright, almost harsh colors: green, red, and blue.

---

[1] Prus' description of a stone-built royal palace seems to have been inspired by Egyptian temples, with their pylons and murals of triumphant pharaohs. Actually, from the Old Kingdom onward, stone was generally reserved for tombs and temples, while sunbaked mudbricks were used even for royal palaces, fortresses, the walls of temple precincts and towns, and for subsidiary buildings in temple complexes. (Translator.)

In this hall, with its patterned mosaic floor,[2] stood—silent, white-robed, and bare-foot—priests, the highest officials of the Kingdom, Minister of War Herhor, and Generals Nitager and Patroklos, summoned to the Pharaoh.

His Holiness Ramses XII, as usual before a conference, was making offerings to the gods in his chapel. This took quite some time. Every few moments, a priest or official ran in from the farther chambers to communicate the progress of the rites.

"The Lord has broken the seal to the chapel ... He is washing the holy god ... He is dressing the god ... He has closed the door ..."

The faces of those present, despite their eminence, registered anxiety. Only Herhor was indifferent, Patroklos impatient, while Nitager from time to time disturbed the solemn quiet with his powerful voice. After each such uncouth utterance of the old commander's, the courtiers stirred like frightened sheep, then looked at one another as if to say: "He's a boor, he's been chasing barbarians all his life, so we may forgive him."

In outlying chambers there rang chimes and a clatter of arms. A dozen or so guardsmen entered the hall, double-file, in gold helmets and breastplates, swords drawn; then two files of priests; and finally the Pharaoh, borne on a throne, enveloped in clouds of incense.

Egypt's ruler, Ramses XII, was a man of nearly sixty, with a wizened face. He wore a white toga and on his head a red-and-white kalpak[3] with a gold serpent, and he held a long staff.

When the entourage appeared, all prostrated themselves on their faces. Only Patroklos, as a barbarian, contented himself with a low bow, and Nitager knelt on one knee but soon stood up.

The litter stopped before a canopied platform bearing an ebony throne. The Pharaoh slowly descended from the litter, looked a moment at those present, then, sitting down on the throne, fixed his eyes on the hall's cornice, which featured a painted rose-colored sphere with blue wings and green serpents.

The Great Scribe posted himself to the right of the Pharaoh, the Great Judge with a staff to the left, both in huge wigs.

At a sign from the Judge, everyone sat down or knelt on the floor, and the Scribe addressed the Pharaoh:

"Our Lord and mighty ruler! Your servant Nitager, the great guard of the eastern border, has come to pay you homage and has brought tribute from the conquered nations: a vase of green stone full of gold, three hundred oxen, a hundred horses, and fragrant teshep wood."[4]

"It is paltry tribute, my lord," said Nitager. "Real treasures, we would find at the

---

[2] Mosaic floor: There were no mosaic floors in 20th-Dynasty Egypt. *(Translator.)*

[3] Kalpak: a Turkish-derived term for a kind of large cap. The word is used here to describe the *Pschent,* the combined crowns of Lower Egypt (the low, red *Deshret* crown) and Upper Egypt (the tall, white *Hedjet* crown). The combined Double Crown was generally referred to as *Sekhemti* ("the Two Powerful Ones"). The Double Crown bore two animal emblems: an Egyptian cobra, known as the *uraeus,* ready to strike, which symbolized the Lower-Egyptian goddess Wadjet; and an Egyptian vulture, representing the Upper Egyptian tutelary goddess Nekhbet. These emblems were fastened to the front of the *Pschent* and were referred to as the "Two Ladies." *(Translator.)*

[4] Teshep wood: the raw material for a famous ancient Egyptian perfume. *(Translator.)*

Euphrates,[5] where the haughty but still weak kings badly need reminding of Ramses the Great."

"Answer my servant Nitager," the Pharaoh told the Scribe, "that his words will be taken under advisement. And now ask what he thinks of the military abilities of my son and Successor, whom he had the honor of engaging yesterday at Pi-Bailos."

"Our ruler, the Lord of the Nine Nations, asks you, Nitager ..." began the Scribe.

To the shock of the courtiers, the general interrupted brusquely: "I can hear what my lord says. And only the Crown Prince can be his lips when he addresses me, not you, Great Scribe."

The Scribe regarded the audacious man with consternation, but the Pharaoh said: "My faithful servant Nitager speaks the truth."

The Minister of War bowed.

The Judge informed all those present—priests, officials, and guardsmen—that they could go out into the courtyard; and he and the Scribe bowed to the throne and left the hall first. There remained only the Pharaoh, Herhor, and the two commanders.

"Lend your ears, Lord, and hear a complaint," began Nitager. "This morning the priest-official who at your behest came to anoint my hair, told me that, when I came to you, I was to leave my sandals in the vestibule. Now, it's known not only in Upper and Lower Egypt but among the Hittites, the Libyans, the Phoenicians, and in the land of Punt[6] that twenty years ago you gave me the right to stand before you sandaled."

"You speak the truth," said the Pharaoh. "Some disorder has crept into my court."

"Only give the word, King, and my veterans will soon put things to rights," said Nitager.

At a sign from the Minister of War, several officials ran in. One brought sandals and helped Nitager into them; others set costly stools before the throne for the Minister and generals.

When the three dignitaries were seated, the Pharaoh asked: "Tell me, Nitager, do you think my son will make a commander? Speak the honest truth."

"By Amon of Thebes, by the glory of my forbears in whom flowed royal blood, I swear that Ramses, your Successor, will be a great commander, the gods willing," replied Nitager. "He is a young boy, barely a stripling, but he showed great skill in gathering his regiments, supplying them, and facilitating their march. What I liked most, though, is that he did not lose his head when I cut him off but led his men in attack. He will be a commander, and he will vanquish the Assyrians, who ought to be beaten today if our grandchildren are not to see them at the Nile."

"What do you say to that, Herhor?" asked the Pharaoh.

"As to the Assyrians, I think His Eminence Nitager troubles himself about them too soon. We have yet to recover from our previous wars and must strengthen ourselves well before starting a new one," said the Minister. "As to the Crown Prince, Nitager says justly that this young man possesses the virtues of a commander: he is prudent as a fox and im-

---

[5] Euphrates River: the longest river of western Asia. With the Tigris River, it defines Mesopotamia (Greek for "the Land between the Rivers"). Originating in eastern Turkey, the Euphrates flows south through Syria and Iraq to join the Tigris in the Shatt al-Arab, which empties into the Persian Gulf. *(Translator.)*

[6] land of Punt: an old kingdom and a trading partner of ancient Egypt, generally thought to have lain southeast of Egypt, likely in the Horn of Africa. Punt exported gold, aromatic resins, African blackwood, ebony, ivory, slaves, and wild animals. *(Translator.)*

petuous as a lion. Nevertheless, yesterday he made many mistakes."

"Which of us doesn't make them!" broke in the hitherto silent Patroklos.

"The Crown Prince," continued the Minister, "led the main corps capably but neglected his staff, as a result of which we marched so slowly and in such disarray that Nitager was able to block our way."

"Maybe Ramses was counting on Your Eminence?" asked Nitager.

"In governance and war, one counts on nobody: one can stumble over a single over-looked pebble," said the Minister.

"If Your Eminence," said Patroklos, "hadn't pushed the column off the highway on account of those scarabs ..."

"Your Eminence is a foreigner and a pagan," replied Herhor, "so you speak that way. But we Egyptians know that when the populace and soldiers stop respecting the scarab, their sons will stop fearing the uraeus. From disregard of the gods will spring rebellion against the pharaoh."

"What are axes for?" interrupted Nitager. "Who would keep his head on his shoulders, had better heed the supreme commander."

"Then what is your final thought about the Successor?" the Pharaoh asked Herhor.

"O living image of the Sun, O son of the gods," replied the Minister, "have Ramses anointed, give him a great chain and ten talents, but do not yet appoint him commander of the Menfi Corps. The Prince is too young, too hotheaded, too inexperienced for the post. Can we deem him the equal of Patroklos, who has trampled the Ethiopians and Libyans in twenty battles? Can we set him beside Nitager, whose very name for twenty years has made our enemies to the east and north turn pale?"

The Pharaoh rested his head in his hand, thought, and said: "Go in peace and in my favor. I shall do as wisdom and justice dictate."

The dignitaries bowed low, and Ramses XII without waiting for his suite repaired to the farther chambers.

When the two commanders found themselves alone in the vestibule, Nitager said to Patroklos:

"I see that here the priests rule as they do on their home turf. But what a strategist this Herhor is! He beat us before we could take the floor, and he won't give the Corps to the Crown Prince."

"He gave me such praise that I dared not speak," said Patroklos.

"He does see far, if he doesn't say everything. Lordlings who ride to war with singing girls would slip into the Corps after the Successor, and they'd take the top posts. Naturally the old officers would slack off in anger at being passed up in promotions; the dandies would slack off for the sake of their revels—and the Corps would fragment without even striking a blow at an enemy. Oh, Herhor is wise!"

"May his wisdom not cost us more than Ramses' inexperience," whispered the Greek.

Through a series of columned and muraled chambers where priests and palace officials made him low bows at every door, the Pharaoh proceeded to his cabinet. This was a two-story hall on whose alabaster walls were depicted, in gold and in bright paints, signal events in the reign of Ramses XII: homage paid him by inhabitants of Mesopotamia, a mission from the king of Bukhten, and the triumphal journey of the god Khonsu through the land of Bukhten.

In this hall was a malachite statuette of Horus with a bird's head, adorned with gold and precious stones; and before it, an altar in the shape of a truncated pyramid, the royal weapons, costly armchairs and benches, and tables covered with bric-a-brac.

When the Pharaoh appeared, one of the priests in attendance burned incense before him, and one of the officials announced the Crown Prince, who presently entered and bowed low to his father. The Prince's expressive face showed feverish anxiety.

"I am glad, Iry-pat," said the Pharaoh, "that you return hale from your arduous journey."

"May Your Holiness live forever and fill both worlds with your works," replied the Prince.

"My military advisors," said the Pharaoh, "were just telling me of your diligence and prudence."

The Prince's face trembled and fluctuated. He fixed his great eyes on the Pharaoh and listened.

"Your deeds will not go unrewarded. You'll receive ten talents, a great chain, and two Greek regiments with which to drill."

The Prince was dumbfounded, but after a moment he asked in a subdued voice: "What about the Menfi Corps?"

"In a year we'll repeat the maneuvers, and if you make no error in leading your force, you'll receive the Corps."

"I know, Herhor did this!" cried the Successor, scarcely controlling his anger.

He looked about and added: "I can never be alone with you, Father. Other people are always with us ..."

The Pharaoh stirred his eyebrows slightly, and his suite vanished like a pack of shades.

"What is it you wish to tell me?"

"Just one thing, Father. Herhor is my enemy ... he accused me to you and exposed me to this shame!"

Despite his humble posture, the Prince was biting his lip and clenching his fists.

"Herhor is my faithful servant, and your friend. It was at his urging that you were named crown prince. It is I who don't entrust the Corps to a young commander who let himself get cut off from his army."

"I rejoined it!" said the Successor. "It was Herhor ordered them to go around two beetles."

"Would you have a priest disregard religion in front of the army?"

"Father," whispered Ramses in a quavering voice, "in order not to spoil the beetles' procession, a canal abuilding was destroyed and a man was killed."

"That man raised his own hand against himself."

"But through Herhor's fault."

"In the regiments which you gathered so ably at Pi-Bailos, thirty men died of exhaustion and several hundred are ill."

The Prince lowered his head.

"Ramses," continued the Pharaoh, "with your lips there speaks not a dignitary of the Kingdom who is concerned for the integrity of the canals and the lives of the workers, but an angry man. And anger is incompatible with justice, as the hawk is incompatible with the dove."

"Oh, Father!" the Successor burst out, "if I'm angry, it's because I see the ill will of Herhor and the priests toward me."

"Why, you are the grandson of a high priest; priests were your teachers. You learned more of their secrets than any other prince."

"I learned of their insatiate pride and lust for power. And since I'm going to curb it ... they're already my enemies ... Herhor won't even give me a corps, since he'd rather rule the entire army ."

Having uttered the reckless words, the Prince took fright. But the Lord looked at him genially and replied calmly:

"I rule the army and the Kingdom. It is from me that all orders and decrees emanate. I am the scales of Osiris[7] in this world, and I myself weigh the affairs of my servants—of Crown Prince, Minister, and people. It would be an injudicious man who thought I don't know all the weights that are in the scales."

"Still, Father, had you watched the maneuvers with your own eyes ..."

"Maybe," interrupted the Pharaoh, "I would have seen the commander at the decisive moment abandoning the army and chasing an Israelite girl in the bushes. But I don't care to know about such trifles."

The Prince fell to his father's feet, whispering, "Thutmose told you about it, Lord?"

"Thutmose is a child like you. He's already running up debts as chief of staff of the Menfi Corps, and thinks in his heart[8] that the pharaoh's eye won't reach his affairs in the desert."

---

[7] scales of Osiris: As depicted in *The Book of the Dead*, a deceased person was judged in the "Weighing of the Heart" ritual. The deceased was led by the wolf-headed (formerly thought jackal-headed) god Anubis into the presence of the god Osiris, the lord of the underworld. There the deceased recited the "Negative Confession," swearing that he had not committed any of the 42 sins. His heart was then weighed in a pair of scales against the goddess Maat, embodying truth and justice. Maat was often represented by an ostrich feather, the hieroglyphic sign for her name. If the scales balanced, it meant the deceased had led a good life; Anubis would then take him to Osiris, and the deceased would find his place in the afterlife. If the heart was out of balance with Maat, then a fearsome beast, Ammit (the Devourer), would eat it, thereby ending the deceased's afterlife. *(Translator.)*

[8] The Egyptians regarded the heart, rather than the brain, as the seat of the mind. *(Translator.)*

CHAPTER 7

A few days later Prince Ramses was summoned into the presence of his most worshipful mother, Nikotris, who was the Pharaoh's second wife but today the greatest lady in Egypt.

The gods had not erred in singling her out to be the mother of a king. She was tall, fairly full of form and, despite her forty years, still beautiful. Above all, in her eyes, face, and entire person there was such majesty that, even when she walked unattended in the simple attire of a priestess, people bowed their heads before her.

Her Eminence received her son in a faience-tiled cabinet. She sat on an incrusted chair beneath a palm. At her feet, on a small table, lay a little puppy; at her other side knelt a black slave girl with a fan. The royal consort wore a muslin coat embroidered in gold, and on her wig a circlet studded with jewels in a lotus design.

As the Prince made a low bow, the puppy sniffed him over and lay down again, and the lady nodded and asked: "Why did you request audience of me, Ramses?"

"It has been two days, Mother."

"I knew you were busy. Today we both have time, and I can hear you out."

"You speak to me, Mother, as if the powerful desert wind had blown on me and I no longer had courage to present my request."

"Then no doubt it's about money?"

Ramses lowered his head in confusion.

"How much do you need?"

"Fifteen talents ..."

"Oh, gods!" exclaimed the lady. "Just a couple of days ago you received ten talents from the treasury. Take a walk in the garden, my dear, you must be tired," said the Queen to the black slave girl. When the Queen and her son were alone, she asked the Prince:

"Your Jewess is that demanding?"

Ramses blushed but raised his head. "You know, Mother, that it's not so," he replied. "I promised the army a reward ... and I can't make good on it!"

The Queen was contemplating him with quiet pride.

"How bad it is," she said after a while, "when a son makes decisions without consulting his mother. Remembering your age, I wanted to give you a Phoenician slave girl whom Tyre sent me, with ten talents' dowry. But you preferred a Jewess."

"I liked her. There isn't as beautiful a girl among your servants, Mother, or even among His Holiness' women."

"But she's Jewish!"

"Don't be prejudiced, Mother, I beg you. It's a lie that Jews eat pork and kill cats."

Her Eminence smiled. "You speak like a boy from the lowest priest school," she shrugged, "and you forget the words of Ramses the Great: 'The yellow people[1] are more numerous and wealthier than we; let us act against them, but carefully, lest they become yet stronger.' I don't think a girl of that people is suitable as the first mistress of the Pharaoh's Successor."

"Can Ramses' words apply to the daughter of a miserable tenant farmer?" cried the Prince. "Where are the Jews in our land, anyway? It's been three centuries since they left Egypt, and today they're creating a ridiculous kingdom governed by priests."

"I see," Her Eminence frowned slightly, "that your mistress isn't losing any time. Be careful, Ramses! Mind that their leader Messu[2] was a renegade priest who is cursed in our temples to this day. Mind that the Jews carried more treasures out of Egypt than their labor of several generations was worth: they took not only our gold[3] but our faith in the One God and our sacred laws, which they now proclaim as their own.[4] Finally, know," she added forcefully, "that the daughters of this people prefer death to the bed of a foreigner. If they give themselves even to enemy commanders, it's only to win them to their own politics or to kill them."[5]

"Believe me, Mother, all these stories are spread by the priests. They don't want to admit, to the footstool of the throne, people of a different faith who might serve the pharaoh against them."

The royal consort rose from her chair and, crossing her arms on her breast, regarded her son with astonishment.

"So it's true, what I've been told, that you're an enemy of the priests," she said. "You, their beloved pupil?"

"I must still have traces of their canes on my back!"[6] said the Prince.

"Why, your grandfather—my father dwelling with the gods, Amenhotep—was a high priest and held extensive power in the land."

"It's because my grandfather was a man of power and my father is one, that I can't abide Herhor's power."

"He was raised to his post by your grandfather, holy Amenhotep."

"I'll remove him from it."

The mother shrugged. "And you," she said sadly, "want to command an army corps?

---

[1] Prus explains in his introduction that "The native Egyptians boasted their copper-colored skins and disdained the black Ethiopians [an ancient name for the peoples of all the lands, including Nubia, Sudan, and modern Ethiopia, lying south of Egypt], yellow Semites [including Jews], and white Europeans." A mural preserved at London's British Museum illustrates this ancient Egyptian view of skin color. (*Translator.*)

[2] Messu: presumably an Egyptian form of the biblical name *Moses*. (*Translator.*)

[3] A reference to passages in the biblical *Book of Exodus*. (*Translator.*)

[4] *Pharaoh* anticipated by 42 years Sigmund Freud's thesis, in *Moses and Monotheism* (1937), that Moses and the Old Testament Jews adopted monotheism from the Egyptians. (*Translator.*)

[5] Cf. the Old Testament story of the Jewess, Judith, who decapitates the enemy Assyrian general Holofernes. A similar case, but with a change in the victim's ethnicity, is that of Samson (judge of Israel), destroyed by Delilah, employed by the Philistines. (*Translator.*)

[6] *Pharaoh*'s author, Prus, may have received canings in primary school. (*Translator.*)

Why, you're a spoiled girl, not a man and a commander."

"How's that?" interrupted the Prince, scarcely suppressing an outburst.

"I don't recognize my son ... I don't see in you the future master of Egypt! In your person the Dynasty will be like a Nile boat without a rudder. You'll drive the priests from court, and who will remain by you? Who will be your eye in the Lower and Upper Lands and abroad? The pharaoh must see all that is illuminated by the divine ray of Osiris."

"The priests will be my servants, not ministers."

"They *are* the most faithful servants. Thanks to their prayers, your father has reigned thirty-three years and avoided wars which could have been disastrous."

"For the priests."

"For the Pharaoh, for the Kingdom!" she interrupted. "Do you know what is happening in our treasury, from which in a single day you take ten talents and demand fifteen more? Do you know that, but for the generosity of the priests, who take genuine gems for the treasury even from the gods and replace them with imitations—do you know the royal estates would already be in the hands of the Phoenicians?"

"One successful war will flood our coffers as the rising Nile floods our fields."

The great lady burst into laughter. "No, Ramses," she said, "you're still such a child that your impious words can't even be reckoned sinful. Please attend to the Greek regiments and get rid of the Jewish girl ... and leave politics to us."

"Why should I get rid of Sara?"

"Because if you were to have a son by her, it might complicate matters for the Kingdom, which has troubles enough as it is. You're free to be angry at the priests," added the Lady, "so long as you don't offend them publicly. They know much must be forgiven a crown prince, especially one with such a tempestuous character. But time will soothe everything, to the glory of the Dynasty and the well-being of the Kingdom."

The Prince reflected. Suddenly he said: "Then I can't reckon on money from the treasury?"

"In no case. The Great Scribe would have had to suspend disbursements today if I hadn't given him the forty talents Tyre sent me."

"What shall I do about the army?" said the Prince, impatiently rubbing his forehead.

"Send away the Jewess and ask the priests. Maybe they'll give you a loan."

"Never! I'd rather get it from the Phoenicians."

The Lady shook her head. "You are Iry-pat, do as you like. But be warned, you have to put down large security; and once a Phoenician becomes your creditor, he'll never let you go. They're more insidious than the Jews."

"A small part of my income will cover the debts."

"We'll see. I truly would like to help you, but I can't," said the Lady, sadly spreading her hands. "So do as you will, but remember that Phoenicians on our estates are like rats in the granaries: when one of them slips through a chink, others follow."

Ramses tarried.

"Is there something more you would tell me?" she asked.

"I'd just like to ask ... my heart guesses, Mother, that you have plans in regard to me. What might they be?"

The Queen stroked his face. "Not just yet ... not just yet! Today you're free like any young noble in this country, so make the most of it. But, Ramses, the time will come when you'll have to take a wife whose children will be princes of royal blood—and her son, your successor. It's of those times that I'm thinking."

"And?"

"Nothing definite as yet. In any event, political wisdom tells me your wife should be the daughter of a priest."

"Herhor's, maybe?" laughed the Prince.

"What would be objectionable in that? Herhor will very soon become high priest in Thebes, and his daughter is only fourteen."

"And she would agree to take the place of a Jewess at my side?" asked Ramses ironically.

"You would need to have today's error forgiven you."

"I kiss your feet, Mother, and depart," said Ramses, clutching his head. "So many strange things have I heard here, I begin to fear lest the Nile start flowing toward the Cataracts,[7] or the Pyramids cross over to the Eastern Desert."

"Don't blaspheme, child," whispered the Lady, looking at her son in alarm. "Stranger wonders have been seen in this land."

"Such," smiled the son wryly, "as the walls of the royal palace listening in on their masters?"

"Such as the deaths of pharaohs after a few months' reign, and the falls of dynasties which ruled Nine Nations."

"Because those pharaohs neglected the sword for the censer," replied the Prince.

He bowed and went out.

As the Successor's footsteps died away in the enormous vestibule, Her Eminence's face changed: majesty was replaced by pain and fear, and tears glistened in her great eyes.

She ran over to a statue of a goddess, knelt, sprinkled Indian incense on the coals, and spoke:

"O Isis, Isis, Isis! thrice I pronounce your name. O Isis who brings forth snakes, crocodiles, and ostriches, thrice may thy name be praised! O Isis who protects the grains from deadly winds, and the bodies of our fathers from the destructive work of time, O Isis, take pity and protect my son. Thrice may thy name be pronounced, here ... and there ... and there ... Today and forever, and world without end, while the temples of our gods shall view themselves in the waters of the Nile."

Praying thus and sobbing, the Queen bent over and touched the floor with her forehead. Just then a quiet whisper wafted overhead:

"The voice of the just is always heard."

Her Eminence jumped up and looked about in astonishment. There was no one in the room. Only painted flowers looked out at her from the walls—and from the altar, the statue of the goddess, full of unearthly tranquility.

---

[7] The Cataracts of the Nile are shallow lengths of the Nile River—between Aswan, in southern Egypt, and Khartoum, to the south in Sudan—where the surface of the water is broken by boulders, stones, and many rocky islets. The six primary Cataracts are numbered successively from north to south. The First, Second, and Fourth Cataracts were submerged by dams built in the 20th and 21st centuries. *(Translator.)*

CHAPTER 8

The Prince returned to his villa, distressed, and summoned Thutmose.

"You must teach me," said Ramses, "how to get money."

"Ah!" laughed the dandy. "That's a wisdom they don't teach at the highest priest schools, but in which I could be a prophet."

"There they lecture on not borrowing money," said the Prince.

"Did I not fear impiety staining my lips, I'd say that some priests waste their time ... Poor men, if holy! They eat no meat, they content themselves with one wife or avoid women altogether—and they don't know what it is to borrow. I'm pleased, Ramses," spoke Thutmose, "that you'll get to know this manner of wisdom by my counsel. Already you know the sufferings which a lack of money begets. A man in need of money has no appetite, starts in his sleep, looks at women perplexed as if asking: 'What use are they?' In the chilliest temple, his face is afire; in the greatest desert heat, he shivers with cold. He stares before him like a man deranged, he doesn't hear what is said to him, he generally goes about in a twisted wig which he's neglected to perfume, and he calms himself only with a flagon of strong wine, and that not for long. For hardly does the poor wretch regain his senses, when he again feels as if the earth were parting underfoot.

"I can see," continued the dandy, "by your restless walk and by the way you toss your hands that right now you're experiencing despair brought on by lack of money. But soon you'll know other feelings, as if the Great Sphinx[1] had been lifted from your chest. Later you'll succumb to sweet oblivion about your previous troubles and present creditors, and then ...

"Ah, lucky Ramses, what extraordinary surprises await you! For when the term expires and the creditors start visiting you under pretext of paying their respects, you'll be like a stag pursued by dogs or like an Egyptian girl drawing water from the river who spots the gnarly back of a crocodile."

"All that is well and good," laughed Ramses, "but it doesn't bring a single drachma."

"Say no more!" said Thutmose. "I'm going straight to the Phoenician banker Dagon[2] and by evening, even if he hasn't yet given you the money, you'll have regained your peace of mind."

---

[1] Great Sphinx: monumental limestone statue of a reclining sphinx on the Giza Plateau, at the west bank of the Nile, near Cairo. The Sphinx is commonly thought to have been built in the reign of the Old Kingdom pharaoh Khafre and to bear his features. It shares the Giza Plateau with the Great Pyramid of Khufu (or Cheops) and the Pyramids of Khafre and Menkaure. *(Translator.)*

[2] Dagon: name borrowed from a Phoenician and Philistine god of agriculture and the earth. *(Translator.)*

He ran out, climbed into a small litter and, surrounded by servants and other frivolers like himself, disappeared into the alleys of the park.

Before sunset the Phoenician Dagon, the foremost banker of Memphis, arrived at the Successor's house. He was a man in prime of life, yellow-complected, spare but well built. He wore a blue tunic and over it a sheer white coat, his own copious natural hair confined by a gold circlet, and a large black beard, likewise natural. His hair and beard looked impressive next to the wigs and false beards of the Egyptian dandies.

The Successor's rooms were aswarm with aristocratic youth. Some were bathing downstairs and rubbing themselves with oil, others were playing chess and checkers on the first floor, others were drinking under the tents on the terrace in the company of several dancing girls. The Crown Prince was not drinking, playing at a game, or conversing with the girls but was pacing one side of the terrace, impatiently looking out for the Phoenician. When he saw him ride out of an alley in a litter on two donkeys, he went down to the first floor to an unoccupied room.

After a moment Dagon appeared in the door, knelt on the threshold, and cried:

"I salute you, O new sun of Egypt! May you live forever, and may your fame reach the distant shores that are touched by Phoenician ships!"

At the Prince's bidding he rose, and spoke with vehement gesticulation:

"When His Eminence Thutmose alighted before my hut (my house is a hut next to your palaces, Iry-pat!), his face was so radiant that I shouted to my wife: 'Tamar,[3] His Eminence Thutmose does not come on his own behalf but on behalf of someone higher than himself, as the Lebanon[4] is higher than the coastal sands.' And my wife asks: 'My lord, how do you know His Eminence Thutmose does not come on his own behalf?' 'Because he could not have come with money because he has none, and he hasn't come for money because I have none.' We bowed to His Eminence Thutmose. And when he told us Your Eminence desires fifteen talents from his slave, I asked my wife: 'Tamar, did my heart teach me wrong?' 'Dagon, you are so wise that you should be advisor to the Successor,' answered my wife."

Ramses was seething with impatience but listened to the banker. He, who fumed before his own mother and the Pharaoh!

"When we had taken thought," spoke the Phoenician, "and realized Your Lordship desires my services, such joy entered our household that I ordered our servants given ten pitchers of beer, and my wife Tamar asked me to buy her a pair of earrings. My rejoicing reached such a pitch that, as I was riding over, I forbade the donkey driver to beat the donkeys. And when my unworthy feet touched the Prince's floor, I took out a gold ring[5] (bigger than the one His Eminence Herhor gave Ennana!) and presented the gold ring to your slave who poured water on my hands. By Your Eminence's leave, what is the provenance of the silver pitcher from which they poured water on my hands?"

---

[3] Tamar: a female name of Hebrew origin—meaning "date" (the fruit), "date palm," or "palm tree"—that is borne by several Old Testament individuals. It was also the name of a Georgian sky goddess before the Christianization of Georgia, in the Caucasus. Variants of *Tamar* include *Tamara* and, more recently, *Tammy*. *(Translator.)*

[4] The Lebanon (Mount Lebanon) is a mountain range that runs the length of the modern Near Eastern country of Lebanon, north of Israel. *(Translator.)*

[5] Gold ring: Prus represents gold rings as a form of ancient Egyptian currency. *(Translator.)*

"Azariah,[6] son of Gaber,[7] sold it to me for two talents."

"A Jew? Your Eminence does business with Jews? What will the gods say?"

"Azariah is a merchant like you," replied the Successor.

Dagon clutched his head in his hands, spat, and moaned:

"O Baal Tammuz![8] O Baaleth![9] O Astoreth![10] Azariah, son of Gaber, a Jew, is a merchant like me! O my legs, why did you bring me here? O heart, why do you suffer such pain and ridicule? Eminence," shouted the Phoenician, "beat me, cut off my hand if I counterfeit gold, but do not say a Jew can be a merchant. Sooner Tyre will fall, sooner sand will replace Sidon, than a Jew will become a merchant. They can milk their scrawny goats, or mix clay with straw under an Egyptian lash, but never do business. Pish! ... Unclean nation of slaves! Robbers, thieves!"

For some unknown reason the Prince boiled up in anger—but soon calmed down, which seemed strange to Ramses himself, who had never thought it necessary to restrain himself in front of anyone.

"So, worthy Dagon," said the Successor suddenly, "will you lend me fifteen talents?"

"O Astoreth! ... fifteen talents? ... That's such a burden, I'd have to sit down to think it through."

"Then sit down."

"For a talent," said the Phoenician, seating himself comfortably in a chair, "one can have twenty gold chains, or sixty fine milk cows, or ten laborer slaves, or a slave who can play the flute or paint or maybe even treat illnesses. A talent is a tremendous fortune!"

The Prince's eyes flashed. "Well, if you don't have fifteen talents ..." interrupted the Prince.

The alarmed Phoenician suddenly slid off his chair onto the floor.

"Who in this city," he cried, "hasn't money at your bidding, O Son of the Sun? True, I'm a beggar whose gold, gems, and aggregate leases aren't worth the Prince's glance. But when I go round to our merchants and tell them who sent me, by tomorrow we'll dig up the fifteen talents, if need be out of the ground. Iry-pat, if you stepped up to a withered fig tree and said, 'Give me money!'—the tree would pay the ransom. Only don't look at me that way, O son of Horus, for it causes me pain in the pit of my heart and confuses my mind," beseeched the Phoenician.

"Have a seat, have a seat ..." smiled the Prince.

Dagon got up off the floor and sprawled still more comfortably in the chair.

"For how long will the Prince need the fifteen talents?" he asked.

"Probably a year."

"Let's make it three years. Only His Holiness could return fifteen talents in a year, not a

---

[6] Azariah: name borrowed from several individuals in the Hebrew Bible and Jewish history. *(Translator.)*

[7] Gaber: alternative spelling of the male Arabic name *Jaber*, or *Jabir*. *(Translator.)*

[8] Baal Tammuz: an ancient Near Eastern god. *(Translator.)*

[9] Baaleth: "goddess." *(Translator.)*

[10] Astoreth: a goddess worshipped in the Near East from the Bronze Age through classical antiquity also under various other names, including Astarte (Hellenized name), Ishtar (East Semitic), and Inanna, as worshipped in Mesopotamia. The goddess was revered among the Canaanites and Phoenicians and also came to be celebrated in Egypt. *(Translator.)*

young Prince who must daily entertain merry noblemen and beautiful women ... Ah, those women! By Your Eminence's leave, is it true the Prince has taken Sara, daughter of Gideon, into his house?"

"How much interest do you want?" interrupted the Prince.

"A trifle about which your holy lips need not speak. For the fifteen talents, the Prince will pay five talents a year, and over the course of the three years I'll collect everything myself."

"You will give me fifteen talents today, and in three years you'll collect thirty?"

"Egyptian law permits the sum of interests to equal the loan," replied the Phoenician in confusion.

"But isn't it too much?"

"Too much?" shouted Dagon. "Every great lord has a great court, a great estate, and pays only great interests. I would be ashamed to take less from the Crown Prince; he might have me caned and driven out if I dared take less."

"When will you bring the money?"

"Bring? ... Oh, gods! that's more than one man can do. I'll do better: I'll take care of all the Prince's disbursements so Your Eminence won't need to think about such wretched matters."

"Do you know my disbursements?"

"I know some," replied the Phoenician casually. "The Prince wants to send six talents for the Eastern Army, which will be done by our bankers in Khetem and Migdol.[11] Three talents to His Eminence Nitager, and three to His Eminence Patroklos—that will be taken care of on the spot. And I can pay Sara and her father Gideon through that Jew Azariah. That will be even better, because they would cheat the Prince in the accounts."

Ramses impatiently began pacing the room. "Then I'm to give you a promissory note for thirty talents?" he asked.

"What promissory note? ... Why a promissory note? What would I have from a promissory note? The Prince will give me three-year leases on his farms in the nomes of Ta-seti,[12] Ses, Neha-Khent,[13] Neha-Pekhu,[14] Sebt-Het,[15] Am-Khent[16] ..."

"Leases?" said the Prince. "I don't like it ..."

"Then how will I get back my money ... my thirty talents?"

"Wait. I must first ask the steward of barns how much these estates bring me annually."

---

[11] Migdol: a place in the northeastern Nile Delta, in the 23rd or 14th nome of Lower Egypt. The word *Migdol* appears in a number of biblical contexts: as the name of several places and of various objects, including forts and a fortified gate-house at the Temple of Ramses III at Medinet Habu. *(Translator.)*

[12] Ta-seti: 1st nome of Upper Egypt. Its capital was Abu, or Yebu (also called Elephantine). Prus calls Ta-seti *Takens. (Translator.)*

[13] Neha-Khent: perhaps a misspelling of the 20th nome of Upper Egypt, Atef-Khent. Prus here calls it *Neha-Ment. (Translator.)*

[14] Neha-Pekhu: perhaps a misspelling of the 21st nome of Upper Egypt, Atef-Pehu. Prus calls it *Neha-Pechu. (Translator.)*

[15] Sebt-Het: perhaps a misspelling of the 11th nome of Lower Egypt, Ka-heseb. *(Translator.)*

[16] Am-Khent: the 18th Nome of Lower Egypt. Prus calls it *Habu. (Translator.)*

"Why should Your Eminence go to all the trouble? What does the steward know? He doesn't know a thing, as I'm an honest Phoenician. Each year there's a different harvest and a different income ... I could lose on this deal, and then the steward isn't going to make good my losses ..."

"But you see, Dagon, it seems to me these estates bring in far more than ten talents a year."

"The Prince doesn't wish to trust me—all right. At your behest I can forgo the farms in Ses ... Is the Prince still unsure of my heart? Well, then I'll also waive Sebt-Het. But what need is there of the steward? Is he going to teach the Prince wisdom? ... Oh, Astoreth! I would lose sleep and appetite if some steward, a serf and slave, dared correct my gracious lord. All that is needed here is a scribe to write down that Your Eminence leases to me, for three years, farms in this, this, and this nome. Also needed are sixteen witnesses to my being thus honored by the Prince. But why should the servants know their master is borrowing money from me? ..."

The bored Successor shrugged. "Tomorrow," he said, "bring the money and your scribe and witnesses. I don't want to think about it."

"Ah, what wise words!" cried the Phoenician. "May Your Eminence live forever ..."

CHAPTER 9

On the left bank of the Nile, at the northern peripheries of Memphis, lay the farm that the Successor had given as an abode to Sara, daughter of the Jew Gideon.

It was a property of twenty hectares,[1] forming a modest square viewable from the top of the house as on the palm of one's hand. The farm's lands were distributed over four tiers on a hill. The two lowest and broadest, which the Nile invariably flooded, were devoted to grains and vegetables. On the third tier, which sometimes escaped inundation, grew palms, figs, and other fruit trees. On the fourth, the highest, was a garden planted with olives, grapevines, nut trees, and chestnuts, in the midst of which stood the house.

The house was wooden, one-story, with the usual terrace topped by a canvas tent. Downstairs lived Ramses' black slave; upstairs, Sara with her relative and servant Taphath.[2] The house was surrounded by a mudbrick wall, some distance out from which were buildings for cattle, farmhands, and overseers.

Sara's rooms were modest-sized but exquisite. Carpets covered the floors; curtains in varicolored stripes hung in the doors and windows. There were carved beds and chairs, encrusted clothes chests, and tripod and unipod tables bearing vases of flowers, slender wine pitchers, caskets of perfume vials, gold and silver winecups and goblets, faience tureens and bowls, bronze oil lamps. The smallest stick of furniture and vessel was embellished with carving or color drawing; every article of clothing—with embroidery and fringes.

Sara had been living ten days in this remote place, hiding from people in fear and shyness so that hardly any of the farm servants had seen her. In her curtained boudoir she sewed, wove linen on a small loom, and fashioned floral garlands for Ramses. Sometimes she stole out onto the terrace and, cautiously parting the tent flaps, looked out at a Nile full of boats whose oarsmen sang merry songs; or she lifted her eyes with dread to the pylon towers of the royal castle which, silent and brooding, dominated the opposite bank of the river. Then she would run back to her work and call Taphath.

"Sit here, mother," she would say. "What have you been doing downstairs?"

"The gardener brought fruit, and they've sent bread, wine, and poultry from the city; I had to collect them."

---

[1] Twenty hectares: in the original Polish, "thirty-five *mórgs*." *(Translator.)*

[2] Taphath: a biblical Old Testament name belonging to Solomon's daughter, who was the wife of one of her father's twelve regional administrators. Prus calls her *Tafet*. *(Translator.)*

"Stay here and talk; I'm terrified ..."

"Silly child!" laughed Taphath. "The first day, I too saw some terror lurking in every corner; but when I went outside the wall, it all ended. Whom should I fear, with everyone falling to his knees before me? Before you, they'd probably stand on their heads! Go into the garden, it's beautiful as paradise. Take a look at the field where they're harvesting wheat ... Get into a carved boat whose ferrymen long to see you and carry you about the Nile ..."

"I'm scared."

"Of what?"

"I don't know. While I sew, I think I'm in our little valley and Father will soon be home. But when the wind parts the curtain in the window and I look down at this great ... great land, it seems to me ... You know what? ... That a vulture has carried me off to its eyrie on a rock from which there's no getting down."

"Oh, you ... you! ... If you saw what a bathtub the Prince sent over today, a copper bathtub! And what a tripod for the fireplace, what pots and spits! And I set two hens today and we'll soon have chicks ..."

After sunset, when no one could see her, Sara was sometimes bolder. She would go up onto the terrace and view the river. When a boat appeared in the distance, illumined by torches that carved sanguineous and fiery streaks into the black water, Sara clutched with both hands her poor heart, which trembled like a trapped bird.

There was Ramses sailing over to her, and she could not have said what she felt: joy at the approach of the handsome youth whom she had met in the little valley; or dread that she would again set eyes on the great lord and master who made her timid.

One Sabbath eve her father came to the farm for the first time since her settling there. Sara, weeping, flung herself on him; she personally washed his feet, and poured fragrances on his head, covering him with kisses. Gideon was an already grizzled man, with austere features. He wore an ankle-length tunic with a bottom trim of colored embroidery, and over it a yellow sleeveless kaftan, a kind of robe draping his chest and back. He covered his head with a small cap which narrowed at the top.

"You're here? ... You're here!" cried Sara, again kissing his hands and head.

"I myself wonder that I'm here!" replied Gideon sadly. "I stole into the garden like a thief. All the way from Memphis, it seemed to me that all the Egyptians were pointing at me and every Jew was spitting."

"But, Father, you yourself gave me to the Prince?" whispered Sara.

"I did. What was I to do? Anyway, it only seems to me that they point at me and spit. The Egyptians who know me, bow the lower to me, the higher they are themselves. Since you've been here, our Lord Sezofris has said my house must be enlarged; Lord Khaires has given me a cask of the best wine; and His Eminence our Nomarch has sent a confidential servant to ask me: are you well, and would I be his steward?"

"What about the Jews?" asked Sara.

"The Jews! They know I didn't give in willingly. Anyway, everybody would like to have just such an outrage done to him. May the Lord God judge us all. Now tell me: how have you been?"

"At the bosom of Abraham she won't have it better," said Taphath. "All day long they bring us fruit, wine, bread, and meat—everything the soul can desire. And what a bathtub we've got! ... all copper. And what kitchenware! ..."

"Three days ago," interrupted Sara, "a Phoenician, Dagon, came here. I didn't want to see him, but he insisted ..."

"He gave me a gold ring," broke in Taphath.

"He told me," said Sara, "that he's my lord's tenant and gave me two anklets, a pair of pearl earrings, and a casket of perfumes from the land of Punt."

"What did he give you this for?" asked the father.

"Nothing. He only asked me to think well of him and occasionally tell my lord that Dagon is his most faithful servant."[3]

"You'll very quickly collect a whole chest of earrings and bracelets," smiled Gideon. "Ah," he added after a moment, "collect a great fortune quickly, and let's flee to our land, because here it's always misery for us. Misery when things are bad, worse misery when they're good."

"But what would my lord say?" asked Sara sadly.

The father shook his head. "Before a year is out, your lord will leave you, and others will help him. If you were Egyptian, he would take you into his house—but a Jewess ...?"

"He'll leave me?" sighed Sara.

"Why worry about the days to come, which are in God's hand? I've come to pass the Sabbath with you ..."

"I have excellent fish, meat, cakes, and kosher wine," said Taphath quickly. "I also bought a seven-branched candelabrum[4] and wax candles in Memphis. It will be a better supper than at Lord Khaires' himself."

Gideon went out onto the terrace with his daughter. When they were alone, he said:

"Taphath tells me you stay inside all the time. Why? You should at least go out into the garden."

Sara shuddered. "I'm afraid to," she whispered.

"Why should you be afraid of your garden? You are the lady here, the great lady ..."

"One time I went into the garden in the daytime ... Some people saw me and said, 'Look, that's the Successor's Jewess who causes the flood to be delayed!'"

"They are fools," said Gideon. "Hasn't the Nile been as much as a whole week late in flooding? So for now go out in the evening."

Sara shuddered still more violently. "I don't want to ... I don't want to!" she cried. "Another day I went out in the evening, over there among the olive trees. Suddenly, like shades, two women slipped out from a side path. Frightened, I wanted to run ... But one of them, the younger and shorter one, grabbed my arm, saying, 'Don't run away, we must have a look at you.' And the other, the older and taller one, came to within a few paces of me and looked into my eyes ... Oh, Father, I thought I would turn to stone ... What a woman she was ... what a look she gave me!"

"Who could it have been?" asked Gideon.

"The older one looked like a priestess."

"She said nothing to you?"

---

[3] A similar encounter between Sara and Dagon will take place in Chapter 13. *(Translator.)*

[4] Seven-branched candelabrum: known as the Temple menorah (having been used in the Temple in Jerusalem), it has served since antiquity as a symbol of the Jewish people and Judaism. A nine-branched menorah variant is used in the eight-day festival of Hanukkah. *(Translator.)*

"No. But when they were leaving and had disappeared behind the trees, I heard probably the older one, who said only: 'Of a truth, she is pretty ...'"

"Maybe," mused Gideon, "they were great ladies from court."

The sun was setting, and on both banks of the Nile thick crowds of people were gathering, impatiently awaiting the signal announcing the flood, which was in fact delayed. For two days already the wind had blown from the sea, and the river had turned green; the sun had already passed the star Sothis,[5] but in the priests' Nilometer[6] in Memphis the water had not risen by so much as a finger's width.[7] People were concerned, especially since in Upper Egypt, according to signals, the flood was going well and even promised to be excellent.

"What, then, is holding it up at Memphis?" asked the worried husbandmen, as they anxiously awaited the signal.

When the first stars appeared in the heavens, Taphath covered the dining-room table with a white cloth, placed the candelabrum with seven lit candles, drew up three chairs, and announced that she would presently serve the Sabbath supper.

Gideon covered his head and, lifting both hands over the table, spoke gazing into the heavens:

"God of Abraham, Isaac, Jacob, Who led our people out of the land of Egypt, Who gave a homeland to slaves and exiles, Who made an eternal covenant with the sons of Judah ... God Jehovah, God Adonai, permit us to sinlessly partake of the fruits of a hostile land, deliver us from the sorrow and fear in which we dwell, and return us to the banks of the Jordan,[8] which we departed for Thy glory ..."

At that moment, from across the garden wall, there spoke a voice: "His Eminence Thutmose, the most faithful servant of His Holiness and the Crown Prince ..."

"May they live forever!" said several voices from the garden.

"His Eminence," spoke the single voice again, "sends his compliments to the fairest rose this side of the Lebanon!"[9]

A harp and flute sounded.

---

[5] Sothis: the Greek transcription of the Egyptian name, *Sopdet*, for the star Sirius. Each year the "heliacal rising" of Sirius occurred within about a month of the start of the annual Nile flood. For more about this, please see the note on "Sirius" in Prus' introduction. *(Translator.)*

[6] Nilometer: a structure for measuring the Nile's level during the annual late-summer flood season. A notable example of a Nilometer is on Elephantine Island, at Aswan, which marked Egypt's southern border. The ability to predict the volume of the coming flood was part of the mystique of ancient Egypt's priesthood and was used to determine the levels of taxes to be paid. A moderate flood was vital to agriculture: an insufficient flood caused famine, while an excessive flood was equally disastrous. In pharaonic times, an average of one year out of five saw an insufficient or excessive flood. Egypt's Nilometers functioned from pharaonic times until made obsolete by the two successive Aswan dams completed in 1902 and 1970. *(Translator.)*

[7] Finger's width (also "finger" or "finger's breadth"): any of several units of measure that approximate the width of an adult human finger. *(Translator.)*

[8] Jordan River: a 250-kilometer-long river in the Near East that flows roughly north to south through the Sea of Galilee and on to the Dead Sea. The river is now bordered on the east by the country of Jordan and the Golan Heights, and on the west by the West Bank and Israel. *(Translator.)*

[9] The Lebanon (Mount Lebanon) is a mountain range that runs the length of the modern Near Eastern country of Lebanon, north of Israel. *(Translator.)*

"Music!" exclaimed Taphath, clapping. "We're going to celebrate the Sabbath to music!"
Sara and her father, at first terrified, broke into laughter and sat down to the table.

"Let them play," said Gideon. "Their music won't spoil our appetites."

The flute and harp played a motif, followed by a tenor voice singing:

"You are fairer than all the girls who view themselves in the waters of the Nile. Your hair is blacker than the raven's feathers; your eyes gaze gentler than those of the hind pining for her fawn. Your stature is as that of the palm, and the lotus envies your charm. Your breasts are like the grapes whose juice intoxicates kings."

Flute and harp again, followed by song:

"Come and rest in the garden. Your servants will bring numerous dishes and every kind of beer. Come, we'll celebrate this night and the dawn that follows. In my shade, the shade of the fig tree that bears sweet fruit, your lover will sit at your right hand; and you shall make him drunk and be docile to all his wishes ..."

Flute and harp—followed again by song:

"I am discreet and never speak of what I see. I do not spoil the sweetness of my fruit with idle chatter ..."[10]

---

[10] Authentic. *(Author.)* The text beginning "Come and rest in the garden" is from the ancient Egyptian text, "The Trees in the Garden," published by Gaston Maspero and by Adolf Erman. *(Translator.)*

CHAPTER 10

Suddenly the singing was drowned out by tumult and by sounds as of many persons running.

"Pagans! Enemies of Egypt!" called someone. "You sing while we're all plunged in distress, and you praise the Jewess whose spells are holding back the Nile ..."

"Woe betide you!" called another. "You tread the land of the Successor! Death will befall you and your children!"

"We'll give way, but let the Jewess come out so we may tell her our grievances ..."

"Let's flee!" shouted Taphath.

"Where to?" asked Gideon.

"Never!" replied Sara, her gentle face flushed with anger. "Don't I belong to the Successor, before whom these people prostrate themselves on their faces?"

Before father or servant could collect themselves, she ran out onto the terrace, all in white, calling to the crowd outside the wall: "Here I am! What do you want of me?"

For a moment the noise abated, then menacing voices spoke again: "Damn you, foreign woman whose sin holds back the waters of the Nile!"

Several rocks, thrown blindly, whistled through the air; one of them struck Sara's forehead.

"Father!" she cried, clutching her head.

Gideon snatched her in his arms and carried her off the terrace. In the night, naked men in white caps and aprons could be seen clambering over the wall.

Downstairs Taphath was shouting at the top of her lungs, while the Negro slave grabbed an ax and placed himself in the sole door to the house, vowing to smash the head of anyone who tried to enter.

"Give us rocks for that Nubian dog!" the men on the wall called to the crowd.

But the crowd suddenly hushed when, from the depths of the garden, there emerged a shaven-headed man wearing a leopard skin.

"A prophet! ... A holy father!" murmured the crowd.

Those sitting on the wall proceeded to jump off.

"People of Egypt," said the priest calmly, "by what right do you lift your hand against the property of the Crown Prince?"

"The unclean Jewess lives there who holds back the flood of the Nile ... Alas! ... misery and famine hang over Lower Egypt."

"People of bad faith or weak minds," said the priest, "where did you hear that one woman can thwart the will of the gods? Each year the Nile starts rising in the month of

Thoth and grows until the month of Choiak. Has it ever been otherwise, though our land has always been full of foreigners, sometimes alien priests and princes who, moaning in slavery and at hard labor, might have cast the most terrible curses out of grief and anger? They surely desired to bring every kind of misfortune down on our heads, and more than one would have given his life that either the sun not rise over Egypt at the morning hour or the Nile not rise at the start of the year. And what ever came of their prayers? Either they went unheard in the heavens, or the foreign gods were powerless against ours. So how could a woman who is content among us bring about a calamity which our most powerful enemies could not?"

"The holy father speaks the truth! Wise are the words of the prophet!" said voices in the crowd.

"Yet Messu,[1] the Jewish chieftain, made darkness and pestilence[2] in Egypt!" objected a voice.

"Whoever said that, let him come forward!" called the priest. "I bid him come forward if he be not an enemy of the Egyptian people ..."

The crowd murmured like a strong wind flowing from afar between the trees; but no one came forward.

"Truly I say," continued the priest, "bad people move among you like hyenas in a sheep-fold. They do not take pity on your misery but want to goad you into destroying the Successor's house and into rebellion against the Pharaoh. But if their nefarious plot succeeded and if blood began flowing from your breasts, these same people would hide from the spears as they now hide from my call."

"Heed the prophet! Bless you, man of the gods!" called the crowd, bowing their heads. The more pious prostrated themselves.

"Hear me, people of Egypt ... For your faith in the words of a priest, for your obedience to the Pharaoh and Successor, for the reverence which you accord a servant of the gods, a favor will be granted you. Go to your homes in peace, and perhaps before you've descended this hill, the Nile will begin to rise."

"May it be so!"

"Go! The greater your faith and piety, the sooner will you behold the sign of grace."

"Let's go! ... Let's go! ... Bless you, prophet, son of prophets ..."

They began to disperse, kissing the priest's robe.

Suddenly someone shouted: "A miracle! A miracle is coming to pass!"

"They've lit a beacon on the tower in Memphis! The Nile is rising! Look, more and more lights! ... Truly, a most holy man spoke to us... Live forever!"

They looked about for the priest, but he had vanished into the shadows.

The crowd, lately angry and the moment before amazed and overwhelmed with gratitude, forgot both their anger and the wonder-worker priest. A tremendous joy took hold of them, and they dashed for the riverbank, where many fires already burned and there rang the singing of the gathered populace:

"Welcome, O Nile, sacred river that issues from the earth to bring life to Egypt. O concealed god that scatters darkness and waters the meadows to nourish the cattle. O dew

---

[1] Messu: presumably an Egyptian form of the biblical name *Moses*. *(Translator.)*

[2] This is a reference to the biblical Plagues of Egypt described in the Book of Exodus. *(Translator.)*

that falls from heaven to water the land, O friend of bread that gladdens the huts ... Lord of fish, that makes the waterfowl go upstream; that makes barley and wheat to grow; that gives rest to the hands of unhappy millions, and forever preserves the temples."[3]

Meanwhile the Successor's illuminated boat had sailed over from the opposite bank amid the shouting and singing. The same people who half an hour earlier had wanted to break into the Prince's villa, now prostrated themselves before him on their faces or jumped into the water to kiss the oars and the sides of the vessel that had brought the son of Egypt's ruler.

Merry, surrounded by torches, Ramses, accompanied by Thutmose, proceeded to Sara's house.

At the sight of him, Gideon told Taphath: "Afraid though I am for my daughter, I do not wish to meet her lord."

He jumped over the wall and in the dark, through garden and fields, struck out for Memphis.

In the courtyard Thutmose called: "Greetings, fair Sara! I trust you will receive us well after the music I sent you ..."

Sara appeared in the door, her head bound, supported by the Negro and her servant Taphath.

"What's this?" asked the astonished Prince.

"It's terrible!" cried Taphath. "Pagans attacked your house, and one of them hit Sara with a rock ..."

"What pagans?"

"Oh, those ... Egyptians!" clarified Taphath.

The Prince cast her a look of contempt. But presently he became furious.

"Who hit Sara? Who threw the rock?" he shouted, grabbing the Negro's arm.

"Them by the river," said the slave.

"Hey, overseers!" cried the Prince, "arm all the men on the farm—we're going after that bunch!"

The Negro picked up his ax, the overseers began calling the farmhands out of the buildings, and several soldiers in the Prince's suite reflexively adjusted their swords.

"For the love of God, what do you mean to do?" whispered Sara, draping herself on the Prince's neck.

"I mean to avenge you," he said. "Who smites my belonging, smites me."

Thutmose turned pale and shook his head. "Listen, lord," he said, "how at night and in a crowd can you tell who committed the crime?"

"I don't care ... The mob did it, and the mob will answer for it!"

"No judge would say that," admonished Thutmose. "And you are to become the supreme judge ..."

The Prince pondered; Thutmose continued:

"Consider what our Lord the Pharaoh would say tomorrow. And what joy would reign among Egypt's enemies east and west if they heard that the Crown Prince attacks his people at night, practically outside the royal palace ..."

---

[3] Authentic. *(Author.)* The text is drawn from "Hymn to the Nile," published by Gaston Maspero and by Adolf Erman. *(Translator.)*

"Oh, if Father gave me half the army, our enemies in all the quarters of the world would be silenced forever!" whispered the Prince, stamping his foot.

"Finally ... remember the peasant who hanged himself. You felt sorry for him because an innocent man had died, and now ... Could you kill innocent people yourself?"

"Enough!" interrupted the Successor quietly. "My anger is like a pitcher brimful of water ... Woe betide him on whom it overflows! Let's go in ..."

The frightened Thutmose stepped aside. The Prince took Sara's arm and conducted her up to the first floor. He seated her by the table with the unfinished supper, brought up the candelabrum, and stripped the bandage from her head.

"Oh," he cried, "it's not a wound, only a bruise!"

He was scrutinizing Sara. "I'd never have thought you could bruise," he said. "It changes your face ..."

"You don't like me anymore?" asked Sara quietly, her great eyes full of fear.

"That's not what I mean! Anyway, it will pass ..."

He called Thutmose and the Negro and inquired about the evening's events.

"He defended us," said Sara. "He stood in the door with an ax ..."

"Did you?" the Prince asked the slave, looking him in the eye.

"I couldn't let people break into your house, lord."

The Prince patted his kinky hair. "You acted like a man of courage," he said. I'm giving you your freedom. Tomorrow you'll receive a reward and can return to your people."

The Negro reeled and rubbed his eyes, whose whites glistened. Suddenly he fell to his knees, struck his forehead on the floor, and cried: "Don't drive me away from you, lord!"

"All right," said the Successor. "Remain with me, but as a free soldier. That's the kind of people I need," he added, glancing at Thutmose. "He can't talk like the keeper of a house of books, but he's prepared to fight."

He asked about further details of the incursion. When the Negro told him about the priest and his miracle, the Prince clutched his head, crying:

"I'm the most pitiable man in Egypt! Soon I'll be finding priests even in my bed ... Where's he from? Who is he?"

The Negro did not know. But he said the priest's conduct had been very friendly toward the Prince and Sara; and that the attack had been led not by Egyptians but by people the priest had called enemies of Egypt and had vainly called on to come forward.

"Wonder of wonders!" mused the Prince, throwing himself on a bed. "My black slave is a brave soldier and a man of good sense ... A priest defends a Jewess because she's mine ... Who is this singular priest? ... The Egyptian people, who kneel before the Pharaoh's dogs, attack the Successor's house, led by enemies of Egypt? I must look into this myself ..."

CHAPTER 11

The month of Thoth had ended, and the month of Phaophi was starting—the second half of July.[1] The Nile waters had turned from greenish to white, then red, and kept rising. The royal Nilometer at Memphis was filled to nearly the height of two men, and the river rose daily by two hands.[2] The lowest grounds were flooded; higher up, flax, grapes, and a kind of cotton were being cleared in. Where it was still dry in the morning, waves splashed by evening.

A violent if unseen gale seemed to be blowing in the depths of the river. It plows broad swathes, fills the furrows with foam, briefly smooths the water's surface, and a moment later twists it into precipitous whirls.

Again it plows, smooths, twists, drives up fresh swells of water, fresh streaks of foam, and continually raises the swishing river, capturing new stretches of soil. Every so often, on reaching a verge, the water crosses it, pours into a hollow, and forms a shiny little lake where withered grasses had been crumbling to dust.

Though the flood had reached barely a third of its extent, the entire bank was already awash. Every hour some hilltop farm became an island, cut off by a narrow strait which gradually widened, increasingly separating the homestead from its neighbors. Many a person who set off for work on foot, returned by boat.

More and more boats and rafts plied the Nile. From some, people netted fish; in others, they transported crops and bellowing cattle to barns; in yet others, they visited friends to inform them amid laughter and shouting that (as all could plainly see) the Nile was rising. Sometimes boats, clustered like ducks, scattered in all directions before a broad raft bearing, downstream, huge stone blocks hewn out of the riverside quarries of Upper Egypt.

The air was filled with the swish of rising water, the cries of frightened fowl, and the gay singing of people. The Nile is rising, there will be plenty of bread!

All that month, investigation was conducted into the attack on the Successor's house. Each morning a boatload of officials and police landed at some farm. People were torn away from their work, showered with tricky questions, caned. Toward evening, two boats returned to Memphis: one with officials, the other with prisoners.

In this way several hundred culprits were rounded up, half of whom knew nothing while the other half faced prison or several years' labor in the quarries. However, nothing

---

[1] Actually, the ancient Egyptian month of Phaophi lay between October 11 and November 9, unless the previous Coptic year was a leap year. *(Translator.)*

[2] Hand: an Egyptian unit of length based on the breadth of a human hand. *(Translator.)*

was learned either of the attack's leaders or of the priest who had prevailed on the populace to disperse.

Prince Ramses combined some exceptionally contradictory traits. He was impetuous as a lion and stubborn as an ox. He also had great good sense and a deep sense of justice.

Seeing that the investigation conducted by the officials was producing no results, the Prince sailed to Memphis and visited the prison.

It stood on a hill, surrounded by a high wall, and comprised many stone, brick, and wooden buildings. The greater part of these structures were entrances or warders' quarters. The prisoners were lodged underground in caves hollowed out of the limestone.

On passing through the gate, the Successor saw a small group of women washing and feeding a prisoner. The near-naked man, resembling a skeleton, sat on the ground, his hands and feet confined in four openings in a square board in lieu of manacles.[3]

"How long has this man been suffering like that?" asked the Prince.

"Two months," said the warden.

"How much longer is he in for?"

"A month."

"What did he do?"

"He insulted a tax collector."

The Prince turned and saw another group, comprising women and children. With them was an old man.

"Are those people prisoners?"

"No, Eminence. That is a family waiting for the remains of a criminal who is to be strangled ... Oh, they're taking him to the chamber now," said the warden.

Turning to the little group, he said: "Be patient just a bit longer, dear people, you will soon have the body."

"Thank you very much, honorable sir," replied the old man, likely the delinquent's father. "We left home yesterday evening, our flax stayed in the field, and here the river is rising!"

The Prince turned pale and stopped. "You know," he said to the warden, "that I have power of clemency?"

"Yes, Iry-pat," answered the warden with a bow, adding: "By law, in commemoration of your visit here, O Son of the Sun, well-behaved prisoners convicted of offenses against religion or the state should be granted clemency. A list of those persons will be laid at your feet within a month."

"What about the man who is to be strangled right now? Isn't he eligible for my clemency?"

The warden spread his hands and bowed in silence.

They moved on and passed through several courtyards. In cramped wooden cages on the bare ground swarmed criminals sentenced to imprisonment. In one building there rang terrible shouts: people were being beaten to extract statements.

"I want to see those accused in the attack on my house," said the deeply affected Successor.

---

[3] "confined in four openings in a square board": This is a stocks, a device generally used for physical punishment involving public humiliation. It is mentioned in the biblical Old Testament's *Book of Job* and was used well into modern times. *(Translator.)*

"There are upwards of three hundred of them," replied the warden.

"Choose those you deem guiltiest and question them in my presence. However, I don't want them to recognize me."

The Successor was ushered into a chamber where an investigator was at work. The Prince bade him take his usual place, and himself sat down behind a pillar.

Presently the accused began appearing one at a time. All were thin; they had grown long hair and beards, and their eyes held an expression of subdued derangement.

"Dutmose," said the investigator, "tell me how you attacked the house of His Eminence the Iry-pat."

"I'll tell the truth as at the court of Osiris. It was the evening of the day the Nile was supposed to start flooding. My wife says to me: 'Come, father, let's go up on the hill, the better to see the signal in Memphis.' So we went up on the hill, the better to see the signal in Memphis. Then a soldier approaches my wife and says: 'Come with me into this garden, and we'll find some grapes or something.' So my wife went into the garden with the soldier, and I got very angry and looked over the wall. But whether they threw rocks at the Prince's house, I can't say because I saw nothing on account of the trees and the dark."

"How could you let your wife go with the soldier?" asked the investigator.

"By Your Eminence's leave, what was I to do? I'm only a peasant, and he's a warrior and soldier of His Holiness ..."

"Did you see the priest who spoke to you?"

"It wasn't a priest," said the peasant with conviction. "It must have been the god Khnum,[4] because he came out of a fig stump and had a ram's head."

"Did you see that he had a ram's head?"

"By your leave, I don't rightly remember whether I saw it myself or whether people said so. I was blinded by concern over my wife."

"Did you throw rocks into the garden?"

"Why should I throw them, O lord of life and death? If I'd hit my wife, I would have made myself trouble for a whole week; and if I'd hit the soldier, I would've gotten a fist in the belly to make my tongue stick out. I'm only a peasant, and he's a warrior of our eternally living Lord."

The Successor leaned out from behind the column. Dutmose was led away, and Anupa was brought in. He was a short peasant with pale cane scars on his back.

"Anupa," began the investigator again, "tell me about the attack on the Successor's garden."

"O eye of the sun," replied the peasant, "O vessel of wisdom, you know I didn't attack anything. What happened was, my neighbor came over and says: 'Anupa, let's go up on the hill, the Nile is rising.' And I say: 'Is it rising?' And he says: 'You're more stupid than a donkey, because a donkey would hear the music on the hill, and you don't.' And I answer: 'Stupid I am, because I haven't learned to write; but if you please, music is one thing, and the flood is another.' And he says: 'If it weren't flooding, people would have nothing to be happy, or play music, or sing about.' So, Your Justice, we went up on the hill, and there

[4] Khnum: one of the earliest Egyptian deities, originally the god of the source of the Nile. Later he was described as having molded the other deities. Usually depicted with a ram's head, Khnum presided over the annual flood of the Nile. Sacred to Khnum were two riverside sites, Elephantine Island and Esna. Prus here calls him *Num. (Translator.)*

they've driven away the musicians and they're pitching rocks into the garden."

"Who was pitching them?"

"I couldn't tell. They didn't look like peasants; sooner like unclean openers of dead bodies."

"Did you see a priest?"

"By your leave, O Watchfulness, it wasn't a priest but probably some spirit that watches over the house of the Prince Successor (may he live forever!)."

"Why a spirit?"

"Because sometimes I saw him, and sometimes I lost sight of him."

"Maybe people got in the way?"

"No doubt sometimes people got in the way. But then, one time he was taller;[5] and another time, shorter."

"Maybe he climbed up a hill and back down again?"

"No doubt he must have climbed up and back down, but maybe he became taller and shorter, because he was a great wonder-worker. Hardly did he say, 'The Nile will soon flood,' when the Nile started flooding."

"Did you throw rocks, Anupa?"

"Would I dare throw rocks into the Successor's garden? I'm a simple peasant, and my arm would wither to the elbow for such sacrilege."

The Prince stopped the interrogations. When the accused had been led away, he asked the investigator: "These people are among the guiltiest?"

"Yes, lord," replied the investigator.

"In that case, they must all be released today. People can't be jailed for wanting to find out whether the sacred Nile is flooding, or for listening to music."

"The utmost wisdom speaks with your lips, Iry-pat," said the investigator. "I was told to find the guiltiest persons, so I chose from among those that I found. But it's not in my power to restore them to freedom."

"Why not?"

"Look at this chest, Your Eminence. It holds the papyri that document the case. The judge in Memphis receives daily reports on its progress and informs His Holiness. What would become of the work of so many learned scribes and great men if the accused were released?"

"But they're innocent!" cried the Prince.

"There was an attack, so there was a crime. Where there is a crime, there must be criminals; and once a person has gotten into the hands of the authorities and been entered in the records, he can't depart without some result. In a tavern, a person drinks and pays; at the fair, he sells and receives; in the field, he sows and reaps; at the graves, he receives the blessings of his deceased ancestors. How, then, could someone go to a court of law and return with nothing, like a traveler who stops halfway and turns his steps homeward without having achieved his goal?"

"Wisely spoken," replied the Successor. "Tell me, though, would His Holiness not have a right to release these people?"

---

[5] "... one time he was taller": This passage may have been inspired by the phenomenon of *elongation*, simulated by some Spiritualist mediums, including Eusapia Palladino, whose séances Prus had witnessed in Warsaw in 1893. *(Translator.)*

The official crossed his arms and bowed his head.

"He, the equal of the gods, may do whatsoever he pleases: release the accused, even the convicted, and even destroy the records of a case, which if done by an ordinary person would be sacrilege."

The Prince bade farewell to the investigator and asked the warden to feed those accused in the attack better, at the Prince's expense. Next, exasperated, he sailed across the constantly widening river to the palace to ask the Pharaoh to dismiss the miserable case.

That day, however, His Holiness had many religious ceremonies and a conference with his ministers, so the Successor was unable to see him. The Prince therefore went to the Great Scribe, the most influential person at court after the Minister of War. The old official, a priest at one of the Memphis temples, received the Prince politely but coolly and, on hearing him out, replied:

"I find it strange that Your Eminence would disturb our Lord with such matters. It is as if you asked that the locusts that have descended upon the field not be destroyed."

"But these are innocent people!"

"We cannot know that, Eminence, since it is the law and the law court that pass upon guilt or innocence. To me, one thing is certain: the state cannot suffer a person's garden to be invaded, let alone a hand to be raised against the belongings of the Crown Prince."

"Justly spoken—but where are the guilty parties?" asked the Prince.

"Where there are no guilty parties, there must at least be punished ones. It's not guilt, but the punishment which follows upon a crime, that teaches others that this mustn't be done."

"I can see," interrupted the Successor, "that Your Eminence will not back my request with His Holiness."

"Wisdom flows from your lips, Iry-pat," answered the dignitary. "I could never offer my Lord advice that would jeopardize respect for authority."

The Prince returned home pained and astonished. He felt that several hundred people were being wronged, and he saw that he could not save them. Any more than he could have extricated a man trapped under a fallen obelisk or temple column.

"My hands are too weak to lift this edifice," thought the Prince with an ache in his soul. For the first time he sensed that there was a force infinitely greater than his will: the interest of the state, which was recognized even by all-powerful Pharaoh and to which he himself, the Crown Prince, must bow!

Night fell. Ramses told the servants to admit no one and walked the terrace of his villa by himself, thinking:

"Incredible! Out there Nitager's invincible regiments parted before me—and here a prison warden, an investigator, and the Great Scribe stand in my way ... Who are they? ... Wretched servants of my father (may he live forever!) who can at any moment reduce them to slaves and send them to the quarries. Why shouldn't my father pardon innocent people? It's the will of the state! ... And what is the state? ... What does it eat, where does it sleep, where are its hands and sword, of which everyone stands in dread?"

He looked at the garden and, among the trees on the summit of the hill, saw the gigantic silhouettes of the pylon towers, on which burned the torches of the watch. It occurred to him that the watch never slept and the pylon towers never ate, yet were. Centuries-old[6] towers, mighty as the ruler who erected them, Ramses the Great.

To move those edifices and hundreds like them; to beguile that watch and thousands of others which stood guard over Egypt's safety; to flout the laws bequeathed by Ramses the Great and other, still greater rulers before him, and which twenty dynasties had hallowed with their respect ...

In the Prince's soul, for the first time in his life, there began to take form a vague but gigantic concept—that of the state. The state was something more magnificent than the temple at Thebes, something greater than the pyramid of Cheops, something more ancient than the undergrounds of the Sphinx,[7] something more durable than granite. In that immense if invisible edifice, people were like ants in a rock crevice, and the pharaoh was like an itinerant architect who had barely time to set a single stone in a wall before he departed. And the walls grew from generation to generation, and the process of building continued.

Never had the royal scion so felt his smallness as now when his eyes ranged in the night above the Nile, among the pylon towers of the Pharaoh's castle and the indistinct but mighty silhouettes of the Memphis temples.

Suddenly, from among the trees whose boughs touched the terrace, there spoke a voice:

"I know your concern, and I bless you. The court will not release the accused peasants. But their case may be dismissed, and they may return home in peace, if the steward of your farm does not press charges in the attack."

"Then it was my steward who turned in the complaint?" asked the Prince in surprise.

"Yes, he submitted it in your name. But if he doesn't appear in court, there will be no plaintiff; and where there is no plaintiff, there is no crime."

The bushes rustled.

"Wait!" cried Ramses. "Who are you?"

No one answered. But the Prince thought that, in a streak of light from a torch burning on the first floor, he glimpsed a shaven head and a leopard skin.

"A priest?" whispered the Successor. "Why does he hide?"

Then it occurred to him the priest might answer gravely for furnishing advice that impeded the administration of justice.

---

[6] "Centuries-old towers ... erected [by] Ramses the Great": Ramses II (the Great) was born ca. 1303 BCE—little more than two centuries before *Pharaoh*'s present time. *(Translator.)*

[7] There are no spaces within or beneath the Great Sphinx. Originally, a temple stood *in front of* the Sphinx, built when the Sphinx was carved. *(Translator.)*

CHAPTER 12

R amses spent the greater part of the night in fevered visions. One moment he saw
the state as an immense labyrinth with massive impenetrable walls. Then again he
saw the shade of the priest whose utterance had shown him a way out of the labyrinth. Thus, most unexpectedly, two powers presented themselves to him: the interest of
the state, which he had never been aware of though he was crown prince—and the priesthood, which he wanted to crush and make his servant.

It was a hard night. The Prince tossed on his bed and asked himself, had he not been
blind and had he not just regained sight, only to learn of his own foolishness and nothingness? How differently, in these hours, he viewed his mother's cautions, his father's re-
straint in pronouncing the supreme will, and even the stern conduct of Minister Herhor.

"Kingdom and clergy!" repeated the Prince, half-asleep, bathed in a cold sweat.

Only the gods in heaven know what might have ensued, had the thoughts that germi-
nated this night in the Prince's soul had time to develop and mature. Perhaps on becoming
pharaoh he might have been among the happiest and longest-reigning sovereigns. Perhaps his name, carved in underground and surface temples, might have passed down to
posterity invested with the utmost glory. Perhaps he and his dynasty might not have lost
the throne, and Egypt might have been spared a great shock at the worst time.

But daylight scattered the visions circling the Prince's fevered head, and ensuing days
greatly altered his ideas about the inflexibility of state interests.

The Prince's visit to the prison did not pass without results for the accused. The investigating official immediately submitted a report to the Supreme Judge; the Judge reviewed
the case again, personally examined several of the accused and, over a couple of days,
released the greater part of them and speedily placed the rest on trial.

And when the plaintiff failed to appear on behalf of the Prince, despite paging in the
courtroom and marketplace, the case in the attack was dismissed and the rest of the accused were released.

One of the judges did remark that, under the law, the steward of the Prince's farm
ought to stand trial for false complaint and, if convicted, suffer the same punishment that
had faced the accused. However, the question was passed over in silence.

The steward of the farm disappeared from the court's view, sent by the Crown Prince
to the nome of Ta-Seti, and presently the chest containing the dossier in the attack disappeared.

Learning of this, Prince Ramses went to the Great Scribe and asked him with a smile:

"Your Eminence, the innocent have been released, the dossier has been sacrilegiously destroyed, yet respect for authority does not seem to have been compromised?"

"My Prince," replied the Great Scribe with his wonted coolness, "I did not realize you turn in complaints with one hand and choose to withdraw them with the other. Your Eminence was offended by the mob, so it was our duty to punish it. However, if you have forgiven, then the state has nothing to add."

"The state! ... The state!" said the Prince. "The state," he narrowed his eyes, "is *us*."

"Yes, the state is the pharaoh ... and his most faithful servants," answered the Scribe.

The conversation with so high a dignitary sufficed to expunge from the Successor's soul the powerful if inchoate concept of "the state." The state was not an eternal, immovable edifice to which each pharaoh should add a stone of glory, but rather a heap of sand that each ruler shifted as he pleased. In the state there were not those tight doors called laws, passing through which everyone must bow his head, whoever he be, peasant or crown prince. In that edifice there were diverse entrances and exits: narrow for the small and weak, commodious for the strong.

"If that is so," thought the Prince, "then I'll set up an order that will be to my liking!"

He recalled two persons: the Negro freedman who, without waiting to be told, had been ready to lay down his life for the Prince's belongings; and the unknown priest.

"If I had more people like them, my will would count for something in Egypt and abroad!" he told himself, and he felt an irresistible urge to find the priest.

He was probably the same who had stopped the mob from attacking the Prince's house. On one hand, he had an excellent knowledge of the law; on the other, he knew how to handle mobs.

"A priceless man! I must find him."

In a small boat with a single rower, the Prince began visiting the huts near his farm. Wearing a tunic and great wig, and carrying a calibrated staff, the Prince looked like an engineer monitoring the Nile's flood.

The peasants gladly informed him about changes in the contours of the land due to the flood, and asked that the government devise easier means of drawing water than the shadoof. They also described the attack on the Successor's farm and said they didn't know the people who had thrown rocks. Finally, they recalled the priest who had prevailed on the crowd to disperse; but who he might be, they did not know.

"There is a priest in our vicinity," said a peasant, "who treats the eyes; there is one who treats wounds and sets broken arms and legs. There are a couple of priests who teach reading and writing; there's one who plays the double flute, and nicely too. But the one who showed up in the Successor's garden is none of them, nor do they know anything about him. It must certainly have been the god Khnum or some spirit that watches over the Prince, may he live forever and always have a good appetite."

"Maybe it really was a spirit!" thought Ramses. In Egypt, good and evil spirits were always more readily encountered than rain.

The Nile's water turned from red to dark brown and in August, in the month of Athyr,[1] attained half its maximum height. Sluices were opened in dikes, and water gushed in to

---

[1] Actually, the ancient Egyptian month of Athyr lay between November 10 and December 9 of the modern, Gregorian calendar. *(Translator.)*

replenish the canals and the vast artificial Lake Moeris in Fayum Province, renowned for its beautiful roses. Lower Egypt seemed an arm of the sea, thickly dotted with hills bearing gardens and houses. Land communication had ceased entirely, and such profusion of boats, white, yellow, red, and dusky, plied the water that they looked like so many autumn leaves. On the highest points of the countryside, the harvesting of a kind of cotton and the second mowing of clover were being concluded, and the plucking of tamarind fruit and olives was beginning.

One day, as his boat was passing some flooded farms, the Prince observed an unusual commotion. Among the trees on one of the transient islets, women were shouting. "Someone must have died," thought the Prince.

From another isle a couple of small boats were carrying away quantities of grain and several head of cattle, while people standing at the farm buildings were threatening and cursing those in the boats. "A neighbors' dispute," the Successor told himself.

At several farms farther along it was quiet and the residents, instead of working or singing, sat on the ground in silence. "They must have finished work and are resting."

At another islet a boat had pushed off with several wailing children aboard, and a woman standing waist-deep in the water was threatening with her fists. "They're taking the children to school," thought Ramses.

Nevertheless, the incidents began to intrigue him.

On a neighboring isle, there was more shouting. The Prince shaded his eyes with his hand and saw a man lying on the ground, being caned by a Negro.

"What's going on here?" Ramses asked the rower.

"Can't you see, lord, that they're caning the miserable peasant?" laughed the boatman. "He must have done something, and now his bones are aching for it."

"And what are you?"

"Me?" replied the oarsman proudly. "I'm a free fisherman. And so long as I turn over His Holiness' share of the catch, I have free run of the whole Nile from the First Cataract[2] to the sea. A fisherman is like a fish or a wild goose; a peasant is like a tree: he feeds his masters with his fruit and can't flee, but only creaks, when the overseers tear up his bark.

"Oh, my! ... Won't you look there!" cried the contented fisherman. "Hey ... Father! Don't drink up all the water, or there'll be a bad harvest!"

The merry cry referred to a group of persons engaged in a very original activity. Several near-naked men were holding another man by the legs and immersing him head-first in the water up to the neck, to the chest, finally to the waist. At the side stood a gentleman with a cane, wearing a stained tunic and a sheepskin wig. Somewhat farther off, a woman was screaming at the top of her lungs, and men were holding her arms.[3]

Caning was as ubiquitous in the happy kingdom of the pharaohs as eating and

---

[2] First Cataract: This was, until modern times, the first of six Nile cataracts (shallow lengths of the river), numbered from north to south, that lay between Aswan and Khartoum (now the capital of Sudan). The First Cataract was chosen for construction of the Aswan Low Dam (1899-1902). The Second Cataract, in Nubia (now Sudan), was submerged under Lake Nasser when the Aswan High Dam was built (1958-70). (Translator.)

[3] This scene of water torture was inspired by an ancient Egyptian text that will be quoted at length in Chapter 44. (Translator.)

sleeping. Children and adults, peasants, craftsmen, soldiers, officers, and officials—all were caned. Everyone was caned except for the priests and the highest dignitaries, for there was no one left over to cane them. Thus the Prince had watched the caning of the peasant with some equanimity; but the immersing of this peasant captured his attention.

"Oh, boy!" laughed the rower, "aren't they watering him! He'll get so big around, his wife will have to let out his loincloth."

The Prince told him to make shore. Meanwhile the peasant was retrieved from the river, allowed to cough up the water, and again seized by the legs despite the inhuman screams of his wife, who began biting her captors.

"Stop!" shouted the Prince to the torturers who were dragging away the peasant.

"Carry on!" called the gentleman in the sheepskin wig nasally. "Who do you think you are, who impudently dare ..."

The Prince smashed him over the head with his gauge, which fortunately was light. Even so, the owner of the stained tunic landed on the ground and, after palpating his wig and head, regarded his assailant hazy-eyed.

"I gather," he said in his natural voice, "that I have the honor to be speaking with a distinguished personage ... May good humor always attend thee, my lord, and choler[4] never overflow your bones ..."

"What are you doing with this man?" interrupted the Prince.

"You ask, my lord," replied the gentleman, again nasally, "like a foreigner unfamiliar with the local customs and people, whom he addresses too familiarly. Know, then, that I am tax collector to His Eminence Dagon, the foremost banker of Memphis. And if you are not yet pale, then know that His Eminence Dagon is the lessee, plenipotentiary, and friend of the Crown Prince (may he live forever!) and that you have, as my people will attest, perpetrated violence within the estates of Prince Ramses ..."

"Then these ..." interrupted the Prince, suddenly stopping himself. "Then what right have you to be torturing the Prince's peasant like this?"

"The scoundrel won't pay his taxes, and the Crown Prince's treasury is in need."

The agent's assistants, in view of the catastrophe that had befallen their master, had released their victims and stood by helpless like members of a decapitated body. The freed peasant again spat up water and shook it out of his ears, while his wife ran over to their deliverer.

"Whoever you are," she moaned, clasping her hands before the Prince, "whether a god or a messenger of the pharaoh, hear our plight. We are peasants of the Crown Prince (may he live forever!) and we've paid all our taxes: in millet, wheat, blossoms, and cattle hides. But last decade[5] this man comes and tells us to give him another seven measures of wheat ...

"'By what right?' asks my husband, 'The taxes have been paid.' And he knocks my husband to the ground, kicks him, and says, 'By this right, that His Eminence Dagon said so.'— 'Where will I get it?' answers my man, 'We have no grain, and we've been living a month

---

[4] Choler: yellow bile. In ancient and medieval medicine, it was considered one of four bodily *humors* (the others were black bile, phlegm, and blood). Each humor corresponded to one of four traditional temperaments; choler was responsible for anger and aggression. *(Translator.)*

[5] decade: Each of the 12 Egyptian months was divided into three 10-day "decades," together making 360 days. The 365-day Egyptian calendar was rounded out at year's end with five extra days. *(Translator.)*

now on lotus seeds and roots, and even those are getting harder to come by because great lords like to play with lotus blossoms.'"[6]

She became short of breath and began weeping. The Prince waited patiently for her to calm down.

The peasant who had been immersed muttered: "The woman will bring misfortune on us with her talk. I've said I don't like women meddling in my affairs."

Meanwhile the agent had sidled over to the rower and asked him quietly, indicating Ramses: "Who's the squirt?"

"May your tongue wilt!" replied the rower. "Can't you see he must be a great lord? He pays well, and he gives a good drubbing."

"I could tell right off," whispered the agent, "that he must be someone great. I passed my youth at feasts with distinguished lords."

"Aha! You've still got the sauces on your clothes to show for it," muttered the rower.

Having had a good cry, the woman continued:

"And today this scribe comes with his men and tells my husband: 'Since you've got no wheat, give us your two little boys, and His Eminence Dagon will not only forgive you this tax but he'll pay a drachma a year for each boy.'"

"Woe is me!" screamed the peasant who had been immersed. "You'll ruin us all with your talk ... Don't listen to her, good lord," he said to Ramses. "As a cow thinks she'll drive off the flies with her tail, so the woman thinks she'll drive off the tax collectors with her tongue. They don't know they're both stupid ..."

"You're the one that's stupid!" interrupted the woman. "Solar lord of regal presence ..."

"You're my witnesses that the woman blasphemes," said the agent in an undertone to his men.

"Fragrant blossom whose voice is like the sound of the flute, hear me!" the woman implored Ramses. "So my husband told the agent: 'I'd rather lose two bullocks, if I had them, than turn over my boys, even if you paid me four drachmas a year for each. When a child leaves home to go into service, no one ever sees him again ...'"

"Would I'd drowned! Would the fish were eating my body at the bottom of the Nile!" moaned the peasant. "Woman, you'll ruin the whole farm with your complaints ..."

The agent, seeing he had the support of the party chiefly concerned, stepped forward and began again nasally:

"Ever since the sun first rose behind the royal palace and set over the pyramids, various wonders have taken place in this land. In the reign of Pharaoh Semerkhet,[7] marvels were seen around the Pyramid of Kahun[8] and a plague descended upon Egypt. In the reign

---

[6] Lotus: The seeds of some Nile lotuses are edible. Additionally, the Egyptian blue lotus, or blue water lily, *Nymphaea caerulea*, has mild sedative and psychotropic properties, was important in religion and mythology, and often appears in Egyptian iconography, including party and funerary scenes. It has also been used since ancient times to produce perfume, tea, and wine, and is a likely candidate for the lotus plant eaten by the Lotus-Eaters in Homer's *Odyssey*. *(Translator.)*

[7] Pharaoh Semerkhet: According to the 3rd century BCE Egyptian historian Manetho, the reign of this penultimate First Dynasty pharaoh was marked by many disasters. Semerkhet was known to the Greeks as *Semempses*—the name by which Prus calls him. *(Translator.)*

[8] Pyramid of Kahun (or Lahun): the pyramid of the 12th Dynasty pharaoh Senusret II, also known as Sesostris II. It is located near the workers' village of Kahun (or Lahun) in Egypt's Fayum province. *(Translator.)*

of Boethos, the ground parted at Bubastis[9] and swallowed many people.[10] In the reign of Neferkhes,[11] for eleven days the Nile waters ran sweet as honey. These things have been seen, and many others of which I know, for I am full of wisdom. But never has a stranger been seen to come from the water and forbid the collecting of taxes on the estates of His Eminence the Crown Prince ..."

"Silence!" shouted Ramses, "and get out of here! No one," he said to the woman, "will take your sons."

"It's easy for me to get out," said the tax collector, "for I have a swift boat and five rowers. But, Your Eminence, give me a sign for my Lord Dagon ..."

"Take off your wig and show him the sign on your head," said the Prince. "Tell Dagon I'm going to give him identical signs over all his body!"

"Do you hear the profanity?" whispered the tax collector to his men, as he withdrew to the water's edge amid low bows.

He climbed into his boat; and when his helpers had pushed off and made several dozen paces, he stretched out his arm and called:

"Rebels, blasphemers, may your entrails cramp! I'm going straight to the Crown Prince and tell him what's going on in his estates!"

He picked up a cane and belabored his people for not having come to his aid.

"The same will happen to you!" he threatened Ramses.

The Prince regained his own boat and furiously told the rower to pursue the usurer's insolent agent. But the gentleman in the sheepskin wig dropped his cane and grabbed a pair of oars; and his men helped him so zealously that the chase became unlikely.

"Sooner will the owl overtake the swallow than we'll overtake them, my bonny lord," laughed Ramses' rower. "But as for you, you're no surveyor but an officer, maybe even in His Holiness' guard. Right off you hit them over the head! I know: I was in the army myself for five years. I would always hit them over the head or in the belly, and I got along well enough in the world. And if someone knocked me down, I immediately knew he must be great. Our Egypt (may the gods never forsake it!) is terribly crowded: city next to city, house next to house, man next to man. To move about in the throng, you need to hit them over the head."

"Are you married?" asked the Prince.

"H'm! when I've got a woman and room for a person and a half, then I'm married, but otherwise I'm a bachelor. I've been in the army, and I know that a woman is good once a day, and then not always. Gets in the way."

"How about joining my service? Who knows whether you'd regret it."

"By Your Eminence's leave, I could tell right away that you might command a regiment, despite your youthful face. But I'm not entering anyone's service. I'm a free fisherman; my grandfather was (saving Your Eminence) a herdsman in Lower Egypt, but my folks are of

[9]Bubastis: Greek name for the city of *Per-Bast*, or *Pi-Bast* ("House [of the goddess] Bast"). It was the capital of Am-Khent, the 18th Nome of Lower Egypt. Prus, farther on, calls the city *Pi-Bast*. *(Translator.)*

[10] "In the reign of Boethos, the earth ... swallowed many people ...": Manetho recounts that, during the 38-year reign of Boethos (the Greek name for Hotepsekhemwy, the first pharaoh of the Second Dynasty), a chasm opened at Bubastis, causing many to perish. *(Translator.)*

[11]Neferkhes: Greek name of a Second Dynasty pharaoh mentioned by Manetho—possibly the last one, Khasekhemwy. *(Translator.)*

Hyksos stock. To be sure, we're giving rise to stupid Egyptian peasants, but that makes me laugh. The peasant and the Hyksos, Your Eminence, are like the ox and the bull. A peasant can walk behind or in front of a plow, but a Hyksos won't serve anyone. Except maybe in His Holiness' army, because that's an army."

The merry boatman talked on, but the Prince was no longer listening to him. Quite new, very painful questions were asserting themselves within his own soul. So these islets belonged to his estates? Strange, he'd had no idea where his farms were or what they looked like. So Dagon had imposed new taxes on the peasants in the Prince's name, and these peculiar doings that he had been watching were the collecting of taxes? Evidently the peasant being caned had been unable to pay. The children wailing in the boat had been sold for a drachma a head for a year. And the woman who had gone waist-deep into the water and cursed was their mother.

"Women are very excitable," the Prince told himself. "Sara is the calmest of women, but other women love to talk, cry, and shout."

He was put in mind of the peasant who had tried to mollify his wife's transports. They had been near drowning him, and he hadn't been angry; they had done nothing to her, and she had shouted.

"Women are very excitable! Yes, even my worshipful mother ... What a difference between Father and Mother! His Holiness doesn't care to know that I abandoned the army for a girl, but the Queen is fascinated by my having taken a Jewess into my house. Sara is the calmest woman I know. But Taphath talks, cries, and shouts for four women."

Then the Prince recalled the peasant's wife saying that for a month they had been eating no grain, only lotus seeds and roots. The seeds were like poppy seeds; the roots, so-so. He wouldn't have eaten the stuff for three days running. And the priest-physicians recommended a varied diet. At school he had been told that one should eat meat alongside fish, dates alongside wheat, figs alongside barley. To subsist for a whole month on lotus seeds! Well, but what about horses and cows? Horses and cows like hay, and barley noodles have to be shoved down their gullets. By the same token, peasants doubtless preferred lotus seeds and had no taste for wheat cakes or barley cakes, or for fish or meat. And the most pious priests, the wonder-workers, never touched meat or fish. Apparently magnates and royal sons needed meat like lions and eagles; peasants, grass like oxen.

Only ... what about that ducking for taxes? Oh, well, hadn't he, swimming with friends, pushed them under and dived under himself? How much laughter had attended it ... ducking was fun! As for canings, hadn't he been caned at school? ... It was painful, but evidently not to all creatures. A beaten dog howled and bit; a beaten ox didn't even look around. Likewise a great lord might find caning painful, but a peasant shouted merely for the pure joy of shouting. Then, too, not everyone did shout; soldiers and officers sang under the cane.

These wise reflections nevertheless failed to still a slight but gnawing uneasiness in the Successor's heart. The fact was, his lessee Dagon had imposed an unjust tax which the peasants were unable to pay!

Just now the Prince was not concerned about the peasants but about his mother. She must know about the Phoenician's management of the estates. What would she say about it to her son, how would she look at him, how would she smirk? She wouldn't be a woman if she didn't say to him: "Ramses, didn't I tell you this Phoenician would ruin your estates?"

"If those traitors the priests," thought the Prince, "offered me twenty talents today, tomorrow I would drive out Dagon, my peasants wouldn't be caned and ducked, and my mother wouldn't taunt me. A tenth ... a hundredth of the riches that repose in the temples and feed the greedy eyes of the baldpates would make me independent of the Phoenicians for years."

A peculiar idea flashed to Ramses' soul: that there existed a deep conflict between the peasants and the priests.

"It was because of Herhor," he thought, "that the peasant at the edge of the desert hanged himself. Some two million Egyptian populace toil for the upkeep of the priests and temples. If the estates of the priests were the pharaoh's property, I wouldn't be needing to borrow fifteen talents and my peasants wouldn't be so dreadfully oppressed. That is the source of Egypt's misfortunes, and of the weakness of her kings!"

The Prince felt the peasants were being wronged, and so he felt no little relief to discover that the culprits were the priests. It did not cross his mind that his judgment might be mistaken and unfair.

In any event, he was not judging; he was angry. And a man's anger never turns upon himself; like a hungry leopard, it does not devour its own body but, twisting its tail and pricking its ears, looks about for prey.

CHAPTER 13

The Successor's quest for the priest who had saved Sara and given him legal advice produced an unexpected result.

The priest had not turned up, but legends about Ramses began circulating among the Egyptian peasants.

A man skiffed evenings from village to village, telling the peasants that the Successor had freed the persons who, because of the attack on his house, had been threatened with the mines. He had also struck an agent trying to exact an unjust tax from the peasants. The stranger added, finally, that Prince Ramses enjoyed the special favor of the god Amon of the Western Desert, who was his father.

The simple populace avidly listened to these tidings, first because they accorded with facts; second, because the man relating them seemed himself to be a spirit: he skiffed in from nowhere, and disappeared.

Prince Ramses did not discuss his peasants with Dagon, or even summon him. He was mortified at having had to borrow money from the Phoenician, from whom he might need to do so again.

But a few days after the encounter with Dagon's scribe, the banker called on the Successor, carrying a wrapped object in his hands. On entering the Prince's room, he knelt, undid the white cloth, and took out an exquisite gold winecup.

It was encrusted with stones of various colors and covered with low reliefs depicting, on the base, the harvesting and pressing of grapes, and on the bowl a feast.

"Your Eminence, accept this winecup from your slave," said the banker, "and use it a hundred ... a thousand years ... to the end of the ages."

The Prince saw through the Phoenician. Forbearing to touch the golden gift, he said stern-faced: "Dagon, do you see the purple sheen within the cup?"

"Indeed," replied the banker, "how could I not but see the purple sheen, which shows that the cup is purest gold?"

"And I tell you that that is the blood of children taken from their parents," retorted the Successor.

He turned and stalked out of the room.

"Oh, Astoreth!" groaned the Phoenician. His lips went livid, and his hands shook so badly that he barely managed to wrap the winecup back in the white cloth.

A couple of days later, Dagon sailed with his winecup to Sara's farm. He wore gold-threaded robes, in his thick beard a small glass sphere which seeped perfumes, and two feathers affixed to his head.

"Beautiful Sara," he began, "may Jehovah pour as many blessings upon your family as there is water flowing today in the Nile. We Phoenicians and you Jews are neighbors and brothers. And I burn with such fervent love for you that, if you did not belong to His Eminence our Lord, I would give Gideon (may he be well!) ten talents for you and take you for my lawful wife. So passionate am I!"

"God keep me," replied Sara, "lest I need have another lord than the one I have. But, worthy Dagon, whence your wish to visit our lord's servant today?"

"I'll tell you the truth as if you were my wife Tamar who, though a native daughter of Sidon and though she brought me a big dowry, is now old and unworthy to remove your sandals ..."

"In the honey flowing from your lips there is much wormwood,"[1] broke in Sara.

"Let the honey be for you," said Dagon, sitting down, "and let the wormwood poison my heart. Our lord Prince Ramses (may he live forever!) has the lips of a lion and the cunning of a vulture. He was pleased to lease me his estates, which filled my stomach with joy; but he so distrusts me that from anguish I do not sleep nights but heave sighs and pour tears on my bed, where I wish you lay with me, Sara, instead of my wife Tamar, who can no longer excite my lust."

"That isn't what you meant to say," interrupted Sara, blushing.

"I no longer know what I mean to say ever since I set eyes on you and since our lord, watching my activities on the farms, caned and broke the health of my scribe who was collecting a tax from the peasants. The tax isn't for me, Sara, but for our lord. Not I will eat the figs and wheat breads from those estates but you, Sara, and our lord ... I've given our lord money, and you gems, so why should the wretched Egyptian peasants impoverish our lord and you, Sara? And so you may know how powerfully you excite my blood for you, and that I want nothing from our lord's estates but give everything to him and to you, Sara, take this winecup of pure gold, encrusted with gems and covered with sculpture which the very gods would admire ..."

With that, Dagon took from its white cloth the winecup that had been rejected by the Prince.

"Sara," he said, "I do not want you to keep this gold winecup in your house and give our lord drink from it. You give this cup of pure gold to your father Gideon, whom I love as a brother. And, Sara, you tell your father these words: 'Dagon, your twin, the hapless lessee of the Successor's estates, is ruined. So drink, my father, from this winecup and think of your twin Dagon, and ask Jehovah that our lord Prince Ramses not beat up Dagon's scribes or stir rebellion among the peasants, who refuse to pay the tax, as it is.' And know, Sara, that should you ever admit me to intimacy with you, I would give you two talents and your father a talent. And I would be ashamed that I give you so little, for you are worthy to be caressed by the Pharaoh himself and by the Successor, and by His Eminence Minister Herhor, and by the most valiant Nitager, and by the richest Phoenician bankers. You're so delectable that when I see you I swoon, and when I don't see you I close my eyes and lick my lips. You are sweeter than figs, more fragrant than roses ... I'd give you five talents ... Take the cup, Sara ..."

---

[1] Wormwood: any of several aromatic plants of genus *Artemisia*, especially *Artemisia absinthium*, yielding a bitter extract that is used in flavoring certain wines. Medicinal use of wormwood dates to ancient Egypt and is mentioned in the Ebers Papyrus of herbal knowledge, ca. 1550 BCE. *(Translator.)*

Sara backed away with downcast eyes. "I won't," she said, "because my lord forbids me to accept gifts from anyone."

Dagon was dumbfounded and regarded her with astonished eyes. "Perhaps, Sara, you don't know what this cup is worth? Anyway, I'm giving it to your father, to my brother ..."

"I can't accept it," whispered Sara.

"Good heavens!" shouted Dagon. "Then, Sara, you'll pay me for the cup a different way, without telling your lord. A beautiful woman like you needs gold and jewels and should have a banker of her own to give her money when she likes, not just when it pleases her lord?"

"I can't!" whispered Sara, with unconcealed disgust for Dagon.

In the blink of an eye, the Phoenician changed his tone and laughed: "Very good, Sara! I just wanted to see whether you're faithful to our lord. And I see you are, though stupid people will talk ..."

"What?" Sara burst out, throwing herself at Dagon clenched-fisted.

"Ah! ha! ha!" laughed the Phoenician. "What a pity our lord didn't hear and see this. But I'll tell him sometime, when he's in a good mood, that you're not only as faithful to him as a dog but wouldn't even accept a gold winecup because he forbids you to accept gifts. And this cup, believe me, Sara, would tempt more than one woman ... no small woman, too ..."

Dagon stayed a while longer, admiring Sara's virtue and obedience, then took a very tender leave of her, boarded his boat equipped with tent, and sailed off for Memphis. The farther the boat receded from the farm, the more the smile faded from the Phoenician's face, replaced by an angry expression. When Sara's house had disappeared behind the trees, Dagon rose and, lifting his hands, called:

"O Baal Sidon,[2] O Astoreth! Avenge this affront on the accursed daughter of Judah! May her treacherous beauty perish like a raindrop in the desert ... May diseases waste her body, and madness possess her soul ... May her master drive her from his house like a mangy pig ... And as today she pushed away my winecup, so may the time come when people will push away her withered hand as she begs, thirsty, for a cup of turbid water ..."

Then he spat repeatedly and muttered incomprehensible but terrible expressions until a black cloud momentarily concealed the sun, and the water near the boat became troubled, swelling into large waves. When he had finished, the sun came out again but the river remained troubled, as though stirred by a new flood.

Dagon's rowers became frightened and stopped singing but, separated from their master by the wall of the tent, they did not see what he was about.

Henceforth the Phoenician did not show himself to the Successor. But one day when the Prince returned to his villa, he found in the bedroom a beautiful sixteen-year-old Phoenician dancing girl wearing only a gold circlet on her head and a gossamer shawl on her shoulders.

"Who are you?" asked the Prince.

"I'm a priestess and your servant. Lord Dagon sent me to exorcise the anger you bear for him."

"How do you do that?"

"Like this ... Sit here," she said, placing him in an armchair. "I'll stand on tiptoe to make

---

[2] Baal Sidon: a Phoenician god, the patron (*baal*, "lord") of the city of Sidon. *(Translator.)*

myself taller than your anger, and with this consecrated shawl I'll drive the evil spirits from you. Begone! ... Begone!" she whispered, dancing around Ramses. "Let my hands take the gloom from your hair ... let my kisses restore a bright look to your eyes ... let the beating of my heart fill your ears with music, O lord of Egypt ... Begone! ... Begone! ... He's not yours but mine ... Love needs such quiet that even anger must be stilled ..."

Dancing, she played with Ramses' hair, embraced his neck, kissed his eyes. At last, tired, she sat down at the Prince's feet and, leaning her head on his knees, gazed at him, panting with parted lips.

"You're not angry anymore at your servant Dagon?" she whispered, stroking the Prince's face.

Ramses tried to kiss her lips but she sprang away from his knees, crying: "Oh, no, you mustn't!"

"Why not?"

"I'm a virgin and a priestess of the great goddess Astoreth. You would have to love and revere my patroness very much before you might kiss me."

"But you're allowed to?"

"I am allowed anything, because I'm a priestess and have sworn to preserve my chastity."

"Then why did you come here?"

"To drive away your anger. I've done that, and I'm leaving. Be well and always be good!" she added with a piercing look.

"Where do you live? ... What's your name?" asked the Prince.

"My name is Cuddles. And I live ... Oh, why should I say? You won't soon be coming over."

She waved and disappeared, and the stunned Prince did not move from his armchair. When after a moment he looked out the window, he saw a sumptuous litter being rapidly borne by four Nubians toward the Nile.

Ramses did not regret her departure: she had surprised him but had not swept him off his feet.

"Sara is calmer than her," he thought, "and prettier. Besides ... it seems to me this Phoenician girl must be cold, and her caresses studied."

Still, the Prince ceased being angry with Dagon, especially after peasants came one time when he was at Sara's and, thanking him for his help, said the Phoenician was no longer making them pay the new tax.

So it was outside Memphis. But at the Prince's more distant farms, his lessee recouped his losses.

CHAPTER 14

n the month of Choiak, from mid-September to mid-October,[1] the Nile waters crested and
began dropping slightly. In gardens, tamarind fruit, dates, and olives were harvested,
and trees blossomed a second time.

His Holiness Ramses XII departed his solar palace outside Memphis and sailed for Thebes with a great suite in several dozen festive ships to thank the local gods for a good flood[2] and to make offerings at the tombs of his eternally living forbears.[3]

His Holiness had taken a very gracious leave of his son and Successor; but he had entrusted affairs of state for the duration of his absence to Herhor.

Prince Ramses was so affected by this evidence of the monarch's lack of confidence in him that for three days he did not leave his villa or eat but only wept. Then he stopped shaving and moved to Sara's farm in order to avoid contact with Herhor and to vex his mother, whom he considered the cause of his misfortunes.

On his second day in this out-of-the-way place he was visited by Thutmose trailing two boats of musicians and dancing girls and a third laden with baskets of food and flowers and with pitchers of wine. The Prince sent the musicians and dancing girls packing, took Thutmose into the garden, and said:

"I expect that my mother (may she live forever!) sent you here to get me away from the Jewess? Well, you tell Her Eminence that, even were Herhor to become not only my father's viceroy but his son, I will do as I like. I know what they're up to. Today they want

---

[1] Actually, the ancient Egyptian month of Choiak lay between December 10 and January 8 of the modern, Gregorian calendar, or between December 11 and January 9 immediately after a Coptic leap year. *(Translator.)*

[2] This was the Beautiful Festival of Opet (in Egyptian, *heb nefer en Ipet*), or Opet Festival, celebrated annually in Thebes. It actually took place not in the Fourth Month of the Flood Season, Choiak, but in the Second Month, Phaophi. It became a major festival in the early New Kingdom following the expulsion of the Hyksos. The central event was a procession of the ceremonial barque of the god Amon-Ra, carrying his statue, from the Temple of Karnak to the Temple of Luxor. There the pharaoh was ceremonially reborn and confirmed as intermediary between the gods and Egyptian society. This was crucial to ensuring *Maat* (truth, balance, order, harmony, law, morality, justice) as personified by the goddess Maat; and, among other things, to ensuring optimal (neither too scant nor too excessive) annual flooding of the Nile. *(Translator.)*

[3] This was the Beautiful Festival of the Valley (in Egyptian, *heb nefer en inet*), from the Middle Kingdom period cekebrated in Thebes annually in the *shemu* (summer) low-water season. In the Festival's central event, the sacred barque of Amon-Ra left the Temple of Karnak to visit the funerary temples of deceased royalty on the Nile's west bank and their shrines in the Theban necropolis. *(Translator.)*

to deprive me of Sara; tomorrow, of power ... I'm going to show them I'm not giving up anything."

The Prince was exercised; Thutmose shrugged and at length replied:

"As a gale sweeps a bird out into the desert, so anger casts a man onto the verge of injustice. Are you surprised at the priests' displeasure with the Crown Prince binding his life to a woman of a different land and faith? It's true they don't like Sara, especially as she's your only woman; if you had several women like all the young nobles, no one would pay attention to the Jewess. But, then, what harm have they done her? ... None. Indeed, a priest even defended her from an angry mob of assailants whom it has pleased you to get released from jail."

"What about my mother?" broke in the Successor.

Thutmose burst out laughing. "Your worshipful mother," he said, "loves you like her own eyes and heart. Sure enough, she doesn't like Sara either; but do you know what Her Eminence told me one time? ... To take Sara away from you! ... Do you appreciate her joke? I answered likewise with a joke: Ramses gave me a pack of hunting dogs and two Syrian horses when he grew tired of them; so maybe one of these days he'll give me his mistress, whom I'll doubtless have to accept along with a bonus."

"Perish the thought! I wouldn't give Sara to anybody today precisely because it was on her account that my father didn't name me viceroy."

Thutmose shook his head. "You're very mistaken," he said. "So mistaken, it frightens me. Could it be you really don't understand the causes of disfavor, which are common knowledge with every enlightened person in Egypt?"

"I don't know a thing."

"More's the pity," said Thutmose, concerned. "Then you don't know that since the maneuvers the soldiers, especially the Greeks, have been drinking your health in every tavern."

"That's what they got the money for."

"Yes, but not so they would go shouting at the tops of their voices that when you succeed His Holiness (may he live forever!) you're going to start a great war, after which there will be changes in Egypt. What changes? ... And who dares speak in the pharaoh's lifetime about the plans of his successor?"

The Prince turned somber.

"That's one thing, and I'll tell you another," said Thutmose, "for evil, like a hyena, never walks alone. Do you know that the peasants are singing songs about you, about how you freed the assailants from jail—and what's worse, they're again saying that when you succeed His Holiness, taxes will be abolished? It should be added that every time there's been talk among the peasants about injustice and taxes, disturbances have always followed. And either an external enemy has invaded the weakened Kingdom, or Egypt has split into as many parts as there were nomarchs. Finally, judge for yourself: is it proper that in Egypt any name be pronounced oftener than the pharaoh's? Or that anyone should stand between the people and our Lord? ... And if I may, I'll tell you how the priests view the matter."

"Go on."

"A very learned priest who observes the heavenly revolutions from the top of the Temple of Amon has come up with an allegory:

"The pharaoh is the sun, and the crown prince is the moon. When the moon follows the radiant god at a distance, we have light in the daytime and at night. When the moon seeks to get too close to the sun, the moon disappears and nights are dark. But if the moon happens to stand in front of the sun, there occurs an eclipse—a great fright for the world."

"And all this prattle," interrupted Ramses, "reaches the ears of His Holiness? Woe is me! Would I'd never been the King's son!"

"The Pharaoh, as a god on earth, knows about everything; but he is too powerful to attend to the drunken cries of the soldiers or the whispers of the peasants. He knows that every Egyptian would give his life for him, you foremost."

"That's true!" said the Prince. "But I see all this as an outrageous new hypocrisy of the priests," he added, growing animated. "I conceal our Lord's majesty by releasing innocent people from jail and by forbidding my lessee to torment the peasants with an unjust tax. But when His Eminence Herhor runs the army, names the commanders, treats with foreign princes, and has my father spend his days in prayer ..."

Thutmose covered his ears and, stamping his feet, cried:

"Silence, silence! Your every word is blasphemy! His Holiness alone rules the Kingdom, and whatever happens on earth stems from his will. Herhor is the Pharaoh's servant and does the Lord's bidding ... One day you'll find out for yourself ... May my words not be taken wrong!"

The Prince turned so somber that Thutmose broke off the conversation and took a hasty farewell of his friend. When he had boarded his canopied and curtained boat, he drew a deep breath, drained a generous cup of wine, and ruminated:

"Brr! I thank the gods for not having given me a character like Ramses'. He's the unhappiest of men in the happiest of circumstances. He could have the most beautiful women in Memphis but keeps to one in order to annoy his mother! Whereas it's not his mother he's annoying but all the virtuous maidens and faithful wives who languish because the Crown Prince, who's a gorgeous boy, won't take away their virginity or make them unfaithful. He could not only drink but bathe in the finest wines, but instead he prefers wretched soldiers' beer and a dry cake rubbed with garlic. Why these peasant tastes? I don't get it, unless the worshipful Lady Nikotris happened to watch workers eating during the most vulnerable time.[4]

"He could also do nothing from dawn to dusk. If he liked, he could be fed personally by the foremost lords and their wives, sisters, and daughters. But he not only reaches for his food himself but, to the mortification of the young nobles, washes and dresses by himself, while his barber spends his days snaring fowl and wasting his skills.

"Oh, Ramses! Ramses!" sighed the dandy. "How can a style develop around such a prince? We've been wearing the same aprons for a year now, and wigs remain in fashion only thanks to the court dignitaries, because Ramses just won't wear a wig, which is a great humiliation for the nobility.

"And all this ... brr! ... is the doing of damned politics! Oh, how glad I am I don't have to guess what they're thinking in Tyre or Nineveh, trouble myself over pay for the army, calculate how many people Egypt has gained or lost, and how much can be raised in taxes. It's a terrible thing to tell myself that my peasant doesn't pay me as much as I need and

---

[4] A superstition holds that things viewed by an expectant mother can affect the child's subsequent traits. (Translator.)

spend but as much as the Nile's flood allows for. Father Nile doesn't ask my creditors how much I owe them."

Thus reflected the elegant Thutmose, as he fortified his distressed spirit with golden wine. Before the boat reached Memphis, he was overcome by such a heavy slumber that the slaves had to carry their master ashore to the litter.

Following Thutmose's decampment, the Successor pondered deeply and became afraid.

The Prince was a skeptic, as an alumnus of the highest priest schools and a member of the highest aristocracy. He knew that while some priests prepared through months-long fasts and mortifications to conjure spirits, others called spirits a delusion[5] or fraud. He had also seen the sacred Apis bull, before which all Egypt prostrated itself on its face, receive hidings from the lowest priests who brought it fodder and cows for servicing.

He knew, finally, that his father Ramses XII, who to the commonalty was an eternally living god and almighty Lord of the World, was actually a man like others, only a little sicklier than other old people and very constrained by the priests.

The Prince knew all this and mocked many things in his mind, and even publicly. But all his freethinking was futile before the hard fact that no one may make light of the pharaoh's titles!

Ramses knew his country's history and remembered that in Egypt much was forgiven the great. A great lord could ruin a canal, furtively kill a man, privately mock the gods, take gifts from envoys of foreign powers ... but two sins were inadmissible: betrayal of priestly secrets, and betrayal of the pharaoh. The man who committed either of these would vanish, sometimes after a year's time, from amid servants and friends. But what became of him and where, no one dared even to speak of.

Ramses felt he had been on such an incline ever since the army and peasants had started uttering his name and holding forth about supposed plans of his, about changes in the Kingdom, and about future wars. Thinking about it, the Prince had the impression that a nameless mob of wretches and rebels was shoving him, the Crown Prince, to the top of the tallest obelisk, from which one could only fall and be smashed to a pulp.

When eventually he succeeded his father as pharaoh, he would have the right and means to do many things that no one in Egypt could contemplate without dread. But today he must truly be on his guard lest he be pronounced a traitor and rebel against the fundamental laws of the Kingdom.

In Egypt there was one overt ruler: the pharaoh. He ruled, he willed, he thought for everyone, and woe betide him who dared doubt aloud the pharaoh's omnipotence or speak of plans of his own or of changes in general.

Plans were made in but one place: the hall where the pharaoh heard the views of his privy councilors and told them his opinions. Any changes could come only thence. It was there that the sole visible lamp of state wisdom burned, illuminating all of Egypt. But about that, too, it was safer to be silent.

All these thoughts swept at gale speed through the Successor's head as he sat on a

---

[5] Prus here uses the word *przywidzenie*, which non-psychiatric Polish dictionaries (Prus was not a psychiatrist) define, often simultaneously, by several words, including ones that individually translate into English as "illusion," "delusion," and "hallucination." Each of the latter English terms refers to a distinctly different psychiatric phenomenon. *(Translator.)*

stone bench in Sara's garden, under a chestnut tree, and looked out over the surrounding countryside.

The water of the Nile had fallen a bit and was beginning to turn crystal-clear. But the whole country still looked like a gulf of the sea densely strewn with islands bearing buildings, vegetable and fruit gardens, and here and there clumps of great ornamental trees.

Ranged around all the islands were shadoofs with which copper-colored men in dirty loincloths and caps were drawing water from the Nile and pouring it into successively higher wells.

One such spot in particular impressed itself on Ramses. It was a steep hillside on which three shadoofs were at work: one drew water from the river and poured it into the lowest well; the second drew water from the lowest well and raised it a couple of cubits[6] to the middle well; and the third lifted water from the middle well to the highest well, atop the hill. There several more half-naked men drew water into buckets and watered the vegetable beds or sprinkled the trees with watering pots.

The shadoofs' down-and-up movements, the inclinations of the buckets, and the streams from the watering pots were so rhythmic that the men who produced them might have been thought automatons. None of them spoke to his neighbor, changed place, or looked about, but only bent over and straightened up, ever the same way, from morning to evening, from one month to the next, doubtless from childhood to death.

"And it's creatures like these," thought the Prince, watching the husbandmen at work, "creatures like these that want to make me the agent of their delusions! What changes can they ask for in the Kingdom? That the man who lifts water to a lower well be promoted to a higher one? Or that the man who waters the vegetable beds with a bucket, instead sprinkle the trees with a watering pot?"

It angered and humiliated him to think that he, the Crown Prince, had not become viceroy due to the tales of such beings that rocked away their whole lives over wells of muddy water!

Just then he heard a quiet rustling among the trees, and delicate hands came to rest on his shoulders.

"What do you say, Sara?" said the Prince without turning his head.

"You're sad, my lord?" she replied. "Moses was not as happy to see the Promised Land as I was to hear you say you were coming here to live with me. But we've been together a day now, and I've yet to see you smile. You don't even speak to me but go about gloomy, and at night you don't caress me but heave sighs."

"I have worries."

"Tell them to me. A worry is like a treasure entrusted for safekeeping. While we alone mind the worry, even sleep eludes us, and it becomes easier only when we find a second keeper."

Ramses embraced her and seated her beside him on the bench.

"When a peasant," he smiled, "can't finish clearing the field before the flood, his wife helps him. She also helps him milk the cows, brings him food from the house, washes him

---

[6] The cubit, a unit of length, is the distance from the elbow (in Latin, *cubitum*, "elbow") to the tip of the middle finger. The cubit was used in many parts of the world from antiquity into early modern times. The "royal cubit," the earliest known standard measure, dates at least from the construction of pharaoh Zoser's Step Pyramid, about 2700 BCE. *(Translator.)*

when he returns from work. Hence the belief that a woman can ease a man's troubles."

"You don't believe it, lord?"

"A prince's cares," said Ramses, "can't be helped by a woman, even so astute and masterful a woman as my mother."

"By God! what are they, tell me!" insisted Sara, snuggling against the Successor's arm. "In our traditions, Adam left Paradise for Eve; and he was surely the greatest king of the most beautiful kingdom."

The Prince mused: "Our sages likewise teach that more than one man has given up dignities for a woman. But one doesn't hear of a man gaining anything great through a woman: except maybe a commander to whom a pharaoh gave his daughter along with a big dowry and a high office. But a woman can't help a man out of his troubles, let alone to a higher station."

"Maybe she doesn't love him as I love your lordship," whispered Sara.

"I know you love me wondrous well. You've never asked me for gifts or favored those who don't hesitate to seek a career even under the beds of princes' mistresses. You're gentler than a lamb and quiet as a night on the Nile; your kisses are like perfumes from the land of Punt, and your embrace is sweet as the sleep of the weary. I have no measure for your beauty or words for your virtues. You're a wonder among women whose lips are full of discord and whose love costs dear. But with all your perfection, how can you ease my cares? Can you make His Holiness send a great expedition against the East, with me in command? Can you give me the Menfi Corps, which I've requested, or make me the Pharaoh's viceroy for Lower Egypt? Can you make all His Holiness' subjects think and feel as do I, his most faithful subject?"

Sara dropped her hands into her lap and whispered sadly: "It's true, I can't ... I can't do anything!"

"Yes, you can. You can cheer me up," smiled Ramses. "I know you learned to dance and play music. Take off this trailing dress suitable for priestesses who tend the fire and put on diaphanous muslin—like the Phoenician dancing girls—and dance and caress me like them."

Sara grabbed his hands and, eyes ablaze, shouted:

"You associate with such harlots? Tell me ... let me know my misfortune. Then send me back to my father, to our desert valley where I wish I'd never set eyes on you!"

"Now, now ... calm down," said the Prince, toying with her hair. "I can't help seeing dancing girls, if not at feasts then at royal observances or temple services. But all of them together don't interest me as much as you. Which of them is your equal? You have a body like an ivory statue of Isis, while each of them has some flaw. Some are fat, others have skinny legs or ugly hands, yet others wear false hair. Which of them is like you? If you were Egyptian, all the temples would vie for you as their chorister. What do I say? If you showed up right now in Memphis in a diaphanous dress, the priests would make their peace with you, provided you agreed to take part in their processions."

"We daughters of Judah may not wear immodest dresses ..."

"Or dance or sing? ... Then why did you learn to?"

"Our women and girls dance in praise of the Lord, not to sow the fiery seeds of lust in men's hearts. And we sing ... Wait, my lord, I'll sing for you."

She rose from the bench and walked off toward the house. Soon she reappeared, followed by a young girl with frightened black eyes who carried a harp.

"Who's the girl?" asked the Prince. "Wait, I think I've seen that look before ... Yes, last time I was here, this frightened girl watched me out of the bushes ..."

"This is my relative and servant Esther,"[7] said Sara. "She's been living with me a month now, but she fears your lordship, so she runs off. She may have watched you out of the bushes."

"You may go, my child," said the Prince to the petrified girl. When she was hidden by the trees, he added: "Is she Jewish too? And that watchman of your house, who also looks at me like a sheep at a crocodile?"

"That is Samuel,[8] son of Ezra,[9] likewise my relative. I hired him in place of the Negro your lordship manumitted. You did let me choose the servants?"

"Of course. And I suppose the overseer of farmhands is also a Jew, as he has a yellow complexion and likewise so humble a look as no Egyptian could manage."

"That," answered Sara, "is Ezekiel,[10] son of Ruben,[11] a relative of my father's. Are you displeased, my lord? They are very faithful servants of yours."

"Displeased!" said the Prince glumly, drumming the bench with his fingers. "He's not here to please me but to watch your farm. Anyway, these people don't concern me ... Sing, Sara."

Sara knelt on the grass at the Prince's feet, plucked a couple of chords on the harp, and began:

"Who is without care? Who, when retiring to sleep, can say: 'I've passed this day without sorrow'? Who, when going to his grave, can say: 'My life has passed without pain and fear like a fair evening on the Jordan'?

"But many each day sprinkle their bread with tears, and their homes are full of sighs!

"The wail is man's first voice on the earth; the moan, his last farewell. Full of distress he enters life; full of sorrow he descends to his resting place, and none ask him where he would abide.

"Who hasn't known life's bitter? Is it the child whose mother has passed, or the infant whose rightful breast has been sucked dry by hunger?

"Who is sure of his fate and looks unblinking to his morrow? Is it the husbandman who directs not rain nor locust? Is it the merchant who consigns his wealth to fickle winds, and his life to waves that swallow all and return nought?

---

[7] Esther: name borrowed from the Jewish heroine of the biblical *Book of Esther*. According to the Hebrew Bible, Esther was a queen of the Persian King Ahasuerus, who is variously identified with Xerxes I or his son Artaxerxes. Esther's story is the basis for the Jewish Feast of Purim. *(Translator.)*

[8] Samuel: name borrowed from a prophet in the Hebrew Bible who played a key role in the transition from the period of the biblical judges to the institution of a kingdom under Saul, and in the transition from Saul to David. Samuel is venerated as a prophet by Jews, Christians, and Muslims. *(Translator.)*

[9] Ezra: name borrowed from a Jewish scribe and priest (flourished 480-440 BCE) who, according to the Hebrew Bible, returned from Babylonian exile and reintroduced the Torah in Jerusalem. *(Translator.)*

[10] Ezekiel: name borrowed from the protagonist of the Hebrew Bible's *Book of Ezekiel*. He is acknowledged as a prophet by Jews, Christians, and Muslims. Jews and Christians consider him the 6th-century BCE author of the *Book of Ezekiel*, which prophesied the destruction of Jerusalem, the restoration to the land of Israel, and the Third Temple. *(Translator.)*

[11] Ruben: name borrowed from the biblical Reuben or Re'uven, eldest son of Jacob with Leah, and founder of the Israelite Tribe of Reuben. *(Translator.)*

"Who is at ease? Is it the hunter who pursues a deer and meets a lion that laughs at arrows? Is it the soldier who strives for glory but finds sharp spears and bronze swords thirsty for blood? Is it the king who wears heavy armor beneath the purple, sleeplessly tracks the hosts of mighty neighbors, and snatches sounds lest treachery fell him in his tent?

"Man's heart ever brims with dread. In the desert threaten lion and scorpion; in caves, dragon; amid blossoms, poisonous viper. In daylight, greedy neighbor schemes to steal his land; at night, crafty burglar gropes at the door. In childhood, man is awkward; in old age, feeble; in prime, beset by danger like the whale by the abyss.

"Wherefore, O Lord my Creator, to Thee turns man's weary soul. Thou brought it into this world abounding in snares, Thou implanted it with fear of death, Thou sealed off all avenues to peace save that which leads to Thee. And as the infant clutches its mother's dress so as not to fall, wretched man stretches his hands to Thy mercy and frees himself from doubt."

Sara fell silent. The Prince mused:

"You Jews are a gloomy people. If Egypt believed what your song teaches, no one would laugh on the banks of the Nile. The powerful would cower in temple basements; and the populace, instead of working, would flee to the caves, there to await a deliverance that would never come.

"Our world is different: you can have anything, but you must do everything yourself. And our gods don't help snivelers. They descend to earth only when a hero who has ventured a superhuman deed exhausts all his powers. Thus it was when Ramses the Great plunged into the midst of twenty-five hundred enemy chariots, each carrying three warriors. Only then did his immortal father Amon lend him a hand and complete the rout.[12] Had Ramses, instead of fighting, waited for deliverance by your god, the Egyptian would long since be walking the banks of the Nile only with bucket and brick, and the wretched Hittite with papyrus and cane!

"That, Sara, is why your charms will dispel my cares sooner than your song. If I did as the Jewish sages teach and awaited help from heaven, wine would flee my lips, and women my houses.

"Above all, I could not be the Pharaoh's successor, like my half brothers, one of whom can't cross the room unsupported by two slaves, and the other spends his days up in the trees."

[12] Ramses is speaking of the Battle of Kadesh, ca. 1274 BCE, two centuries before *Pharaoh*'s present time. It was fought, on the Orontes River in Syria, between Ramses II's Egyptian Empire and Muwatalli II's Hittite Empire. Ramses II fell into a Hittite ambush and was saved only by the last-minute arrival of Egyptian reinforcements. He later represented the resulting military draw, on monuments including Egypt's far-southern Temple of Abu Simbel, as a resounding Egyptian victory. The Battle of Kadesh was history's first battle for which details of tactics and formations are known and was probably history's largest chariot battle. Sixteen years later, the Egyptian-Hittite borderland conflicts were ended with history's first known international peace treaty. *(Translator.)*

CHAPTER 15

Next day Ramses sent his Negro to Memphis with orders; and about noon, coming from the direction of the city, a large boat landed at Sara's farm, full of Greek soldiers in tall helmets and shining armor.

On command, sixteen men armed with shields and short spears debarked and formed two ranks. They were about to march to Sara's house when they were intercepted by a second messenger from the Prince, bidding the soldiers remain on the bank and summoning only their commander Patroklos.

They stood stock-still like two rows of columns sheathed in burnished metal. Patroklos followed the messenger, in plumed helmet and a purple tunic topped by gold armor emblazoned on the chest with an image of a woman's head bristling with serpents in lieu of hair.[1]

The Prince received the illustrious general at the garden gate. Ramses did not smile as was his wont or even acknowledge Patroklos' low bow but said with a cool mien:

"Your Eminence, tell the Greek soldiers of my regiments that I won't be drilling with them until His Holiness our Lord reappoints me as their commander. They have lost this honor by uttering, in taverns, cries worthy of drunkards and offensive to myself. The Greek regiments, Your Eminence, are insufficiently disciplined. The soldiers publicly hold forth on politics, on some possible war, which sounds like treason. These things may be spoken of only by His Holiness the Pharaoh and the members of the Supreme Council. We soldiers and servants of our Lord, whatever our stations, may only carry out the orders of our most gracious Lord—and always be silent. I ask that Your Eminence convey these remarks to my regiments, and I wish Your Eminence every success."

"Very good, Your Eminence," replied the Greek. He turned on his heel and, erect, clanked off to his boat.

He knew of the soldiers' discussions in the taverns, and now he realized that some unpleasantness had befallen the Crown Prince, whom the men worshipped. On reaching the handful of armed men standing on the bank, he put on a very angry visage and, furiously flailing his arms, cried:

"Valiant Greek soldiers!—Mangy dogs, may you rot with leprosy! If from now on any Greek utters the Successor's name in a tavern, I'll smash a pitcher on his head and stuff the shards down his throat—and out of the regiment you go! You'll tend pigs for an Egyptian

---

[1] "an image of a woman's head bristling with serpents in lieu of hair": This is a representation of the Greek mythical Medusa. *(Translator.)*

peasant, and hens will lay eggs in your helmets. That's the fate of stupid soldiers who can't keep a hold on their tongues. Now, left—about face!—to the boat march, a plague on you! A soldier of His Holiness should drink first of all to the health of the Pharaoh and the prosperity of His Eminence Minister of War Herhor. May they live forever!"

"May they live forever!" repeated the soldiers.

They embarked somber. But around Memphis Patroklos cleared his brow and had the men sing a ballad about a priest's daughter who was so fond of the army that she used to place a doll in her bed and spend all night in a sentry box.

It was in time to this ballad that the men marched best and the oars struck most briskly.

Toward evening a second boat landed at Sara's farm, debarking the general manager of Ramses' estates.

The Prince received this dignitary as well at the garden gate: perhaps from sternness, or perhaps to spare him entering the house of the Prince's concubine and Jewess.

"I wanted to tell you," said the Successor, "that there is unseemly talk going around among my peasants about lowering the taxes, or something of the sort. I want the peasants to know I'm not going to lower their taxes. And if, despite warning, any of them persist in their folly and talk about taxes, they are to be caned."

"Maybe it would be better to fine them—a deben or a drachma, as Your Eminence will," said the general manager.

"Very well, they can be fined," said the Prince after a moment's hesitation.

"How about now caning some of the more unruly ones, that they may better remember the gracious order?" whispered the manager.

"Yes, the more unruly ones may be caned."

"If I might be so bold, Your Eminence," whispered the manager, still bowing, "the peasants did for a time talk about abolishing the taxes, stirred up by some stranger. But a couple of days ago they suddenly became quiet."

"Well, then they needn't be caned," observed Ramses.

"Except perhaps preventively?" broke in the manager.

"Isn't it a waste of canings?"

"That's a commodity we'll never run out of."

"Anyway ... in moderation," admonished the Prince. "I don't want ... I don't want His Holiness hearing that I needlessly torment the peasants. Rebellious talk must be met with canings and monetary penalties; but when there is no need of those, we may be magnanimous."

"I understand," replied the manager, looking the Prince in the eye. "Let them shout just enough so they don't whisper blasphemies."

The two conversations, with Patroklos and with the estate manager, made the rounds of Egypt.

After the manager's departure, the Prince yawned and, looking about with a bored expression, told himself: "I've done what I could ... Now I'll do nothing, if I can."

Just then he heard, from the direction of the farm buildings, quiet groans and thick blows. Ramses turned his head and saw the overseer of farmhands, Ezekiel, son of Ruben, caning a subordinate while quieting him: "Be quiet! Shut up, you filthy swine!"

The farmhand, lying on the ground, was holding his hand over his mouth in order not to cry out.

The Prince at first lunged like a leopard toward the buildings, but suddenly stopped. "What can I do?" he whispered. "This is Sara's farm, and that Jew is her relative ..."

He bit his lip and hid among the trees, particularly as punishment was now concluded.

"So that's how the humble Jews manage the farm?" thought the Prince. "So that's how? He looks at me like a frightened dog, but he beats the farmhands? Are they all like that?"

For the first time, Ramses began wondering whether Sara's gentleness, too, might be disingenuous.

Sara had in fact been going through changes, particularly in her thinking and emotions.

From her initial encounter with the Prince in the desert valley, she had liked Ramses. But that feeling had suddenly been swamped by the stunning news that the handsome boy was the Pharaoh's son and successor. And when Thutmose had arranged with Gideon for her to be taken to the Prince's house, Sara had lapsed into bewilderment.

Not for the world, not for dear life would she have given Ramses up—though she could not be said to have loved him at that point. Love requires freedom and time to give forth its most beautiful blossoms; she had been allowed neither time nor freedom. One day she had met the Prince, the next she had been carried off, almost without a by-your-leave, to a villa outside Memphis. And a couple of days later she had become a mistress, surprised, frightened, not comprehending what was happening to her.

Then, before she had had a chance to get used to the novel sensations, she had been terrified by the hostility of the local populace to her, a Jewess; then by the visit of the unknown ladies; and finally by the attack on the farm.

Ramses' wanting to go after the assailants had frightened her still more. She swooned at the thought that she was in the hands of so impetuous and powerful a man who, if he wished, could spill people's blood, could kill.

Sara had momentarily lapsed into despair; it seemed to her she would go mad listening to the Prince fiercely calling the servants to arms. But then a few words had restored Sara to her senses and redirected her feelings.

The Prince, thinking her wounded, had stripped the bandage from her head and, seeing the contusion, had exclaimed: "It's just a bruise? How it changes your face!" At this, Sara had forgotten her pain and fear. A new anxiety had overwhelmed her: she had changed so much that it surprised the Prince? ... And he was only surprised!

The bruise had disappeared after a couple of days, but previously unknown feelings remained and grew in Sara's soul. She began to be jealous of Ramses and to fear he might leave her.

One more thing distressed her: she felt herself a servant and slave to the Prince. She was, and wanted to be his most faithful servant, his most devoted slave, inseparable as a shadow. But at the same time she wished that, at least in their more intimate moments, he did not act the lord and master.

After all, she was his and he was hers. Why, then, did he not show that he belonged to her at least a little, instead of indicating with every word and gesture that there was some gulf separating them? ... What gulf? ... Did she not hold him in her arms? Did he not kiss her lips and breasts?

One day the Prince had sailed over with a dog. He had stayed only a couple of hours, but all that time the dog had lain at the Prince's feet, in Sara's place; and when she tried to sit there, it had growled at her. The Prince had laughed and sunk his fingers in the unclean animal's fur just as he had in her hair. And the dog had looked into the Prince's eyes just like her, only perhaps more boldly.

She could not calm down and had come to detest the clever animal which took part of Ramses' caresses away from her without caring about them, and which behaved toward its master with a familiarity she could not muster. She could not even have managed such an indifferent expression, or have looked away, with the Successor's hand on her head.

Recently the Prince had mentioned dancing girls. Sara had burst out: He let himself be caressed by the naked, shameless women? And Jehovah, seeing this from on high, did not hurl a thunderbolt at the monstrous women?

True, Ramses had told her she was dearer to him than all other women. But his words had not reassured Sara; they had only determined her to think of nothing outside the compass of her love.

Never mind about tomorrow ... When, at the Prince's feet, she had sung of the tribulations afflicting humankind from cradle to grave, she had expressed the state of her own soul and her final hope—in God.

Today Ramses was with her, and she was content; she had all the happiness that life could afford her. But it was just here that the bitterest part began for Sara.

The Prince dwelled with her under the same roof, walked with her in the garden, sometimes took her boating on the Nile. But he did not become a hairsbreadth more accessible to her than when he had been on the other side of the river, within the precincts of the royal park.

He was with her but his thoughts were elsewhere, and Sara could not begin to guess where. He embraced her or played with her hair, but looked Memphis-ward at the enormous pylon towers of the pharaoh's castle—or who knows where.

Sometimes he did not even respond to her questions, or suddenly looked at her as though just wakened, as though surprised to see her beside him.

CHAPTER 16

S uch were the—fairly rare—moments of the greatest intimacy between Sara and
her lover the Prince. Having issued the orders to Patroklos and the general manager of his estates, the Successor spent the greater part of the day away from the
farm, usually in a boat. Either he netted the fish that teemed in their thousands in the
blessed Nile; or he made his way to the marshes and, concealed among the tall stalks of
lotus,[1] shot his bow at the wildfowl, noisy flocks of which swarmed thick as flies. But even
then ambitious thoughts did not leave him, and he turned the hunt into a kind of augury or
divination. Spotting a flock of yellow geese on the water, he would draw his bow and say:

"If I hit my mark, I'll be another Ramses the Great..."

The missile swished quietly, and the transfixed bird, fluttering its wings, uttered an-
guished cries that threw the entire marsh into commotion. Clouds of geese, ducks, and
storks sprang up, wheeled in a great circle over their dying comrade, and settled down
elsewhere.

When it had quieted, the Prince carefully moved the boat on, guiding himself by the
swaying of the reeds and the intermittent cries of the birds. And when amidst the green he
saw a patch of clear water and a new flock, he drew his bow again and said:

"If I hit my mark, I'll be pharaoh. If not..."

This time the arrow struck the water, skipped several times, and vanished into the
lotus. The impassioned Prince let fly missile after missile, killing birds or merely stamped-
ing flocks. At the farm, they knew where he was by the screaming clouds of fowl that kept
springing up and circling over his boat.

When toward evening he returned tired to the villa, Sara would be waiting at the door
with a basin of water, a pitcher of light wine, and rose garlands. The Prince would smile at
her, stroke her face but, looking into her tender eyes, think:

"I wonder whether she could thrash Egyptian peasants like her ever-frightened
relatives? Oh, Mother is right, distrusting the Jews; though, who knows, maybe Sara is
different."

Once, returning unexpected, he saw numerous near-naked children playing merrily in
the front yard. All were yellow-complexioned and, at sight of him, scattered shrieking like

---

[1] "tall stalks of lotus": Egyptian lotuses do not have tall stalks; the confusion may be with papyrus,
likewise an aquatic flowering plant but with a very talk stalk. Egyptian lotuses are one of several distinct
genera of plants that are commonly referred to as "lotuses." It is not certain where the Land of the Lotus-
Eaters, in Homer's *Odyssey*, was supposed to have been located—or what sort of "lotus" they would have
eaten. *(Translator.)*

the wild geese in the swamp. Before he had climbed to the terrace of the house, they had vanished without trace.

"What mites are those," he asked Sara, "who run away from me?"

"Those are children of your servants," she replied.

"Of the Jews?"

"Of my brothers ..."

"Gods! how this people multiplies!" the Prince burst out laughing. "And who's that now? ..." he added, indicating a man who was looking timidly across the wall.

"That is Aod, son of Barak,[2] a relative of mine. He wishes to serve your lordship. May I hire him?"

The Prince shrugged. "It's your farm," he said, "you may hire whomever you like. Only, if these people keep multiplying like that, they'll soon take over Memphis ..."[3]

"You hate my brothers?" whispered Sara, looking fearfully at Ramses and slipping down to his feet.

The Prince looked at her, surprised. "I don't even think about them," he said proudly.

These slight incidents, which fell in fiery drops onto Sara's soul, did not change Ramses toward her. He was always uniformly kind and caressed her as usual, though increasingly his eyes strayed to the other side of the Nile to lodge on the mighty pylon towers of the castle.

Soon he noticed that he was not pining alone in his self-imposed exile. One day an elegant royal barge set off from that bank, sailed the Nile toward Memphis, then circled so close to the farm that Ramses could recognize the persons seated in it.

He recognized under the purple canopy his mother among ladies-in-waiting and, opposite her on a low bench, Viceroy Herhor. To be sure, they were not looking at the farm, but the Prince guessed they saw him.

"Aha!" he chuckled. "My worshipful mother and His Eminence the Minister would like to lure me away from here before His Holiness returns."

The month of Tybi arrived—late October and early November.[4] The Nile fell the height of one and a half men, daily exposing new patches of soggy black soil. Where the waters retreated, there soon appeared a narrow wooden plow drawn by two oxen. Behind the plow walked a half-naked plowman, beside the oxen a driver with a short whip, and behind him a sower who, sinking to his ankles in mud, scattered handfuls of wheat from an apron.

Egypt's most beautiful season was commencing—winter. The temperature did not exceed fifteen degrees Celsius,[5] and the ground was rapidly being covered with an emerald verdure that gushed forth narcissus and violets. Their fragrance was increasingly in evidence amid the raw smells of land and water.

---

[2] Barak: name (meaning "lightning") borrowed from a pre-monarchic ruler of ancient Israel who, as a military commander in the biblical *Book of Judges*, defeated, with the prophetess Deborah, Canaanite armies led by Sisera. *(Translator.)*

[3] This may be an echo of God's biblical exhortation to Adam and Eve (*Genesis* 1:28), and to Noah and his sons (*Genesis* 9:7), to "be fruitful and multiply." (Translator.)

[4] Actually, the ancient Egyptian month of Tybi lay between January 9 and February 7 of the modern, Gregorian calendar. (Translator.)

[5] Fifteen degrees Celsius = 59 degrees Fahrenheit. *(Translator.)*

The ship bearing the worshipful Lady Nikotris and Viceroy Herhor had appeared several times near Sara's abode. Each time, the Prince had seen his mother gaily conversing with the Minister while they ostentatiously avoided looking his way, as if to demonstrate their disregard for him.

"Just you wait!" whispered the angry Crown Prince, "I'll show you I'm not bored either!"

One day shortly before sunset, when the golden royal barge appeared offshore, ostrich plumes flying at the corners of its purple tent, Ramses had a two-person boat readied and told Sara he was taking her out in it.

"Jehovah!" she cried, clasping her hands. "But your mother and the Viceroy are out there."

"And the Crown Prince will be over here. Bring your harp, Sara."

"The harp too?" she asked, trembling. "What if your worshipful mother wants to talk to you? I'd throw myself in the water!"

"Don't be a child, Sara," laughed the Prince. "His Eminence the Viceroy and my mother are very fond of songs. You might win them over with a nice Jewish song. Something about love ..."

"I don't know any," answered Sara, heartened by the Prince's words. Maybe those powerful people really would like her singing, and then?

Aboard the royal ship, the Successor was observed climbing with Sara into a simple boat and himself rowing.

"Do you see, Eminence?" the Queen whispered to the Minister, "he's rowing out toward us with his Jewess ..."

"The Crown Prince comported himself so properly in regard to his soldiers and peasants, and showed such contrition in departing the palace precincts, that Your Honor may forgive him this slight lapse," replied the Minister.

"Oh, if it weren't him sitting in that shell, I'd have it smashed!" said Her Eminence angrily.

"Why?" asked the Minister. "The Prince would not be a scion of high priests and pharaohs if he did not champ at the bit that, alas, is imposed on him by law and by our perhaps mistaken customs. In any case, he has shown a capacity for self-control in important matters. He is even able to acknowledge his errors, which is a rare quality and priceless in a crown prince.

"And the fact that the Prince seeks to annoy us with his ladylove, shows that he is pained by the disfavor he has incurred, albeit from the noblest of motives."

"But the Jewess!" whispered the lady, rumpling her fan of feathers.

"My mind is at ease about her already today," said the Minister. "She is a pretty but silly creature who neither wishes nor would know how to exploit her influence with the Prince. She accepts no gifts and sees no one, shut up in her none too expensive cage. Maybe in time she would learn to exploit her position as the Prince's mistress and diminish his treasury by ten or twenty talents. But before that happens, Ramses will tire of her."

"Would that omniscient Amon speaks with your lips."

"I'm certain of it. The Prince was never for a moment mad about her, as will happen with our young lords, whom a designing woman can divest of wealth and health and even hale before a court of law. The Prince dallies with her as a mature man dallies with a slave girl. And since Sara is with child ..."

"Is she?" exclaimed the lady. "How do you know?"

"Which neither His Eminence the Crown Prince nor even Sara knows," smiled Herhor. "We have to know everything. Anyway, this secret was not hard to obtain. Sara has with her a relative named Taphath, a woman of unequalled talkativeness."

"Have they called in a physician?"

"I repeat, Sara knows nothing about it; and the worthy Taphath, who fears the Prince losing interest in her charge, would gladly smother the secret. But we won't allow it. After all, this will be the child of a prince."

"But what if it's a boy, Your Honor? You know, he could cause a lot of trouble," said the lady.

"All is anticipated," said the priest. "If it's a girl, we'll give her a dowry and an upbringing befitting a young lady of high birth. If it's a boy, he'll become a Jew ..."

"My grandson a Jew!"

"Ladyship, do not lose heart to him too soon. Our envoys report that the Israelites are beginning to desire a king. Before the boy is grown, their demands will mature ... and we'll give them a ruler—one of truly exquisite blood!"

"You are like the eagle, which takes in east and west at a single glance!" said the Queen, regarding the Minister with admiration. "I feel my aversion to the girl starting to decline."

"The least drop of pharaonic blood should be exalted over the nations like a star over the earth," said Herhor.

The Successor's boat was now barely a few dozen paces from the court barge, and the Pharaoh's consort concealed herself behind her fan and regarded Sara through the feathers.

"In truth, she is pretty!" she whispered.

"This is the second time Your Worship has said that."

"Oh, so you know about that too?" smiled Her Eminence.

Herhor looked down.

A harp sounded in the little boat, and in a quavering voice Sara began her song:

"How great is the Lord, how great is the Lord thy God, O Israel!"

"An exquisite voice!" whispered the Queen.

The high priest listened intently.

"His days have no beginning," sang Sara, "and His house has no bounds. The eternal heavens change beneath His eye like the robes a man dons and doffs. The stars light and expire like hardwood sparks, and the earth is like a brick that a passerby treads once, passing ever on.

"How great is thy Lord, O Israel. None may tell Him, 'Do this!' nor any womb bring Him forth. He made the infinite voids over which He soars whither He will. From darkness He extracts light—and from the earth's dust, creatures that give forth sound.

"To Him, fierce lions are locusts; the huge elephant is trifling; and the whale is an infant.

"His tricolor bow cleaves the heavens in twain and rests on the ends of the earth. What gate can match His greatness? Nations tremble at the thunder of His chariot, and nought under the sun can withstand His flickering arrows.

"His breath is the north wind that refreshes the languid trees; His puff is the khamsin that sears the earth.

"When He draws His hand over the waters, they turn to stone. He shifts seas from place to place as a woman pours leaven into a kneading trough. He rips open the earth like rotten cloth, and covers bald mountain tops with silver snow.

"In a grain of wheat He secretes a hundred other grains, and He causes birds to hatch. From the dormant chrysalis He extracts the golden butterfly, and He makes people's bodies await resurrection in graves ..."

Engrossed in the song, the rowers had lifted their oars, and the purple royal ship was slowly drifting with the current. Suddenly Herhor rose and cried: "Turn for Memphis!"

The oars struck; the ship pivoted on the spot and, with a rushing sound, began forcing its way upriver. After it sped Sara's waning song:

"He sees the beating of the aphid's heart, and the hidden paths of the most private human thought. But no one can search His heart and guess His intentions.

"Before the radiance of His raiment, great spirits hide their faces. Before His gaze, the gods of mighty cities and nations shrivel like a withered leaf.

"He is might, He is life, He is wisdom, He is thy Lord, thy God, O Israel!"

"Why did Your Eminence move our ship away?" asked Her Worship Nikotris.

"Does your ladyship know what song that is?" said Herhor in a language understood only by priests. "Why, the silly girl sings in the middle of the Nile a psalm that may be recited only in the innermost sanctums of our temples."

"Then it's blasphemy?"

"Happily there's but one priest on board," said the Minister. "I did not hear it and, though I had, I should forget. I fear, though, that the gods may place their hand on the girl."

"But how did she come to know this dread psalm? Surely Ramses couldn't have taught her?"

"The Prince is not to blame. But, ladyship, don't forget that the Jews carried more than one such treasure out of our Egypt. That is why we treat them, of all the nations of the world, as sacrilegists."

The Queen took the high priest's hand. "But nothing bad," she whispered, looking him in the eye, "will happen to my son?"

"I assure your ladyship that nothing bad will happen to anyone, as I did not hear and do not know. But the Prince must be separated from the girl ..."

"Separated gently ... right, Viceroy?" asked the mother.

"As gently, as gradually as possible, but it must be done. It seemed to me," spoke the high priest as if to himself, "that I had foreseen everything ... Everything but an action for blasphemy which, with this strange woman by him, hangs over the Crown Prince!"

Herhor mused: "Yes, Your Worship! One may laugh at many of our prejudices; nonetheless, the fact is, the pharaoh's son should not ally himself with a Jewess."

CHAPTER 17

A fter the evening when Sara sang in the boat, the court barge appeared no more on the Nile, and Prince Ramses began to be bored in earnest.

The month of Mechir, December,[1] was approaching. The waters were falling, the ground was extending ever broader, the grass was daily taller and thicker, and amid it, like colorful sparks, were lighting up flowers of the most diverse colors, of unmatched scent. Like islands in a sea of green, in the course of a single day there appeared floral clusters: white, blue, yellow, pink, or motley carpets that exuded an intoxicating fragrance.

In spite of this, the Prince was bored—and anxious. Since his father's departure he had not been to the palace, nor had anyone from there visited him, including Thutmose who, after their last conversation, had vanished like a snake in the grass. Were they respecting his privacy, were they trying to annoy him, were they afraid to visit a Prince who was in disfavor? Ramses did not know.

"Maybe Father will bar me from the throne, as he did my older brothers?" the Successor sometimes thought, sweat coming to his brow and his feet growing cold.

What would he do then?

In addition, Sara was unwell: she was growing thin and pale; her great eyes were sinking; some mornings she complained of nausea.

"Someone must have cast spells on the poor girl!" moaned Taphath, whom the Prince could not stand for her talkativeness and very poor husbandry.

On a couple of evenings, for example, the Successor had seen Taphath send out to Memphis huge hampers of food, linens, even kitchenware. The next day she would be complaining to high heaven of a domestic shortage of flour, wine, or pots. Ever since the Successor had moved in to the farm, ten times more of various products had been running out than before.

"I'm sure," thought Ramses, "that the garrulous woman is plundering me for her Jews, who disappear from Memphis in the daytime but at night swarm the dirtiest back alleys like rats!"

The Prince's only diversion now was watching the harvesting of dates.

A near-naked peasant would go up to a tall, branchless palm tree, encircle the trunk and himself with a loose band of rope, and climb the tree on his heels, his whole body arched backward and held taut against the tree by the rope. He then advanced the rope

---

[1] Actually, the ancient Egyptian month of Mechir lay between February 8 and March 9 of the modern, Gregorian calendar. *(Translator.)*

band a few inches² higher, climbed, advanced the rope again, and this way, at the constant risk of a broken neck, climbed as high as a couple of stories, to the top, where grew a clump of fronds and some dates.

Witnessing these gymnastics was not only the Prince but the Jewish children. At first they weren't there. Then, between the bushes and over the wall, there appeared little curly heads and black shiny eyes. Then, seeing that the Prince wasn't shooing them off, the children emerged from hiding and very slowly approached the tree being harvested. The boldest girl lifted a beautiful date from the ground and handed it to Ramses. One of the boys ate the smallest date, and next the children began now eating the fruit, now offering them to the Prince. At first they brought him the choicest dates, later worse ones, finally quite spoiled ones.

The future Lord of the World mused: "They'll get in everywhere, and they'll always treat me like this: with good as enticement, and rotten as thanks!"

He rose and walked off glumly, and the children of Israel descended like a swarm of birds upon the handiwork of the Egyptian peasant who, high overhead, hummed a tune, little thinking of his bones and unaware that he wasn't harvesting for himself.

Sara's inexplicable illness, her frequent tears, the decline of her charms, and above all the Jews who, ceasing to hide, ran the farm more and more blatantly, blighted this beautiful corner of the earth for the Prince. He no longer boated, hunted, or watched the date harvest, but glumly wandered the garden or, from the terrace, observed the royal castle.

Uncalled he would never return to court, but he was beginning to think of going to his seaside estates in Lower Egypt.

Such was the Successor's frame of mind when Thutmose arrived one day in a grand court barge with a summons for the Successor from the Pharaoh.

His Holiness was returning from Thebes and desired that the Successor sail out to greet him.

The Prince trembled, blanched, and blushed as he read the gracious letter from the lord and master. He was so excited that he did not even notice Thutmose's colossal new wig which gave off fifteen different scents, his tunic and coat finer than mist, or his sandals garnished with gold and beads.

After a while Ramses cooled down and said, not looking at Thutmose: "Why did you stay away so long? Were you put off by the disfavor I'd fallen into?"

"Gods!" exclaimed the dandy. "When were you ever in disfavor, and with whom? Each of His Holiness' couriers has inquired about you, and the worshipful Lady Nikotris and His Eminence Herhor sailed up to your house several times, expecting you would go a hundred paces toward them when they'd gone a couple of thousand. There's hardly need to speak of the army. The soldiers of your regiments keep silent as palm trees during drill and don't leave their barracks, and His Eminence Patroklos drinks and curses days on end out of grief."

So the Prince had not been in disfavor; or if he had been, it was now over! The thought affected Ramses like a cup of good wine. He quickly bathed and rubbed himself with oil, put on fresh linens, donned a military tunic and plumed helmet, and went to Sara who lay, pale, under Taphath's care.

²Inch: Prus uses the word *cal*, denoting a former Polish unit of measure that was equal to 2.4 centimeters. The British and United States inch equals 2.54 centimeters. *(Translator.)*

Sara cried out, seeing the Prince dressed this way. She sat up, embraced his neck, and whispered: "You're leaving, my lord? You won't come back!"

"Why is that?" asked the Successor. "Haven't I been away before and come back?"

"I remember you dressed this way in our valley," said Sara. "Oh, where are those times! They passed so quickly, and so long ago."

"I'll come back, and I'll bring you the best physician there is."

"What for?" broke in Taphath. "She's all right, is my peahen ... all she needs is rest. The Egyptian physicians would drive her into a real illness."

The Prince didn't even glance at the loquacious woman.

"This has been my happiest month with you," said Sara, snuggling up to Ramses, "but it hasn't been kind to me."

A trumpet sounded aboard the royal ship, repeating a signal given upriver.

Sara shuddered. "Oh, do you hear those terrible sounds, lord? You do, and you smile ... and, alas, you tear yourself from my arms. When trumpets call, nothing will keep you, least of all your slave ..."

"Would you want me to always be listening to the clucking of the farm hens?" interrupted the Prince impatiently. "Be well and wait for me in good spirits."

Sara released him from her arms and looked at him so piteously that the Successor relented and stroked her.

"Now, relax," he said. "Our trumpets frighten you ... Were they a bad omen back then?"

"Lord," said Sara, "I know they're going to keep you there. So do me a last favor ... I'm going to give you," she sobbed, "I'm going to give you a cage of doves. They were born and raised here. Whenever you think of your servant, open the cage and release one of the birds ... It will bring me word of you ... and I'll kiss it ... I'll caress it as ... as ... Well, go now!"[3]

The Prince hugged her and went out to the ship, instructing his Negro to wait for Sara's doves and overtake him in a skiff.

At sight of the Crown Prince, drums and fifes sounded and the village raised a great cheer. Finding himself among soldiers, the Prince drew a deep breath and stretched his arms as though freed from bonds.

"I was getting tired," he told Thutmose, "of the women and the Jews ... Osiris! ... better roast me over a slow fire than set me down once again on a farm."

"Yes," assented Thutmose, "love is like honey: you can taste of it, but hardly wallow in it. Brr! It makes my flesh creep to think you've spent close to two months being fed kisses in the evening, dates in the morning, and donkey's milk at noon."

"Sara is a very good girl," said the Prince.

"I'm not speaking of her but of the Jews who've filled up the farm as papyrus fills the marshes. Do you see them, they're still looking your way and maybe sending their fond farewells," said the courtier.

The Prince turned away in displeasure, and Thutmose winked merrily at the officers, as if to intimate that Ramses would not soon be quitting their company.

The farther they sailed upriver, the thicker were the crowds on both banks and the

[3] Doves: Some varieties of doves and pigeons (the two terms are often used synonymously) are notable for their ability to find their way home over long distances, and have been used to carry messages for peaceful or belligerent purposes. In 43 BCE, Decimus Junius Brutus Albinus broke Marc Antony's siege of Mutina (Modena, in northern Italy) by sending letters to Rome's consuls via pigeon. *(Translator.)*

boats on the Nile, and the more flowers, garlands, and bouquets, cast at the Pharaoh's ship, floated in the water.

A mile outside Memphis stood throngs with banners, gods, and music, and there rang a great tumult like the howl of a storm.

"There's His Holiness!" exclaimed Thutmose joyously.

A singular view presented itself to the eyes of the beholders. Down the middle of a wide bend sailed the Pharaoh's enormous ship, its prow raised like a swan. To the right and left of it, like two gigantic wings, moved countless boats of his subjects and behind it, spread out in a rich fan, the entourage of Egypt's ruler.

Every living soul cheered, sang, clapped, or threw flowers to the feet of the Lord, whom no one even saw. It sufficed that a red-and-blue banner, the sign of the pharaoh's presence, streamed over the gold tent and tufts of ostrich plumes.

The people in the boats seemed drunk; those on the banks, mad. Every few moments, some boat bumped into or capsized another and someone fell into the water, from which the crocodiles had fortunately fled, frightened off by the uncommon din. On the banks, people jostled, no one looking out for neighbor, father, or child, but everyone gluing his distracted eyes to the ship's golden prow and royal tent. Even those who were trampled— whose ribs were mindlessly crushed, and joints wrenched, by the unruly crowd—had no other cry than: "Live forever, our Lord ... Shine on, sun of Egypt!"

Soon the frenzy of greeting was imparted as well to the Successor's boat: the officers, soldiers, and oarsmen, jammed into a single crowd, cheered to outdo each other; and Thutmose, oblivious of the Successor, climbed the ship's tall prow and all but fell into the water.

Suddenly a trumpet sounded on the royal ship, answered a moment later by a trumpet on Ramses' ship. Another signal—and the Successor's boat came alongside the Pharaoh's great ship.

An official summoned Ramses. A cedar bridge with carved handrails was thrown between the ships—and the Prince found himself in the presence of his father.

The sight of the Pharaoh, or the storm of cheers raging all round, so stunned the Prince that he could utter nary a word. He fell to his father's feet, and the Lord of the World clasped Ramses to his divine bosom.

A moment later the side flaps of the tent were lifted, and all the populace on both banks of the Nile beheld their ruler on the throne and Prince Ramses kneeling on the highest step, his head on the paternal bosom.

Such a hush fell that the flutter of the ships' banners was audible. Then suddenly a tremendous cry burst forth, greater than any before. With it the Egyptian people celebrated the reconciliation of father and son; saluted their present, and greeted their future, Lord.

If anyone had reckoned on discord within the Pharaoh's holy family, today he could see that the new royal branch held fast to the trunk.

His Holiness looked very poorly. After the affectionate greeting, he bade his son sit beside the throne and said:

"My soul yearned the more for you, Ramses, the better the news that I had of you. Today I see that you are not only a lion-hearted youth but a prudent man who is capable of judging his own behavior and restraining himself, and has a sense of state interests."

As the moved Prince held his peace and kissed the paternal feet, the Lord continued:

"You did well in renouncing the two Greek regiments, for you deserve the Menfi Corps, of which you are henceforth the commander."

"My father!" whispered the trembling Successor.

"Moreover, in Lower Egypt, on three sides exposed to enemy attack, I need a brave and judicious man who will see everything, weigh it in his heart, and act quickly in emergencies. That is why I am naming you my viceroy for that half of the Kingdom."

Copious tears streamed from Ramses' eyes. With them he took leave of his youth and greeted the power for which he had so long been anxiously yearning.

"I am weary and in poor health," said the ruler, "and but for concern about your youth and the future of the Kingdom, I would today ask my eternally living forbears to call me to my glory. But with each day things are harder for me and so, Ramses, you will begin now sharing with me the burden of power. As the hen teaches its brood to seek grains and to shelter from the hawk, so I shall teach you the demanding art of governing the Kingdom and tracking the moves of enemies. May you, in the fullness of time, descend upon them like an eagle upon skittish partridges!"

The royal ship and its festive entourage arrived at the palace. The weary Lord climbed into a litter, while the Successor was approached by Herhor.

"Eminence," said Herhor, "permit me to be the first to rejoice in the Prince's elevation. May you with equal success command the army and govern the most important region of the Kingdom, to the glory of Egypt."

Ramses firmly clasped his hand. "You did this, Herhor?" he asked.

"You deserved it," replied the Minister.

"You have my gratitude, and you'll find that it's worth something."

"You have already rewarded me, saying that," answered Herhor.

The Prince was about to leave when Herhor detained him. "A word more," he said. "Successor, advise your woman Sara not to sing religious psalms."

When Ramses looked at him in surprise, Herhor added:

"During the ride on the Nile, the girl sang our most sacred hymn, which may be heard only by the pharaoh and high priests. The poor child might have paid dearly for her skill in song and for her ignorance of what it is she sings."

"It would have been blasphemy?" asked the Prince in confusion.

"Inadvertent blasphemy," answered the high priest. "Fortunately only I heard it, and I think the similarity between the song and our hymn is quite remote.

"In any event, she shouldn't sing it anymore."

"Yes, and she ought to cleanse herself," said the Prince. "Will it suffice a foreign woman to offer the Temple of Isis thirty cows?"

"Certainly, let her do so," replied Herhor with a slight grimace. "The gods do not take offense at offerings."

"And I hope," said Ramses, "that Your Eminence will accept the wonderful shield that I received from my holy grandfather ..."

"Me? ... Amenhotep's shield?" exclaimed the Minister, moved. "Am I worthy of it?"

"You equal my grandfather in wisdom, and you shall equal him in station."

Herhor silently made a deep bow. Apart from its great pecuniary value, the bejeweled gold shield also had value as an amulet; it was therefore a regal gift.

But of greater moment were the Prince's words—that Herhor would equal Amenhotep in station. Amenhotep had been the Pharaoh's father-in-law. Had the Successor decided to wed Herhor's daughter?

That was a fond dream of the Minister and Queen Nikotris. But truth be told, in speaking of Herhor's future dignities Ramses had hardly meant marrying Herhor's daughter— only giving him new offices, of which there were plenty at the temples and at court.

CHAPTER 18

The day he became viceroy of Lower Egypt, an extremely onerous life began for Ramses, such as he had never imagined though he had been born and bred at the royal court.

He was tyrannized outright, and his tormentors were parties of diverse sorts and social classes.

The very first day, seeing the crowd that pressed and pushed, inadvertently trampling his lawns, breaking trees, even damaging the garden wall, the Successor ordered a guard detail for his villa. But on the third day he had to flee to the palace proper where, due to the heavy guard and especially the high walls, access was difficult for ordinary people.

In the decade[1] preceding Ramses' departure, representatives of all Egypt, if not the entire contemporary world, passed before his eyes.

First to be admitted were the great. There came to salute him high priests of temples, ministers, envoys—Phoenician, Greek, Jewish, Assyrian, Nubian—whose very costumes he could not keep straight. Then came the heads of adjacent nomes, judges, scribes, ranking officers of the Menfi Corps, and landowners.

These persons requested nothing but simply expressed their joy. But the Prince, hearing them from morning to noon and from noon to evening, felt a confusion in his head and a trembling in all his members.

Then came representatives of the lower classes with gifts: merchants with gold, amber, foreign fabrics, perfumes, and fruits. Then bankers and moneylenders. Next, architects with plans for new structures, sculptors with designs for statues and bas reliefs, stonemasons, manufacturers of earthenware vessels, carpenters, cabinetmakers, blacksmiths, foundrymen, tanners, winemakers, weavers, even openers of dead bodies.

The procession of homage-payers had not even ended when there drew up an army of supplicants. Invalids, widows, and orphans of officers requested pensions; nobles—court offices for their sons. Engineers brought proposals for new irrigation schemes; physicians—remedies for every ailment; foretellers—horoscopes. Relatives of convicts petitioned for commutations of sentence; convicts who had been sentenced to death—for their lives; the ill begged the Successor to touch them or grant them some of his saliva.

Finally, beautiful women and mothers of comely daughters presented, humbly

[1]Decade (from the Greek and Latin for "ten"): here, a period of 10 days—the ancient-Egyptian "week." *(Translator.)*

importuning the Viceroy to accept them into his house. Some specified a requested allowance and extolled their virginity and talents.

After ten days of constantly viewing new persons and faces and hearing requests that might have been satisfied only by the wealth of the entire world and by divine providence, Prince Ramses was exhausted. He could not sleep; he was so tense that he would be irritated by the buzzing of a fly; and at times he did not understand what was said to him.

In this situation Herhor again came to his aid. He had the powerful informed that the Prince was receiving no more callers; and against the populace who kept waiting despite repeated orders to disperse, he sent a company of Numidian[2] soldiers with canes. They succeeded with incomparably greater ease than Ramses in satisfying human cupidity. Before an hour was out, the supplicants had vanished like a mist, and for the next couple of days some of them applied compresses to their heads or other battered parts.

After this essay at wielding supreme power, the Prince felt a deep contempt for people and sank into apathy.

For two days he lay on a couch, hands under head, vacantly gazing at the ceiling. He no longer wondered at his holy father passing his time at the altars of the gods, but he could not understand how Herhor managed with an onslaught of similar interests which, like a storm, not only exceeded a man's strength but could crush him.

"How do you carry out your plans, with a mob of supplicants trammeling your will, devouring your thoughts, drinking your blood? After ten days I'm ill; after a year, I must surely lose my mind! In this office, it's impossible to make any plans; it's all you can do to preserve your sanity!"

He was so terrified by his powerlessness as a ruler that he sent for Herhor and plaintively recounted his plight.

The statesman listened smiling to the laments of the young helmsman of the ship of state and finally said:

"Does your lordship know that this enormous palace in which we are dwelling was reared by just one architect, named Senebi[3]—and that he died before completing it? And surely you will understand how that eternally living architect could execute his plan without ever tiring or losing his good cheer."

"How?"

"He did not do everything himself: he did not hew the beams or stones; he did not press the bricks; he did not carry them to the scaffolds; he did not lay them or join them. He only drew up the plan, and even for that he had assistants.

"But the Prince wanted to do everything himself; to hear and settle every matter himself. That exceeds human capacity."

---

[2] *Numidia* was a Berber kingdom lying *west* of Egypt, in what is now northern Algeria and parts of Tunisia and Libya, from the 3rd to the 1st century BCE. Thus, mention of Numidia here is an anachronism; Prus may have been thinking of *Nubia*, which lay *south* of Egypt. *(Translator.)*

[3] *Senebi*: name borrowed from a Middle Kingdom royal treasurer, under 13th Dynasty pharaohs Neferhotep I and Sobekhotep IV (about 1750 BCE). As treasurer, Senebi was the most powerful official at court next to the vizier. (The English word "vizier" comes from the Arabic *wazir*, meaning "viceroy.") Later, under the New Kingdom—*Pharaoh*'s time period—Egypt had two viziers: one each for Upper and Lower Egypt. *(Translator.)*

"How could I do otherwise, when the supplicants included the wronged and the unrewarded? After all, the foundation of the Kingdom is justice," replied the Successor.

"How many persons can the Prince hear in a day without tiring?" asked Herhor.

"Say ... twenty ..."

"You're lucky. I hear at most six to ten; however, they're not supplicants but great scribes, stewards, and ministers. They bring me not trivia but the most important things that are happening in the army, in the pharaoh's estates, in religious affairs, in the law courts, in the nomes, in the movements of the Nile. They bring me no trivia because each of them, before coming to me, has had to hear ten lesser scribes. Each lesser scribe and steward has collected information from ten under-scribes and under-stewards; and they in turn have heard reports from ten lower officials.

"This way His Holiness and I, speaking with only ten persons a day, know everything of importance that has happened at a hundred thousand points in the land and the world.

"A policeman who watches part of a Memphis street sees only a couple of buildings. The decurion knows the whole street; the centurion, a city quarter; the chief, the whole city. And the pharaoh stands above them all, as it were atop the pylon of the Temple of Ptah, and sees not only Memphis but also the cities of Khem,[4] On,[5] Kher-aha,[6] Turra,[7] Tetaui,[8] their vicinities, and part of the Western Desert.

"From that height, it is true, His Holiness does not notice the wronged or the unrewarded, but he will make out a gathering crowd of unemployed laborers. He won't see a soldier in a tavern, but he will know whether the regiment is performing its drills. He does not see what a peasant or townsman is cooking for dinner, but he will spot a fire starting in the district.

"This order of the Kingdom," spoke Herhor, growing animated, "is our glory and power. And when Zoser,[9] the first pharaoh of the Third Dynasty, asked a certain priest what kind of monument to erect for himself, the priest answered:

"'Draw a square on the ground, Lord, and place in it six million rough stones—they will represent the populace. On that layer, place sixty thousand hewn stones—these will be your lower officials. On that, put six thousand dressed stones—these will be the higher officials. On that, set sixty pieces covered with sculpture—these will be your closest

---

[4] Khem: an ancient city near Cairo; capital of the 2nd Nome of Lower Egypt. Prus calls it *Sochem*. *(Translator.)*

[5] On: the biblical Hebrew name for the ancient Egyptian city of Iunu (located within modern Cairo), which the Greeks called *Heliopolis* ("City of the Sun") because it was the principal site of sun worship. *(Translator.)*

[6] Kher-aha ("Field of Battle"): a city on the east bank of the Nile, south of Cairo. Prus calls it *Cherau*. *(Translator.)*

[7] Turra (properly, *T-ro-aw*): a city in the 1st Nome of Lower Egypt, on the east bank of the Nile, south of Cairo. Near Turra, in ancient times, were quarries of Egypt's finest and whitest limestone. *(Translator.)*

[8] Tetaui (properly *Iti-taui*, "Taking Both Lands"): a city on the border between Upper and Lower Egypt, on the west bank of the Nile, south of Memphis. *(Translator.)*

[9] Zoser: Prus here misattributes the Step Pyramid to Snofru, the first pharaoh of the 4th Dynasty, whom Prus calls "a pharaoh of the very first dynasty." The Step Pyramid was actually built by Zoser, the first pharaoh of the Third Dynasty. Snofru, however, built three other famous pyramids: the Meidum Pyramid and, at Dahshur, the Bent Pyramid and the Red Pyramid. *(Translator.)*

advisors and commanders; and on the summit, place a single block with a gold image of the sun—that will be yourself.'

"Pharaoh Zoser did so. Thus came into being the oldest pyramid, the Step Pyramid—a true picture of our Kingdom—which gave birth to all the others. These are immovable structures whose peaks command the ends of the earth, and which will be the wonder of the remotest generations.

"In this order, as well," continued the Minister, "rests our preponderance over our neighbors. The Ethiopians[10] were as numerous as we. But their king personally looked after his cattle, personally caned his subjects, and neither knew how many he had nor was able to muster them when our armies marched in. There was no one Ethiopia but a great mass of unorganized people. So today they are our vassals.

"The Libyan prince personally judges every case at law, particularly those involving the wealthy, and devotes so much time to them that he can barely look about him. And so whole gangs of bandits spring up at his side, whom we eradicate.

"Know too, lord, that if Phoenicia had one ruler in common who knew what was going on and laid down the law in all the cities, that country would not pay us a single deben of tribute. And how fortunate for us that the kings of Nineveh and Babel[11] have but one minister apiece and are as exhausted by the onslaught of business as you are today! They want to see, judge, and dispose of everything themselves, and as a result they have tangled up affairs of state for the next century. But were some renegade Egyptian scribe to go there, explain to the kings their errors in governance, and introduce our hierarchy of officials— our pyramid—in ten or twenty years' time Judea and Phoenicia would fall into the hands of the Assyrians; and in a few dozen years, from the east and north, by land and by sea, powerful armies would descend upon us, which we might not be able to fend off."

"Then let's attack them today, taking advantage of their disarray!" cried the Prince.

"We have yet to recover from our previous victories," said Herhor coldly, readying to take his leave.

"Have our victories weakened us?" the Successor burst out. "Did we not bring back treasure?"

"Does an ax not become damaged in felling trees?" asked Herhor, going out.

It was clear now to the Prince that the Minister wanted peace at all costs, though he was the head of the army.

"We shall see!" he whispered to himself.

A couple of days before his departure, Ramses was summoned to His Holiness. The Pharaoh sat alone in an armchair in a marble hall whose four entrances were guarded by Nubian sentries.

Beside the royal armchair were a stool for the Prince and a small table covered with papyrus[12] documents. On the walls were colored low reliefs depicting farm labors; and in

---

[10] Ethiopians: The term "Ethiopia" was used by ancient authors, including Herodotus, not only for Ethiopia proper but for *all* the lands lying south of Egypt, including Nubia. *(Translator.)*

[11] *Babel* is the biblical Hebrew name for Babylon. *(Translator.)*

[12] Papyrus was a material, made from the pith of a wetland sedge, *Cyperus papyrus*, that was used in ancient Egypt, throughout the Mediterranean region, and in the kingdom of Kush. Papyrus served as a writing surface (*papyrus* is the source of the word "paper") and, in Egypt, also as material for production of mats, rope, sandals, baskets, and reed boats. *(Translator.)*

the corners, stiff statues of Osiris with a melancholy smile on his lips.

When at his father's behest the Prince had seated himself, His Holiness said: "Here are the Prince's credentials as commander and Viceroy. Well, I gather your first days in power tired you?"

"I shall find strength in Your Holiness' service."

"Flatterer!" smiled the Lord. "Mind, I don't want you overworking yourself. Have fun, youth needs its diversions ... But that doesn't mean you don't have important matters to attend to."

"I'm ready."

"To begin with ... To begin with, let me tell you my concerns. Our treasury is in bad shape: the tax revenues decline with each year, especially in Lower Egypt, while expenditures multiply ..."

The Lord mused. "The women ... the women, Ramses, drain the wealth not only of mortals but mine as well. I have several hundred women, and each wants to have lots of maids, seamstresses, hairdressers, litter bearers, chamber slaves, horses, rowers, even her own favorites and children ... The little children! When I returned from Thebes, one of these ladies whom I don't even recall stopped me and, presenting a stout three-year-old boy, demanded that I set aside an estate for him, as he is supposed to be my son—a three-year-old son, do you hear, Eminence? Obviously I couldn't argue with the woman, especially in such a delicate matter. But it's easier for a man of noble birth to be polite than to find money for every such fancy ..."

He nodded, paused, and continued: "Meanwhile, since the start of my reign, my revenues have fallen by half, particularly in Lower Egypt. I ask what it means. They tell me the populace have grown poor, we've lost many inhabitants, the sea has buried some land in the north, the desert has buried land in the east, there have been several years of poor harvests—in a word, one disaster after another, and the treasury becomes ever shallower ...

"So I'm asking you to clear up this matter for me. Look around, get to know some well-informed, truthful people, and form them into a commission of inquiry. When they start submitting their reports, don't trust the papyrus too much but check this and that personally. I hear you have the eye of a commander; if that's so, then a single glance will tell you how accurate are the reports of the commission's members. But don't rush your judgment—and above all, don't announce it. Write down every important conclusion that comes into your head today, and after a few days look into the same matter again and write down your conclusion again. That will teach you caution in judging and accuracy in observing."

"It will be as Your Holiness says," said the Prince.

"Your second mission is more difficult. Something is happening in Assyria that is beginning to concern my government.

"Our priests tell that across the Northern Sea there is a pyramidal mountain, usually covered in verdure at the bottom and snow at the top, which has strange habits. After many years of quiet, it suddenly starts smoking, shaking, thundering, then disgorges from within itself as much liquid fire as there is water in the Nile. The fire flows down several channels in the mountain's flanks and ruins the work of the husbandmen over a huge area.

"Assyria, my Prince, is such a mountain. For centuries, peace and quiet reign there, then suddenly an internal storm springs up and great armies pour from out of nowhere and destroy Assyria's peaceful neighbors.

"Today, around Nineveh and Babel, there is an audible seething: the mountain is smoking. You must find out whether the smoke portends a tempest—and devise remedies."

"Will I manage?" asked the Prince quietly.

"One must learn to look," said the Lord. "If you would know something well, don't content yourself with the evidence of your own eyes, but secure the aid of several other pairs.

"Don't limit yourself to the views of Egyptians, for every person and nation has its own specific way of seeing things and does not grasp the entire truth. Listen to how the Assyrians are viewed by the Phoenicians, Jews, Hittites, and Egyptians—and carefully weigh in your heart what is common to their views about Assyria.

"If they all tell you there is danger coming from Assyria,[13] you will know there is. But if they speak variously, then likewise be on the alert, for wisdom requires anticipation of evil rather than good."

"Your Holiness speaks like the gods!" whispered Ramses.

"I'm old, and from the height of the throne one sees things that mortals do not suspect. If you asked the sun what it thought of the world's affairs, it would tell still more interesting things."

"Father, among the people whose views I'm to seek concerning Assyria, you did not mention the Greeks," said the Successor.

The Lord nodded with an indulgent smile. "The Greeks! ... The Greeks!" he said. "That people has a great future. Next to us they are still children, but what a soul dwells within them ...

"Do you remember that statue of me by the Greek sculptor? It's a second me, a living man! For a month I kept it at the palace—but finally gave it to the temple at Thebes. Would you believe: I was terrified lest this stone *me* rise from its seat and claim half my power. What confusion would arise in Egypt![14]

"The Greeks! Have you seen the vases they mold, the villas they build? From that clay and stone emanates something that cheers my old age and bids me forget my ill health ...

"And their speech? ... Oh, gods, why, it's music and sculpture and painting. Truly I say, if Egypt could die like a person, her legacy would be taken over by the Greeks. They would even convince the world that all this was their doing—that we never were. Yet they are only pupils in our elementary schools: for, as you know, we are not allowed to confer higher learning on foreigners."

"Still, Father, you seem to distrust the Greeks?"

"They are a peculiar people: neither they nor the Phoenicians can be believed. When the Phoenician wants to, he sees and tells the solid, Egyptian truth. But you never know when he wants to. Whereas the Greek, guileless as a child, would always tell the truth—but simply isn't able to.

"They see the whole world differently than we. To their strange eyes, everything is shiny, shimmery, and colorful like Egypt's sky and water. So how can we rely on their opinion?

---

[13] Such a test of the truth of a proposition was in 1840 dubbed "consilience" by the English polymath and scientist William Whewell. Consilience—also termed "convergence of evidence" or "concordance of evidence"—is the principle that evidence from independent, unrelated sources can "converge" on strong conclusions. (*Translator*.)

[14] Prus is anachronistically describing sculpture of the Greek Classical period, rather than sculpture of the earlier, Greek Archaic period contemporary with *Pharaoh*'s present time. *(Translator.)*

"During the Theban Dynasty,[15] far to the north there was a little town called Troy whose likes, in our land, number twenty thousand. Various Greek vagabonds kept attacking this chicken coop, and they harassed its few residents so badly that, after ten years' troubles, the residents burned down their little fort and moved elsewhere.

"A case of banditry, pure and simple! But look what stories the Greeks sing about the Trojan wars. We laugh at these marvels and heroics because our government had accurate reports of events. We see the glaring lies ... yet we listen to these songs like a child to its nanny's tales—and we can't tear ourselves away from them!

"Those are the Greeks: born liars but agreeable and, yes, brave. To a man, they would rather lay down their lives than tell the truth. Not for profit like the Phoenicians, but from a spiritual need."

"And what am I to think of the Phoenicians?" asked the Successor.

"They are clever people of great industry and daring, but traders: their whole life revolves around profit—the bigger, the better! The Phoenician is like water: he brings much and takes much away, and gets in everywhere. We should give them as little as possible, and above all see that they don't sneak into Egypt through the chinks.

"If you pay them well and give them prospects for still greater profit, they will be choice agents. What we know today of Assyria's secret moves, we know through them."

"What about the Jews?" whispered the Prince, lowering his eyes.

"A sharp people, but gloomy fanatics and born enemies of Egypt. Only when they feel the hobnailed Assyrian sandal on their necks, will they turn to us. May it not be too late. But they can be made use of. Of course, not here but in Nineveh and Babel."

The Pharaoh was tired. The Prince prostrated himself on his face and, after receiving the paternal embrace, went to see his mother.

The lady, seated in her cabinet, was weaving sheer linen for raiment for the gods, and her ladies-in-waiting were sewing and embroidering garments and fashioning bouquets. A young priest was burning incense before the statue of Isis.

"I come," said the Prince, "to thank you, Mother, and to take my leave."

The Queen rose, embraced her son's neck, and said with tears:

"How you've changed... You're now a man!... I see you so seldom, I might forget your features did I not see them always in my heart... Bad boy! I sailed so many times up to the farm with the highest dignitary of the Kingdom, thinking you'd finally end your ill feeling, and you brought out your concubine..."

"I'm sorry ... I'm sorry!" said Ramses, kissing his mother.

The lady led him out to a small garden planted with extraordinary flowers; and when they were alone without witnesses, she said:

"I'm a woman, so women and mothers are a concern of mine. Do you intend to take the girl with you on the journey? Mind you, the noise and commotion that will surround you could harm her and the child. The best thing for pregnant women is peace and quiet."

"Are you speaking of Sara?" asked Ramses in surprise. "Is she pregnant? She didn't mention it to me..."

---

[15] Theban Dynasty: presumably the 18th Dynasty. The Egyptian city that the Greeks called *Thebes* was Egypt's capital during most of the 18th Dynasty (ca. 1549-1292 BCE). Most scholars who believe that the stories of the Trojan Wars reflect a specific historical conflict, date it to the 12th or 11th century BCE. *(Translator.)*

"Maybe she's bashful, maybe she herself doesn't know," replied the Queen. "Anyway, a journey ..."

"But I have no intention of taking her along!" cried the Prince. "Only ... why is she keeping this from me ... as if the child weren't mine?"

"Now, don't be suspicious!" the lady rebuked him. "It's the ordinary bashfulness of young girls. And maybe she concealed her condition from fear that you would leave her ..."

"I certainly won't take her to my court!" interrupted the Prince, so impatiently that the Queen's eyes smiled, but she concealed them with her lashes.

"Well, it wouldn't do to push away too roughly a woman who has loved you. I know you've made provisions for her. We too will give her something. And a child of royal blood must have a proper upbringing and an estate ..."

"Of course," replied Ramses. "My first-born son, though he won't have princely rights, must be so situated that I needn't be ashamed of him and he won't bear me a grudge."

After taking leave of his mother, Ramses wanted to sail over to Sara's and, to that end, returned to his rooms.

He was stirred by two emotions: anger with Sara for concealing from him the cause of her indisposition—and pride that he was to be a father.

A father! This title lent him a dignity which, as it were, bolstered his offices as commander and viceroy. A father—he was no longer a youngster who must regard his elders with deference.

The Prince was thrilled and delighted. He wanted to see Sara, reproach her, then hug her and shower her with gifts. But on returning to his part of the palace he found there two Lower-Egyptian nomarchs who had come to report on the nomes. By the time he had heard them out, he was tired. Moreover, he was holding an evening reception to which he did not want to be late.

"Once again I won't be able to visit her," he thought. "Poor girl, she hasn't seen me in nearly two decades."

He called in the Negro. "Do you have the cage Sara gave you the time we were greeting His Holiness?"

"Yes," replied the Negro.

"Take out a dove and release it."

"The doves have been eaten."

"By whom?"

"Your Eminence. I told the cook the birds were from Lady Sara; so he made them into roasts and pies just for Your Eminence."

"May a crocodile devour you!" exclaimed the distraught Prince.

He sent for Thutmose and asked him to go at once to Sara. Recounting the story of the doves, he continued:

"Take her a pair of emerald earrings, a pair of anklets and bracelets, and two talents. Tell her I'm angry that she concealed her pregnancy from me but that I'll forgive her if the baby is healthy and comely. And if she has a boy, I'll give her a second farm!" he laughed.

"Only ... only get her to send away some of the Jews and hire at least a couple of Egyptian men and women. I don't want my son coming into the world in that company and maybe playing with Jewish children. They would teach him to hand his father the worst dates!"

CHAPTER 19

T he foreign quarter of Memphis lay in the northeast corner of the city, near the Nile. It numbered several hundred buildings and over ten thousand inhabitants: Assyrians, Jews, Greeks; most of all, Phoenicians.

It was a prosperous district. The main artery was a street thirty paces wide, fairly straight, paved with flagstones. On either side there rose brick, sandstone, and limestone buildings three to five stories tall. In the basements were stores of raw materials; on the ground floors, shops; on the first floors, apartments of the well-to-do; higher up, weavers', sandal-makers', jewelers' workshops; and highest, the cramped quarters of the workers.

Most of the buildings in the quarter, as in the whole city, were white. Still, there were tenements green as a meadow, yellow as a stand of wheat, blue as the sky, or red as blood.

Many façades were adorned with murals showing the inhabitants' occupations.[1]

On a jeweler's house, long series of drawings advertised that its owner sold chains and bracelets of his manufacture to admiring foreign kings. A merchant's huge palace was covered with paintings recounting the travails and dangers of mercantile life. On the sea a man is seized by terrible monsters with fishes' tails; in the desert, by winged fire-breathing dragons; and on remote islands he is harassed by giants with sandals bigger than a Phoenician ship.

Shown on a physician's office were persons who, with his help, were regaining lost arms and legs, even teeth and youth. And pictured on the building of the quarter's administrative authorities was a barrel into which people were dropping gold rings; a scribe into whose ear someone was whispering; and a penitent stretched out on the ground, to whom two other men were administering a hiding.

The street was full. The walls were lined with litter bearers, fan bearers, messengers, and laborers ready to offer their services. Down the middle stretched an unbroken chain of goods carried by porters, donkeys, and oxcarts. On the sidewalks circulated shrill peddlers of fresh water, grapes, dates, and smoked fish; and among them, hucksters, flower girls, musicians, and various kinds of performers.

In this human stream which flowed, shoved, bought, and sold, shouting in many voices, the policemen stood out. Each had a knee-length tan tunic, bare legs, an apron in blue and red stripes, and a short sword at his side, and held a stout cane. This functionary strolled

---

[1] The murals described by Prus may have been suggested by murals on buildings in Warsaw's medieval-Renaissance Old Town. *(Translator.)*

down the sidewalk, occasionally conferred with a colleague, but generally stood on a road-side stone, the better to view the throng spilling over at his feet.

In the face of such vigilance, street thieves had to act with great circumspection. Usually two would start fighting; and when a crowd had gathered and the police were caning combatants and onlookers alike, their confederates stole.

Nearly midway down the street stood the caravansary of a Phoenician from Tyre, Asarhadon,[2] where, for their easier surveillance, all arrivals from abroad were required to put up. It was a great square building with over a dozen windows on a side, and it touched no other building so that it was possible to go all the way around it and spy from every side. Over the main portal hung a model of a ship, and the façade bore pictures showing His Holiness Ramses XII making offerings to the gods and extending his protection to foreigners, among whom the Phoenicians were distinguished by their great stature and intensely red color.

The windows were narrow, always open and, only as need arose, screened with shades of canvas or colored reeds. The lodgings of the host and travelers took up three floors; on the ground floor were a wineshop and restaurant. Sailors, porters, craftsmen, and poorer travelers generally, ate and drank in the court, with its mosaic floor and canvas awnings hung from posts, so that all the guests could be watched. The more well-to-do and better born dined in a gallery surrounding the court.

In the court, guests sat on the ground at rocks in lieu of tables. In the galleries, where it was cooler, were tables, benches, and chairs, even low pillow couches for napping.

In each gallery was a great table covered with bread, meat, fish, and fruit, as well as earthen casks of beer, wine, and water. Negro men and women carried dishes round to the guests, removed empty casks, and brought full ones up from the cellars; and scribes watching over the tables scrupulously recorded every piece of bread, every garlic bulb and cup of water. In the middle of the court, on an elevation, stood two overseers with canes who, on one hand, kept an eye on the servants and scribes, and on the other—with their canes—soothed disputes among the poorer guests of various nationalities. Thanks to this arrangement, thefts and fights occurred rarely; more often, in fact, in the galleries than in the court.

The inn's host, the famous Asarhadon, a man past fifty, grizzled, dressed in a long tunic and muslin cape, walked among the guests to see that each had what he needed.

"Eat and drink, my sons," he said to some Greek sailors, "there isn't pork or beer like this in all the world. I hear a storm buffeted you off Raphia?[3] You should make the gods a generous offering for saving you! In Memphis you can live out your life without seeing a storm, but on the sea a thunderbolt is commoner than a copper deben. I have honey, flour, and incense for sacred offerings, and over in the corners stand gods of all the nations. At my inn a man can be well fed and pious for very small money."

He turned and entered the gallery among the merchants.

"Eat and drink, honorable sirs," he encouraged them, bowing. "Times are good! His Eminence the Crown Prince, may he live forever, is going to Pi-Bast with a huge retinue,

---

[2]Asarhadon: a variant of *Esarhaddon*, the name of a 7th century BCE Assyrian king. The choice of this name for a Phoenician is incongruous, since Assyria emerges as the Phoenicians' *bête noire*. *(Translator.)*

[3]Raphia: Ancient Greek name for a city near the Mediterranean Sea, first recorded in an inscription of Pharaoh Seti I from 1303 BCE. The city is now the Palestinian city of Rafah in the southern Gaza Strip. *(Translator.)*

and a gold shipment has come in from the Upper Kingdom on which more than one of you will turn a tidy profit.[4] We have partridges, goslings, fish straight from the river, and excellent roast venison. And what a wine they've sent me from Cyprus! May I be a Jew if a cup of this nectar isn't worth two drachmas! But, my fathers and good sirs, I'll give it to you today for a drachma. Just today, to make a start."

"Make it half a drachma a cup, and we'll try it," said a merchant.

"Half a drachma?" repeated the restaurateur. "Sooner the Nile will flow toward Thebes than I'll let such ambrosia go for half a drachma. Except ... for you, Lord Belezis, who are the pearl of Sidon. Hey, slaves! ... bring our gentlemen here a large pitcher of Cyprus wine."

When Asarhadon had left, the merchant named Belezis told his companions:

"My hand will wither if this wine is worth half a drachma. But, confound it, let it be! We'll have less trouble with the police."

Conversation with the guests of all nationalities and stations did not prevent the host from watching the scribes who recorded food and drink, the overseers who minded the servants and scribes, and above all a traveler who, having seated himself in the front gallery on cushions with his legs tucked under, dozed over a handful of dates and a cup of pure water. The traveler was about forty, with bushy raven hair and beard, meditative eyes, and strangely noble features which seemed never to have been wrinkled by anger or distorted by fear.

"That's a dangerous rat!" thought the host, watching him out of the corner of his eye. "He has the air of a priest but goes about in a dark hooded cloak ... He deposited a talent's worth of jewels and gold with me, but eats no meat and drinks no wine ... He must be a great prophet or a great thief!"

Two near-naked snake charmers entered the court from the street with a bagful of venomous reptiles and started a show. The younger played a pipe, while the elder proceeded to wind small and large snakes about himself, any one of which would have sufficed to scatter the guests out of "The Ship" inn. The pipe sounded more and more shrilly; the charmer gyrated, foamed at the mouth, quivered convulsively, and continually goaded the reptiles. Finally one of the snakes bit his hand, a second his face, and a third—the smallest—the charmer swallowed alive.

The guests and servants watched the charmer's play with anxiety. They trembled as he goaded the reptiles, closed their eyes when snake bit man. But when the charmer swallowed the snake—they howled their joy and wonder.

Only the traveler in the front gallery did not leave his cushions, or even bother to watch the show. When the charmer approached for a gratuity, the traveler threw two copper debens on the floor, motioning him not to come closer.

The show had lasted half an hour. When the snake charmers had left the court, a Negro attending the guest rooms ran up to the host and whispered something in a fluster. Then a police decurion appeared from out of nowhere, led Asarhadon to a distant alcove, and had a long conversation with him, while the inn's venerable proprietor beat his breast, wrung his hands, and clutched his head. Finally he kicked the Negro in the stomach, ordered a

---

[4] The source of Egypt's gold was Nubia, south of Egypt. New Kingdom pharaohs had conquered gold-bearing portions of Nubia. *(Translator.)*

baked goose and pitcher of Cyprus wine for the decurion, and approached the guest in the front gallery, who still seemed to doze with open eyes.

"I have sad news for you, good sir," said the host, sitting down beside the traveler.

"The gods send down rain and sadness on people at their pleasure," replied the guest indifferently.

"As we were watching the snake charmers here," continued the host, tugging at his grizzled beard, "thieves got onto the second floor and stole your things—three bags and a chest, no doubt a very expensive one!"

"You must inform the law court of my loss."

"Why the law court?" whispered the host. "In our land the thieves have their own guild. We'll send for the elder and assess the things, you'll pay him twenty percent of the value, and everything will turn up. I can help you."

"In our land," said the traveler, "no one treats with thieves, and neither will I. I'm staying with you, I entrusted my belongings to you, and you are responsible for them."

The venerable Asarhadon began scratching himself between the shoulder blades.

"Man from a distant land," he said in a lowered voice, "you Hittites and we Phoenicians are brothers, so I sincerely advise you not to become involved with an Egyptian law court, because it has only one door, by which to enter, and none by which to leave."

"The gods will lead an innocent man out through a wall," replied the guest.

"Innocent! Who of us is innocent in the land of bondage?" whispered the host. "Look—over there, a police decurion is finishing a goose; a choice goose that I would gladly have eaten myself. And do you know why I gave up this dainty morsel, taking it away from my own lips? Because the decurion came asking questions about you."

With that, the Phoenician frowned at the traveler; but the latter had not lost his composure even for a moment.

"He asks me," continued the host, "the decurion asks me: 'Who's that dark one who's been sitting two hours over a handful of dates?' I tell him: 'A very honorable man, the lord Phut.'[5]—'Where's he from?'—'From the land of Hatti,[6] from the city of Harran;[7] he has a handsome three-story house there, and ample fields.'—'Why's he come here?'—'He's come,' I tell him, 'to get back five talents that his father lent to a certain priest.'

"And do you know, honorable sir," said the restaurateur, "what the decurion answered me? These words: 'Asarhadon, I know you are a faithful servant of His Holiness the Pharaoh, and that you have good food and unadulterated wines, so I tell you beware! Beware of foreigners who make no friends, avoid wine and all pleasures, and say nothing. This Phut from Harran may be an Assyrian spy.'

"My heart turned faint when I heard this," continued the host. "But nothing matters to you!" he said indignantly, seeing that even the terrible imputation of espionage had not ruffled the Hittite's calm.

"Asarhadon," said the guest after a moment, "I entrusted myself and my possessions to you. So see that my bags and chest are returned, or I shall complain against you to that same decurion who is eating your goose."

---

[5] Phut: name borrowed from the biblical third son of Ham, who was a son of Noah. *(Translator.)*

[6] Hatti: the Hittite Kingdom. *(Translator.)*

[7] Harran: a major ancient city, in Upper Mesopotamia, whose site is now in southeastern Turkey. *(Translator.)*

"Well ... then let me pay the thieves just fifteen percent of the value of your things," cried the host.

"You have no right to pay them."

"Give them at least thirty drachmas ..."

"Not a deben."

"Give the poor beggars at least ten drachmas ..."

"Go in peace, Asarhadon, and ask the gods to restore your wits," replied the traveler, ever with the same calm.

The host sprang up from the cushions, panting with anger.

"The reptile!" he thought. "He hasn't come here just to collect a debt. He's also going to turn his hand to some sort of business. My heart tells me he must be a rich merchant, or maybe even a restaurateur who will open another inn somewhere nearby in partnership with priests and judges. Heavenly fire burn you up first! Leprosy consume you! Miser, cheat, thief off whom an honest man can't make any profit!"

The worthy Asarhadon had not yet managed to allay his anger when a flute and tabor rang out in the street and a moment later four almost naked dancing girls ran into the court. The porters and sailors greeted them with cries of joy, and the respectable merchants in the galleries looked on with interest and commented on their beauty. The girls greeted all with waves and smiles. One of them began playing a double flute, another accompanied her on the tabor, and the two youngest danced around the court in such a way that there was hardly a guest but was brushed by their muslin scarves.

Those who were drinking began singing, shouting, and inviting the girls over, and among the commonalty there ensued a fray which, however, the overseers easily quelled, raising up their canes. Only a Libyan, provoked by the sight of a cane, drew a knife; but two Negroes grabbed his arms, relieved him of several copper rings in payment for food, and cast him out into the street. Meanwhile a dancing girl remained with the sailors, two went among the merchants who offered them wine and pastries, and the eldest began going round the tables, soliciting contributions.

"For the temple of divine Isis!"[8] she called. "Pious foreigners, give to the temple of Isis, the goddess who looks after all creatures. The more you give, the more happiness and blessings will you receive ... For the temple of mother Isis!"

Little coils of copper wire, now and then a small grain of gold, were dropped onto her tabor. A merchant asked whether he could visit her, to which she nodded with a smile.

When she entered the front gallery, the Harranian Phut reached into a leather bag and took out a gold ring, saying:

"Ishtar[9] is a great and good goddess, accept this for her temple."

The priestess looked at him briskly and whispered: "Anael, Sakhiel."

"Amabiel, Abalidot," answered the traveler in the same tone of voice.

---

[8] Isis: the Greek name for Aset, one of the Egyptian sky goddesses, daughter of the sky goddess Nut and the earth god Geb; wife of the god Osiris, and mother of the god Horus. *(Translator.)*

[9] Ishtar was the Babylonian and Assyrian goddess of love, sex, fertility, and war. She was a counterpart to the Sumerian goddess Inanna and was cognate with the northwest Semitic goddess Astoreth, also known by the Hellenized name Astarte. The name Astoreth is particularly associated with her worship in the ancient Levant among the Canaanites and Phoenicians. She was also celebrated in ancient Egypt after the introduction there of Levantine cults during the 18th Dynasty. *(Translator.)*

"I see that you love mother Isis," said the priestess aloud. "You must be rich and are generous, so it is worth telling your fortune."

She sat down next to him, ate a couple of dates and, looking at the palm of his hand, said: "You come from a distant land from Bretor and Hagit.[10] You have had a good journey ...

"For several days the Phoenicians have been watching you," she added more quietly. "You come for money though you are not a merchant. Come over today after sunset ...

"Your demands," she said aloud, "should be fulfilled ...

"I live on the Street of Tombs, at the sign of the Green Star,"[11] she whispered.

"Just beware of thieves with designs on your property," she finished, seeing that the worthy Asarhadon was listening.

"There are no thieves in my house!" the host burst out. "If anybody steals, it's those who come in off the street!"

"Don't be angry, old man," said the priestess sarcastically. "It brings a red streak to your neck, which portends a bad death."

At this, Asarhadon spat thrice and silently recited a spell against ill omens. When he had moved away down the gallery, the priestess began flirting with the Harranian. She gave him a rose from her garland, hugged him in farewell, and went off to the other tables.

The traveler beckoned to the host. "I want that woman to visit me," he said. "Have her shown up to my room."

Asarhadon looked him in the eye, clapped his hands, and burst out laughing.

"Typhon[12] has possessed you, Harranian!" he exclaimed. "If something like that were to happen in my house involving an Egyptian priestess, they would drive me out of the city. Only foreign women may be received here."

"In that case I will go to her," said Phut. "She is a wise and pious woman and will advise me in many matters. You will give me a guide after sunset so I do not lose my way."

"All the evil spirits have entered your heart," answered the host. "Do you know that this acquaintance will cost you two hundred, maybe three hundred drachmas, not counting what you must give the servant women and the temple? And for that sum—for five hundred drachmas—you can get to know a young and virtuous woman, my daughter, who is already fourteen and, being a sensible girl, is collecting herself a dowry. So don't wander at night in an unfamiliar city where you will fall into the hands of the police or the thieves, but take advantage of what the gods offer you at home ... All right?"

"Will your daughter go with me to Harran?" asked Phut.

The host regarded him in astonishment. Suddenly he slapped himself on the forehead as though he had guessed a secret, grabbed the traveler's arm, and pulled him into a quiet alcove.

---

[10] Spirits of the northern and eastern region of the world. *(Author.)* A wife of the biblical David bears the name *Haggith*; this has become *Hagit*, a common female given name in Israel. *(Translator.)*

[11] Green Star: the name of the house may have been suggested by the green-star emblem of the Esperanto movement. Esperanto, the most successful constructed international language, was created in the late 19th century by Ludwik Zamenhof, a Jewish-Polish ophthalmologist. Prus' personal library, which he bequeathed to the Warsaw Public Library, holds a book on Esperanto. *(Translator.)*

[12] Typhon: the deadliest monster of Greek mythology. He was identified by the ancient Greeks with Set, the Egyptian god of the desert, storms, foreigners, darkness, chaos, and evil. Typhon's name may have given rise to the word "typhoon." *(Translator.)*

"Now I know everything!" he whispered, indignant. "You traffic in women. But mind, for carrying away a single Egyptian woman you'll forfeit all your property and go to the mines. Unless ... you make me your partner, because I know all the ways here."

"In that case, you will tell me the way to the priestess' house," replied Phut. "See that I have a guide after sunset and my bags and chest tomorrow, or I'll complain to the law court."

With that, Phut left the restaurant and went up to his room.

Beside himself with anger, Asarhadon approached a table where Phoenician merchants were drinking and called aside one of them, Cush.[13]

"Nice guests you place into my care!" said the host, unable to control the tremor in his voice. "This Phut hardly eats, he tells me to ransom his stolen things from the thieves, and now, as in derision of my house, he's going to an Egyptian dancing girl instead of dowering my women."

"What's strange about that?" laughed Cush. "He could get to know Phoenician girls in Sidon, here he prefers Egyptian girls. It's a foolish man who, when in Cyprus, drinks Tyrian beer instead of trying Cyprus wine."

"And I tell you," interrupted the host, "he's a dangerous man. He pretends to be a townsman, but he has the demeanor of a priest!"

"You look like a high priest, Asarhadon, but you're only an innkeeper! A bench doesn't stop being a bench for being covered in lion skin."

"But why does he go to priestesses? I'll swear it's a ruse and, instead of to a feast with the women, this Hittite boor will go to a gathering of conspirators."

"Anger and greed have dimmed your mind," said Cush earnestly. "You're like a man who seeks a pumpkin on a fig tree and doesn't see the fig. To any merchant it's obvious that if Phut is to get back five talents from a priest, he has to curry favor with all those who hang around the temples. But you wouldn't understand."

"My heart tells me he must be an Assyrian agent with designs for His Holiness' ruin."

Cush was eyeing Asarhadon with contempt. "Then watch him, watch his every step. And if you discover something, maybe you'll get part of his property."

"Ah, now you're making sense!" said the host. "Let this rat go to the priestesses, then to a place unknown to me. But I'll send my eyes after him, from which nothing can hide!"

---

[13] Cush: name borrowed from the biblical eldest son of Ham, who was a son of Noah. *(Translator.)*

CHAPTER 20

About nine in the evening, Phut left the caravansary at the sign of The Ship, accompanied by a Negro carrying a torch. Half an hour earlier, Asarhadon had sent a trusted man to the Street of Tombs, telling him to watch closely whether the Harranian slipped out of the house at the Green Star and, if so, where to.

A second trusted man of the host's followed Phut at a distance. In the narrower streets, he hid against the buildings; in wider ones, he feigned a drunk.

The streets were empty; the porters and peddlers slept. There were lights only in the apartments of working craftsmen and of wealthy persons feasting on the flat roofs. In various parts of the city there rang harps and flutes, song, laughter, hammer blows, rasp of carpenters' saws. An occasional drunken shout, now and then a cry for help.

The streets that Phut and the slave passed through were for the most part narrow, crooked, full of potholes. The nearer to the destination, the lower were the tenements, and the more numerous the one-story houses and the gardens, or rather palms, figs, and scrawny acacias which leaned out from between walls as though with intent to escape.

On the Street of Tombs the view suddenly changed. The tenements gave way to expansive gardens containing elegant villas. Before one of the gates, the Negro stopped and put out his torch.

"This is the Green Star," he said; and, making Phut a low bow, he turned homeward.

The Harranian knocked at the gate. After a moment a porter appeared. He carefully surveyed the arrival and muttered: "Anael, Sakhiel ..."

"Amabiel, Abalidot," answered Phut.

"Welcome," said the porter, quickly opening the gate.

Passing a score of paces between the trees, Phut found himself in the villa's vestibule, where he was greeted by his acquaintance the priestess. In the depths stood a man with black beard and hair, so like the Harranian that the arrival could not hide his astonishment.

"He will replace you in the eyes of those who watch you," smiled the priestess.

The man disguised as the Harranian placed a rose garland on his head and, accompanied by the priestess, went up to the first floor, where presently there rang a flute and the clink of winecups. Meanwhile two junior priests led Phut to a bath in the garden. There they bathed him and dressed his hair, then clothed him in white raiment.

From the bathhouse all three re-emerged among the trees; they passed through several gardens and at last found themselves in an empty square.

"Over there," one of the priests told Phut, "are the old tombs, over there the city, and here the temple. Go where you will; may wisdom point you the way, and holy words keep you from harm."

The two priests withdrew into the garden, and Phut remained alone. The moonless night was fairly clear. In the distance, wrapped in fog, glimmered the Nile, and above it sparkled the seven stars of the Great Bear. Over the traveler's head stood Orion, and over the dark pylon towers shone the star Sirius.

"In our land the stars shine brighter," thought Phut. He began whispering prayers in an unknown language and headed toward the temple.

When he had gone off a few dozen paces, a man leaned out from a garden and watched the traveler. But almost at the same moment such a thick fog descended that nothing could be seen in the square except for the temple roofs.

After a while the Harranian came upon a high wall. He looked at the sky and proceeded west. Every now and again nocturnal birds and great bats flew overhead. The fog became so thick that he had to grope his way along the wall so as not to lose it. Some time had passed when suddenly Phut found himself before a low wicket studded with many bronze nails. He began counting them from the upper left, firmly pressing down on some and twisting others.

When in this fashion he had moved the last nail at the bottom, the door quietly opened. The Harranian advanced several steps and found himself in a narrow, completely dark recess.

He carefully tested the ground with his foot until he found, as it were, the edge of a well, from which blew a chill draft. Here he sat down and boldly lowered himself into the shaft, though this was his first time in this place and in this land.

The shaft was not deep. Phut alighted on an inclined floor and began descending a narrow corridor with such surefootedness as though he had long known the way.

At the corridor's end was a door. The arrival groped for the knocker and knocked three times. In response a voice spoke seemingly from out of nowhere:

"You who at a night hour disturb the peace of a holy place, have you the right to enter?"

"I have harmed no man, woman or child ... My hands are unstained by blood ... I have not eaten of unclean foods ... I have not taken another's property ... I have not lied or betrayed a great secret," answered the Harranian calmly.

"Are you he whom they await, or he whom you give yourself out to be?" asked the voice after a moment.

"I am he who was to come from the brethren in the East but the other name is mine as well, and I have a house and land in the northern city as I told the others," answered Phut.

The door opened, and the Harranian entered a spacious cellar lit by a small lamp burning on a table before a purple curtain. The curtain was embroidered, in gold, with a winged sphere flanked by two serpents.

At the side stood an Egyptian priest in white raiment.

"You that have entered," said the priest, indicating Phut, "do you know the meaning of the emblem on the curtain?"

"The sphere," said the arrival, "represents the world on which we dwell, and the wings indicate that the world soars in space like an eagle."

"And the serpents?" asked the priest.

"The two serpents remind the wise man that he who would betray this great secret will die twice—in body and in soul."

After a moment's silence, the priest asked:

"If you are indeed Berossus"[1]—he bowed his head—"the great prophet of Chaldea"[2]—he bowed his head again—"for whom there are no secrets on earth or in heaven, please tell your servant: which star is the strangest?"

"A strange star is Hor-set,[3] which makes a circuit of the heavens in twelve years, because it is circled by four smaller stars. But more strange is Horka,[4] which makes a circuit of the heavens in thirty years. For it has not only stars subordinate to it, but also a great ring that sometimes disappears."

At this, the Egyptian priest prostrated himself on his face before the Chaldean. Then he handed him a purple sash and a muslin veil, showed him where the incense was kept, and left the cavern amid low bows.

The Chaldean remained alone. He placed the sash on his right shoulder, covered his face with the veil, took a gold ladle, poured incense into it, and lit the incense at the lamp before the curtain. Whispering, he turned three times in place, and the incense girdled him in a triple ring.

Meanwhile a strange unrest had come over the empty cavern. The ceiling seemed to be going up, and the walls receding. The purple curtain on the altar swayed as if moved by hidden hands. The air undulated as if flocks of invisible birds were flying through it.

The Chaldean parted his raiment at the chest and took out a gold medal covered with arcane signs. The cavern shuddered, the sacred curtain moved more violently, and small flames appeared at various points in the chamber.

The magus lifted up his hands and spoke:

"Heavenly Father, gracious and merciful, cleanse my soul ... Send Thy blessings upon an unworthy servant and extend Thy almighty arm upon rebellious spirits so that I may show Thy might..."

"Behold the sign that I touch in your presence ... Lo, I am foreseeing and fearless, supported by divine assistance ... Lo, I am powerful and invoke and conjure you ... Come here, obedient, in the name of Aye, Saraye, Aye, Saraye ..."

Now voices spoke on various sides. A bird flew by the lamp, then a russet robe, next a man with a tail, finally a crowned cock which settled on the table before the curtain.

The Chaldean spoke again: "In the name of the almighty and eternal God ... Amorul, Tanekha, Rabur, Latisten ..."

Distant voices spoke a second time.

"In the name of the real and eternally living Eloy, Arkhima, Rabur, I conjure and invoke you ... By the name of the star that is the Sun, by this its sign, by the glorious and terrible name of the living God ..."[5]

---

[1] Berossus: name borrowed from a Babylonian writer, priest of Bel Marduk, and astronomer who would be active at the beginning of the 3rd century BCE. He wrote in Koine Greek, which—after the conquests of Alexander the Great—was for centuries the *lingua franca* of much of the Mediterranean region and Near East. Prus calls him *Beroes. (Translator.)*

[2] Chaldea was a marshy land in southeastern Mesopotamia which briefly came to rule Babylon. *(Translator.)*

[3] The planet Jupiter. *(Author.)*

[4] The planet Saturn. *(Author.)*

[5] Spells of magi. *(Author.)*

Suddenly all became still. Before the altar there appeared a crowned specter holding a scepter and seated on a lion.

"Berossus! ... Berossus!" called the specter in a muffled voice, "wherefore do you invoke me?"

"I wish my brethren at this temple to receive me with a sincere heart and to lend ear to the words that I bring them from the brethren in Babylon," answered the Chaldean.

"So be it," said the specter, and vanished.

The Chaldean remained motionless like a statue, head thrown back, arms upraised. He stood thus for over half an hour in a position impossible for an ordinary man.

Meanwhile a piece of the cavern wall receded, and three Egyptian priests entered. At sight of the Chaldean, who seemed to lie in the air, his back resting on an invisible support, the priests looked at one another in astonishment. The eldest said:

"We used to have such people; but today no one can do it."

They walked all around him, touched his stiff limbs, and peered anxiously into his face, yellow and bloodless as a corpse's.

"Is he dead?" asked the youngest.

At this, the Chaldean's backward-tilted body righted. A slight blush colored his face, and the upraised arms fell. He sighed, rubbed his eyes like a man wakened from sleep, looked at the arrivals, and after a moment said:

"You"—he turned to the eldest—"are Mephres,[6] High Priest of the Temple of Ptah in Memphis ... You are Herhor, High Priest of Amon in Thebes, the most powerful man in the Kingdom after the king ... You"—he indicated the youngest—"are Pentuer, Second Prophet at the Temple of Amon and advisor to Herhor."

"And you undoubtedly are Berossus, the great Babylonian priest and wise man whose coming was made known to us a year ago," replied Mephres.

"You have said the truth," said the Chaldean. He embraced each in turn, and they bowed their heads before him.

"I bring you great words from our mutual homeland, which is wisdom," said Berossus. "Please hear them and act as required."

At a sign from Herhor, Pentuer withdrew into the depths of the cavern and brought out three light wooden armchairs for the elder priests and a low stool for himself. He sat down near the lamp and took from his bosom a stylus and a wax-covered tablet.

When all three had taken their armchairs, the Chaldean began:

"To you, Mephres, speaks the Supreme College of Priests in Babylon. Egypt's holy priesthood is in decline. Many priests gather money and women and lead lives of pleasure. Wisdom is neglected. You have no power over the invisible world or even over your own souls. Some of you have lost the higher faith, and the future is concealed from your eyes. Worse, many priests, feeling their spiritual resources exhausted, have taken to the path of lies and are deceiving the simple folk with clever tricks.

"This is what the Supreme College says: if you would return to the true path, Berossus shall abide with you for several years in order to kindle a genuine light at the Nile with the spark brought from the great altar of Babylon."

---

[6] Mephres: name borrowed from an 18th Dynasty pharaoh identical with Thutmose I, as found in Manetho's *History of Egypt*, composed in the 3rd century BCE . *(Translator.)*

"All is as you say," replied Mephres sadly. "Therefore abide among us for several years, that the young may be reminded of your wisdom."

"Now, Herhor, the words of the Supreme College for you ..."

Herhor bowed his head.

"Owing to neglect of the great secrets, your priests have failed to divine that bad years are coming for Egypt. You are threatened with internal disasters that only virtue and wisdom can avert. Worse, if during the next ten years you were to start a war with Assyria, her armies would rout yours, come to the Nile, and destroy all that has existed here since time immemorial.[7]

"Such an ominous conjunction of stars as today impends over Egypt occurred for the first time during the Fourteenth Dynasty, when your country was conquered and pillaged by the Hyksos. It will recur a third time in five or six hundred years from the direction of Assyria and the Parsa people[8] who live east of Chaldea."

The priests listened, terrified. Herhor was pale; Pentuer's tablet fell from his hands. Mephres took hold of an amulet hanging on his chest and prayed with parched lips.

"So beware of Assyria," continued the Chaldean, "for today is her hour. They are a savage people! They scorn work and live by war. They impale or flay the vanquished; they destroy captured cities and take the population into bondage. Their pastime is to hunt fierce animals; and their sport,[9] to shoot bows at captives or to gouge out their eyes. They turn other people's temples to rubble; they use the vessels of the gods at their feasts; and they make the priests and wise men their fools. The ornaments of their walls are the skins of live people; and of their tables, the gory heads of enemies."

When the Chaldean had finished, the venerable Mephres spoke:

"Great prophet, you have cast fear upon our souls, and you indicate no deliverance. It may be—and surely is, since you say so—that fate will for a time be unpropitious to us; but how is this to be avoided? There are dangerous places in the Nile where no boat can survive; so the wisdom of the helmsmen bypasses the dangerous whirlpools. Likewise with the misfortunes of nations. The nation is the vessel, and time the river, which in certain periods is disturbed by whirlpools. And if a little fishing shell can evade disaster, then why should not millions of people in like circumstances escape destruction?"

"Your words are wise," replied Berossus, "but I can answer them only in part."

"Don't you know all that is to happen?" asked Herhor.

"Ask me not about what I know but cannot say. The most important thing for you is to maintain a ten-year peace with Assyria, and that lies within your power.

"Assyria still fears you, knows nothing about the convergence of bad fortunes over your land, and wants to begin a war with the peoples of the North and East who inhabit the shores of the sea. So you could make an alliance with her today."

---

[7] In fact, Assyria's King Esarhaddon will invade Egypt in 671-669 BCE, but will not hold the country. *(Translator.)*

[8] Parsa people: the Persians, who will conquer and rule Egypt in the 6th-5th centuries BCE and again, briefly, in the 4th century BCE. *Parsa* is the Old Persian name for Persia and Persepolis ("the City of the Persians"), the ceremonial capital of the First Persian Empire (ca. 550-330 BCE). *Pharaoh*'s Polish text spells it *Paras*, perhaps a typographical error. *(Translator.)*

[9] "sport": The word is used here and elsewhere in *Pharaoh* in a sense of "pastime," "amusement," "recreation," "play," or "fun." *(Translator.)*

"On what terms?" asked Herhor.

"Very good ones. Assyria will let you have the land of Israel as far as the city of Akko,[10] and the land of Edom[11] as far as the city of Elath.[12] Thus, without war, your borders will advance ten days' march to the north and ten days to the east."

"What about Phoenicia?" asked Herhor.

"Beware of temptation!" cried Berossus. "Were the pharaoh to extend his hand today for Phoenicia, in a month the Assyrian armies meant for the north and east would turn south; and before a year was out, their horses would be bathing in the Nile."

"But Egypt can't give up her sway over Phoenicia!" Herhor burst out.

"If she doesn't, she will be preparing her own doom," said the Chaldean. "I repeat the words of the Supreme College: 'Tell Egypt'—instructed the brethren in Babylon—'to hug her land like a partridge for ten years, because the hawk of ill fortune lurks. Tell her we Chaldeans hate the Assyrians more than do the Egyptians, for we endure the burden of their rule; but in spite of that we counsel Egypt peace with this bloodthirsty people. Ten years—it's a short period of time, after which you can not only regain your previous positions but also rescue us.'"

"It's true!" said Mephres.

"Only consider," continued the Chaldean. "If Assyria makes war on you, it will drag in Babylon, which hates war, exhaust our wealth, and halt the work of wisdom. Even if you do not succumb, your country will be devastated for years to come and will lose not only much population but these fertile lands which, absent your labor, the sand will bury within a year."

"We understand that," broke in Herhor, "and so we do not think to tangle with Assyria. But Phoenicia ..."

"What harm is it to you," said Berossus, "if the Assyrian bandit squeezes the Phoenician thief? Our merchants and yours will profit by it. And if you want to have the Phoenicians, let them settle on your shores. I am sure the wealthiest and cleverest among them will escape from the power of the Assyrians."

"What would become of our fleet if Assyria took over Phoenicia?" asked Herhor.

"It is not really your fleet but the Phoenicians'," replied the Chaldean. "When you no longer have Tyrian and Sidonian ships, you shall start building your own and training Egyptians in the art of sailing. If you have good sense and an intrepid spirit, you will wrest the entire western trade away from the Phoenicians."

Herhor tossed his hand dismissively.

"I have said what I was told to," said Berossus, "you do as you like. But, mind, ten ominous years impend over you."

"I think, holy man," said Pentuer, "that you also spoke of internal disasters threatening Egypt in the future. What will they be? ... If you could tell your servant."

"About that, do not ask me. You should know these things better than I, a stranger.

---

[10] Akko: Acre—known locally as Akko (in Hebrew) or Akka (in Arabic)—is an extant ancient city in northern Israel's Western Galilee, at the northern extremity of Haifa Bay. *(Translator.)*

[11] Edom: a Semitic-inhabited historic region of the Southern Levant, south of Judea and the Dead Sea. It is mentioned in the Bible as a 1st century BCE Iron Age kingdom of Edom. *(Translator.)*

[12] Elath: a city, mentioned in the Hebrew Bible, that is located at the northern tip of the Gulf of Aqaba. The Gulf separates the Sinai Peninsula, to the west, from the Asian continent. *(Translator.)*

Prudence will show you the illness, and experience will provide the medicines."

"The populace are terribly oppressed by the great!" whispered Pentuer.

"Piety has fallen!" said Mephres.

"Many people hanker for war abroad," added Herhor. "Whereas I have long seen that we can't conduct a war. Possibly in ten years ..."

"Then you will make a treaty with Assyria?" asked the Chaldean.

"Amon, who knows my heart," said Herhor, "knows how I loathe such a treaty ... Not so long ago, the wretched Assyrians were paying us tribute! But, holy father, if you and the Supreme College say that fate is against us, then we must make a treaty."

"That is true, we must!" added Mephres.

"In that case, let the College in Babylon know your decision, and they will see that King Assar[13] sends you an envoy. Trust me, this pact is very advantageous: you increase your possessions without war! Our College of Priests deliberated over the pact."

"May all the blessings flow down on you: abundance, power, and wisdom," said Mephres. "Yes, we must restore our priesthood; and you, holy Berossus, shall help us."

"We must above all ease the misery of the populace," said Pentuer.

"The priests! ... The populace!" said Herhor, as though to himself. "Above all, we must restrain those who yearn for war. True, His Holiness the Pharaoh is behind me, and I think I've gained some influence over the heart of His Eminence the Crown Prince (may they live forever!). But Nitager, for whom war is as necessary as water is to a fish ... and the commanders of the mercenary regiments, who matter in our land only in wartime ... and our aristocracy, who think war will pay off the Phoenician debts and bring them wealth ..."

"Meanwhile the peasants are collapsing under their workloads, and the public laborers are seething at being fleeced by their bosses," said Pentuer.

"Him and his everlasting peasants and laborers!" said Herhor, lost in thought. "Pentuer, you go on and think about the peasants and laborers; Mephres, you about the priests. I don't know what you'll succeed in doing—but I swear that, if my own son were to push Egypt toward war, I would rub out my own son."

"Do so," said the Chaldean. "If anyone wants to make war, let him, so long as it's not in those parts where he's liable to run afoul of Assyria."

With that, the session came to an end. The Chaldean placed the sash on his shoulder, and the veil on his face; Mephres and Herhor took their places to either side of him, and Pentuer behind them, all facing the altar.

As Berossus whispered, his arms crossed on his chest, an agitation again came over the cellar, and something like a distant commotion could be heard, which surprised the assistants. Then the magus spoke loudly:

"Baralanensis, Baldachiensis, Paumachiae, I call on you to witness our compacts and to support our aims."

Trumpets rang out, so distinctly that Mephres bowed down to the ground, Herhor looked about in astonishment, and Pentuer knelt, trembling, and covered his ears.

The purple curtain on the altar lurched, and its folds assumed the shape of a man seeking to emerge from behind it.

---

[13]King Assar: Actually, the Assyrian king contemporary with Eygpt's last Ramesside pharaohs was Tiglath-Pileser I. *(Translator.)*

"Bear witness," called the Chaldean in a transformed voice, "O heavenly and infernal powers. And who would break the agreement or betray its secret, may he be confounded ..."

"Confounded!" repeated a voice.

"And destroyed ..."

"And destroyed!"

"In this visible and in that invisible life. By the ineffable name of Jehovah, at whose sound the earth trembles, the sea ebbs, fire goes out, the elements of nature disintegrate ..."

A veritable storm came over the cavern. Sounds of trumpets mingled with seeming distant thunder. The curtain on the altar lifted almost horizontally, and beyond it, amid flickering lightning flashes, appeared strange creatures, half human, half plant and animal, heaped and jumbled together.

Suddenly all became still, and Berossus slowly ascended into the air over the heads of the three assisting priests.[14]

‡

At eight in the morning Phut the Harranian returned to the Phoenician caravansary at the sign of The Ship, where his bags and chest, taken by thieves, had turned up. A few minutes later one of Asarhadon's confidential servants returned, and the host took him down into the cellar and asked curtly: "Well?"

"All night long," replied the servant, "I was in the square before the Temple of Set. About ten in the evening, three priests came out of a garden five properties from the house at the Green Star. One of them, with a black beard and hair, directed his feet across the square to the Temple of Set. I ran after him, but a fog descended and I lost sight of him. Whether he returned to the Green Star, or when, I don't know."

The host of the inn slapped himself on the forehead and muttered to himself:

"My Harranian, if he dresses in a priest's outfit and goes to a temple, must be a priest. If he wears a beard and hair, he must be a Chaldean priest. And if he sees local priests in secret, then there's some mischief in play. I won't tell the police, because I might get in trouble. But I'll let one of the great Sidonians know, because there may be profit to be made from this, if not for me then for our people."

Before long the host's other man returned. Asarhadon took him as well down to the cellar, and heard the following account:

"I stood all night opposite the house at the Green Star. The Harranian was there, got drunk, and became so loud that a policeman admonished the doorman."

"Eh?" asked the host. "The Harranian was at the Green Star all night, and you saw him?"

"Not just me, the policeman too ..."

Asarhadon brought in the first servant and asked each man to repeat his story. They faithfully did so. And it transpired that Phut the Harranian had partied all night at the Green Star without ever leaving the place—and at the same time, late in the evening, had set out for the Temple of Set, from which he had not returned.

<hr>

[14] This and other scenes in *Pharaoh* were influenced by Spiritualist séances conducted by the Italian medium Eusapia Palladino which Prus attended in Warsaw in 1893, before beginning the novel in 1894. *(Translator.)*

"Oh!" muttered the Phoenician, "there's some very great mischief in all this. I must inform the elders of the Phoenician community that this Hittite is able to be in two places at once. And I'll ask him to get out of my inn ... I don't like people who have two persons: one their own, and one for spare. A man like that is either a great thief or a sorcerer or a conspirator."

Since Asarhadon feared these things, he secured himself against spells with prayers to all the gods adorning his tavern. Then he ran downtown, where he informed the elder of the Phoenician community and the elder of the thieves' guild of what had happened. Next, returning home, he called in the police decurion and told him Phut may be a dangerous man. Finally he demanded of the Harranian that he leave the inn, to which he was bringing no profit but only suspicions and losses.

Phut willingly agreed to the proposal and told the host that he would sail for Thebes that evening.

"May you not return from there!" thought the hospitable host. "May you rot in the mines or fall into the river, prey for the crocodiles."

CHAPTER 21

The Crown Prince's journey began during the most beautiful season of the year, in the month of Phamenoth (late December, early January).[1]

The water had fallen by half, revealing ever new expanses of land. Numerous rafts were sailing from Thebes to the sea with wheat; in Lower Egypt, clover and senna were being harvested. Orange and pomegranate trees were in bloom, and fields were being sown in lupine, flax, barley, beans, broad beans, cucumbers, and other crops.

Seen off to the Memphis harbor by priests, the highest officials of the Kingdom, the guard of His Holiness the Pharaoh, and crowds of populace, about ten in the morning Viceroy Ramses boarded a golden barge. Beneath the deck, on which stood sumptuous tents, twenty soldiers plied the oars; and the best river pilots were stationed at the mast and at either end of the ship. Some supervised the sails, others commanded the rowers, others steered the ship.

Ramses had invited aboard the most venerable High Priest Mephres and the holy father Mentesuphis,[2] who were to accompany him in the journey and in the exercise of governance. He had also invited aboard the Nomarch of Memphis, who was seeing the Prince off to the border of his province.

A few hundred paces ahead of the Viceroy sailed the beautiful ship of His Eminence Otoes, the Nomarch of Khensu,[3] the province adjoining Memphis. Arrayed behind the Prince were countless ships carrying courtiers, priests, officers, and officials.

The provisions and servants had left earlier.

---

[1] Actually, the ancient Egyptian month of Phamenoth lay between March 10 and April 8 of the modern, Gregorian calendar. *(Translator.)*

[2] Mentesuphis (Prus spells it *Mentezufis*): name given by the 3rd century BCE Egyptian historian Manetho to Pharaoh Nemtyemsaf II, the sixth and penultimate king of the 6th Dynasty, who reigned in the first half of the 22nd century BCE. In the Abydos King List, he bears the throne name Merenre. Less than three years after his one-year reign, the Old Kingdom ended and the chaos of the First Intermediate Period began, marked by the collapse of royal power and the rise of the provincial nomarchs. Book Two of Herhodotus' *Histories* records a legend that a Queen Nitocris avenged the murder of her brother-and-husband, allegedly Nemtyemsaf II, by drowning his murderers at a banquet. The name *Nitocris* may actually be a conflation and distortion of the name of the male Pharaoh Neitiqerty Siptah, who succeeded Nemtyemsaf II. *(Translator.)*

[3] Khensu: the 2nd Nome of Lower Egypt. Prus calls it *Aa*. The nome's capital was Khem, which Prus calls *Sochem*. *(Translator.)*

The Nile flows to Memphis between two belts of hills. Farther along, the hills turn east and west, and the river splits into several branches whose waters flow to the sea across a great plain.

When the ship had left the harbor, the Prince wished to speak with High Priest Mephres. Just then, however, such a cry went up from the crowd that the Successor had to come out of his tent and show himself to the populace.

But the uproar, instead of subsiding, mounted. On either bank there stood and continually grew crowds of half-naked laborers and festively dressed townsfolk. A great many wore garlands on their heads; nearly all carried green branches. Some groups sang; in others rang the clatter of drums and the piping of flutes.

The shadoofs thickly ranged along the river stood idle. The Nile itself swarmed with small boats, whose occupants threw flowers at the Successor's barge. Some jumped from the boats into the water and swam after the Prince's ship.

"Why, they greet me as if I were His Holiness!" thought the Prince.

His heart swelled with pride at the sight of so many festive boats which he could have stopped with a single gesture, and of the thousands of people who had dropped their labors and braved crippling, even death, to look upon his divine countenance.

Ramses was intoxicated particularly by the crowd's immense, ceaseless clamor. It filled his bosom, rushed to his head, lifted him up. The Prince felt that, were he to jump off the deck, he would not even reach the water because the people's enthusiasm would sweep him up and carry him into the heavens like a bird.

The ship neared the left bank somewhat, the figures in the crowd became more distinct, and the Prince noticed something unexpected. While the first ranks of populace clapped and sang, in farther ranks canes were falling thick and fast upon invisible backs.

The Viceroy turned in surprise to the Nomarch of Memphis. "Look over there, Eminence ... Canes at work?"

The Nomarch shaded his eyes with his hand, and his neck reddened. "Pardon me, lord, but I have poor eyesight ..."

"Canes at work ... I'm sure of it," said the Prince.

"That's possible," replied the Nomarch. "It's probably police apprehending a band of thieves."

None too satisfied, the Successor went aft among the pilots, who suddenly veered into midstream, and from there looked toward Memphis.

The banks up the Nile were nearly deserted; the small boats had disappeared; the shadoofs were at work as though nothing had happened.

"Are the festivities over?" the Prince asked a pilot, pointing upriver.

"Yes ... People have gone back to work," said the pilot.

"Pretty fast!"

"They have to make up for lost time," said the pilot carelessly.

The Successor winced and glared at the speaker. But he soon calmed down and went back to his tent. He no longer cared about the shouting. He had turned somber and silent. After the earlier access of pride, he felt contempt for a crowd which passed so quickly from enthusiasm to shadoofs drawing mud.

In this area the Nile starts branching. The ship of the Nomarch of Khensu turned west and, after an hour's sail, made shore. The crowds were still more numerous than at Memphis. There had been set up many bannered posts and verdure-twined triumphal gates. Increasingly in evidence among the populace were foreign faces and dress.

When the Prince debarked onto shore, priests approached with a canopy, and His Eminence Nomarch Otoes said to him:

"Welcome, Viceroy of divine Pharaoh, to the Nome of Khensu. In token of your favor, which to us is celestial dew, be pleased to make offering to our patron the god Ptah, and accept into your care and rule this nome with its temples, officials, populace, cattle, grain, and all that is found here."

Next the Nomarch presented to him a group of fragrant, rouged young dandies dressed in gold-embroidered attire. They were close and distant relatives of the Nomarch: the local aristocracy.

Ramses scrutinized them. "Ah!" he cried. "I thought these lords lacked something, and now I see. They don't have wigs."

"Since the Prince doesn't use a wig, our young men have sworn off this apparel," replied the Nomarch.

After this explanation, a young man with a fan, another with a shield, and a third with a spear took their places behind the Prince, and a procession began. The Successor walked beneath the canopy, preceded by a priest with a canister of burning incense and by several young girls who strewed roses in the Prince's path.

The populace, festively dressed, branches in hand, formed a lane and cheered, chanted, or prostrated themselves on their faces before the Pharaoh's deputy. But the Prince saw that, despite the loud expressions of joy, the faces were lifeless and troubled. He also noticed that the crowd was divided into groups which were directed by some people, and that the rejoicing was taking place on command. Once again he felt in his heart a chill contempt for the rabble that was incapable even of joy.

Slowly the entourage approached a masonry column demarcating the nome of Khensu from the Memphis nome. Three sides of the column bore inscriptions pertaining to the province's area, population, and number of cities; at the fourth side stood a statue of the god Ptah, wound from chest to foot in swaddling bands, an ordinary cap on his head, a staff in his hand.

One of the priests handed the Prince a gold spoon with burning incense. The Successor, reciting the prescribed prayers, extended the censer to the level of the god's face and bowed low several times.

The cries of the populace and priests intensified still more, while smirks and jibes could be seen among the aristocratic youth. The Prince, who since his reconciliation with Herhor had shown great respect for the gods and priests, frowned slightly, and the youths instantly changed their demeanor. They all turned serious, and some prostrated themselves on their faces before the column.

"It's true!" thought the Prince, "the noble-born are better than the rabble! Whatever they do, they do it with their hearts, not like those who yell in my honor but can't wait to get back to their cowbarns and workshops."

Better than ever, he appreciated the distance that separated him from the simple folk. He now understood that the aristocracy was the only class with which he shared a commonality of sentiment. If suddenly these stylish young men and beautiful women, whose ardent gazes followed his every move to immediately serve him and do his bidding—if they were to vanish, the Prince would feel, amid the countless throngs of the populace, more alone than if he had been in the desert.

Eight Negroes brought a litter whose canopy was decorated with ostrich feathers, and the Prince climbed in and rode to the nome's capital, Khem,[4] where he took up residence at the government palace.

Ramses' sojourn in this province, barely a few miles distant from Memphis, went on for a month. All that time passed in entertaining requests, receiving homage, meeting officials, and taking part in feasts.

The feasts were twofold: one in the palace, in which only the aristocracy partook; the other, in an outer court, where oxen were roasted whole, hundreds of breads were consumed, and hundreds of pitchers of beer were quaffed. In the latter, the Prince's servants and the lower nome officials regaled themselves.

Ramses was impressed with the generosity of the Nomarch and the devotion of the great lords who surrounded the Viceroy day and night, attentive to his every beck and ready to do his bidding.

At last, wearied of the revels, the Prince told His Eminence Otoes that he wished to become acquainted with the province's economy; for such was the charge that he had received from His Holiness the Pharaoh.

His wish was granted. The Nomarch invited the Prince to take a seat in a litter borne by two porters and, with a great retinue, conducted him to the temple of the goddess Hathor. There the retinue remained in the vestibule, while the Nomarch had the porters carry the Prince to the top of the pylon and accompanied him up.

The six-story tower—from which the priests observed the heavens and, using colored flags, communicated with adjacent temples in Memphis, Athribis, and Iunu—commanded, within a several-mile radius, nearly the entire province. His Eminence Otoes showed the Prince where the pharaoh's fields and vineyards lay; which canal was being cleared; which dam was being repaired; where were located the bronze foundries, the royal granaries, the marshes full of lotus and papyrus; which fields had been buried by sand, and so on.

Ramses was enthralled by the beautiful view and warmly thanked Otoes for the pleasure thus experienced. But on returning to the palace and starting to note down his impressions in accordance with his father's advice, he found that his knowledge of the economic condition of the nome of Khensu had not been enhanced.

After a couple of days he again asked Otoes for information on the administration of the province. Whereupon His Eminence ordered all the officials to assemble and parade before the Prince, who sat on an elevation in the main court.

There passed before the Viceroy great and petty treasurers; scribes in charge of grain, wine, cattle, and textiles; foremen of masons and diggers; civil and hydraulic engineers; physicians who treated diverse illnesses; officers of workers' regiments; police scribes, judges, prison wardens; even openers of dead bodies and execution-

---

[4] Khem (known to the Greeks as Letopolis): capital of Khensu, the 2nd Nome of Lower Egypt. The modern site of Khem's remains is known as Ausim. The city was a center of worship of the deity Khenty-irty or Khenty-khem, a form of the god Horus. The site and its deity are mentioned in texts from as far back as the Old Kingdom, but the only extant monuments date to the reigns of Late Period pharaohs. Prus calls Khem *Sochem*. *(Translator.)*

ers. Next the Nomarch presented Ramses' own officials in the province. The Prince learned, to his no small surprise, that in the nome of Khensu and the city of Khem he had a charioteer; an archer; shield-, spear-, and ax-bearers; a dozen litter-bearers; a couple of cooks, cupbearers, and barbers; and many other servants distinguished by their devotion and loyalty, though Ramses did not know them and had never so much as heard their names.

Wearied and bored by the fruitless review of functionaries, the Prince became despondent. He was terrified by the thought that he understood nothing and was therefore incapable of governing the Kingdom. But he feared to admit this even to himself.

For if he could not govern Egypt, and if others saw this, then what would remain for him? ... Only death. Ramses felt that, apart from the throne, there could be no happiness for him; that, without power, he could not exist.

But after he had rested a couple of days, insofar as that was possible amid the chaos of court life, he summoned Otoes again and said to him:

"I asked Your Eminence to initiate me into the governance of your nome. You've shown me the land and the officials, but still I know nothing. Indeed, I'm like someone in the undergrounds of our temples who sees about him so many paths that he's unable to emerge back into the world."

The Nomarch was disconcerted. "What am I to do?" he cried. "What do you wish of me, Lord? Only give the word, and I'll relinquish to you my office, my fortune, even my head."

Seeing the Prince receptive of these assurances, he went on:

"During your journey you saw the populace of the nome. You may say that not all were there. Granted. I can order the whole population out, all two hundred thousand men, women, elderly, and children. You were pleased to view our territory from the pylon. But if you wish, we can view from close up every field, every village, and every street in Khem.

"Finally, I showed you the officials, though it's true that the lowest were missing. However, give the order and tomorrow all of them will appear and lie before you on their stomachs.

"What more can I do? ... Please tell me, Lord! ..."

"I believe in your loyalty," replied the Prince. "Tell me two things: Why have His Holiness' revenues declined? And what do you do in the nome?"

Otoes was taken aback.

The Prince quickly added: "I want to know what you do and how you govern, because I'm young and only beginning to govern."

"But you have the wisdom of an old man!" whispered the Nomarch.

"Then it's proper," said the Prince, "that I should question those who are experienced, and that you should lend me instruction."

"I'll show and tell Your Eminence everything," said Otoes. "But we must get out to someplace it's not so noisy."

Indeed, at the palace occupied by the Prince the inner and outer courts were thronged like a fairground. People ate, drank, sang, wrestled, and ran races, all in honor of the Viceroy whom they served.

Accordingly about three in the afternoon the Nomarch called for horses, and he and the Prince rode west out of the city. The courtiers remained at the palace and made still merrier.

The day was beautiful and cool; the earth was covered in greenery and blossoms. Bird-song rang overhead; the air was filled with fragrance.

"How nice it is here!" exclaimed Ramses. "For the first time in a month, I can collect my thoughts. I was starting to believe a regiment of war chariots had taken up residence in my head and were doing drills from morning to night."

"Such is the lot of the world's potentates," replied the Nomarch.

They stopped on a hill. At their feet lay a vast meadow traversed by an azure stream. To north and south bleached the walls of small towns; beyond the meadow, as far as the horizon, stretched the red sands of the Western Desert, from which now and again wafted an oven-hot wind.

Grazing in the meadow were countless herds of domestic animals: horned and horn-less cattle, sheep, goats, donkeys, antelopes, even rhinoceroses. Visible here and there were marshes covered with water plants and shrubs and teeming with wild geese, ducks, pigeons, storks, ibises, and pelicans.

"Behold, lord," said the Nomarch, "that is a picture of our land of Kemet,[5] our Egypt. Osiris took a fancy to this strip of land between deserts and filled it with vegetation and animals, that he might benefit from them. Then the good god assumed human form and was the first pharaoh. And when he felt his body withering, he left it and entered that of his son, then that of his son's son.

"This way, since time immemorial Osiris has been living among us as pharaoh and has been benefiting from Egypt and its bounties, which he himself created. The Lord has grown like a mighty tree. Its boughs are all the Egyptian kings; its branches, the nomarchs and priests; its twigs, the nobility. The visible god sits upon the earthly throne and receives his due income from the country; the invisible god receives offerings in the temples and pronounces his will with the lips of the priests."

"Yes," said the Prince, "so it is written."

"Since Osiris-Pharaoh," continued the Nomarch, "cannot personally attend to earthly husbandry, he has commissioned us nomarchs, who are descended of his blood, to look after his wealth."

"That is true," said Ramses. "Sometimes the solar god is even incarnated in a nomarch and gives rise to a new dynasty. Thus began the Memphite,[6] Elephantinian,[7] Theban,[8] and Xoite[9] Dynasties ..."[10]

---

[5] Kemet: Egypt's "black land", the fertile black soil of the Nile flood plains, as distinct from the *deshret*, the "red land" of the desert. Prus calls Kemet *Queneh*. *(Translator.)*

[6] Memphite Dynasty: This term could apply to any of Dynasties 3-8, which all had their capitals at Memphis. *(Translator.)*

[7] Elephantinian Dynasty: Manetho wrote that Egypt's 5th Dynasty kings ruled from Elephantine Island, in the Nile River in northern Nubia (the island is now part of southern Egypt's city of Aswan); but archeologists have found evidence that those kings' palaces were still located at Memphis. *(Translator.)*

[8] Theban Dynasty: Thebes was Egypt's capital during part of the 11th Dynasty (during the Middle King-dom) and most of the 18th Dynasty (during the New Kingdom). *(Translator.)*

[9] Xoite Dynasty: According to Manetho, the 14th Dynasty's kings ruled from Xois, near the center of the Nile Delta, on an island formed by the Nile's Sebennytic and Phatnitic branches. However, most Egyp-tologists now believe that the 14th Dynasty was based at Avaris, in the eastern Delta. *(Translator.)*

[10] The religious ideology of pharaonic power described here is essentially correct. In the coronation cer-

"Yes, lord," Otoes went on. "And now I will answer your question.

"You were asking what I do in the nome. I watch the property of Osiris-Pharaoh and my little share in it. Look at these herds: you see a variety of animals. Some provide milk; others, meat; still others, wool and hides. Likewise Egypt's populace: some provide grains; others, wines, textiles, furnishings, buildings. My task is to collect from each what he owes and lay it at the feet of the pharaoh.

"I couldn't look after such numerous herds all by myself; therefore I've picked myself vigilant dogs and competent herdsmen. Some milk the animals, shear them, skin them; others see that the thief doesn't make off with them, nor the beast of prey savage them. It's the same with a nome: I wouldn't have time to collect all the taxes and warn the people against evil; so I have officials who do what is needed and tender me accounts of their activities."

"All that is true," interrupted the Prince, "I know that and understand it. What I can't make out is why His Holiness' revenues have declined despite being so looked after."

"Please bear in mind, Eminence," replied the Nomarch, "that the god Set, though he is the brother of solar Osiris, hates him, fights him, and spoils all his works. He visits deadly illnesses on people and cattle, he causes the Nile's flood to be too scant or too violent, he casts billows of sand upon Egypt in the hot season.

"When the year is good, the Nile reaches to the desert; when it is bad, the desert comes up to the Nile, and then the royal revenues must be smaller.

"Behold, Your Honor," he said, indicating the meadow. "These herds are numerous, but in my youth they were more numerous. And who is to blame? None other than Set, whom men are powerless to oppose. This meadow, today enormous, was once still greater, and from this spot one did not see the desert, which today terrifies us.

"Where gods fight, man can do nothing; where Set vanquishes Osiris, who can stand in his way?"

His Eminence Otoes was done; the Prince hung his head. He had heard not a little in school about the beneficence of Osiris and the wickedness of Set, and while yet a child he had been angry that accounts had not been squared with Set.

"When I grow up," he had thought, "and can carry a spear, I'll seek Set out and try my hand!"

Today here he was looking at the immense expanse of sands, the realm of the sinister god who was decreasing Egypt's incomes; but he did not think to fight him. How does one fight a desert? ... One can only go around it or perish in it.

---

emony, the pharaoh was transformed into a god through his union with the royal *ka*, or life-force of the soul, which had been possessed by all previous pharaohs. This made him the son of the gods Ra, Horus, Osiris, and, from the Middle Kingdom, Amon. At his death the pharaoh became fully divine, assimilated with Osiris and Ra. *(Translator.)*

CHAPTER 22

The Crown Prince's sojourn in the nome of Khensu so wearied him that, to get some rest and collect his thoughts, he ordered an end to all festivities in his honor and asked that the people not come out to greet him anywhere on his travels.

The Prince's retinue was taken aback. But the order was carried out, and Ramses regained a measure of privacy. He now had time to drill the troops, which was his favorite activity, and could begin gathering his distracted thoughts.

Ensconced in the remotest corner of the palace, the Prince pondered to what extent he had carried out his father's charges.

With his own eyes he had viewed the nome of Khensu: its fields, towns, people, and officials. He had verified that the eastern edge of the province had suffered from encroachment by the desert. He had observed that the working populace was apathetic and stupid and did only what it was told to, and that reluctantly. Finally, he had discovered that truly loyal and loving subjects were to be found only among the aristocracy. These were either related to the pharaonic line or belonged to the nobility and were scions of soldiers who had fought under Ramses the Great.

In any case, these people sincerely cleaved to the dynasty and were ready to serve it with genuine zeal: unlike the peasants who, having shouted out a greeting, hurried back to their swine and oxen.

But the main goal of his mission remained unresolved. Ramses not only did not see clearly the causes of the decline in the royal incomes, he did not even know how to formulate the question: why were things bad—and how could they be improved? He only felt that the legendary war between the gods Set and Osiris explained nothing and offered no remedies.

The Prince, as pharaoh-to-be, wanted to have great revenues like Egypt's past rulers. He seethed at the thought that, on mounting the throne, he might be as poor as his father, if not more so. "Never!" cried the Prince, clenching his fists.

In order to enlarge the royal estates, he was ready to hurl himself, sword in hand, at the god Set and hack him to pieces as Set had his brother Osiris. But instead of the cruel god and his legions, he saw about himself emptiness, silence, and the unknown.

Influenced by these tussles with his own thoughts, he approached High Priest Mephres.

"Tell me, holy father versed in all manner of wisdom: why are the Kingdom's revenues declining, and how could they be increased?"

The High Priest lifted up his hands. "Blessed be the spirit," he cried, "that whispered these thoughts to Your Eminence! Oh, may you follow in the steps of the great pharaohs who covered Egypt with temples and enlarged her fertile lands with dams and canals!"

The old man was so moved that he burst into tears.

"First of all," said the Prince, "answer my question. Surely there can be no thought of building canals or temples when the treasury is empty. The greatest misfortune has befallen Egypt: her rulers are threatened with poverty. That above all must be investigated and remedied, and the rest will follow."

"About that the Prince will learn only in the temples, at the foot of the altar," said the High Priest. "Only there can your noble curiosity be satisfied."

Ramses jumped impatiently. "The temples blind Your Eminence to the entire country, even to the pharaoh's treasury! I'm a pupil of the priests, I grew up in the shadow of the temples, I'm familiar with the spectacles in which you present the malice of Set and the death and rebirth of Osiris, and of what use is it to me? When Father asks me how the treasury may be filled, I'll have no answer. Or rather, I should urge him to pray still longer and oftener than he has been!"

"The Prince blasphemes because he does not know the high rites of the religion. If he knew them, he could answer many questions that trouble him. And if he'd seen what I have! ... He would believe that the most important matter for Egypt is to elevate her temples and priests."

"Old people become children once again," thought the Prince, breaking off the conversation. High Priest Mephres had always been very pious; but lately he had taken it to the point of eccentricity.

"I'd make a fine spectacle," Ramses told himself, "putting myself into the hands of the priests to assist at their childish rituals. Mephres might have me as well stand for whole hours before an altar with my arms upraised, as he supposedly does in the expectation of miracles!"

In the month of Pharmouthi (late January—early February)[1] the Prince took his leave of Otoes in order to transfer to the nome of Heq-At.[2] He thanked the Nomarch and lords for their splendid hospitality but was sad at heart, fearing he would be unable to carry out his father's charge.

Seen off by Otoes' family and court, the Viceroy crossed with his retinue to the right bank of the Nile, where he was welcomed by His Eminence Nomarch Ranuzer and his lords and priests. When the Prince stepped onto the soil of Heq-At, the priests lifted up statues of Atum,[3] the province's patron god; the officials prostrated themselves on their faces; and the Nomarch handed Ramses a gold sickle, asking that as the Pharaoh's deputy he inaugurate the harvest: this was the season to bring in the barley.

Ramses accepted the sickle, cut a couple handfuls of ears, and burned them together with incense before the tutelary god at the border. Then the Nomarch and great lords followed suit, and finally the peasants began the harvest. They gathered only the ears, which were stuffed into sacks; the straw was left in the field.

---

[1] Actually, the ancient Egyptian month of Pharmouthi lay between April 9 and May 8 of the modern, Gregorian calendar. *(Translator.)*

[2] Heq-At: the 13th Nome of Lower Egypt; Prus calls it *Hak*. Its capital was Iunu. *(Translator.)*

[3] Atum: In the Heliopolitan creation myth, Atum was the first god, having created himself. He was associated with the sun god Ra. *(Translator.)*

After hearing a religious service, which bored him, the Prince mounted a chariot. A detachment of soldiers went forward; then the priests; then two lords who led the Successor's horses by the bridles; then, in a second chariot, Nomarch Ranuzer, followed by a huge retinue of lords and court servants. The populace, obedient to Ramses' wishes, did not come out; but peasants working in the fields prostrated themselves on their faces at sight of the procession.

In this way, crossing several pontoon bridges thrown over Nile branches and canals, by nightfall the Prince reached Iunu, the province capital.[4]

For several days there were welcoming feasts, homage-paying to the Viceroy, and presentations of officials. Finally Ramses ordered an end to festivities and asked the Nomarch to acquaint him with the wealth of the nome.

The review began next day and lasted a couple of weeks. Each day various craft guilds, under command of their guild officers, came to the courtyard of the palace where the Successor was staying to show him their wares.

Arms makers brought swords, spears, and axes; makers of musical instruments—fifes, trumpets, drums, and harps. They were followed by the great carpenters' guild, which showed chairs, tables, couches, litters, and wagons, adorned with rich designs, inlaid with many-colored woods, mother-of-pearl, and ivory. Next to be brought in were metal kitchen utensils: grills, spits, and two-handled pots and shallow stewpans with covers. Jewelers showed off marvelous gold rings; bracelets and anklets of electrum, an alloy of gold and silver; and chains: all finely sculpted and set with precious stones or colored enamels.

The procession was closed by potters bearing over a hundred varieties of earthen vessels. There were vases, pots, bowls, pitchers, and cruses, of the most varied shapes and sizes, covered with paintings, adorned with heads of birds and beasts.

Each guild presented the Prince with its most beautiful wares. Though there were no two alike, they filled a large hall.

At the close of the interesting if exhausting exhibition, His Eminence Ranuzer asked the Prince whether he was satisfied.

"I've seen more beautiful things," mused the Successor, "perhaps only in temples or in my father's palaces. But since only the wealthy can afford them, I don't know whether the Kingdom's treasury has very great revenues from them."

The Nomarch was surprised at the young Lord's indifference to works of art and disturbed by his concern over revenues. But wishing to satisfy Ramses, he began taking him on tours of royal factories.

They visited mills where slaves ground grain into flour in several hundred querns and mortars; bakeries which produced bread and biscuits for the army; and a factory which made fish and meat preserves.

They viewed great tanneries and sandal workshops; foundries that produced bronze for vessels and weapons; brickworks; and weavers' and tailors' guilds.

These establishments were located in the east of the city. At first Ramses inspected

---

[4] Iunu (Egyptian for "Place of Pillars") was one of the oldest cities of ancient Egypt, and capital of Heq-At, the 13th Nome of Lower Egypt; Prus calls the city *Anu*. The ancient Greeks called it *Heliopolis* ("City of the Sun") because it was the principal seat of the sun god Ra and of the related god Atum. The Hebrew Bible calls the city *On*. Its site is now at the northeast edge of Cairo; little remains of the ancient city, whose temples and other buildings were quarried to build medieval Cairo. *(Translator.)*

them with interest; but he very soon became disgusted with the sight of the frightened, thin workers with their sickly complexions and cane-scarred backs.

He did not linger at the factories; he preferred viewing the environs of Iunu. Visible far to the east was the site of the previous year's desert maneuvers between his corps and Nitager's. As on the palm of his hand, he saw the highway down which his regiments had marched; the spot where, due to the scarabs, the military engines had turned into the desert; and perhaps the very tree on which the peasant who had been digging the canal had hanged himself.

From yonder peak, accompanied by Thutmose, he had viewed the blossoming land of Goshen and denounced the priests. And there, between the hills, he had met Sara, who had captured his heart.

Today, what changes! He had ceased hating the priests ever since, through Herhor's good offices, he had received the corps and the viceroyship. And he had lost interest in Sara as a mistress but was taking an ever livelier interest in the child whose mother she was to be.

"I wonder what she's doing," thought the Prince. "It's been a while since I've had word from her."

As Ramses contemplated the eastern hills and recalled the recent past, Nomarch Ranuzer, standing at the head of the Prince's suite, was sure the Prince had noticed irregularities at the factories and was meditating on ways to punish him.

"I wonder what he saw," thought the Nomarch. "Is it that half the bricks have been sold to the Phoenician merchants? Or that ten thousand sandals are missing from the warehouse? Or maybe a vile wretch whispered something to him about the metal furnaces?"

Ranuzer's heart was filled with great misgivings.

Suddenly the Prince turned around to the suite and called Thutmose, who was obliged always to be near his person.

Thutmose ran up, and the Successor took him still farther aside. "Listen," he said, indicating the desert. "Do you see those hills?"

"We were there last year," sighed the courtier.

"I was just thinking of Sara ..."

"I'll burn incense to the gods!" cried Thutmose. "I was beginning to think that, ever since Your Eminence became viceroy, you've forgotten your faithful servants."

The Prince looked at him and shrugged. "Choose," he said, "from the gifts presented to me, some of the most beautiful furnishings, fabrics, and especially bracelets and chains, and take them to Sara ..."

"Live forever, Ramses," whispered the dandy, "you're a noble lord ..."

"Tell her," continued the Prince, "that my heart is ever full of favor for her. Tell her I want her to watch her health and care for the child that is to come into the world. And tell Sara that when delivery nears and I've carried out my father's instructions, she'll come and live in my house. I can't have the mother of my child languishing in solitude. Go, do as I've said, and bring back good news."

Thutmose prostrated himself on his face before the noble Lord and immediately set out on his way. The Prince's retinue, unable to guess the substance of their conversation, envied Thutmose his lord's favor, and His Eminence Ranuzer felt a growing anxiety in his soul.

"May I," he thought in his distress, "not need to raise my hand against myself and, in prime of life, orphan my house ... Oh, wretch that I am, in appropriating to myself the goods of His Holiness the Pharaoh, why did I not think of the hour of judgment?"

His face turned ashen, and his legs swayed beneath him. But the Prince, swept up in a wave of reminiscence, did not notice his trepidation.

CHAPTER 23

Now in the city of Iunu a series of feasts and entertainments took place. His Eminence Ranuzer brought the best wines up from his cellars; and the most beautiful dancing girls, most famous musicians, and most extraordinary performers assembled from three adjacent nomes. Prince Ramses' time was perfectly filled. In the morning there was drilling of troops and receiving of dignitaries; later, a feast, spectacles, hunts, and another feast.

But no sooner was the Nomarch of Heq-At sure that the Viceroy had wearied of administrative and economic questions, than the Prince called him in and asked:

"Your Eminence's nome is one of the wealthiest in Egypt?"

"Yes ... though we've had several difficult years," replied Ranuzer, his heart again sinking and his legs quaking.

"What I don't understand," said the Prince, "is that His Holiness' revenues keep declining year after year. Could you explain it to me?"

"Lord," said the Nomarch, bowing deeply, "I see that my enemies have sown distrust in your soul; whatever I say, you'll not be convinced. Therefore let me say no more. Rather, let scribes come with documents which you can touch and examine for yourself."

The Prince was surprised at the unexpected outburst but accepted the suggestion. Indeed, he welcomed it: he thought the scribes' reports would explain to him the secrets of administration.

Next day the Great Scribe of the Nome of Heq-At came with his assistants, bringing more than a dozen papyrus scrolls written over on both sides. When they were unfurled, they formed a band three spans[1] wide by sixty paces long. The Prince had never seen such a gigantic document, describing only a single province for a single year.

The Great Scribe sat down on the floor with his legs tucked under and began:

"'In the thirty-third year of the reign of His Holiness Mer-amen-Ramses, the Nile was late in flooding. The peasants, ascribing this misfortune to the sorcery of foreigners residing in the province of Heq-At, demolished the houses of infidel Jews, Hittites, and Phoenicians, and in the process several persons were killed. His Eminence the Nomarch ordered the culprits tried, and twenty-five peasants, two masons, and five sandal-makers were sentenced to the mines, and a fisherman was strangled.'"

"What document is this?" interrupted the Prince.

---

[1] Span: the distance between the tips of the human thumb and little finger. In ancient times, a span was considered equal to half a cubit. A cubit, from the Latin *cubitum* ("elbow"), is the length of the forearm from the elbow to the tip of the middle finger. *(Translator.)*

"This is the judicial report destined for the feet of His Holiness."

"Put it away and read about the treasury revenues."

The Great Scribe's assistants rolled up the discarded document and handed him another. The official began again:

"'On the fifth day of the month of Thoth, six hundred measures of wheat were delivered to the royal granaries, for which the chief keeper issued a receipt.

"'On the seventh day of Thoth, the Great Treasurer learned and verified that a hundred forty-eight measures of wheat were missing from last year's harvest. During the inspection, two workers stole a measure of grain and concealed it among bricks. When this was discovered, they were put on trial and sent to the mines for lifting their hands to the property of His Holiness.'"

"What about the hundred forty-eight measures?" asked the Successor.

"Mice ate them," answered the Scribe, and he read on:

"'Delivered on the eighth of Thoth were twenty cows, eighty-four sheep for slaughter, which the overseer of cattle directed be issued to the Sparrow Hawk Regiment in exchange for the proper receipt ...'"

In this fashion the Viceroy learned, day by day, how much barley, wheat, beans, and lotus seeds had been delivered to the granaries, how much had been sent to the mills, how much had been stolen, and how many workers had as a result been sentenced to the mines. The report was so boring and chaotic that at the middle of the month of Phaophi[2] the Prince stopped the reading.

"Tell me, Great Scribe," asked Ramses, "what do you make of this? What does it tell you?"

"Whatever Your Eminence will ..."

And he began over again from the beginning, but now from memory:

"On the fifth day of the month of Thoth, six hundred measures of wheat were delivered to the royal granaries ..."

"Enough!" cried the angry Prince, and he ordered them to get out.

The scribes prostrated themselves on their faces, quickly gathered up the papyrus scrolls, prostrated themselves again, and hastily cleared out of the room.

The Prince called in Nomarch Ranuzer. He came, hands clasped on chest, but with a calm face: he had learned from the scribes that the Viceroy had been unable to make anything of the reports and had not even heard them through.

"Tell me, Eminence," began the Successor, "do they read you the reports?"

"Daily ..."

"Do you understand them?"

"Pardon me, Lord, but ... could I govern the nome if I didn't?"

The Prince was disconcerted. Could it really be that he alone was so incompetent? If so, what would become of his rule?

"Have a seat," he said after a moment, indicating to Ranuzer a chair. "Have a seat and tell me how you rule the nome."

His Eminence turned pale and his eyes inverted, whites up. Ramses saw it and proceeded to explain:

"Don't think I lack confidence in your wisdom ... Indeed, I know of no man who could exercise power better than you. But I'm young and wish to understand the art of governance. So I'm asking you to share with me some crumbs of your experience. You govern the nome, that I know! Now tell me how one governs."

The Nomarch breathed again. "I will tell Your Eminence the whole course of my life, so that you may know how demanding is my work.

"In the morning, after my bath, I make offerings to the god Atum and then call in the treasurer and ask him whether His Holiness' taxes are being properly collected. If he says they are, I praise him; if he says that so-and-sos haven't paid, I order the disobedient persons jailed.

"Next I call in the keeper of royal barns, to learn how much the grain stocks have increased. If much, I praise him; if little, I order those guilty to be flogged.

"Later the Great Scribe comes and tells me which of His Holiness' goods are needed by the army, the officials, and the workers—and I order these issued in exchange for receipts. If he issues less, I praise him; if more, I start an investigation.

"In the afternoon, Phoenician merchants come to me and I sell them grain and deposit the money in the Pharaoh's treasury. Then I pray and confirm the sentences of the courts; and toward evening the police inform me of events. Just the other day, people from my nome crossed into the province of Ka-khem[3] and desecrated a statue of the god Sobek.[4] In my heart I was pleased, because that is not our patron; nonetheless I sentenced a couple of those guilty to be strangled, many to the mines, and all to be flogged.

"And so, peace and good order prevail in my nome and the taxes flow in daily."

"But the Pharaoh's revenues have declined here as well," said the Prince.

"That is true, Lord," sighed His Eminence Ranuzer. "The priests say the gods are angry with Egypt over the influx of foreigners; but I see that the gods don't spurn Phoenician gold and precious stones ..."

Just then, preceded by the duty officer, the priest Mentesuphis entered the room to invite the Viceroy and Nomarch to a public religious ceremony. Both dignitaries accepted the invitation, Nomarch Ranuzer with a show of piety that astonished the Prince.

When Ranuzer had left, bowing repeatedly, the Viceroy asked the priest: "Holy Prophet, as you are the most venerable Herhor's deputy to me, please explain something that fills my heart with concern."

"Will I be able?" replied the priest.

"You will, because you are full of learning, of which you are the servant. Only consider what I shall say to you.

"You know why His Holiness the Pharaoh has sent me here."

"So that the Prince may acquaint himself with the wealth and governance of the country," said Mentesuphis.

"That's what I'm doing. I question the nomarchs, I inspect the country and the people, I hear the reports of the scribes, but I understand nothing, and that poisons my life and perplexes me.

---

[3] Ka-khem: Lower Egypt's 10th Nome. Prus calls it "Ka." *(Translator.)*

[4] Sobek: the crocodile god and god of the Nile, depicted as a crocodile or as a man with a crocodile's head. Prus calls him *Sebak. (Translator.)*

"When I'm dealing with the military, I know everything: how many men, horses, chariots there are; which officers drink or neglect their duties, and which carry them out. I also know what to do with an army. If an enemy corps stands in a plain, in order to defeat it I need two corps. If the enemy is in a defensive position, I won't set out without three corps. If the enemy is untrained and fights in disorganized mobs, I can field five hundred of our soldiers against his thousand and I'll beat him. If the other side has a thousand axmen and I have a thousand, I'll attack and defeat them if I have a hundred slingers in support.

"With the army, holy father," continued Ramses, "one sees everything like the fingers on his hands, and to every question one has a ready answer which my mind grasps. But in the governance of nomes I not only see nothing, but I have such a confusion in my head that I sometimes forget why I've come here.

"So tell me frankly, as a priest and an officer: what does it mean? Are the nomarchs deceiving me, or am I incompetent?"

The holy prophet pondered. "I don't know whether they would dare deceive Your Eminence," he replied, "because I've not examined their deeds. But I suspect the reason they can't explain anything to the Prince is that they don't understand anything themselves.

"The nomarchs and their scribes," continued the priest, "are like decurions in the army: each knows his ten-man unit and keeps superior officers informed about it. Each also commands his little unit. But the decurion doesn't know the overall plan that is drawn up by the army's commanders.

"The nomarchs and scribes record all that happens in their province and send the reports to the feet of the Pharaoh. But it's the Supreme Council that extracts from them the honey of wisdom."

"It's that honey that I want!" cried the Prince. "Why won't they give it to me?"

Mentesuphis shook his head. "Knowledge of governance is a priestly secret and therefore may be obtained only by a man consecrated to the gods; whereas Your Eminence, despite your education by the priests, is most definitely moving away from the temples."

"Then if I don't become a priest, you won't explain it to me?"

"There are things which Your Eminence may learn even now, as Iry-pat; there are those which you will learn as pharaoh. But there are also those which only a high priest may know."

"Every pharaoh is a high priest," said the Prince.

"Not every. And then, between high priests there are differences."

"Then," exclaimed the angry Successor, "you're concealing the Kingdom's governance from me ... And I won't be able to carry out my father's charges."

"What the Prince needs to know," said Mentesuphis calmly, "he can learn, for he possesses the lowest priestly orders. However, these things are concealed in the temples, behind a veil which no one will venture to lift without the necessary preparations."

"I'll lift it! "

"May the gods preserve Egypt from such a calamity!" replied the priest, raising up his hands. "Doesn't Your Eminence know that lightning will strike anyone who touches the veil without the proper rites? Prince, have a slave or convict taken to a temple, and let him but reach out his hand and he will instantly die."

"Because you'll kill him."

"Each of us would die like the commonest criminal, were he to approach the altars sacrilegiously. To the gods, my Prince, pharaoh and priest mean no more than slave."

"Then what am I to do?" asked Ramses.

"Seek the answer to your query at a temple, after first cleansing yourself with prayer and fasting," replied the priest. "In Egypt no ruler has ever acquired knowledge of governance any other way."

"I'll think about it, holy prophet," said the Prince, "though I see that you and the most venerable Mephres want to draw me into religious ceremonies as my father has been drawn."

"Not at all. Were Your Eminence to limit yourself as pharaoh to commanding the army, you would need take part in religious ceremonies barely a few times a year, for high priests would stand in for you at other times. But if you would learn the secrets of the temples, you must revere the gods, for they are the font of wisdom."

CHAPTER 24

R amses now knew that either he would fail of the Pharaoh's charge, or he must submit to the will of the priests, which filled him with animus toward them.

He was in no hurry to get at the secrets concealed in the temples. There would
be time enough for fasting and piety. He began taking an all the more avid part in the feasts
being held in his honor.

Thutmose, past master of all pastimes, had just returned, bringing the Prince good
news of Sara. She was well and looked lovely, which was now of less interest to Ramses.
But the Prince was delighted with the horoscope the priests had cast for his future child.

They held it would be a boy highly gifted of the gods and that, if his father loved him,
he would attain great honors in life.

The Prince laughed at the second part of the prediction. "Their learning is strange," he
told Thutmose. "They know it will be a boy, which I don't though I'm the father: but they're
not sure I will love him, though it's easy to guess I would love the child even if it were a girl.

"As to honors for him, they needn't worry. I'll see to that!"

In the month of Pachon (January-February)[1] the Crown Prince moved on to the Nome
of Ka-khem, where he was welcomed by Nomarch Sofra.[2] The city of Iunu lay seven hours'
way by foot from Athribis,[3] but the journey took the Prince three days. At the thought of the
prayer and fasting that awaited at his initiation into the secrets of the temples, Ramses felt
a growing desire to party; his retinue guessed as much, so revel followed revel.

Once again, on the highways leading to Athribis, there appeared cheering crowds with
flowers and music. Enthusiasm reached a particular apex outside the city. A giant worker
dove under the Viceroy's chariot. When Ramses stopped the horses, over a dozen young
women stepped out of the crowd and entwined his whole chariot in flowers.

"They do love me!" thought the Prince.

In the province of Ka-khem he did not ask the nomarch about the Pharaoh's revenues,

[1] Actually, the ancient Egyptian month of Pachon lay between May 9 and June 7 of the modern, Gregorian calendar. *(Translator.)*

[2] Sofra: Prus might have drawn this character's name from the Turkish word *sofra*, denoting a low dining table. The word had been imported from Ottoman Turkish into the Crimean Tatar, Romanian, and Serbo-Croatian languages. *(Translator.)*

[3] Athribis was the chief town of the 10th (Athribite) Nome of Lower Egypt. Athribis stood on the eastern bank of the Nile's Tanitic branch (now silted up), near where that branch diverged from the Nile main-stream. *(Translator.)*

visit factories, or have reports read to him. He knew he would not understand anything, so he set these matters aside pending his initiation at a temple. However, when he saw a temple of the god Sobek perched on a tall hill, he expressed a desire to climb its pylon tower and view the vicinity.

His Eminence Sofra immediately fulfilled the Successor's wish, and Ramses spent a couple of hours on the tower with great pleasure.

The province of Ka-khem was a fertile plain. It was crisscrossed in all directions by a score of canals and Nile branches as by a network of silver and azure ropes. Melons and wheat, sown in November, were ripening. The fields swarmed with half-naked people harvesting cucumbers and sowing cotton. All about the land were buildings, which at a score of points clustered into towns.

Most of the buildings, especially those amid fields, were mud huts thatched with straw and palm fronds. In the cities, the buildings were of masonry, flat-roofed, and looked like white cubes pierced for doors and windows. Very often atop one such cube there stood a second cube, somewhat smaller, and on top of that a third, still smaller, each story painted a different color. Beneath Egypt's fiery sun, the buildings looked like great pearls, rubies, and sapphires scattered amid the green of the fields and surrounded by palms and acacias.

From this vantage, Ramses remarked something curious: the handsomest houses stood near the temples, and the most people moved about in the fields adjacent.

"The farms of the priests are the wealthiest!" he recalled, and once more ran his eyes over the temples and chapels, a score of which were visible from the pylon tower.

Having, however, made his peace with Herhor, and needing the services of the priests, he did not wish to dwell on the matter.

In the following days His Eminence Sofra organized a series of hunts for the Prince, ranging eastward out of Athribis. Over the canals, the participants shot at birds with bows, caught them in huge nets that swept up dozens at a time, and released falcons at birds in free flight. When the Prince's retinue entered the Eastern Desert, there began great hunts with dogs and a leopard for quadrupeds, a couple hundred of which were killed or captured over several days.

When His Eminence Sofra saw that the Prince had had his fill of sport under the open heavens, and of bivouacs in tents, he broke off the hunts and returned his guests by the shortest routes to Athribis.

They arrived at four in the afternoon, and the Nomarch invited everyone to his palace for a feast.

He personally conducted the Prince to the bath, assisted at the ablutions, and brought perfumes from his own chest for Ramses. Then he oversaw the barber who dressed the Viceroy's hair, and finally he knelt and begged the Prince to accept a new set of garments.

There was a freshly woven shirt covered in embroidery, an apron sewn with pearls, and a coat threaded with gold, very strong yet so fine that it could be enclosed in two hands.

The Successor graciously accepted these, saying he had never before received such a beautiful gift.

The sun had set, and the Nomarch conducted the Prince to the ballroom.

This was a large colonnaded court with a mosaic floor. All the walls were painted with scenes from the lives of Sofra's forebears: wars, sea voyages, and hunts. Over the building, in lieu of roof, was a gigantic butterfly with multicolored wings which were flapped by concealed slaves to refresh the air.

In bronze cressets affixed to the columns torches burned brightly, giving off fragrant smoke.

The hall was divided into two parts: one empty, the other filled with tables and chairs for the banqueters. In the depths rose a dais on which, under a sumptuous tent with flaps drawn, stood a table and bed for Ramses.

At each table were potted palms, acacias, and fig trees. The Successor's table was sur-rounded with coniferous plants that poured a fragrant balm into the hall.

The assembled guests greeted the Prince with joyous cheering; and when Ramses had taken his place under the canopy, which gave out onto the entire hall, his retinue sat down to their tables.

Harps sounded, and ladies entered in rich muslin attire, bare-breasted, aglitter with jewels. The four most beautiful surrounded Ramses; the others seated themselves beside the dignitaries of his retinue.

A fragrance of roses, lilies-of-the-valley, and violets wafted in the air, and the Prince felt pulses in his temples.

Slave men and women in white, pink, and blue tunics distributed pastries, roast fowl and venison, fish, wine, and fruit, as well as floral garlands, which the feasters placed on their heads. The huge butterfly flapped its wings ever faster, and a show began in the emp-ty half of the hall. By turns there performed dancing girls, gymnasts, clowns, jugglers, and fencers; and when one of them gave an extraordinary display of skill, the spectators threw him flowers from their garlands, or gold rings.

The feast went on for several hours, punctuated by cheers in honor of the Prince, the Nomarch, and his family.

Ramses, half-recumbent on a bed covered in a lion skin with gold talons, was served by the four ladies. One fanned him, another changed the garlands on his head, the other two drew the dishes nearer. Toward the end of the feast, the lady with whom the Prince most enjoyed speaking brought him a chalice of wine. Ramses downed half, handed the rest to her and, when she had drained it, kissed her lips.

Then slaves quickly began dousing the torches, the butterfly stopped flapping its wings, and night and silence descended over the hall, broken by the nervous titter of women.

Suddenly there rang out rapid footsteps of several persons, and a terrible cry: "Let me go!" called a hoarse male voice. "Where's the Successor? Where's the Viceroy?"

The hall seethed. Women wept, terrified; men shouted: "What's this? ... An attempt on the Successor! ... Hey, guards!"

There were sounds of shattering dishes and smashing chairs.

"Where's the Successor?" bellowed the stranger.

"Guards! ... Protect the Successor!" came an answer from the hall.

"Bring torches!" spoke the youthful voice of the Successor. "Who seeks me? I'm over here."

Torches were brought in. Overturned and broken furniture was piled up in the hall, concealing the feasters. On the dais the Prince was tearing himself free of the women who, shouting, entwined his arms and legs. Beside the Prince, Thutmose in disheveled wig, bronze pitcher in hand, was prepared to smash the head of anyone who approached. In the door to the hall, several soldiers appeared with drawn swords.

"What is this? ... Who's there?" called the terrified Nomarch.

At last the instigator of the commotion was made out. A mud-caked giant with bloody welts on his back knelt on the dais steps, stretching out his hands to the Successor.

"That's a murderer!" screamed the Nomarch. "Take him!"

Thutmose raised his pitcher, the soldiers ran in from the door. The bloodied man prostrated himself on his face on the steps, crying: "Mercy, O sun of Egypt!"

The soldiers were about to seize him when Ramses tore himself free of the women and approached the wretch.

"Don't touch him!" he called to the soldiers. "What do you want, man?"

"I want to tell you of the wrongs done to us, lord."

Sofra approached the Prince and whispered: "He's a Hyksos. Look at his shaggy beard and hair, Your Eminence. And the audacity with which he burst in here shows that this criminal is not a native Egyptian."

"Who are you?" asked the Prince.

"I am Bakura, a worker with the diggers' regiment in Khem. We have no work now, so Nomarch Otoes told us ..."

"He's a drunkard and a madman!" whispered Sofra excitedly. "How he speaks to your lordship ..."

The Prince gave the Nomarch a look that made the dignitary back away, bent over double.

"What did His Eminence Otoes tell you?" the Viceroy asked Bakura.

"He told us, Lord, to walk along the Nile, swim in the river, stand at the roadsides, and make noise in your honor. He promised that in return he would give us what we are owed —because, Lord, we haven't received anything for two months now—not barley cakes, nor fish, nor oil to rub our bodies."

"What do you say to that, Eminence?" the Prince asked the Nomarch.

"He's a dangerous drunkard ... an ugly liar," replied Sofra.

"How did you make noise in my honor?"

"As ordered," said the giant. "My wife and daughter shouted with the others, 'May he live forever!' and I jumped into the water and threw garlands at Your Eminence's ship, for each of which I was to have been paid a deben. And when Your Honor was graciously pleased to ride into Athribis, I was chosen to dive under the horses and stop the chariot."

The Prince began laughing. "As I live," he said, "I never thought we'd conclude the feast so merrily! How much were you paid for diving under my chariot?"

"I was promised three debens, but neither my wife nor daughter nor I were paid anything. Likewise the whole regiment hasn't received anything to eat for two months."

"What have you been living on?"

"By begging or on what we could earn from the peasants. In our dire misery we rebelled three times and wanted to go home. But the officers and scribes either promised to pay us or had us caned."

"To make noise for me?" laughed the Prince.

"That's right, Your Honor. Yesterday was the biggest rebellion, and His Eminence

Nomarch Sofra had us decimated.[4] Each tenth man was caned, and I got the most because I'm big and have three mouths to feed: my wife's, my daughter's, and my own. Caned, I escaped from them to prostrate myself on my stomach before your lordship and tell you our grievances. Cane us if we're at fault, but let the scribes give us what we're owed, or we'll starve to death—we, our wives, and our children ..."

"He's a man possessed!" cried Sofra. "Look at all the damage he's done me, Your Eminence ... I wouldn't get ten talents for these tables, bowls, and pitchers."

A murmur began among the banqueters who had regained their senses.

"He's a bandit!" they said. "Look, he really is a Hyksos. The accursed blood of his ancestors who invaded and ravaged Egypt, still churns in him. Such expensive furniture ... such beautiful dishes, smashed to bits!"

"One rebellion by unpaid workers damages the Kingdom more than these valuables are worth," said Ramses sternly.

"Holy words! They ought to be inscribed on monuments," said guests immediately. "Rebellion distracts people from their work and saddens His Holiness' heart. It's not right for workers to go unpaid for two months."

The Prince looked with undisguised contempt at the courtiers changeable as clouds, and addressed the Nomarch:

"I'm turning over to you," he said sternly, "this pitilessly flogged man. I'm sure that not a hair will fall from his head. And tomorrow I want to see his regiment and find out whether he was telling the truth."

With that, the Viceroy went out, leaving the Nomarch and guests greatly troubled.

Next day the Prince, as he was dressing with Thutmose's help, asked him: "Have the workers come?"

"Yes, lord. Since dawn they've been awaiting your orders."

"And this ... this Bakura, is he among them?"

Thutmose made a wry face and replied: "A strange thing has happened. His Eminence Sofra ordered him locked in an empty cellar of his palace. Well, this rogue, a very strong man, broke down a door into another cellar, where there was wine, knocked over several very expensive pitchers, and got himself so drunk that ..."

"That what?" asked the Prince.

"He died."

The Successor sprang up from his chair. "And you believe," he exclaimed, "that he drank himself to death?"

"I have to believe it, because I have no evidence he was killed," answered Thutmose.

"I'll look for it!" the Prince burst out.

He ran about the room, spitting like an angry young lion.

When the Prince had calmed somewhat, Thutmose said: "Lord, don't seek guilt where it's not to be seen, because you'll not even find witnesses. If someone in fact strangled this worker on the Nomarch's instructions, he's not going to admit it. The deceased himself isn't talking either, and anyway how much weight would his complaint against the Nomarch carry! In these circumstances, no court will want to open an investigation."

---

[4] To decimate (from the Latin verb *decimare*, itself derived from the adjective *decimus*, "tenth") is "to punish every tenth person." Decimation was practiced as early as 471 BCE by the Roman army, which on occasion punished mutinous or cowardly units by executing one in ten men, chosen by lot. *(Translator.)*

"What if I order it?" asked the Viceroy.

"In that case, they'll investigate and find Sofra innocent. Your lordship will be embarrassed, and all the nomarchs and their kin and servants will become your enemies."

The Prince was standing in the middle of the room, thinking.

"Finally," said Thutmose, "everything seems to speak to the unfortunate Bakura having been a drunkard or a madman—above all, a man of foreign descent. Would a native Egyptian in his right mind, though he'd gone unpaid for a year and received twice as many cane strokes, have dared burst into the Nomarch's palace and call for you so raucously?"

Ramses lowered his head and, seeing courtiers in the next room, said in a lowered voice: "You know, Thutmose, ever since I set out on this journey, Egypt has been seeming to me somehow different. Sometimes I ask myself, am I in a foreign country? Then, again, my heart grows uneasy, as if I had a veil over my eyes—beyond which, villainies are taking place which I can't make out."

"Then don't look for them, or you'll end up thinking we should all go to the mines," laughed Thutmose. "Remember that the nomarchs and officials are the herdsmen of your flock. If one of them draws a measure of milk for himself or slaughters a sheep, you're not going to kill him or drive him out. Sheep you have aplenty, while shepherds are hard to find."

The Viceroy, now dressed, passed to the waiting hall, where his entourage of priests, officers, and officials was gathered. Next, together with them, he left the palace and repaired to an external yard.

This was a large space planted with acacias, in whose shade the workers awaited the Prince. At the sound of a trumpet, the whole crowd sprang up from the ground and formed five ranks.

Ramses, surrounded by his glittering retinue of dignitaries, suddenly stopped in order to first survey the diggers' regiment from a distance. They were near-naked men in white caps and loincloths. Readily distinguishable in the ranks were tan Egyptians, black Negroes, yellow Asiatics, and white natives of Libya and of Mediterranean islands.

The first line of diggers had pickaxes; the second, mattocks; the third, shovels. The fourth rank comprised porters, each with a pole and two buckets; the fifth, likewise porters, but with great boxes each tended by two men. The porters carried away excavated soil.

Every dozen or so paces in front of the ranks stood foremen: each carried a stout cane and a large wooden compass or square.

At the Prince's approach, they cried in unison, "May you live forever!" and, kneeling, struck the ground with their foreheads. The Successor bade them rise and scrutinized them again.

They were healthy, robust men who hardly looked as if they had been living two months by begging.

Nomarch Sofra, with his retinue, approached the Viceroy. But Ramses, taking no notice of him, turned to a foremen:

"Are you diggers from Khem?" he asked.

The foreman prostrated himself on his face and was silent.

The Prince shrugged and called to the workers: "Are you from Khem?"

"We are diggers from Khem!" they answered in unison.

"Have you been paid?"

"We have been paid—we are well-fed and happy—servants of His Holiness," replied the chorus in measured cadences.

"About-face!" commanded the Prince.

They turned around. Nearly all had deep, serried cane scars on their backs; but there were no fresh welts.

"They're deceiving me!" thought the Successor. He ordered the workers to their barracks and, without acknowledging the Nomarch, returned to the palace.

"Will you also tell me," he said on the way to Thutmose, "that those men are workers from Khem?"

"They said so themselves," replied the courtier.

The Prince called for a horse and rode off to the troops camped outside the city.

All day long he drilled the regiments. About noon, several dozen porters under command of the Nomarch appeared on the drill ground with tents, furniture, food, and wine. But the Prince sent them back to Athribis; and when mealtime rolled around for the troops, he called for and consumed oatcakes with dried meat.

These were mercenary Libyan regiments. In the evening, when the Prince had them put away their weapons and proceeded to take farewell, the men and officers seemed to go mad. Shouting "Live forever!" they kissed his hands and feet, fashioned a litter from spears and coats, with chanting carried the Prince to the city, and on the way quarreled over the honor of bearing him on their shoulders.

The Nomarch and province officials, seeing the enthusiasm of the barbarian Libyans and the Successor's favor for them, became frightened.

"That's a ruler for you!" the great scribe whispered to Sofra. "If he wished, those men would put us and our children to the sword."

The distressed Nomarch sighed to the gods and commended himself to their merciful protection.

Late in the night Ramses found himself at his palace, where the servants told him his bedroom had been changed.

"Why is that?"

"A venomous snake was seen in the other bedroom, and it hid and could not be found."

The new bedroom was in a wing adjacent to the Nomarch's house. It was a rectangular room surrounded by columns. The alabaster walls were covered with painted low reliefs depicting, at the bottom, potted plants, and higher up, garlands of olive and laurel leaves.

Almost in the middle stood a great bed inlaid with ebony, ivory, and gold. The room was lit by two fragrant torches; next to the colonnade stood tables with wine, viands, and rose garlands.

In the ceiling there was a large rectangular opening covered with a cloth.

The Prince bathed and reclined on the soft bedding; his servants withdrew to the outer rooms. The torches began dimming, and through the room there wafted a cool breeze laden with a fragrance of blossoms. Soft strains of harp music sounded overhead.

Ramses lifted his head. The ceiling's cloth had moved away, and through the opening he could see the constellation Leo containing the bright star Regulus. The harp music intensified.

"Will the gods be paying me a call?" thought Ramses with a smile.

A broad streak of light flashed in the opening; it was strong, yet gentle. A moment later, there appeared overhead a litter in the shape of a golden boat bearing a small bower of blossoms: the posts were twined in rose garlands; the roof was of violets and lotuses.

On ropes wrapped in verdure the golden boat silently descended into the bedchamber. It alighted on the floor, and from beneath the flowers there emerged a naked woman of uncommon beauty. Her body had the tone of white marble; from the amber wave of her hair there wafted an intoxicating fragrance.

Descending from her airborne litter, the woman knelt before the Prince.

"You are Sofra's daughter?" asked the Successor.

"Yes, lord ..."

"In spite of that, you've come to me?"

"To beg forgiveness for my father. He's miserable! Since noon, he's been pouring tears and rolling in ashes ..."

"If I don't forgive him, will you go away?"

"No," she whispered.

Ramses drew her to him and kissed her passionately. His eyes gleamed.

"Then I'll forgive him," he said.

"Oh, how good you are!" she cried, cuddling up to the Prince. She added cajolingly: "Will you have them make good his losses caused by that crazy worker?"

"I will ..."

"And you'll take me into your house ..."

Ramses looked at her. "I will, because you're beautiful."

"Really?" she replied, embracing his neck. "Take a better look at me ... I'm only fourth among the beautiful women of Egypt."

"What do you mean?"

"Your first lives in Memphis or thereabouts ... fortunately, only a Jewess! The second is in Khem ..."

"I know nothing about it," broke in the Prince.

"Oh, you dove! Then I suppose you don't know about the third one, in Iunu, either ..."

"Does she also belong to my house?"

"Ingrate!" she exclaimed, striking him with a lotus blossom. "In a month you're liable to say the same of me. But I won't be wronged ..."

"Like father, like daughter."

"Haven't you forgiven him yet? ... Mind, I'll go away ..."

"No, stay ... stay!"

Next day the Viceroy was pleased to accept homage and a feast from Nomarch Sofra. He publicly praised Sofra's administration of the province and, to make good the damages done by the drunken worker, presented to Sofra half the vessels and furniture he had received in Iunu.

The other half went to the Nomarch's daughter, the fair Abeb, as a lady of the Prince's court. She also had herself paid five talents from Ramses' coffers for clothes, horses, and slave girls.

In the evening, with a yawn, the Prince told Thutmose: "His Holiness my father imparted to me a great lesson—that women are expensive!"

"It's worse without them," said the dandy.

"But I have four, and I'm not even sure how I came by them. I could give you two of them."

"Including Sara?"

"Not her, especially not if she has a boy."

"If Your Eminence provides these turtledoves nice dowries, husbands will turn up for them."

The Prince yawned again.

"I don't like talk of dowries," he said. "Ahhh! What a piece of luck that I'll be getting away from all of you and moving in with the priests ..."

"Are you really going to?"

"I have to. Maybe at last I'll find out from them why the pharaohs are growing poor ... Ahhh! ... and I'll get some rest."

CHAPTER 25

That same day, in Memphis, His Eminence Dagon, the Crown Prince's Phoenician banker, lay on a couch on the veranda of his palace. He was surrounded by aromatic potted conifer shrubs. Two black slaves fanned the wealthy man as he played with a young monkey and listened to accounts being read him by his scribe.

At that moment a slave outfitted with sword, helmet, spear, and shield (the banker fancied military dress) announced His Eminence Rabsun, a Phoenician merchant residing in Memphis.

The guest entered, bowed low, and looked down in such a way that His Eminence Dagon ordered the scribe and slaves off the veranda. Then, prudent man that he was, he looked into all the corners and told the guest: "We can talk."

Rabsun began without introduction: "Does Your Eminence know that Prince Hiram[1] has arrived from Tyre?"

Dagon bolted upright on the couch. "May leprosy visit him and his principality!" he screamed.

"He mentioned," continued the guest calmly, "that the two of you have a misunderstanding ..."

"What misunderstanding?" shouted Dagon. "That pirate robbed me, destroyed me, ruined me! When I sent my ships west for silver after some other Tyrian ships, that scoundrel Hiram's helmsmen threw fire at them to drive them into the shoals. And my ships returned empty, charred, and battered! Heavenly fire burn him up!" concluded the furious banker.

"What if Hiram has a good proposition for Your Eminence?" asked the guest phlegmatically.

The storm raging in Dagon's breast instantly subsided. "What proposition can he have for me?" he said in a completely calm voice.

"He will tell Your Eminence that himself, but first of course he has to see you."

"Well, then let him come here."

"He thinks Your Eminence should go to him. After all, he is a member of the Supreme Council in Tyre."

"He can drop dead if I'm going to him!" shouted the banker, angry again.

The visitor drew his chair up to the couch and patted the rich man's thigh.

---

[1] Hiram: name borrowed from two kings of Tyre. Hiram I was Phoenician king of Tyre, 980-947 BCE. Hiram II was king of Tyre, 739-730 BCE, under the Assyrian ascendancy. *(Translator.)*

"Dagon," he said, "be reasonable."

"Why am I not reasonable, Rabsun, and why do you not call me 'Eminence'?"

"Dagon, don't be stupid!" remonstrated the guest. "If you don't go to him and he doesn't come to you, then how are you going to make a deal?"

"You're the one that's stupid, Rabsun!" the banker burst out again. "If I go to Hiram, may my hand wither if I don't lose half the profit by that courtesy."

The guest thought and replied: "Now you're making sense. So I tell you what. You come to my place, and Hiram will come to my place, and the two of you will talk over this business there."

Dagon tilted his head, slyly narrowed his eye, and asked: "Hey, Rabsun! Come clean: how much did he give you?"

"For what?"

"For my going to your place and doing business with this Jew."

"This business is for all of Phoenicia, so I don't need to make profit on it," said Rabsun indignantly.

"May your debtors pay you if that's the truth!"

"May they not, if I make any profit on this! May Phoenicia only not be the loser!" shouted Rabsun angrily.

They parted.

Toward evening His Eminence Dagon climbed into a litter borne by six slaves. He was preceded by two runners with staffs and two with torches; after the litter came four servants armored from head to foot. Not for safety, but because Dagon had taken to surrounding himself with men-at-arms like a knight.

He alighted from the litter with great pomp and, supported by two men (a third carried a parasol over him), entered Rabsun's house.

"Where is this ... Hiram?" he asked the host proudly.

"He's not here."

"How's that? ... I'm to wait for him?"

"He's not in this room but in a third room, with my wife," replied the host. "Right now he's calling on my wife."

"I'm not going there!" said the banker, seating himself on a couch.

"You'll go into the second room, and he'll go in there at the same time."

After brief resistance, Dagon yielded and a moment later, at a sign from the master of the house, entered the second chamber. At the same time, from the farther rooms there entered a rather short man with a gray beard, wearing a gold toga and a gold circlet on his head.

"This," said the host, standing in the middle, "is His Grace Prince Hiram, member of the Tyrian Supreme Council. ... This is His Eminence Dagon, banker to the Crown Prince and Viceroy of Lower Egypt."

The two Eminences bowed to each other, hands clasped on their chests, and sat down at separate tables in the middle of the room. Hiram slightly parted his toga to show a great gold medal on his neck; in answer to which, Dagon began toying with a thick gold chain which he had received from Prince Ramses.

"I, Hiram," said the old man, "greet you, Lord Dagon, and I wish you a large fortune and success in your ventures."

"I, Dagon, greet you, Lord Hiram, and I wish you what you wish me ..."

"You want to quarrel already?" said Hiram, annoyed.

"How am I quarrelling? ... Rabsun, you tell me, am I quarrelling?"

"Your Eminences better talk business," said the host.

After a moment's reflection, Hiram began: "Your friends in Tyre send their salutations."

"Is that all they send me?" asked Dagon sarcastically.

"What do you want them to send you?" said Hiram in a raised voice.

"Quiet! ... Accord!" said the host.

Hiram breathed deeply several times and said: "It's true we need accord. Hard times are coming for Phoenicia ... "

"Has the sea flooded Tyre or Sidon?" smirked Dagon.

Hiram spat and asked: "Why are you so testy today?"

"I'm always testy when they don't call me Eminence."

"Why don't you call me Grace? ... I'm a prince!"

"Maybe in Phoenicia," replied Dagon. "But in Assyria you cool your heels in a satrap's² vestibule three days for an audience, and when they admit you, you lie on your belly like any Phoenician trader."

"What would *you* do, with a savage who can have you impaled?" shouted Hiram.

"What I would do, I don't know," said Dagon. "But in Egypt I sit on the same couch with the Crown Prince, who today is Viceroy."

"Accord, Your Eminence! ... Accord, Your Grace!" the host admonished them.

"Accord! ... according to me, this man is an ordinary Phoenician trader who won't give me respect!" cried Dagon.

"I have a hundred ships!" shouted Hiram.

"His Holiness the Pharaoh has twenty thousand cities, towns, and villages ..."

"Your Eminences will sink this business and all of Phoenicia!" said Rabsun, now in a raised voice.

Hiram clenched his fists but fell silent and rested.

"But Your Eminence must admit," he said after a moment to Dagon, "that His Holiness doesn't really have many of those twenty thousand cities."

"Your Grace means to say," replied Dagon, "that seven thousand belong to the temples, and seven thousand to the great lords? Still, that leaves His Holiness with seven thousand, free and clear."

"Not very! When Your Eminence takes away some three thousand pledged to the priests, and some two thousand leased to our Phoenicians ..."

"Your Grace speaks the truth," said Dagon. "But that still leaves His Holiness with some two thousand very wealthy cities."

"Has Typhon³ possessed the two of you?" shouted Rabsun in his turn. "Now you'll be enumerating the Pharaoh's cities, may he ..."

² Satrap: the governor of a province in ancient Media and Persia, beginning in the 7th century BCE, four centuries after *Pharaoh*'s present time. The term's use here is therefore an anatopism and an anachronism. *(Translator.)*

³ Typhon: Greek mythology's deadliest monster, which the ancient Greeks identified with Set, Egypt's god of the desert, storms, foreigners, darkness, chaos, and evil. Some etymologists suggest *Typhon* as the ultimate source—possibly via the Arabic language, and perhaps alongside the Chinese *tai-fung*—for the word *typhoon*. *(Translator.)*

"Hist!" whispered Dagon, springing up from his chair.

"When disaster hangs over Phoenicia!" finished Rabsun.

"Will you tell me, what disaster?" said Dagon.

"Well, let Hiram talk, and you'll find out," replied the host.

"Go on ..."

"Does Your Eminence know what happened at The Ship Inn, at our brother Asarhadon's?" began Hiram.

"I have no brothers among the tavernkeepers!" interjected Dagon sarcastically.

"Shut up!" shouted Rabsun furiously, grabbing the hilt of his dagger. "You're as stupid as a dog that barks in its sleep ..."

"What's he angry about, this ... this rag-and-bone merchant?" replied Dagon, likewise reaching to his knife.

"Quiet! ... Accord!" the hoary Prince quieted them, likewise lowering his lean hand to his waist.

For a moment, the nostrils of all three quivered and their eyes shone. Finally Hiram, the first to calm down, resumed as if nothing had happened:

"A couple of months ago a certain Phut, from the city of Harran, put up at Asarhadon's inn ..."

"He was to get back five talents from a priest," broke in Dagon.

"Go on," said Hiram.

"He found favor with a priestess and on her advice went to seek his debtor in Thebes."

"You have the mind of a child and the talkativeness of a woman," said Hiram. "This Harranian isn't a Harranian but a Chaldean, and his name isn't Phut but Berossus ..."

"Berossus? ... Berossus?" repeated Dagon, trying to recall. "I've heard the name somewhere ..."

"You've heard it!" said Hiram contemptuously. "Berossus is the most learned priest in Babylon, and advisor to the Assyrian princes and to the king himself."

"What if he is, so long as he's not the pharaoh's advisor, what do I care?" said the banker.

Rabsun rose from his chair, threatened Dagon's nose with his fist, and cried:

"You hog fattened on the pharaoh's swill! You care as much about Phoenicia as I do about Egypt ... If you could, you'd sell your native land for a drachma ... Leprous dog!"

Dagon turned pale and replied in a calm voice:

"What's this huckster saying? My sons are in Tyre, training to be sailors; my daughter is living in Sidon with her husband ... I lent half my fortune to the Supreme Council, though I haven't even ten percent for it. And this huckster says I don't care about Phoenicia! ...

"Rabsun, listen to me," he added after a moment. "I wish your wife and children, and the shades of your ancestors, that you may care about them as much as I do about every Phoenician ship, about every stone in Tyre, Sidon, even Zarpath[4] and Achzib[5]."

"Dagon speaks the truth," said Hiram.

"I don't care about Phoenicia!" continued the banker, warming to the subject. "How many Phoenicians have I brought here to make their fortunes—and what do I have for it? I don't care! ... Hiram ruined two of my ships and deprived me of great profits, but when it comes to Phoenicia I sit down with him in the same room ..."

---

[4] Zarpath: a city south of Sidon, in Phoenicia. *(Translator.)*

[5] Achzib: a city near Tyre, in Phoenicia. *(Translator.)*

"Because you thought you would be talking about swindling someone," said Rabsun.

"May you think the same way about dying, stupid!" replied Dagon. "As if I'm a child and don't know that when Hiram comes to Memphis, it's not to buy and sell. Oh, Rabsun! You should sweep my stables for two years ..."

"Enough!" cried Hiram, striking the table with his fist.

"We'll never finish with this Chaldean priest," muttered Rabsun as calmly as if he had not been the object of vituperation the moment before.

Hiram cleared his throat and began:

"This man really does have a house and land in Harran, where he is called Phut. He got letters from the Hittite merchants to the Sidonian merchants, so our caravan took him along. He speaks good Phoenician, pays honestly, makes no special demands, so our people actually took a liking to him.

"But," said Hiram, scratching his chin, "when a lion dons an oxhide, part of the lion's tail is still bound to show. This Phut was terribly wise and self-assured; so the caravan's captain made a secret search of his things. And he came up with nothing except for a medal of Astoreth. The medal stung the caravan's captain to the quick. How did the Hittite come by a Phoenician medal?

"So when they arrived in Sidon, he immediately reported this to the elders, and from then on our secret police kept an eye on this Phut.

"But he's so cunning that, after he had been in Sidon a few days, everyone came to love him. He prayed and made offerings to Astoreth, paid in gold, didn't borrow or lend money, associated only with Phoenicians. And he so beguiled everyone that the watch over him slackened, and he arrived uneventfully in Memphis.

"Here our elders again placed him under surveillance, but uncovered nothing; they only surmised that he must be a great lord, and not a simple Harranian townsman. It was only Asarhadon who accidentally discovered—or rather stumbled on indications—that this supposed Phut spent a whole night at the old Temple of Set, which counts for a lot here."

"Only high priests go there for important conferences," said Dagon.

"Even that would be nothing," said Hiram. "But one of our merchants returned a month ago from Babylon with strange information. In exchange for a large present, a courtier of the Babylonian satrap's told him that disaster hangs over Phoenicia!

"'You will be taken over by the Assyrians,' the courtier told our merchant, 'and the Israelites will be taken over by the Egyptians. The great Chaldean priest Berossus has gone to the Theban priests in the matter, and he will conclude a treaty with them.'

"You need to know," continued Hiram, "that the Chaldean priests consider the Egyptian priests their brothers. And since Berossus is very important at King Assar's court, the information about this treaty may well be true."

"What do the Assyrians want with Phoenicia?" asked Dagon, biting his nails.

"What does a thief want with someone's granary?" rejoined Hiram.

"What significance can Berossus' treaty with the Egyptian priests have?" mused Rabsun.

"Are you stupid!" replied Dagon. "The pharaoh does only what the priests decide."

"There will be a treaty with the pharaoh too, have no fear!" interrupted Hiram. "In Tyre we know for certain that an Assyrian envoy, Sargon, is going to Egypt with a great suite and gifts. Ostensibly he wants to see Egypt and get the ministers not to write in the Egyptian records that Assyria pays the pharaohs tribute. But actually he is coming to make a treaty for the division of the lands that lie between our sea and the river Euphrates."

"May the earth swallow them up!" cursed Rabsun.

"What do you think about it, Dagon?" asked Hiram.

"What would you do if Assar did attack you?"

Hiram shook with anger. "What would we do? We'll take ship with our families and treasures and leave to those dogs the rubble of our cities and the rotting corpses of the slaves. Don't we know of lands greater and fairer than Phoenicia where a new homeland can be established, richer than the present one?"[6]

"May the gods save us from such an extremity!" said Dagon.

"That is what's at stake—to save today's Phoenicia from destruction," said Hiram. "And there is much you can do in this matter, Dagon ..."

"Like what?"

"Can you find out from the priests whether Berossus met with them, and whether he made such a compact with them?"

"That will be terribly hard!" whispered Dagon. "But maybe I can find a priest who will tell me."

"Can you," Hiram went on, "prevent a treaty with Sargon at the pharaoh's court?"

"Very hard ... I won't manage it by myself."

"I'll be with you, and Phoenicia will supply the gold. They're raising a tax right now."

"I gave two talents!" whispered Rabsun.

"I'll give ten," said Dagon. "But what do I get for my trouble?"

"Oh ... ten ships," said Hiram.

"How many do you get?" asked Dagon.

"Not enough? ... All right, you'll get fifteen ..."

"I'm asking: what are you getting?" persisted Dagon.

"We'll give you ... twenty. Is that enough?"

"All right. But you'll show me the way to the land of silver?"

"We will."

"And where you get tin from?"[7]

"Yes ..."

"And where amber is from,"[8] concluded Dagon.

"Drop dead!" replied the gracious Prince Hiram, extending his hand. "You'll no longer harbor a bad heart toward me on account of those two scows?"

Dagon sighed. "I'll try to forget. But ... what a fortune I would have had if you hadn't driven me off back then!"

"Enough!" said Rabsun. "Talk Phoenicia."

"Through whom will you find out about Berossus and the treaty?" Hiram asked Dagon.

---

[6] Soon, during the first millennium BCE, the Phoenicians will develop a Mediterranean empire, with its capital at Carthage, which will become the deadly rival of the Roman Republic in the second half of the first millennium BCE, finally leading to the three Punic Wars (264 -146 BCE). *(Translator.)*

[7] Tin: From ancient times a major source of tin, used as a raw material in the production of bronze, was Cornwall in extreme southwest England. *(Translator.)*

[8] Amber was traded south, down the Amber Road, to Egypt, Greece, Rome, and other ancient civilizations from the Baltic seacoast of what, two millennia later, would become Prus' Polish homeland. *(Translator.)*

"Let that be. It's dangerous to say, because it will involve the priests."

"Whom could you use to wreck the treaty?"

"I think ... I think probably the Crown Prince. I have a lot of his notes."

Hiram raised his hand and replied: "The Crown Prince—very good, because he will become pharaoh, maybe soon ..."

"Hist!" interrupted Dagon, striking the table with his fist. "May you lose power of speech for such talk!"

"Hog!" cried Rabsun, threatening the banker's nose.

"Stupid huckster!" sneered Dagon. "Rabsun, you should peddle dried fish and water in the streets, not meddle in business between kingdoms. An ox's hoof smeared with Egyptian mud has more sense than you who have lived five years in Egypt's capital! May the pigs eat you ..."

"Quiet! ... Quiet!" broke in Hiram. "You're not letting me finish ..."

"Speak, for you are wise and my heart understands you," said Rabsun.

"Dagon, if you have influence with the Crown Prince, that's very good," continued Hiram. "If he decides on a treaty with Assyria, there will be a treaty, written in our blood on our hides. But if the Crown Prince wants war with Assyria, he will make war, though the priests call in all the gods against him."

"Hist!" broke in Dagon. "If the priests want it very much, there will be a treaty. But maybe they won't want it ..."

"That, Dagon," said Hiram, "is why we must have all the commanders with us."

"It can be done."

"And the nomarchs ..."

"That too can be done."

"And the Crown Prince," said Hiram. "But if you alone push him to war with Assyria, it's no use. A man, like a harp, has many strings, which must be played with all ten fingers; while you, Dagon, are but one finger."

"I can't tear myself in ten."

"But you can be one hand which has five fingers. You should see that no one knows you want war, but that the Crown Prince's every cook wants war, his every barber wants war, all his bath attendants, litter bearers, scribes, officers, charioteers—that they all want war with Assyria and that the Crown Prince hears about it from morning to night, and even when he sleeps ..."

"It can be done."

"Do you know his mistresses?" asked Hiram.

Dagon tossed his hand. "Stupid girls," he said. "All they think about is dressing up and putting on makeup and perfumes. But where the perfumes come from and who brings them to Egypt, they don't know."

"He must be given a mistress who does know," said Hiram.

"Where to find her?" asked Dagon. "Ah ... I have it!" he exclaimed, slapping his forehead. "Do you know Kama,[9] the priestess of Astoreth?"

"What?" interrupted Rabsun. "A priestess of Astoreth is to become mistress to an Egyptian?"

---

[9] Kama: name possibly taken from the Sanskrit word for "love," "desire," "wish," or "longing." It may refer to pleasure, esthetic enjoyment, affection, or love, with or without sexual connotations. *(Translator.)*

"You'd rather she became yours?" sneered Dagon. "She'll even become a high priestess, when she needs to be brought close to court."

"You speak the truth," said Hiram.

"But that's sacrilege!" objected Rabsun.

"And so a priestess who commits it may die," said the hoary Hiram.

"If only that Jewess Sara doesn't get in the way," said Dagon after a moment's silence. "She's expecting, and the Prince is already attached to the child. Were she to have a boy, the Prince would abandon all other girls."

"We'll have money for Sara too," said Hiram.

"She won't take anything!" Dagon burst out. "The wretched girl rejected an expensive gold cup which I brought her ..."

"She thought you wanted to trick her," said Rabsun.

Hiram nodded. "There's nothing to worry about," he said. "Where gold won't work, a father, mother, or mistress will. And where a mistress won't work ..."

"A knife ..." hissed Rabsun.

"Poison ..." whispered Dagon.

"A knife is a very messy affair," concluded Hiram.

He smoothed his beard, thought a moment, finally rose and took from his bosom a purple band threaded with three gold amulets featuring an image of Astoreth. He took the knife from his belt, cut the band in three, and handed a piece with amulet, each, to Dagon and Rabsun.

Then all three men went from the middle of the room over to a corner where stood a statue of a winged goddess; they clasped their hands on their chests, and Hiram began in a lowered voice but distinctly:

"To Thee, O mother of life, we pledge to faithfully keep our compacts and not to rest until the holy cities have been secured against enemies, may they be confounded by famine, pestilence, and fire.

"Should any of us break the pledge or betray the secret, may every misfortune and disgrace befall him ... May hunger rack his bowels and sleep elude his bloodshot eyes ... May the hand wither that would hasten to his aid, taking pity on his misery ... May the bread on his table turn to rot, and the wine to fetid ichor ... May his children die, and his house be filled with bastards who will spit upon him and drive him out ... May he die moaning many a day alone, and may neither earth nor water accept his degraded corpse, may fire not burn it up nor wild beasts devour it ...

"So be it!"

After the terrible oath, which Hiram had begun and from midway all three had shouted out, their voices quavering with rage, the three Phoenicians rested, out of breath. Then Rabsun invited them to a feast where, with wine, music, and dancing girls, they forgot for the moment the work awaiting them.

CHAPTER 26

N ear the city of Pi-Bast[1] was a great temple of the goddess Hathor.[2]
    In the month of Payni (March-April),[3] on the day of the vernal equinox, about
nine in the evening as the star Sirius was approaching the west, two traveling
priests and a penitent stopped at the temple gate. The penitent walked barefoot, head
strewn with ashes, draped in a coarse cloth with which he concealed his face.

Despite the clear night, the travelers' physiognomies could not be made out, as the
men stood in the shadow of two gigantic statues of the cow-headed goddess that guarded
the temple entrance and, with kindly eye, protected the nome of Am-Khent[4] from pestilence, bad flood, and southern winds.

Having rested a bit, the penitent prostrated himself on his chest and prayed a long
while. Then he rose, took up the copper knocker, and struck. The powerful metallic clang
swept all the courts, reverberated from the temple's thick walls, and sped over wheat
fields, peasants' clay huts, and the silvery waters of the Nile, where it was answered by the
feeble cries of wakened fowl.

After a long while, behind the gate there was a murmur and the question: "Who wakes us?"

"A slave of the gods: Ramses," said the penitent.

"Wherefore have you come?"

"For the light of wisdom."

"What license have you?"

"I have received minor orders and carry a torch at great processions in the temple."

The gate opened wide. In the middle stood a priest in white raiment who extended his
hand and said slowly and distinctly:

---

[1] Pi-Bast: otherwise, *Per-Bast* ("House of [the cat goddess] Bast"); in Greek, *Bubastis*. The city was the
capital of Am-Khent, the 18th nome of Lower Egypt, and was situated in the Nile Delta on the eastern
shore of the river's Pelusiac branch. *(Translator.)*

[2] Hathor was a cow-headed, horned sky goddess associated with joy, beauty, music, dance, feminine love,
fertility, motherhood, foreign lands, and mining. In a complicated set of contradictory relationships,
she was variously the mother, daughter, or wife of Ra and, like Isis, at times the mother of Horus, and
associated with the feline goddess Bast. The ancient Greeks identified Hathor with Aphrodite; the
Romans, with Venus. *(Translator.)*

[3] Actually, the ancient Egyptian month of Payni lay between June 8 and July 7 of the modern, Gregorian
calendar. *(Translator.)*

[4] Nome of Am-Khent: the 18th Nome of Lower Egypt. Prus calls it *Habu. (Translator.)*

"Enter. As you cross this threshold, may divine peace inhabit your soul, and may the wishes be fulfilled that you beg of the gods in humble prayer."

When the penitent fell to the priest's feet, the priest made some signs over his head and whispered: "In the name of Him who is, was, and will be ... Who created all ... Whose breath fills the visible and the invisible world and is life eternal ..."

When the gate had closed, the priest took Ramses' hand and led him through the twilight, between the enormous columns of the vestibule, to his assigned lodging. This was a small cell lit by an oil lamp. On the stone floor lay a bundle of dry grass; in a corner was a pitcher of water, and beside it a barley cake.

"I see I'll really get some rest here after the nomarchs' receptions!" cried Ramses merrily.

"Think on eternity," said the priest, withdrawing.

The Prince found the reply disagreeable. Though hungry, he did not feel like eating the barley cake or drinking the water. He sat down on the grass, looked at his feet cut up on the journey, and asked himself: Why had he come here? Why had he freely surrendered his dignity?

The cell's walls and poverty brought back his boyhood years spent at priest school. How many canings he had experienced there! How many nights spent on a stone floor as punishment! Even now Ramses felt his earlier hatred for, and fear of, the dour priests who had answered all his questions and requests ever with the same "Think on eternity!"

After several months' hubbub, to plunge into such silence, to exchange a prince's court for darkness and solitude and, in lieu of feasts, women, and music, to experience all around and overhead the weight of the walls ... "I've gone mad! ... I've gone mad! ..."

For a moment he wanted to leave the temple at once, but it occurred to him they might not open the gate. The sight of his dirty feet, of the ashes sifting down from his hair, the coarseness of his penitent's cloth—all filled him with revulsion. If at least he had his sword! But, in this dress and place, would he have dared use it?

He felt an overwhelming dread, and this restored his senses. He recalled that the gods visited dread on people in temples, and that it was supposed to be the preliminary to wisdom.

"I'm the Pharaoh's Viceroy and Successor," he thought, "what can harm me here?"

He rose and went outside his cell. He was in a great court surrounded by columns. The stars shone brightly and he saw, at one end of the court, the gigantic pylon; at the other end, the open entrance to the temple.

He went to the entrance. From the doorway in, there was gloom; while, somewhere very far in, burned several lamps, seemingly floating in the air. Looking closely, he made out between the entrance and the lights a whole forest of serried thick columns whose tops melted away into the dark. Indistinctly visible in the depths, perhaps a couple of hundred paces from him, were the gigantic legs of a seated goddess and her hands resting on her knees, which faintly reflected the lamplight.

Suddenly he heard a murmur. In the distance, from a side nave, there emerged a file of small white figures walking in pairs. It was a nocturnal procession of priests venerating the statue of the goddess, as they chanted in two choruses:

Chorus I. "I am He that created heaven and earth and made all the creatures contained within."

Chorus II. "I am He that made the waters and created the great flood; He that sired the bull."

Chorus I. "I am He that created heaven and the secrets of its horizons and placed within them the souls of the gods."

Chorus II. "I am He that, when He opens his eyes, it becomes light; and when He closes them, it becomes dark."

Chorus I. "The waters of the Nile flow at His behest ..."

Chorus II. "But the gods know not His name."[5]

The voices, at first indistinct, waxed until each word was audible; then, when the procession had disappeared, the voices scattered among the columns, waning. At last they fell still.

"These people," thought Ramses, "don't just eat, drink, and gather wealth. They really do carry out their duties, even at night. Though—much good will it do the statue!"

The Prince had seen statues of border gods that had been splattered with mud by residents of a different nome or shot up with bows and slings by soldiers of foreign regiments. If the gods took no offense at desecrations, they must also care little about prayers and processions.

"Anyway, who has seen the gods!" the Prince said to himself.

The temple's vastness, its countless columns, the lights burning before the statue, all drew Ramses. He wanted to look about the mysterious expanse and went forward.

Suddenly it seemed to him that a hand had gently touched the back of his head. He looked about, there was no one there, so he went on.

Now two hands took hold of his head, and a third large one rested against his back ...

"Who's there?" cried the Prince, throwing himself between the columns.

He stumbled and all but fell: something had grabbed his legs.

Ramses was again overwhelmed by fear, greater than in the cell. He began running frantically, knocking into columns which blocked his way, while darkness enveloped him on all sides.

"O holy goddess, save me!" he whispered.

Suddenly he stopped: a few paces in front of him was the temple's great doorway, framing a starry sky. He turned his head: amid the forest of gigantic columns there burned lamps, their light faintly reflecting from the bronze knees of holy Hathor.

The Prince returned to his cell, agitated and contrite; his heart tossed within him like a snared bird. For the first time in many a year, he prostrated himself on his face and fervently prayed for mercy and forgiveness.

"You shall be heard!" spoke a dulcet voice above him.

Ramses suddenly lifted his head, but there was no one in the cell: the door was closed, the walls were thick. He prayed still more fervently and so fell asleep, face on the stones and arms outstretched.

When he woke next day, he was a different man: he had experienced the might of the gods and had received a pledge of grace.

Henceforth for many a day, with a will and with faith, he gave himself over to pious devotions. He spent long hours in his cell praying, let his hair be shaved, donned priest's garb, and four times a day attended the choir of youngest priests.

His past life of revelry and sport repelled him, and the unbelief that he had acquired

---

[5] Authentic. *(Author.)*

among dissolute youths and foreigners horrified him. Today, given a choice between the throne and a priestly office, he would have hesitated.

One day the Great Prophet of the temple summoned him and reminded him that he had come there not exclusively for prayer, but to learn. He praised Ramses' pious life, said he was now cleansed of worldly soils, and bade him acquaint himself with the schools at the temple.

More from obedience than curiosity, the Prince repaired from the Great Prophet's directly to an outer court, to the department of reading and writing.

This was a great hall illuminated by an opening in the roof. On mats sat several dozen near-naked pupils holding wax-covered tablets. One wall was of smooth alabaster; before it stood the teacher, writing characters in variously colored chalks.

When the Prince entered, the pupils (nearly all his age) prostrated themselves on their faces. The teacher bowed and broke off the lesson to deliver the boys a lecture on the surpassing importance of learning.

"Dear boys!" he said, "'The man who has no heart for learning must engage in manual labor and strain his eyes. But he who understands the value of the learned disciplines and studies them can attain any authority, any court office. Bear that in mind.'

"Consider the wretched lives of people who cannot write. 'The blacksmith is grimy, has callused fingers, and works day and night. The stonecutter tears off his arm to fill his stomach. The mason who builds lotus capitals sometimes gets knocked off the roof by a high wind. The weaver has bent knees; the armsmaker is constantly on the road: hardly does he get home in the evening when he must leave again. The house painter's fingers stink, and his time passes in cutting up rags. And the courier, when saying goodbye to his family, should leave a last will, for he risks meeting wild beasts or Asiatics.

"'I have shown you the lot of various trades because I want you to love the art of writing, which is your mother, and now I shall tell you its beauties. It is not an empty word on the earth; it is more important than any other occupation. He who cultivates the art of writing is esteemed from childhood; he carries out great commissions. But he who does not partake in it, lives in want.

"'School lessons are heavy as mountains; but a day of them will suffice you for all eternity. Therefore get to know and love them as quickly as possible. The scribe's station is a princely station; his inkwell and book bring him pleasures and wealth!'"[6]

After this high-flown speech on the dignity of learning, which Egyptian pupils had heard without change for three thousand years,[7] the master picked up a chalk and proceeded to write the alphabet on the alabaster wall. Each letter was expressed by several hieroglyphic symbols or several demotic signs.[8] A drawing of an eye, a bird, or a feather denoted the letter *A*; a sheep or flowerpot, *B*; a standing man or a boat, *K*; a snake, *R*; a

---

[6] Authentic. *(Author.)* The citation is from "The Instruction of Duauf." *(Translator.)*

[7] "three thousand years": actually, some *two* thousand years. Hieroglyphs arose around the 32nd century BCE, with the first decipherable Egyptian-language sentence dating to the 28th century BCE. *(Translator.)*

[8] Demotic signs: demotic script, which derived from hieratic script, came into use only in the 7th century BCE, some four centuries after *Pharaoh*'s present time; therefore mention of demotic script here is an anachronism. The ancient Egyptian scripts had no signs for vowels, only consonants; therefore most transcriptions depend, for reconstruction, on the Coptic language (the latest stage of the Egyptian language) or are theoretical in nature. *(Translator.)*

seated man or a star, *S*. The abundance of signs expressing each letter made the study of reading and writing very tedious.

Ramses grew weary just listening. The sole relief occurred when the teacher told a pupil to draw or name a letter and caned him when he erred.

Taking his leave of the teacher and pupils, the Prince went from the school of scribes to the school of surveyors. Here youths were taught to plot fields, mostly rectangular-shaped, and to level the ground, using two leveling staffs and a square. Also taught in this department was the writing of numbers, an art no less complex than that of the hieroglyphic and demotic scripts. The simplest arithmetic operations constituted an advanced course and were performed using pellets.

Ramses had had enough, and only after several days agreed to visit the school of physicians.

This was simultaneously a hospital, or rather a great garden planted with a multitude of trees and sown with fragrant herbs. The ill spent their days out in the air and sun on beds of stretched canvas in lieu of mattresses.

When the Prince entered, activity was running at its peak. Several patients were bathing in a pool of running water, one was being rubbed with fragrant salves, another was being censed. Several had been put to sleep by use of the eyes and hand motions; one was moaning after the setting of a dislocated leg.

A gravely ill woman was receiving a cup of a concoction from a priest, who was saying:

"Come, medicine, come expel this from my heart, from these my members, O medicine strong in sorcery."[9]

Next the Prince accompanied the Great Physician to the dispensary, where one of the priests was preparing medicines from herbs, honey, oil, snake and lizard skins, bones, and animal fats. To a question from Ramses, the apothecary did not take his eyes from his work but continued weighing and grinding materials while reciting a prayer:

"It cured Isis, it cured Isis, it cured Horus ... O Isis, great sorceress, cure me, free me from all evil, harmful, red things, from the god's fever and the goddess' fever ...

"Schauagat', eenagate', O son! Erukate'! Kauaruschagate'! Paparuka paparaka paparura ..."[10]

"What is he saying?" asked the Prince.

"It's a secret," replied the Great Physician, placing a finger to his lips.

When they had gone out into a vacant court, Ramses asked the Great Physician:

"Tell me, holy father: what is the physician's art, and what do its practices consist in? I've heard that illness is an evil spirit which settles inside a person and torments him from hunger until it receives its proper sustenance. And that one evil spirit, or illness, feeds on honey, another on oil—and another, on animal excrement. Thus the physician first needs to know what spirit has taken residence in the ill person—and next, what sustenance that spirit needs in order not to torment the person."

The priest pondered and replied:

"What illness is, how it comes to afflict the human frame, I cannot tell you, Ramses. But since you have been cleansed, I shall explain to you what guides us in the dispensing of medicines.

"Say a person has a liver ailment. Well, we priests know that the liver is under the influence

---

[9] Authentic. *(Author.)*

[10] Authentic. *(Author.)*

of the star Peneter-Deva[11] and that the treatment must depend on that star.

"But here the wise men fall into two schools. Some hold that the person with a liver ailment should be given everything that is governed by Peneter-Deva, which is to say: copper, lapis-lazuli, floral decoctions—especially of verbena and valerian—and various parts of the turtledove and goat. However, other physicians believe that when the liver is afflicted, it should be treated with exactly the opposite agents. And since the opposite of Peneter-Deva is Sebeg,[12] the medicines will be: quicksilver, emerald and agate, hazel and coltsfoot, and parts of the frog and owl, ground to a powder.

"But that is not all. One must also bear in mind the day, month, and time of day, for each of these timespans is influenced by a star that can support or vitiate the effect of the medicine. Finally, one must bear in mind which star and which sign of the zodiac governs the patient. Only when the physician has taken all these things into account, can he prescribe an infallible medicine."

"Are you able to help all the patients at the temple?"

The priest shook his head. "No," he said. "The mind of man, which must compass all the details which I have mentioned, very easily errs. What is worse, envious spirits—genii of other temples, jealous of their fame—time and again thwart the physician and spoil the effect of the medicines. Thus the final outcome may vary: one patient recovers completely, another only improves, and a third remains without change. But occasionally patients get still worse or even die ... The will of the gods!"

The Prince listened attentively but admitted to himself that he understood little. Then, recalling his purpose in coming to the temple, he suddenly asked the Great Physician:

"You holy fathers were supposed to show me the secret of the Pharaoh's treasury. Would these things that I have seen, be it?"

"By no means," answered the physician. "We are not versed in matters of governance. The holy priest Pentuer, a man of great learning, is to come here, and he will lift the veil from your eyes."

Ramses took his leave of the physician, still more curious about what he was to be shown.

---

[11] The planet Venus. *(Author.)*

[12] The planet Mercury. *(Author.)*

CHAPTER 27

The Temple of Hathor received Pentuer with great reverence, and its junior priests went out half an hour's way to welcome the distinguished guest. Many prophets, holy fathers, and sons of the gods had come from all the miraculous places in Lower Egypt to hear the words of wisdom. A couple of days later, High Priest Mephres and the prophet Mentesuphis had arrived.

Pentuer was paid homage not only because he was advisor to the Minister of War and, despite his youth, a member of the Supreme College, but because the priest was renowned throughout Egypt. The gods had given him superhuman memory, eloquence, and above all a wonderful gift of clairvoyance. In every thing and matter, he perceived aspects concealed from other people and knew how to present these in ways that were comprehensible to all.

More than one nomarch or high official of the Pharaoh, on learning that Pentuer was to officiate at a religious event in the Temple of Hathor, envied the humblest priest his hearing the man inspired of the gods.

The clerics who went out onto the highway to welcome Pentuer were sure the distinguished visitor would appear in a court carriage or in a litter borne by eight slaves. How great, then, was their surprise when they beheld a thin bareheaded ascetic, dressed in a coarse cloth, who traveled alone on a she-ass and greeted them with great humility.

When he had been escorted into the temple, he made an offering to the goddess and immediately went to inspect the site for the ceremony.

Henceforth he was seen no more. But extraordinary activity set in at the temple and its adjoining courts. Grains, apparel, and costly furnishings were gathered, and several hundred peasants and laborers were brought in, with whom Pentuer sequestered himself in the court assigned to him and made his preparations.

After eight days' work, he notified the high priest of Hathor that all was ready.

Throughout that time Prince Ramses, secluded in his cell, had been giving himself over to prayer and fasting. Finally, one day at three in the afternoon, a score of priests in two files came and summoned him to the ceremony.

In the temple vestibule the Prince was greeted by the high priests, and together they burned incense before the gigantic statue of Hathor. Then they turned into a low, narrow side corridor at the end of which burned a fire. The air in the corridor was redolent of tar boiling in a kettle.

Near the kettle, through an opening in the floor, there issued a man's terrible wailing and curses.

"What's this?" Ramses asked a priest walking beside him.

The priest made no answer; the faces of all present, insofar as they could be made out, registered horror.

High Priest Mephres took up a ladle, drew hot tar from the kettle, and said in a raised voice: "May thus perish every betrayer of holy secrets!"

He poured the tar into the opening in the floor, and a scream rose from below ...

"Kill me ... if you have the least mercy in your hearts!" wailed the voice.

"May vermin consume your body!" said Mentesuphis, pouring tar into the opening.

"Dogs! ... Jackals!" wailed the voice.

"May your heart be burned up, and the ashes cast into the desert," said the next priest, following suit.

"Oh, gods! How can one suffer so much?" came answer from below.

"May your soul, with the image of its shameful crime, wander about places dwelled by happy people," said another priest, pouring in a ladle of tar.

"May the earth swallow you up! ... Mercy! ... Let me breathe ..."

Before Ramses' turn came, the underground voice had been stilled.

"Thus do the gods punish traitors!" the temple's high priest said to the Prince.

Ramses stopped and glared at him. It seemed he would burst out and quit the torturers; but he felt a fear of the gods and followed the others in silence.

The proud Successor now realized there was a power before which pharaohs bowed. He was nearly overcome with despair and felt like fleeing and renouncing the throne. But he held his peace and went on, surrounded by priests chanting prayers.

"Now I know," he thought, "what happens to those who displease the servants of the gods!"

The thought did nothing to reduce his horror.

Leaving the narrow smoke-filled corridor, the procession found itself again under the open heavens, on an elevation. Below lay an enormous court surrounded on three sides by a ground-floor building in lieu of wall. From where the priests stood, there descended a kind of amphitheater of five broad tiers on which one could walk the length of the court or descend into it.

There was no one in the court, but some people were looking out from the buildings.

High Priest Mephres, as the most eminent of the company, introduced Pentuer to the Prince. Ramses was struck by the contrast between the ascetic's gentle face and the horrors that he had witnessed in the corridor. To say something, he remarked to Pentuer: "I believe we have met before, pious father?"

"Last year at the Pi-Bailos maneuvers. I was there with His Eminence Herhor," said the priest.

Pentuer's sonorous, calm voice intrigued the Prince. He had heard that voice before too, in unusual circumstances. But when and where?

In any event, the priest had made a pleasant impression on Ramses. If only he could forget the cries of the man who had been tarred!...

"We may begin," said High Priest Mephres.

Pentuer slipped out to the fore of the amphitheater and clapped. A troupe of dancing girls ran out of the buildings, and priests came out with musicians and a statuette of the goddess Hathor. The musicians went at the head, followed by the dancing girls performing a sacral dance, and finally by the statuette enveloped in incense. In this fashion they made a circuit of the court, stopping every few paces to request the goddess' blessing and to ask evil spirits to quit the site of a religious event full of secrets.

When the procession had returned to the buildings, Pentuer stepped forward. The distinguished audience, twenty or thirty in number, gathered round.

"By the will of His Holiness the Pharaoh," began Pentuer, "and with the concurrence of the highest priestly authorities, we are to initiate Crown Prince Ramses into certain details of the life of the Egyptian Kingdom that are known only to the gods, the country's rulers, and the temples. I know that any of you distinguished fathers could explain these matters better to the young Prince, for you are full of learning and the goddess Mut speaks with your lips. However, since this duty has fallen to me, who am but a disciple and dust next to you, permit me to carry it out under your reverend guidance and supervision."

A murmur of satisfaction swept the priests thus honored. Pentuer turned to the Prince:

"For several months, servant of the gods Ramses, as a lost traveler seeks his way in the desert, so you have sought an answer to the question: why have the holy pharaoh's revenues been declining? You have questioned the nomarchs and, while they have explained the matter to the best of their ability, you have not been satisfied, though theirs is the utmost in human wisdom. You have turned to the great scribes, but despite their best efforts they, like birds trapped in a net, have been unable to extricate themselves from perplexity; for the mind of man, even of one educated in the school of scribes, is incapable of grasping the enormity of these things. Finally, wearied of fruitless explanations, you examined the nome lands, their people, and their handiworks, but you saw nothing. For there are things about which people are silent as stones, but about which even a stone will tell you if the light of the gods falls upon it.

"When all earthly wisdom and powers had thus failed you, you turned to the gods. Barefoot, head strewn with ashes, you came as a penitent to this great temple, where with prayer and mortification you cleansed your body and fortified your spirit. The gods, particularly powerful Hathor, have heard your pleas and will, by my unworthy lips, give you an answer—may you inscribe it deep in your heart!"

"How does he know," thought the Prince, "about my questioning the scribes and nomarchs? ... Ah, Mephres and Mentesuphis told him ... Anyway, they know everything!"

"Listen," spoke Pentuer, "and I shall reveal to you, with the assent of Their Eminences here present, what Egypt was four hundred years ago, in the reign of the most glorious and pious Nineteenth, the Theban, Dynasty and what she is today ...

"When the first pharaoh of that dynasty, Menpehtire Ramesses,[1] took power in this land, the revenues of the Kingdom's treasury in grain, cattle, beer, hides, metals, and sundry manufactures came to a hundred thirty thousand talents. If there were a people that could exchange all those goods for us into gold, the pharaoh would annually have a hundred thirty-three thousand minas[2] of gold. And since a soldier can carry on his back a weight of twenty-six minas, the transporting of this gold would require the use of some five thousand soldiers."

---

[1] Menpehtire Ramesses: also known as Ramses I. Prus calls him *Ramen-pehuti-Ramessu*. *(Translator.)*

[2] A mina was 1½ kilograms. *(Author.)* The mina was an ancient Near Eastern unit of weight and currency. *(Translator.)*

The priests whispered in astonishment. The Prince forgot about the man who had been tortured to death.

"Today," said Pentuer, "His Holiness' annual income in all the products of this land is worth only ninety-eight thousand talents: which might bring a quantity of gold whose transporting would require only four thousand soldiers."

"I know the Kingdom's revenues have declined greatly," said Ramses, "but why is that?"

"Be patient, servant of the gods," replied Pentuer. "Not only His Holiness' revenues have declined ...

"Under the Nineteenth Dynasty, Egypt had a hundred eighty thousand men under arms. Had the gods turned each soldier into a grape-size pebble ..."

"That is impossible," whispered Ramses.

"For the gods, anything is possible," said High Priest Mephres austerely.

"Better yet," said Pentuer, "if each soldier had placed a pebble on the ground, there would have been a hundred eighty thousand pebbles; and behold, fathers, the pebbles would have occupied this much space ..."

He indicated a reddish rectangle on the floor of the court.

"This figure would have accommodated the pebbles dropped by all the soldiers in the time of Ramses I. The figure is nine paces long by about five wide. The figure is red, the body color of Egyptians, because at that time all our soldiers were exclusively Egyptians."

The priests whispered again. The Prince turned somber, for he took this for an allusion to his preference for foreign troops.

"Today," continued Pentuer, "it might be possible to scrape together a hundred twenty thousand warriors. If each dropped his pebble on the ground, the pebbles might form this figure ... Behold, Eminences ..."

Beside the first rectangle lay a second, equally tall but with a much shorter base. Also, it was not of a uniform color but comprised several strips of different colors.

"This figure is about five paces wide but only six paces long. The Kingdom has lost a huge number of soldiers—a third of those we once had."

"Of greater use to the Kingdom than soldiers is the wisdom of prophets such as you," broke in High Priest Mephres.

Pentuer bowed to him and continued:

"In this new figure representing today's army of the pharaohs Your Eminences see, besides the red color which signifies native Egyptians, also three other stripes: black, yellow, and white. They represent mercenary troops: Ethiopians; Asiatics; and Libyans and Greeks. There are some thirty thousand of them altogether, but they cost as much as fifty thousand Egyptians."

"The foreign regiments should be abolished without delay!" said Mephres. "They're expensive, they're useless, and they teach our people godlessness and insolence. Already today many Egyptians no longer prostrate themselves on their faces before the priests; yea, many a one has taken to plundering temples and tombs.

"So, down with the mercenaries ..." spoke Mephres earnestly. "Egypt has only harm from them, and our neighbors suspect us of hostile intentions!"

"Down with the mercenaries! ... Drive out the rebellious pagans!" said the priests.

"Years hence, Ramses, when you ascend the throne," said Mephres, "you'll discharge this sacred duty to the Kingdom and the gods."

"Yes, do! ... Free your people of the unbelievers!" called the priests.

Ramses lowered his head in silence. The blood drained away to his heart; he felt the ground swaying beneath his feet.

He was expected to disband the finest part of the army! He, who would like to have twice as large an army, and four times as many valiant mercenary regiments!

"They're merciless with me!" he thought.

"Speak, heaven-sent Pentuer," said Mephres.

"And so, holy men," continued Pentuer, "we have learned two of Egypt's misfortunes: the decline of the pharaoh's revenues and of his army."

"Never mind the army!" muttered the High Priest, contemptuously shaking his hand.

"And now, by grace of the gods and by your leave, I will show you why this has happened and why the treasury and army will continue to decline in the future."

The Prince lifted his head and regarded the speaker. He was no longer thinking of the man murdered in the undergrounds.

Pentuer proceeded a dozen paces along the amphitheater, followed by the dignitaries.

"Do you see at your feet this long, narrow band of green ending in a broad triangle? To either side of the band are limestone, sandstone, and granite; and beyond these, expanses of sand. Down the middle flows a stream which divides at the triangle into several branches ..."

"That's the Nile! ... That's Egypt!" cried the priests.

"Mark this, now," interrupted Mephres emotionally. "I bare my arm. Do you see the two blue veins coursing from the elbow to the fist? Isn't that the Nile and its canal, which starts opposite the Alabaster Hills[3] and flows to the Fayum? ... Now regard the top of my fist: there are as many veins here as the sacred river divides into branches beyond Memphis. And my fingers—don't they recall the number of branches by which the Nile flows to the sea?"

"It's true!" called the priests, examining their own arms.

"Well, I tell you," continued the High Priest fervently, "that Egypt is ... the imprint of Osiris' arm ... Here on this land the great god rested his arm: his divine elbow lay in Thebes, his fingers reached to the sea, and the Nile is his veins ... Is it any wonder that we call this land blest!"

"Obviously," said the priests, "Egypt is the clear imprint of Osiris' arm ..."

"Does Osiris," asked the Prince, "have seven fingers to his hand? The Nile flows to the sea by seven branches."[4]

There followed a dead silence.

"Young man," replied Mephres with good-natured irony, "do you think Osiris could not have seven fingers if he so pleased?"

"Naturally!" assented the priests.

"Speak on, excellent Pentuer," said Mentesuphis.

---

[3] Alabaster Hills: hills at the Nile's eastern bank in the 6th Nome of Upper Egypt. *(Translator.)*

[4] Seven Nile branches: In ancient times, seven Nile branches flowed north through the Delta: viewed from west to east, the Canopic (or Herakleotic), Bolbitine, Sebennytic, Phatnitic (or Phatmetic), Mendesian, Tanitic, and Pelusiac branches. Today, due to flood control since the construction of the Aswan Dam and due to silting, there are only two main Nile branches: in the west, the Rosetta branch (corresponding to the Bolbitine); and in the east, the Damietta branch (corresponding to the Phatnitic). *(Translator.)*

"Your Eminences are right," resumed Pentuer. "This stream with its branches is a picture of the Nile; the narrow band of turf hemmed in by stones and sand is Upper Egypt; and the triangle traversed by little veins of water is an image of Lower Egypt, the largest and richest part of the Kingdom.

"At the start of the Nineteenth Dynasty the whole of Egypt, from the Nile's cataracts to the sea, comprised five hundred thousand measures of land.[5] And each measure was home to sixteen people: men, women, and children. But over the next four hundred years, with almost every generation, Egypt lost fertile land."

The speaker gave a sign. A dozen young priests ran out of the building and proceeded to pour sand on various points of the turf.

"With each generation," continued the priest, "fertile land was lost, and the narrow band became ever narrower.

"Today," he raised his voice, "instead of five hundred thousand measures, our country has only four hundred thousand ... Over the reigns of two dynasties, Egypt has lost land that once fed nearly two million people!"

A horrified murmur again rose from the gathering.

"And do you know, servant of the gods Ramses, what became of those fields where once wheat and barley grew or herds of cattle grazed? ... You know they were buried by the desert sands. But have you been told why this happened? ... It was because peasants were lacking to battle the desert from dawn to night with bucket and plow. And do you know why those godly workers were lacking? What had become of them? What swept them from the land? ... It was foreign wars. Our knights vanquished their foes, our pharaohs immortalized their venerable names as far as the banks of the Euphrates, while our peasants, like beasts of burden, carried provisions, water, and other loads after them and died on the way by the thousands.

"Thus, in exchange for their bones scattered over the eastern deserts, the western sands have devoured our lands, and today it will take immense labor and many generations to reclaim the black Egyptian soil from its tomb of sands."

"Hear, hear!" cried Mephres, "some god speaks with this man's lips. Yes, our triumphant wars were Egypt's grave ..."

Ramses could not collect his thoughts. It seemed to him that those mountains of sand were now pouring down upon his head.

"I've said," spoke Pentuer, "that great effort will be required to dig Egypt out and to restore her former wealth which war has consumed. But have we the strength to carry out this endeavor?"

He moved another dozen or so paces along the amphitheater, followed by his audience. Never had anyone so tellingly depicted Egypt's adversities, though everyone knew of them.

"Under the Nineteenth Dynasty, Egypt had a population of eight million. If every man, woman, old person, and child at the time had dropped a bean here, the beans could have formed a figure like this ..."

He indicated the court, where in two rows, next to each other, lay eight great squares formed of red beans.

---

[5] Measure of land: presumably the *setat*, which was a square *khet* (a *khet*, in turn, being 100 cubits). *(Translator.)*

"This figure is sixty paces long, thirty wide, and as you see, pious fathers, consists of uniform beans—like the population at the time, when everyone was of Egyptian descent.

"But today—look! ..."

He moved on and indicated another set of squares, of diverse colors.

"You see a figure that is likewise thirty paces wide, but only forty-five long. Why? Because it contains only six squares—because today's Egypt no longer has eight million but only six million inhabitants.

"Note as well that, while the previous figure consisted exclusively of red Egyptian beans, this present one contains enormous swaths of black, yellow, and white beans. As in our army, so among the people generally there are today very many foreigners: black Ethiopians, yellow Syrians and Phoenicians, white Greeks and Libyans ..."

Pentuer was interrupted. The priests hugged him; Mephres wept.

"Never has there been such a prophet!" someone called.

"It's inconceivable when he could have carried out such calculations!" said the best mathematician at the Temple of Hathor.

"Fathers!" said Pentuer, "do not exaggerate my accomplishments. At our temples, in the past, the Kingdom's economy was always represented in this way ... I have merely rediscovered what later generations forgot a little."

"But the calculations?" asked the mathematician.

"Calculations are continually carried on in all the nomes and temples," replied Pentuer. "The overall sums are to be found at His Holiness' palace."

"But the figures? ... The figures!" called the mathematician.

"Our fields are divided into such figures, and the Kingdom's geometers study them at school."

"I don't know what to admire more in this man: his learning or his humility!" said Mephres. "Oh, the gods have not forgotten us if we have such a man ..."

Just then a watchman on the temple's tower called everyone to prayer.

"In the evening I shall conclude my remarks," said Pentuer. "For now I'll say just a few more words.

"Your Reverences may ask why, in these pictures, I have used seeds. It is because, as a seed cast into the ground brings its husbandman a harvest each year, so each year a man pays taxes to the treasury.

"If, in a given nome, two million fewer beans were to be sown than in previous years, the nome's next harvest would be markedly reduced and the husbandmen would have poor incomes. It is likewise with the Kingdom: when two million people are lost, the flow of taxes must decline."

Ramses listened attentively and went away in silence.

CHAPTER 28

When the priests and Crown Prince returned to the courtyard in the evening, several hundred torches had been lit and it was bright as day.

At a sign from Mephres, the procession of musicians, dancing girls, and junior priests again appeared with the statuette of the cow-headed goddess Hathor. When the evil spirits had been driven off, Pentuer resumed his sermon.

"Your Eminences have seen that, since the Nineteenth Dynasty, we have lost a hundred thousand measures of land and two million people. That explains why the Kingdom's revenues have fallen by thirty-two thousand talents, and we all know about that. But that is only the beginning of the adversities of Egypt and the treasury. It would seem that His Holiness still has ninety-eight thousand talents of income. But do you think the Pharaoh receives all that income?

"As an example, I will tell you what His Eminence Herhor discovered in the Hare Nome.[1]

"Under the Nineteenth Dynasty, the nome had a population of twenty thousand people, who paid three hundred fifty talents in annual taxes. Today barely fifteen thousand people live there, and naturally pay the treasury only two hundred seventy talents. But instead of two hundred seventy talents, the Pharaoh receives only a hundred seventy!

"'Why?' asked His Eminence Herhor, and this is what investigation showed.

"Under the Nineteenth Dynasty there were about a hundred officials in the nome, and each received a thousand drachmas' annual salary. Today, despite the loss of population, there are over two hundred officials, who each receive two thousand five hundred drachmas a year.

"His Eminence Herhor does not know whether it is so in every nome. What is certain, though, is that the Pharaoh's treasury, instead of ninety-eight thousand talents a year, receives only seventy-four thousand ..."

"Say it, holy father: fifty thousand ..." broke in Ramses.

"That, too, I shall explain," said the priest. "In any case, bear in mind, Prince, that today the Pharaoh's treasury gives the officials twenty-four thousand talents, whereas under the Nineteenth Dynasty it gave them only ten thousand."

---

[1] Hare Nome: *Un*, the 15th Nome of Upper Egypt, with its capital at Khemenu (a city later known to the Romans as Hermopolis Magna). Each of Egypt's forty-two nomes (twenty in northern, or Lower Egypt; twenty-two in southern, or Upper Egypt) was named for an object, animal, direction, or god: e.g., Lower Egypt's Nomes 1-3 were, respectively, "White Walls," "Cow's thigh," and "West." *(Translator.)*

There was a great silence among the dignitaries: more than one had a relative in office—in lucrative office.

But Pentuer was undaunted. "Now, Successor," he said, "I will show you the lives of the officials, and the lot of the populace, in former years and today."

"Isn't it a waste of time? ... Everybody can see it for himself," murmured the priests.

"I want to know about it," said the Successor firmly.

The murmuring subsided. Pentuer descended the amphitheater steps into the court, followed by the Prince, High Priest Mephres, and the other priests.

They stopped before a long screen of mats that formed a kind of fence. At a cue from Pentuer, a dozen young priests ran up with burning torches. Another cue—and part of the screen dropped.

The audience cried out in astonishment. Before them was a brightly illuminated *tableau vivant*[2] of about a hundred figures.

The tableau comprised three tiers: a lower, of peasants; a middle, of officials; and the highest, bearing the pharaoh's gold throne supported by two lions whose heads were the armrests.

"This," said Pentuer, "is how things were under the Nineteenth Dynasty. See the husbandmen. Their plows are drawn by oxen or donkeys; their hoes and shovels are bronze and therefore sturdy. See what robust people they are! Today their like may be found only in His Holiness' guard. Powerful arms and legs, swelling chests, smiling faces. All are bathed and rubbed with oil. Their wives occupy themselves preparing food and clothes or washing the dishes for the family; the children play or attend school.

"The peasant of that time, as you see, ate wheat bread, broad beans, meat, fish, and fruit, and drank beer and wine. See how beautiful were the pitchers and bowls. Look at the caps, aprons, and capes of the men: all adorned with many-colored embroidery. Still more beautifully embroidered were the shifts of the women ... And mark what pains the women took doing their hair; what pins, earrings, rings, and bracelets they wore. These ornaments are of bronze and colored enamel; but occasionally there is gold, if only in the form of wire.

"Now lift your eyes to the officials. They wear capes, but every peasant used to don the same kind on holidays. They eat just like the peasants—adequately but frugally. Their furnishings are a little more finely decorated than those of the peasants, and gold rings occur oftener in their chests. They travel by donkey or oxcart."

Pentuer clapped, and the living picture came alive. The peasants began passing to the officials baskets of grapes; sacks of barley, peas, and wheat; pitchers of wine, beer, milk, and honey; and large numbers of livestock and of white and colored cloths. The officials accepted these, kept part for themselves, but moved the most beautiful and costliest items up for the throne. The platform bearing the symbol of the pharaoh's power was piled high with goods.

"Your Eminences see," said Pentuer, "that when the peasants were well-fed and prosperous, His Holiness' treasury could barely accommodate all the gifts of his subjects. Now see how things are today ..."

Another cue, another part of the screen dropped, and a second picture appeared, similar in broad outline to the previous one.

---

[2] *Tableau vivant:* French for "living picture." *(Translator.)*

"These are today's peasants," said Pentuer, his voice ringing with indignation. "They are skin and bones; they look ill; they are dirty and never rub themselves with oil. Their backs are wounded from canes.

"There are no oxen or donkeys to be seen; but what need of them, when the wife and children draw the plow? The hoes and shovels are of wood, which is easily damaged, increasing the peasants' work. They have no clothes to speak of, other than the coarse shifts of the women, who even in their dreams never see the embroideries that adorned their grandfathers and grandmothers.

"See what the peasant eats. Sometimes barley and dried fish, always lotus seeds, seldom a wheat cake, never meat, beer, or wine. You ask what has become of his crockery and furniture. He has none except for a water pitcher, and no more would fit inside the hovel he inhabits.

"Forgive me what I will now bring to your attention. Over there several children are lying on the ground: it means they are dead. Strange thing how often peasant children die nowadays—of hunger and toil! And those are the fortunate ones; the others, who remain alive, go under the cane of the overseer or are sold like lambs to the Phoenicians ..."

Emotion stopped his voice. He paused a moment, then continued amid the angry silence of the priests.

"Now see the officials: how hale, rouged, beautifully dressed they are! Their wives wear gold bracelets and earrings, and raiment so sheer that princes might well envy them. There is not an ox or a donkey to be seen among the peasants; but the officials travel on horses or in litters. And they drink only wine—good wine!"

He clapped, and again there was movement. The peasants passed sacks of grain, baskets of fruit, wine, and animals up to the officials. The officials set these beside the throne as before—but in much smaller quantities. On the royal tier there was no longer a great mound of products. But the tier of the officials was piled high.

"This is today's Egypt," said Pentuer. "Wretched peasants, wealthy scribes, the treasury not so full as in the past. And now ..."

He gave a cue, and an unexpected thing happened. Hands began taking grain, fruit, and cloths from the platforms of the pharaoh and officials. And when the quantities of goods had greatly diminished, the same hands began seizing and leading away peasants and their wives and children.

The astonished spectators watched the peculiar doings of the mysterious persons. Suddenly someone cried: "Those are the Phoenicians! ... They fleece us like that!"

"That's right, holy fathers," said Pentuer. "Those are the hands of the Phoenicians concealed among us. They fleece the king and the scribes; and they take the peasants into bondage when nothing more can be extracted from them ..."

"Yes! ... The jackals! ... Confound them! ... Expel the villains!" shouted priests. "They do the greatest harm to the Kingdom!"

But not all the priests shouted this way.

When it had quieted down, Pentuer had the torches borne to another part of the court and conducted his audience there. Here were no tableaus but a kind of industrial exposition.

"Pray look, Eminences," he said. "Under the Nineteenth Dynasty, foreigners used to send us these things: from the land of Punt, perfumes; from Syria, gold, iron weapons, and war chariots. That was all.

"But at that time Egypt produced ... See these huge pitchers: how many shapes there are here, what variety of colors! ...

"And how about the furniture: this little chair is inlaid with ten thousand pieces of gold, mother-of-pearl, and colored woods ... See the apparel of the time: what embroidery, what delicacy of fabrics, what variety of colors ... And how about the bronze swords, pins, bracelets, earrings, agricultural and craft implements ... All this was produced in Egypt under the Nineteenth Dynasty."

He moved on to the next group of objects.

"But today—look. The pitchers are small and nearly devoid of ornament; the furniture is plain; the fabrics are coarse and all alike. Not one of today's manufactures can compare in size, durability, or beauty with the earlier ones. Why is that?"

He moved on again a few steps and, surrounded by torches, spoke:

"These are the great many goods that the Phoenicians bring us from various parts of the world. Several dozen kinds of perfumes, variously colored glass, furniture, crockery, fabrics, vehicles, ornaments—all this comes to us from Asia and is purchased by us.

"Eminences, do you understand now what it was that the Phoenicians took the grain, fruit, and cattle from the scribes and Pharaoh for? It was for these foreign manufactures which have ruined our craftsmen as the locusts ruin our fields."

The priest paused, then continued:

"Foremost among the goods supplied by the Phoenicians to His Holiness, the nomarchs, and the scribes is gold. This trade best illustrates the calamities that these Asiatics inflict upon Egypt.

"When someone takes a talent of gold from them, after three years he is obliged to return two talents. As a rule, though, the Phoenicians, under pretext of easing the debtor's troubles, supplant him in the repayment of the loan by having him lease them for three years, for each talent borrowed, thirty-two people and two measures of land ...

"Behold, Eminences," he said, indicating a better illuminated part of the court. "That square of land a hundred eighty paces on a side is two measures; and that group of men, women, and children comprises eight families. All this, people and land, together goes for three years into a terrible bondage. During that time their owner—the pharaoh or nomarch—does not have the use of them; and at the end of the term he gets back the land exhausted ... and at most twenty people ... The rest have been worked to death!"

The audience muttered their horror.

"I have said that, in return for lending a talent of gold, the Phoenician takes a three-year lease on two measures of land and thirty-two people. See what a piece of land that is, what a large group of people—and now look at my hand ...

"This bit of gold that I'm holding, this little lump smaller than a chicken's egg, is a talent!

"Do Your Eminences appreciate the full infamy of the Phoenicians in such a barter? This little bit of gold actually has no valuable properties: it is yellow, is heavy, does not tarnish—that is all. A man cannot clothe himself in gold or slake his hunger or thirst with it. If I had a piece of gold the size of a pyramid, I would still be as much of a wretch as a Libyan wandering a Western Desert devoid of dates and water.

"And look, in exchange for a little lump of this barren stuff, the Phoenician takes a piece of land that can feed and clothe thirty-two people; and more than that, he takes the people as well! For three years he gains power over beings that can till and sow, harvest grain, produce flour and beer, weave clothing, build houses and furniture ...

"For three years, the pharaoh or nomarch is deprived of the services of those people. They pay him no taxes, they carry no burdens for the army; instead they toil for the profit of a greedy Phoenician.

"Your Eminences know that at present there is not a year but a rebellion breaks out in this or that nome among famished, overworked, caned peasants. Some of them die, others are sent to the mines, and the country becomes ever more depopulated, all because a Phoenician gave someone a small lump of gold! Can one imagine a greater calamity? ... And in such circumstances, will Egypt not continue each year losing land and people? Victorious wars have sapped our country; the Phoenician gold trade is finishing it off."

The priests' faces were very pictures of satisfaction: they preferred hearing about the perversity of the Phoenicians rather than about the excesses of the scribes.

Pentuer rested a moment, then turned to the Prince.

"For several months, servant of the gods Ramses," he said, "you have been asking with concern why His Holiness' revenues have declined. The wisdom of the gods has shown you that not only the treasury has declined but so also has the army, and that both these sources of royal power will continue to decline. And either this will end in the utter ruin of the Kingdom—or the heavens will send Egypt a ruler who will stem the flood of disasters which for several centuries have been inundating our land.

"The treasury of the pharaohs was full when we had a lot of land and population. Therefore we must wrest from the desert the fertile lands that it has devoured, and remove from the populace the burdens that weaken them and reduce their numbers."

The priests became concerned again lest Pentuer touch a second time on the scribal class.

"The Prince has seen with his own eyes, in the presence of witnesses, that in the age when the populace were well-fed, handsome, and content, the royal treasury was full. Conversely, when the populace became unsightly, when their wives and children had to harness themselves to the plow, when lotus seeds replaced wheat and meat, the treasury became impoverished. Therefore if you would restore the Kingdom to the power that it possessed before the wars of the Nineteenth Dynasty, if you desire that the pharaoh, his scribes, and the army should enjoy affluence, then assure many years of peace to Egypt, and prosperity to her populace. Let adults again eat meat and wear embroidered clothes, and let children, instead of moaning under the lash and dying of toil, play or attend school.

"Finally, bear in mind that Egypt carries a venomous serpent at her breast."

The audience listened with curiosity and dread.

"That serpent, which sucks the blood of the populace, the wealth of the nomarchs, the power of the pharaoh, is the Phoenicians!"

"Down with them!" called the audience. "Cancel all the debts ... Bar their merchants and ships ..."

They were quieted by High Priest Mephres who, with tears in his eyes, addressed Pentuer:

"I doubt not that sacred Hathor has spoken to us with your lips. Not only because no man could be so wise and all-knowing as you, but also because I observed little horn-shaped flames over your head.

"I thank you for the great words with which you have dispelled our ignorance. I bless you and I ask the gods, when they shall call me to my judgment, to name you as my successor ..."

A protracted cheer from the audience seconded the high dignitary's blessing. The priests were the more pleased, as the fear had hung over them incessantly lest Pentuer touch a second time on the question of the scribes. But the sage knew moderation: he had pointed out the Kingdom's internal lesion but had not inflamed it, and so had carried off a complete triumph.

Prince Ramses did not thank Pentuer but hugged the prophet's head to his chest. No one doubted, however, that the great prophet's discourse had shaken the Successor's soul and was the seed from which might spring Egypt's glory and prosperity.

Next day at sunrise Pentuer, without taking farewell, departed the temple and rode off for Memphis.

For several days Ramses spoke with no one: he remained in his cell or walked the shady corridors, thinking. His soul was at work.

At bottom, Pentuer had said nothing new: everyone complained about Egypt's loss of land and population, about the peasants' misery, the scribes' abuses, and the Phoenicians' exploitativeness. But the prophet's discourse had organized the Prince's inchoate information, had given it tangible forms, and had highlighted certain facts.

The Phoenicians terrified the Prince: he had not appreciated the enormity of the misfortunes wrought by them upon his Kingdom. His horror was heightened by the fact that he had let his own peasants out to Dagon—and had witnessed the way the banker exacted his due from them!

But the Prince's implication in the Phoenicians' depredations produced a curious result: Ramses did not want to think about the Phoenicians; and every time that his anger at them flared up, it was extinguished by a feeling of shame. In some measure, he was their accomplice.

The Prince appreciated, however, the importance of the loss of land and population, and it was on these points that he placed the chief emphasis in his solitary meditations.

"If we had those two million people whom Egypt has lost," he told himself, "with their help we could reclaim the fertile lands from the desert, even expand them. And then, notwithstanding the Phoenicians, our peasants would be better off and the Kingdom's revenues would rise ..."

But where to get the people?

A chance occurrence suggested an answer. One evening as the Prince was strolling in the temple gardens, he came upon a group of slaves whom General Nitager had seized on the eastern border and sent to the goddess Hathor. They were superbly built, worked harder than Egyptians and, since they were well fed, were actually content with their lot.

At the sight of them, a flash of lightning illuminated the Successor's mind: he nearly passed out from excitement. Egypt needed people, lots of people, hundreds of thousands, even a million or two million ... And here they were! ... One need but foray into Asia, grab everyone who was encountered on the way, send them to Egypt, and not end the war until so many people had been gathered that every Egyptian peasant could have a slave of his own.

Thus was conceived a simple, colossal plan by which the Kingdom could gain population; the peasants, help in their labors; and the pharaoh's treasury, an inexhaustible source of revenue.

The Prince was enthralled, but the next day he was assailed by doubt.

Pentuer had greatly emphasized, and still earlier Herhor had likewise maintained, that the source of Egypt's misfortunes was her victorious wars.

Which would imply that Egypt could not be restored by means of a new war.

"Pentuer is a great sage, and so is Herhor," thought the Prince. "If they think war harmful, and if High Priest Mephres and the other priests think so too, then maybe war really is a dangerous thing ...

"And so it must be, since so many wise and holy men hold it to be."

The Prince was deeply distressed. He had thought of a simple way to restore Egypt, and the priests held that precisely that could complete Egypt's ruin.

The priests were the wisest and holiest of men!

But an incident cooled somewhat the Prince's faith in the veracity of the priests; or rather, revived his earlier distrust of them.

He happened to be going with a certain physician to the library. The way led through a narrow, dark corridor from which the Successor recoiled in disgust. "I'm not going this way!" he said.

"Why?" asked the physician, surprised.

"Don't you remember, holy father, at the end of this corridor is a cellar where you cruelly tortured a traitor to death ..."

"Ah!" replied the physician. "There is a cellar into which, before Pentuer's sermon, we poured molten tar ..."

"And you killed a man ..."

The physician smiled. He was a good-hearted, cheerful man. Seeing the Prince's indignation, he mused:

"That's true, no one may betray holy secrets ... Of course ... Before every major ceremony, we remind our novices of that ..."

His tone was so peculiar that Ramses demanded an explanation.

"I must not betray secrets," said the physician, "but ... but if Your Eminence promises to keep it to yourself, I'll tell you a story ..."

Ramses promised, and the physician proceeded:

"An Egyptian priest visiting temples in the pagan land of Aram[3] met at one of them a man who seemed very well-nourished and contented though he was shabbily dressed.

"'Tell me,' the priest asked the jolly wretch, 'how it is that, though you are poor, your body looks as if you were the temple superior.'

"The man looked about to see whether anyone else might be listening and replied:

"You see, I have an exceeding doleful voice and I'm the temple martyr. When the populace gather for a service, I get down in the cellar and moan for all I'm worth; in exchange for which, they give me plenty of food all year round and a pitcher of beer for each day of martyrdom.'

"So it is in the pagan land of Aram," concluded the physician, putting a finger to his lips. "Remember your promise to me, Prince, and think of our molten tar what you will."

The Prince was relieved that a man had not been murdered at the temple, but all his old suspicions about the priests were aroused anew.

---

[3] Land of Aram: any of several ancient lands so named which appear in history and in the Bible, including one near the central Euphrates River. *(Translator.)*

He knew they deceived the simple folk. He remembered a procession of the sacred Apis bull when he was at priest school. The populace were certain Apis was leading the priests, but every pupil knew the divine beast went where the priests wanted it to.

So who could say whether Pentuer's discourse had not been such an Apis procession staged for his benefit? It was easy enough to pour red and other-colored beans on the ground; nor was it difficult to stage living pictures. He had seen much more magnificent spectacles, such as Set's battle with Osiris, which had involved several hundred persons ... Had the priests not deceived then as well? Ostensibly it had been a battle between gods, but had been conducted by costumed men. In it Osiris had perished, but the priest playing him remained healthy as a rhinoceros. What marvels had not been shown! ... Water had risen, lightning had struck, the earth had trembled and spewn fire. And all this had been deception. So why should Pentuer's presentation be true?

The Prince saw strong evidence for an intent to deceive him. One fraud had been the man moaning in the cellar, ostensibly tarred by the priests. But never mind him. The important thing was what the Prince had found more than once: that Herhor did not want war. Neither did Mephres, and Pentuer was the aide of one, a favorite of the other.

A struggle was under way within the Prince: now he thought he understood everything, now he was compassed by darkness; now he was full of hope, now he doubted all. Hour by hour, day by day, his soul rose and fell like the waters of the Nile over the span of the year.

Slowly, though, Ramses regained an equipoise; and by the time he was to leave the temple, he had some views formulated.

First of all, he grasped clearly what it was that Egypt needed: more land and more people.

Secondly, he believed that the simplest way to get people was through war with Asia. Pentuer, though, had told him war could only increase the Kingdom's woes. Which raised the question: had Pentuer spoken the truth, or had he lied?

If he had spoken true, he plunged the Prince into despair: for Ramses saw no other way to restore the Kingdom save through war. Absent war, Egypt would from year to year lose population, and the pharaoh's treasury would grow in debt. Until the whole process ended in some terrible catastrophe, maybe as soon as the next reign.

But what if Pentuer had lied? Why should he? Obviously, put up to it by Herhor, Mephres, and all the priesthood. But why did the priests oppose war? What was their motive for doing so? Every war brought them and the pharaoh the greatest profits.

Anyway, could the priests be deceiving him in such a momentous matter? True, they had done so very often, but in small matters, not when it was a question of the Kingdom's future and existence. Nor could it be said that they deceived always. They were, after all, servants of the gods, and custodians of great secrets. Spirits dwelled in their temples, as Ramses had discovered his first night here.

And if the gods did not allow the profane to approach their altars, if they watched that closely over the temples, then why should they not watch over Egypt, which was their greatest temple?

When a few days later, following a solemn service, Ramses was leaving the Temple of Hathor amid the blessings of the priests, two questions stood uppermost in his mind:

Could war with Asia really harm Egypt?

Could the priests be deceiving him, the Pharaoh's Successor, in the matter?

CHAPTER 29

Horseback, accompanied by a couple of officers, the Prince rode for Pi-Bast, famed capital of the nome of Am-Khent.[1]

The month of Payni had passed; Epiphi (April-May)[2] was starting. The sun stood high, ushering in Egypt's worst, hot season. Several times already, the terrible desert wind had sprung up; people and animals were collapsing from the heat, and a gray vegetation-killing dust was settling upon the fields and trees.

Roses had been harvested and were being processed into rose oil;[3] grains and the second mowing of clover had been gathered in. Shadoofs worked overtime, pouring dirty water onto the ground to prepare for a new sowing. The plucking of figs and grapes was starting.

The Nile waters had fallen; the canals were shallow and fetid. Over the whole country, amid the streams of burning sunlight, hung a fine dust.

Still, the Prince rode content. He was weary of the penitent's life at the temple and longed for feasts, women, and noise.

Moreover the area, though flat and uniformly traversed by a network of canals, was interesting. In the nome of Am-Khent lived a different population: not native Egyptians but descendants of the valiant Hyksos who had conquered Egypt and ruled it for several centuries.[4]

The native Egyptians disdained this remnant of the expelled conquerors: but Ramses looked upon them with pleasure. They were tall, strong people of proud bearing and man-

---

[1] Nome of Am-Khent: the 18th Nome of Lower Egypt. Prus calls it *Habu. (Translator.)*

[2] Actually, the ancient Egyptian month of Epiphi lay between July 8 and August 6 of the modern, Gregorian calendar. *(Translator.)*

[3] Rose oil: the essential oil extracted from rose petals. Rose oils are still perhaps the most widely used essential oils in perfumes. *(Translator.)*

[4] "the ... Hyksos who had conquered Egypt": The Hyksos, a mixed group of Asiatic peoples from Western Asia, had taken over the eastern Nile Delta, ending Egypt's 13th Dynasty and initiating the Second Intermediate Period. That Period lasted from the end of the Middle Kingdom to the start of the New Kingdom—from ca. 1650 to ca. 1550 BCE (a century, not "several centuries" as Prus has it). During their ascendancy, which ended with the inception of the New Kingdom, the Hyksos introduced into Egypt new musical instruments and foreign loan words; new techniques of bronze-working and pottery; new animal breeds and crops; and, in warfare, the horse and chariot, the composite bow, improved battle axes, and advanced fortification techniques. Because of these advances, Hyksos rule was decisive to Egypt's later empire in the Near East. *(Translator.)*

ly, energetic face. They did not prostrate themselves on their faces before the Prince and officers like Egyptians; they regarded the dignitaries without hostility but also without fear. And their backs bore no cane scars: scribes respected the Hyksos, knowing that a beaten Hyksos returned the lashes and sometimes killed his tormentor. Finally, the Hyksos had the pharaoh's favor because they furnished the best soldiers.

The closer the Successor's retinue approached Pi-Bast, whose temples and palaces were visible through the haze of dust as through muslin, the more the area bustled. Cattle, wheat, fruit, wine, blossoms, bread, and many other commodities were being transported down a broad highway and nearby canals. The stream of people and goods heading toward the city, as noisy and dense as at Memphis on holidays, was here the norm. At Pi-Bast a fairground hubbub reigned year-round, subsiding only at night.

The reason was simple: the city was home to a famous old temple of Astarte,[5] venerated by all western Asia, which drew in crowds of pilgrims. It is no exaggeration to say that some thirty thousand foreigners camped daily outside Pi-Bast: Shasu[6] or Arabs, Phoenicians, Jews, Philistines, Hittites, Assyrians, and others. The Egyptian government took a friendly attitude to the pilgrims, who brought it considerable income; the priests tolerated them, and the populace of several adjoining nomes plied a brisk trade with them.

The arrivals' huts and tents, pitched on the bare ground, were visible already an hour's way out of the city. The nearer to Pi-Bast, the greater were their numbers and the more densely swarmed their transient residents. Some of them prepared food under the open sky, others purchased the constantly inflowing goods, others went in procession to the temple. Here and there, large groups collected before places of entertainment where animal tamers, snake charmers, athletes, dancing girls, and jugglers performed.

Over this multitude rose the heat and tumult.

At the city gate Ramses was greeted by his courtiers and by the Nomarch of Am-Khent and his officials. The greeting, despite its amicability, was so cool that the surprised Viceroy whispered to Thutmose: "Why do you all look at me as if I had come to mete out punishments?"

"Your Eminence," replied the favorite, "has the visage of one who has communed with the gods."

He spoke the truth. Whether due to the ascetic life or to the company of learned priests, or perhaps to his long deliberations, the Prince had changed. He had lost weight, his complexion had darkened, and his face and bearing projected a tremendous gravity. In a few weeks, he had aged several years.

In one of the city's main thoroughfares, there pressed such a dense crowd of populace that the police had to clear a way for the Successor and his suite. The populace, however, were not greeting the Prince but were gathered about a modest palace as if awaiting someone.

"What's this?" Ramses asked the Nomarch. He was displeased with the crowd's indifference.

"Here lives Hiram," replied the Nomarch, "a Tyrian prince, a man of great compassion. He daily distributes generous alms, and the poor flock here."

The Prince turned about on his horse, looked, and said: "I see royal workers here. Do they also come for alms to the rich Phoenician?"

---

[5] Astarte: a goddess also known as *Ishtar* and *Astoreth*. (*Translator.*)

[6] Shasu: ancient Egyptian name for Semitic-speaking cattle nomads who inhabited lands east of the Nile Delta. The Shasu's misidentification here as "Arabs" is probably due to lifestyle similarities between the two nomadic Semitic groups. (*Translator.*)

The Nomarch held his peace. Fortunately they were nearing the government palace, and Ramses forgot about Hiram.

Over several days there was a series of feasts in honor of the Viceroy, but the Prince was not thrilled with them. They lacked gaiety and were marred by unpleasant incidents.

On one occasion a mistress of the Prince's, while dancing before him, burst into tears. Ramses embraced her and asked what was the matter.

At first she shrank from answering but, emboldened by her master's kindness, she replied with still more copious tears: "We are your lordship's women, we come from great families, and we are deserving of respect!"

"That's right," said the Prince.

"But your treasurer keeps reducing our expenses. He would even like to deprive us of our servant girls, without whom we can't wash ourselves or do our hair."

Ramses summoned the treasurer and told him in no uncertain terms that the women were to have everything to which they were entitled by their birth and high stations.

The treasurer prostrated himself on his face before the Prince and promised to do the women's bidding. But a couple of days later a mutiny broke out among the court slaves, who complained of being denied their wine.

The Successor ordered that they be issued their wine. But next day, during the review of troops, regimental deputations came to him with a most humble complaint that their meat and bread rations had been cut.

The Prince again directed that the petitioners' requests be fulfilled.

A couple of days later he was wakened in the morning by noise outside the palace. Ramses asked the cause, and the duty officer explained that royal workers had gathered and were calling for their back pay.

The treasurer was called in, and the Prince pounced on him in great anger.

"What's going on here?" he cried. "Ever since I arrived, there hasn't been a day without complaints of wrongs. If there's another repetition of this, I'll order an investigation and put a stop to your thievery!"

The trembling treasurer again prostrated himself on his face, moaning: "Kill me, lord! ... But what can I do, when your treasury, barns, and pantries are empty?"

Despite his anger, the Prince recognized that the treasurer might be blameless. He dismissed the man and called Thutmose.

"Listen," Ramses said to his favorite, "things are happening here that I don't understand and that I'm not used to. My women, the slaves, the troops, and the royal workers aren't getting what they're supposed to or are being limited in their expenses. When I asked the treasurer what it meant, he said we have nothing left in the treasury or the barns."

"He spoke the truth."

"How's that?" the Prince burst out. "His Holiness allocated two hundred talents in gold and kind for my journey. Could it all be gone?"

"That's right," said Thutmose.

"How? ... On what?" cried the Viceroy. "Throughout the journey, the nomarchs hosted us ..."

"But we paid them for it."

"Then they're rogues and thieves, if they pretend to host us, then fleece us!"

"Don't be angry," said Thutmose, "I'll explain it all to you."

"Have a seat."

Thutmose sat down. "Do you know," he said, "that for the past month I've been eating from your kitchen, drinking wine from your pitchers, and dressing from your wardrobe?"

"That is your privilege."

"But I never used to: I've lived, dressed, and entertained at my own expense, so as not to burden your treasury. True, you've sometimes paid my debts. But that was only part of my expenses."

"Never mind the debts."

"A dozen or so young nobles of your court," continued Thutmose, "are in a like situation. They used to pay their own way in order to sustain the ruler's splendor; but now, like me, they're living at your expense, because they have no more to spend."

"Sometime I'll make it up to them."

"We're drawing on your treasury," said Thutmose, "because we're in straits—and the nomarchs are doing the same. If they could afford to, they would throw feasts and receptions for you at their own expense; but since they haven't the wherewithal, they're accepting compensation. Now will you still call them rogues?"

The Prince was pacing in thought.

"I condemned them too hastily," he said. "Anger, like smoke, obscured my vision. I'm ashamed of what I said; still, I don't want the court people, the soldiers, or the workers to be wronged.

"And since my resources are exhausted, I must borrow ... A hundred talents should suffice, don't you think?"

"I don't think anyone will lend us a hundred talents," whispered Thutmose.

The Viceroy regarded him haughtily. "Is that how you answer the pharaoh's son?" he asked.

"Banish me," said Thutmose in a sad voice, "but I was telling the truth. Today no one will give us a loan, because there is no one to do it."

"What about Dagon?" asked the Prince, surprised. "Isn't he with my court? Has he died?"

"Dagon is living in Pi-Bast, but he's spending his days with other Phoenician merchants at the Temple of Astarte in penance and prayer."

"Why such piety? Because I've been to a temple, does my banker feel a need to consult the gods?"

Thutmose was fidgeting on his stool. "The Phoenicians are frightened and distressed by rumors."

"Of what?"

"Someone has spread a rumor that when Your Eminence mounts the throne, the Phoenicians will be expelled and their assets will be seized for the treasury."

"Well, then they've still plenty of time," smiled the Prince.

Thutmose hesitated. "It's said," he spoke in hushed tones, "that the health of His Holiness (may he live forever!) has been badly shaken of late ..."

"That's a lie!" interrupted the Prince, alarmed. "I would have known about it ..."

"The priests are holding services in secret for the restoration of the Pharaoh's health," whispered Thutmose. "That I know for certain."

The Prince stopped, astonished. "How's that?" he said. "My father is gravely ill, the priests are praying for him, and they tell me nothing about it?"

"It's said His Holiness' illness may go on for a year."

Ramses tossed his hand. "Bah! ... You listen to fables and upset me. Tell me rather about the Phoenicians; that sounds more interesting."

"I've heard," said Thutmose, "only what everyone has: that Your Eminence learned at the temple about the perniciousness of the Phoenicians and has pledged to expel them."

"At the temple?" repeated the Successor. "Who can know what I learned and decided at the temple?"

Thutmose shrugged in silence.

"Could there be treachery there as well?" whispered the Prince. "Anyway," he said aloud, "you get me Dagon. I must learn the source of these lies and, by the gods, put an end to them!"

"Your lordship will be doing well," said Thutmose, "because all Egypt is concerned. Already there's no one to borrow money from; and if these rumors were to persist, commerce would come to a halt. The aristocracy is already in straits with no prospect of relief, and your lordship's court is also feeling the pinch. In a month, the same could happen at His Holiness' palace ..."

"Silence," interrupted the Prince, "and get me Dagon at once."

Thutmose ran out, but the banker appeared at the Viceroy's only in the evening. He was wearing a white cloth in black stripes.

"Have you gone mad?" exclaimed the Successor at the sight. "I'll soon cheer you up ... I need a hundred talents immediately. Go, and don't show yourself until you've taken care of it."

The banker covered his face and wept.

"What's the meaning of this?" asked the Prince impatiently.

"Lord," replied Dagon, kneeling, "take my fortune, sell me and my family ... take everything, even our lives. But a hundred talents ... where would I get such a fortune today? Not in Egypt, nor in Phoenicia ..." he sobbed.

"Set has possessed you, Dagon," laughed the Successor. "Would you really believe I'm thinking of expelling you Phoenicians?"

The banker again fell at the Prince's feet.

"I know nothing ... I'm an ordinary merchant and your slave. As many days as there are between the new and full moons have sufficed to turn me to dust and my fortune to spit ..."

"Tell me what that means," asked the Successor impatiently.

"I'm unable to say anything; and even if I were able to, I have a great seal on my lips! Today I only pray and weep ..."

"Do Phoenicians pray too?" thought the Prince.

"Unable as I am to be of any service to you, my lord," continued Dagon, "I'll at least offer you a piece of good advice. There is here in Pi-Bast a famous Tyrian prince named Hiram. An old, wise, and terribly rich man ... Call him, Iry-pat, ask for a hundred talents, and maybe he can help Your Eminence ..."

As Ramses could elicit no explanations from the banker, he let Dagon go and promised to send a deputation to Hiram.

CHAPTER 30

The next morning Thutmose, with a great entourage of officers and courtiers, called on the Tyrian prince and invited him to the Viceroy's.

At noon Hiram appeared before the palace in a simple litter borne by eight Egyptian almsmen. He was surrounded by leading Phoenician merchants and by the same crowd that daily stood outside his house.

It was with some surprise that Ramses greeted the old man, whose eyes regarded him with wisdom and whose whole person bespoke dignity. Hiram wore a white coat and, on his head, a gold circlet. He bowed to the Viceroy with decorum and, lifting his hands over Ramses' head, pronounced a short benediction. All present were deeply moved.

When the Viceroy had indicated an armchair to him and dismissed his courtiers, Hiram spoke up:

"Yesterday Your Eminence's servant Dagon told me that the Prince has need of a hundred talents. I immediately sent my couriers to Sabne-Khetam, Sethroe,[1] Xois, and other cities where Phoenician ships lie at anchor, with instructions for them to discharge all their cargoes. I think that in a couple of days Your Eminence will receive this petty sum."

"Petty!" laughed the Prince. "Your Eminence is fortunate if you can call a hundred talents a petty sum."

Hiram nodded. "Your Eminence's grandfather," he said after taking thought, "the eternally living Ramesses-sa-Ptah, honored me with his friendship; I also know His Holiness your father (may he live forever!) and will try to pay my respects to him, if I am admitted ..."

"Why the doubt?" broke in the Prince.

"There are those," replied the guest, "who admit some and not others into the Pharaoh's presence, but never mind ... Your Eminence is not to blame for it, so I shall make bold to ask you a question, as an old friend of your grandfather and father."

"Yes?"

"Why is it," spoke Hiram slowly, "why is it that the Pharaoh's Successor and Viceroy must borrow a hundred talents, when his Kingdom is owed over a hundred thousand talents?"

"How?" exclaimed Ramses.

"How do you mean, how? In tribute from the Asiatic peoples! Phoenicia owes you five thousand, which I guarantee she will pay if nothing untoward happens. Additionally, Israel

---

[1] Sethroe: a town on Lake Manzala, perhaps in the 14th nome of Lower Egypt. *(Translator.)*

owes three thousand, the Philistines[2] and Moabites[3] two thousand each, the Hittites thirty thousand ... I don't remember all the items, but I know the total comes to a hundred and three or a hundred and five thousand talents."

Ramses was biting his lip, impotent anger visible on his expressive face. He lowered his eyes in silence.

"So it's true!" sighed Hiram suddenly, gazing at the Viceroy. "So it's true? Poor Phoenicia, and Egypt too ..."

"What is Your Eminence saying?" frowned the Prince. "I don't understand your lament ..."

"The Prince does know whereof I speak, since he does not answer my question," said Hiram, rising as if to leave. "Still ... I won't withdraw my promise. The Prince shall have the hundred talents."

He bowed low, but the Viceroy made him resume his seat.

"Your Eminence is holding something back," he said in an offended tone. "I want you to tell me what misfortune threatens Phoenicia or Egypt."

"Would Your Eminence not know about it?" asked Hiram hesitantly.

"I don't know a thing. I've spent over a month at a temple."

"That is where one could have learned everything."

"Your Eminence shall tell me!" cried the Viceroy, striking the table with his fist. "I don't like people amusing themselves at my expense!"

"I will tell Your Eminence, if you give me a solemn pledge not to betray this to anyone. Though ... I can't believe the Crown Prince would not have been informed of it!"

"You don't trust me?" asked the Prince incredulously.

"In this matter, I would require a pledge from the pharaoh himself," replied Hiram firmly.

"Very well ... I swear by my sword and by the standards of our armies that I won't tell anyone what Your Eminence discloses to me."

"Good enough," said Hiram.

"I'm listening."

"Does the Prince know what is happening right now in Phoenicia?"

"I don't know even that!" said the Viceroy, annoyed.

"Our ships," whispered Hiram, "are returning from all the ends of the earth to the homeland in order, at the first signal, to transport the people and treasures somewhere across the sea ... to the west."

"Why?" asked the Viceroy.

"Because Assyria is to take us over."

The Prince burst out laughing. "Your Worship has gone mad!" he cried. "Assyria is to take Phoenicia! And what is Egypt's response to that?"

"Egypt has already agreed."

The Viceroy's blood boiled up.

---

[2] Philistines: a people that, as part of the Sea Peoples, appeared, probably from the Aegean region, in Canaan's southern coastal area at the start of the Iron Age—about a century before *Pharaoh*'s present time. The Bible paints them as the most dangerous enemy of the Kingdom of Israel. *(Translator.)*

[3] Moabites: the people of Moab, a mountainous strip of land in Jordan, alongside much of the eastern shore of the Dead Sea. In biblical times, the Moabites were often in conflict with their Israelite neighbors to the west. *(Translator.)*

"The heat scrambles your thoughts, old man," he said to Hiram in a calm voice. "You even forget that such a thing could not take place without the Pharaoh's consent ... and mine!"

"That, too, will follow. Meanwhile the priests have made a pact."

"With whom? ... What priests?"

"With the Chaldean high priest Berossus, empowered by King Assar," replied Hiram. "And on your side? ... I cannot say for certain, but I believe His Eminence Herhor, His Eminence Mephres, and the holy prophet Pentuer."

The Prince turned pale.

"Tyrian," he said, "consider yourself to be accusing the Kingdom's highest dignitaries of treason."

"The Prince is mistaken, it is not treason: Egypt's senior high priest and His Holiness' minister have the right to treat with neighboring potentates. Anyway, how does Your Eminence know that all this is not happening by the Pharaoh's will?"

Ramses had to concede inwardly that such a pact would not be treason ... only a slight to himself, the Crown Prince. So that was how the priests were treating him, who in a year might be pharaoh? So that was why Pentuer had condemned wars, and why Mephres had backed him!

"When and where was this supposed to have happened?" asked the Prince.

"It seems they made the pact at night in the Temple of Set outside Memphis," answered Hiram. "When? I'm not sure, but it seems to have been the day Your Eminence left Memphis."

"The scoundrels!" thought the Viceroy. "So that's how they respect my office? So they deceived me also in describing the state of the Kingdom? Some good god stirred my doubts at the Temple of Hathor ..."

After a moment's inner struggle, he said aloud: "Not likely! ... And I'm not believing what Your Eminence says until you give me proof."

"Proof there will be," replied Hiram. "Any day now, the great Assyrian lord Sargon,[4] a friend of King Assar's, will be arriving in Pi-Bast. He is coming here under pretext of a pilgrimage to the Temple of Astoreth; he will present gifts to the Prince and to His Holiness—then you will conclude a pact. But in reality you will be putting the seal to what the priests have contrived for the doom of the Phoenicians, and maybe also to your own misfortune."

"Never!" said the Prince. "Think what compensation Assyria would have to give Egypt ..."

"Now, that is speech worthy of a king: what compensation would Egypt get? For a kingdom, any pact is good so long as it brings gain. What I find perplexing," continued Hiram, "is that Egypt will be making a bad deal: Assyria takes, in addition to Phoenicia, almost all of Asia, vouchsafing you the Israelites, the Philistines, and the Sinai Peninsula. Of course, in that case the tributes owing to Egypt will be forfeit and the pharaoh will never see those hundred and five thousand talents."

The Viceroy shook his head. "Your Eminence," he said, "doesn't know the Egyptian priests: none of them would accept such a pact."

---

[4] Sargon: name borrowed from three Mesopotamian kings: Sargon of Akkad ("Sargon the Great," reigned ca. 2340—ca. 2284 BCE); and Assyria's Sargon I (reigned ca. 1920—ca. 1881 BCE) and Sargon II (reigned 722—705 BCE). *(Translator.)*

"Why not? A Phoenician proverb says: Better barley in the barn than gold in the desert. If Egypt felt very weak, she might prefer Sinai and Palestine for free, over war with Assyria. But that is what puzzles me ... Today it is not Egypt but Assyria that is vulnerable: she has a conflict going in the northeast and has few forces, and those are of poor quality. If Egypt attacked Assyria, she would destroy that kingdom, take immense treasures from Nineveh and Babel, and once and for all establish her power in Asia."

"So you see, such a pact cannot exist," said Ramses.

"Only in one case could I see such negotiations: if the priests wanted to do away with royal authority in Egypt ... Which has been their goal since the time of the Prince's grand-father."

"Again you're talking nonsense," said the Viceroy. But in his heart he felt uneasy.

"Maybe I am mistaken," said Hiram, looking him smartly in the eye. "But listen, Eminence ..."

He moved his chair closer to the Prince and spoke in a lowered voice: "If the pharaoh made war on Assyria and won, he would have: a great army attached to his person; a hundred thousand talents in back tribute; some two hundred thousand talents from Nineveh and Babel.

"Finally, a hundred thousand talents annually from the conquered countries.

"Such vast treasure would allow him to redeem the estates pledged to the priests, and once and for all put an end to their meddling with power."

Ramses' eyes shone. Hiram went on:

"On the other hand, today the army is subordinate to Herhor and therefore to the priests; in the event of conflict, apart from the foreign regiments, the pharaoh cannot count on it.

"Furthermore, the pharaoh's treasury is empty, and the greater part of his estates are held by the temples. If only to maintain his court, the King has to contract new debts each year; and since you will no longer have the Phoenicians, you will have to take loans from the priests ... This way, in ten years' time His Holiness (may he live forever!) will lose the rest of his estates, and then what?"

Beads of sweat came to Ramses' forehead.

"So you see, Eminence," said Hiram, "in one case the priests could—indeed, would have to—accept the most shameful pact with Assyria: if they meant to humble and bring down the pharaoh's authority. Of course, there could be a second case: if Egypt were so weak that she needed peace at all costs ..."

The Prince sprang up. "Silence!" he cried. "I'd rather the treason of the most faithful servants than such national impotence! Egypt would have to turn Asia over to Assyria ... and within a year Egypt herself would fall under Assyria's yoke, because in signing the disgrace she would be acknowledging her impotence!"

He walked about excitedly, while Hiram watched him with pity or empathy.

Suddenly Ramses stopped before the Phoenician.

"It's a lie!" he said. "Some cunning scoundrel has deceived you with a semblance of the truth, Hiram, and you believed him. If such a treaty existed, it would have been negotiated in the greatest secrecy. In which case, one of the four priests you named would have be-trayed not only the King but his own fellow-conspirators."

"There could have been a fifth person, who listened in," said Hiram.

"And sold you the secret?"

Hiram smiled. "I'm surprised," he said, "that the Prince has not yet learned the power of gold."

"But consider, Eminence, our priests have more gold than you, though you are richer than the rich!"

"Still, I don't mind gaining a drachma. Why should others spurn talents?"

"Because they are servants of the gods," said the Prince fervently, "because they would fear divine retribution."

The Phoenician smiled. "I've seen many temples belonging to various nations," he replied, "and in those temples, statues large and small: wooden, stone, even gold. But gods, I've never encountered ..."

"Blasphemer!" cried Ramses. "I've seen a deity, felt its hand on me, heard its voice ..."

"Where was this?"

"At the Temple of Hathor: in the vestibule and in my cell."

"In the daytime?" asked Hiram.

"At night ..." said the Prince, taking pause.

"At night ... the Prince heard the gods speak ... and felt their hand," repeated the Phoenician, scanning the phrases. "At night, one can see many things. What actually happened?"

"I was grabbed by the head, shoulders, and legs, and I swear ..."

"Hist!" smiled Hiram. "One ought not to swear in vain."

With his perspicacious eyes he fixed Ramses and, seeing doubts stirring in the young man, he said: "I tell you what, lord. You are inexperienced and surrounded by a web of intrigues, while I've been a friend to your grandfather and father. I'll render you a service. Come some night to the Temple of Astoreth ... after pledging secrecy. Come alone, and you'll learn what kind of gods speak and touch us in the temples."

"I will," said Ramses, on reflection.

"Let me know the morning of the day, Prince, and I'll tell you the temple's evening password, and you'll be admitted. Only don't give away me or yourself," said the Phoenician, with a good-natured smile. "The gods sometimes forgive betrayal of their secrets; people, never."

He bowed, lifted his eyes and hands, and began whispering a benediction.

"Hypocrite!" cried the Prince. "You pray to gods in whom you do not believe?"

Hiram finished the benediction and said: "Yes: I don't believe in the Egyptian, the Assyrian, even the Phoenician gods, but I believe in the One God Who dwells in no temples and Whose name is not known."

"Our priests too believe in the One God," said Ramses.

"And so do the Chaldean priests, yet both conspire against us. There is no truth in the world, my Prince!"

After Hiram's departure, the Prince ensconced himself in his remotest room under pretense of reading sacred papyri.

Almost in the blink of an eye, the newly received information took order in his quick mind, and a plan took shape.

First and foremost, he grasped that a quiet life-and-death struggle was under way between the Phoenicians and the priests. Over what? Naturally, over influence and treasure. Hiram had spoken the truth: were the Phoenicians to be no more in Egypt, all the estates of the pharaoh, and of the nomarchs and all the aristocracy, would pass into the power of the temples.

Ramses had never liked the priests and had long known and seen that the greater part of Egypt already belonged to the priests; that their cities were the wealthiest, their fields the best tended, their populace content. He also knew that half the treasures of the temples could deliver the pharaoh from his ceaseless troubles and restore his power.

The Prince knew this and had more than once spoken bitterly of it. But when, through Herhor's good offices, he had become Viceroy and commander of the Menfi Corps, he had made his peace with the priests and had suppressed in his heart his old antipathy toward them.

Today it all revived.

So the priests not only had not told him about their negotiations with Assyria, they had not even alerted him to the mission of that Sargon?

It might be that this question constituted a supreme secret of the temples and Kingdom. But why were they concealing from him the amounts of tribute owing from the various Asiatic nations? ... A hundred thousand talents: why, a sum like that could immediately improve the pharaoh's finances. Why were they concealing what was known even to a Tyrian prince, a member of that city's council?

How mortifying for him, the Crown Prince and Viceroy, to have his eyes opened by foreigners!

But there was something worse: Pentuer and Mephres had used every conceivable argument to convince him that Egypt must avoid war.

Already at the Temple of Hathor this emphasis had seemed to him suspect, because war could provide the Kingdom with many thousands of slaves and raise the general prosperity of the country. Today it seemed the more essential, as Egypt had back sums to collect and new ones to win.

The Prince propped his arms on the table and reckoned:

"We have a hundred thousand talents in tribute to collect. Hiram figures on the sack of Babylon and Nineveh bringing some two hundred thousand. All told, three hundred thousand.

"A sum like that would cover the costs of the greatest war, leaving as profit several hundred thousand slaves and a hundred thousand talents' annual tribute from the reconquered countries.

"And after that," concluded the Prince, "we would square accounts with the priests."

Ramses was feverish. Nevertheless he reflected: "What if Egypt were unable to carry off a victorious war against Assyria?"

But at that question his blood boiled up. How could Egypt fail to crush Assyria, when the army would be headed by him, Ramses—scion of Ramses the Great, who single-handedly hurled himself at the Hittite chariots and routed them!

The Prince could conceive of anything save that he might be defeated—that he might fail to wrest victory from the greatest potentates. He felt within him a boundless daring, and would have been surprised had any foe not fled at the sight of his loosed horses. The gods themselves stood in the pharaoh's chariot to shield him and to strike down enemies with celestial missiles.

"Only ... what was this Hiram telling me about the gods?" thought the Prince. "And what is he to show me at the Temple of Astoreth? ... We shall see."

CHAPTER 31

Hiram was as good as his word. Daily, to the Prince's palace in Pi-Bast, hosts of slaves and long files of donkeys brought wheat, barley, dried meat, textiles, and wine. Gold and precious stones were delivered by Phoenician merchants overseen by agents of Hiram's house.

In this fashion, over five days' time, the Viceroy received the hundred talents promised him. Hiram charged a modest interest: a talent for every four talents per year; and he required no security but contented himself with a note from the Prince, certified by a court of law.

The needs of the Viceroy's court were generously provided for. Each of his three mistresses received a new wardrobe, plenty of exotic perfumes, and several slave girls of different hues. The servants had abundant food and wine; the royal workers received their back pay; the military got extra rations.

The court was especially delighted as, at Hiram's behest, Thutmose and the other young nobles received fairly high loans from the Phoenicians; and the Nomarch of Am-Khent and his higher officials, expensive gifts.

Feast followed feast, revel followed revel, in spite of the constantly rising heat. The Viceroy, in view of the universal happiness, was himself pleased. Only one thing troubled him: the conduct of Mephres and the other priests. The Prince had expected them to upbraid him for contracting such a big loan with Hiram despite what he had learned at the temple. But the holy fathers kept their peace and did not even show themselves at court.

"Why is it," Ramses asked Thutmose, "that the priests aren't admonishing us? We've never indulged in such excesses. There's music from morning to night, and we drink from sunrise and drop off with women in our arms or pitchers under our heads."

"Why should they admonish us?" said Thutmose righteously. "Aren't we abiding in the city of Astarte, for whom the fittest service is revelry and the most suitable offering is love? Anyway, the priests know that, after all the mortifications and fasts, you deserve a rest."

"Did they say that to you?" asked the Prince uneasily.

"More than once. Just yesterday the holy Mephres remarked to me, laughing, that a young man like you cares more for revels than for religion or the demands of ruling a kingdom."

Ramses became thoughtful. So the priests considered him a light-minded youngster even though any day now, thanks to Sara, he was to become a father? So much the better: at the right moment, they would have a surprise in store for them.

If truth be told, the Prince felt some slight pangs of conscience: since leaving the Temple of Hathor, he had devoted not a single day to the affairs of the nome of Am-Khent. The priests might well suppose that he was either completely satisfied with Pentuer's exposition—or had tired of meddling in governance.

"So much the better!" he whispered. "So much the better!"

In his young soul, influenced by the constant intrigues or suspicions of intrigues about him, there was beginning to develop an instinct for dissemblance. Ramses sensed that the priests had no idea what he had discussed with Hiram, or what plans he was spinning. His revels sufficed to convince the blinded priests that the Kingdom's governance would remain in their hands.

"The gods have so muddled their minds," Ramses told himself, "that they don't even ask why Hiram gave me such a big loan. Maybe the wily Tyrian managed to put their suspicious hearts to sleep. So much the better! ... so much the better!"

It gave him a peculiar pleasure to think that the priests had deceived themselves on his account. He decided to keep them in error, and so disported himself like mad.

The priests, above all Mephres and Mentesuphis, had indeed deceived themselves as to both Ramses and Hiram. The cunning Tyrian played the man very proud of his relations with the Successor, and the Prince with no less success played the dissolute youth.

Mephres was even sure the Prince was seriously thinking of expelling the Phoenicians from Egypt, and that in the meantime he and his courtiers were running up debts in order never to repay them.

Meanwhile the Temple of Astarte and its numerous gardens and courts swarmed with the faithful. Daily if not hourly, braving the terrible heat, some company of pilgrims from the depths of Asia arrived at the great goddess's.

They were strange pilgrims. Weary, streaming with sweat, covered in dust, they went with music, while dancing and singing sometimes very bawdy songs. They passed their days in carousal, their nights in unbridled debauchery in honor of the goddess Astoreth. Each such company could be not only recognized but smelled from afar: they carried huge bouquets of fresh flowers—and bundles containing cats that had died in the course of the year.

The pious turned the cats over for embalming or stuffing to embalmers who lived outside Pi-Bast, then toted them back home as venerated relics.[1]

In early Mesore (May-June)[2] Prince Hiram notified Ramses that he could come that evening to the Phoenician Temple of Astoreth. After sunset, when the streets had grown dark, the Viceroy fastened on a short sword, donned a hooded cloak and, unseen by any of the servants, slipped out to Hiram's house.

The old magnate was awaiting him.

"Well," he smiled, "does Your Eminence not fear going into a Phoenician temple where cruelty presides at the altar and is served by perversity?"

"Fear?" asked Ramses, regarding him almost scornfully. "Astoreth isn't Baal, nor I a child that can be tossed into the burning belly of your god."

---

[1] Cats were also deliberately bred in catteries, to be killed and mummified for sale as objects of veneration. *(Translator.)*

[2] Actually, the ancient Egyptian month of Mesore lay between August 7 and September 5 of the modern, Gregorian calendar. *(Translator.)*

"And the Prince believes all that?"

Ramses shrugged. "A credible eyewitness told me about your child sacrifices. One time a storm wrecked a dozen of your ships. The Tyrian priests immediately announced a service, and a crowd gathered for it."

The Prince spoke with visible indignation.

"Before the temple of Baal, on a platform, sat a huge bronze statue with the head of an ox. Its belly was fired red-hot. At the behest of your priests, stupid Phoenician mothers laid the most beautiful infants at the feet of the cruel god ..."

"Only boys," broke in Hiram.

"Yes, only boys," said the Prince. "The priests sprinkled each with fragrances and dressed him in flowers, then the statue seized him in its bronze hands, opened its mouth, and devoured the screaming infant. Each time, flames belched from the god's mouth ..."

Hiram was chuckling. "And Your Eminence believes this?"

"I repeat, I was told this by a man who never lies."

"He said what he in fact saw," replied Hiram. "Was he not surprised, though, that none of the mothers whose sons were burned, wept?"

"Indeed he was struck by this indifference in women who are always ready to shed tears, even over a dead chicken. It goes to show the great cruelty of your people."

The old Phoenician was nodding his head. "When was this?" he asked.

"Several years ago."

"Well," spoke Hiram slowly, "should Your Eminence ever visit Tyre, I will be honored to show you such a ceremony ..."

"I don't want to see it!"

"And next we'll go into another court at the temple, where the Prince will see a very beautiful school and in it, hale and hearty, the same boys who were burned several years ago."

"What!" exclaimed Ramses. "Then they didn't die?"

"They live and grow into sturdy sailors. When Your Eminence becomes Your Holiness— may you live forever!—some of them may be operating your ships."

"Then you deceive your people?" laughed the Prince.

"We deceive no one," replied the Tyrian solemnly. "He deceives himself, who does not ask for explanation of a ceremony which he does not understand."

"What is the explanation?" asked Ramses.

"We in fact have a custom," said Hiram, "whereby needy mothers who wish to secure a good life for their sons, offer them to the service of the state. The children are indeed seized by the statue of Baal, which contains a red-hot furnace. The ceremony does not mean that the boys are actually burned—but that they have become property of the temple and have perished to their mothers as though they had fallen into fire.

"In reality, they do not go into the furnace but to wet nurses and nannies who rear them for several years. When they are a bit older, they are taken and educated by a school of the priests of Baal. The most gifted of the fosterlings become priests or officials; the less gifted enter the merchant marine and sometimes attain great wealth.

"Now maybe the Prince will understand why the Tyrian mothers do not mourn their sons. Furthermore, now your lordship will know why our laws hold no punishments for parents who kill their offspring, as sometimes happens in Egypt."

"There are bad persons everywhere," said the Viceroy.

"But in our land there are no infanticides," continued Hiram, "because in our land children whose mothers can't feed them are cared for by the state and the temple."

The Prince reflected. Suddenly he hugged Hiram and exclaimed: "You're much better than those who tell such terrible stories about you. I'm very glad."[3]

"In us, too, there is not a little evil," said Hiram, "but we will all be your lordship's faithful servants when you call upon us."

"Will you?" asked the Prince, looking him steadily in the eye.

The old man placed his hand over his heart. "I swear to you, Successor to the Egyptian Throne and future Pharaoh, that whenever you open the struggle against our common enemies, all Phoenicia will hasten to your aid as one man.

"Here—take this as a memento of our conversation today."

He retrieved from his robes a gold medal covered with arcane characters and, whispering prayers, suspended it on Ramses' neck.

"With this amulet," said Hiram, "you can travel the whole world over and wherever you encounter a Phoenician, he will serve you with advice, gold, even the sword. And now let us be off."

Several hours had elapsed since sunset, but visibility was good as the moon had risen. The awful daytime heat had yielded to coolness; the clean air held none of the gray dust that poisoned the breath and stung the eyes. Here and there in the heavens shone stars melting away in a flood of moonlight.

Movement had ceased in the streets, but all the rooftops were full of merrymakers. Pi-Bast seemed a single hall filled edge-to-edge with music, song, laughter, and the clink of winecups.

The Prince and the Phoenician walked rapidly for the city outskirts, taking the less illuminated sides of the streets. Nevertheless, now and again feasters on the terraces spotted them and, having done so, invited them to come up or showered flowers on their heads.

"Hey, you nocturnal vagabonds there!" they called from the roofs. "If you're not thieves whom the night lures out for profit, come on up! We have good wine and friendly women ..."

The two wanderers did not respond to the gracious invitations as they hurried on their way. At last they reached a part of town with fewer buildings and more gardens, whose trees, thanks to the moist sea breezes, grew taller and more luxuriant than in Egypt's southern provinces.

"Not far now," said Hiram.

The Prince lifted his eyes and saw, above the trees' dense foliage, a square bluish tower and, on it, a slimmer white one. It was the Temple of Astoreth.

Soon they entered a garden which afforded a view of the whole edifice.

It comprised several tiers. The first was a square terrace four hundred paces on a side;

---

[3] Ancient Greek and Roman stories about Phoenician infant-sacrifices have been variously interpreted as anti-Phoenician propaganda, as references to cremated remains of stillborn infants, or as accounts of actual child sacrifices. Urns containing cremated remains of children and animals have been found in the central Mediterranean—in North Africa (Carthage), Sicily, and Sardinia—but actually *not* in Phoenician localities to the east in the Levant (Phoenicia proper, where Prince Hiram hails from) or to the west in Spain. *(Translator.)*

it rested on a wall several meters high, painted black. At the east face was a projection to which, from two sides, led broad stairways. Along the other faces stood small towers, ten at each face; between each pair of towers were five windows.

More or less in the middle of the terrace there rose another square building, two hundred paces on a side. It had a single stairway, towers at the corners, and was colored purple.

On that structure's flat roof stood another square terrace, a couple of meters high, gold-colored; and on that, one atop the other, two towers: a blue, and a white.

The whole looked as if someone had placed on the ground a great black block; on it, a smaller purple one; on that, a gold; higher up, a blue; and at the top, a silver. To each level there led stairways, either twin lateral ones or a single frontal one, always on the east side.

At the stairways and doors there stood, alternately, great Egyptian sphinxes and winged, human-headed Assyrian bulls.

The Viceroy regarded with pleasure the edifice, resplendent in the moonlight, against a backdrop of lush vegetation. It was reared Chaldean-style and differed markedly from Egyptian temples—first, in its system of tiers; second, in its vertical walls.[4] All important Egyptian buildings had sloping, tapered walls.

The garden was not empty. At various points stood houses and villas, burned lights, rang singing and music. Between the trees, from time to time, there flashed a shadow of a pair of lovers.

Suddenly they were approached by an old priest. He exchanged a few words with Hiram, made Ramses a low bow, and said: "Pray come with me, lord."

"And may the gods watch over Your Eminence," added Hiram, leaving them.

Ramses followed the priest. A little to the side of the temple, in the densest thicket, was a stone bench; and perhaps a hundred paces from it, a villa outside of which there was singing.

"Are they praying over there?" asked the Prince.

"No!" said the priest disapprovingly. "Those are devotees of Kama, our priestess who tends the fire before the altar of Astoreth."

"Which will she receive today?"

"None, ever!" said the guide, horrified. "If a priestess who tends the fire broke her vow of chastity, she would have to die."

"A cruel law!" said the Prince.

"Please wait on this bench, lord," said the Phoenician priest coldly. "When you hear three bronze tones, go to the temple and climb to the terrace, then go into the purple building."

"By myself?"

"Yes."

The Prince sat down on the bench, in the shade of an olive tree, and listened to a woman's laughter pealing in the villa.

"Kama?" he thought. "Nice name! ... She must be young and may be beautiful, and the stupid Phoenicians threaten her with death if ... Do they mean, this way, to assure themselves a dozen virgins out of a whole country?"

He chuckled but was sad. For some reason, he pitied the unknown woman for whom love was the entrance to the grave.

---

[4] Prus is describing a ziggurat, a massive religious structure in ancient Mesopotamian cities. *(Translator.)*

"I can imagine Thutmose, were he made a priestess of Astoreth! The poor fellow would have to die before a single lamp had burned out before the goddess ..."

Just then, outside the villa, a flute began a wistful melody accompanied by women crooning, lullaby-fashion: "Aha-a! ... aha-a!"

The flute and women fell still, and a handsome male voice sang in Greek:

"When your raiment flashes on the balcony, stars dim, nightingales fall still, and my heart hushes like the earth at daybreak ..."

"Aha-a! ... aha-a! ... aha-a!" crooned the women, and the flute played a refrain.

"When, engrossed in prayer, you go to the temple, violets enclose you in fragrance, butterflies circle your lips, palms bow to your beauty ..."

"Aha-a! ... aha-a! ... aha-a! ..."

"When I see you not, I search the sky to recall the sweet serenity of your face. Lost labor! The sky hasn't your serenity, and its heat is cold to the flames that burn my heart."

"Aha-a! ... aha-a! ..."

"One day I stood amid the roses which your gaze invests in white, scarlet, and gold. Each leaf recalled an hour—each blossom, a month—spent at your feet. The dewdrops were my tears that the desert wind imbibes.

"Give the word, and we will sail to my homeland. Myrtle groves will conceal our caresses, and kindly gods will watch over our happiness."

"Aha-a! ... aha-a! ..."

Ramses half-closed his eyes and dreamed. Through his lashes he no longer saw the garden, only a flood of moonlight imbued with black shadows and with the song of the unknown man to the unknown woman. At moments the song took such hold of him, forced its way so deep into his psyche, that Ramses was moved to wonder: was it not he himself singing—nay, was he not the love song?

At this moment his title, power, and weighty questions of state all seemed to him wretched trifles next to the moonlit night and the outcries of an enamored heart. Were he given the choice of all the pharaoh's power or this present mood in which he found himself, he would have preferred this reverie in which the whole world, he himself, even time vanished and there remained a longing flying into eternity upon wings of song.

Suddenly the Prince came to; the singing had stopped, the lights had gone out in the villa, and the black, empty windows stood out starkly against the white walls. It might have been supposed no one had ever lived there. The garden had become desert and still; even the light breeze had ceased fluttering the leaves.

One! ... two! ... three! ... Three powerful bronze tones rang from the temple.

"Oh, I have to go!" thought the Prince, without quite knowing where he was to go or why.

However, he set off toward the temple, whose silvery tower dominated the trees as if beckoning him.

He went stupefied, full of strange fancies. He felt confined among the trees: he wanted to climb to the top of the tower, breathe, and take in a broader horizon. Then, recalling that it was the month of Mesore, that a year had already passed since the desert maneuvers, he felt a longing for the desert. How gladly he would have mounted his light two-horse chariot and flown someplace where the air would be fresher and trees did not conceal the horizon.

He was now at the foot of the temple, and climbed to the terrace. All was quiet and desert, as though everyone had died; only a fountain murmured in the distance. On the second stairway he dropped his burnoose and sword, looked once more at the garden as though loath to part with the moon, and entered the temple. Above him towered three more tiers.

The bronze doors were open; at either side of the entrance stood a winged figure of a human-headed bull with a proud, serene face. "Assyrian kings," thought the Prince, scrutinizing their beards plaited into little braids.

The temple interior was black as blackest night, the darkness accentuated by white streaks of moonlight plunging in through tall, narrow windows.

In the depths burned two lamps before a statue of the goddess Astoreth. Some peculiar overhead lighting rendered the statue perfectly visible. Ramses looked. She was a gigantic woman with ostrich wings, wearing a long pleated gown and a pointed cap, and holding a pair of doves in her right hand. Her lovely face and downcast eyes, with their expression of sweetness and innocence, astonished the Prince: this was the patroness of vengeance and of the most unbridled debauchery.

Phoenicia had shown him yet another of her secrets.

"A peculiar nation!" he thought. "Their man-eating gods eat no one, and their debauchery is in the care of virgin priestesses and of a goddess with a child's face!"

Suddenly he felt something like a great snake pass swiftly over his feet. Ramses stepped back and into a streak of moonlight. "An illusion!" he told himself.

Almost the same moment, he heard a whispered "Ramses! ... Ramses! ..."

There was no telling whether the voice was male or female or whence it came.

"Ramses! ... Ramses! ..." came a whisper, as from the floor.

The Prince moved to an unlit spot and, listening, bent over. Suddenly he felt two delicate hands on his head.

He sprang up to catch them but grasped only air.

"Ramses! ..." came a whisper from above.

He lifted his head and felt a lotus flower on his lips; when he extended his hands for it, someone leaned lightly on his shoulders.

"Ramses! ..." called a voice from the altar.

The Prince turned around and was stunned. In a light streak a couple of paces off stood a gorgeous man exactly like him. The same face, eyes, youthful facial hair; the same bearing, movements, and dress.

For a moment the Prince thought he was standing before a great mirror such as even the Pharaoh did not own. But he soon realized that his look-alike was not an image but a living man.

At that moment he felt a kiss on his neck. He again turned around but no one was there, and meanwhile his double had vanished.

"Who's there? ... I want to know!" cried the angry Prince.

"It's me ... Kama," answered a dulcet voice.

In a light streak there appeared a gorgeous woman, naked but for a gold loincloth.

Ramses ran up and grabbed her arm. She did not flee.

"You're Kama? No, you're ... Yes, Dagon sent you over one time, but then your name was Cuddles."

"I am also Cuddles," she answered naively.

"You touched me with your hands?"

"Yes."

"How did you do it?"

"Like so ..." she answered, throwing her arms round his neck and kissing him.

Ramses grabbed her in his arms, but she pulled free with a strength unsuspectable in so slight a figure.

"So you're the priestess Kama? ... It was you the Greek sang to today..." said the Prince, passionately squeezing her hands. "Who is the singer?"

Kama shrugged contemptuously. "He's with our temple."

Ramses' eyes were afire, his nostrils flared, his head buzzed. The same woman had made little impression on him a few months earlier, but today he was ready to do madness for her. He envied the Greek, and at the same time felt an indescribable regret at the thought that, were she to became his mistress, she would have to die.

"How beautiful you are," he said. "Where do you live? ... Oh, I know, in that villa. May I visit you? ... Naturally, if you receive visits from singers, you have to receive me as well. Are you really a priestess who tends the fire?"

"Yes."

"And your laws are so cruel that they won't let you love? ... Oh, those are just threats! ... For me you'll make an exception."

"All Phoenicia would curse me, the gods would wreak vengeance," she laughed.

Ramses again drew her to him; she again pulled free.

"Beware, Prince," she said with a defiant look. "Phoenicia is powerful, and her gods ..."

"What do I care about your gods or Phoenicia! If a hair fell from your head, I'd trample Phoenicia like a vicious reptile!"

"Kama! ... Kama!" spoke a voice from the statue.

She was terrified. "Oh, you see, they're calling me. Maybe they even heard your blasphemies ..."

"May they not hear my anger!" burst out the Prince.

"The anger of the gods is more terrible ..."

She sprang away and vanished into the temple's shadows. Ramses lunged after her but suddenly drew back; the whole temple between the altar and him was flooded by an enormous blood-red flame in which there appeared monstrous figures: great bats, human-faced reptiles, shades ...

The flame came straight at him the full width of the building, and the Prince, bewildered by the unfamiliar sight, backed away. Suddenly fresh air blew on him. He turned his head—he was now outside the temple, and the bronze doors slammed shut before him.

He rubbed his eyes and looked about. The moon, from its zenith in the heavens, was already sinking toward the west. Beside a column, Ramses found his sword and burnoose. He picked them up and descended the stairs as though drunk.

When the Prince returned late to the palace, Thutmose, seeing his pale face and dull expression, cried out in alarm: "By the gods! ... Where've you been, Iry-pat? All your court are up, worried."

"I was having a look at the town. Nice night out."

"You know," added Thutmose quickly, as if in fear of someone forestalling him, "you know, Sara has borne you a son."

"Really?...I don't want any of the retinue worrying about me any time I go out for a walk."

"Alone?"

"If I couldn't go where I liked alone, I'd be the most miserable slave in the Kingdom," said the Viceroy tartly.

He turned his sword and burnoose over to Thutmose and went to his bedroom without calling anyone. Only yesterday, news of the birth of a son would have filled him with joy. But now he received it with indifference. His entire soul was filled with memories of this evening, the strangest he had yet experienced in his life.

He still saw the moonlight; the Greek's song still sounded in his ears. And that Temple of Astarte!...

He could not fall asleep until morning.

CHAPTER 32

N ext day the Prince rose late, bathed and dressed by himself, and sent for Thutmose. Decked out and perfumed, the dandy appeared at once, scrutinizing the Prince to learn his mood and adjust his own expression accordingly.

But Ramses' face showed only weariness. "Are you sure," he yawned, "that it's a boy?"

"That's the word I have from the holy Mephres."

"Oho! How long have the prophets been taking an interest in my household?"

"Ever since Your Eminence started showing them his favor."

"Is that so?" asked the Prince, plunging into thought. He had recalled the previous day's scene at the Temple of Astoreth and was comparing it with similar phenomena at the Temple of Hathor.

"I was called to at both temples," he told himself, "But there my cell was thick-walled and cramped, while here the person calling, which is to say Kama, could hide behind a column and whisper ... And here it was terribly dark, whereas my cell was light."

Suddenly he asked Thutmose: "When did it happen?"

"When was His Eminence your son born? I understand some ten days ago ... Mother and child are fine and look very well. Menes, physician to your worshipful mother and His Eminence Herhor, attended the birth."

"Well, well ..." said the Prince.

"At both temples," thought Ramses, "I was touched with equal dexterity ... Was there a difference? I think so, maybe because here I was prepared for a miracle and there I wasn't. But here I was shown a second *me*, which they weren't able to do there ... The priests are very clever! ... I wonder who impersonated me so well, a god or a man? ... The priests are very clever, and I hardly know which it's better to believe: ours or the Phoenicians'.

"Listen, Thutmose ..." he said aloud, "listen, Thutmose, they must come here. After all, I must see my son ... Now no one will be able to think himself my better."

"Are Her Eminence Sara and her son to come at once?"

"The sooner, the better; as soon as their health is up to it. Within the palace precincts there are many comfortable buildings. We must choose a place among the trees, quiet and cool, as the hot season is coming on ... And I'll show my son to the world!"

Ramses mused again, somewhat to Thutmose's discomfiture.

"Yes, they're clever!" thought Ramses. "That they deceive the populace, even by crude means, I knew. Poor sacred Apis! How many jabs he gets during processions while the peasants lie before him on their stomachs ... But that they should deceive me, I wouldn't have believed. The voices of gods, the invisible hands, the tarring of that man were preludes! ... to be followed by Pentuer's song about the loss of land and population, about the officials, about the Phoenicians—all to make me hate war.

"Thutmose," he said suddenly.

"At your service ..."

"We must start bringing the regiments down from the coastal cities. I want to review them and reward their loyalty."

"What about us nobility, aren't we loyal to you?" asked Thutmose.

"The nobility and the army are one."

"What about the nomarchs, the officials? ..."

"You know, Thutmose, even the officials are loyal," said the Prince. "What am I saying—even the Phoenicians! But there are traitors in many other places ..."

"By the gods, not so loud!" whispered Thutmose, looking anxiously into the next room.

"Oho!" laughed the Prince, "why so jumpy? I see it's no secret to you either that we have traitors."

"I know of whom Your Eminence speaks," replied Thutmose, "because you have always been prejudiced."

"Against whom?"

"Against whom! ... I have a good notion. But I thought that after your reconciliation with Herhor, after your long stay at the temple ..."

"What of the temple? There, as everywhere in this land, I've always found the same thing: that the best lands, bravest populace, and immense wealth are not the pharaoh's ..."

"Not so loud!" whispered Thutmose.

"But I'm always keeping quiet, I've always got a cheerful face—why won't you at least let me say my piece? Even in the Supreme Council I would have a right to say that, in this Egypt which belongs indivisibly to my father, I, his Successor and Viceroy, had to borrow a hundred talents from some Tyrian princeling ... What a disgrace!"

"Why these thoughts today?" whispered Thutmose, intent on bringing a swift close to the dangerous conversation.

"Why these thoughts today?" repeated the Prince, again lapsing into silence.

"It would matter little," thought Ramses, "if they deceived only me: I'm but the pharaoh's successor and can't be privy to every secret. But who can assure me that they haven't been treating my venerable father the same way? For thirty-odd years he's trusted them boundlessly, he's humbled himself before wonders, he's made generous offerings to the gods ... so that his wealth and power would pass into the hands of ambitious rogues. And no one has opened his eyes! For, unlike me, the Pharaoh can't go at night to Phoenician temples, as no one has access to His Holiness.

"And who can assure me the priesthood aren't bent on abolishing the throne, as Hiram said? Father told me the Phoenicians are most truthful when they have a stake. And certainly they do have a stake: not to be expelled from Egypt and fall into the power of Assyria ... Assyria is a pack of raging lions! ... Where they pass, nothing remains but ruins and corpses, as after a fire!"

Suddenly Ramses raised his head: he heard distant flutes and horns.

"What's that?" he asked Thutmose.

"Important news!" smiled the courtier. "The Asiatics are welcoming a distinguished pilgrim from far-off Babylon."

"From Babylon? ... Who is it?"

"His name is Sargon."

"Sargon?" interrupted the Prince. "Sargon!... ah! ha! ha!" he broke into laughter. "Who is he?"

"He's supposedly a great dignitary at the court of King Assar. He's bringing along ten elephants, lots of the most beautiful desert steeds, and droves of slaves and servants."

"Why is he coming here?"

"To make obeisance to the goddess Astoreth, who is revered by all of Asia," said Thutmose.

"Ha! ha! ha!" laughed the Prince, recalling Hiram's prediction about the mission of the Assyrian envoy. "Sargon ... ha! ha! ... Sargon, kinsman to King Assar, is suddenly become so pious that he goes on a several months' arduous journey just to worship Astoreth in Pi-Bast! When in Nineveh he would find greater gods and more learned priests ... ha! ha! ha!"

Thutmose was watching the Prince in bewilderment. "What's with you, Ramses?"

"It's a wonder," said the Prince, "surely without like in the chronicles of any temple! Just think, Thutmose, at the very moment you're racking your mind how to nab a thief who keeps robbing you—just then the thief again sticks his hands into your chest, before your very eyes, before a thousand witnesses ... ha! ha! ha! ... Sargon—a pious pilgrim!"

"I don't understand you ..." whispered Thutmose, perplexed.

"Nor need you," replied the Viceroy. "Just remember that Sargon has come to sacred Astoreth for pious devotions."

"It seems to me," said Thutmose, lowering his voice, "that you're talking about very dangerous matters."

"So don't mention them to anyone."

"I daresay the Prince can be sure I won't, but I don't know about you. You're quick as lightning ..."

The Successor placed his hand on Thutmose's shoulder. "Don't worry," he said, looking him in the eye. "Just keep faith with me, you nobility and military, and you'll see strange things happen ... and hard times will end for you!"

"You know we'll go to our deaths at your bidding," said Thutmose, placing his hand on his chest.

In his face there was such uncommon earnestness that the Prince realized, not for the first time, that the frivolous dandy concealed a brave man whose sword and mind could be depended on.

The Prince never again held such a strange conversation with Thutmose. But the faithful friend and retainer guessed that Sargon's arrival concealed great matters of state that were being high-handedly decided by the priests.

For some time, all of Egypt's aristocracy, the nomarchs, the higher officials, and the commanders had been very quietly, but ever so quietly, whispering that important events were coming. The Phoenicians had been telling them, under oaths of secrecy, about treaties with Assyria whereby Phoenicia would perish and Egypt would cover herself with ignominy and likely someday fall vassal to Assyria.

Indignation ran high among the aristocracy, but no one gave himself away. At the Successor's court and at the nomarchs' courts in Lower Egypt, revelry was the order of the day. It might have been supposed that, along with the heat, a madness not merely of conviviality but of debauchery had settled upon them. There was not a day without games, feasts, and triumphal processions; not a night without illuminations and shouting. Not only in Pi-Bast but in every city, it became the fashion to run through the streets with torches, music, and above all with brimming pitchers. Houses were burst into, and the sleeping inhabitants were dragged out for carousal; and since Egyptians had a great penchant for revelry, every living soul made merry.

During Ramses' stay at the Temple of Hathor, the panic-stricken Phoenicians had spent their days praying and had denied everyone credit. But after Hiram's conversation with the Viceroy, piety and caution had suddenly abandoned the Phoenicians and they had begun giving loans to the Egyptian lords more bountifully than ever.

The oldest people could not recall such abundance of gold and goods, or such low interest rates, as now prevailed in Lower Egypt.

The austere, sage priesthood noted the madness of the highest social classes. But they erred in their assessment of its sources; and the holy Mentesuphis, who sent Herhor a report every few days, kept writing that the Crown Prince, wearied of the religious devotions at the Temple of Hathor, was now disporting himself like mad, and with him all the aristocracy.

The Minister did not even respond to these remarks, which indicated that he regarded the Prince's revels a natural, and perhaps even a useful, thing.

From this mood of his closest milieu Ramses gained a great deal of freedom. Almost each evening, as the wine-bemused courtiers were passing out, the Prince stole out of the palace.

Draped in an officer's dark burnoose, he ran through the deserted streets and out of the city, to the gardens of the Temple of Astoreth.

There he sought out his bench opposite Kama's villa and, concealed among the trees, watched the torches burning, listened to the priestess' admirers singing—and dreamed of her.

The moon was rising ever later, approaching its new phase; nights were drab, the light effects were lost; but Ramses still saw the brightness of that first night and heard the passionate strophes of the Greek.

At times he rose from the bench, intending to go straight to Kama's rooms; but he would be overcome with shame. He felt it would be unseemly for the Crown Prince to be seen in the house of a priestess who was visited by any pilgrim who gave the temple a generous offering. Stranger yet, he feared that the sight of Kama surrounded by pitchers and lovelorn admirers might expunge his wonderful vision of that moonlit night.

When Dagon had sent her over to allay the Prince's anger, Kama had seemed to Ramses a fairly attractive young girl, but one over whom a man need hardly lose his head. But when for the first time in his life he, Viceroy and commander, had had to sit outside a woman's house; when he had been beguiled by the night; when he had heard the fervent suit of another man, then, again for the first time in his life, a peculiar feeling had arisen within him: a compound of desire, longing, and envy.

Could he have had Kama at his beck and call, she would very soon have palled on him and he might not even have sought her. But death lurking at the threshold to her bedchamber, the enamored singer, and finally this humbling stance of the highest dignitary in relation to a priestess—all this created a situation hitherto unfamiliar to Ramses, and therefore alluring.

That was why, almost each evening for ten days, he had been coming to the gardens of

Astoreth, concealing his face from passers-by.

One evening, after having had a good deal of wine at a feast in his palace, Ramses slipped out with a firm resolve. He told himself that today he would enter Kama's rooms—and, for all he cared, her admirers could sing away outside her windows.

He walked rapidly through the town, but in the temple gardens he slowed his step: he was again feeling embarrassed.

"Who ever heard," he thought, "of the pharaoh's successor running after women like a poor scribe with no one to lend him ten drachmas? Women have always come to me, and so should this one ..."

He was about to turn back. "But this one can't," he thought, "because they would kill her ..."

He stopped and hesitated.

"Who would kill her? ... Hiram, who doesn't believe in anything; or Dagon, who's not to be believed in anything? ... Yes, but there are many other Phoenicians here, and hundreds of thousands of fanatical, wild pilgrims pass through here. In the eyes of those fools, if Kama visited me, she'd be committing sacrilege."

He again went toward the priestess' villa. It hardly occurred to him he might be in danger here. He who, without drawing his sword, could with a mere glance bring the whole world prostrate to his feet. He, Ramses, in danger!

When the Prince emerged from the trees, he saw that the priestess' house was more brightly lit and noisier than usual. There were many guests in the rooms and on the terraces, and a crowd was milling around outside the villa.

"What bunch is this?" thought the Prince.

It was no everyday gathering. Nearby stood a huge elephant bearing on its back a gilded howdah with purple curtains. Next to the elephant there neighed, squealed, and generally fretted a dozen or more horses with thick necks and legs, tails bound at the bottom, and metal pseudo-helmets on their heads.

Among the restive, almost wild animals there milled several dozen men such as Ramses had never seen. They had shaggy hair, great beards, and peaked caps with earflaps. Some wore ankle-length garments of thick woolen cloth; others, trousers and short overcoats; and some, knee boots. All were armed with swords, bows, and spears.

At sight of the foreigners, powerful, ungainly, laughing coarsely, stinking of suet,[1] and speaking an unfamiliar harsh language, the Prince boiled up. As a lion, though not hungry, yet readies to spring on sighting a strange animal, so Ramses, though these men had never done him harm, felt a terrible hatred for them. He was irritated by their language, their dress, their smell, their very horses. His blood boiled up and he reached for his sword, intending to fall upon the men and kill them and their animals. But he came to his senses.

"Has Set cast a spell on me?" he thought.

Just then an Egyptian clad only in cap and loincloth was passing by. The Prince thought him agreeable, even dear just now, because he was an Egyptian. Ramses took from a bag a gold ring worth over a dozen drachmas and gave it to the slave.

"Listen," he asked, "who are those people?"

"Assyrians," whispered the Egyptian, his eyes flashing hatred.

---

[1] Suet is the fat of beef, lamb, or mutton found around the loins and kidneys. It is used as an ingredient in cooking and to make tallow, the raw material for soaps. *(Translator.)*

"Assyrians!" repeated the Prince. "Those are Assyrians? ... What are they doing here?"

"Their master Sargon is courting a priestess, the holy Kama, and they're guarding him ... May leprosy consume the sons of swine!"

"You may go."

The near-naked man bowed low to Ramses and ran off, doubtless to a kitchen.

"So those are Assyrians?" thought the Prince, watching the outlandish figures and listening to the hateful if incomprehensible speech. "So the Assyrians are already at the Nile to fraternize with us or deceive us, and their dignitary Sargon is courting Kama?"

He turned back homeward. His reverie had expired in the glare of a new, if only stirring, passion. A noble, gentle man, he was feeling a mortal hatred for Egypt's age-old enemies, whom he had encountered for the first time.

When, after leaving the Temple of Hathor and speaking with Hiram, he had begun contemplating war with Asia, it had been only speculation. Egypt needed people, the Pharaoh needed treasure, and since war was the easiest way to obtain both, and since it promised to gratify his need of glory, he had planned himself a war.

But right now he was not concerned with treasure, slaves, or glory, because the voice of hatred, more powerful than aught else, had spoken within him. The pharaohs had fought the Assyrians for so long, both sides had shed so much blood, conflict had sunk such deep roots into hearts, that the Prince reached for his sword at the mere sight of Assyrian soldiers. It seemed as though all the spirits of fallen warriors, all their travails and sufferings, had been resurrected in the soul of the royal scion and called out for vengeance.

On returning to the palace, the Prince summoned Thutmose. The one was in his cups; the other, in high dudgeon.

"Do you know what I just saw?" said the Prince to his favorite.

"A priest?" whispered Thutmose.

"Assyrians ... O gods! What I felt! ... What vile people: their bodies, wrapped head to foot in wool like those of wild beasts, stink of stale suet; and what speech, beards, hair! ..."

He walked rapidly about the room, breathless, feverish.

"I had thought," said Ramses, "that I despised the thievery of the scribes, the cant of the nomarchs, that I hated the cunning, ambitious priests ... I detested the Jews and feared the Phoenicians. But today I realize that those were playthings. Only now do I know what hatred is, after I've seen and heard Assyrians; now I know why the dog tears into the cat that crosses the dog's path."

"Your Eminence is used to the Jews and Phoenicians. You've encountered Assyrians for the first time," said Thutmose.

"Never mind the Phoenicians!" the Prince went on, as if to himself. "The Phoenician, the Philistine, the Shasu, the Libyan, even the Ethiopian are like members of our family. When they don't pay their tributes, we get angry at them; when they pay up, we forgive and forget ..."

"But the Assyrian is something so alien, so hostile ... I won't be content till I see a field covered with their corpses, till I count a hundred thousand severed hands ..."

Thutmose had never seen Ramses like this.

CHAPTER 33

A couple of days later, the Prince sent Thutmose with a summons to Kama. She arrived immediately in a tightly curtained litter.

Ramses received her in a private room.

"The other evening," he said, "I was outside your house."

"O Astoreth!" cried the priestess. "To what do I owe the supreme favor? And what prevented Your Eminence from deigning to call your slave?"

"There were some brutes there. I gather, Assyrians."

"Your Eminence troubled yourself in the evening? I'd never have dared suppose our ruler was a few paces from me under the open heavens."

The Prince blushed. How surprised she would have been to learn that the Prince had spent some ten evenings outside her windows!

But perhaps she did know, to judge by her half-smiling lips and slyly downcast eyes.

"So now, Kama," said the Prince, "you're entertaining Assyrians?"

"He's a great magnate!" cried Kama. "He is Sargon, kinsman to the king, and he offered five talents to our goddess."

"And you will return the favor, Kama," taunted the Successor. "And since he's such a generous magnate, the Phoenician gods won't punish you with death."

"What are you saying, lord?" she replied, clasping her hands. "Don't you know that an Asiatic, though he found me in the desert, wouldn't lift a hand to me, even were I to offer myself to him? They fear the gods ..."

"Then why does this stinking ... this pious ... Asiatic visit you?"

"He wants to get me to move to the Babylonian temple of Astoreth."

"And will you?"

"Yes ... if your lordship bids me go," answered Kama, veiling her face.

The Prince silently took her hand. His lips trembled.

"Don't touch me, lord," she whispered. "You are the master and mainstay of myself and all the Phoenicians in this land ... but be merciful ..."

The Viceroy released her and proceeded to pace the room.

"Hot day, isn't it?" he said. "I hear there are countries where, in the month of Mechir, a white fluff falls from the sky onto the ground and, in fire, turns to water and produces cold. Oh, Kama, ask your gods to send me some of that fluff! ... Though, what am I saying? ... Were they to cover all Egypt with it, all that fluff would turn to water but it wouldn't cool my heart."

"That is because you are as the god Amon, you are the sun in human guise," replied Kama. "Darkness flies whence you turn your face, and flowers grow in the radiance of your gaze."

The Prince again approached her.

"But be merciful," she whispered. "You are a good god and cannot harm your priestess."

The Prince moved away again and shook himself as if to cast off a burden. Kama watched him from beneath lowered eyelids and smiled slightly.

When the silence had lasted overlong, she said: "Your Lordship bade me summoned. I am here and await your pleasure."

"Aha!" the Prince roused himself. "Tell me, now, priestess ... Aha! ... Who was that looka-like of mine whom I saw in your temple that time?"

Kama placed a finger to her lips. "It's a holy secret," she whispered.

"One thing is a secret, another is forbidden," replied Ramses. "At least tell me which it was: a man or a spirit?"

"A spirit."

"And this spirit sang outside your windows?"

Kama smiled.

"I don't want to violate the secrets of your temple ..." continued the Prince.

"Your lordship promised that to Hiram," interjected the priestess.

"All right ... all right!" interrupted the exasperated Viceroy. "I won't talk with Hiram or anyone else about this wonder, just you. Well, Kama, you tell this spirit or man who looks so much like me to leave Egypt with all speed and not to show himself to anybody. You see, no kingdom can have two successors to the throne."

Suddenly he slapped his forehead. He had been speaking this way to aggravate Kama, but now a quite serious thought had come to him.

"I wonder," he said, looking sharply at Kama, "why your countrymen showed me my living image. Do they mean to warn me that they have a replacement for me? ... Truly I am astonished."

Kama fell to his feet. "Oh, lord!" she whispered. "You who wear our highest talisman on your chest, can you suppose the Phoenicians would do anything to harm you? But only think ... If you were in danger or wanted to mislead your enemies, might such a man not be useful? That is all that the Phoenicians wanted to show you in the temple."

The Prince reflected and shrugged. "Yes," he told himself. "As if I needed anyone's help! ... Do the Phoenicians think I can't manage on my own? If so, they've picked them-selves the wrong patron."

"Lord," whispered Kama, "don't you know that Ramses the Great had two doubles for his enemies? Those two royal shades perished, and he lived."

"Enough!" interrupted the Prince. "Kama, so that the peoples of Asia may know they enjoy my favor, I'm allotting five talents for games in honor of Astoreth, and a sumptuous cup for her temple. You'll receive this today."

He nodded good day to the priestess.

After her departure, a new stream of thought came over him:

"The Phoenicians are indeed cunning. If this living image of mine is a man, they could make me a great gift of him, and someday I could work wonders unheard-of in Egypt.

The Pharaoh resides in Memphis but simultaneously turns up in Thebes or Tanis![1] The Pharaoh advances with an army on Babylon, the Assyrians mass their main forces there—while the Pharaoh captures Nineveh with a second army. I expect the Assyrians would be very surprised at such a turn of events."

Once again he felt a blind hatred for the powerful Asiatics, and saw his triumphal chariot crossing a battlefield full of Assyrian corpses, and baskets full of severed hands.

War had now become as much a necessity to his soul as bread was to his body. Through war he could not only enrich Egypt, fill the treasury, and win everlasting glory—but he could satisfy a hitherto dormant, today powerfully aroused, instinct to destroy Assyria.

Until he had seen those warriors with the shaggy beards, he hadn't thought about them. But now they were in his way. The world was too small for both him and them. Someone had to give way: it was him or them.

He did not realize the role that Hiram and Kama had played in his present mood. He only felt that he must have war with Assyria, as a bird of passage feels it must fly north in the month of Pachon.

The passion for war gripped the Prince quickly. He spoke less, smiled less often, sat brooding at feasts, and increasingly consorted with the military and the aristocracy. Seeing the favors that the Viceroy lavished on those who bore arms, noble youths and even older men began enlisting in regiments. This drew the attention of the holy Mentesuphis, who epistled Herhor:

"Since the arrival of the Assyrians in Pi-Bast, the Successor has been feverish, and his court very bellicosely disposed. They drink and play dice as before, but all have cast off their sheer apparel and wigs and, notwithstanding the awful heat, go about in soldiers' caps and tunics.

"I fear lest this armed readiness offend His Eminence Sargon."

Herhor immediately answered:

"There is no harm in our effeminate nobility taking a fancy to things military during the stay of the Assyrians, as it will give them a better opinion of us. His Eminence the Viceroy, evidently enlightened by the gods, has divined that this is the time to rattle swords when we have among us the envoys of such a warlike nation.

"I am sure this brave disposition of our young men will give Sargon pause and make him more amenable in the negotiations."

For the first time a young Egyptian prince had beguiled the vigilance of the priests. To be sure, behind him stood the Phoenicians, along with the secret of the treaty with Assyria, acquired by the Phoenicians—something that the priests did not even suspect.

But the Successor's best mask vis-a-vis the priestly dignitaries was his desultoriness. Everyone remembered how easily, the previous year, he had shifted from the Pi-Bailos maneuvers to Sara's quiet farm; and how, of late, he had enthused by turns over feasts, administrative affairs, and piety, to return again to feasts. Thus, except for Thutmose, no one would have believed that this desultory youth had a plan, a watchword for which he would strive with indomitable resolve.

This time, new evidence of the lability of Ramses' fancies was not long in coming.

---

[1] Tanis: an ancient city in the northeastern Nile Delta, on the Nile's long-since silted-up Tanitic branch. (Translator.)

Despite the heat, Sara arrived in Pi-Bast with the whole court and her son. She was a little thin, the infant a little sickly or tired, but both looked lovely.

The Prince was delighted. He gave Sara a house in the most beautiful part of the palace garden and sat practically whole days at his son's cradle.

Shelved were feasts, maneuvers, and Ramses' broodings. The gentlemen of his retinue had to drink and party by themselves, very quickly ungirded their swords, and changed into their best finery. The change of dress was the more essential as the Prince would take several of them at a time to Sara's to show off his son.

"See, Thutmose," he said to his favorite, "what a beautiful child he is: a veritable rose petal. And this little mite is going to grow into a man! Someday this pink nestling will walk, talk, and learn in the priest schools.

"Do you see his little hands, Thutmose?" cried Ramses in rapture. "Remember these little hands, to tell of them someday when I give him a regiment and have him carry my ax after him ... And this is my son, my very own son!"

Little wonder, when the lord spoke this way, that his courtiers regretted they could not become nannies, even wet nurses, to the infant, which, though possessed of no dynastic rights, was nevertheless the first-born son of the future pharaoh.

But the idyl ended very soon, as it did not comport with the interests of the Phoenicians.

His Eminence Hiram came one day to the palace with a great entourage of merchants, slaves, and Egyptian almsmen, and addressed the Successor:

"Our gracious lord! To give evidence that your heart abounds in favor as well for us Asiatics, you have granted us five talents to organize games in honor of the goddess Astoreth. Your will is accomplished, we have prepared the games, and now we come to beg you to honor them with your presence."

With that, the gray-haired Tyrian Prince knelt before Ramses and presented him, on a gold tray, a gold key to an amphitheater box.

Ramses gladly accepted the invitation, and the holy priests Mephres and Mentesuphis had nothing against the Prince taking part in festivities honoring the goddess Astoreth.

"In the first place," His Eminence Mephres told Mentesuphis, "Astoreth corresponds to our Isis and the Chaldeans' Ishtar. Secondly, since we let the Asiatics build a temple on our soil, it behooves us to extend an occasional courtesy to their gods."

"Indeed, we have an obligation to do the Phoenicians a small good turn after making such a treaty with Assyria!" laughed His Eminence Mentesuphis.

The amphitheater to which the Viceroy repaired with the nomarch and foremost officers at four in the afternoon stood in the garden of the Temple of Astoreth. It comprised a circular arena enclosed by a fence the height of two men, with numerous boxes and benches rising amphitheatrically outside the fence. The structure had no roof, but stretched over the boxes were varicolored sheets shaped like butterfly wings, sprinkled with fragrant water, which were flapped to cool the air.

When the Viceroy appeared in his box, the Asiatics and Egyptians in the amphitheater raised a great cheer. Then the show began with a procession of musicians, singers, and dancing girls.

The Prince looked about. On his right was the box of Hiram and the leading Phoenicians; on his left, the box of the Phoenician priests and priestesses, among whom Kama, in one of the first places, drew attention by her rich costume and beauty. She wore a diaphanous gown adorned with multicolored embroidery, gold bracelets and anklets, and a headband with a lotus blossom artfully fashioned in precious stones.

Kama, having made the Prince a deep bow with her colleagues, turned to the box on the left and struck up a lively conversation with a foreigner of splendid bearing and somewhat graying hair. He and his companions had hair and beards plaited into a host of little braids.

Ramses, who had come to the amphitheater almost straight from his son's room, had been in a cheerful mood. But when he saw Kama conversing with the stranger, he turned somber.

"Do you know," he asked Thutmose, "who that ruffian is that the priestess is making up to?"

"That is the distinguished Babylonian pilgrim, His Eminence Sargon."

"What an old man!" said the Prince.

"He's no doubt older than the two of us put together, but he's a handsome man."

"Can such a barbarian be handsome?" objected the Viceroy. "I'm sure he stinks of suet!"

They both fell silent: the Prince, from anger; Thutmose, from dismay at having praised a man his lord disliked.

Meanwhile, in the arena, spectacle followed spectacle. By turns, there performed gymnasts, snake charmers, dancers, jugglers, and clowns, eliciting the spectators' cries of applause.

But the Viceroy was somber. Two dormant passions had revived in his soul: hatred of the Assyrians, and jealousy over Kama.

"How," he thought, "can that woman ogle an old man with a face the color of tanned leather, restless dark eyes, and a goat's beard?"

Only once did the Prince give much attention to the arena.

Several half-naked Chaldeans had entered. The eldest planted three short spears in the ground, sharp end up, and with motions of his hands he put the youngest to sleep. Then the others picked up the latter and laid him across the spears so that one spear supported his head, another the small of his back, the third his legs.

The sleeping man was stiff as a board. The old man made several more passes over him with his hands—and removed the spear supporting his legs. After a moment he pulled out the spear holding up his back, and finally he knocked away the one on which rested his head.

And it came to pass in broad daylight, before several thousand witnesses, that the sleeping Chaldean lay in the air without any support, a couple of cubits above the ground. Finally the old man pushed him to the ground and roused him.

Astonishment reigned in the amphitheater; no one dared to shout or clap. Flowers were thrown from a couple of boxes.

Ramses, too, was amazed. He leaned over to Hiram's box and whispered to the old Prince: "Could you work this wonder at the Temple of Astoreth?"

"I don't know all the secrets of our priests," he replied in confusion, "but I know the Chaldeans are very cunning."

"We all saw the young man lie in the air."

"If a spell was not cast on us," said Hiram grudgingly, losing his humor.

After a brief intermission during which fresh flowers, cold wine, and pastries were distributed to the dignitaries' boxes, the main spectacle began—the bullfights.

To trumpets, drums, and flutes, a stout bull was led into the arena with a cloth over its head so it would not see. Then several near-naked men ran in with spears, and one with a short sword.

At a sign from the Prince the attendants ran off, and one of the armed men pulled the cloth off the bull's head. For a few moments the beast stood dazed, then it began chasing the spearmen who goaded it with their weapons.

The futile combat dragged on for a quarter of an hour. The men tormented the bull, and the bull, angry and bloodied, reared and chased its foes over the arena, unable to catch them.

At last it fell amid the laughter of the public.

The bored Prince, rather than watch the arena, was looking at the box of the Phoenician priests. And he saw that Kama, having taken a seat closer to Sargon, was conducting an animated conversation with him. The Assyrian was devouring her with his eyes, and she, smiling and abashed, at times whispered with him, leaning in so that her hair mingled with the shaggy barbarian's, at times turned away from him in mock anger.

Ramses felt a pain in his heart. It was the first time that a woman had given another man precedence over him. An almost old man, too, an Assyrian!

Meanwhile a murmur spread among the public. In the arena the swordsman asked to have his left arm bound to his chest, the spearmen looked over their weapons—and a second bull was brought in.

When one of the armed men pulled the cloth from its eyes, the bull turned and looked about as though to tally its opponents. When they began jabbing it, it drew back to the fence to secure its rear. Then it lowered its head and followed the movements of the men harassing it.

At first the armed men cautiously stole up from the sides to jab it. But as the beast continued motionless, they became bolder and began darting ever closer in front of it.

The bull lowered its head still more but stood seemingly rooted to the ground. The public began laughing, but suddenly its mirth transmuted into a cry of horror. The bull had picked the moment, lunged heavily, struck a spearman, and with a single blow of its horns had tossed him into the air.

The man fell to the ground with shattered bones, and the bull cantered over to the other side of the arena to resume a defensive stance.

The spearmen again surrounded and goaded it, while amphitheater attendants ran into the arena to pick up the injured man, who was groaning. The bull, despite redoubled spear thrusts, stood stock-still; but when three attendants had lifted the fainted warrior to their arms, it hurled itself like a whirlwind at the group, knocked them down, and proceeded to kick them savagely.

The public was plunged into turmoil: women wept; men cursed and threw at the bull whatever was to hand. Canes, knives, even bench boards rained into the arena.

The swordsman ran up to the enraged beast. But the spearmen lost their heads and failed to back him properly, and the bull knocked him down and began chasing the others.

Something unheard-of in amphitheaters had happened: five men lay in the arena; the others fled the beast, defending themselves poorly; and the public howled their anger or horror.

Suddenly a hush fell, the spectators rose and leaned forward, a terrified Hiram turned pale and spread his hands. Two men had jumped into the arena from the dignitaries' boxes: Prince Ramses with a drawn sword, and Sargon with a hatchet.

The bull ran round the arena, head lowered and tail cocked, kicking up a cloud of dust. It headed straight for the Prince but, seemingly deflected by the majesty of the royal scion, passed Ramses by, hurled itself at Sargon—and fell on the spot. The dextrous, tremendously strong Assyrian had dropped it with a single hatchet blow between the eyes.

The public howled their delight and showered Sargon and his victim with flowers. Ramses stood by with his drawn sword, astonished and angry, watching as Kama snatched flowers from her neighbors to throw at the Assyrian.

Sargon received the public adulation with indifference. He nudged the bull with his foot to see whether it might still be alive, then approached to within a couple of steps of the Prince and, pronouncing something in his own language, bowed with the dignity of a great lord.

A sanguineous fog passed before Ramses' eyes: he would gladly have plunged his sword into the victor's chest. But he mastered himself, thought a moment and, taking the gold chain from round his neck, handed it to Sargon.

The Assyrian bowed again, kissed the chain, and placed it on his own neck. The Prince, his cheeks livid, proceeded to the performers' gate and, amid the cheers of the public, deeply humiliated, left the amphitheater.

CHAPTER 34

I t was now the month of Thoth (late June, early July).[1] The influx of people to Pi-Bast and the vicinity had begun falling off due to the heat. Ramses' courtiers still disported themselves and talked of the events in the amphitheater.

The courtiers extolled the Prince's daring, the maladroit admired Sargon's strength, the priests whispered with serious mien that the Crown Prince should not have involved himself in the bullfights. There were other people, paid to do that kind of work and hardly favored with public esteem.

Ramses either did not hear the various opinions or paid no attention to them. Two episodes from the amphitheater were fixed in his memory: the Assyrian had snatched victory over the bull from him—and had flirted with Kama, who had received his attentions very favorably!

Since it would have been unseemly to bring the Phoenician priestess to his quarters, he wrote her, saying he wanted to see her and asking when she would receive him. By return messenger Kama replied that she would await him that evening.

Hardly had the stars appeared when the Prince in the greatest secrecy, as he thought, slipped out of the palace.

The garden of the Temple of Astoreth was nearly deserted, particularly in the vicinity of the priestess' villa. The house was quiet, and barely a couple of small lights burned inside.

When the Prince knocked diffidently, the priestess personally opened the door. In the dark entry she kissed his hands, whispering that she would have died had the enraged beast in the arena harmed him.

"But now you must be easy," retorted the Successor, "since your lover saved me."

When they entered an illuminated room, the Prince saw that Kama was crying.

"What's this?" he asked.

"My lord's heart has turned away from me," she said. "And maybe rightly."

The Successor laughed out bitterly. "Then are you already his mistress, or are you going to be, you holy virgin?"

"Mistress? ... Never! ... But I may become wife to this terrible man."

Ramses sprang up from his seat. "Am I dreaming?" he cried, "or has Set cast a spell on me? You, a priestess who tends the fire at the altar of Astoreth and must remain virgin on pain of death—you're to marry? Truly, Phoenician lies are worse than people say!"

---

[1] Actually, the ancient Egyptian month of Thoth lay between September 11 and October 10 of the modern, Gregorian calendar. *(Translator.)*

"Hear me out, lord," she said, wiping her tears, "and condemn me if I deserve it. Sargon wants to take me as his wife, as his first wife. Under our laws, in very exceptional cases a priestess may marry, but only a man descended of royal blood. And Sargon is kin by marriage to King Assar."

"And you'll marry him?"

"If the Supreme Council of Tyrian Priests orders me to, then what can I do?" she replied, again dissolving in tears.

"What does the Council care about Sargon?" asked the Prince.

"Apparently it cares a great deal," she sighed. "The Assyrians are expected to take over Phoenicia, and Sargon is supposed to become her satrap."[2]

"You're out of your mind!" exclaimed the Prince.

"I'm telling you what I know. Already prayers are starting at our temple for the second time to avert disaster from Phoenicia. The first time we held them was before your lordship arrived here."

"Why again now?"

"Reportedly the Chaldean priest Istubar has lately arrived in Egypt with letters in which King Assar names Sargon his envoy plenipotentiary to make a treaty with you for the annexation of Phoenicia."

"But I ..." interrupted the Prince.

He was going to say "know nothing about it" but checked himself. He started to laugh and replied: "Kama, I swear to you on my father's honor that, so long as I live, Assyria isn't going to take over Phoenicia. Is that good enough?"

"Oh, lord! ... lord! ..." she cried, falling to his feet.

"So now you won't marry this boor?"

"Oh!" she shuddered. "Need you ask?"

"You'll be mine," whispered the Prince.

"Do you want my death?" she said, terrified. "Well! If that is your wish, I'm ready ..."

"I want you to live," he whispered passionately. "To live and be mine ..."

"That's impossible."

"What about the Supreme Council of Tyrian Priests?"

"It can only give me in marriage."

"You'll enter my house ..."

"If I entered it not as your wife, I would die. But I'm ready ... even not to see tomorrow's sun."

"Don't worry," answered the Prince solemnly. "Whoever possesses my favor, will never know harm."

Kama again knelt before him. "How can it happen?" she asked, clasping her hands.

Ramses was so excited, had so forgotten his office and obligations, that he was ready to promise the priestess marriage. He was prevented from taking that step only by some sheer instinct.

"How can it be? ... How can it be?" whispered Kama, devouring him with her eyes and kissing his feet.

---

[2] Satrap: the governor of a province in ancient Media and Persia, beginning in the 7th century BCE—four centuries after *Pharaoh*'s present time. Use of the term "satrap" here is thus an anatopism and an anachronism. *(Translator.)*

The Prince lifted her up, seated her at a distance from him, and replied with a smile:

"You ask how it can be ... I'll tell you. My last teacher before I came of age was an old priest who knew by heart many curious stories about the lives of gods, kings, priests, even lowly officials and peasants.

"This old man, famous for his piety and wonder-working, for some reason disliked women—indeed, feared them. He would describe women's perversity and once, to illustrate what a powerful hold you have over menfolk, he told me this story:

"A poor young scribe without a copper deben in his bag—all he had was a barley cake—was wending his way from Thebes down to Lower Egypt in search of remunerative work. He'd been told that the richest lords and merchants lived in that part of the Kingdom and that, with a bit of luck, he might find a position in which he would make his fortune.

"So he was walking along the Nile (he lacked boat fare) and was thinking:

"'How improvident are those who inherit a talent, two talents, maybe ten, from their fathers and, instead of multiplying their wealth by trading in goods or by lending out at high interest, squander their fortunes on who knows what! Now, if I had a drachma ... No, a drachma is too little. But if I had a talent or better yet a bit of land, I would increase it from year to year and by the end of my life I would be as rich as the richest nomarch.

"'But what's to be done!' he sighed. 'The gods clearly look out only for fools; whereas I'm full of wisdom from my wig down to my bare heels. If in my heart there be a bit of stupidity, then it's in this one respect, that truly I wouldn't know how to squander away a fortune—I wouldn't know how to begin going about such a godless deed!'

"Thus meditating, the poor scribe was passing a mud hut before which sat a man, neither young nor old, with very keen eyes that saw to the depths of the heart. The scribe, who was wise as a stork, immediately realized that this must be a god, and he bowed and said:

"'I greet you, worshipful owner of this beautiful house, and I regret that I have no wine or meat to share with you in token that I esteem you and that all that I have is yours.'

"Amon (he it was in human guise) liked the courtesy of the young scribe. He looked at him and asked:

"'Of what were you thinking as you were coming here? I see wisdom in your brow, and I am one who gathers words of truth as the partridge gathers grains of wheat.'

"The scribe sighed. 'I was thinking,' he said, 'of my poverty and of those improvident rich who squander fortunes who knows on what or how.

"'You wouldn't squander one?' asked the god in human guise.

"'Look at me, lord,' said the scribe. 'I wear a tattered robe and have lost my sandals on the way, but papyrus and inkwell I always carry with me like my heart. For as I rise and as I lay me down to sleep, I repeat that indigent wisdom is better than stupid wealth.

"'If that is how I am—if I can express myself in the two scripts[3] and carry out the most complex calculations, if I know all the plants and animals under heaven—then can you suppose that I, who am possessed of such knowledge, would be capable of frittering away a fortune?'

"The god reflected and said: 'Your speech flows as smoothly as the Nile at Memphis, but if you truly are so learned, then write for me in the two scripts: "Amon."'

---

[3] "The two scripts": presumably meant are hieroglyphic script and hieratic script. The two writing systems developed concurrently, beginning in Egypt's Proto-Dynastic Period. A later development of hieratic script was demotic script. *(Translator.)*

"The scribe took out his inkwell and brush, and in a short time he had written on the door of the hut in the two scripts, 'Amon,' so clearly that even the dumb animals stopped to pay their respects to the Lord.

"The god was well-pleased and added:

"'If you are equally proficient at calculating as at writing, then calculate me the following transaction: If for one partridge they give me four chicken eggs, then how many chicken eggs should they give for seven partridges?'

"The scribe collected some pebbles, laid them out in rows, and before the sun had set he answered that seven partridges should bring twenty-eight chicken eggs.

"Almighty Amon smiled to see before him a sage of such uncommon measure, and he said:

"'I see that you spoke the truth about your learning. If you prove equally constant in virtue, I will make you happy to the end of your life, and following your death your sons will place your shade in a beautiful tomb. Now say what wealth you desire which you not only would not squander but would multiply.'

"The scribe fell to the feet of the beneficent god and replied: 'If I but possessed this hut and four measures of land, I would be rich.'

"'Alright,' says the god, 'but first look around and see whether this will suffice you.'

"He conducted him into the hut and said:

"'You have here four caps and aprons, two cloaks for inclement weather, and two pairs of sandals. Here is a fireplace, here a bench to sleep on, a mortar for grinding wheat, and a trough for kneading dough.'

"'What is that?' asked the scribe, indicating a figure draped in linen.

"'That,' said the god, 'is the one thing you mustn't touch, or you will lose all your fortune.'

"'Oh!' shouted the scribe. 'It can stand there a thousand years, and I won't touch it. By Your Honor's leave: what manor do I see over there?'

"He leaned out the window of the hut.

"'Wisely spoken,' said Amon. 'That is indeed a manor, and a nice one too. There is the spacious house, fifty measures of land, over a dozen head of cattle, and ten slaves. If you'd rather have that manor ...'

"The scribe fell to the feet of the god. 'Is there,' he asked, 'anyone under the sun who wouldn't prefer a wheat roll over a barley cake?'

"At this, Amon pronounced a spell, and instantly they found themselves in the grand manor house.

"'You have here,' said the god, 'a carved bed, five tables, and ten chairs. You have here embroidered clothes, wine vats and wine glasses, you have here an oil lamp and a litter ...'

"'What is that?' asked the scribe, indicating a figure that stood in a corner, draped in muslin.

"'That is the one thing you mustn't touch,' replied the god, 'if you're not to lose all your fortune.'

"'Should I live ten thousand years,' cried the scribe, 'I'll never touch it! For, after learning, I consider wealth to be the next best thing.

"'But what do I see over there?' he asked after a moment, indicating a huge palace within a garden.

"'That is a princely estate,' replied the god. 'There is the palace, five hundred measures of land, a hundred slaves, and a couple of hundred head of cattle. It's a great estate, but if you think your wisdom equal to it ...'

"The scribe again fell to Amon's feet, dissolving in tears of joy.

"'Oh, Lord!' he called. 'What madman would not prefer a vat of wine over a cup of beer?'

"'Your words are worthy of a sage who solves the most difficult calculations,' said Amon.

"He pronounced the great words of a spell, and they found themselves inside the palace.

"'You have here,' said the good god, 'a dining hall with gilt couches and chairs, and tables inlaid with many-colored woods. Down below is a kitchen for five cooks, a pantry stocked with every sort of meat, fish, and cake, and a cellar of the finest wine. You have here a bedroom with a mobile roof with which your slaves will cool you as you sleep. Note the bed, which is of cedar and rests on four lion's paws artfully cast in bronze. You have here a dressing room full of linen and woolen garments; and in the chests you'll find rings, chains, and bracelets ...'

"'What is that?' asked the scribe suddenly, indicating a figure draped in a veil embroidered in gold and purple.

"'That is what you should most beware of,' replied the god. 'If you touch it, your enormous fortune will be lost. And truly I tell you, there are not many such estates in Egypt. For I must add that the treasury holds ten talents in gold and precious stones.'

"'My Lord!' shouted the scribe. 'Let me put your holy statue in the foremost place in this palace, and three times daily I will burn incense before it.'

"'Only avoid that!' replied Amon, indicating the veiled figure.

"'I must needs lose my mind and be worse than a wild pig for which wine is as hogwash,' said the scribe. 'Let the figure in the veil languish there a hundred thousand years, and I won't touch it if that be your will ...'

"'Mind, you would lose everything!' cried the god, vanishing.

"The fortunate scribe proceeded to walk about his palace and look out the windows. He inspected the treasury and weighed the gold in his hands: it was heavy; he looked at the precious stones—they were genuine. He ordered food: immediately slaves ran in, bathed him, shaved him, and dressed him in sheer garments.

"He ate and drank his fill as never before: his hunger combined with the excellence of the viands to produce one prodigious gusto. He lit incense before the statue of Amon and dressed it in fresh flowers. Then he sat down at a window.

"A pair of horses harnessed to a carved chariot were neighing in the courtyard. Elsewhere a group of men with spears and nets were calming the unruly hunting dogs eager for the chase. In front of the granary, a scribe was taking receipt of grain from husbandmen; in front of the cattle barn, another scribe was receiving an account from the overseer of herders.

"Visible in the distance were an olive grove, a tall grape-covered hill, stands of wheat, and date palms planted thickly about all the fields.

"'Forsooth!' he told himself, 'today I am wealthy even as I deserved to be. What amazes me is that I could endure so many years in abasement and privation. And I must own,' he continued, 'I don't know whether I'll be able to increase this enormous fortune, for neither do I need more, nor will I have time to pursue speculations.'

"However, he began to be bored in the rooms, so he inspected the garden, rode about the fields, talked to the servants, who prostrated themselves before him on their stomachs though they were so dressed that only yesterday he would have deemed it an honor to have kissed their hands. But being bored there as well, he returned to the palace and looked over his pantry and cellar and the furnishings in the rooms.

"'This is nice,' he told himself, 'but solid-gold furniture and pitchers fashioned of precious stones would have been more beautiful.'

"His eyes turned involuntarily to the corner where the figure in the embroidered veil stood—sighing.

"'Go ahead and sigh!' he thought, taking a censer to burn incense before the statue of Amon.

"'It's a good god,' he thought, 'who appreciates the attainments of sages, even barefoot ones, and does justice by them. What a beautiful estate he's given me! Well, it's true, I honored him, writing the name 'Amon' in the two scripts on the door of the hut. And how beautifully I calculated for him how many chicken eggs he would get for seven partridges. My teachers were right when they said that learning opens the mouths even of the gods.'

"He glanced again at the corner. The veiled figure heaved another sigh.

"'I wonder,' said the scribe to himself, 'why my friend Amon forbade me to touch that little thing standing over in the corner? Well, for an estate like this he had a right to set me conditions; though I wouldn't do anything like that to him. Because if this entire palace is my property, if I may use everything that's here, then why may I not so much as touch that thing?

"'That's what they always say: mustn't touch! But one may at least have a look.'

"He approached the figure, carefully removed the veil, looked ... it's something very pretty. Like a beautiful young boy, only not a boy. It has knee-length hair, petite features, and a sweet gaze.

"'What are you?' he says to the figure.

"'I am Woman,' the figure answers him, in a voice so thin that it insinuated itself into his heart like a Phoenician dagger.

"'Woman?' thinks the scribe. 'They didn't teach me about that at priest school.' ... 'Woman?' he repeated. 'What's this you have here?'

"'Those are my eyes.'

"'Eyes? ... What can you see with eyes like that, which could melt away from the faintest light?'

"'My eyes are not for me to look with, but for you to look into,' answered the figure.

"'Strange sort of eyes!' said the scribe to himself, walking about the room.

"He again stopped in front of the figure, and asked: 'And what's this you have here?'

"'That is my mouth.'

"'By the gods! You'll starve to death,' he cried, 'you can't eat your fill with such a small mouth!'

"'It's not for eating with,' replied the figure, 'but for you to kiss.'

"'Kiss?' repeated the scribe. 'They didn't teach me that either at priest school. And this here ... what's this you have here?'

"'Those are my handkins.'

"'Handkins? It's good you didn't say they're hands, because you couldn't get anything done with hands like that, not even milk a ewe.'

"'My handkins aren't for doing work.'

"'Then what are they for?' said the perplexed scribe, spreading her fingers."

("As I'm spreading yours, Kama," said the Successor, fondling the priestess' little hand.)

"'Then what are such hands for?' the scribe asked the figure."

"'For me to embrace your neck with.'"

"'You mean, take me by the scruff of the neck?" shrieked the terrified scribe, whom the priests had always grabbed by the scruff of the neck when he was to be caned.

"'No, not the scruff of the neck,' said the figure, 'but like so ...'

"And," continued the Prince, "she embraced his neck like so ..." (He placed the priestess' arms round his neck.) "And she snuggled him to her breast like so ..." (He snuggled up to Kama.)

"What are you doing, lord?" whispered Kama. "That is my death ..."

"Don't worry," replied the Prince, "I'm just showing you what the figure did with the scribe ...

"... Suddenly the earth trembled, the palace vanished, the dogs, horses, and slaves vanished. The grape-covered hill turned to bedrock, the olive trees to briars, the wheat to sand ...

"When the scribe woke in the arms of his mistress, he realized he was as poor as he had been the day before on the highway. But he didn't regret the loss of his wealth, because he had a woman who loved and caressed him."

"Everything vanished except for her!" exclaimed Kama naively.

"Merciful Amon left her to him as a consolation," said the Prince.

"Then Amon was merciful only to the scribe," replied Kama. "But what's the point of the story?"

"Guess. You heard what the poor scribe gave up for a woman's kiss."

"But he wouldn't give up the throne!" interrupted the priestess.

"Who knows? ... if he were asked to very nicely ..." whispered Ramses passionately.

"Oh, no!" cried Kama, tearing herself from his embrace. "He'd better not give up the throne, or what would become of his promises to Phoenicia?"

They looked into one another's eyes a long, long time. The Prince felt as it were a wound in his heart, and from that wound a certain feeling as it were escaped him. Not passion, for passion remained—but respect for and faith in Kama.

"These Phoenician women are strange," thought the Successor, "you can go mad about them, but there's no trusting them."

He felt weary and bade Kama goodnight. He looked about the room as though he found it difficult to part with; and as he was leaving, he told himself: "Still you'll be mine, and the Phoenician gods won't kill you if they care for their temples and priests."

Scarcely had Ramses left Kama's villa when into the priestess' room there burst a young Greek, strikingly handsome and a striking look-alike of the Egyptian Prince. His face was a picture of fury.

"Lykon!"[4] cried Kama, terrified. "What are you doing here?"

"Snake in the grass!" replied the Greek in his sonorous voice. "It's not been a month

[4] Lykon (properly *Lykaon*; also spelled *Lycon*): name borrowed from a character in Homer's *Iliad*—a son of Troy's King Priam who was captured and sold by Achilles. On Lykaon's redemption and return to Troy, he is slain in battle by a wrathful Achilles who is mourning the death of his friend Patroklos. *(Translator.)*

since the evening you swore you loved me, that you would elope with me to Greece, and already you're flinging yourself on another lover's neck ... Have the gods died, or has justice forsaken them?"

"Jealous madman," interrupted the priestess, "you'll be the death of me!"

"Certainly it will be me who will kill you, not that stone goddess of yours. With these hands, "he cried, extending hands like talons, "I'll strangle you, if you become his mistress."

"Whose mistress?"

"How would I know! Probably both the old Assyrian's and this princeling's, whose head I'll smash with a rock if he keeps coming here ... The Prince! ... He's got all the women of Egypt and he still hankers after foreign priestesses. Priestesses are for priests, not foreigners ..."

Kama had regained her composure. "Aren't you a foreigner to us?" she said haughtily.

"Viper!" the Greek burst out again. "I can't be a foreigner to you, when I turn my god-given voice to the service of your gods. How often have you used my person to deceive the stupid Asiatics into believing that the Egyptian Crown Prince secretly professes your faith? ..."

"Hush! ... Hush!" hissed the priestess, stopping his mouth with her hand.

There must have been something spell-binding in her touch, for the Greek calmed down and spoke more quietly:

"Listen, Kama. Soon now a Greek ship skippered by my brother will be arriving in the Bay of Sebennytos. Get the high priest to send you to Xois, and from there we'll elope to northern Greece, to a place which has never seen Phoenicians."

"It will see them, if I take refuge there," interrupted the priestess.

"If a hair fell from your head," whispered the furious Greek, "I swear that Dagon ... that all the Phoenicians here will give their heads or die in the mines! They'll find out what a Greek is made of."

"And I tell you," replied the priestess in the same tone of voice, "that until I've collected twenty talents, I'm not budging from here. And I only have eight ..."

"Where will you get the rest?"

"From Sargon and the Viceroy."

"Sargon, alright, but not the Prince!"

"Silly Lykon, don't you see why I like that youngster a bit? ... He looks like you!"

The Greek became completely calm. "Now, now!" he muttered. "I know that when a woman has a choice between the Successor and a singer like me, I have nothing to fear. But I'm jealous and impulsive, so please don't encourage familiarities from him."

He kissed her, slipped out of the villa, and disappeared into the dark garden.

Kama extended after him her clenched fist. "Wretched clown!" she whispered, "You could barely be my singing slave!"

CHAPTER 35

hen Ramses went next day to visit his son, he found Sara melting in tears. He asked the cause. At first she answered that nothing was the matter; then, that she was sad; finally, she fell to Ramses' feet with great weeping.

"Lord! ... Lord mine!" she whispered, "I know you no longer love me, but at least don't put yourself in danger!"

"Who said I no longer love you?" asked the surprised Prince.

"You have three new women in your house ... ladies of great family ..."

"Oh, so that's it."

"And now you're putting yourself in danger for a fourth ... a perverse Phoenician woman."

The Prince was taken aback. How could Sara have found out about Kama and guessed that she was perverse?

"As dust works its way into a chest, so evil talk finds its way into the most peaceable houses," said Ramses. "Who's been talking to you about a Phoenician woman?"

"I don't know. A bad prophecy and my heart."

"There are prophecies?"

"Terrible prophecies! One old priestess learned, apparently from a crystal ball, that we will all perish on account of the Phoenicians, or at least me and my son!" burst out Sara.

"And you who believe in the one God, in Jehovah, you fear the tales of some stupid, maybe scheming, old woman? Where's your great God?"

"My God is only mine; the others are yours and I have to respect them."

"So this old woman was telling you about Phoenicians?" asked Ramses.

"She prophesied to me before, outside Memphis, that I should beware of a Phoenician woman," replied Sara. "But it's only here that everybody's talking about a Phoenician priestess. I don't know, maybe I'm just going mad from worry. They even said that if it hadn't been for her spells, your lordship wouldn't have jumped into the arena that time ... Oh, if the bull had killed you! ... Even now, when I think about the misfortune that might have met you, my heart grows faint."

"Laugh it off, Sara," interrupted the Prince gaily. "Whomever I befriend, stands so high that no fear should reach him ... let alone foolish talk."

"But what of misfortune? Is there a mountain so high that it's beyond reach of misfortune's missile?"

"Motherhood has tired you, Sara," said the Prince, "and the heat unsettles your thoughts, and so you fret needlessly. Relax and watch over my son. A man," he mused, "whoever he be, Phoenician or Greek, can harm only beings like himself, not us who are the gods of this world."

"What did you say about a Greek? ... What Greek?" asked Sara anxiously.

"Did I say 'Greek'? ... I don't know anything about it. Maybe the expression did pass my lips, or maybe you misheard."

He kissed Sara and his son and took his leave. He had not allayed her anxiety.

"No two ways about it," he thought. "In Egypt nothing can remain a secret. I'm watched by the priests and by my courtiers, even when they're drunk or pretend to be, and Kama is watched by the serpents' eyes of the Phoenicians. If up to now they haven't concealed her from me, they must care little about her virtue. Anyway, in relation to whom? Me, to whom they've revealed the frauds in their temple? ... Kama will be mine. They have too much at stake to want to bring my anger down on them."

A couple of days later the Prince was visited by the holy priest Mentesuphis, assistant to His Eminence Herhor at the Ministry of War. From the prophet's pale face and downcast eyes, Ramses guessed that he too knew about Kama and might choose, in his priestly capacity, to admonish Ramses. But this time Mentesuphis did not touch on the Successor's affairs of the heart.

After with an official mien greeting the Prince, the prophet took the seat indicated and began:

"I have been advised by the Memphis palace of the Lord of Eternity about the arrival in Pi-Bast of the great Chaldean priest Istubar, court astrologer and advisor to His Majesty King Assar."

The Prince was tempted to prompt Mentesuphis as to the purpose of Istubar's arrival but bit his lip and kept silent.

"And His Excellency Istubar," continued the priest, "has brought documents empowering His Eminence Sargon—kinsman and satrap to His Majesty King Assar—as envoy plenipotentiary, to Egypt, of that mighty king."

Ramses all but burst into laughter. The solemnity with which Mentesuphis deigned to disclose secrets long since known to the Prince, filled him with mirth—and contempt.

"So this juggler,"[1] thought the Successor, "doesn't even sense in his heart that I know all their impositions?"

"His Eminence Sargon and the venerable Istubar," said Mentesuphis, "shall be proceeding to Memphis to kiss the feet of His Holiness. First, however, Your Eminence as Viceroy will be so gracious as to receive the two dignitaries and their suite."

"Very gladly," replied the Prince, "and I'll take the occasion to ask them when Assyria will pay us her back tribute."

"Your Eminence would do that?" said the priest, looking him in the eye.

"That above all! Our treasury needs the tribute."

Mentesuphis suddenly rose from his seat and said in a solemn if lowered voice:

"Viceroy of Our Lord and Bestower of Life: in the name of His Holiness, I forbid you to speak with anyone about tribute, above all with Sargon, Istubar, or any of their suite."

---

[1] Juggler: in this context, the word means a trickster—a person who practices trickery to deceive or cheat. (Translator.)

The Prince turned pale. "Priest," he said, likewise rising, "on what basis do you address me in the tone of a superior?"

Mentesuphis parted his habit and took from his neck a chain with one of the Pharaoh's rings.

The Viceroy examined the ring, kissed it piously, and returned it to the priest, saying: "I will carry out the orders of His Holiness, my Lord and father."

They resumed their seats, and the Prince asked the priest:

"Could Your Eminence tell me why Assyria should not pay us tribute which would immediately deliver the Kingdom's treasury from its straits?"

"Because we cannot compel Assyria to pay us tribute," said Mentesuphis coldly. "We have an army of a hundred twenty thousand men, while Assyria has an army of about three hundred thousand men. I'm telling Your Eminence this in strict confidence."

"Very good. But why has the Ministry of War, in which you serve, reduced our valiant army by sixty thousand men?"

"To increase the income for His Holiness' court by twelve thousand talents," said the priest.

"Aha! Tell me, Your Eminence," continued the Prince, "what is the reason for Sargon traveling to the feet of the Pharaoh?"

"I don't know."

"Aha! But why shouldn't I know—I, the Crown Prince?"

"There are state secrets which barely a few dignitaries know."

"And which even my most venerable father might not know?"

"Certainly," replied Mentesuphis, "there are things which even His Holiness might not know, did he not possess the highest priestly orders."

"Strange thing!" mused the Prince. "Egypt is the property of the pharaoh, yet things can happen in the Kingdom unbeknown to the pharaoh? ... Explain that to me, Eminence."

"Egypt is above all—even solely and exclusively—the property of Amon," said the priest. "Therefore it is essential that only those should know the supreme secrets, to whom Amon reveals his will and plans."

As he listened, the Prince felt as if he were being rolled over a bed of daggers, with a fire being set underneath.

Mentesuphis made to rise; the Viceroy detained him.

"Just another word," he said mildly. "If Egypt is so weak that Assyrian tributes may not even be mentioned ..."

He was breathless. "... If she is so wretched," he continued, "then what assurance is there that the Assyrians won't attack us?"

"We can safeguard ourselves against that with treaties," said the priest.

The Successor tossed his hand dismissively. "There are no treaties for the weak!" he said. "The borders won't be protected by silver tablets inscribed with treaties, if there are no spears and swords to back them."

"Who told Your Eminence there won't be?"

"You did. A hundred twenty thousand men must yield to three hundred thousand. And once the Assyrians entered Egypt, our land would become a desert."

Mentesuphis' eyes lit up. "If they entered Egypt," he cried, "their bones would never see their native soil! We'd arm all the nobility, the workers' regiments, even the criminals in the mines! We'd gather treasure from all the temples! Assyria would meet with five hundred thousand Egyptian warriors!"

Ramses was thrilled with the priest's patriotic outburst. He grabbed Mentesuphis' arm and said:

"If we can have such an army, then why don't we attack Babylon? Hasn't the great warrior Nitager been begging us for several years to do so? Isn't His Holiness concerned about the ferment in Assyria? If we let them gather strength, the fight will be harder; but if we start it ourselves ..."

The priest interrupted him. "Does the Prince know," he said, "what is war? War, moreover, to which one must march through desert? Who can say whether, before we had reached the Euphrates, half our army and porters wouldn't have died off from their travails?"

"We would even it out in one battle," said Ramses.

"Battle!" repeated the priest. "Does the Prince know what is battle?"

"I expect so!" replied the Successor proudly, clapping his sword.

Mentesuphis shrugged. "I tell your lordship you do not know what is battle. Indeed, you have a quite false idea of it from the maneuvers, where you were always the victor though sometimes you should have been the vanquished."

The Prince turned somber.

The priest slipped his hand into his habit and suddenly said: "Your Eminence, guess what I'm holding."

"What?" repeated the Prince, surprised.

"Guess quickly and well," said the priest. "If you err, two of your regiments will perish ..."

"You're holding the ring," said the Successor, brightening.

Mentesuphis opened his hand: in it was a piece of papyrus.

"Now what am I holding?" asked the priest again.

"The ring."

"No, it's an amulet of Hathor," said the priest.

"You see, lord," he went on, "that is battle. During a battle, fate is each moment extending its hand to us and bidding us guess as quickly as possible the surprises enclosed. We err or we guess aright, but woe to him who errs oftener than he's right. And hundredfold woe to those whom fate turns away from and compels to err!"

"Still, I believe, I feel it here ..." cried the Successor, striking his chest, "that Assyria must be crushed!"

"Would that Amon speaks with your lips," said the priest. "Indeed," he added, "Assyria shall be brought low, perhaps even by your lordship's hand, but not right away ... not right away!"

Mentesuphis took his leave; the Prince remained alone. His heart and head were in tumult.

"So Hiram was right, they are deceiving us," thought Ramses. "Now I too am sure that our priests have made a pact with the Chaldean priests which His Holiness will have to confirm. Have to! ... What an unheard-of monstrosity! ... He, the Lord of the Living and Western Worlds, has to sign pacts concocted by schemers!"

He was breathless.

"Come to think of it, though, the holy Mentesuphis has given himself away. If need be,

Egypt can field a half-million-man army? I never dreamed of such strength! And they think I'm going to be put off by stories about fate posing us riddles. Give me just two hundred thousand men trained like our Greek and Libyan regiments, and I'll undertake to solve every riddle on earth and in heaven."

Meanwhile the prophet Mentesuphis, as he wended his way to his cell, was telling himself:

"He's hotheaded, quarrelsome, a womanizer—but what a powerful character he's got. After today's weak pharaoh, I daresay he'll remind us of the times of Ramses the Great. In ten years' time the bad stars will change, and he will mature and crush Assyria. Nineveh will be reduced to rubble, sacred Babylon will regain its rightful dignity, and the one supreme God, the God of the Egyptian and Chaldean prophets, will reign from the Libyan Desert all the way to the most sacred River Ganges.

"May our youngster only not make a laughingstock of himself with his nightly excursions to the Phoenician priestess! Were he seen in the garden of Astoreth, people might think the Successor is lending his ear to the Phoenician faith. And Lower Egypt needs little more to repudiate the old gods ... What a hodgepodge of peoples it is!"

A few days later, His Eminence Sargon officially notified the Prince of his capacity as Assyrian envoy, declared a desire to meet the Successor, and requested an Egyptian escort to accompany him with all safety and honors to the feet of His Holiness the Pharaoh.

The Prince held off for two days before responding and set Sargon an audience after two more days. The Assyrian, used to eastern slowness in travel and business, did not worry in the least or waste his time. He drank from morning to evening, played dice with Hiram and other rich Asiatics, and in his free time, like Ramses, slipped out to see Kama.

An older and practical man, at each visit he brought the priestess costly presents. And he expressed his feelings for her as follows:

"Kama, why do you stay in Pi-Bast and grow thin? While you are young, service at the altars of Astoreth amuses you; but when you get old, a wretched fate awaits you. They'll strip the costly vestments off you and take a younger girl in your place, and you'll have to earn a handful of parched barley telling fortunes or tending women in childbed.

"Now," continued Sargon, "if in their malice the gods had made me a woman, I'd rather myself be in childbed than nurse such women.

"That is why, as a man of good sense, I tell you: leave the temple and join my harem. I'll give, for you, ten talents in gold, forty cows, and a hundred measures of wheat. The priests at first will fear divine retribution in order to wheedle more out of me. But since I won't go them another drachma—at most, I'll throw in a few sheep—they'll hold a solemn service, and celestial Astoreth will promptly appear to them and release you from your vows, provided I throw in a gold chain or cup."

Kama, listening to these views, bit her lip to keep back the laughter, while he continued:

"And when you go with me to Nineveh, you will be a great lady. I'll give you a palace, horses, a litter, servant girls, and slaves. You'll pour more perfumes on yourself in a month than you offer here to their goddess in a whole year.

"And who knows," he concluded, "maybe King Assar will take a shine to you and decide to take you into his harem. In that case you'll be happier, and I'll recoup what I spent on you."

On the day appointed for Sargon's audience, Egyptian troops and a crowd avid for spectacle stood outside the Successor's palace.

About noon, at the height of the scorching heat, the Assyrian cortege appeared. At the head went police armed with swords and staffs, followed by several half-naked runners and three horsemen. These were trumpeters and a crier. At each street corner the trumpeters sounded a flourish, and the crier announced in a booming voice:

"Here comes the envoy-plenipotentiary of the mighty King Assar: Sargon, kinsman to the King, master of great estates, victor in battles, governor of a province. People, pay him the respect due a friend of His Holiness the ruler of Egypt!"

The trumpeters were followed by a score of Assyrian cavalry in peaked caps, jackets, and tight-fitting trousers. Their shaggy, sturdy mounts wore brass scale-armor on their heads and chests.

Then came infantry in helmets and ground-length coats. One little detachment was armed with maces, the next with bows, a third with spears and shields. In addition, all wore swords and armor.

After the soldiers came Sargon's horses, wagons, and litters, surrounded by attendants in white, red, and green liveries. Then there appeared five elephants bearing howdahs: in one rode Sargon, in another the Chaldean priest Istubar.

The procession was closed by more foot and horse and by piercing Assyrian music played on trumpets, drums, brasses, and shrill flutes.

Prince Ramses, surrounded by priests, officers, and nobility colorfully and richly attired, awaited the envoy in the great audience hall, which was open on all sides. The Successor was in good humor, knowing that the Assyrians were bearing gifts which might pass in the eyes of the Egyptian people for tribute. But when he heard the crier's booming voice in the courtyard extolling Sargon's power, the Prince turned somber. And when he heard the phrase about King Assar being a friend of the Pharaoh, he became angry. His nostrils flared like those of a provoked bull, and his eyes flashed. Seeing this, the officers and nobility scowled and adjusted their swords. The holy Mentesuphis noticed their restiveness and cried:

"In the name of His Holiness, I command the nobility and officers to receive His Eminence Sargon with the respect due the envoy of a great king!"

The Successor frowned and began impatiently pacing the dais bearing his viceregal chair. But the disciplined officers and nobility settled down, knowing that Mentesuphis, assistant to the Minister of War, was not a man to trifle with.

Meanwhile in the courtyard the huge, heavily clad Assyrian soldiers drew themselves up in three ranks opposite the agile, half-naked Egyptian soldiers. The two sides eyed each other like a pack of tigers and a herd of rhinoceroses. An ancient hatred smoldered in the hearts of both. But hatred was held in check by discipline.

Just then the elephants lumbered in, Egyptian and Assyrian trumpets blared, the two formations presented arms, the populace prostrated themselves on their faces, and the Assyrian dignitaries Sargon and Istubar descended from their howdahs.

In the hall Prince Ramses seated himself in the elevated armchair under the canopy, and the crier appeared at the entrance.

"Most gracious Lord!" he addressed the Successor. "The envoy-plenipotentiary of the great King Assar, His Excellency Sargon, and his companion, the pious prophet Istubar, desire to greet you and to pay honor to you, Viceroy and Successor of the Pharaoh, may he live forever!"

"Bid Their Eminences enter and rejoice my heart with their sight," replied the Prince.

With a clatter and clank, Sargon entered the hall in a long green robe thickly embroidered in gold. Beside him, in a snow-white coat, strode the pious Istubar; and they were followed in by elegant Assyrian lords bearing gifts for the Prince.

Sargon approached the dais and said in Assyrian, an interpreter immediately repeating in Egyptian:

"I, Sargon, commander, satrap, and kinsman by marriage of the most mighty King Assar, come to greet you, Viceroy of the most mighty Pharaoh, and in token of eternal friendship to offer you gifts ..."

The Successor rested his hands on his knees and sat motionless like the statues of his royal forbears.

"Interpreter," said Sargon, "did you misspeak my courteous greeting to the Prince?"

Mentesuphis, standing beside the dais, turned to Ramses. "Lord," he whispered, "His Eminence Sargon awaits your gracious response ..."

"Then tell him," the Prince burst out, "that I don't understand by what right he addresses me as if he were my equal in station."

Mentesuphis fell into confusion, which further angered the Prince, whose lips began twitching and whose eyes flashed again.

The Chaldean Istubar, who understood Egyptian, quickly told Sargon: "Prostrate yourself on your face!"

"Why should I?" asked Sargon indignantly.

"Prostrate yourself, if you don't want to lose our King's favor, and maybe your head as well!"

With that, Istubar fell full-length onto the floor, Sargon beside him.

"Why should I lie on my belly in front of this squirt?" he muttered indignantly.

"Because he's Viceroy," replied Istubar.

"Haven't I been viceroy to my lord?"

"But he's going to be king, and you're not."

"What are the envoys of the most mighty King Assar arguing about?" the appeased Prince asked the interpreter.

"About whether they are to show Your Eminence the gifts for the Pharaoh, or only present those sent for you," replied the quick-witted interpreter.

"I indeed want to see the gifts for my holy father," said the Prince, "and I give the envoys leave to rise."

Sargon got up, red with anger or fatigue, and sat down on the floor, legs tucked under him.

"I didn't know," he cried, "that I, relative and plenipotentiary of the great Assar, would have to wipe the dust from the Egyptian Viceroy's floor with my robes!"

Mentesuphis, who knew Assyrian, without consulting Ramses ordered two carpeted benches brought at once, on which presently the breathless Sargon and the serene Istubar seated themselves.

His breath recovered, Sargon asked for a great glass cup and a steel sword to be brought him, and for two gold-caparisoned horses to be brought around to the front of the porch. When his bidding had been done, he rose, bowed, and said to Ramses:

"My lord King Assar sends the Prince a pair of wonderful steeds—may they carry you only to victories. He sends a chalice, from which may joy ever flow to your heart—and a sword such as you won't find outside the armory of the mightiest ruler."

He unsheathed a fairly long sword which shone like silver and proceeded to bend it in his hands. The sword gave like a bow, then suddenly sprang back.

"That's indeed a wonderful weapon!" said Ramses.

"If I may, Viceroy, I'll show you another of its virtues," said Sargon who, able to show off a choice Assyrian weapon, had forgotten his anger.

At his request, one of the Egyptian officers drew his bronze sword and held it as if to attack. Then Sargon raised the steel sword and struck, lopping off a piece of his opponent's weapon.

A murmur of amazement swept the hall, and a strong blush colored Ramses' face.

"This foreigner," thought the Prince, "took the bull from me in the arena, wants to marry Kama, and shows me a weapon that slices our swords into shavings!"

He felt a still worse hatred for King Assar, for all Assyrians in general, and for Sargon in particular.

In spite of that, he strove to master himself and most courteously asked the envoy to show him the gifts for the Pharaoh.

Presently huge crates fashioned of fragrant wood were brought in, from which ranking Assyrian officials took out lengths of patterned cloths, winecups, pitchers, steel weapons, ibex-horn bows, gold armor, and bucklers encrusted with precious stones.

The most splendid gift, however, was a model of King Assar's palace fashioned of silver and gold. It looked like four successively smaller buildings stacked one atop another, each densely colonnaded, and had a terrace in lieu of roof. Each entrance was guarded by lions or winged bulls with human heads. At either side of a stairway stood statues of the king's vassals bearing gifts; at either side of a bridge were horses sculpted in the most varied poses. Sargon displaced a wall of the model, revealing sumptuous rooms filled with priceless furnishings. Particular admiration was roused by an audience hall containing figures of the king, on a high throne, and his courtiers, soldiers, and vassals paying homage.

The whole model was the length of two men and nearly the height of a man. The Egyptians whispered that this one gift of King Assar's was worth a hundred fifty talents.

When the crates had been carried away, the Viceroy invited the two envoys and their retinue to a feast, during which the guests were lavished with gifts. Ramses took his courtesy so far that, when Sargon took a liking to one of the Prince's women, he presented her to the envoy, subject of course to her agreement and her mother's consent.

Thus he was courteous and generous, but he did not clear his brow. When Thutmose asked him, "Did King Assar not have a beautiful palace?" the Prince answered: "I would find more beauty in its rubble amid the smoldering ruins of Nineveh."

The Assyrians were very abstemious at the feast. Despite the abundance of wine, they drank little and uttered equally few cries. Sargon did not once burst into his wonted thunderous laughter; lowering his eyelids, he pondered deeply in his heart.

Only the two priests, the Chaldean Istubar and the Egyptian Mentesuphis, were at peace like men who are given knowledge of the future and power over it.

CHAPTER 36

After the reception at the Viceroy's, Sargon tarried in Pi-Bast, awaiting the Pharaoh's letters from Memphis, and meanwhile strange rumors began circulating again among the officers and nobility.

The Phoenicians had been telling them, naturally in the greatest secrecy, that for unknown reasons the priests had not only forgiven Assyria her back tribute, had not only released Assyria once and for all from paying tribute but moreover, to give the Assyrians a free hand in a northern war, had concluded a long-term treaty of peace with them.

"The Pharaoh," said the Phoenicians, "was taken still more ill on learning of the concessions being made to the barbarians. Prince Ramses is worried and goes about sad, but both have to defer to the priests, uncertain as they are of sentiment among the nobility and the army."

That was what most upset the Egyptian aristocracy.

"How's that?" whispered the debt-ridden magnates among themselves, "the Dynasty no longer trusts us? The priests are bent on disgracing and ruining Egypt? Clearly, if Assyria has a war going somewhere in the far north, then now is the time to attack her and use the spoils to lift the impoverished royal treasury and aristocracy."

A few of the young lords made bold to ask the Successor what he thought of the Assyrian barbarians. The Prince kept his peace, but his flashing eyes and clenched lips adequately expressed his feelings.

"Obviously," whispered the lords, "the Dynasty is priest-ridden and distrusts the nobility, and Egypt is threatened with great misfortunes."

The quiet angers soon turned into quiet discussions of a conspiratorial cast. But while many persons took part in them, the self-assured or blinded priesthood knew nothing about them; and Sargon, though sensing hatred, attached no weight to it.

He realized Prince Ramses was ill-disposed toward him, but ascribed it to the incident in the amphitheater—and still more so, to jealousy over Kama. However, confident in his diplomatic immunity, he drank, feasted, and almost each evening stole out to the Phoenician priestess', who was receiving his suit and gifts with growing favor.

Such was the mood in the highest circles when one night the holy Mentesuphis burst into Ramses' rooms and announced that he must see the Prince at once.

The courtiers answered that the Prince was with one of his women, so they dared not disturb him. But when Mentesuphis insisted with mounting urgency, they called the Successor.

After a moment the Prince appeared, not even angry.

"What is it?" he asked the priest. "Are we at war, that Your Honor troubles himself at so late an hour?"

Mentesuphis scrutinized Ramses and drew a deep breath. "The Prince hasn't been out all this evening?" he asked.

"Not a pace."

"May I give my priestly word for that?"

"I hardly think," said the Successor proudly, "that your word is necessary, as I have given mine. What is the meaning of this?"

They went to another room.

"Does your lordship know," said the priest excitedly, "what happened perhaps an hour ago? His Eminence Sargon was set upon and caned by some young men!"

"What young men? ... Where?"

"Outside the villa of a Phoenician priestess named Kama," continued Mentesuphis, scrutinizing the Successor's face.

"Brave boys!" shrugged the Prince. "To take on such an athlete! I daresay more than one bone must have cracked."

"But to attack an envoy! Consider, Your Eminence, an envoy shielded by the majesty of Assyria and Egypt," said the priest.

"Oh, my!" laughed the Prince. "King Assar sends his envoys to Phoenician dancing girls?"

Mentesuphis was taken aback. Suddenly he slapped his forehead and laughed:

"Prince, see what a simpleton I am, unversed in diplomatic protocol. I forgot that Sargon wandering nights outside the house of a suspect woman is not an envoy but an ordinary man!"

However, after a moment he added: "In any event, this isn't good ... Sargon may take an aversion to us."

"Priest! ... Priest! ..." the Prince shook his head. "You forget something far more important: that Egypt needn't care about, let alone fear, the good or bad disposition of Sargon or even King Assar."

Mentesuphis was thrown into such confusion by the aptness of the royal youth's remarks that, rather than reply, he bowed, muttering:

"The gods have given the Prince the wisdom of a high priest ... blessed be their names! I was about to order the young brawlers tracked down and tried; but now I'd rather get your advice, for you are a sage among sages.

"Tell me, then, lord, what are we to do about Sargon and these insolent young men?"

"Above all, wait till tomorrow," said the Successor. "As a priest, you know best that divine sleep often brings good counsel."

"What if I don't think of something by tomorrow?" asked Mentesuphis.

"In any case, I will call on Sargon and try to expunge this little incident from his memory."

The priest took a most respectful leave of Ramses. Wending his way home, he reflected:

"I'll let my heart be ripped from my chest if the Prince was party to this: he neither wielded a cane nor put others up to it, nor even knew of it. One who judges a matter this coolly and aptly can't be complicit. In which case, I can proceed with an investigation and, if we can't placate the shaggy barbarian, I'll put the rowdies on trial. Nice treaty of friendship between two countries that starts with abuse of the envoy!"

Next day His Excellency Sargon lay until noon on felt bedding, as happened with him fairly often—after every drinking bout. Beside him, on a low sofa, sat the pious Istubar, his eyes fixed on the ceiling, whispering prayers.

"Istubar," sighed the dignitary, "are you sure none of our court know of my mishap?"

"Who can know, if no one saw you?"

"But the Egyptians!" groaned Sargon.

"Of the Egyptians, Mentesuphis and the Prince know—and, of course, those madmen, who will long remember your fists."

"Maybe a little ... maybe! ... But it seems to me the Crown Prince was among them and has a busted if not broken nose!"

"The Crown Prince's nose is intact and he wasn't there, I assure you."

"In that case," sighed Sargon, "the Prince ought to have several of them impaled. After all, I'm an envoy! ... My person is sacred!"

"And I tell you," counseled Istubar, "cast anger from your heart and don't even make a complaint. If the rowdies go on trial, the whole world will learn that the envoy of His Majesty King Assar consorts with Phoenicians and, worse, visits them alone by night. And how shall you answer when your mortal enemy Chancellor Lik-Bagus asks you: 'Sargon, what Phoenicians did you see, and what did you speak about with them, outside their temple at night?'"

Sargon was sighing, if sounds akin to the growlings of a lion can be called sighs.

Suddenly an Assyrian officer ran in. He knelt, struck the floor with his forehead, and said to Sargon:

"Light of Our Lord's eyes! There's a lot of Egyptian magnates and dignitaries in front of the porch, headed by the Crown Prince himself. He wants to come in here, apparently to pay his respects to you."

Before Sargon could issue any instructions, the Prince appeared in the door to the room. He brushed aside the huge Assyrian who stood guard and quickly approached the felts where the bewildered envoy, his eyes open wide, did not know what to do: flee naked to another room, or hide under the bedding.

Several Assyrian officers stood on the threshold, aghast at the Successor's breach of etiquette. But Istubar gave them a sign, and they disappeared behind a curtain.

The Prince was alone; he had left his suite in the courtyard.

"Greetings," he said, "envoy of a great king, and guest of the Pharaoh. I have come to visit you and to inquire whether there is anything you may be in need of. And should your time and inclination permit, I desire you to ride with me about the town on a horse from my father's stable, surrounded by our retinue. As befits an envoy of mighty Assar, may he live forever!"

Sargon listened, recumbent and comprehending nary a word. After Istubar had interpreted the Prince's speech for him, the envoy became so ecstatic that he pounded his head on the felts while repeating the words "Assar and Ramses."

When he had calmed down and apologized to the Prince for the wretched state in which the illustrious guest found him, he added:

"Do not hold it against me, O Lord, that the earthworm and footstool of the throne that

I am shows his joy at your visit in so unusual a way. I am doubly rejoiced. First, because a celestial honor has befallen me; second, because I had thought in my foolish and wretched heart that Your Lordship was the author of my misfortune of yesterday. It had seemed to me that, among the canes falling on my back, I felt your cane, coming down indeed hard!"

The serene Istubar interpreted this, phrase by phrase, for the Prince.

The Successor replied with truly regal dignity: "You were mistaken, Sargon. Had you not recognized your error, I would have ordered you immediately given fifty cane strokes, that you might remember that persons such as I do not attack a single man in a group or at night."

Before the learned Istubar had finished interpreting the reply, Sargon had crawled over to the Prince and embraced his legs, crying:

"O great lord! ... O great king! ... Glory to Egypt that has such a ruler."

"What is more, Sargon," said the Prince, "if you were attacked yesterday, I assure you none of my courtiers was involved. I expect that a powerful man like you must have cracked more than one skull; while my intimates are whole."

"He speaks truly and wisely!" Sargon whispered to Istubar.

"But," continued the Prince, "though the ugly deed was not of my doing or my court's, I feel obliged to assuage your grievance against a city where you have been so disgracefully received. That is why I am personally calling at your bedchamber; that is why I am opening my house to you at any hour you may wish to visit me. That is why I am asking you to accept from me this little gift ..."

The Prince reached under his tunic and took out a chain studded with rubies and sapphires.

The huge Sargon burst into tears, which moved the Prince but did not affect Istubar's indifference. The priest knew that Sargon, as the envoy of a wise king, had tears, joy, and anger on call.

The Viceroy tarried briefly. As he was taking his leave of the envoy, he reflected that the Assyrians, despite their barbarity, were not bad people, as they were capable of appreciating magnanimity.

Sargon, for his part, was so excited that he ordered wine brought and drank—drank from noon into the evening.

Well past sunset the priest Istubar left Sargon's chamber for a moment, and returned by a secret door. He was followed in by two men in dark cloaks. When they drew the hoods from their faces, Sargon recognized High Priest Mephres and the prophet Mentesuphis.

"Distinguished plenipotentiary, we bring you good news," said Mephres.

"May I give you the same!" cried Sargon. "Be seated, holy Eminences. And though my eyes are red, speak to me as if I were completely sober. I have my wits about me even when drunk, maybe even better ones ... Eh, Istubar?"

"Speak," agreed the Chaldean.

"Today," said Mentesuphis, "I have received a letter from His Eminence Minister Herhor. He writes that His Holiness the Pharaoh (may he live forever!) awaits your mission at his wonderful palace outside Memphis, and that His Holiness (may he live forever!) is well disposed to concluding a treaty with you."

Sargon swayed on the felt mattresses, but his eyes were almost sentient.

"I will go," he replied, "to His Holiness the Pharaoh (may he live forever!), I will put my seal to the treaty in my lord's name, provided it's written on bricks in cuneiform[1] because I don't understand your script. I will lie, if need be, all day on my belly before His Holiness (may he live forever!) and I'll sign the treaty. But how you'll carry it out ... ha! ha! ha! ... I don't know ..." he concluded with raucous laughter.

"How dare you, servant of the great Assar, doubt the good will and faith of our ruler?" exclaimed Mentesuphis.

Sargon sobered somewhat. "I'm not speaking of His Holiness," he replied, "but of the Crown Prince ..."

"He is a wise young man who will unhesitatingly carry out the will of his father and the Supreme Priestly Council," said Mephres.

"Ha! ha! ha!" laughed the drunken barbarian. "Your Prince ... oh, gods, wrench my limbs if I speak untrue: I'd like Assyria to have such a crown prince! Our Assyrian crown prince is a wise man, a priest. Before he sets out for war, he first looks at the stars in the heavens, then under chickens' tails. Yours would look to see how many troops he has, find out where the enemy is camped, and swoop down on him like an eagle on a sheep. That's a commander! ... That's a king! ... He isn't one who listens to the advice of priests. He'll consult his sword, and you must carry out his orders!

"And that is why, though I'll sign the treaty with you, I'll tell my master that, aside from the ailing King and the learned priests, there is here a young Crown Prince, a lion and a bull in one ... with honey on his lips and thunderbolts in his heart."

"Do that, and you will be telling a falsehood," broke in Mentesuphis. "Our Prince—though impetuous and somewhat of a rake, like most young men—respects the counsels of the wise men, and the highest offices in the land."

Sargon nodded. "Oh, you wise men! ... versed in script! ... learned in the revolutions of the stars!" he sneered. "I'm a simple man, an ordinary general who can't reliably grave his name without his seal. You're wise men, I'm a simple man, but by my King's beard I wouldn't swap you for your wisdom!

"You're men to whom the world of bricks and papyri has opened up but this real one in which we all live has closed. I'm a simple man! ... but I have the nose of a dog. And as a dog will sniff out a bear from afar, so with my red nose I can tell a hero.

"You're going to advise the Prince! Why, he's already got you charmed as the snake charms the pigeons. I at least don't deceive myself and, though the Prince is as good to me as if he were my father, I feel in my bones that he despises me and my Assyrians as the tiger despises the elephant ... Ha! ha! ... Just you give him an army, and in three months' time he'll be at Nineveh, provided that, along the way, soldiers are born instead of dying."

"Even if you spoke the truth," interrupted Mentesuphis, "even if the Prince did want to march on Nineveh, he won't."

"Who will stop him, once he's pharaoh?"

"We will."

"You? ... You?! ... Ha! ha! ha! ..." laughed Sargon. "You still think the youngster has no

---

[1] Cuneiform is one of the world's earliest writing systems, invented by the Sumerians. "Cuneiform" means "wedge-shaped": the script comprised wedge-shaped marks impressed on clay tablets with a blunt reed stylus. Cuneiform was adopted and developed by many Near Eastern peoples, until it was gradually replaced by the Phoenician alphabet in the early first millennium BCE. Cuneiform script became extinct by the second century CE. *(Translator.)*

inkling of our treaty? And I ... I ... ha! ha! ha! ... I'll let myself be flayed and impaled if he isn't on to everything already.

"Would the Phoenicians be this calm if they weren't sure the young Egyptian lion will protect them from the Assyrian bull?"

Mentesuphis and Mephres exchanged furtive glances. They were almost terrified at the genius of the barbarian who boldly uttered what they had not taken into account.

Indeed, what if the Crown Prince had guessed their intents and even meant to foil them?

However, they were rescued from their momentary troublement by the hitherto silent Istubar.

"Sargon," he said, "you're meddling in matters that are none of your business. Your charge is to conclude the treaty with Egypt that our Lord wants. What their Crown Prince knows, doesn't know, will do, won't do, is none of your business. Since the eternally living Supreme Priestly Council assures us that the treaty will be carried out, it will be. How it's done, is not our problem."

The cold tone in which Istubar pronounced this, settled the Assyrian plenipotentiary's boisterous gaiety. Sargon nodded and muttered:

"In that case, I'm sorry for the boy! ... He's a great warrior, a generous lord ..."

CHAPTER 37

After their visit to Sargon, the holy Mephres and Mentesuphis, having carefully wrapped themselves in their burnooses, were returning home steeped in thought.

"Who knows," said Mentesuphis, "whether that drunkard Sargon isn't right about our Crown Prince."

"In that case, Istubar will be more right," answered Mephres flintily.

"Still, let's not prejudge. The Prince should be sounded out," replied Mentesuphis.

"Do so, Your Honor."

Next day the priests called on the Crown Prince with very serious mien, asking to speak in confidence.

"What's happened?" asked the Prince, "has His Eminence Sargon discharged another nocturnal mission?"

"Regrettably, it's not to do with Sargon," replied the high priest. "There are rumors among the people that Your Eminence is maintaining close relations with infidel Phoenicians."

The Prince began to guess the purpose of the prophets' visit, and his blood boiled up. But he judged this to be the start of a game between him and the priesthood and, as became a royal scion, mastered himself. His face took on an expression of interested naïvete.

"And the Phoenicians are dangerous people, born enemies of the Kingdom!" added Mephres.

The Successor smiled. "If you holy men," he said, "lent me money and had pretty girls at your temples, I'd have to see you oftener. As it is, I have no alternative but to be on friendly terms with the Phoenicians!"

"They say Your Eminence visits this Phoenician woman at night."

"And so I must until the girl comes to her senses and moves to my house. But have no fear, I carry my sword, and should anyone stop me ..."

"But because of this Phoenician woman, Your Eminence has taken on a dislike for the Assyrian king's plenipotentiary."

"Not because of her, but because Sargon stinks of suet! Anyway, what's your point? You holy fathers aren't my women's keepers. I doubt that His Eminence Sargon has entrusted you with his."

Mephres' confusion brought a blush to his shaven head.

"Your Eminence speaks the truth," he replied. "Your love life is not our concern. But there is something worse: people are surprised that the cunning Hiram so easily lent you a hundred talents, without collateral."

The Prince's lips quivered, but he spoke calmly:

"It's not my fault if Hiram trusts my word more than do wealthy Egyptians! He knows I'd sooner give up the armor I inherited from my grandfather than default on my debt to Hiram. He seems unconcerned, too, about interest, as he didn't even mention it.

"I won't make it a secret that Phoenicians are more clever than Egyptians. Before a rich Egyptian would lend me a hundred talents, he'd make sour faces, moan and groan, make me wait a month, and finally demand huge collateral and still bigger interest. But the Phoenicians, who have a better understanding of princes' hearts, give us money without even a judge and witnesses."

The high priest was so irked by Ramses' calm scoffing that he fell silent and clenched his lips.

Mentesuphis suddenly asked: "What would Your Eminence say if we made a treaty with Assyria, giving her northern Asia and Phoenicia?"

He fixed his eyes on the Successor's face.

The Prince replied calmly: "I would say that only traitors could urge such a treaty on the Pharaoh."

Mephres lifted up his hands. Mentesuphis clenched his fists.

"What if the security of the Kingdom required it?" pressed Mentesuphis.

"What do you want of me?" the Prince burst out "You meddle with my debts and women, you surround me with spies, you presume to admonish me, and now you ask me a loaded question. Well, I'll tell you: if you threatened me with poison, I still wouldn't sign such a treaty. Fortunately, its ratification depends not on me but on His Holiness, whose will we must all obey."

"What would Your Eminence do as pharaoh?"

"What the honor and interest of the Kingdom required."

"Of that I have no doubt," said Mentesuphis. "But what does Your Eminence consider to be the Kingdom's interest? Where should we seek guidance?"

"Why don't you ask the Supreme Council?" cried the Prince with feigned anger. "You say it's a body of wise men. Well, let them take responsibility for the treaty, which I consider the disgrace and doom of Egypt!"

"How does Your Eminence know," replied Mentesuphis, "that that isn't what your divine father did?"

"Then why ask me about it? What sort of inquest is this? What gives you the right to delve into my heart?"

Ramses affected such indignation that the priests backed off.

"The Prince," said Mephres, "speaks as befits a good Egyptian. Such a treaty would pain us as well, but the Kingdom's security sometimes requires temporary submission to circumstances."

"But what compels it?" cried the Prince. "Have we lost a great battle, have we no army?"

"The oarsmen of the ship on which Egypt sails the river of eternity are the gods," replied the high priest in solemn tones, "and the steersman is the Supreme Lord of all creation. Sometimes they stop the ship or turn it to avoid dangerous vortices which we do not even perceive. In such cases, only patience and obedience are needed on our part to bring us, sooner or later, a generous reward surpassing all that mortal man can conceive."

With that, the priests took their leave of the Prince, confident that, though he was angry at the treaty, he would not break it but would ensure Egypt the requisite period of peace.

Following their departure, Ramses called in Thutmose. When he found himself alone with his favorite, his pent-up anger and despondence burst out. The Prince threw himself on a couch, writhed like a snake, pummeled his head with his fists, and wept.

The frightened Thutmose waited for the Prince's tantrum to pass. Then he handed Ramses water with wine, censed him with soothing fragrances, and finally sat down beside him and asked the cause of his unmanly despair.

"You know," said the Successor without rising, "I'm now sure our priests have made a disgraceful treaty with Assyria. Without war, without even demands from the other side! Can you guess how much we lose?"

"Dagon was telling me Assyria wants to take over Phoenicia. But the Phoenicians are less frightened now, since King Assar has a war on his northeastern borders. There are very numerous, valiant peoples there, so there's no telling how it will end. In any event the Phoenicians will have a couple of years of peace, which will suffice them to prepare a defense and find allies."

The Prince impatiently tossed his hand. "You see," he interrupted, "even Phoenicia will arm herself, and maybe all her neighbors as well. Whereas we will lose at least the back tributes from Asia, which come to—imagine!—over a hundred thousand talents!"

"A hundred thousand talents," said the Prince. "Gods! A sum like that would immediately fill the pharaoh's treasury. And if we attacked Assyria at the right moment, just in Nineveh, in Assar's palace alone, we'd find inexhaustible treasures. Now think how many slaves we could take. Half a million ... a million ... tremendously strong people, and so wild that slavery in Egypt, the hardest work at the canals or mines, would seem sport[1] to them.

"The fertility of the land would rise within a few years, our populace would get some rest, and before the last slave had died, the Kingdom would have regained its former power and wealth. And all this, the priests will bring to nought with a few inscribed silver tablets and a few bricks incised with wedge-shaped marks[2] that none of us understand!"

Thutmose rose from his chair, carefully checked the adjacent rooms to see whether anyone was listening in, then sat down again beside Ramses and whispered:

"Be of good cheer, lord! To my knowledge, all the aristocracy, all the nomarchs, all the senior officers have heard something about this treaty and are outraged. Just give the sign, and we'll smash the treaty bricks on Sargon's head and even Assar's."

"That would be rebellion against His Holiness," replied the Prince as quietly.

Thutmose made a sad face. "I wouldn't want to make your heart bleed," he said, "but your father equal to the highest gods is gravely ill."

"That's not true!" exclaimed the Prince.

"It is, only don't let on that you know. His Holiness is very weary of his sojourn on this earth and wishes to depart. But the priests detain him, and they don't summon you to Memphis, so that they may sign the pact with Assyria unhindered."

"The traitors! ... The traitors!" whispered the furious Prince.

"That's why you'll have no trouble breaking the pact once you take power after your father (may he live forever!)."

"It's easier," mused the Prince, "to sign a treaty than to break it."

---

[1] Sport: the word is used here in the sense of a "pastime" or "amusement." *(Translator.)*

[2] Wedge-shaped marks: cuneiform script, produced on clay tablets with a blunt reed stylus. *(Translator.)*

"Breaking it is easy too!" smiled Thutmose. "Aren't there unruly tribes in Asia which will violate our borders? Doesn't godly Nitager stand guard with his army to repulse them and carry war to their lands? And do you think Egypt will lack for men to take up arms, or treasure to make war? We'll all go, because everyone has something to gain and a living to secure for himself. The treasures are in the temples ... and in the Labyrinth!"

"Who will get them out?" asked the Prince dubiously.

"Who? Any nomarch, any officer, any nobleman will do it, so long as he has an order from the pharaoh ... and junior priests will show us the way to the vaults."

"They won't dare ... Divine retribution ..."

Thutmose tossed his hand scornfully. "Are we peasants or herdsmen, that we should fear gods who are mocked by the Jews, Phoenicians, and Greeks, and whom the mercenary soldier desecrates with impunity?

"The priests thought up all the nonsense about gods whom they themselves don't believe in. You know that at the temples they recognize only the One God. And they work wonders which they ridicule. The peasant, as of old, prostrates himself on his forehead before the statues. But the laborers are doubting the omnipotence of Osiris, Horus, and Set; the scribes deceive the gods in the accounts; and the priests use the gods as lock and chain to secure their treasuries.

"Oh, gone are the times," continued Thutmose, "when all Egypt believed every report emerging from the temples. Today we insult the Phoenician gods, the Phoenicians insult ours, and no one gets struck by lightning."

The Viceroy was scrutinizing Thutmose. "Why these thoughts today?" he asked. "Not that long ago, you would grow pale at mention of the priests."

"I was alone. But now that I've found that all the nobility are of the same mind, I'm in better fettle."

"Who's been telling you and the nobility about treaties with Assyria?"

"Dagon and the other Phoenicians," said Thutmose. "They've even offered, when the time comes, to stir up the Asiatic tribes so our army will have a pretext to cross the border. And once we're bound for Nineveh, the Phoenicians and their allies will join up with us. You'll have an army such as Ramses the Great never had!"

The Prince did not like the fervor of the Phoenicians; but he kept his peace. Instead he asked: "What if the priests find out about all your talk? Truly, none of you will escape with your lives!"

"They won't find out anything," said Thutmose jauntily. "They have too much faith in their power, they pay their spies poorly, and they've alienated all Egypt with their greed and overweening. The aristocracy, the army, the scribes, the laborers, even the junior priests only wait word to break into the temples, seize the treasures, and lay them at the foot of the throne. When the holy men are bereft of treasure, they'll lose all their power. They'll even stop working wonders, for that too requires gold rings."

The Prince turned the conversation to other matters, then let Thutmose go.

The Successor would have been delighted with the nobility's animus toward the priests and with the warlike instincts of the highest classes, had their fervor not burst out so suddenly and had the Phoenicians not been behind it.

This gave him pause: the Prince realized that in Egyptian affairs it was better to trust in the patriotism of the priests than in the friendship of the Phoenicians.

But he recalled his father's words, that the Phoenicians were truthful and loyal when their interests were at stake. Without question the Phoenicians had a vital interest: not to fall into the clutches of the Assyrians. They could be depended on as allies in the event of war, because an Egyptian defeat would first and foremost affect Phoenicia.

On the other hand, Ramses did not think the priests, even in making such an ugly treaty with Assyria, were committing treason. No, they weren't traitors, only lazy dignitaries. They liked peace because peace allowed them to multiply their treasures and increase their power. They did not want war because war would expose them to heavy expenses and enhance the pharaoh's power.

Thus the young Prince, despite his inexperience, realized that he must be cautious, must avoid haste, must condemn no one, but must also not trust anyone too much. He had decided on war with Assyria not because the nobility and the Phoenicians wanted it, but because Egypt needed treasure and slaves.

Having, however, decided on war, he wanted to act with deliberation. He wanted to slowly win the priesthood over to the idea—and only in the event of resistance, to crush them, using the army and nobility.

And just when the holy Mephres and Mentesuphis were joking about Sargon's prediction that the Successor would not submit to the priests but would compel them to obey him, the Prince already had a plan for subjugating them and saw the means at his disposal. He left the opening of the struggle and the manner of its conduct to the future.

"Time brings the best advice!" he told himself.

He felt at ease and content like a man who, after long hesitation, knows what he is to do and has faith in his capacity. To shake off the last traces of his late agitation, he went to Sara's.

Play with his infant son soothed his cares and filled his heart with cheer.

He passed the garden, entered the villa of his first mistress—and found her again in tears.

"Oh, Sara!" he cried, "if you had the Nile in your breast, you'd manage to cry it out."

"I won't anymore," she replied, a still more copious stream flowing from her eyes.

"What is it?" asked the Prince. "Has another fortuneteller been frightening you with Phoenician women?"

"It's not Phoenician women I fear, but Phoenicia," she said. "Oh, your lordship doesn't know what vile people they are."

"Do they burn children?" laughed the Viceroy.

"You think they don't?" she answered, regarding him with her great eyes.

"Fables! I have it from Prince Hiram that those are fables."

"Hiram?!" shouted Sara. "Why, Hiram is the greatest criminal. Ask my father, lord, he'll tell you how Hiram lures young girls from distant lands onto his ships, then sets sail and carries them off to sell them. We had a fair-haired slave girl whom Hiram had kidnapped. She went mad longing for her homeland but couldn't even say where it was. And she died! That's what Hiram, what that wretch Dagon and all those villains are like."

"Maybe, but how does that concern us?" asked the Prince.

"It does, very much," said Sara. "Your lordship is listening to Phoenician advice, while our Jews have discovered that Phoenicia wants to provoke war between Egypt and Assyria. It seems the leading Phoenician merchants and bankers have pledged themselves to it with terrible oaths."

"Why should they want war?" asked the Prince with feigned indifference.

"Why!" exclaimed Sara. "They'll supply you and the Assyrians with weapons, goods, and intelligence, and for everything they'll have themselves paid ten times over. They'll strip the dead and wounded on both sides. They'll buy up booty and slaves from your soldiers and the Assyrians ... Isn't that enough? Egypt and Assyria will ruin themselves, while Phoenicia builds new storehouses for her wealth."

"Who taught you this wisdom?" smiled the Prince.

"You think I don't hear my father, our relatives, and friends whispering, as they look about in fear that someone may overhear? And don't I know the Phoenicians? They lie on their stomachs before your lordship, and you don't see their hypocritical looks, but I've seen their eyes green with greed or yellow with choler.[3]

"Oh, beware the Phoenicians, lord, as you would a venomous viper!"

Ramses regarded Sara and, despite himself, compared her genuine love with Kama's interestedness; Sara's tender outbursts, with Kama's insidious coolness.

"The Phoenicians truly are venomous reptiles!" he thought. "But if Ramses the Great used a lion in war,[4] why shouldn't I use a viper against Egypt's enemies?"

The more vividly he pictured Kama's perversity, the more he desired her. Heroic souls are wont to seek danger.

He took his leave of Sara and suddenly, for some obscure reason, recalled that Sargon had suspected him of having had a hand in the attack.

The Prince slapped his forehead. "Could it have been that double of mine," he said, "who organized the brawl for the envoy? If so, who put him up to it? ... The Phoenicians? ... And if they wanted to involve my person in such a dirty business, then Sara is right that they're villains whom I ought to shun."

His anger aroused again, the Prince decided to resolve the question at once. As evening was just falling, Ramses went directly to Kama's villa.

He cared little if he were recognized; in the event of danger, after all, he had his sword.

There was light in the priestess' villa, but none of the servants were about the entry.

"Up to now," he thought, "Kama has sent away her servants when I was to come over. Today does she have a presentiment, or is she receiving a lover more fortunate than me?"

He climbed to the first floor, stopped before Kama's room, and suddenly pulled the curtain. Inside were Kama and Hiram, whispering together.

"Oh! I've come at a bad time," laughed the Successor. "Well, Prince, are you also courting a woman who, on pain of death, may not be kind to men?"

Hiram and the priestess both sprang up from their stools.

"Evidently, lord," said the Phoenician Prince, bowing, "some good spirit alerted you that we were speaking of you."

"Are you readying me a surprise?" asked the Viceroy.

"Maybe! ... Who knows?" said Kama, eyeing him provocatively.

The Prince replied coolly, "Those who wish to go on making me surprises had better

---

[3] Choler, or yellow bile, was one of four "humors" that were thought in antiquity to determine people's temperaments. Choler was believed to cause anger when secreted by the liver in excess. *(Translator.)*

[4] James Henry Breasted writes (*A History of Egypt*, 1905): "Ramses II ... was followed on his campaigns by a tame lion who trotted beside his chariot ..." Ramses III imitated Ramses II in this, as in many other ways. *(Translator.)*

not get their necks in the way of an ax or noose. That might surprise them more than their doings could surprise me."

Kama's smile froze on her half-parted lips. Hiram turned pale and said humbly: "How have we earned the anger of our lord and patron?"

"I want the truth," said the Prince, sitting down and regarding Hiram sternly. "I want to know who organized the attack on the Assyrian envoy, and involved in that villainy a man who resembles me as my right hand resembles my left."

"You see, Kama," said Hiram, aghast, "I said that scoundrel's familiarity with you could bring a great misfortune ... And here you are! ... It wasn't a long wait."

Kama threw herself to the Prince's feet. "I'll tell your lordship everything," she moaned, "only cast ill feeling for Phoenicia from your heart! Kill me, jail me, but don't be angry with them."

"Who attacked Sargon?"

"Lykon, a Greek who sings at our temple," said the kneeling Kama.

"Aha! ... So he sang outside your house, and he bears such a resemblance to me?"

Hiram bowed his head and placed his hand over his heart.

"We paid this man generously," he said, "for resembling your lordship. We thought his wretched person might prove of use to you ..."

"And so it did!" interrupted the Successor. "Where is he? I want to see this excellent singer ... this living image of me."

Hiram spread his hands. "The scoundrel has run off, but we'll find him," he replied. "Excepting he turns into a fly or an earthworm."

"Will you forgive me, lord?" whispered Kama, leaning on the Prince's knees.

"Much is forgiven women," said the Successor.

"You won't take vengeance on me?" she asked Hiram fearfully.

"Phoenicia," replied the old man deliberately, "will forgive the greatest offense on the part of him who possesses the favor of our lord Ramses—may he live forever!

"As far as Lykon is concerned," he added, "your lordship shall have him, dead or alive."

With that, Hiram bowed low and departed the room, leaving the priestess with the Prince.

Ramses embraced the kneeling Kama and whispered: "You heard His Eminence Hiram ... Phoenicia will forgive you the greatest offense! That man truly is loyal to me. And if he said that, then what excuse can you find?"

Kama kissed his hands, whispering: "You've won me ... I'm your slave. But today let me be ... respect a house that belongs to the goddess Astoreth."

"Then you'll move to my palace?" asked the Prince.

"Oh, gods, what did you say? Ever since the first sunrise and sunset, there's never been a case of a priestess of Astoreth ... But there's nothing for it! Phoenicia gives your lordship a token of reverence and devotion that none of her own sons has ever received ..."

"Then ..." interrupted the Prince, embracing her.

"Only not today and not here," she begged.

CHAPTER 38

Learning from Hiram that the Phoenicians were giving him the priestess, the Successor wanted to have her in his house as soon as possible, not because he could not live without her but because she constituted a novelty for him.

But Kama delayed her arrival, begging the Prince to let her be until the influx of pilgrims abated; above all, until the most prominent ones had left Pi-Bast. If she became the Prince's mistress during their sojourn, the temple's income could drop and the priestess would be in danger.

"Our wise and great people," she told Ramses, "will forgive me the betrayal. But the common folk will call the vengeance of the gods upon my head, and your lordship knows the gods have long arms ..."

"May they not lose them, reaching under my roof!" replied the Prince.

He did not insist, however, having his attention at this time very occupied.

The Assyrian envoys Sargon and Istubar had left for Memphis to sign the treaty. At the same time the Pharaoh had called on Ramses to submit a report on his journey.

The Prince instructed scribes to describe in detail all that had happened since his departure from Memphis: inspections of craftsmen, visits to factories and fields, conversations with nomarchs and officials. He designated Thutmose to deliver the report.

"In the presence of the Pharaoh," the Prince told him, "you shall be my heart and lips. And here's what you're to do:

"When His Eminence Herhor asks what I think the causes of the poverty of Egypt and the treasury, advise the Minister to consult his aide Pentuer, who shall explain my views as he did at the Temple of Hathor.

"When Herhor asks my opinion of the treaty with Assyria, answer that it's my duty to carry out the orders of our Lord."

Thutmose nodded his head.

"But," continued the Viceroy, "when you stand before my father (may he live forever!) and find that no one is listening in, fall to his feet in my name and say as follows:

"'Our Lord, these are the words of your son and servant, miserable Ramses, to whom you gave life and power:

"'The cause of Egypt's misfortunes is the loss of arable land to the desert, and the loss of populace, who are dying from overwork and privation.

"'But know, our Lord, that no less harm than by death and the desert is inflicted on your treasury by the priests. Not only are their temples full of gold and gems that could pay off all the debts, but the holy fathers and prophets have the best farms, bravest peasants and laborers, and far more land than the god-pharaoh.

"'Thus says your son and servant Ramses, who throughout the journey had his eyes constantly open like a fish, and his ears pricked like a prudent donkey.'"

The Prince paused, while Thutmose rehearsed the Prince's words in his mind.

"When," resumed the Viceroy, "His Holiness asks my opinion of the Assyrians, prostrate yourself on your face and answer:

"'Your servant Ramses, by your leave, ventures that the Assyrians are big, strapping men and have excellent weapons but are plainly ill-trained.

"'At Sargon's heels walked the best Assyrian warriors—bowmen, axmen, spearmen— but there were not six who could march in step together. Also, they hold their spears askew; their swords are poorly attached; and they carry their axes like carpenters or butchers. Their clothing is heavy; their thick sandals chafe their feet; and their shields, though sturdy, will be of little service to them as the soldier is clumsy.'"

"That's true," said Thutmose. "I noticed the same things, and I hear the same from our officers, who hold that Assyrian troops like the ones they saw here would put up weaker resistance than the Libyan hordes."

"Also," continued Ramses, "tell our Lord who bestows life on us that all the nobility and the Egyptian army are outraged at the very word that the Assyrians might take over Phoenicia. Phoenicia is Egypt's port, and the Phoenicians are the best sailors in our fleet.

"Finally say that I've heard from the Phoenicians that (as His Holiness is doubtless aware) Assyria is today weak: she has a war in the north and east, and all of western Asia against her. If we attacked her today, we could take great treasures and hosts of slaves to help our peasants in their labors.

"Conclude, however, that my father's wisdom surpasses that of all people and that therefore I will do as he bids me, so long as he doesn't hand Phoenicia over to Assar, else we shall perish. Phoenicia is the bronze door to our treasury, and who would turn his door over to a thief?"

Thutmose departed for Memphis in the month of Phaophi (July, August).[1] The Nile was rising, reducing the influx of Asiatic pilgrims to the Temple of Astoreth. The local populace were out in the fields, clearing in grapes, flax, and a kind of plant that produced cotton.

In a word, the area had settled down, and the gardens surrounding the Temple of Astoreth were almost deserted.

At this time Prince Ramses, free of partying and of state duties, gave himself over to the matter of his love for Kama. He conferred in secret with Hiram, who on Ramses' behalf presented the Temple of Astoreth with twelve talents in gold, a statuette of the goddess wonderfully carved in malachite, fifty cows, and a hundred fifty measures of wheat. It was so generous an offering that the Temple's high priest personally called on the Viceroy, prostrated himself on his stomach, and thanked him for this boon, which he said would never be forgotten by the peoples who loved the goddess Astoreth.

---

[1] Actually, the ancient Egyptian month of Phaophi lay between 11 October and 9 November of the modern, Gregorian calendar, unless the previous Coptic year was a leap year. (Translator.)

Having settled with the Temple, the Prince summoned the Chief of Police of Pi-Bast and spent a good hour with him. A few days later, the city was rocked by extraordinary tidings.

Kama, priestess of Astoreth, had been abducted—and had vanished like a grain of sand in the desert!

The incredible incident had occurred in the following circumstances:

The high priest of the Temple had sent Kama to the city of Sabne-Khetam, on Lake Menzaleh, with offerings for the local chapel of Astoreth. The priestess had been journeying by boat at night to avoid the summer heat and the curiosity and homage of the populace.

Toward morning as the four weary oarsmen dozed, boats manned by Greeks and Hittites had suddenly slipped out of the reeds, had surrounded the boat carrying the priestess, and had abducted Kama. The attack had been so swift that the Phoenician oarsmen had put up no resistance; and evidently the priestess' mouth had been stopped, as she had not even managed to cry out.

Having done the sacrilegious deed, the Hittites and Greeks had disappeared into the reeds, next to make their way to the sea. And to prevent pursuit, they had capsized the boat belonging to the Temple of Astoreth.

Pi-Bast was soon abuzz like a beehive: no one spoke of anything else. There were conjectures as to the crime's perpetrators. Some suspected the Assyrian, Sargon, who had offered Kama the title of wife if she would leave the Temple and go with him to Nineveh. Others suspected the Greek, Lykon, a singer of Astoreth who had long burned with passion for Kama. He was wealthy enough to hire Greek thugs, and godless enough not to hesitate about abducting a priestess.

Understandably, a council was immediately convoked at the Temple of Astoreth, of the goddess' wealthiest and most pious faithful. The council's first order of business was to release Kama from her priestess' duties and to lift from her the curses encumbering virgins who lost their innocence in the service of the goddess.

This was a holy and wise dispensation: if someone had forcibly abducted the priestess and deprived her of her holy orders against her will, it would not be right to punish her.

A couple of days later, to sounds of horns, it was announced to the faithful in the Temple of Astoreth that the priestess Kama had died; and should anyone encounter a woman resembling her, he had no right to exact vengeance or to reproach her. The priestess had not abandoned the goddess but had been abducted by evil spirits, which would be punished.

That same day His Eminence Hiram called on Prince Ramses and presented him with a gold case containing a parchment bearing a profusion of priestly seals and the signatures of the most prominent Phoenicians.

It was the decree of the ecclesiastical court of Astoreth, releasing Kama from her vows and lifting from her the curse of the heavens, provided she relinquished her priestly name.

With this document, when the sun had set, the Prince made his way to an isolated villa in his garden. He opened the door by a secret means and climbed to a small room on the first floor.

By the light of a sculpted cresset burning fragrant oil, the Prince saw Kama.

"At last!" he exclaimed, handing her the gold case. "You've got everything you wanted!"

Kama was feverish; her eyes blazed. She grabbed the case, looked it over, and threw it to the floor.

"You think it's gold?" she said. "I'll bet my necklace the case is copper and only plated inside and out with gold."

"Is that how you greet me?" asked the Prince, taken aback.

"I know my brethren," she replied. "They counterfeit not only gold, but rubies and sapphires."

"Woman ..." interrupted the Successor, "your safety is in the case."

"What do I care about safety!" she replied. "I'm bored and scared ... I've been cooped up here for four days as in a prison!"

"Do you lack for anything?"

"I lack for light ... for air ... for laughter, song, people! O vengeful goddess, how cruelly you punish me!"

The Prince listened astounded. In the furious woman, he did not recognize the Kama whom he had seen in the temple—the woman over whom had soared the passionate song of the Greek.

"Tomorrow," said the Prince, "you can go out into the garden. And when we go to Memphis and Thebes, you'll enjoy yourself as never before. Look at me. Don't I love you, and isn't belonging to me honor enough for a woman?"

"Yes," she pouted, "but you had four others before me."

"If I love you best ..."

"If you loved me best, you'd make me your first woman, you'd place me in the palace occupied by that Jewess Sara, and you'd give me the guard instead of her. Before the statue of Astoreth, I was the first. Those who worshipped the goddess, kneeling before her, looked at me! And here? ... The army sounds the drums and flutes, and the officials clasp their hands on their chests and bow their heads, before the house of the Jewess."

"Before my first-born son," interrupted the Prince impatiently, "and he's not a Jew."

"Oh, yes, he is!" screamed Kama.

Ramses jumped. "Are you mad?" he said, suddenly calm. "Don't you know my son can't be a Jew..."

"And I tell you he is!" she shouted, striking the table with her fist. "He's a Jew like his grandfather, like his uncles, and his name is Isaac!"[2]

"What did you say, woman? Do you want me to drive you out?"

"Very well, drive me out if a lie passed my lips. But if I spoke the truth, drive her out ... the Jewess and her spawn ... and give me the palace. I want, I deserve to be the first woman in your house. Because she deceives you ... mocks you. And I've denied my goddess for you ... I risk her vengeance!"

"Prove it, and the palace is yours ... No, it's a lie!" said the Prince. "Sara wouldn't commit such a crime. My first-born son ..."

"Isaac! ... Isaac! ..." shouted Kama. "Go to her and find out for yourself."

Ramses, half out of his mind, ran out of Kama's villa, heading for Sara's. Despite the starry night, he lost his way and wandered a time in the garden. But the cool air restored him to his senses, he found his way again, and he entered Sara's house almost composed.

Despite the late evening, the household was still up. Sara was personally washing her son's diapers, while her servants passed the time eating, drinking, and making music.

---

[2] Isaac: name borrowed from the biblical *Book of Genesis*. Isaac was one of the three patriarchs of the Israelites; he was the son of Abraham and Sara, the father of Jacob, and grandfather of the twelve tribes of Israel. Many modern scholars doubt the historicity of the Genesis figures, including Isaac. *(Translator.)*

When Ramses stepped onto the threshold, pale with emotion, Sara cried out but soon calmed down.

"Greetings, lord," she said, wiping her wet hands and bowing deeply.

"Sara, what is your son's name?" he asked.

The terrified woman grabbed her head.

"What is your son's name?" he repeated.

"Why, you know, lord, it's Seti,"[3] she replied in a barely audible voice.

"Look me in the eye ..."

"Oh, Jehovah!" whispered Sara.

"See, you're lying. And now I'll tell you: my son, the son of Egypt's crown prince, is named Isaac ... and is a Jew ... a wretched Jew!"

"God! ... God! ... Mercy!" she called, throwing herself to the Prince's feet.

Ramses did not even for a moment raise his voice, but his face was ashen.

"I was warned," he said, "not to take a Jewess into my house. My stomach turned as I saw the farm fill with Jews. But I curbed my disgust because I trusted you. And you and your Jews have stolen my son."

"The priests ordered that he become a Jew,"[4] whispered Sara, sobbing at the Prince's feet.

"Priests? ... What priests?"

"His Eminence Herhor ... His Eminence Mephres ... They said it was necessary because your son must become the first Jewish king ..."

"Priests? ... Mephres? ..." repeated the Prince. "Jewish king? Why, I told you your son could become the commander of my archers, my scribe ... I told you! ... and, wretched woman, you thought that a Jewish king ranks with my archer and scribe? Mephres! ... Herhor! ... The gods be thanked that at last I understand Their Eminences and know what fate they propose for my offspring."

For a moment he pondered, biting his lip. Suddenly he cried in a powerful voice: "Hey! ... Servants ... soldiers!"

In the twinkling of an eye, the room began filling with Sara's weeping servant women, the scribe and steward of her house, then slaves, and finally several soldiers and an officer.

"Death!" shouted Sara in a piercing voice.

She flung herself to the crib, grabbed her son, and went to a corner of the room, crying, "Kill me ... but I'm not giving him up!"

Ramses smiled. "Centurion," he said to the officer, "take this woman and her child to the slaves' house. The Jewess will no longer be mistress here, but the servant of her who will take her place.

"And you, steward," he added, turning to the official, "see that tomorrow morning the Jewess remembers to wash the feet of her mistress, who will presently come here. Should this servant prove refractory, then at her mistress' discretion she is to be flogged.

---

[3] Seti: name borrowed from two New Kingdom pharaohs. Seti I, the second pharaoh of the 19th Dynasty, was the son of Ramses I and the father of Ramses II ("the Great"). Seti II was the fifth pharaoh of the 19th Dynasty. *Seti* means "of Set," indicating that its bearer was consecrated to the god Set. *(Translator.)*

[4] It is not clear how the infant would have "become a Jew." Prus may have been thinking of circumcision; but, by *Pharaoh*'s present time, circumcision had already been practiced by the Egyptians, apparently as a rite of passage to adulthood, for over twelve centuries, since at least 2300 BCE. *(Translator.)*

"Take this woman to the servants' quarters!"

The officer and steward approached Sara but stopped, daring not touch her. There was no need. Sara wrapped the whimpering babe in a cloth and left the room, whispering: "God of Abraham, Isaac, Jacob, have mercy on us."

She bowed low to the Prince, silent tears flowing from her eyes. Ramses still heard her sweet voice in the entry: "God of Abraham, Isaac ..."

When all was still, the Viceroy said to the officer and steward: "You shall go with torches to the house among the fig trees ..."

"Yes, lord," replied the steward.

"And you shall immediately bring here the woman who lives there."

"Very good."

"That woman will henceforth be your mistress and the mistress of the Jewess Sara, who each morning is to wash her mistress' feet, pour water on her, and hold the mirror for her. That is my will and command."

"Very good," replied the steward.

"Tomorrow morning you'll tell me whether the new servant is refractory."

Having issued his instructions, the Viceroy returned home, but he did not sleep all night. The fire of vengeance was growing deep in his soul.

He felt that, without raising his voice even for an instant, he had crushed Sara, the wretched Jewess who had dared deceive him. He had punished her like a king who, with a single flick of an eyelid, casts people from the heights into the abyss of servitude. But Sara had been only a tool of the priests; and the Successor had too keen a sense of justice, having broken the tool, to forgive the true culprits.

His fury was made the greater by the untouchability of the priests. The Prince could banish Sara and the infant in the dead of night to the servants' quarters, but he could not deprive Herhor of his power, or Mephres of his high-priesthood. Sara had fallen at his feet like a trampled worm; but Herhor and Mephres, who had snatched his first-born son from him, loomed over Egypt and (for shame!) over him, over the future pharaoh, like the pyramids.

For who knows which time this year, he recalled the wrongs he had suffered at the hands of the priests. At school they had caned him till his back was ready to split; or had starved him till his belly cleaved to the small of his back. At the previous year's maneuvers, Herhor had spoiled his whole plan, then had laid the blame on him and had withheld command of the Menfi Corps from him. The same Herhor had procured him the disfavor of His Holiness for having taken Sara into his house; and had not restored him to his honors until the humiliated Prince had spent a couple of months in self-imposed exile.

It might have seemed that, when he became Corps commander and Viceroy, the priests would cease oppressing him with their attentions. But precisely now they had come out with redoubled force. They had made him Viceroy, to what end? To distance him from the Pharaoh and to conclude a humiliating treaty with Assyria. They had forced him to go for information about the state of the Kingdom, as a penitent, to a temple; there they had deceived him with the aid of wonders and terrors and had given him utter misinformation.

Then they had meddled with his distractions, mistresses, relations with the Phoenicians, debts; and finally, to humiliate him and render him a laughingstock in Eygpt's eyes, had made his first-born son a Jew!

What peasant, what slave, what prisoner in the mines, what Egyptian could not say: "I am your better, Viceroy, for no son of mine has been a Jew."

While feeling the onus of the humiliation, Ramses at the same time realized that he could not immediately avenge it. He therefore decided to defer the matter to the future. At priest school he had learned self-control; at court, patience and dissimulation. These attributes would be his shield and armor in the struggle with the priesthood. For a time, he would lead them astray; then, when the right moment came, he would strike so that they would never rise again.

Outside, dawn was breaking. The Successor fell fast asleep. When he woke, the first person he beheld was the steward of Sara's palace.

"What about the Jewess?" asked the Prince.

"Pursuant to Your Eminence's order, she washed her new mistress' feet," replied the official.

"Was she refractory?"

"She was full of humility but not dexterous enough, so the angry mistress kicked her between the eyes."

The Prince jumped. "And what did Sara do?" he asked quickly.

"She fell to the floor. When the new mistress told her to clear out, she left, weeping softly."

The Prince began pacing the room. "How did she spend the night?"

"The new mistress?"

"No!" interrupted the Successor. "I'm asking about Sara ..."

"As ordered, Sara went with the infant to the servants' quarters. There, out of pity, the women let her have a fresh mat, but Sara did not lie down to sleep but sat up all night with the babe in her lap."

"How is the child?" asked the Prince.

"He is well. This morning, when the Jewess went on duty to the new mistress, the other women bathed the tot in warm water, and a herdsman's wife who likewise has an infant suckled him."

The Prince stopped in front of the steward.

"It is bad," he said, "when a cow, instead of suckling her calf, goes to the plow and is caned. So, although the Jewess has committed a great offense, I don't want her innocent issue to suffer. Therefore Sara will no longer wash the new mistress' feet and will not be kicked by her in the eyes. You shall give her a separate room in the servants' house, a couple pieces of furniture, and food appropriate for a woman lately in childbed. And let her nurse the child in peace."

"May you live forever, our Lord!" replied the steward, running off to do the Viceroy's bidding.

All the servants liked Sara, and a couple of hours had sufficed them to detest the irascible and shrill Kama.

CHAPTER 39

The Phoenician priestess brought Ramses little happiness.

When he came to visit her for the first time in the villa hitherto occupied by Sara, he expected to be greeted with delight and gratitude. Instead, Kama received him almost angrily.

"What's this?" she cried, "after just half a day you've restored the wretched Jewess to favor?"

"Isn't she housed with the servants?" replied the Prince.

"But my steward says she's no longer to wash my feet."

The lord felt distaste. "I see you're not satisfied," he said.

"And I won't be," she burst out, "until I've humbled the Jewess! Until she forgets, as she serves me and kneels at my feet, that she was once your first woman and the mistress of this house. Until my servants stop looking at me with fear and mistrust, and at her with pity!"

Ramses was liking the Phoenician woman less and less.

"Kama," he said, "consider what I will say to you. If a servant in my house kicked a suckling bitch in the teeth, I would drive him out. You kicked a woman and mother between the eyes. And in Egypt, Kama, 'mother' is a great word, for a good Egyptian reveres three things above all else on earth: the gods, the pharaoh, and his mother."

"Alas!" cried Kama, throwing herself on the bed. "This is my reward, wretch that I am, for denying my goddess! Only a week ago, they were laying flowers at my feet and burning incense before me, and now ..."

The Prince quietly slipped out of the room and visited Kama again only after several days.

He once more found her in ill humor.

"I beg you, lord," she shouted, "care for me a bit more! Now the servants too are starting to ignore me, the soldiers are looking askance, and I fear that in the kitchen someone may poison my food."

"I was busy with the army," replied the Prince, "so I couldn't visit you."

"Oh, yes!" retorted Kama. "Yesterday you were in front of my porch, and then you went off toward the servants' quarters, where the Jewess lives ... you wanted to show me ..."

"Enough!" interrupted the Successor. "I visited neither your porch nor the servants' quarters. If you thought you saw me, it means that your lover the scurvy Greek not only hasn't left Egypt but dares circulate in my garden."

Kama listened, terrified. "Astoreth!" she suddenly shouted, "save me ... Earth, hide me! If that wretch Lykon is back, I'm in great danger!"

The Prince burst into laughter, but he had no patience for the ex-priestess' laments.

"Don't worry," he said, leaving, "and don't be surprised if one of these days they bring your Lykon trussed up like a jackal. His insolence has exhausted my patience."

Returning to his rooms, the Prince immediately sent for Hiram and the Chief of Police of Pi-Bast. He told them his look-alike, the Greek Lykon, was haunting the palace grounds and ordered him apprehended. Hiram swore that when the Phoenicians joined forces with the police, the Greek must fall into their hands. But the Police Chief proceeded to shake his head.

"You doubt it?" the Prince asked him.

"Yes, lord. In Pi-Bast live many very pious Asiatics in whose opinion a priestess who abandons the altar deserves to die. If this Greek has pledged to kill Kama, they will aid him, conceal him, and facilitate his escape."

"What do you say to that, Prince?" the Successor asked Hiram.

"His Eminence the Chief of Police is very astute," replied the old man.

"But you lifted the curse from Kama!" cried Ramses.

"I vouch," replied Hiram, "that the Phoenicians won't touch Kama and will give chase to the Greek. But what's to be done about the other adherents of Astoreth?"

"I daresay," spoke the Chief of Police, "that the woman is in no immediate danger. And were she brave, we could use her to lure the Greek and catch him here in Your Eminence's palace precincts."

"Then go tell her your plan," said the Prince. "If you catch the scoundrel, I'll give you ten talents."

When the Successor had taken his leave of them, Hiram said to the Chief of Police:

"Eminence, I know that you are versed in the two scripts and are no stranger to priestly learning. When you want to, you hear through walls and see in the dark. Thus you know the thoughts alike of the peasant who works the bucket, the craftsman who brings sandals to market, and the great lord who feels as safe among his servants as the babe in its mother's womb."

"Your Honor speaks the truth," replied the official, "the gods have granted me a wonderful gift of clairvoyance."[1]

"And thanks to your preternatural abilities," continued Hiram, "you have doubtless already divined that the Temple of Astoreth will give you twenty talents if you catch this wretch who dares assume the likeness of our lord the Prince. Additionally, in any event, the Temple offers you ten talents if word of the wretched Lykon's resemblance to the Successor is not bruited about Egypt. It's unseemly and unmeet for a common mortal to resemble a person who is descended from the gods.

"Therefore let what you hear of the wretched Lykon, and our whole search for the godless man, not leave our hearts."

"Understood," replied the official. "Such a criminal could lose his life before we turned him over to the courts."

---

[1] Clairvoyance (also known as "second sight") is an alleged ability to perceive things that are out of the natural range of human senses. A person who is claimed to have such ability is called a clairvoyant (from the French for "one who sees clearly"). *(Translator.)*

"You said it," said Hiram, clasping his hand. "And any assistance that you may request of the Phoenicians will be tendered you."

They parted like two friends hunting big game who know that it matters not whose spear strikes the quarry, but that the quarry be well struck and not fall into other hands.

After several days Ramses visited Kama again and found her in a state verging on madness. She hid in the most cramped room of her villa, hungry, uncombed, unwashed, issuing the most contradictory orders to her servants. One moment she bade them all assemble, the next moment she drove them away. At night she called the soldiers of the watch, then a moment later fled to the attic, shouting that they wanted to kill her.

In view of such behavior, love vanished from the Prince's soul, leaving only a sense of bewilderment. He grabbed his head as the officer and the villa's steward told him of these prodigies, and he whispered: "I was wrong to take the woman from her goddess. Only the goddess could have patiently borne her caprices!"

Nevertheless he went to Kama and found her gaunt, disheveled, trembling.

"Woe is me!" she cried. "I live among enemies. My wardrobe maid wants to poison me, and my hairdresser wants to visit a grave illness on me. The soldiers only wait for a chance to plunge their spears and swords into my breast; and in the kitchen, I'm sure, instead of food, magical herbs are cooking. They all seek my life!"

"Kama ..." interrupted the Prince.

"Don't call me that!" she whispered, terrified, "it will bring me misfortune!"

"Where do you get these thoughts?"

"Where!? In the daytime I see strangers outside the villa who disappear before I can call the servants. And at night I hear whispers across the wall ..."

"You're imagining things."

"Confound all of you!" she wailed. "You all say I'm imagining things. But just the other day some criminal hand planted a veil in my bedroom, and I wore it for half a day before I realized it wasn't mine ... that I never had one like it."

"Where is the veil?" asked the Prince, concerned now.

"I burned it, after first showing it to my servant girls."

"Well, what if it wasn't yours, what harm has it done you?"

"None yet. But if I'd kept that rag in the house for a couple of days, I'd surely have been poisoned or come down with an incurable disease. I know the Asiatics and their ways!"

Bored and irritated, the Prince hurried away despite her pleas that he remain. However, when he asked the servants about the veil, the wardrobe maid allowed that it had not been Kama's but had been dropped off by someone.

The Prince ordered the guard doubled in and around the villa and, despairing, made his way back to his rooms.

"I'd never have believed," he thought, "that one puny woman can cause so much commotion! Four freshly captured hyenas couldn't match her disquietude!"

In his rooms the Prince found Thutmose, only returned from Memphis, who had just bathed and changed after his journey.

"What have you to report?" the Prince asked his favorite, guessing he had not brought good news. "Did you see His Holiness?"

"I saw the solar god of Egypt," replied Thutmose, "and these were his words to me ..."

"Speak them," said the Successor.

"Thus saith our Lord," continued Thutmose, clasping his hands on his chest and bowing his head. "Thus saith the Lord: 'For thirty-four years have I driven the heavy wagon of Egypt, and I am weary and long for my great forbears who dwell in the Western Land. Soon I will depart this land, and my son Ramses shall mount the throne and shall do with the Kingdom as wisdom dictates to him.'"

"My holy father said that?"

"Those are his words, faithfully repeated," replied Thutmose. "The Lord told me distinctly several times that he leaves you no instructions for the future so that you may rule Egypt as you shall choose."

"Oh, holy one! Is his infirmity really so grave? Why won't he let me go to him?" asked the Prince disconsolately.

"You have to be here, because you may be needed here."

"What about the treaty with Assyria?" asked the Successor.

"It is concluded in the sense that Assyria can, without hindrance from us, conduct war in the east and north. But the matter of Phoenicia remains in abeyance pending your accession to the throne."

"O blessed one! ... O holy ruler!" cried the Prince. "What a terrible legacy you've spared me!"

"So Phoenicia remains in abeyance," said Thutmose. "But that aside, a bad thing has happened because His Holiness, to give Assyria earnest that he won't interfere in her war with the northern peoples, has ordered our army cut by twenty thousand mercenary troops."

"What did you say?" shouted the astounded Successor.

Thutmose shook his head sadly. "I'm telling the truth," he said, "and four Libyan regiments have already been disbanded."

"Why, that's madness!" the Successor all but howled, wringing his hands. "Why are we weakening ourselves like that, and where will those men go?"

"That's just it, they've gone into the Libyan Desert, and either they'll attack the Libyans, which will make trouble for us, or they'll join up with them and together strike at our western borders."

"I've heard nothing about it! What have they done? ... And when did they do it? ... No word has reached us!" cried the Prince.

"The disbanded mercenaries went into the desert from Memphis, and Herhor forbade anyone to be told about it."

"Then not even Mephres and Mentesuphis know about it?" asked the Viceroy.

"They do," said Thutmose.

"They do, and I don't!?"

The Prince suddenly became quiet and pale, and a terrible hatred appeared on his young countenance. He grabbed both his confidant's arms and, squeezing them powerfully, whispered: "Listen ... By the holy heads of my father and mother ... by the memory of Ramses the Great ... by all the gods, if any there be, I swear that if—during my reign—the priests don't bend to my will, I'll crush them!"

Thutmose listened, terrified.

"It's them or me!" said the Prince. "Egypt can't have two masters."

"Usually it's had only one: the pharaoh," broke in the confidant.

"Then you'll keep faith with me?"

"Me, all the nobility, and the army, I swear it!"

"Enough," concluded the Successor. "Let them go discharging mercenary regiments ... let them sign treaties ... let them hide from me like bats, and let them deceive us all. But the time will come ...

"And now, Thutmose, rest up from your journey and come to my feast this evening. These people have me so trammeled that all I can do is party ... And so I shall. But someday I'll show them who rules Egypt: they or I ..."

That day the feasts resumed. The Prince, as though ashamed of the army, did not drill with it. Instead his palace swarmed with nobility, officers, assorted performers, and singing girls, and at night there were great orgies at which the sounds of harps mingled with the shouts of drunken banqueters and the spasmodic laughter of women.

Ramses invited Kama to attend a feast but she declined. The Prince took her refusal in bad part; noticing which, Thutmose said, "I've been told Sara has lost your lordship's favor?"

"Don't mention the Jewess to me," replied the Successor. "I suppose you know what she did with my son?"

"I do," said the favorite, "but it seems to me it wasn't her fault. I heard in Memphis that your worshipful mother Lady Nikotris and His Eminence Minister Herhor made your son a Jew so he might rule one day over the Israelites."

"But the Israelites don't have a king, only priests and judges!" said the Prince.

"They don't have one, but they want to. They, too, are sick of government by priests."

The Successor tossed his hand scornfully. "His Holiness' charioteer counts for more than any king, let alone an Israelite king who doesn't yet exist."

"At any rate, Sara isn't that much to blame," said Thutmose.

"Well, if you want to know, someday I'll also repay the priests."

"In this case, neither are they so much to blame. His Eminence Herhor did this from a desire to enhance the glory and power of your dynasty. Moreover, he was acting with the knowledge of Lady Nikotris."

"And why is Mephres meddling in my affairs?" asked the Prince. "Surely he ought to be minding the temples, not influencing the fate of pharaonic issue."

"Mephres is an old man grown crotchety. Today all His Holiness' court are mocking Mephres on account of his practices, about which I myself knew nothing though I've been seeing the holy man almost daily."

"That's interesting ... What does he do?"

"Several times a day," said Thutmose, "he holds a solemn service in the most secret part of the temple and instructs his priests to watch whether the gods lift him into the air during prayer."

"Ha! ... ha! ... ha!" laughed the Successor. "And all this is happening here in Pi-Bast, under our very noses, and I know nothing ..."

"It's a priestly secret."

"A secret that everyone in Memphis is talking about! Ha! ... ha! ... ha! ... At the amphitheater, I saw a Chaldean juggler[2] lie in the air ..."

"So did I," said Thutmose, "but that was a trick, whereas Mephres actually means to ascend into the air on the wings of his piety."

---

[2] A "juggler," in this context, is a person who practices trickery in order to deceive or cheat. *(Translator.)*

"Unheard-of buffoonery!" said the Prince. "What do the other priests think of it?"

"It seems that the sacred papyri mention our having had prophets who possessed the gift of ascending into the air, so the priests aren't surprised at Mephres wanting to. And since, as you know, in our country subordinates see what pleases their superiors, some holy men hold that, during prayer, Mephres actually does ascend into the air, by a couple of fingers!"

"Ha! ... ha! ... ha! ... The whole court is amusing itself with this great secret, while we here, like peasants or diggers, do not even suspect the wonders being wrought at our side. Miserable lot of the Successor to the Egyptian Throne!" laughed the Prince.

When he had settled down, at Thutmose's repeat request he ordered Sara and the infant transferred from the servants' quarters to the villa which Kama had initially occupied.

The Successor's servants were delighted with the decision, and all the servant women, slave women, and even the scribes saw Sara off to her new home with music and jubilation.

Kama, hearing the noise, asked the cause. Told that Sara had been restored to the Successor's good graces and been moved from the slave women's house back to the palace, the infuriated ex-priestess sent for Ramses.

The Prince came.

"This is how you treat me?!" screamed an out-of-control Kama. "This is how? ... You promised I would be your first woman, but before the moon has crossed half the sky you've broken your promise? Do you think Astoreth's vengeance falls only upon priestesses and doesn't reach princes?"

"Tell your Astoreth," replied the Successor calmly, "never to threaten princes, or she too will wind up in the servants' quarters."

"I see," cried Kama. "I'll go to the servants' quarters, maybe even to prison, and you'll be spending the nights with your Jewess! For my having denied the gods for you ... for my having brought their curse upon my head ... for my not having a quiet hour, for my wasting my youth, my life, my very soul for you, this is how you repay me?"

The Prince owned in his heart that Kama had in fact sacrificed a great deal for him, and he felt contrite.

"I haven't been seeing Sara, nor will I," he said. "But what harm is it to you if the unfortunate woman regains some comfort and can nurse her infant?"

The Phoenician woman shook. She raised her clenched fists, her hair bristling and her eyes lighting with the dirty fire of hatred.

"Is that how you answer me? The Jewess is unfortunate because you banished her from the palace, but I must be content though the gods have banished me from all their temples. And what of my soul ... the soul of a priestess drowning in tears and fear, doesn't it mean more to you than that Jewish spawn, that child ... may it live no more, may it ..."

"Silence!" shouted the Prince, stopping her mouth.

She backed away, frightened.

"May I not even complain of my misery?" she asked. "But if you care so much for the child, why did you steal me from the temple, why did you promise I would be your first woman?

"Beware," she raised her voice again, "lest Egypt learn my fate and call you faithless!"

The Prince shook his head, smiling. Finally he sat down and said:

"My teacher was right, warning me about women. You're like a ripe peach to the eyes of a man whose tongue is parched with thirst. But only to appearances. For woe betide the fool who ventures to bite into the beautiful fruit: instead of a cooling sweetness, he'll find a nest of wasps which will wound not only his lips but his heart."

"Complaining already? You won't spare me even this shame? For my having sacrificed for you my station as a priestess, and my virtue!"

The Prince was shaking his head, smiling.

"I'd never have thought," he said after a moment, "that a peasants' bedtime story could come true. But I see that it's so. Listen, Kama, and maybe you'll take thought and won't force me to withdraw the favor that I bear for you."

"Now he'll be telling stories!" said the priestess bitterly. "You told me one before, and much good it did me."

"This one certainly will do you good, if you but try to understand it."

"Will there be anything in it about Jewish brats?"

"About priestesses too, just listen closely: Once upon a time, in this very city of Pi-Bast, in the square before the Temple of Ptah, Prince Setne[3] saw a very beautiful woman. She was more beautiful than any he had ever encountered; and what's more, she was wearing a great deal of gold.

"The Prince took a tremendous fancy to her. He inquired about her; and on being told she was the daughter of the high priest in Pi-Bast, he sent his equerry to her with an offer:

"'I will give you ten gold rings if you spend an hour with me.'

"The equerry went to the beautiful Tabubu[4] and repeated Prince Setne's words to her. The lady heard him out politely and answered as becomes a young lady of good breeding:

"'I am the daughter of a high priest; I am an innocent and respectable girl. Therefore if the Prince wishes the pleasure of my acquaintance, let him come to my house, where all will be in readiness and our acquaintance will not expose me to the talk of all the gossips in the street.'

"So Prince Setne followed Lady Tabubu to the top floor to her rooms, whose walls were inlaid with lapis lazuli and pale-green enamel.[5] There were many beds covered with regal linen, and not a few unipod tables bearing gold winecups. One of these being filled with wine and handed to the Prince, Tabubu said, 'Please have a drink.' To which the Prince replied, 'You know I did not come for wine.' Nevertheless they sat down to a feast, during which Tabubu wore a long opaque gown fastened up to the neck. When the intoxicated Prince tried to kiss her, she pushed him away and replied:

"'This house will be yours. Mind you, though, I am no streetwalker but an innocent

---

[3] The name "Setne" (Prus calls him *Satni*) is a distortion of "*setem*," a high rank of priesthood that was used as the name of the hero of a cycle of stories dating to Egypt's later, Greco-Roman period. The real-life Setne was Prince Khamwese, *sem*-priest of Ptah, and Ramses the Great's fourth son—one of several crown princes whom Ramses outlived, and the best known of his sons. Khamwese was remembered as a wise man and has been called "the first Egyptologist" for his efforts to identify and restore historic buildings, tombs, and temples. Prus here retells one of the stories of the Setne cycle, "The Story of Setne and Tabubu." *(Translator.)*

[4] Tabubu (Prus calls her *Tbubui*) is the heroine of "The Story of Setne and Tabubu." *(Translator.)*

[5] Enamel: The use of enameled tiles as wall decoration was common in Mesopotamia rather than in Egypt. *(Translator.)*

woman. Therefore if you would have me be docile to you, pledge me your troth and sign your fortune over to me.'

"'Then get a scribe,' cried the Prince. And when the scribe had been brought, Setne had him draw up a marriage contract and a deed of gift whereby he signed over all his money, chattels, and real property to Tabubu.

"An hour later, the servants informed the Prince that his children were waiting downstairs. Tabubu then left him, but soon returned wearing a dress of diaphanous gauze. Setne again tried to embrace her, but she pushed him away, saying:

"'This house will be yours. But since I am no harlot but an innocent maiden, if you would possess me then let your children make out a quitclaim so that they will not later bring litigation against my children.'

"Setne called his children upstairs and told them to sign a quitclaim, which they did. But when, intoxicated by her long resistance, he tried to approach Tabubu, she again stopped him.

"'This house will be yours,' she said. 'But I am not just anybody; I am a chaste virgin. Therefore if you love me, have your children killed so they will not someday wrest the estate from mine.'"

"What a long story!" interrupted Kama impatiently.

"It's almost over," replied the Successor. "And, Kama, do you know what Setne said: 'If that be your wish ... then let the deed be done!'

"Tabubu did not need to be told twice. She had the children killed in front of their father's eyes and threw their bloodied members out the window to the dogs and cats. Only then did Setne enter her room and recline on her ebony bed inlaid with ivory."[6]

"Tabubu did well, distrusting the assurances of men," said the irritated Kama.

"But Setne," said the Successor, "did still better: he woke ... for his terrible crime had been only a dream.

"Remember, Kama: the surest way to rouse a man from love's intoxication is to cast curses on his son."

"Don't worry, lord, I'll never again mention to you either my misfortune or your son," answered Kama glumly.

"And I won't withdraw my favor from you, and you shall be happy," concluded Ramses.

---

[6] Authentic story. *(Author.)*

CHAPTER 40

Ominous tidings about the Libyans had begun spreading as well among the populace of Pi-Bast. It was said that the barbarian soldiers disbanded by the priests had, in returning to their homeland, at first begged, then stolen, and finally had begun looting and burning Egyptian villages and murdering their inhabitants.

Thus, over several days' time, had been attacked and destroyed the towns of Khinensu, Per-Medjed,[1] and Saka,[2] south of Lake Moeris. Thus had perished a caravan of Egyptian merchants and pilgrims returning from the oasis of Ut-Mehet.[3] The Kingdom's whole western border was in peril, and the inhabitants had begun fleeing even from Terenuthis.[4] For in that area, too, from the direction of the sea, Libyan bands had appeared, rumored to have been sent out by the fearsome chieftain Musawasa,[5] who was expected to declare holy war against Egypt throughout the desert.

So if, of an evening, the western heavens remained red too long, the residents of Pi-Bast would be gripped with fear. People gathered in the streets, and some went up onto the flat roofs or climbed trees—and announced that they saw a fire in Menuf[6] or Sekhem. Some, despite the dusk, even made out fleeing inhabitants or Libyan hosts marching for Pi-Bast in long black files.

Despite the people's alarm, the rulers of the nome behaved apathetically, for they had received no instructions from the central authorities.

Prince Ramses knew about the anxiety of the crowds and saw the apathy of the Pi-Bast dignitaries. He was furious at receiving no instructions from Memphis and at neither Mephres nor Mentesuphis speaking with him about the alarums to the Kingdom.

But since the two priests did not present themselves to him—indeed, seemed to be avoiding conversation with him—the Viceroy did not seek them out either or make any military preparations.

[1] Per-Medjed: a city on the west bank of the Nile, south of the Fayum Oasis; capital of the 19th Nome of Upper Egypt. It was known to the Greeks as Oxyrhynchus. Prus calls it *Pimat*. *(Translator.)*

[2] Saka: a city on the west bank of the Nile, south of Per-Medjed; capital of the 17th Nome of Upper Egypt. It was known to the Greeks as Cynopolis. Prus calls it *Kasa*. *(Translator.)*

[3] Ut-Mehet ("Northern Oasis"): an oasis in the Libyan Desert. Prus calls it *Uit-Mehe*. *(Translator.)*

[4] Terenuthis: Greek name of a town in Egypt's western Delta, on the west bank of the Nile's Bolbitine branch. *(Translator.)*

[5] Musawasa: name formed from that of the *Meshwesh*, an ancient Libyan tribe. *(Translator.)*

[6] Menuf: a town in the western Delta, in the 4th Nome of Lower Egypt. *(Translator.)*

Finally he stopped visiting the regiments stationed outside Pi-Bast and instead, gathering all the young nobility at the palace, disported himself and feasted, stifling in his heart his outrage at the priests and his fears for the Kingdom.

"You'll see!" he told Thutmose. "The holy prophets will get us into such a fix that Musawasa will take Lower Egypt and we'll have to flee to Thebes, if not to Syene,[7] assuming the Ethiopians haven't chased us out of there."

"That's true," replied Thutmose, "our rulers are acting like traitors."

The first day of Athyr (August-September) saw the greatest feast at the Successor's palace. The revels began at two in the afternoon, and by sunset everyone was drunk. It ended in men and women wallowing on a floor awash in wine and strewn with flowers and potsherds.

The Prince was the most sentient of the company. He was not yet supine but sat in a chair, holding on his knees two beautiful dancing girls, one of whom plied him with wine while the other poured strong fragrances on his head.

Just then an aide entered the hall, clambered over several drunken revelers, and approached the Successor.

"Your Eminence," he whispered, "the holy Mephres and Mentesuphis wish to speak with you at once."

The Successor pushed away the girls and, flushed, in stained tunic, tottered up to his room.

At sight of him, Mephres and Mentesuphis exchanged glances.

"What do you want, Eminences?" asked the Prince, dropping into a chair.

"I don't know whether Your Eminence will be able to hear us out," said Mentesuphis.

"Ah! ... You think I'm drunk?" cried the Prince. "Fear not ... Today all Egypt is so mad or stupid that the most sense remains in her drunkards."

The priests frowned, but Mentesuphis began:

"Your Eminence is aware that our Lord and the Supreme Council have decided to discharge twenty thousand mercenary troops ..."

"Well, not really," broke in the Successor. "You didn't see fit to ask my advice in such a wise decision, or to inform me that four regiments have already been disbanded and that those men are attacking our cities from hunger!"

"It seems to me Your Eminence is judging the orders of His Holiness the Pharaoh," said Mentesuphis.

"Not His Holiness'!" cried the Prince, stamping his foot, "but the orders of traitors who are taking advantage of the illness of my father and Lord to sell the Kingdom out to the Assyrians and Libyans!"

The priests were dumbfounded. No Egyptian had ever uttered such words.

"Let us come back in a couple of hours, Prince ... when you are calmer," said Mephres.

"No need. I know what's happening on our western border. Or rather I don't, but my cooks, stableboys, and scullery maids do. So maybe now, reverend fathers, you would care to initiate me as well into your plans?"

---

[7] Syene: ancient Greek name for the city now called Aswan, in southern Egypt. Prus here calls the city *Sunnu. (Translator.)*

Mentesuphis assumed a noncommittal expression. "The Libyans," he said, "have rebelled and are massing hosts with the intent of attacking Egypt."

"I see."

"Therefore," continued Mentesuphis, "by the will of His Holiness and the Supreme Council, Your Eminence is to gather the armies of Lower Egypt and destroy the rebels."

"Where's the order?"

Mentesuphis took from his bosom a parchment bearing seals and handed it to the Prince.

"So from this moment I am commander-in-chief and the supreme authority in this province?" asked the Crown Prince.

"That is so."

"And I may hold a council of war with you?"

"Certainly," said Mephres. "Though right now ..."

"Sit," said the Prince.

The priests obeyed.

"I ask you, because it is necessary to my plans: why were the Libyan regiments disbanded?"

"Others, too, will be," said Mentesuphis. "The Supreme Council wants to get rid of twenty thousand of the most expensive troops in order to provide His Holiness' treasury with four thousand talents a year, without which the royal court may find itself in straits ..."

"Which do not threaten the most wretched Egyptian priest!" broke in the Prince.

"Your Eminence forgets that it is unseemly to call a priest 'wretched,'" replied Mentesuphis. "And the fact that none of them is at risk of straits is due to the frugality of their lives."

"In that case, it must be the statues that drink the wine delivered daily to the temples, and the stone gods that deck their women in gold and precious stones," scoffed the Prince. "But never mind your frugality! The Priestly Council doesn't disband twenty thousand men and open the gates of Egypt to bandits in order to replenish the pharaoh's treasury!"

"Then why?"

"To ingratiate itself to King Assar. And since His Holiness declined to hand Phoenicia over to the Assyrians, you want to weaken the Kingdom another way: by disbanding the mercenaries and provoking war on our western border."

"The gods are my witness that Your Eminence astounds us!" exclaimed Mentesuphis.

"The shades of the pharaohs would be more astounded to hear that, in this same Egypt where royal power has been trammeled, a Chaldean fraud sways the fate of the Kingdom!"

"I don't believe my ears!" said Mentesuphis. "What is Your Eminence saying about a Chaldean?"

The Viceroy laughed sarcastically.

"I'm speaking of Berossus ... If you haven't heard of him, holy man, ask the venerable Mephres; and if he too has forgotten, let him consult Herhor and Pentuer.

"It's a great secret of your temples! A foreign vagabond who got into Egypt like a thief, imposes on members of the Supreme Council a treaty so disgraceful that we might sign it only after defeats in battle, after the loss of all the regiments and both capitals.[8]

"And to think that one man did this, most likely a spy of King Assar's! And our wise men

---

[8] "both capitals": presumably Memphis in Lower, and Thebes in Upper, Egypt. *(Translator.)*

let themselves be so charmed by his eloquence that, since the Pharaoh wouldn't let them give up Phoenicia, they at least disband regiments and provoke war on the western border.

"Did you ever hear the like?" continued Ramses, no longer in control of himself. "At the best time to build up the army to three hundred thousand men and send it against Nineveh, these pious madmen scatter twenty thousand men and set fire to their own house."

Mephres listened to the cruel taunts, stiff and pale. At last he spoke:

"Your Eminence, I know not from what source you draw your information. May it be as pure as the hearts of the Supreme Council! Let us suppose, however, that you are right and that a Chaldean priest did prevail on the Council to sign an onerous pact with Assyria. Well, if that were so, how would you know that the priest was not an emissary of the gods, who through his lips warned us of impending dangers to Egypt?"

"Since when have the Chaldeans enjoyed such trust on your part?" asked the Prince.

"Chaldea's priests are the elder brethren of Egypt's," interjected Mentesuphis.

"Then perhaps Assyria's king is master to the pharaoh?" said the Prince.

"Do not blaspheme, Eminence," Mephres rebuked him. "You are rummaging recklessly in the holiest secrets, and that has been dangerous even for men greater than yourself!"

"Very well, I won't rummage! But how can you tell that one Chaldean is an emissary of the gods; and another, a spy of King Assar's?"

"By miracles," replied Mephres. "If at the Prince's bidding this room filled with spirits, if invisible powers lifted you into the air, we should say that you were an instrument of the immortals and we would heed your advice."

Ramses shrugged. "I, too, have seen spirits: a young girl produced them. And at the amphitheater I saw a juggler lie in the air."

"But you did not detect the fine strings that his four assistants held in their teeth," said Mentesuphis.

The Prince again broke into laughter and, recalling what Thutmose had told him about Mephres' rituals, he said sarcastically:

"In the reign of King Cheops, a certain high priest wanted very badly to fly in the air. With that in view, he prayed to the gods and bade his subordinates watch whether invisible forces lifted him. And, holy men, what do you suppose? There wasn't a day but the prophets assured the high priest that he was rising into the air; not much, to be sure, only a finger off the floor. But ... what's that to Your Eminence?" he suddenly asked Mephres.

As he listened to his own story being rehearsed, the high priest reeled in his chair and would have fallen off had he not been held up by Mentesuphis.

Ramses was disconcerted. He gave the old man water to drink, rubbed his forehead and temples with vinegar, and cooled him with a fan.

Shortly the holy Mephres came to. He rose from his chair and said to Mentesuphis: "I suppose we may go?"

"I should think so."

"What should I do?" asked the Prince, sensing that something bad had happened.

"Carry out the duties of commander-in-chief," replied Mentesuphis coldly.

The two priests bowed ceremoniously to the Prince and went out. The Viceroy was now quite sober, and a great weight descended upon his heart. He realized now that he had committed two grave errors: he had revealed to the priests that he knew their great secret—and he had mercilessly taunted Mephres.

He would have given a year of his life to expunge the whole drunken conversation from their memories. But it was too late.

"It's no use," he thought, "I've given myself away and bought myself some mortal enemies. Too bad. The struggle begins at the most inopportune moment for me. But let's go on. More than one pharaoh has fought the priesthood and defeated it, without even having very strong allies."

Nevertheless, he so felt the peril of his situation that he swore by the holy head of his father never again to drink wine in quantity.

He sent for Thutmose. The confidant appeared at once, quite sober.

"We have a war, and I'm commander-in-chief," said the Successor.

Thutmose made a deep bow.

"And I'll never get drunk again," added the Prince. "Do you know why?"

"A commander should avoid wine and intoxicating fragrances," replied Thutmose.

"I forgot that ... and I blabbed to the priests ..."

"Blabbed what?" cried Thutmose, alarmed.

"That I despise them and laugh at their miracles."

"No harm done. They surely never reckon on human love."

"And that I know their political secrets," added the Prince.

"Ay!" hissed Thutmose. "Now, that was unnecessary."

"Never mind," said Ramses. "Send couriers at once to the regiments, for their commanders to assemble tomorrow morning for a council of war. Order beacons lit so all the armies of Lower Egypt will march out tomorrow for the western border. Go tell the Nomarch to inform the other nomarchs of the need to gather provisions, clothing, and weapons."

"We'll have trouble with the Nile," said Thutmose.

"Have all the boats and ships on the Nile branches commandeered for troop ferrying. We must also call on the nomarchs to see about preparing reserve regiments."

Meanwhile Mephres and Mentesuphis were returning to their rooms at the Temple of Ptah. When they were alone in a cell, the high priest lifted up his hands and cried:

"Trinity of immortal gods: Osiris, Isis, and Horus—save Egypt from destruction! Never has any pharaoh uttered as many blasphemies as we heard today from this child. What am I saying—pharaoh? ... No enemy of Egypt, no Hittite, Phoenician, Libyan would dare to so affront priestly untouchability."

"Wine makes a man transparent," replied Mentesuphis.

"Why, there's a surging nest of vipers inside that young heart. He holds the priesthood in contempt, scoffs at miracles, disbelieves in the gods."

"What most gives me concern, though," mused Mentesuphis, "is how he found out about your talks with Berossus. Because I'll swear he does know about them."

"There has been a terrible betrayal," replied Mephres, clutching his head.

"Strange thing! There were the four of you ..."

"No. Others also knew about Berossus: the elder priestess of Isis, the two priests who pointed his way to the Temple of Set, and the priest who received him at the gate ... Wait, now!" said Mephres. "That priest was in the undergrounds all the time. Maybe he listened in?"

"Anyway, he didn't sell the secret to the child but to someone more consequential. And that's dangerous!"

There was a knock at the cell, announcing the high priest of the Temple of Ptah, the holy Sem.[9] "Peace be with you," he said, entering.

"A blessing on your heart."

"I come because you speak in such raised voices as though there had been some misfortune. Surely you're not frightened of the war with the wretched Libyan?" said Sem.

"What might Your Honor think of the Crown Prince?" Mentesuphis interrupted him.

"I think," replied Sem, "that he must be very pleased with the war and the commander-in-chief-ship. He's a born hero! When I look at him, I'm put in mind of Ramses' lion. The boy is ready to hurl himself single-handed at all the Libyan hosts—and he just may rout them."

"The boy," said Mephres, "may overturn all our temples and wipe Egypt from the face of the earth."

The holy Sem quickly took out a gold amulet he wore on his chest and whispered:

"Begone, evil words, into the desert. Depart and do no harm to the just!... Whatever is Your Eminence talking about!" he said louder, in a tone of reproach.

"His Eminence Mephres speaks the truth," said Mentesuphis. "Your head would ache, and your stomach too, if human lips could repeat the blasphemies we heard today from this youngster."

"Do not jest, prophet," said High Priest Sem indignantly. "I would sooner believe that water burns and that air extinguishes, than that Ramses perpetrates blasphemies."

"He did so ostensibly while drunk," said Mephres spitefully.

"Even so. I won't deny the Prince is light-minded and a carouser, but a blasphemer!"

"That's what we thought too," said Mentesuphis. "And we felt so sure we knew his character that, when he returned from the Temple of Hathor, we discontinued surveillance of him."

"You grudged the gold to pay the agents," said Mephres. "You see what consequences a seemingly slight neglect can bring!"

"But what has happened?" asked Sem impatiently.

"In brief: the Crown Prince mocks the gods ..."

"Oh!"

"Judges the orders of the Pharaoh ..."

"Can it be?"

"Calls the Supreme Council traitors ..."

"But ..."

"And he found out from someone about the arrival of Berossus, and even about his having seen Mephres, Herhor, and Pentuer at the Temple of Set."

High Priest Sem grabbed his head in both hands and began running about the cell.

"It can't be!" he said. "It can't be! ... Someone must have cast a spell on the young man. Maybe that Phoenician priestess whom he stole from the temple?"

The remark seemed to Mentesuphis so apt that he glanced at Mephres. But the incensed high priest would not be diverted from his course.

"We shall see," he replied. "First, though, we must investigate what the Prince did, day by day, after his return from the Temple of Hathor. He had too much freedom, too many

---

[9] Sem: The name may have been suggested by the title, "*sem*," held by many high priests of the god Ptah, such as Prince Khamwese, fourth son of Ramses II (the Great). A *sem* priest wore a short wig with a side-lock, and a leopard skin. A different *Sem* was the biblical *Sem* (in English, oftener *Shem*), mentioned in *Genesis 10:21* and *11:10*, who gave his name to the Near East's Semitic peoples. *(Translator.)*

relations with infidels and enemies of Egypt. And, Sem, Your Eminence shall help us."

Accordingly, the very next day High Priest Sem had the people summoned to a solemn service at the Temple of Ptah.

Priestly heralds went out to streetcorners, squares, even to fields and, with the help of trumpets and flutes, called the people together. When a sufficient audience was gathered, the heralds announced that for three days prayers and processions would be held at the Temple of Ptah, that the good god might bless the Egyptian arms and confound the Libyans. And that he might visit leprosy, blindness, and madness on their leader Musawasa.

It came to pass as the priests proposed. From morning till late at night, the simple populace of all walks of life gathered outside the temple walls, the aristocracy and rich townspeople assembled in the outer vestibule, and local priests and those of adjacent nomes made offerings to the god Ptah and sent up prayers in the most sacred chapel.

Three times daily a solemn procession went out, with the god's venerable statue carried in a curtained golden boat; and the populace prostrated themselves on their faces and confessed aloud their misdeeds while prophets, thickly scattered among the crowd, facilitated their contrition with suitable questions. The same happened in the temple vestibule. However, since the eminent and wealthy disliked inculpating themselves aloud, the holy fathers took penitents aside and quietly dispensed counsel and admonitions to them.

At noon the service was at its most solemn. At that hour the troops marching westward came to receive the blessing of the high priest and to renew the power of their amulets which attenuated enemy blows.

Sometimes thunder rang within the temple, and at nighttime lightning flashed over the pylon. This was a sign that the god had heard someone's prayers or was communing with the priests.

By the end of the solemnities, when Their Eminences Sem, Mephres, and Mentesuphis assembled for a conference, the situation had been cleared up.

The service had brought the temple some forty talents' income; but some sixty talents had been spent on gifts or in payment of debts of various aristocrats and ranking military.

And the following information had been gleaned:

Among the military there circulated a rumor that, as soon as Prince Ramses mounted the throne, he would begin a war with Assyria which would assure its participants great profits. The lowliest soldier, it was said, would not return from the expedition without a thousand drachmas or better. Among the populace, it was whispered that when the pharaoh returned from Nineveh after his victory, he would gift all the peasants with slaves and would forgive Egypt's taxes for a number of years.

The aristocracy thought the new pharaoh would, above all, take from the priests and restore to the nobility all the estates that had become temple property in forfeit of contracted debts. It was also said the future pharaoh would govern autocratically, without the participation of the Supreme Priestly Council.

Finally, at all social strata there prevailed a conviction that Prince Ramses, in order to secure the help of the Phoenicians, had converted to the goddess Ishtar and was showing her his special devotion. In any case, it was certain that one night the Crown Prince had visited the Temple of Ishtar and had there seen wonders. Additionally, rumors among the wealthy Asiatics had it that Ramses had made great gifts to the temple and in return had received from there a priestess who was to confirm him in the faith.

All this information had been gathered by His Eminence Sem and his priests. And the holy fathers Mephres and Mentesuphis communicated to him another piece of news, which had come to them from Memphis.

It was that the Chaldean priest and wonderworker Berossus had been received in the undergrounds of the Temple of Set by the priest Osochor,[10] who two months later, when giving his daughter in marriage, had presented her with costly gems and had bought the newlyweds a big farm. And since Osochor did not have that substantial an income, the suspicion arose that the priest, having listened in to Berossus' conversation with the Egyptian dignitaries, had next sold the secret of the treaty to the Phoenicians and received from them a great fortune.

On hearing this out, High Priest Sem said, "If the holy Berossus really is a wonderworker, then above all ask him whether Osochor betrayed the secret."

"The wonderworker Berossus was asked about it," replied Mephres, "but the holy man said he wished to remain silent in the matter. He added that, even if someone did listen in to their negotiations and inform the Phoenicians about it, Egypt and Chaldea will suffer no harm. Therefore, if the culprit is found, he ought to be accorded mercy."

"A holy man! ... He truly is a holy man!" whispered Sem.

"What does Your Eminence think," Mephres asked Sem, "of the Crown Prince and the unrest his conduct has provoked?"

"I will say the same as Berossus: the Crown Prince will do Egypt no harm, so we should be forbearing."

"This youngster scoffs at the gods and miracles, visits foreign temples, stirs the populace to rebellion ... Those are no small things!" spoke Mephres bitterly, unable to forgive Ramses' brutal mockery of his rituals.

High Priest Sem liked Ramses, and replied with an indulgent smile:

"What Egyptian peasant wouldn't like to have a slave, so that he might give up his own hard work for sweet idleness?"

"And is there in the world a man who does not dream of not paying taxes? For what he pays to the treasury, his wife, he himself, and the children could have attractive clothes and enjoy a variety of pleasures."

"Idleness and excessive expenditures spoil a man," said Mentesuphis.

"What soldier," Sem went on, "would not like a war and would not desire a profit of a thousand drachmas or better?"

"Further, I ask you, fathers: what pharaoh, what nomarch, what nobleman gladly pays his contracted debts and does not look askance at the wealth of the temples?"

"That is a godless coveting!" whispered Mephres.

"Finally," said Sem, "what crown prince has not dreamt of limiting the authority of the priests? What pharaoh, at the start of his reign, has not wanted to shake off the tutelage of the Supreme Council?"

"Your words are full of wisdom," said Mephres, "but where are they supposed to lead us?"

---

[10] Osochor: name borrowed from Osochor (usually called "Osorkon the Elder"), the fifth pharaoh of Egypt's 21st Dynasty, and the first pharaoh of Libyan extraction. The 21st Dynasty, which succeeded the 20th Dynasty featured in *Pharaoh*, ruled Lower Egypt from Tanis, and is therefore called the "Tanite Dynasty." The rest of the country was effectively ruled from Thebes by the High Priests of Amon. *(Translator.)*

"To your not lodging a complaint against the Crown Prince with the Supreme Council. No court would condemn the Prince because the peasants would fain not pay taxes or because the soldiers desire war. Indeed, you could meet with reproof; for had you watched the Prince day in, day out, and curbed his little antics, there would not today be a pyramid of accusations—of completely unsubstantiated accusations.

"In such matters, the evil is not in people's propensity to sin, for they have had that always. What is dangerous is that we did not watch them. Our sacred river, the mother of Egypt, would very quickly silt up the canals if the engineers stopped watching her."

"What will Your Eminence say of the insults the Prince perpetrated in speaking with us? Will you forgive his hideous mocking of miracles?" asked Mephres. "This youngster has gravely insulted my piety."

"Who speaks with a drunkard, insults himself," replied Sem. "Your Eminences had no business discussing the most important matters of state with an inebriated Prince. Indeed, you erred in naming an intoxicated man commander of an army, for a commander must be sober."

"I humble myself before your wisdom," said Mephres, "but I vote for lodging a complaint against the Successor with the Supreme Council."

"I vote against," replied Sem energetically. "The Council must learn of the Viceroy's doings but not in the form of a complaint, only of an ordinary report."

"I too am against a complaint," said Mentesuphis.

High Priest Mephres, seeing two votes against him, abandoned his demand for a complaint against the Prince. But he would not forget the insult to him, and he concealed his animus in his heart.

He was a learned and pious old man, but vengeful. He would sooner have forgiven having his hand cut off than having his priestly dignity offended.

CHAPTER 41

On the advice of astrologers, the headquarters were to move out of Pi-Bast on the seventh day of Athyr. For that day was "good, good, good." The gods in heaven, and the people on earth, rejoiced in the victory of Ra over his enemies; and whoever came into the world on that day was destined to die in advanced age, surrounded with respect.

It was also a propitious day for pregnant women and cloth merchants, and bad for frogs and mice.

From the moment of his appointment as commander-in-chief, Ramses had feverishly thrown himself to work. He personally received each incoming regiment, inspecting its weapons, clothing, and camps. He personally welcomed recruits and urged them to master the drills, to the downfall of the enemy and the glory of the pharaoh. He presided over every council of war, was present at the interrogation of every spy and, as intelligence came in, with his own hand marked on a map the movements of the Egyptian armies and the positions of the enemy.

He rode from place to place so swiftly that he was expected everywhere, yet swooped down suddenly as a hawk. In the morning he was south of Pi-Bast inspecting provisions; an hour later, he showed up north of the city and discovered that the Yeb[1] Regiment was a hundred fifty men short. Toward evening he overtook the advance guard, was present at the crossing of a Nile branch, and inspected two hundred chariots.

The holy Mentesuphis, who as Herhor's plenipotentiary was well versed in the art of war, could not contain his admiration.

"Your Eminences know," he told Sem and Mephres, "that I've disliked the Crown Prince ever since I discovered his spitefulness and perversity. But may Osiris be my witness, the young man is a born commander. I'll tell you something incredible: we will have our forces gathered at the border three or four days sooner than could have been expected. The Libyans have already lost the war, though they have yet to hear the whistle of our arrow."

"The more dangerous to us, such a pharaoh," said Mephres, with the doggedness of the old.

Toward evening on the sixth day of Athyr, Prince Ramses bathed and told the staff that on the morrow, two hours before dawn, they would be moving out.

"And now I want to get some sleep," he concluded.

---

[1] Yeb (in Prus' Polish text, *Jeb*): name possibly borrowed from one of the ancient names for Elephantine Island, in the Nile River at southern Egypt's border with Nubia. *(Translator.)*

That, however, was easier said than done.

The whole city teemed with soldiers, and a regiment encamped next to the Successor's palace ate, drank, and sang with no thought of rest.

The Prince repaired to his most secluded room, but even there he was not allowed to undress. Every few minutes, some aide would rush in with a trivial report or for orders in matters that could have been settled by the regimental commander. Spies were brought in who had no new intelligence; great lords reported with small bands of men to offer their volunteer services. Phoenician merchants came soliciting orders for the army, and purveyors complained about the demands of generals.

Nor was there a shortage of soothsayers and astrologers who, at the last moment before the outbound march, wanted to cast the Prince's horoscope; or of conjurors with infallible amulets to sell against projectiles.

All these people simply burst into the Prince's room, for each believed that the war's outcome rested in his hands and that, under the circumstances, etiquette must give way.

The Successor dealt patiently with them. But when one of his women slipped in after an astrologer, complaining that Ramses clearly didn't love her since he hadn't told her goodbye, and when a quarter-hour later he heard another mistress sobbing outside his window, the Successor had had enough.

He called in Thutmose and told him:

"Stay in this room and, if you feel so inclined, console the women of my house. I'm going to hide out in the garden, or I won't get any sleep and tomorrow I'll look like a chicken that's been rescued from a well."

"Where am I to look for you, if need arise?" asked Thutmose.

"Don't look for me anywhere!" laughed the Prince. "I'll turn up by myself at reveille."

He threw on a long, hooded cloak and slipped out into the garden.

But soldiers, cooks' helpers, and other servants of the Successor's were wandering about the garden: order had vanished from the palace precincts, as usual before a departure for war. Seeing this, Ramses headed for the densest part of the park, found a small vine-grown bower, and contentedly threw himself down on a bench.

"They won't find me here," he muttered, "not the priests, nor the women."

Soon he was asleep like a rock.

For several days Kama had been feeling unwell. To her irritability had been joined a peculiar indisposition and joint pains. Also her face itched, particularly her forehead over the eyebrows.

She found these slight afflictions so disturbing that she stopped fearing for her life and instead sat continually before a mirror, having told the servants they could do what they liked, so long as they let her be. She now thought about neither Ramses nor the hateful Sara; all her attention was occupied by spots on her forehead which an unpracticed eye would not even have noticed.

"A spot ... yes, there are spots," she told herself anxiously. "Two ... three ... O Astoreth, you wouldn't punish your priestess that way! Better, death ... But, again, what nonsense. When I rub my forehead with my fingers, the spots get redder. Something must have stung me, or I rubbed on impure oil. I'll wash, and by tomorrow the spots will have gone."

Tomorrow came, but the spots had not gone away.

She called a servant girl. "Listen," said Kama, "take a look at me ..."

With that, she sat down in a less illuminated part of the room.

"Listen," she said in a subdued voice. "Do ... do you see spots on my face? Only ... don't come near!"

"I don't see a thing," said the servant.

"Beneath my left eye? ... Over the eyebrows?" asked Kama with growing irritation.

"Could your ladyship please sit with your divine face to the light?" said the servant girl.

Naturally the request infuriated Kama. "Get out, you wretch!" she cried, "and don't show yourself to me!"

When the servant girl had fled, her mistress threw herself feverishly to the dressing table, opened a couple of jars and, with a small brush, painted her face a pink color.

Toward evening, still feeling joint pains and an anxiety worse than the pains, she asked for a physician to be summoned. When told that he had come, she looked in the mirror— and a new attack of madness seemed to overtake her. She threw the mirror to the floor and wailed that she did not want the physician.

During the sixth of Athyr, she did not eat all day and wouldn't see anyone.

When after sunset a slave girl entered with a light, Kama wrapped her head in a shawl and lay down on the bed. She told the girl to get out quickly, then seated herself in an armchair at a distance from the lamp and passed several hours in a drowsy stupor.

"There are no spots," she thought, "or if there are, it's not those ... It's not leprosy!

"Gods!" she shouted, throwing herself to the floor, "it can't be! Gods, save me! I'll go back to the temple ... I'll atone with the rest of my life ..."

She calmed down again, and thought:

"There are no spots. I've been rubbing my skin for several days, so it's reddened. Anyway, did anyone ever hear of a priestess and crown prince's woman coming down with leprosy? ... Gods! ... It's never been ... It's only fishermen, convicts, and wretched Jews! Oh, that vile Jewess! Send leprosy down on her, O celestial powers ..."

A shadow flashed in the first-floor window. Then there was a swishing sound and, from outside, Prince Ramses jumped into the middle of the room.

Kama was dumbstruck. Suddenly she grabbed her head, boundless terror in her eyes.

"Lykon?" she whispered. "Lykon, you're here? ... You'll be killed! ... They're after you ..."

"I know," said the Greek, laughing sarcastically. "All the Phoenicians and all His Holiness' police are after me.

"Still," he added, "here I am, and I've been to your lord's."

"You've been to the Prince's?"

"Yes, in his own room. And I would've left a dagger in his breast if evil spirits hadn't removed him. Evidently your lover went to another woman."

"What do you want here? ... Flee!" whispered Kama.

"With you," he replied. "There's a wagon in the street waiting to take us to the Nile, where I have a barge ..."

"You're mad! The city and roads are crawling with troops."

"That's how I was able to get into the palace and we'll easily slip away," said Lykon. "Collect your valuables ... I'll soon be back for you!"

"Where are you going?"

"I'm going to seek out your master," he said. "I'm not departing without leaving him a keepsake ..."

"You're mad!"

"Shut up!" he broke in, pale with anger. "Are you going to defend him?"

Kama fell to thinking; she clenched her fists, and an ominous light flashed in her eyes. "What if you don't find him?" she asked.

"I'll kill a couple of his sleeping soldiers ... set fire to the palace ... I don't know ... But I'm not going away without leaving a keepsake!"

Kama's great eyes held such a baleful expression that Lykon was taken aback. "What's with you?" he asked.

"Nothing. Listen. You've never looked more like the Prince! If you want to do something good ..."

She brought her face to his ear and whispered.

The Greek listened, astounded. "Woman," he said, "the worst spirits speak through you! Yes, suspicion will fall on him ..."

"Better than the dagger," she laughed, "eh?"

"I'd never have thought of it! ... How about both of them?"

"No! ... Let her live ... This will be my revenge."

"What a wicked soul!" whispered Lykon. "But I like you ... We'll pay them back royally!"

He withdrew to the window and disappeared. Kama leaned out after him and listened feverishly, oblivious of self.

Perhaps a quarter hour after Lykon's departure, from the direction of the fig grove there rang a woman's piercing scream. It repeated a couple of times and fell still.

Instead of the expected joy, Kama was overcome with terror. She dropped to her knees and peered distraughtly into the dark garden.

There was a quiet sound of running; a porch post creaked; and Lykon reappeared in the window in a dark cloak. He was panting violently, and his hands shook.

"Where are the jewels?" he whispered.

"Let me be," she said.

The Greek grabbed the scruff of her neck. "You wretch!" he said, "don't you understand that before sunrise they'll jail you, and strangle you in a couple of days?"

"I'm ill ..."

"Where are the jewels?"

"Under the bed."

Lykon went into the room, by lamplight retrieved a small heavy chest, threw a cloak on Kama, and tugged her arm.

"Get going. Where's the door used by that ... master of yours?"

"Leave me ..."

The Greek bent over her and whispered:

"Ah! You think I'm going to leave you here? I now care as much for you as for a bitch that's lost her nose. But you have to come with me. Your master needs to learn he has a better. He stole a priestess from a goddess, I'm taking a mistress from him."

"I tell you I'm ill ..."

The Greek took out a slender dagger and poised it on the back of her neck. She shuddered and whispered, "I'm coming ..."

Through a hidden door they went out into the garden. They heard, from the direction of the Prince's palace, a murmur of soldiers at their fires. Here and there lights were visible between the trees; from time to time, some servant of the Successor's passed them. At the gate they were challenged by a sentry: "Who goes there?"

"Thebes," said Lykon.

They passed into the street and vanished into the alleys of Pi-Bast's foreign quarter.

Two hours before dawn, trumpets and drums sounded in the city. Thutmose still lay steeped in deep slumber when Prince Ramses pulled the cloak off him and laughed merrily: "Rise, vigilant commander! The regiments have set out."

Thutmose sat up on the bed and rubbed his sleepy eyes. "Oh, it's you, lord?" he yawned. "Did you sleep well?"

"Never better!" replied the Prince.

"I could sleep a bit longer."

They bathed, donned tunics and cuirasses, and mounted horses which tore from the grooms' hands.

Soon the Successor left the city along with a small retinue, on the way passing lazily marching columns of troops. The Nile had flooded, and the Prince wanted to be present at the crossings of the canals and fords.

By sunrise the last of the train was well out of the city, and His Eminence the Nomarch of Pi-Bast[2] was telling his servants:

"I'm going to get some sleep now, and woe betide whoever wakes me before the evening feast! Even the divine sun rests at the end of each day, and I haven't lain down since the first of Athyr."

Before he had finished extolling his vigilance, a police officer entered and requested a private hearing in a very important matter.

"May the earth swallow you up!" muttered His Eminence. Nevertheless he ordered the officer admitted and asked him gruffly: "Can't it wait a few hours? Surely the Nile isn't making off ..."

"There's been a great misfortune," replied the officer. "The Crown Prince's son has been killed ..."

"What? ... Whose son?" shouted the Nomarch.

"The son of Sara the Jewess."

"Who killed him? ... When?"

"Last night."

"Who could have done it?"

The officer bowed his head and spread his hands.

"I ask, who killed him?" repeated His Eminence, more terrified than angry.

"Lord, please conduct the investigation yourself. My lips will not repeat what my ears have heard."

The Nomarch's terror mounted. He ordered Sara's servants brought in, and sent for High Priest Mephres. Mentesuphis, representative of the Minister of War, had departed with the Prince.

Mephres came, surprised. The Nomarch briefed him about the killing of the Successor's son and about the police officer not daring to give any details.

---

[2] Nomarch of Pi-Bast: more correctly, "Nomarch of *Am-Khent*". Pi-Bast was the capital of the Nome of Am-Khent, the 18th Nome of Lower Egypt. *(Translator.)*

"Are there witnesses?" asked the High Priest.

"They are at Your Eminence's disposal, holy father."

Sara's doorman was brought in.

"Have you heard," the Nomarch asked him, "that your lady's infant has been killed?"

The man dropped to the floor and answered: "I even saw His Eminence's remains, which had been smashed against a wall, and I stopped our lady who ran screaming into the garden."

"When was this?"

"Last night after midnight. Just after His Eminence the Successor came to our lady ..." replied the doorman.

"How's that? The Prince was at your lady's last night?" asked Mephres.

"Yes, great prophet."

"That's strange!" Mephres whispered to the Nomarch.

The second witness was Sara's cook; the third, a servant girl. Both said that, past midnight, the Crown Prince had gone upstairs to Sara's room, had stayed a moment, then had quickly run out into the garden, followed shortly after by a screaming lady Sara.

"But the Crown Prince didn't leave his room at the palace all night ..." said the Nomarch.

The police officer shook his head and said several palace servants were waiting in the anteroom.

They were called in, the holy Mephres questioned them—and it transpired that the Successor had not slept in the palace. He had left his room before midnight and gone into the garden, returning when the first trumpets sounded reveille.

When the witnesses had been led out and the two dignitaries remained alone, the Nomarch, groaning, threw himself to the floor and told Mephres that he was gravely ill and would rather lose his life than conduct an investigation. The High Priest was very pale and moved but replied that the killing must be cleared up and, in the Pharaoh's name, bade the Nomarch go with him to Sara's apartment.

It was not far to the Successor's garden, and the two dignitaries were soon at the scene of the crime.

On climbing up to the room, they found Sara kneeling at the cradle in the attitude of nursing the infant. The wall and floor were stained with blood.

The Nomarch turned so faint that he had to sit down, but Mephres was composed. He approached Sara, touched her shoulder, and said: "Your ladyship, we come in the name of His Holiness ..."

Sara suddenly sprang to her feet and, seeing Mephres, cried out in a frightful voice:

"A curse on you! You wanted a Jewish king, and here is your king! Oh, wretch that I am, why did I heed your treacherous advice?"

She reeled and dropped back to the cradle, moaning:

"My son ... my little Seti! He was so beautiful, so clever. He'd just extended his hands to me ... Jehovah!" she shouted, "give him back to me, it's in your power ... Egyptian gods, Osiris ... Horus ... Isis ... Isis, you were a mother! It can't be that no one in heaven will hear my prayer. Such a little child ... a hyena would take pity on him ..."

The High Priest lifted her to her feet. The room had filled with police and servants.

"Sara," said the High Priest, "in the name of His Holiness the Lord of Egypt, I conjure and command you to say who murdered your son."

She looked before her like a madwoman while rubbing her forehead. The Nomarch gave her some water with wine, and one of the women present sprinkled her with vinegar.

"Sara, in the name of His Holiness," repeated Mephres, "I command you to name the killer."

Those present began backing away toward the door; the Nomarch desperately covered his ears.

"Who killed him?" said Sara in a choked voice, sinking her eyes into Mephres' face. "Who killed him, you ask? ... I know you priests! ... I know your justice ..."

"Who was it, then?" insisted Mephres.

"Me!" shouted Sara in an unhuman voice. "I killed my baby because you made him a Jew!"

"That's a lie!" hissed the High Priest.

"Me! ... Me! ..." repeated Sara. "Hey, you people who see and hear me," she turned to the witnesses, "know that it was me who killed him ... me ... me ... me!" she shouted, beating her breasts.

At her clear self-inculpation, the Nomarch came around and regarded Sara compassionately; the women sobbed; the doorman wiped away his tears. The holy Mephres, however, clenched his livid lips. At last he said distinctly to the police officials:

"Servants of His Holiness, I am turning over to you this woman, whom you are to take to the courthouse."

"With my son!" broke in Sara, throwing herself to the cradle.

"With your son ... with your son, poor woman," said the Nomarch, covering his face.

The dignitaries left the room. A police officer summoned a litter and saw Sara downstairs with signs of the utmost respect. The unfortunate woman took the gory bundle from the cradle and, unresisting, got into the litter.

All the servants followed her to the courthouse.

As Mephres and the Nomarch were returning home through the garden, the province chief said emotionally: "I'm sorry for the woman!"

"She will be justly punished ... for lying," replied the High Priest.

"Your Eminence thinks ..."

"I am sure the gods will find and judge the true murderer."

At the garden gate they were met by the steward of Kama's villa, who called: "The Phoenician woman is gone! She disappeared last night."

"Another misfortune ..." whispered the Nomarch.

"Fear not," said Mephres, "she followed the Prince ..."

From Mephres' utterances the Nomarch concluded that the High Priest hated the Prince—and the Nomarch's heart sank. For if Ramses were proven to have killed his son, the Successor would never mount his father's throne, and the heavy priestly yoke would settle yet more oppressively over Egypt.

His Eminence's sorrow grew when he was told in the evening that two physicians from the Temple of Hathor, on examining the infant's corpse, had stated that the killing could have been carried out only by a man. Someone, they said, had taken the infant's legs in his right hand and dashed its head against the wall. Sara's hand could not encompass the two legs, which moreover showed traces of large fingers.

Following this clarification, High Priest Mephres, accompanied by High Priest Sem, went to Sara at the jail and conjured her by all the Egyptian and foreign gods to state that she was not guilty of her child's death and to describe the crime's perpetrator.

"We will credit your words," said Mephres, "and you shall be free at once."

But Sara, instead of being moved by this evidence of goodwill, became angry.

"Jackals," she cried, "are two victims not enough for you, that you desire more? I did it, wretch that I am! Who else would be so despicable as to kill a baby? ... A little baby that never harmed anyone."

"Stubborn woman, do you know what you face?" asked the holy Mephres. "For three days you shall hold your child's body in your arms, then you shall go to prison for fifteen years."

"Only three days?" she repeated. "But I don't want to part from him ever, from my little Seti. And I'll not go to prison but follow him to the grave, and my lord will have us buried together."

When the high priests had left Sara, the most pious Sem said: "I've had occasion to see and judge infanticide mothers; none of them were like her."

"That's because she didn't kill her child," said Mephres angrily.

"Then who did?"

"He whom the servants saw enter Sara's house and run off a moment later. He who, setting out against the enemy, took with him the Phoenician priestess Kama who had defiled the altar. He, finally," concluded Mephres passionately, "who drove Sara from her house and made her a slave because her son had become a Jew ..."

"Those are terrible words!" replied Sem, appalled.

"The crime is worse, and will be detected despite the stubbornness of the stupid woman."

Little did the holy man suppose how soon his prophecy would be fulfilled.

It came to pass as follows:

Prince Ramses, setting out with his army from Pi-Bast, had not yet left the palace when the Chief of Police already knew about the killing of Sara's child, about Kama's flight, and about Sara's servants having seen the Prince enter Sara's house in the night. The Police Chief was a shrewd man; he surmised who might have committed the crime and, rather than investigate on the spot, hurried out of town in pursuit of the culprits, having alerted Hiram to what had happened.

And even as Mephres was seeking to extract a statement from Sara, the bravest agents of the Pi-Bast police and all the Phoenicians, led by Hiram, were already out after the Greek Lykon and the priestess Kama.

On the third night following the Prince's departure, the Police Chief returned to Pi-Bast with a large cloth-draped cage containing a woman who was shouting at the top of her voice. Without retiring to sleep, the Chief called in the investigating officer and attentively heard his report.

At sunrise the two high priests Sem and Mephres, and the Pi-Bast Nomarch, were most humbly requested to come at once, if they would, to the Police Chief's office. All three arrived at the same hour; and the Police Chief, bowing low, begged them to tell him all they knew about the killing of the Successor's son.

The Nomarch, though a great dignitary, turned pale at the humble request and answered that he knew nothing. High Priest Sem said practically the same, adding for his part that Sara seemed to him innocent. When the turn came for the holy Mephres, he said:

"I don't know whether Your Eminence has heard that, the night of the crime, one of the Prince's women, by the name of Kama, ran off?"

The Chief of Police seemed very surprised.

"Also," continued Mephres, "I don't know whether Your Eminence has been told that the Successor did not spend the night at the palace, and that he went to Sara's house. The doorman and two servant women recognized him, as it was a fairly clear night."

The Police Chief's amazement seemed to reach a peak.

"It's a great shame," concluded the High Priest, "that Your Eminence was away from Pi-Bast for a couple of days."

The Chief bowed very low to Mephres and turned to the Nomarch: "Could Your Honor graciously tell me how the Prince was dressed that evening?"

"He was wearing a white tunic and a purple apron with gold fringe," replied the Nomarch. "I remember well, as I was one of the last to speak with the Prince that evening."

The Police Chief clapped, and Sara's doorman entered the office.

"You saw the Prince," the Chief asked him, "when he entered your lady's house in the night?"

"I opened the gate for His Eminence, may he live forever!"

"Do you remember how he was dressed?"

"He wore a tunic in yellow and black stripes, a matching cap, and a blue-and-red apron," answered the doorman.

It was now the turn of the two priests and the Nomarch to be surprised. When Sara's two servant women were brought in separately and repeated exactly the same description of the Prince's dress, the Nomarch's eyes lit up with joy, while the holy Mephres' face showed confusion.

"I'll swear," said the Nomarch, "that the Prince was wearing a white tunic and a purple-and-gold apron."

"And now," said the Police Chief, "if Your Worships would come with me to the jail, we shall there see one more witness."

They descended into an underground hall where, next to a window, stood a great cage draped in a cloth. The Police Chief threw the cloth back with a stick, and they saw a woman lying in a corner.

"Why, that's the lady Kama!" exclaimed the Nomarch.

It was indeed Kama, ill and very changed. When, seeing the dignitaries, she rose and stepped into the light, they beheld her face covered with copper spots. Her eyes had a deranged look.

"Kama," said the Police Chief, "the goddess Astoreth has touched you with leprosy ..."

"It wasn't the goddess!" she said in an altered voice. "The vile Asiatics planted a tainted veil on me. Oh, I'm miserable!"

"Kama," continued the Police Chief, "our leading high priests, the holy Sem and Mephres, have taken pity on your misfortune. If you tell the truth, they will pray for you—and maybe almighty Osiris will reverse the calamity. There is yet time, the illness is only beginning, and there is much our gods can do."

The ill woman fell to her knees and, pressing her face to the bars, spoke in a broken voice:

"Have pity on me ... I've renounced the Phoenician gods, and I'll devote the rest of my life to serving the great gods of Egypt. Only free me of this ..."

"Tell the truth," said the Police Chief, "and the gods will not deny you their mercy: Who killed the child of the Jewess Sara?"

"The double-crossing Greek, Lykon. He was a singer with our temple and said he loved me. And now he's abandoned me, the villain, taking my jewels!"

"Why did Lykon kill the child?"

"He wanted to kill the Prince, but not finding him in the palace, he ran to Sara's house and ..."

"How did the criminal gain access to the guarded house?"

"Why, doesn't your lordship know that Lykon looks like the Prince? They are as alike as two fronds on the same palm tree."

"How was Lykon dressed that night?" asked the Police Chief.

"He had ... he had a tunic in yellow and black stripes ... a matching cap, and a red-and-blue apron. Don't torment me anymore ... restore my health ... have pity ... I'll be faithful to your gods. Are you leaving already? Oh, merciless ones!"

"Poor woman," said High Priest Sem, "I'll send you a powerful wonderworker, and maybe ..."

"Oh, may Astoreth bless you ... No, may your almighty and merciful gods bless you ..." whispered the sorely tormented woman.

The dignitaries left the jail and returned to the office. The Nomarch, seeing High Priest Mephres' still downcast eyes and compressed lips, asked him:

"Holy man, are you not glad of these wonderful discoveries made by our renowned Chief of Police?"

"I have no cause for joy," replied Mephres brusquely. "The matter, instead of getting simpler, becomes complicated. Sara still maintains she killed the child, and the Phoenician woman responds as though she had been coached."

"Your Eminence does not believe her?" broke in the Police Chief.

"I have never seen two people so alike that one might be taken for the other. Much less have I heard of there being a man in Pi-Bast who could impersonate our Crown Prince (may he live forever!)."

"This man," said the Police Chief, "was in Pi-Bast at the Temple of Astoreth. The Tyrian Prince Hiram knew him, and our Viceroy saw him with his own eyes. Indeed, not long ago the Viceroy ordered me to apprehend him and even promised a large reward."

"Oho!" cried Mephres. "I see, esteemed Chief of Police, that the highest secrets of state are starting to concentrate around you. Permit me, however, not to believe in this Lykon until I have seen him for myself."

He left the office in a huff, followed by the holy Sem shrugging.

When their footsteps had died away in the corridor, the Nomarch looked sharply at the Police Chief and said: "How about that!"

"Truly," replied the Chief, "the holy prophets are now starting to meddle even into matters that were never their province."

"And we must suffer it!" whispered the Nomarch.

"For the time being," sighed the Police Chief. "Insofar as I know men's hearts, all His Holiness' military and officials, and all the aristocracy, are indignant at the high-handedness of the priests. All things must have an end."

"Those are great words," answered the Nomarch, pressing his hand, "and some inner voice tells me I shall yet see you as supreme police chief to His Holiness."

Another couple of days passed. During that time, the openers of dead bodies secured the remains of Ramses' infant son against corruption, while Sara remained in jail awaiting trial, sure that she would be condemned.

Kama likewise remained in jail, in the cage, feared as one touched with leprosy. A wonder-worker physician visited her, recited prayers, and gave her all-healing[3] water to drink. In spite of this, Kama's fever did not abate, and the copper spots over her eyebrows and on her cheeks became increasingly distinct. The Nomarch's office therefore ordered her transported to the Eastern Desert, where there was an isolated leper colony.

One evening the Chief of Police came to the Temple of Ptah, saying he wished to speak with the high priests. With him were two agents and a man covered from head to foot in a sack.

After a while he was told that the high priests awaited him in the sanctuary, by the statue of the god.

The Police Chief left the agents outside the gate, took the man in the sack by the arm and, led by the priest, proceeded to the sanctuary. On entering, he found Mephres and Sem in high priests' vestments, with silver plates on their chests.

He prostrated himself before them and said: "At your behest I bring you holy men the criminal Lykon. Do you wish to see his face?"

When they assented, the Police Chief rose and pulled the sack off the man accompanying him.

The two high priests cried out in astonishment. The Greek looked so much like Crown Prince Ramses that the illusion was irresistible.

"You are Lykon, singer at the pagan Temple of Astoreth?" the holy Sem asked the bound Greek.

Lykon sneered.

"And you murdered the Prince's son?" added Mephres.

The Greek turned livid with anger and attempted to break his bonds.

"Yes!" he cried, "I killed the whelp because I couldn't find his father the wolf... Heavenly fire burn him up!"

"Criminal, what harm has the Prince done you?" asked Sem indignantly.

"What harm!? He stole Kama from me and plunged her into an illness with no cure. I was free, I could have escaped with fortune and life, but I decided to avenge myself, and here you have me. It's his good fortune that your gods are more powerful than my hatred. Now you can kill me... the sooner, the better."

"He is a great criminal," said High Priest Sem.

Mephres said nothing as he looked into the Greek's eyes smoldering with rage. He was admiring Lykon's courage and was pondering. Suddenly he said to the Police Chief:

"Your Eminence may go; this man is ours."

"This man," replied the indignant Chief, "is mine... I apprehended him, and I will have the Prince's reward."

Mephres rose and retrieved a gold medal from beneath his chasuble.

"In the name of the Supreme Council, of which I am a member," said Mephres, "I order you to give us this man. Remember that his existence is a supreme secret of state, and

---

[3] "all-healing"—otherwise, "panacea" (from the ancient Greek for "cure-all"). *(Translator.)*

indeed it will be hundredfold better for you to completely forget that you left him here."

The Police Chief again prostrated himself—and left, stifling his anger.

"Our lord the Crown Prince will pay you back for this when he's pharaoh!" he thought. "And I'll get my bit in too, you'll see ..."

The agents standing outside the gate asked him where the prisoner was.

"The hand of the gods," he replied, "is upon the prisoner."

"What about our reward?" asked the senior agent diffidently.

"The hand of the gods is upon your reward as well," said the Chief. "Therefore imagine you dreamed this prisoner, and you will feel more secure in your service and health."

The agents hung their heads in silence. In their hearts they swore vengeance on the priests who had deprived them of such a pretty profit.

After the Police Chief's departure, Mephres called in several priests and whispered something into the ear of the eldest. The priests surrounded the Greek and conducted him out of the sanctuary. Lykon did not resist.

"I think," said Sem, "that this man, as a murderer, should be turned over to the courts."

"Never!" replied Mephres peremptorily. "This man is culpable of an incomparably worse crime: he resembles the Successor."

"What will Your Eminence do with him?"

"I will keep him for the Supreme Council," said Mephres. "Where the Successor visits pagan temples and steals their women; where the country is threatened with a dangerous war, and priestly authority with rebellion—Lykon may come in useful."

Next day at noon, High Priest Sem, the Nomarch, and the Police Chief went to the jail to see Sara. The poor woman had not eaten in several days and was so weak that she did not even rise from her bench at the sight of so many dignitaries.

"Sara," said the Nomarch, whom she had known earlier, "we bring you good news."

"News?" she repeated apathetically. "My son is dead, that's the news! My breasts are full to overflowing with milk, but my heart is still more full of grief."

"Sara," said the Nomarch, "you are free. You didn't kill the child."

Her lifeless features came alive. She sprang up from the bench and shouted: "It was me ... me who killed him ... no one else!"

"Your son—listen, Sara—was killed by a man, a Greek named Lykon, lover of the Phoenician woman Kama."

"What are you saying?" she whispered, grabbing his hands. "Oh, that Phoenician woman! I knew she would be the ruin of us. But a Greek? ... I don't know any Greek ... Anyway, how could my son have offended the Greeks?"

"I don't know," continued the Nomarch. "The Greek is now dead. But listen, Sara. This man looked so much like Prince Ramses that, when he entered your room, you thought it was our lord. And you preferred to accuse yourself rather than your lord and ours."

"Then it wasn't Ramses?" she cried, grabbing her head. "And, wretch that I am, I let a stranger take my son from his cradle. Ha! ... ha! ... ha! ..."

She laughed more and more softly. Suddenly, as if her legs had been cut from under her, she collapsed to the floor, tossed her arms a couple of times and, laughing, died.

But on her face there remained an expression of fathomless grief which even death could not banish.

CHAPTER 42

Egypt's western border for over seven hundred kilometers[1] comprises a wall of naked limestone hills a couple of hundred meters high, pierced by ravines. The wall parallels the Nile at a distance of seven kilometers, sometimes as little as a kilometer.

If one were to climb one of the hills and face north, he would behold a most singular view. Below on the right he would have a narrow but green meadow sliced through by the Nile; and on the left he would behold an endless yellow plain speckled white or brick-color.

The monotony of the view, the irritating yellowness of the sand, the heat, and above all the endless expanse: these are the most general characteristics of the Libyan Desert stretching away to the west of Egypt.

On closer viewing, however, the desert would appear less monotonous. Its sands do not lie flat but form series of dunes reminiscent of huge waves. It is, as it were, a rolling sea that has congealed.

However, if one dared walk out upon this sea for an hour or two, sometimes a day, ever westward, he would behold a new sight. There appear on the horizon hills, sometimes rocks and cliffs of the strangest shapes. The sand becomes ever shallower underfoot, and from beneath it there begins to emerge limestone, as it were land.

This is indeed a land, even a country, amid the sandy sea. Visible next to the limestone hills are valleys; in the valleys, river- and streambeds; farther on, a plain, and within the plain a lake with a wavy shoreline and concave bottom.

But not a blade of grass grows on these plains and hills; there is not a drop of water in the lake; nothing flows in the riverbed. This is a landscape actually quite varied in respect to land formations, but a landscape from which all the water has fled, in which the slightest moisture has dried up, a dead landscape where all the vegetation has perished and even the fertile layer of soil has been ground to a powder or has sunk into the bedrock.

In these places the most terrible catastrophe conceivable has occurred: nature has perished, leaving only her skeleton and dust, which the heat decomposes and the torrid wind tosses from place to place.

Beyond this dead but unburied land there stretches again a sea of sand with, visible here and there, tapering cones rising sometimes story-high. Each such cone is topped by a tuft of dusty gray leaves which can barely be said to be alive; they are merely unable to wither away.

---

[1] The Polish text gives this as "over a hundred geographical miles." *(Translator.)*

The strange cone signifies that at this spot the water has not yet dried up but has taken underground refuge from the scorching heat and is sustaining, so-so, the ground's moisture. Here a tamarind seed has dropped, and with great effort a plant has begun to grow.

But the master of the desert, Typhon,[2] has spotted it and begun slowly burying it in sand. The higher the little plant climbs, the higher rises the cone of sand choking it. The stray tamarind in the desert looks like a drowning man vainly stretching his hands to heaven.

And the endless yellow sea rolls on, with its waves of sand and its plant-world castaways unable to expire. Suddenly there appears a rocky wall, containing gate-like fissures.

Incredible! Visible beyond one of the gates is a spacious green valley, hosts of palms, the blue waters of a lake. Visible, too, are grazing sheep, cattle, and horses, with people bustling among them; in the distance, on the rock slopes, rises a whole town, and the summits are topped by the white walls of temples.

This is an oasis, an island amid the sandy ocean.

In the times of the pharaohs, there were very many, perhaps several dozen, such oases. They formed a chain of desert islands along Egypt's western border. They lay seventy-five, a hundred, or a hundred fifty kilometers from the Nile, and each covered an area of from a dozen to several dozen square kilometers.

The oases, sung by the Arab poets, really never were gateways to paradise. Their lakes are generally swamps; their springs flow with warm, sometimes fetid and disgustingly brackish, water; the vegetation cannot compare with Egypt's. Still, these remote spots seemed a miracle to desert travelers who found in them a little verdure for the eye, and some coolness, moisture, and dates.

The populations of these islands amid the sandy ocean varied widely: from a few hundred to a score thousand persons, depending on surface area. They were all Egyptian, Libyan, or Ethiopian desperados or their descendants: into the desert fled those with nothing to lose—convicts from the mines, criminals sought by police, peasants oppressed by the corvée,[3] and workers who preferred danger over work.

The greater part of the fugitives perished pathetically in the desert. Some, after indescribable hardships, managed to reach an oasis, where they lived miserable but free lives and were always ready to raid Egypt for dishonest gain.

Between the desert and the Mediterranean Sea stretched a very long, if none too broad, zone of fertile land inhabited by various tribes which the Egyptians called Libyans. Some of these tribes pursued agriculture; others, fishing and seafaring; but each tribe included ruffians who preferred theft, war, and pillage over systematic work. This bandit population continually perished in squalor or in warlike ventures, but also kept being replenished by a regular influx of Shardana (Sardinians) and Shekelesh

---

[2]Typhon: This was Greek mythology's deadliest monster, which the ancient Greeks identified with Set, Egypt's god of the desert, storms, foreigners, darkness, chaos, and evil. Some etymologists suggest that *Typhon* became the source—possibly via Arabic, and perhaps alongside the Chinese *tai-fung*—for the word *typhoon*, designating a northwestern-Pacific hurricane. *(Translator.)*

[3] corvée: labor extracted by a local authority for little or no pay or in lieu of taxes. *(Translator.)*

(Sicilians),[4] who in that period were still greater barbarians and bandits than the native Libyans.

Since Libya abutted on the western border of Lower Egypt, the barbarians had often pillaged His Holiness' land—and had been terribly chastised. But finding that war with the Libyans led nowhere, the pharaohs, or rather the priests, had seized upon a different policy. They let respectable Libyan families settle on Lower Egypt's littoral marshes, and they recruited the bandits and adventurers for the army, thereby obtaining first-class soldiers.

In this way the Kingdom had secured peace for itself on its western border. The police, field guard, and a couple of regular regiments stationed along the Nile's Canopic branch sufficed to keep individual Libyan brigands in line.

This state of affairs had persisted for nearly a hundred eighty years; the last war against the Libyans had been conducted by Ramses III, who had cut great heaps of hands of fallen enemies and had brought thirteen thousand slaves into Egypt. After that, no one had feared attack from Libya, and only toward the close of Ramses XII's reign did the peculiar policies of the priests reignite conflict in those parts.

It broke out from the following causes:

His Eminence Herhor, Minister of War and high priest, had, due to the opposition of His Holiness the Pharaoh, been unable to conclude a treaty with Assyria for the partitioning of Asia. But wishing, in accordance with Berossus' warnings, to maintain a long-term peace with the Assyrians, Herhor had assured Sargon that Egypt would not interfere with their prosecution of war against the eastern and northern Asiatics.

Since King Assar's plenipotentiary seemed distrustful of these assurances, Herhor had decided to give him material proof of good will and to that end had ordered the immediate discharge of twenty thousand mercenary troops, mostly Libyans.

For the discharged, entirely blameless, ever loyal soldiers, this decision was a calamity all but tantamount to a sentence of death. Before Egypt there loomed up a threat of war with Libya, which could not possibly give refuge to such a mass of men accustomed only to military drill and to ease, and not to work and penury. But Herhor and the priests did not let themselves be hampered by details when the great interests of the Kingdom were at stake.

The expulsion of the Libyan mercenaries actually did bring large benefits.

First and foremost, Sargon and his companions signed and swore to observe a ten-year interim treaty with Egypt, during which period, according to the prophecies of the Chaldean priests, ill fortune was to impend over the holy land.

Secondly, the expulsion of twenty thousand men from the army brought the royal treasury four thousand talents in savings—a very important consideration.

Thirdly, war with Libya on the western border would be an outlet for the heroic instincts of the Crown Prince and might for long divert his attention from Asiatic affairs and

[4] The *Shardana* (also called *Serden* or *Sherden*) and the *Shekelesh* (whom Prus calls *Shakalusha*) were two of the "Sea Peoples," who are thought to have been a confederation of seafaring raiders possibly originating from western Anatolia (now Turkey) or southern Europe. Toward the end of the Bronze Age, the Sea Peoples invaded Anatolia, Syria, Canaan, Cyprus, and Egypt. These peoples, whose actual identities and origins remain enigmatic, are documented during Egypt's late 19th Dynasty and especially in the reign of Ramses III (the second pharaoh of the 20th Dynasty), when they tried to enter or control Egyptian territory. *(Translator.)*

the eastern border. His Eminence Herhor and the Supreme Council very astutely supposed that several years would pass before the Libyans, having spent themselves in guerrilla warfare, would sue for peace.

It was a reasonable plan, but its authors made one mistake: they failed to sense, in Prince Ramses, the makings for a warrior of genius.

The dissolved Libyan regiments, plundering along the way, very soon reached their homeland; the more easily, as Herhor ordered no impediment put in their way. And the first of the exiles to set foot on Libyan soil brought their compatriots incredible tidings.

According to their account, dictated by anger and self-interest, Egypt was now as weak as when the Hyksos had invaded nine hundred years earlier.[5] The pharaoh's treasury was so depleted that the ruler equal to the gods had had to disband them, the Libyans, who had constituted the best, if not only, part of the army worth speaking of. Indeed, there hardly was any army, save for a second-rate handful on the eastern border.

Furthermore, discord reigned between His Holiness and the priests; the workers were unpaid and the peasants were being choked outright with taxes, and as a result the masses were ready to revolt if only help were found. Nor was that all: the nomarchs, who had once been independent rulers and had from time to time reasserted their rights, today, seeing the government's weakness, were preparing to overthrow the Pharaoh and the Supreme Priestly Council.

These tidings swept the Libyan coast like a flock of birds—and immediately found credence. The bandits and barbarians were always ready to go on a raid, the more so now when His Holiness' ex-soldiers and ex-officers assured them that pillaging Egypt would be very easy. The well-to-do and sensible among the Libyans likewise believed the expelled legionaries: it had, for many years, been no secret to them that the Egyptian nobility were becoming impoverished, that the pharaoh had no power, that the peasants and workers were rebelling in their misery.

And so enthusiasm broke out in all of Libya. The expelled soldiers and officers were greeted as bearers of glad tidings. And since Libya was a poor country lacking in resources to entertain guests, war was immediately declared with Egypt in order to get rid of the arrivals as quickly as possible.

Even the wily Libyan Prince Musawasa[6] let himself get swept up in the general current. He, however, was not convinced by the immigrants but by some respectable and eminent men—in all likelihood, agents of the Egyptian Supreme Council.

These dignitaries, ostensibly displeased with the state of things in Egypt and offended at the pharaoh and the priests, had arrived in Libya from the direction of the sea, hid from the populace, avoided the expelled soldiers, and told Musawasa in the greatest secrecy, with evidence in hand, that now was the time for him to attack Egypt.

"You will find there," they said, "a bottomless treasury and larder for yourself, for your people, and for the grandsons of your grandsons."

---

[5] Actually, the Hyksos had invaded Egypt closer to 600 years earlier. They had ruled the country during the Second Intermediate Period (i.e., between the Middle and New Kingdoms), ca. 1650 – ca. 1550 BCE., as Egypt's 15th Dynasty. *Pharaoh*'s present time is at the fall of the 20th Dynasty in the first decades of the 11th century BCE. *(Translator.)*

[6] Musawasa: name derived from that of the Meshwesh, an ancient Libyan tribe from beyond Cyrenaica, where, according to Egyptian references, lived the Libu and the Tehenu. *(Translator.)*

Musawasa, though a shrewd commander and diplomat, took the bait. An energetic man, he immediately declared holy war against Egypt and, having thousands of brave warriors to hand, pushed the first corps eastward under the command of his son, twenty-year-old Tehenna.[7]

The old barbarian was versed in warfare and knew that he who would be victorious, must act swiftly, must strike the first blows.

The Libyan preparations took very little time. His Holiness' ex-soldiers had, to be sure, come without weapons but they knew their craft, and in those times weapons posed no difficulty. A couple of straps or cords for a sling; a spear or sharpened stick; an ax or club; a bag of stones, and another of dates—that was all that was required.

So Musawasa gave his son Tehenna two thousand ex-soldiers and some four thousand Libyan riffraff, bidding him dash into Egypt, take what plunder he could, and prepare supplies for the army proper. And himself gathering more substantial forces, he sent messengers round the oases, calling all who had nothing to lose to his standards.

Not in a long time had there been such a stir in the desert. From every oasis came contingent after contingent of such dreadful proletarians that, though nearly naked, they deserved the name of tatterdemalions.

Relying on the judgment of his advisors, who only a month earlier had been officers of His Holiness, Musawasa quite reasonably supposed that his son would pillage several hundred villages and towns from Terenuthis to Senti-Nofer[8] before encountering substantial Egyptian forces. He had received word that, at first news of the Libyan movements, not only had all the workers fled the great glassworks, but the troops manning the small forts at Sechet-Hemau,[9] on the Natron Lakes,[10] had withdrawn.

This was a very good omen for the barbarians, as the glassworks were a major source of revenue for the pharaonic treasury.

Musawasa had fallen into the same error as the Supreme Priestly Council: he had failed to sense the martial genius in Ramses. And an extraordinary thing happened: before the first Libyan corps had reached the Natron Lakes area, the Successor's army, twice as strong, was already there.

The Libyans could not be accused of negligence. Tehenna and his staff had set up a very competent intelligence service. Their spies had repeatedly been to Melcatis,[11] Naucratis,[12]

---

[7] Tehenna: name derived from that of the Tehenu, one of the generic Egyptian terms for "Libyan." *(Translator.)*

[8] Senti-Nofer: a city in Lower Egypt's Nile Delta. *(Translator.)*

[9] Sechet-Hemau ("Field of Natron"): ancient Egyptian name for Wadi El Natrun ("Natron Valley"), located west of the Delta. In the region are eight lakes that produce natron salt. *(Translator.)*

[10] Natron Lakes: In summer, the Natron Lakes dried up, and natron was collected—a mixture of sodium salts that were used in many applications, including cleansers, antiseptics, as a drying agent in mummification, and for the production of Egyptian faience and of a color called "Egyptian blue." *(Translator.)*

[11] Melcatis: Possibly meant is *Metelis*, the Greek name for Senti-Nofer. *(Translator.)*

[12] Naucratis: a city in the western Delta, in the 3rd Nome of Lower Egypt, west of the Nile's Bolbitine branch. It was a Greek colony in ancient Egypt's Late Period (and therefore its mention in *Pharaoh* is an anachronism). *(Translator.)*

Sai,[13] Menuf, and Terenuthis, and had sailed the Canopic and Bolbitine branches of the Nile.[14] Nowhere had they encountered troops, whose movements would have been paralyzed by the flood, whereas nearly everywhere they had seen the panicked populace fleeing the border villages.

So they brought their commander the best of tidings. Meanwhile Prince Ramses' army eight days after setting out, despite the flood, reached the edge of the desert and, supplied with water and provisions, vanished into the hills abutting the Natron Lakes.

Could Tehenna have soared like an eagle over his host's positions, he would have been appalled to see that all the ravines in the area concealed Egyptian regiments—and that at any moment his corps would be surrounded.

---

[13] Sai (in Greek, *Sais*): a city in the western Delta, on the east bank of the Nile's Bolbitine branch. Under the 20th Dynasty, it was the capital of the 5th Nome of Lower Egypt. Under the 26th Dynasty, in the 7th and 6th centuries BCE, it would be the capital of the Egyptian Kingdom. *(Translator.)*

[14] Canopic and Bolbitine branches of the Nile: The Canopic branch was the westernmost of the seven ancient branches of the Nile. The Bolbitine branch was the second from the west. *(Translator.)*

CHAPTER 43

From the moment the armies of Lower Egypt had left Pi-Bast, the prophet Mente-suphis, accompanying the Prince, had been receiving and sending out several dispatches daily.

He conducted one correspondence with Minister Herhor. Mentesuphis reported to Memphis on the army's movements and on the Successor's actions, for which he did not conceal his admiration; His Eminence Herhor commented to the effect that the Successor should be given every latitude—and that, should Ramses lose the first skirmish, the Supreme Council would not be unduly concerned.

"A minor defeat," wrote Herhor, "would be an object lesson in caution and humility for Prince Ramses who, though he is yet to accomplish anything, already regards himself as the equal of the most seasoned warriors."

When Mentesuphis answered that it was hard to suppose the Successor would know defeat, Herhor intimated that in that case the triumph[1] should not be excessive.

"The Kingdom," he said, "will lose nothing by the bellicose and impulsive Successor having a plaything for a few years on the western frontier. He will gain proficiency in the art of war, and our indolent and insolent soldiers will be suitably occupied."

Mentesuphis conducted a second correspondence with the holy father Mephres, and this one seemed to him the more important. Mephres, who had been offended by the Prince, now, in connection with the killing of Sara's infant, bluntly accused the Successor of the infanticide, carried out under the influence of Kama. When in the course of a week Ramses' innocence came to light, the high priest, more provoked than ever, did not cease maintaining that the Prince was capable of anything, as an enemy of the native gods and an ally of the wretched Phoenicians.

The matter of the killing of Sara's infant looked so suspicious in the first few days that even the Supreme Council in Memphis asked Mentesuphis what he thought about it. Mentesuphis replied that he had been observing the Prince for days but did not for a moment suppose he might be a murderer.

Such correspondences circled about Ramses like birds of prey as he sent scouting parties out toward the enemy, conferred with commanders, or urged the troops to march quickly.

On the fourteenth of Athyr, the Successor's whole army was concentrated south of the city of Terenuthis. To the Prince's great joy, Patroklos arrived with the Greek regiments;

---

[1] "Triumph" is understood here as the celebration of a victory, rather than as the victory itself. *(Translator.)*

and with him, the priest Pentuer, sent by Herhor as a second observer with the commander-in-chief.

The profusion of priests in camp (there were others as well) did not delight Ramses. But he decided to pay no attention to them, and at councils of war he did not seek their opinions.

Somehow relations were assuaged: Mentesuphis, in accordance with Herhor's instructions, did not impose himself on the Prince. Pentuer busied himself organizing medical aid for casualties.

The game began.

First Ramses had agents spread a rumor in many border villages that the Libyans were advancing in great force and would be laying waste and murdering. As a result, the terrified populace fled east—and ran into the Egyptian regiments. The Prince drafted the men to carry loads for the army and sent the women and children inland.

Next the commander-in-chief sent spies to determine the strength and order of battle of the approaching Libyans. The spies soon returned with accurate intelligence on the location, but very exaggerated intelligence on the numbers, of the enemy. They also held erroneously, if with great assurance, that the Libyan hosts were being led personally by Musawasa, accompanied by his son Tehenna.

The Prince Commander-in-chief fairly blushed with pleasure at the thought that in his first war he would have so seasoned an opponent as Musawasa.

Consequently he overrated the risk of the encounter and redoubled his precautions. And to have all the odds on his side, he resorted to a stratagem. He sent trusted men to pose as deserters, infiltrate the Libyan camp—and draw away Musawasa's greatest strength: the expelled Libyan soldiers.

"Tell them," Ramses instructed his agents, "that I have axes for the insolent, and mercy for the humble. If in the coming battle they drop their weapons and desert Musawasa, I will reinstate them in His Holiness' army and pay their back wages as though they had never left the service."

Patroklos and the other generals endorsed this measure as very prudent; the priests kept their counsel, and Mentesuphis sent a dispatch to Herhor and received an answer within a day.

The Natron Lakes lay within a valley several dozen kilometers long, hemmed in by two belts of hills running southeast to northwest. At its widest, the valley did not exceed ten kilometers; and there were considerably narrower places, almost ravines.

Down the whole length of the valley stretched a series of some ten swampy lakes of brackish water. Here grew wretched shrubs and herbs, constantly being buried by the sand, constantly withering, which no animal would take into its mouth. On either side rose jagged limestone hills or huge sand drifts which could swallow a person.

The whole landscape of yellows and whites had about it a horrible deadness that was intensified by the heat and silence. No bird sang here, and if ever there was a sound, it would be that of a tumbling rock.

More or less at mid-valley stood two clusters of buildings separated by several kilometers. They were, on the east, a small fort; on the west, a glassworks that was supplied with fuel by Libyan merchants. Both these places had been abandoned due to the wartime unrest. Tehenna's corps was tasked with occupying these two points, which would secure the way into Egypt for Musawasa's army.

The Libyans slowly advanced south from the city of Glaukus[2] and, by evening of the fourteenth of Athyr, found themselves at the entrance to the valley of the Natron Lakes, confident that they would pass through it in two marches, unimpeded. That same day, just at sunset, the Egyptian army set out for the desert and, marching over forty kilometers across the sands in twelve hours, next morning reached the hills between the fort and the glassworks and concealed itself in the many ravines.

If that night someone had told the Libyans that palms and wheat had grown up in the valley of the Natron Lakes, they would have been less astonished than that the Egyptian army should bar their way.

After a brief rest, during which the priests managed to discover and dig several small wells of passably potable water, the Egyptian army began occupying the northern hills stretching the length of the valley.

The Successor's plan was simple: he meant to cut the Libyans off from their homeland and drive them south into the desert, where heat and hunger would finish off the scattered foe.

To that end, he deployed his army along the north side of the valley, divided into three bodies. The right wing, nearest Libya, commanded by Patroklos, was to cut off the invaders' retreat to their city of Glaukus. The left wing, nearest Egypt, commanded by Mentesuphis, was to block the Libyan advance. Command of the center, around the glassworks, was taken personally by the Successor, accompanied by Pentuer.

On the fifteenth of Athyr, about seven in the morning, several dozen Libyan horsemen cantered down the valley. They rested briefly at the glassworks, looked about and, seeing nothing suspicious, turned back to the Libyan force.

At ten in the morning, amid a scorching heat that seemed to drink up men's sweat and blood, Pentuer told the Successor: "The Libu[3] have entered the valley and are passing Patroklos' force. In an hour they will be here."

"How do you know?" asked the surprised Prince.

"The priests know everything!" smiled Pentuer.

He carefully climbed a rock, took from a bag a very shiny object, turned toward the holy Mentesuphis' force, and proceeded to make signals with his hand. "Now Mentesuphis too is informed," he added.

The Prince could not get over his amazement. "My eyesight is better than yours," he said, "and I doubt that my hearing is worse, but I don't see or hear anything. How do you make out the enemy and communicate with Mentesuphis?"

Pentuer bade the Prince watch a particular distant hill on whose summit loomed blackthorn bushes. Ramses gazed there and suddenly covered his eyes: something had flashed powerfully in the bushes.

"What's that unbearable glare?" he shouted. "You could go blind!"

"That's the priest assisting His Eminence Patroklos, signaling us," said Pentuer. "You see, Eminence, we too can be useful in war."

They heard a murmur down in the valley—at first soft, gradually more and more distinct. At the sound, Egyptian soldiers hugging the slope of the hill began jumping up, look-

---

[2] Glaukus: the Latin name for the Greek city of Glaukos, an important Mediterranean port west of the Nile Delta, in Libya. (Translator.)

[3] Libu: an ancient Libyan tribe which gave its name to Libya. (Translator.)

ing over their weapons, whispering. But a curt order from the officers quieted them, and stillness once again settled over the northern rocks.

The murmur down in the valley intensified and passed into a tumult which mingled the conversations of thousands of men with the sounds of song, flutes, creaking wagons, neighing horses, and shouting commanders. Ramses' heart began pounding; unable any longer to contain his curiosity, he climbed a crag that commanded a good part of the valley.

Shrouded in clouds of yellowish dust, the Libyan corps slowly advanced like a several-verst-long[4] serpent speckled blue, white, and red.

At the fore marched a score of riders, one of whom, white-robed, sat his horse like a bench, both legs dangling on the left. The riders were followed by a contingent of slingers in gray tunics, then by a dignitary in a litter shaded by a large parasol. Farther on came a unit of spearmen in blue and red tunics; then a great band of near-naked men armed with clubs; more slingers and spearmen, and again slingers, followed by a red unit with scythes and axes. They marched more or less four abreast; but despite the officers' exhortations, the array kept breaking down, and successive fours kept bunching up.

Singing and conversing noisily, the Libyan snake slowly crept into the widest part of the valley, opposite the glassworks and the lakes. Here the procession fell into still greater disarray. Those marching at the head halted, having been told there would be a rest stop here; while succeeding columns quickened their pace, the sooner to arrive and rest. Some broke ranks, lay down their weapons, and jumped into a lake or drew its fetid water in their hands; others sat down on the ground and took dates out of a bag or drank water with vinegar from earthen bottles.

High overhead circled several vultures.

At this sight, Ramses was overcome with an indescribable sorrow and dread. Tiny flies began darting before his eyes; he lost his presence of mind, and for the blink of an eye he felt he would have given up the throne, not to be in this place and not to see what was about to happen. He slipped down from the crag and stared distraughtly before him.

Suddenly Pentuer approached and tugged his arm. "Snap out of it, commander," he said. "Patroklos awaits orders."

"Patroklos?" repeated the Prince, looking about.

Before him stood Pentuer, pale but calm. A couple of paces farther, Thutmose, equally pale, held an officer's whistle in his trembling hands. From beyond the hill soldiers were leaning out, their faces marked by deep emotion.

"Ramses," repeated Pentuer, "the army waits ..."

With desperate determination, the Prince looked at the priest and said in a stifled whisper: "Commence ..."

Pentuer lifted up his shiny talisman and with it traced several signs in the air. Thutmose softly blew his whistle, the sound was repeated in outlying ravines to right and left—and Egyptian slingers proceeded to climb the hills.

It was about twelve noon.

Ramses slowly cooled down from his first sensations and looked about more attentively. He saw his staff, a unit of spearmen and axmen commanded by veteran officers,

---

[4] verst: an obsolete Russian unit of distance, equal to 1.07 kilometer. (Prus' part of partitioned Poland was governed by the Russian Empire.) *(Translator.)*

finally slingers lazily climbing the rock. He was sure not one of these men wanted to fight or move, let alone die, in the frightful heat.

Suddenly, from one of the hills, there rang a powerful voice mightier than a lion's roar: "Soldiers of His Holiness the Pharaoh, smash the Libyan dogs! The gods are with you!"

The preternatural voice was answered by two no less powerful: the drawn-out cry of the Egyptian army, and the immense uproar of the Libyans.

The Prince, no longer needing to hide, climbed a hill with a good view of the enemy. Before him stretched a long chain of Egyptian slingers seemingly sprung out of the ground; and a couple of hundred paces off, swarming in clouds of dust, the Libyan host. There rang trumpets, whistles, and curses of barbarian officers mustering their men. Those who had been sitting, sprang up; those who had been drinking water, grabbed their weapons and ran to their units; the chaotic crowds began forming ranks, all amid shouting and tumult.

Meanwhile the Egyptian slingers each cast several projectiles a minute, calmly, systematically as if at drill. The decurions[5] indicated to their little units the enemy groups to be hit, and for a couple of minutes the men showered them with a hail of stones and lead balls. The Prince saw, after such a salvo, a little Libyan group scatter, very often leaving one of their number behind.

Despite that, the Libyan ranks formed up and drew back beyond range of the projectiles, and Libyan slingers stepped forward and set about answering the Egyptians with equal speed and composure. Sometimes, in their chain. laughter and cries of glee erupted, when an Egyptian slinger fell.

Soon stones were whirring and whizzing over the heads of the Prince and his retinue. One, deftly cast, struck and broke an aide's arm; another knocked off a second aide's helmet; a third fell at the Prince's feet, shattered on the rock, and showered the commander's face with fragments hot as boiling water.

The Libyans were laughing loudly as they shouted something; they were probably cursing the commander.

Dread, especially sorrow and pity, all in a single instant forsook Ramses. He no longer saw men threatened with suffering and death, only ranks of wild beasts to be exterminated or subdued. Reflexively he reached for his sword to lead the spearmen awaiting orders, but was stopped by a feeling of disdain. Why should he stain himself with the blood of that rabble? What were soldiers for?

Meanwhile the battle went on, and the valiant Libyan slingers, shouting, even singing, began to advance. From both sides, projectiles buzzed like May bugs,[6] hummed like a swarm of bees, occasionally collided mid-air; and every couple of minutes, on either side, a warrior withdrew to the rear, groaning, or fell dead on the spot. But that did not spoil the others' humor: they fought on with a spiteful glee that gradually turned to rage and unmindfulness of self.

Suddenly, far off in the right wing, there rang trumpets and repeated cries. Fearless Patroklos, drunk since dawn, had attacked the enemy rear guard.

"Forward!" cried the Prince.

[5] decurion: an officer in charge of ten soldiers. *(Translator.)*

[6] May bug: colloquial name for the cockchafer (also known as the doodlebug), a European beetle of the genus *Melolontha*, in the family *Scarabaeidae*. *(Translator.)*

The order was relayed by a trumpet, by a second trumpet ... by a tenth, and a moment later Egyptian centuries[7] began issuing from all the ravines. The slingers scattered over the hills redoubled their efforts, while in the valley, without haste and without disorder, four-rank columns of Egyptian spearmen and axmen arrayed themselves opposite the Libyans and slowly advanced.

"Reinforce the center," said the Successor.

A trumpet relayed the order. Behind the two columns of the first line, two new columns came up. Before the Egyptians had completed this maneuver, constantly under a hail of projectiles, the Libyans, imitating them, had formed eight ranks opposite the main corps.

"Bring up the reserves," said the Prince. He turned to an aide: "See whether the left wing is ready."

The aide, the better to view the valley, ran in among the slingers—and suddenly fell, but gave hand signals. In his stead another officer went forward, and soon ran back to report that both wings of the Prince's sector stood in formation.

From the direction of Patroklos' corps the tumult mounted, and suddenly thick black clouds of smoke rose above the hills. An officer ran over to the Prince with word from Pentuer that the Greek regiments had set fire to the Libyan camp.

"Smash the center," said the Prince.

A dozen or so trumpets, one after another, sounded attack; and when they had fallen still, in the center column there rang a command, rhythmic drumbeats, and the sound of infantry marching slowly, in cadence: One ... two! ... One ... two! ... One ... two! ...

The command was repeated in the right and left wings; drums growled again, and the wing columns went forward: One ... two! ... One ... two! ...

The Libyan slingers started backing away, even as they showered the marching Egyptians with stones. But though soldiers fell, the columns advanced, slowly advanced, in good order: One ... two! ... One ... two! ...

Yellow clouds, constantly thickening, marked the advance of the Egyptian battalions. The slingers could no longer hurl stones, and there ensued a relative stillness, broken by the moans and sobs of wounded warriors.

"They seldom marched this well at drill!" the Prince called to the staff.

"Today they don't fear the cane," muttered an old officer.

The distance between the dustcloud on the Egyptian side and the Libyans was decreasing by the moment; but the barbarians stood firm, and a cloud appeared behind their line. Clearly, reserves were reinforcing the center column, which was threatened with the strongest attack.

The Successor ran down the hill and mounted a horse; the last Egyptian reserves issued from the ravines, formed up, and awaited orders. Behind the infantry, several hundred Asiatic horsemen rode out on small, hardy mounts.

The Prince sped after the troops marching to the attack and, a hundred paces on, found a new hill, not high but with a vantage of the whole battlefield. The retinue, the Asiatic cavalry, and the reserve column followed him.

The Prince impatiently looked toward the left wing, whence Mentesuphis was supposed to come but was not coming. The Libyans stood in place; the situation was looking increasingly serious.

---

[7] century: a unit of 100 soldiers. *(Translator.)*

Ramses' corps was the strongest but had almost the whole Libyan force against it. Numerically the two sides were matched, the Prince did not doubt of victory, but he was concerned about the magnitude of losses against such a valiant opponent.

Moreover, a battle has its caprices. The commander-in-chief's sway over those who had gone to the attack was over. He no longer had them; he had only a reserve regiment and a handful of cavalry. So, were one of the Egyptian columns to be smashed, or were the enemy to suddenly receive new reinforcements?

The Prince wiped his brow: he was feeling now the full responsibility of the commander-in-chief. He was like a gambler who has staked all and cast the dice, and wonders how they will fall.

The Egyptians were a few dozen paces from the Libyan columns. A command ... trumpets ... drums rumbled faster, and the troops set out at the double: one—two—three! ... one—two—three! ... On the enemy side as well, a trumpet sounded, two ranks of spears leveled, drums struck. Charge! ... New clouds of dust rose, then merged into a single huge cloud. A roar of men's voices, a clatter of spears, a clang of scythes; now and again a piercing cry, soon drowned out in the general uproar.

Along the whole battle line, the men, their weapons, the very columns were no longer visible, only a yellow dust stretching away in the shape of a gigantic snake. A thicker cloud marked a clash of columns; a thinner cloud, a gap.

After several minutes of the infernal uproar, the Successor noticed that on the left wing the dustcloud was very slowly bending backward.

"Reinforce the left wing!" he cried.

Half the reserves ran in the indicated direction and vanished into the clouds; the left wing straightened, while the right wing slowly advanced and the center, the strongest and most important sector, continued in place.

"Reinforce the center," said the Prince.

The other half of the reserves went forward and vanished into the dustcloud. The shouting briefly mounted, but there was no visible forward movement.

"The wretches are putting up a terrific fight!" the old officer in the retinue said to the Successor. "It's high time Mentesuphis came in."

The Prince summoned the commander of the Asiatic cavalry.

"There must be a gap over on the right," he said. "Ride in carefully so as not to trample our men, and fall upon the center column of those dogs from the side."

"They must be on a chain, they haven't moved in a good while," laughed the Asiatic.

He left a score of his cavalry with the Prince and trotted off with the rest, crying, "Live forever, our commander!"

The heat was indescribable. The Prince exerted his vision and hearing, trying to penetrate the wall of dust. He waited ... and waited ... Suddenly he cried out for joy: the center cloud had lurched and moved a little forward.

It stopped again, moved again, then proceeded slowly, very slowly, but forward.

The roiling uproar was so intense that there was no telling what it meant: ire, triumph, or defeat.

Suddenly the right wing began oddly bending and backing away. Beyond it appeared a new dustcloud. Pentuer rode up horseback and called: "Patroklos is engaging the Libyan rear!"

The welter on the right wing was mounting and approaching the center of the battle-field. The Libyans were visibly starting to retreat, and panic was overwhelming even their main column.

The Prince's whole staff, excited, feverish, was following the movements of the yellow dust. After several minutes, the turmoil affected as well the left wing. There the Libyans had begun fleeing.

"May I not see tomorrow's sun, if this isn't victory!" cried the old officer.

A messenger arrived with word, from the priests who were following the battle from the tallest hill, that Mentesuphis' ranks were visible on the left wing and that the Libyans were surrounded on three sides.

"They'd be running like hinds now," said the winded messenger, "if the sand didn't impede them."

"Victory! ... Live forever, commander!" shouted Pentuer.

It was just after two.

The Asiatic cavalry burst into boisterous song and loosed arrows into the air in honor of the Prince. The staff officers dismounted, took the Successor by his arms and legs from his saddle, and lifted him up, calling:

"Behold the mighty commander! ... He's trampled Egypt's enemies! Amon is at his right and left hands, so who can oppose him?"

Meanwhile the Libyans, constantly retreating, had climbed onto the sandy south-ern hills, pursued by the Egyptians. Horsemen kept emerging from the dustclouds and rnnning to Ramses.

"Mentesuphis has taken their rear!" shouted one.

"Two centuries have surrendered!" called another.

"Patroklos has taken their rear!"

"Three Libyan standards have been captured: the Sheep, the Lion, and the Sparrow Hawk."

The staff were becoming increasingly crowded: surrounded by bloodied, dust-covered men.

"Live forever! ... Live forever, commander!"

The overwrought Prince by turns laughed, wept, and spoke to his retinue:

"The gods have been merciful. I thought we were about to lose. Miserable lot of a com-mander who doesn't draw his sword or even see anything, but must answer for every-thing."

There were cries of "Live forever, victorious commander!"

"Victory!" laughed the Prince. "I don't even know how it was carried off!"

"He wins battles, then wonders!" shouted one of the retinue.

"I tell you I don't even know what a battle looks like ..." said the Prince.

"Relax, commander," said Pentuer. "You deployed your forces so astutely that the en-emy couldn't but be routed. How it was actually done, is not your business but that of your regiments."

"I didn't even draw my sword! ... I didn't see a single Libyan!" lamented the Prince.[8]

---

[8] Ramses' lament, "I don't even know what a battle looks like," in a way contradicts his earlier insistence to Mentesuphis (Chapter 35) that he *did* "know what a battle is." *(Translator.)*

The southern hills were still roiling, but in the valley the dust had begun to settle and here and there small groups of Egyptian soldiers were visible through the haze, their spears held at rest.

The Successor turned his horse in that direction and rode onto the deserted field where the battle of the center columns had just been played out. It was an area several hundred paces wide, deeply pitted, strewn with bodies of wounded and dead. As the Prince approached, there lay a long row, every few paces, of Egyptians; then, somewhat more densely, Libyans; farther on, Egyptians and Libyans intermingled; and still farther, almost solely Libyans.

In places, body lay next to body: sometimes three or four corpses were gathered at a single spot. The sand was bloodstained dark brown; the wounds were grisly: one warrior was missing both arms, another's head was cloven through to the torso, a third had his entrails coming out. Some writhed in convulsions, and from their sand-filled mouths streamed curses or entreaties to finish them off.

The Successor hurried past them without looking about, though some of the wounded uttered faint cheers in his honor.

Not far from there he came upon the first group of prisoners. They prostrated themselves before him on their faces, begging for mercy.

"Announce quarter for the vanquished and humble," said the Prince to his retinue.

Several riders scattered in various directions. Presently a trumpet sounded, followed by a resonant voice:

"By order of His Eminence the Prince Commander-in-Chief, wounded and prisoners are not to be killed!"

The announcement was answered with confused cries, doubtless of prisoners.

"By order of the Commander-in-Chief," sang another voice elsewhere, "wounded and prisoners are not to be killed!"

Meanwhile, on the southern hills, fighting had ceased and the two largest groups of Libyans had laid down their arms before the Greek regiments.

The valiant Patroklos, due to the heat as he said, or due to libations as others supposed, barely kept his horse. He rubbed his teary eyes and addressed the prisoners:

"Mangy dogs!" he cried, "who have lifted your sinful hands against the army of His Holiness (may vermin eat you!), you'll die like lice beneath the fingernail of a pious Egyptian if you don't say right now where your commander is—may leprosy canker his nostrils and drink his festering eyes!"

Just then the Successor rode up. The general greeted him respectfully but did not interrupt his interrogation:

"I'll have you flayed alive! ... I'll impale you, if I don't find out right now where that venomous reptile is, that wild boar's farrow dropped in manure ..."

"There's our commander!" cried a Libyan, pointing to a small group of horsemen slowly riding into the desert.

"What is it?" asked the Prince.

"That wretch Musawasa is getting away!" replied Patroklos, all but falling from his horse.

"That's Musawasa getting away?" cried Ramses. "Hey, those with good mounts, follow me!"

"Well," laughed Patroklos, "now the sheep thief will do the bleating!"

Pentuer stopped the Prince. "Your Eminence musn't pursue the fugitives!"

"What?" shouted the Successor. "I didn't lift a hand against anyone throughout the battle, and now I'm to give up the Libyan commander? What would the soldiers say whom I sent against spears and axes?"

"The army can't be without a commander ..."

"Patroklos, Thutmose, and Mentesuphis are here. What am I commander for, if I'm not allowed to hunt down the enemy? They're a few hundred paces from us, on tired horses."

"We'll be back with them in an hour. Just a matter of reaching out ..." murmured the Asiatic cavalry.

"Patroklos ... Thutmose ... I'm leaving you in charge of the army," called the Successor. "Get some rest, I'll be right back."

He spurred his horse and rode off at a jog trot, sinking into the sand, followed by a score of cavalry and Pentuer.

"What are you doing, prophet?" asked the Prince. "Get some sleep ... You've given us important services today."

"I may yet be of service," replied Pentuer.

"No, stay ... That's an order ..."

"The Supreme Council bade me not leave Your Eminence's side."

The Successor bristled. "What if we're ambushed?" he asked.

"I won't leave you there either, lord," said the priest.

CHAPTER 44

Thad here was such goodwill in his voice that the surprised Prince said no more and let him ride.

They were in the desert, the army a couple of hundred paces behind them, the fugitives several hundred paces in front. Despite beating the horses and urging them on, fugitives and pursuers alike moved with great effort. The terrible heat of the sun flooded them from on high; a fine sharp dust forced its way into their mouths, noses and, above all, their eyes; and at each step the burning sand sank beneath the horses' legs. A deathly stillness was in the air.

"It can't be like this all the way," said the Successor.

"It will get worse," said Pentuer. "See, Eminence"—he indicated the fugitives—"their horses are sinking knee-deep in the sand."

The Prince broke into a laugh: they had just ridden onto somewhat harder ground and rode for a hundred paces at a trot. But soon the sandy sea again impeded them, and they were again reduced to a crawl.

The men streamed with sweat, the horses were beginning to foam.

"It's hot!" whispered the Successor.

"Listen, lord," said Pentuer. "It's not a good day to be out chasing in the desert. This morning the sacred insects showed great agitation, then became lethargic. Also, my priestly knife dipped very shallow into its clay sheath, which indicates unusual heat. And these together, the heat and the insects' lethargy, may portend a storm. So let's go back, because we've not only lost sight of camp but its sounds no longer reach us."

Ramses gave the priest a near-scornful look.

"Do you think, prophet," he said, "that, after pledging Musawasa's capture, I can return empty-handed from fear of heat and storm?"

They rode on. In one place the ground hardened again, and they came within a sling's cast of the fugitives.

"Hey, you there!" called the Successor, "give yourselves up!"

The Libyans did not even look back, as they floundered arduously over the sand. For a moment it seemed they might be overtaken. But soon the Successor's detachment again came upon deep sand, while the others quickened their pace and disappeared beyond a rise.

The Asiatics cursed; the Prince gritted his teeth.

Finally the horses began sinking ever deeper and stopping; the riders had to dismount and go on foot. Suddenly one of the Asiatics turned red and fell on the sand. The Prince ordered him covered with a cloth and said: "We'll pick him up on the way back."

With great effort they gained the top of a sandy rise and saw the Libyans. For them, too, the way had been deadly: two of their horses had foundered.

The Egyptian army's camp was definitely hidden by the undulant terrain, and if Pentuer and the Asiatics had not known how to guide themselves by the sun, they could not now have found their way back.

A second rider in the Prince's retinue fell, ejecting a bloody foam from his mouth. He too was left, together with his horse.

To make things worse, against the background of the sands there appeared a group of rocks into which the Libyans had disappeared.

"Lord," said Pentuer, "there might be an ambush."

"I don't care if death is there, and if it takes me!" said the Successor in a transformed voice.

Pentuer regarded him with admiration: the priest had not suspected Ramses of such resolve.

It was not far to the rocks, but the way was onerous beyond description. The men had not only to walk but to drag the horses out of the sand. Everyone floundered, sinking to above the ankles; in places, they could sink knee-deep.

In the heavens blazed the sun, the terrible desert sun whose every ray burned, blinded, and stung. The hardiest Asiatics were dropping from fatigue: one had a swollen tongue and lips; another, a ringing in his head and little black spots in his eyes; still another was overcome with drowsiness; all felt pain in their joints and had lost sensation of the heat. Had any of them been asked whether it was hot, he could not have said.

The ground hardened again underfoot, and Ramses' retinue entered the rocks. The Prince, the most alert of the party, heard a horse snort, turned, and saw a group of men lying in the shade of the hill, each as he had dropped. It was the Libyans.

One of them, a young man of twenty, wore an embroidered purple tunic, a gold chain on his neck, and a handsomely mounted sword. He seemed to lie insensate, eyes inverted whites-up, some foam in his mouth. Ramses recognized him for the commander. He approached, plucked the chain from his neck, and detached his sword.

An old Libyan, seemingly less weary than the rest, seeing this, said: "Though you are the victor, Egyptian, respect the prince's son who was commander-in-chief."

"This is Musawasa's son?" asked the Prince.

"Yes," replied the Libyan, "this is Musawasa's son Tehenna, our commander who would make even a worthy Egyptian prince."

"Where is Musawasa?"

"Musawasa is in Glaukus, gathering a great army that will avenge us."

The other Libyans said nothing; they did not even trouble to look at the victors. At the Prince's behest, the Asiatics readily disarmed them—and likewise sat down in the shade of the rock.

There were here no friends or enemies, only mortally weary men. Death was stalking them all, but they wanted only to rest.

Pentuer, seeing Tehenna still unconscious, knelt by him and bent over his head so that no one could see what he was about. Soon Tehenna began sighing and tossing and opened his eyes; then he sat up, rubbing his forehead like one wakened from a deep sleep which has not yet passed.

"Tehenna, commander of the Libyans," said Ramses, "you and your men are prisoners of war of His Holiness the Pharaoh."

"Kill me at once," muttered Tehenna, "if I'm to lose my freedom."

"When your father Musawasa humbles himself and concludes peace with Egypt, you shall yet be free and happy."

The Libyan turned his head away and lay down, apathetic. Ramses sat down beside him and soon slipped into a kind of lethargy; he had probably fallen asleep.

He came to after a quarter-hour, somewhat refreshed. He looked at the desert and shouted in delight: on the horizon he saw a green country, water, dense palms and, somewhat higher, towns and temples.

Everyone around him—Asiatics and Libyans—slept. Pentuer, standing on a rock ledge, was shading his eyes with his hand and looking off somewhere.

"Pentuer! ... Pentuer!" called Ramses. "Do you see the oasis?"

He sprang up and ran to the priest, who had a concerned expression.

"Do you see the oasis?"

"That is no oasis," said Pentuer, "but the spirit of some land that is no longer on the earth, haunting the desert.[1] But that, over there ... is real!" he added, pointing south.

"Mountains?" asked the Prince.

"Take a better look."

The Prince did and suddenly said: "The dark mass seems to be rising. My eyes must be tired."

"That is Typhon," whispered the priest. "Only the gods can save us, if they will ..."

Ramses felt on his face a light breeze which seemed warm even amid the desert heat. At first very delicate, the breeze gained intensity, became ever warmer, while the dark streak rose in the sky with astonishing speed.

"What do we do?" asked the Prince.

"These rocks," said the priest, "will prevent our being buried, but they won't keep out the dust or the heat, which keeps rising. And in a day or two ..."

"Typhon blows that long?"

"Sometimes three or four days. Occasionally it springs up for a couple of hours, then suddenly falls like a vulture pierced by an arrow. But that happens very seldom ..."

The Prince turned somber, though he did not lose courage.

The priest took from his robe a small vial of green glass and said: "Here is an elixir. It should last you several days. Whenever you feel drowsy or frightened, take a drop. It will fortify you, and you will hold out."

"What about you ... and the rest?"

"My fate is in the hands of the One. As for the others ... they aren't successors to the throne!"

"I don't want this liquid," said the Prince, pushing away the vial.

"You must take it!" shouted Pentuer. "Remember that the Egyptian people repose their hopes in you. Remember that their blessing watches over you!"

---

[1] Prus is describing a mirage. *(Translator.)*

The black cloud had now risen halfway up the sky, and the hot gale blew so violently that the Prince and the priest had to get down under the rock.

"The Egyptian people? ... blessing? ..." repeated Ramses. Suddenly he exclaimed: "It was you who spoke to me a year ago at night from the garden? It was right after the maneuvers ..."

"The day you pitied the peasant who hanged himself in despair because his canal had been ruined," said the priest.

"You saved my farm and the Jewess Sara from the mob that wanted to stone her?"

"Yes," said Pentuer. "And soon after, you freed the innocent peasants from jail and wouldn't let Dagon torment your people with new taxes.

"For those people," spoke the priest, "for the mercy that you've always shown them, I bless you yet today. Maybe you alone will survive here, but mind ... mind that it's the oppressed Egyptian people who save you, and who await deliverance by you."

Suddenly it grew dark; a torrent of hot sand rained down from the south, and such a violent gale sprang up that it overturned a horse standing unsheltered. The Asiatics and Libyan prisoners all woke; but each only wedged himself tighter against the rock, mute with terror.

Something terrible was happening in nature. Night had descended upon the earth, and ruddy and black clouds of sand raced furiously across the sky. It seemed as if all the sand in the desert had come alive, had leapt up, and was rushing somewhere with the speed of stones cast from a sling.

The heat was like that in a sudatorium:[2] it cracked the skin of hands and face, parched the tongue, and caused a stinging in the chest. The fine grains of sand seared like sparks.

Pentuer quickly brought the vial to the Prince's lips. Ramses swallowed a couple of drops and felt a curious change: the pain and heat ceased tormenting him, and his mind regained its freedom.

"And this can go on for a couple of days?"

"For four days," replied the priest.

"And you wise men, you confidants of the gods, have no way of rescuing people from such a storm?"

Pentuer mused: "There's only one wise man in the world who could fight evil spirits ... but he's not here!"

Typhon had been blowing half an hour with inconceivable force. It had become almost night. At moments the wind slackened, the black clouds parted, and a bloody sun could be seen in the sky, and on the earth an ominous ruddy light.

But soon the torrid wind gathered force; the dust clouds thickened, the cadaverous light went out, and the air rang with disturbing rustles and murmurs such as the human ear is unwonted to snatch.

It was little short of sunset, and the storm's violence and the unbearable heat kept rising. From time to time, a gigantic bloody stain appeared above the horizon, as though a world conflagration were beginning.

Suddenly the Prince noticed that Pentuer was not at his side. Straining to hear, he made out a voice calling:

"Berossus! ... Berossus! ... If not you, then who will help us? ... Berossus! ... in the name of the One, the Almighty Who has no beginning nor end, I call on you!"

---

[2] sudatorium: a hot room used to induce sweating. *(Translator.)*

A thunderclap rang out in the north of the desert. The Prince was appalled: to an Egyptian, thunder was nearly as rare a phenomenon as the passage of a comet.

"Berossus! ... Berossus!" repeated the priest in a powerful voice.

The Successor strained to see in that direction, and made out a dark human figure with uplifted arms. Light-blue sparks were leaping out from the head, fingers, and even the clothing.

"Berossus! ... Berosssus! ..."

A protracted thunderclap rang closer, and a lightning bolt flashed amid the billows of sand, bathing the desert in a red light. Another thunderclap, and another lightning bolt.

The Prince felt the wind's violence slackening, and the heat declining. The surging sand began to fall to the ground; the sky turned ashen, then ruddy, then milky. Then all was still, and a moment later thunder crashed again and a cool wind blew in from the north.

The sweltering Asiatics and Libyans came to.

"Warriors of the pharaoh," said the old Libyan suddenly, "do you hear that soughing in the desert?"

"Another storm?"

"No, it's rain!"

Indeed several cool drops fell from the sky, then more and more, until at last a downpour broke out, accompanied by lightning.

Ramses' soldiers and their prisoners became delirious with joy. Ignoring thunder and lightning, the thirsty men, a moment before seared by the heat, ran like children beneath the torrents of rain. In the dark, they washed themselves and their horses, caught water in their caps and leather bags—and above all, drank, drank!

"Isn't it a miracle?" cried Prince Ramses. "But for the blessed rain, we would have perished in the desert, in Typhon's hot embrace."

"It will sometimes happen," said the old Libyan, "that the sandy south wind irritates the winds that pass over the sea and brings on a downpour."

Ramses was unhappy with this response, for he had ascribed the cloudburst to Pentuer's prayers. Turning to the Libyan, he asked: "Does it sometimes also happen that sparks shower from the human frame?"

"That happens whenever the desert wind blows," said the Libyan. "This time we saw sparks jump as well from the horses."

His voice rang with such assurance that the Prince approached an officer of his cavalry and whispered: "Watch the Libyans ..."

Hardly had he said it when something milled about in the dark, and a moment later hoofbeats rang out. When a lightning bolt lit the desert, a man was seen escaping on a horse.

"Tie the villains up!" shouted the Prince, "and kill any who resist! Woe betide you, Tehenna, if that scoundrel brings your brethren back here! You'll perish in dire torments, you and your men."

Rain, lightning, and darkness notwithstanding, Ramses' soldiers quickly bound the Libyans, who offered no resistance.

They may have been waiting for an order from Tehenna, but he was too dejected to even think of escape.

Slowly the storm subsided, and the desert's daytime heat yielded to piercing cold.

Men and horses drank their fill, and water bags were replenished; there were dates and biscuits enough to go around, making for good spirits. The thunderclaps became fainter, lightning flashed with diminishing frequency, the clouds began to rend in the northern sky, and here and there stars lit up.

Pentuer approached Ramses. "Let's get back to camp," he said. "We can reach it in a couple of hours, before the one who got away brings back enemies."

"How will we find it in this dark?" asked the Prince.

"Do you have torches?" the priest asked the Asiatics.

There were torches—long ropes impregnated with combustibles—but there was no fire. The wooden tinderboxes were soaked.

"We'll have to wait till morning," said the Prince impatiently.

Pentuer made no answer. He took a small vessel from his bag, and a torch from a soldier, and went aside. A moment later a quiet hissing broke out, and the torch lit.

"This priest is a great sorcerer!" muttered the old Libyan.

"This is the second wonder you've worked before my eyes," the Prince said to Pentuer. "Can you tell me how it's done?"

The priest shook his head. "Ask me anything, lord," he replied, "and I'll answer you to the extent of my knowledge. Only never ask me to disclose secrets of our temples."

"Not even if I made you my advisor?"

"Not even then. I'll never turn traitor; and though I dared to, I would be deterred by the punishments."

"Punishments?" repeated the Prince. "Ah! ... I recall the man in the dungeon at the Temple of Hathor on whom the priests poured molten tar. Did they really? ... Was that man really tortured to death?"

Pentuer was silent, as though he had not heard the question, and slowly took from his wonderful bag a small statuette of a god with outstretched arms. The statuette hung by a string; the priest let it dangle and watched it as he whispered a prayer. The figure swung and turned a number of times, then hung still.

Ramses watched in the torchlight, intrigued. "What are you doing?" he asked the priest.

"I can tell Your Eminence only this much," said Pentuer, "that the god points one hand to the star Eshmun.[3] That is what guides Phoenician ships through the seas at night."

"The Phoenicians also have this god?"

"They don't even know about him. The god who always points one hand to the star Eshmun is known only to us and to the Chaldean priests. And with his help any prophet can find his way, day or night, in fair weather or foul, over sea or desert."[4]

At an order from the Prince, who with a burning torch walked beside Pentuer, the retinue and prisoners set out after the priest, heading northeast. The suspended god swayed but pointed to the position of the holy star, the patron of lost travelers.

---

[3]The Pole Star. *(Author.)* Also known as "Polaris" and "the North Star," the Pole Star is the brightest star in the constellation Ursa Minor (Latin for "Little Bear"). Eshmun was actually the name of a Phoenician god of healing who was the tutelary god of the Phoenician city of Sidon. *(Translator.)*

[4]The magnetic compass, described here, was invented in China for purposes of divination as early as the Han Dynasty (206 BCE—220 CE) and was adopted for navigation under the Song Dynasty in the 11th century CE. Its first recorded use in western Europe and the Islamic world was about 1190 CE. *(Translator.)*

They walked at a good clip, leading the horses. The cold was so sharp that the Asiatics blew into their hands, and the Libyans shivered.

All at once something began crunching and creaking underfoot. Pentuer stooped over.

"The rain has formed a shallow puddle here on the bedrock," he said. "And see, Eminence, what has become of the water."

He picked up and showed the Prince what looked like a small pane of glass, which melted in his hands.

"When it's very cold," he added, "water turns into a transparent stone."

The Asiatics confirmed the priest's words, adding that, far to the north, water very often turned to stone; and steam, to a white salt which was tasteless but pinched the fingers and caused pain in the teeth.[5]

The Prince was in growing awe of Pentuer's learning.

Meanwhile the sky had cleared in the north, revealing the Little Bear,[6] containing the star Eshmun. The priest recited a prayer, returned the guiding god to the bag, and bade the torches extinguished, leaving only a rope smoldering to maintain the fire and, by its gradual burning, to mark the passage of the hours.

The Prince charged vigilance to his party and, taking Pentuer, moved ahead some distance.

"Pentuer," he said, "I'm naming you my advisor, both for now and for when it pleases the gods to grant me the crown of Upper and Lower Egypt."

"How have I earned the favor?"

"You have performed deeds before my eyes which bespeak your great learning and power over spirits. Furthermore, you were ready to save my life. So, although you've decided to conceal many things from me ..."

"Forgive me, Eminence," interrupted the priest. "When you have need of traitors, you will find them in exchange for gold and gems even among the priests. But I don't want to be of their number. For consider: were I to betray the gods, what assurance could you have that I would not treat you the same way?"

"Wisely spoken," mused Ramses. "But I wonder why you, a priest, bear goodwill for me in your heart. A year ago you blessed me, and today you wouldn't let me ride into the desert by myself and are giving me great services."

"The gods have advised me that if Your Eminence so choose, you can lift the unfortunate Egyptian populace out of their misery and abasement."

"How do the populace concern you?"

"I come from among them. My father and brothers drew water from the Nile and were caned."

"How can I help the populace?" asked the Successor.

Pentuer became animated. "Your people are overworked, pay excessive taxes, and suffer misery and oppression. The peasant's lot is a hard one!

"'Vermin have devoured half his harvest, the rhinoceros the other half; the fields teem with mice, swarm with locusts, are trampled by cattle, are stripped by sparrows. What little

---

[5] In Chapter 33, Ramses mentioned "countries where, in ... Mechir, there falls from the sky a white fluff which causes cold and is turned by fire into water." Prus' references, there to snow and here to ice, would have brought a chuckle from readers in Poland, one of the countries alluded to. (*Translator.*)

[6] The Little Bear (in Latin, *Ursa Minor*) is the northernmost constellation and contains the star Polaris—the Pole Star, or North Star. (*Translator.*)

remained on the threshing floor, thieves have made off with. Alas, poor husbandman! Now comes the scribe to the riverbank and demands the harvest. His henchmen bring canes; the Negroes, palm rods. They say, "Give us grain!" "There is none." They beat him, lay him on the ground, bind him, and put him head first into the canal, where he chokes. They bind his wife before him, and his children as well. The neighbors run to save their grain.'"[7]

"I've seen it myself," said the Prince, "and I even drove away such a scribe. But can I be present everywhere to prevent injustice?"

"Your lordship can order that people not be tormented needlessly. You can lower the taxes and designate days of rest for the peasants. You can give each family a small plot of land, the harvest from which will be theirs alone and will serve to feed them. Otherwise they will go on eating lotus, papyrus, and rotting fish, and your people will waste away. But if you show them your mercy, they will lift themselves."

"I will indeed do so!" exclaimed the Prince. "A good husbandman doesn't let his livestock starve to death, work beyond their strength, or receive unjust whippings. This must change!"

Pentuer halted. "Does Your Eminence promise me that?"

"I do!" said Ramses.

"Then I swear you'll be the most famous of the pharaohs, putting Ramses the Great in the shade!" exclaimed the priest.

The Prince fell to thinking. "What can we two do against the priests who hate me?"

"They fear you, lord," answered Pentuer. "They fear lest you start a war too soon with Assyria."

"What do they care, if the war is won?"

The priest bowed his head and spread his hands in silence.

"Then I'll tell you!" shouted the exasperated Prince. "They don't want war because they fear lest I return the victor, loaded down with treasure, driving slaves before me. They fear it because they want every pharaoh to be the weak tool of their hand—a useless implement to be discarded at their pleasure!

"But I won't have it! Either I'll do as I want, which is my right as the son and heir of the gods ... or I'll perish ..."

Pentuer stepped back and whispered a spell.

"Don't speak that way, Eminence," he said, disconcerted, "lest evil spirits that haunt the desert seize upon your words. A word—remember, lord—is like a stone cast from a sling; when it strikes a wall, it rebounds and turns against yourself."

The Prince tossed his hand scornfully. "I don't care," he replied. "There's no value to a life where everyone hampers my will. If it's not the gods, it's desert winds; if not evil spirits, then the priests ... Is that to be a pharaoh's power? I want to do what I want, and to account only to my eternal forbears, not to some baldpate who pretends to explain the will of the gods but actually usurps power and fills his treasuries with my substance!"

Suddenly, a few dozen paces from them, there rang a strange cry, midway between a neighing and a bleating—and a gigantic shadow ran past. It sped like an arrow and, insofar as could be made out, had a long neck and a humped torso.

There was a murmur of horror among the Prince's retinue. "It's a griffin! ... I clearly saw its wings!" said the Asiatics.

---

[7] Authentic description. *(Author.)* This text also inspired the Chapter 12 water-torture scene. *(Translator.)*

"The desert swarms with monsters!" added the old Libyan.

Ramses was disconcerted; it had seemed to him as well that the speeding shadow had the head of a serpent and something like stubby wings.

"Do monsters," he asked the priest, "in fact appear in the desert?"

"No doubt," said Pentuer, "such a desolate place is haunted by evil spirits of the most peculiar shapes. I think, though, that what passed us is actually an animal. It resembles a saddled horse, only it is bigger and fleeter. The denizens of the oases say this animal can go entirely without water, or at least drinks it very seldom. If that is so, future generations could use this strange beast, which now only inspires fear, to cross deserts."

"I wouldn't dare climb onto such a monster's back!" said the Prince, shaking his head.

"Our ancestors said the same of the horse, which helped the Hyksos conquer Egypt and is now indispensable to our army. Time greatly alters people's judgments!" said Pentuer.

The last clouds disappeared from the sky, and a clear night began. Despite the absence of the moon, visibility was so good that the general outlines of objects, even small or very distant ones, could be made out against the white sand.

The bitter cold likewise eased. For a time the entourage marched in silence, sinking to the ankles in sand. Suddenly, among the Asiatics, there arose a new tumult and cries of: "A sphinx! ... Look, a sphinx! ... We'll never get out of the desert alive now, with apparitions showing up all the time!"

The silhouette of a sphinx was in fact very clearly limned atop a white limestone hill: a leonine body, a huge head in an Egyptian cap, and a humanlike profile.

"Settle down, barbarians," said the old Libyan. "That's no sphinx but a lion, and he won't harm you because he's busy eating."

"Why, so it is a lion!" allowed the Prince, stopping. "But how he resembles a sphinx."

"He is the father of our sphinxes," said the priest quietly. "His face recalls human features; and his mane, a wig."

"Our Great Sphinx, too, at the Pyramids?"

"Many centuries before Menes," said Pentuer, "before there were pyramids, there was a limestone outcrop there which resembled a recumbent lion, as if the gods had meant thereby to mark the commencement of the desert.

"The priests of the time directed master artisans to work the rock and supply its defects with masonry. The artisans, more often seeing men than lions, carved a human face, and thus was born the first sphinx."

"Which we revere as divine ..." smiled the Prince.

"And rightly so," said the priest. "For the initial outlines of this work were made by the gods, and were finished by men inspired of the gods. Our Sphinx, by its enormousness and mystery, calls to mind the desert; has the appearance of spirits that haunt the desert; and terrifies people as does the desert. It truly is a son of the gods, and the Father of Terror."[8]

"Come to think of it, everything has an earthly origin," remarked the Prince. "The Nile does not flow out of the heavens but out of mountains on the other side of Ethiopia. The pyramids, which Herhor told me are a picture of our Kingdom, are built in the likeness of rocky peaks. And our temples, with their pylons and obelisks, their darkness and coolness—don't they recall the caves and hills that edge the Nile? Whenever, while hunting,

---

[8]Father of Terror: name given to the Great Sphinx of Giza by the Arabs. *(Translator.)*

I've gotten lost among the eastern rocks, I've come upon some singular formation that put me in mind of a temple. Sometimes, on its rough walls, I've even seen hieroglyphs inscribed by the winds and rain."

"There, Eminence, you have proof that our temples were reared to a plan drawn up by the priest. "As a small seed dropped into the ground gives rise to towering palms, so the image of a rock, a cave, a lion, even a lotus, sown in the soul of a pious pharaoh, brings forth avenues of sphinxes, and temples with their mighty columns. These are divine works, not human; and happy is the ruler who, looking about him, can discover divine thought in earthly things and present it in an understandable way to posterity."

"Only, such a ruler must have power and great wealth," said Ramses caustically, "and not be hobbled by priestly illusions."

Before them stretched a long sandy hill, on which now a couple of riders appeared.

"Ours or Libyans?" said the Prince.

A horn sounded on the hill and was answered in the Prince's retinue. The horsemen rode down as quicky as the deep sand allowed. Approaching, one of them called: "Is the Successor here?"

"He is, and well!" answered Ramses.

They dismounted and prostrated themselves on their faces.

"O Iry-pat!" said their commander. "Your soldiers are tearing their clothes and strewing their heads with ashes, thinking you have perished! All the cavalry have scattered over the desert to find your traces, and the gods have let us unworthy ones be the first to greet you."

The Prince promoted him to centurion and bade him present his subordinates next day for prizes.

CHAPTER 45

Half an hour later the dense fires of the Egyptian army came into view, and presently the Prince's retinue found itself within camp. Trumpets sounded on all sides; the soldiers grabbed their weapons and, shouting, formed ranks. Officers fell to the Prince's feet and, as after the previous day's victory, lifted him to their arms and carried him round the units. The ravine walls trembled to cries of "Live forever, victor! ... The gods have you in their keeping!"

Surrounded by torches, the holy Mentesuphis approached. The Successor wrested himself free of the officers and ran over to the priest.

"You know, holy father," cried Ramses, "we've captured the Libyan commander Tehenna!"

"A meager prize," replied the priest austerely, "for which the commander-in-chief should not have abandoned his army. Especially when a new enemy can come up at any moment."

The Prince felt the entire justice of the reproach, and for that very reason he became angry. His fists clenched, his eyes flashed ...

"By your mother's name, be silent, lord!" whispered Pentuer, standing behind him.

The Successor was so surprised by his advisor's utterance that he instantly cooled down; and having done so, he realized that the proper thing would be to acknowledge his error.

"Your Eminence is right," he said. "The army should never abandon its commander, nor the commander his army. I expected, though, that you, as the representative here of the Minister of War, would stand in for me."

The calm reply assuaged Mentesuphis, and the priest did not remind the Prince of the previous year's maneuvers, when the Viceroy had likewise abandoned the army—and had fallen into disfavor with the Pharaoh.

Suddenly Patroklos approached them with a hue and cry. The Greek general was again drunk, and called to the Prince from afar:

"Successor, look what the holy Mentesuphis has done. You announced pardon for any Libyan soldier who abandoned the invaders and returned to His Holiness' army. These men came over to me, thanks to which I smashed the enemy left wing ... but His Eminence Mentesuphis ordered them all butchered! Nearly a thousand prisoners died—all of them, ex-soldiers of ours who were to have been pardoned!"

The Prince's blood boiled up again; but Pentuer, still standing behind him, whispered: "Be silent, by the gods, be silent!"

Patroklos, however, had no advisor and kept shouting: "Henceforth, for good and all, we've lost the confidence of foreigners—and of our own people! Our army too must lose its cohesion when it learns that traitors are forcing their way to its head."

"Wretched mercenary," replied Mentesuphis coldly, "you dare speak like this of His Holiness' army and confidants? Never before has such blasphemy been heard! I fear lest the gods avenge this insult to them!"

Patroklos broke into coarse laughter. "While I sleep among Greeks, I don't fear the vengeance of nocturnal gods. And whilst I wake, diurnal ones won't harm me!"

"Go sleep, go ... among your Greeks, drunkard," said Mentesuphis, "lest lightning strike our heads because of you!"

"It won't strike your miser's shaven head, because it will take it for something else!" replied the inebriated Greek. But seeing no support coming for him from the Prince, he withdrew to his camp.

"Holy man," Ramses asked the priest, "did you really order the prisoners killed, against my pledge of pardon?"

"Your Eminence wasn't in camp," replied Mentesuphis, "so responsibility for the deed does not rest with you. I observe our laws of war, which require the execution of renegade soldiers. Soldiers who previously served His Holiness, then went over to the enemy, are to be executed immediately—that is the law."

"What if I had been here?"

"As commander-in-chief and son of the Pharaoh, you may suspend the execution of certain laws which I must heed," replied Mentesuphis.

"Could you not have waited till I returned?"

"The law calls for *immediate* execution, and I fulfilled that requirement."

The stunned Prince broke off the conversation and repaired to his tent. There, dropping into an armchair, he told Thutmose:

"I'm already in thrall to the priests! They kill my prisoners of war, they threaten my officers, they flout my obligations! Did you say nothing to Mentesuphis when he ordered the unfortunates killed?"

"He invoked the law of war and new orders from Herhor ..."

"But I'm actually commander here, though I rode out for half a day."

"You clearly left Patroklos and me in command," said Thutmose. "But when the holy Mentesuphis rode up, we had to yield to him because he outranked us."

The Prince reflected that Tehenna's capture had been purchased with excessive misfortunes. At the same time, he appreciated with all his being the import of the regulation forbidding a commander to abandon his army. He had to own that he was in the wrong, but that further galled his pride and filled him with hatred for the priests.

"I'm in thrall," he thought, "even before I've become pharaoh (may my holy father live forever!). So I must this very day begin extricating myself from it—and above all, be silent. Pentuer is right: be silent, ever be silent, and store up your angers like precious gems in memory's treasury. Only when they've gathered ... Oh, prophets, then will you pay me!"

"Your Eminence doesn't ask the result of the battle?" asked Thutmose.

"Oh, yes ... What are the tallies?"

"Over two thousand prisoners, more than three thousand killed, barely a few hundred escaped."

"Then how large was the Libyan army?" said the Prince, surprised.

"Six to seven thousand men."

"Impossible! Could virtually an entire army have been wiped out in such a skirmish?"

"And yet it's so, it was a terrible battle," said Thutmose. "You surrounded them on all sides, and the soldiers—and His Eminence Mentesuphis— did the rest. The tomb inscriptions of the most famous pharaohs don't speak of such a disaster for Egypt's enemies."

"Go sleep, Thutmose, I'm tired," said the Prince, feeling that excessive pride was going to his head.

"Did I carry off such a victory? ... Impossible!" he thought.

He threw himself down on the hides but, despite his mortal weariness, could not sleep.

Only fourteen hours had elapsed since he had ordered commencement of battle. Only fourteen hours? ... Impossible!

Had he won such a battle? Why, he'd seen no battle, only a thick yellow cloud streaming with inhuman shouting. Even now he saw the cloud, heard the uproar, felt the scorching heat, though there was no battle.

Then he saw the immense desert where he had moved with painful effort over the sand. He and his men had the best mounts in the whole army, yet had crawled along like turtles. And what scorching heat! ... No one could possibly endure such heat!

Now Typhon springs up, shrouds the earth, sears, gnaws, chokes! Pale sparks shower from Pentuer's figure. Overhead resound thunderbolts, a phenomenon he had never seen before. Then the still night in the desert ... the speeding griffin, the dark silhouette of the sphinx on the limestone hill.

"I've seen so much, experienced so much," thought Ramses, "I was at the construction of our temples, at the birth of the ageless Great Sphinx. Could all this really have happened in the space of fourteen hours?"

A final thought flashed to the Prince: "A person who has lived this much, cannot have long to live!"

A chill swept him from head to foot—and he fell asleep.

Next day he woke a couple of hours past sunrise. His eyes stung, all his bones ached, he coughed a little, but his mind was clear and his heart was full of daring.

Thutmose stood in the tent door.

"What's happening?" asked the Prince.

"Spies bring strange word from the Libyan border," said the favorite. "A great crowd is approaching our ravine: not an army but unarmed men, women, and children, headed by Musawasa and the foremost Libyans."

"What could it mean?"

"Evidently they want to sue for peace."

"After one battle?" asked the surprised Prince.

"But what a battle! Moreover, fear multiplies our army in their eyes. They feel weak, and fear invasion and death ..."

"We'll see whether it's not a ruse!" mused the Prince. "How are the men?"

"Hale, fed, rested, and in good spirits. Only ..."

"Only what?"

"Patroklos died in the night," whispered Thutmose.

"How did it happen?!" cried the Prince, springing up.

"Some say he drank himself to death ... others, that it was punishment by the gods. His face was livid, and his mouth was full of froth."[1]

"As with that slave in Athribis, you remember him? His name was Bakura, and he burst into the feast hall with complaints against the nomarch. Naturally, that same night he died of drink! ... Eh?"

Thutmose lowered his head. "We must be very careful, lord mine," he whispered.

"We'll try," said the Prince calmly. "I won't even be surprised at Patroklos' death. What's special about the death of a drunkard who insulted the gods ... insulted the priests?"

Thutmose sensed a threat in the taunt.

The Prince had felt great affection for Patroklos, who had been faithful as a dog. He could forget many wrongs done to himself, but he would never forgive Patroklos' death.

Before noon a fresh Theban regiment arrived at the Prince's camp from Egypt, and a couple of thousand men and several hundred donkeys brought tents and great supplies of provisions. At the same time, spies came in again from the direction of Libya with word that the host of unarmed people approaching the ravine was constantly growing.

At the Successor's behest, thick cavalry patrols reconnoitered in all directions to see whether an enemy army lurked anywhere. The priests carried a small chapel of Amon up to the tallest peak and held a service there. On returning to camp, they assured the Successor that, while a crowd of several thousand unarmed Libyans was indeed approaching, there was no army anywhere within a three-mile radius.

The Prince laughed at the report. "I have good vision," he said, "but I wouldn't make out an army at that distance."

After taking counsel, the priests told the Prince that, if he pledged not to speak with uninitiates about what he saw, he would find that it was possible to see very far.

Ramses promised. The priests set Amon's altar up on a hill and prayed. When the Prince had washed, removed his sandals, and offered a gold chain and incense to the god, they conducted him into a small, completely dark cabinet and told him to watch the wall.

After a moment, pious chanting began, during which a small bright circle appeared on the inner wall. Soon the circle turned cloudy; the Prince saw a sandy plain, in it rocks and, at the rocks, Asiatic outposts.

The priests chanted more vigorously, and the picture changed. Another part of the desert appeared, and in it a crowd of people no larger than ants. Nevertheless their movements, dress, and even individual faces were so distinct that the Prince could have described them.

The Successor's amazement knew no bounds. He rubbed his eyes, touched the moving image. Suddenly he turned his head about, the picture vanished, and all was darkness.[2]

When he emerged from the chapel, the elder priest asked him: "Iry-pat, do you believe now in the power of Egypt's gods?"

"Truly," he replied, "you are so learned that all the world ought to give you offerings and homage. If you are equally adept at seeing the future, nothing can oppose you."

[1] Frothing can be a sign of poisoning with strychnine, an alkaloid obtained from certain tropical plants. Strychnine, when inhaled, swallowed, or absorbed through the eyes or mouth, causes muscular convulsions and eventually death by asphyxiation. *(Translator.)*

[2] The first practical telescope would be invented, in the Netherlands, only at the start of the 17th century. Its appearance here is therefore an anachronism and an anatopism. *(Translator.)*

At this, one of the priests entered the chapel and prayed, and soon a voice spoke thence, saying: "Ramses! The fate of the Kingdom is weighed, and before the second full moon you shall be its ruler."

"Oh, gods!" exclaimed the terrified Prince, "is my father so ill?"

He prostrated himself on his face in the sand, and one of the priests in attendance asked whether he would know anything more.

"Tell me, father Amon," he said, "will my plans be fulfilled?"

After a moment, a voice said from the chapel: "If you do not begin a war with the East, if you make offerings to the gods and respect their servants, then a long life and a glorious reign await you."

After these wonders, which had taken place in broad daylight, in the open, the Prince repaired, shaken, to his tent. "Nothing can oppose the priests!" he thought, terrified.

In his tent he found Pentuer.

"Tell me, my advisor," he said, "can you priests read the human heart and reveal its secret plans?"

Pentuer shook his head. "Sooner," he said, "can a man see inside a rock than he can read another's heart. It is closed even to the gods, and only death discloses its thoughts."

The Prince drew a deep breath, but he could not shed his anxiety. When, toward evening, a council of war had to be called, he invited Mentesuphis and Pentuer to attend.

No one mentioned the suddenly deceased Patroklos; perhaps because there were more pressing matters. Libyan envoys had arrived, in Musawasa's name begging mercy for his son Tehenna and offering Libya's surrender and eternal peace with Egypt.

"Evil men," said one of the envoys, "deceived our people, saying that Egypt was weak and its pharaoh the shadow of a ruler. But yesterday we learned how strong is your arm, and we deem it wiser to surrender to you and pay tribute than to expose people to certain death, and our property to destruction."

After the council of war had heard this speech, the Libyans were asked to leave the tent, and Prince Ramses, to the surprise of the generals, asked the holy Mentesuphis his opinion.

"Only yesterday," said the prophet, "I would have counseled rejecting Musawasa's plea, carrying the war into Libya, and destroying that nest of bandits. Today, however, I have received such important news from Memphis that I shall vote for clemency for the vanquished."

"Is my holy father ill?" asked the Prince.

"He is. But until we finish with the Libyans, Your Eminence should not think about it."

When the Successor lowered his head sadly, Mentesuphis added:

"I have another duty to discharge. Yesterday, Prince, I ventured to remark that the commander should not have abandoned the army for so meager a prize as Tehenna. Today I see that I was mistaken: had your lordship not captured Tehenna, we would not so soon have had peace with Musawasa. Your wisdom, Commander-in-chief, proved superior to military law."

The Prince was struck by Mentesuphis' contrition. "Why did he say that?" he thought. "Evidently not only Amon knows that my holy father is ill."

Old feelings were roused again in the Successor's soul: contempt for the priests—and distrust of their miracles.

"So it was not the gods who prophesied to me that I will soon be pharaoh, but the information came from Memphis, and the priests deceived me in the chapel. And if they lied in the one thing, then who can say whether the desert scenes shown on the wall were not also a fraud?"

Since the Prince remained silent—which was ascribed to his sorrow over the Pharaoh's illness—and since the generals dared not speak after Mentesuphis' peremptory words, the council of war was concluded. A unanimous decision was adopted to take the greatest possible tribute from the Libyans, send them an Egyptian garrison—and end the war.

Now everyone expected the Pharaoh to die. And to give the Lord a proper funeral, Egypt needed a profound peace.

Leaving the war-council tent, the Prince asked Mentesuphis: "The valiant Patroklos expired last night: do you holy men intend to honor his remains?"

"He was a barbarian and a great sinner," said the priest. "But he rendered Egypt such distinguished services that he ought to be assured a life beyond the grave. Therefore if Your Eminence permits, we shall today send his body to Memphis to be mummified and taken to Thebes for eternal dwelling among the royal sepulchers."

The Prince agreed with a will, but his suspicions mounted.

"Yesterday," he thought, "Mentesuphis chided me as if I were a lazy pupil, and it was only by grace of the gods that he didn't cane me! But today he speaks to me like an obedient son to his father and all but prostrates himself on his stomach. Is this not a sign that power and the hour of reckoning approach my tent?"

Thus reflecting, the Prince waxed proud, and his heart was filled with ever greater anger at the priests. An anger the worse, because silent as a scorpion which, concealed in the sand, wounds the heedless foot with its venomous sting.

CHAPTER 46

In the night, lookouts passed word that the crowd of Libyans suing for mercy had entered the ravine. The glow from their fires was visible above the desert.

At sunrise, trumpets sounded and the whole Egyptian army stood at arms in the widest spot of the valley. Pursuant to orders from the Prince, who wished to frighten the Libyans still more, peaceable porters were placed in the infantry ranks, and donkey drivers on donkeys were introduced among the cavalry. And it came to pass that day that the Egyptians were as numerous as the desert sands, and the Libyans were as timid as doves over which there circles a hawk.

At nine in the morning, the Prince's golden chariot pulled up before his tent. The horses, caparisoned in ostrich plumes, were so eager that each had to be restrained by two grooms.

Ramses came out of his tent, mounted the chariot, and took the reins himself, while the driver's place beside him was taken by his advisor the priest Pentuer. A general spread a large green parasol over the Prince, and behind and at either side of the chariot walked Greek officers in gilt armor. Some distance behind the Prince's retinue came a small guard detachment and, in its midst, Tehenna, son of the Libyan leader Musawasa.

A few hundred paces from the Egyptians, at the exit from the Glaukus ravine, stood a forlorn gathering of Libyans begging the victor for mercy.

When Ramses rode with his suite onto the hill where he was to receive the enemy delegation, the army raised such a cheer in his honor that the wily Musawasa became still more apprehensive and whispered to the elders standing close to him:

"Truly I tell you, that is the cry of soldiers who love their commander!"

One of the more anxious Libyan princes, a great bandit, said to Musawasa:

"Don't you think that at such a moment it were wiser to trust in the fleetness of our horses than in the mercy of the pharaoh's son? He is said to be a mad lion who tears your skin even when stroking it; and we are as lambs torn from their dam's teats."

"Do as you like," replied Musawasa, "you have the whole desert before you. But the people have sent me to redeem their sins, and there is my son Tehenna, on whom the Prince will pour his wrath if I cannot placate him."

Two Asiatic horsemen galloped up to the Libyans and announced that the Lord awaited their humility.

Musawasa sighed bitterly and proceeded toward the victor's hill. Never had he made such a difficult trek! The coarse penitent's cloth covered his back poorly; the sun tortured his ash-strewn head, the gravel bit into his bare feet, and his heart was crushed by his own sorrow and that of his vanquished people.

He had gone barely a few hundred paces, but had had to stop and rest a couple of times. He also looked back often to make sure the near-naked slaves who carried gifts for the Prince did not steal the gold rings or, worse, the gems. An experienced man, Musawasa knew that people most gladly take advantage of another's misfortune.

"I thank the gods," the wily barbarian comforted himself, "that it has fallen to me to humble myself before a Prince who any day now will don the pharaoh's headdress. Egypt's rulers are magnanimous, especially in victory. So if I manage to move my lord, he will strengthen my standing in Libya and let me collect large taxes. And it's a real miracle that the Crown Prince personally captured Tehenna; for not only will the Crown Prince do him no harm, but he will shower Tehenna with dignities."

Thus he reflected, as he kept looking back. A naked slave can still conceal a gem in his mouth, even swallow it.

Thirty paces from the Successor's chariot, Musawasa and the foremost Libyans with him prostrated themselves on their stomachs and lay in the sand until the Prince's aide bade them rise. Approaching several paces, they again prostrated themselves; they did so thrice, and each time Ramses had to order them to rise.

Meanwhile Pentuer, standing in the Prince's chariot, whispered to his master:

"Let thy countenance show neither fierceness nor joy. Rather, be serene like the god Amon, who scorns his enemies and rejoices not at small triumphs."

At last the penitent Libyans stood before the Prince, who looked at them from his gold chariot like a fierce hippopotamus at ducklings with no place to hide from his might.

"You," asked Ramses suddenly, "are Musawasa, the wise Libyan commander?"

"I am your servant," he replied, again throwing himself to the ground.

When Musawasa had been told to rise, the Prince said:

"How could you commit so grievous a sin and lift your hand against the land of the gods? Did your former prudence forsake you?"

"Lord!" answered the wily Libyan, "grief scrambled the wits of His Holiness' expelled soldiers, and they ran to their doom, dragging me and my people after them. And the gods know how long this ugly war might have dragged on had the god Amon, in your form, not stepped to the head of the eternally living Pharaoh's army. Like a desert wind, you struck when and where you were not expected, and as a bull breaks a reed, so you crushed the benighted enemy. Whereupon all our peoples realized that even the redoubtable Libyan regiments are worth something only so long as your hand wields them."

"You speak wisely, Musawasa," said the Prince, "and you did still better, coming to divine Pharaoh's army without waiting for it to come to you. But I would know how real is your humility."

"Clear thy brow, O great Egyptian ruler," answered Musawasa. "We come to thee as subjects, that thy name be great in Libya and that thou be our sun, as thou art the sun of the Nine Peoples.

"Only command thy subordinates to be just to a people conquered and joined unto thy might. Let thy chiefs govern us conscientiously and justly and not, out of spite, report falsely of us and bring thy disfavor upon us and our children. Command them, O Viceroy of benevolent Pharaoh, to govern us according to thy will, sparing the freedom, property, language, and customs of our fathers and forbears.

"Let thy laws be equal for all thy subject peoples, let thy officials not indulge some and be overharsh with others. Let their judgments be the same for all. Let them collect a payment for thy needs and use, but not raise another from us, in secret from thee, which will not go into thy treasury but will only enrich thy servants and the servants of thy servants.

"Have us governed without prejudice to us or our children, for thou art our god and ruler forever. Imitate the sun, which broadcasts its strength-giving and life-giving radiance for all. We Libyan subjects beg thy favor, and we prostrate ourselves on our brows before thee, Successor to great and mighty Pharaoh."[1]

Thus spoke the artful Libyan Prince Musawasa, and when he had finished he again prostrated himself on his stomach. As the Pharaoh's Successor listened to the sage words, his eyes shone and his nostrils flared like those of a young stallion that, having had his fill of fodder, runs out into the meadow among the mares.

"Rise, Musawasa," said the Prince, "and hear what I shall say to you. Your fate and that of your peoples rests not with me but with the gracious Lord who rises above us all as the heavens rise above the earth. Therefore I advise you and the Libyan elders to go hence to Memphis and there prostrate yourselves on your faces before the ruler and god of this world, and repeat the humble speech that I have heard here.

"I know not what will be the outcome of your pleas; but since the gods never turn away from the contrite and suppliant, I have a presentiment that you will not be ill received.

"And now show me the gifts for His Holiness, that I may judge whether they will move the heart of almighty Pharaoh."

At that moment Mentesuphis gestured to Pentuer, who stood in the Prince's chariot. When Pentuer descended and respectfully approached the holy man, Mentesuphis whispered:

"I fear lest the triumph go too much to our young lord's head. Don't you think it would be prudent to somehow break off the proceedings?"

"On the contrary, don't," replied Pentuer, "and I guarantee he will not have a happy expression on his face during the triumph."

"Will you work a miracle?"

"Hardly. I'll only show him that, in this world, great joy is attended by great sorrow."

"Do as you will," said Mentesuphis, "for the gods have given you wisdom worthy of a member of the Supreme Council."

Trumpets and drums sounded, and the triumphal procession began.

It was headed by near-naked slaves bearing gifts, supervised by prominent Libyans. Carried were gold and silver gods, perfume caskets, enameled vessels, fabrics, furniture, and gold bowls heaped with rubies, sapphires, and emeralds. The slaves bearing them had shaven heads and bands over their mouths so that they could not steal a precious gem.

Prince Ramses rested his hands on the chariot's edge and peered down from the hill at the Libyans and his army like a golden eagle at mottled partridges. Pride filled him from head to foot, and everyone felt that no one could be more powerful than this victorious commander.

In a single instant the Prince's eyes lost their luster, and pained surprise registered on his face. Pentuer, standing behind him, had whispered:

---

[1] Inscription on the tomb of Pharaoh Horemheb, 1470 before Christ. [The latter four paragraphs, beginning, "Clear thy brow, O great Egyptian ruler."] *(Author.)* Actually, Horemheb died 178 years later, in 1292 BCE. *(Translator.)*

"Lend your ear, lord! Since you left Pi-Bast, some strange things have happened there. Your Phoenician woman Kama ran off with the Greek Lykon."

"With Lykon?" repeated the Prince.

"Do not move, lord, or show the thousands of your slaves that you have a sorrow on the day of triumph."

Just then a very long line of Libyans was passing at the Prince's feet, carrying baskets of fruit and bread and huge pitchers of wine and olive oil for the army. At this sight a pleased murmur swept the disciplined soldiers; but Ramses did not notice it, absorbed as he was in Pentuer's account.

"The gods," whispered the prophet, "have punished the faithless woman."

"Was she caught?" asked the Prince.

"Yes, but she had to be sent to the eastern colonies. She had contracted leprosy!"

"Oh, gods!" whispered Ramses. "Am I in danger of it?"

"Don't worry, lord: had you been infected, you would have had it by now."

The Prince felt a chill in all his members. How easily the gods plunged a man from the highest peaks into the abyss of deepest misery!

"What about that wretch Lykon?"

"He is a great criminal," said Pentuer, "such as few that the earth has brought forth ..."

"I know him. He looks like my mirror image," said Ramses.

Now there drew up a troop of Libyans leading extraordinary animals. At the head went a one-humped camel[2] with whitish hair, one of the first to be captured in the desert. After that, two rhinoceroses, a herd of horses, and a tame lion in a cage. Then a great many cages with varicolored birds, little monkeys, and puppy dogs, intended for court ladies. Driven at the end were great herds of cattle and sheep: meat for the army.

The Prince barely gave a glance to the peripatetic zoo, and asked the priest: "Has Lykon been captured?"

"Now, unfortunate lord, I will tell you the worst," whispered Pentuer. "But mind lest Egypt's enemies see your sorrow."

The Successor stirred.

"Your other woman, the Jewess Sara ..."

"Has she run off too?"

"She has died in jail ..."

"Oh, gods! Who dared put her there?"

"She accused herself of killing your son ..."

"What?!"

A great shout broke out at the Prince's feet: Libyan prisoners taken in the battle were being paraded, with a sad Tehenna at their head.

Ramses' heart was now so brimming with pain that he motioned to Tehenna, saying: "Stand by your father Musawasa, that he may touch you and see that you're alive ..."

At these words, all the Libyans and the whole army gave a mighty cry; but the Prince was not listening to it.

---

[2] one-humped camel: the dromedary or Arabian camel, which inhabits the Near East and the Horn of Africa; it is distinguished from the two-humped Bactrian camel of Central Asia, including ancient Bactria. (Translator.)

"My son is dead?" he asked the priest. "Sara accused herself of killing him? ... Did madness possess her soul?"

"The infant was killed by the wretch Lykon ..."

"O gods, give me strength!" groaned the Prince.

"Control yourself, lord, as becomes a conquering commander."

"How does one conquer such pain? ... Oh, merciless gods!"

"The child was killed by Lykon, and Sara accused herself to save you. Seeing the murderer at night, she took him for you."

"And I banished her from my house! ... I made her Kama's servant!" whispered the Prince.

Now Egyptian soldiers appeared, carrying baskets of hands cut from fallen Libyans.

At this sight, Prince Ramses covered his face and wept bitterly.

At once generals surrounded the chariot, comforting the lord. The holy prophet Mentesuphis made a motion, which was adopted without discussion, that the Egyptian army nevermore sever the hands of enemies fallen in battle.

This unforseen event concluded the first triumph of the Successor to the Egyptian Throne. The tears that he had shed over the severed hands bound the Libyans to him more powerfully than the victorious battle. Nor was anyone surprised when Egyptian soldiers and Libyans together sat down around the campfires, breaking bread and sharing wine from the same cups. The war and hatred that were to have lasted for years were replaced by a deep feeling of peace and trust.

Ramses bade Musawasa, Tehenna, and the leading Libyans immediately proceed with the gifts to Memphis; and he gave them an escort, not so much to watch them as to safeguard their persons and the treasures. Then he retired to his tent and did not show himself for several hours. Like a man for whom pain suffices as dearest company, he did not receive even Thutmose.

Toward evening a deputation of Greek officers, headed by Kalipos,[3] came to the Prince. When the Successor asked what they wanted, Kalipos replied:

"We come to beg your lordship that the body of our commander and your servant, Patroklos, not be turned over to the Egyptian priests but be cremated in accordance with Greek custom."

"Surely you know," said the surprised Prince, "that the priests want to make a first-class mummy of Patroklos' remains and deposit it by the tombs of the pharaohs. Can a greater honor meet a man in this world?"

The Greeks hesitated; finally Kalipos mustered up his courage and answered:

"Our lord, permit us to open our hearts to you. We well know that mummification is more advantageous for a man than cremation. For while the soul of a cremated man immediately passes to the eternal lands, the soul of an embalmed man may dwell for thousands of years on this earth and rejoice in its beauty.

"But the Egyptian priests, commander (may this not offend your ears!), hated Patroklos. So who can assure us that the priests, after making his mummy, won't detain his soul on the earth in order to torment it? And what would we be worth if, suspecting vengeance, we didn't protect the soul of our countryman and commander from it?"

---

[3] Kalipos: The name *Kallippos* (sometimes spelled *Callippus*) was borne by several notable Greeks of the 4th and 3rd centuries BCE. *(Translator.)*

Ramses' wonder grew. "Do what you deem necessary," he said.
"What if they don't give us the body?"
"Just ready a pyre, I'll see to the rest."
The Greeks left. The Prince sent for Mentesuphis.

CHAPTER 47

The priest scrutinized the Successor and found him very changed. Ramses was pale; he had almost lost weight within a few hours; and his eyes had lost their luster and looked sunken.

On hearing of the Greeks' concern, Mentesuphis did not hesitate about turning over Patroklos' remains.

"The Greeks are right," said the holy man, "we could torment the deceased Patroklos' shade. But they are fools to suppose any Egyptian or Chaldean priest would perpetrate such a crime.

"Let them take their countryman's body, if they think his afterlife will be happier in the care of their customs!"

The Prince sent an officer with a pertinent order, but detained Mentesuphis. He evidently wanted to tell the priest something, but hesitated.

After a lengthy silence Ramses suddenly said: "Holy prophet, you probably know that one of my women, Sara, has died and her son has been murdered?"

"It happened," responded Mentesuphis, "the night we left Pi-Bast."

The Prince jumped. "By eternal Amon!" he shouted. "It was that long ago, and you told me nothing?! Not even that I was suspected of having killed my son?"

"Lord," said the priest, "on the eve of battle a commander-in-chief has no father, no child, no one at all—only his army and enemy. At such a time, could we disturb you with that kind of news?"

"That's true," mused the Prince. "Were we surprised today, I don't know whether I could lead the army well. In fact, I don't know whether I'll ever regain my peace of mind.

"Such a little ... such a beautiful child! And that woman who sacrificed herself for me after I'd grievously wronged her. I never thought there could be such misfortunes or that the human heart could bear them."

"Time heals all ... Time and prayer," whispered the priest.

The Prince nodded, and such a silence again set in that the sands could be heard falling in the hourglass.

"Tell me, holy father," said the Successor, "if this is not one of the great secrets: what's the real difference between burning a dead person's body and making his mummy? I heard something about it at school, but I don't understand this matter, to which the Greeks attach so much weight."

"We attach far greater weight—the greatest," said the priest. "That is attested by our cities of the dead which occupy the whole edge of the Western Desert. It is attested by the pyramids—the tombs of Old Kingdom pharaohs—and by the huge rock-cut tombs of the kings of our time.

"The funeral and the tomb are a great matter, the greatest of human matters. For while we live fifty or a hundred years in corporeal form, our shades last tens of thousands of years, until completely cleansed.

"The Assyrian barbarians laugh at us for devoting more to the dead than to the living; but they would weep over their neglect of the dead if they knew, as we do, the secret of death and the tomb."

The Prince shuddered. "You frighten me," he said. "Have you forgotten that I have two loved ones among the dead who have not been interred in accordance with Egyptian ritual?"

"Not at all. Their mummies are being made right now. Sara and your son shall have all that may avail them on their long journey."

"Really?" asked Ramses.

"I assure you it is so," said the priest, "and that everything that is needed will be done so that your lordship will find them happy when you too weary of earthly life."

The Successor was very moved.

"Then you think, holy man," he asked, "that someday I will find my son again and will be able to tell the woman, 'Sara, I know I was too severe with you'?"

"I'm as certain of it as that I see Your Eminence."

"Tell me more!" cried the Prince. "A man cares nothing about tombs until he's deposited a bit of himself in one. I've had that misfortune, and just when I was thinking that, except for the Pharaoh, there's no one more powerful than me!"

"Your lordship was asking," began Mentesuphis, "about the difference between burning a dead person's body and making his mummy. It's the same as between destroying a garment and putting it away. When the garment is kept, it may yet be of use; and when you have but one, it were madness to burn it."

"That's what I don't understand," said the Prince. "You don't teach it even in the upper school."

"But we can tell the Pharaoh's Successor.

"Your Eminence knows," continued the priest, "that a human being is made up of three parts: the body, the divine spark, and the shade or *ka*, which unites the body with the divine spark.

"When a person dies, his shade and spark separate from the body. If a man lived without sinning, his divine spark and shade would immediately go among the gods for life eternal. But every person sins, sullies himself in this world, and as a result his *ka* shade must cleanse itself, sometimes over thousands of years. It cleanses itself by invisibly wandering our land, among people, and doing good deeds. However, the shades of criminals commit crimes even in the afterlife and ultimately doom both themselves and the divine spark contained within them.

"As is probably no secret to Your Eminence, the shade, the *ka*, perfectly resembles the person, only it looks as though it were woven of a very fine mist. The shade has a head, arms, and torso; can walk, talk, throw or lift objects; dresses like the person; and even, especially in the first several hundred years following death, must from time to time take sustenance. Later on, images of foods suffice it.

"But the shade draws its chief sustenance from the body's earthly remains. Thus, if we put the body into a grave, it quickly decomposes and the shade must content itself with dust and decay. If we burn the body, the shade has only ashes to sustain it. But when we mummify the body—when we embalm it to last for thousands of years—the shade, the *ka*, is always hale and hearty and passes the period of its cleansing at peace, even pleasantly."

"Remarkable!" whispered the Successor.

"Over millenia of study, the priests have learned very important details of the afterlife. It has been found that, when the entrails remain in the body of the deceased, his *ka* shade has a voracious appetite, needs as much food as the person and, when food is lacking, sets upon the living and sucks their blood. But when the entrails are removed from the remains—as is our practice—then the shade does almost without food: its own body, embalmed and filled with powerful fragrant herbs, suffices it for millions of years.

"It has also been found that, when the tomb of the deceased is empty, the shade longs for the world and roams the earth needlessly. But when we place in the funerary chapel the clothing, furniture, weapons, vessels, and implements that the deceased liked; when we cover the walls with paintings of feasts, hunts, religious ceremonies, wars, and generally the activities in which the deceased took part; and when we also provide him statuettes of his family members, servants, horses, dogs, and cattle, then the shade doesn't venture needlessly into the world, because it finds the world in its own house of the dead.

"Finally, it has been found that many shades, even after undergoing penance, cannot enter the land of eternal bliss because they don't know the proper prayers, spells, and conversations with the gods. We prevent this happening by wrapping the mummy in papyri inscribed with aphorisms—and by placing the *Book of the Dead* in their coffins.

"In a word, our funerary ritual fortifies the shade, protects it from discomfort and from longing after the world, facilitates its entry among the gods—and secures the living from harms that might be inflicted on them by the shades. Our great solicitude for the dead has precisely that purpose; that is why we build virtual palaces for them—and in these, the most ornate apartments."

The Prince mused: "I understand that you render a great service to the powerless, defenseless shades in furnishing them this way. But ... how can I know that shades exist?"

"I know there is a waterless desert," continued the Prince, "because I see it, because I've sunk into its sands and experienced its heat. I also know there are lands where water turns to stone, and steam to a white fluff, because credible witnesses have said so.

"But how do you know about shades, which no one has seen, and about their afterlives, when no person has returned from there?"

"Your Eminence is mistaken," said the priest. "Shades have appeared to people many a time, and have even told them their secrets.

"One may live in Thebes ten years and see no rain; one may live on earth a hundred years and not encounter a shade. But if one lived hundreds of years in Thebes, or thousands of years on earth, he would see more than one rain and more than one shade!"

"Who has lived thousands of years?" asked the Prince.

"The holy priesthood has lived, lives, and shall live," answered Mentesuphis. "Thirty thousand years ago, it settled at the Nile; ever since, it has studied heaven and earth; it has created our learning and has drawn the plans for all the fields, dams, canals, pyramids, and temples."

"That is true," interrupted the Prince. "The priesthood is learned and powerful—but where are the shades? Who has seen them and spoken with them?"

"Know, Lord," discoursed Mentesuphis, "that there is a shade in every living person. And as there are persons notable for their enormous strength or exceptional sharpness of vision, so there are persons who possess a rare ability to send out their shades in their lifetimes.

"Our secret books are replete with the most credible accounts of this kind. Many a prophet has been able to fall into a sleep resembling death. Then his shade has separated from his body and instantly migrated to Tyre, Nineveh, or Babylon, has made required observations, has listened in to conferences of interest to us, and on the prophet's waking has rendered the most accurate account. Many an evil sorcerer has likewise fallen into a sleep, then has sent his shade to the home of a hateful person and has overturned or destroyed furniture and terrified the whole family.

"On occasion, a man harassed by a sorcerer's shade has struck it with a spear or sword. Then bloodstains have appeared in the visited home, and the sorcerer's body has borne the very wound that had been inflicted on the shade.

"More than once, too, the shade of a living person has appeared together with that person, a few paces from him."

"I'm familiar with such shades!" whispered the Prince ironically.

"I must add," continued Mentesuphis, "that not only people but also animals, plants, stones, buildings, and furnishings have the same kinds of shades. Only (strangely enough!) the shade of an inanimate object is not inanimate but is possessed of life: it moves, changes place, even thinks and manifests this by various signs—most often, by tapping.

"After a person dies, his shade lives on and appears to people. Our books record thousands of such cases. Some shades have requested food, others have walked about the house, worked in the garden, or hunted in the hills with the shades of their dogs and cats. Other shades have frightened people, ruined their estates, drunk their blood, even drawn the living into debauchery. But there have also been good shades: shades of mothers caring for children, of fallen soldiers warning of enemy ambush, of priests who have disclosed important secrets to us.

"As late as the Eighteenth Dynasty, the shade of Pharaoh Cheops (who is doing penance for oppressing the people at the building of his pyramid) appeared in the Nubian gold mines, pitied the suffering prisoners, and showed them a new source of water."

"Holy man, you tell of interesting things," said Ramses. "Permit me now to tell you something. One night in Pi-Bast, I was shown 'my shade'. It looked just like me and was even dressed like me. But I soon found that it was no shade but a live man, a certain Lykon, the despicable murderer of my son.

"He began his crimes, frightening the Phoenician woman Kama. I set a reward for his capture but our police not only failed to apprehend him, they let him make off with Kama and kill the innocent child.

"Today I hear Kama has been caught; but I know nothing about that wretch Lykon. No doubt he is at large, hale and hearty and affluent in stolen treasure; he may even be readying a new crime!"

"Too many people are after the villain for him not finally to be apprehended," said Mentesuphis. "And once he falls into our hands, Egypt will pay him for the grief he has caused her Crown Prince. Believe me, lord, you may forgive him all his crimes in advance, for the punishment will be commensurate with them."

"I'd rather have him in my own hands," said the Prince. "A 'shade' like that, in one's lifetime, is always a dangerous thing!"[1]

None too pleased with this close to his exposition, the holy Mentesuphis took leave of the Prince. After him, Thutmose entered the tent to report that the Greeks were building a pyre for their commander and that a dozen Libyan women had agreed to weep at the obsequies.

"We'll attend," said the Successor. "Did you know my son has been killed? ... A little child! When I carried him in my arms, he laughed and reached out to me with his hand-kins! It's inconceivable how much villainy the human heart can hold! If that wretch Lykon had attempted my life, I might have understood, even forgiven. But to murder a baby ..."

"Has your lordship been told of Sara's sacrifice?" asked Thutmose.

"Yes. I think she was the most loyal of my women and that I treated her unfairly. But how is it possible," cried the Prince, striking the table with his fist, "that that villain Lykon hasn't been caught? The Phoenicians swore he would be ... I promised the chief of police a reward.

"There must be more to this!"

Thutmose approached the Prince and whispered: "A messenger has been to me from Hiram, who fears the wrath of the priests and is hiding before he leaves Egypt. It seems Hiram has learned from the chief of police of Pi-Bast that Lykon has been caught ... but hush!" added Thutmose, frightened.

The Prince became angry but quickly regained his composure. "Caught?" he said. "Why the secrecy?"

"The chief of police had to turn him over on the holy Mephres' order in the name of the Supreme Council."

"Aha!" said the Successor. "So the venerable Mephres and the Supreme Council need a man who looks so much like me. They're going to give my son and Sara a beautiful funeral ... they're embalming their remains. But they're concealing the murderer in a safe place.

"And the holy Mentesuphis is a very learned man. Today he told me all the secrets of the afterlife; he explained the whole funerary ritual to me as if I were a priest of at least the third degree. But he made no mention of Lykon having been caught or of Mephres' concealing the killer! Apparently the holy fathers are more solicitous of the little secrets of the Successor than of the great secrets of the afterlife."

"That probably shouldn't surprise you, lord," broke in Thutmose. "You know the priests suspect you of ill will toward them and are on their guard. Especially ..."

"Especially what?"

"Especially since His Holiness is very ill. Very ..."

"Aha! My father is ill, and I have to watch the desert at the head of an army so the sands don't make off. It's good you reminded me! ... Yes, His Holiness must be gravely ill if the

[1] Interestingly, this theory of "shades," on which Egypt's extraordinary solicitude for the dead was probably based, has been revived in Europe. It is expounded at length in Adolf d'Assier's book, *Essai sur l'humanité posthume et le spiritisme, par un positiviste* [An Essay on Posthumous Humanity and on Spiritualism, by a Positivist]. *(Author.)*

priests are being so gracious to me. They show me everything and tell me everything, except that Mephres has concealed Lykon.

"Thutmose," said the Prince suddenly, "do you still think I can count on the army?"

"We'll go to our deaths for you!"

"Can you vouch as well for the nobility?"

"Even as for the army."

"Good," said the Successor. "Let's go render the last service to Patroklos."

CHAPTER 48

During the several months that Prince Ramses had been discharging the duties of Viceroy of Lower Egypt, his holy father's health had been steadily declining. The moment neared when the Lord of Eternity who roused joy in hearts, the ruler of Egypt and all the countries lighted by the sun, would take his place beside his venerable predecessors in the catacombs on the other side of Thebes.[1]

He was not yet of a very advanced age—this mighty ruler, equal to the gods, who bestowed life on his subjects and had the right to take away men's wives according to the desires of his heart. But a thirty-odd-year reign had so wearied him that he longed to rest and to recover his youth and beauty in the Western Land where each pharaoh reigned forever without cares over peoples so happy that no one had ever wanted to return from there.

Only half a year earlier the Holy Lord had been carrying on all the functions of his office, on which depended the safety and prosperity of the whole visible world.[2]

In the morning, hardly had the cock crowed when priests woke the ruler with a hymn to the rising sun. The Pharaoh rose from bed and bathed in rose water in a golden tub. Then his divine body was rubbed with precious fragrances amid murmured prayers that drove off evil spirits.

Thus cleansed and censed by the prophets, the Lord would go to a small chapel. He would break the clay seal on the door and alone enter the sanctuary, where on an ivory bed rested a miraculous statue of the god Osiris. The god had an extraordinary property: every night his arms, legs, and head, which had once upon a time been severed by the evil god Set, fell off; but after the Pharaoh's prayer all the members grew back again without any cause.

When His Holiness found Osiris whole again, he took the statue from its bed, bathed it, dressed it in precious vestments, and, seating it on a malachite throne, burned incense before it. This ceremony was of the utmost importance: if some morning Osiris' divine members failed to grow back, it would be a sign that Egypt, if not the whole world, was threatened with a great calamity.

Having resurrected and dressed the god, His Holiness would leave the chapel door open so that blessings might flow out upon the country. He also assigned priests to

1 "catacombs on the other side of Thebes": the underground tombs in the Valley of the Kings, on the west bank of the Nile opposite Thebes proper. For nearly 500 years (16th-11th centuries BCE) during New Kingdom Dynasties 18-20, pharaohs and some privileged nobles were interred there. *(Translator.)*

2 The pharaoh was responsible for maintaining Egypt's cosmic protection. *(Translator.)*

watch the sanctuary all day, not so much against malice as against human careless-
ness. On more than one occasion a heedless mortal had approached too close to the
sanctuary, exposing himself to an invisible blow that deprived him of consciousness,
if not of life.

The service completed, the Lord went, surrounded by chanting priests, to the great
dining hall, where stood a chair and a small table for him, and nineteen other small
tables in front of nineteen statues representing the nineteen previous dynasties. When
the ruler was seated, young boys and girls ran in with silver plates of meat and pastries,
and with pitchers of wine. The priest supervising the dishes tasted of the first plate and
first pitcher, which were then served on bended knee to the Pharaoh, while the other
plates and pitchers were placed before the statues of the ancestors. When the ruler had
sated his hunger and left the hall, the ancestors' dishes could be consumed by princes
or priests.

From the dining hall, the Lord repaired to the equally great audience hall. Here his
closest government dignitaries and closest family prostrated themselves before him on
their faces, after which Minister Herhor, the Supreme Treasurer, Supreme Judge, and Supreme Chief of Police tendered him reports on the Kingdom's affairs. The readings were
interrupted by religious music and dancing, during which the throne was showered with
garlands and bouquets.

After the audience, His Holiness repaired to an adjacent room, reclined on a couch,
and napped. Then he made offerings of wine and incense to the gods and told the priests
his dreams, in accordance with which the wise men arranged the supreme dispositions in
matters that His Holiness was to settle.

Sometimes, however, when there were no dreams or when the Pharaoh thought their
interpretation wrong, His Holiness smiled benignly—and ordered the matter settled thus
and so. This order was law which none could alter, save perhaps in the execution of details.

In the afternoon His Holiness, borne in a litter, appeared in the courtyard to his faithful
guard, and next he went onto the terrace and looked to the four quarters of the world to
give them his blessing. Banners were hung from the pylon tops, and mighty trumpets rang
out. Whoever heard them, in town or in field, Egyptian or barbarian, prostrated himself on
his face so that a bit of the supreme grace might flow down on his head.

At such a moment, it was forbidden to strike man or beast: the cane poised over a back
descended harmlessly. If a criminal sentenced to death proved that his sentence had been
pronounced during the appearance of the Lord of Heaven and Earth, his sentence was
commuted: before the pharaoh, walked power; after him, mercy.

Having blessed his people, the Lord of all things under the sun went down into his
gardens, among the palms and sycamores, and there sat the longest, receiving the homage
of his women and watching the children of his house at play. When one of them drew his
attention by its comeliness or gracefulness, he called it over and asked:

"Who are you, my little one?"

"I am Prince Binotris,[3] son of His Holiness," answered the boy.

"What is your mother's name?"

---

[3] Binotris: *Binothris* was the name the Egyptian historian Manetho, in the early 3rd century BCE, gave to the
2nd Dynasty pharaoh Nynetjer, who had reigned perhaps from ca. 2760 to ca. 2715 BCE. *(Translator.)*

"My mother is His Holiness' woman, the Lady Ameces."[4]

"What can you do?"

"I can count to ten and write: 'May our father and god, the holy Pharaoh Ramses, live forever!'"

The Lord of Eternity smiled benignly and touched the boastful boy's curly head with his delicate, almost translucent hand. The boy now truly was a prince, though His Holiness continued smiling enigmatically.

Whoever had been touched by the divine hand, could experience no adversity in life but must be exalted above others.

For the midday meal the ruler went to another dining hall and shared his meal with the gods of all the nomes of Egypt, whose statues lined the walls. Whatever the gods did not eat, went to the priests and highest persons at court.

Toward evening His Holiness received a visit from Lady Nikotris, the Crown Prince's mother, watched religious dances, and heard a concert. Then he went again to the bath and, cleansed, entered Osiris' chapel to undress the miraculous god and lay him down to sleep. That done, he closed and sealed the chapel door and, surrounded by a procession of priests, went to his bedroom.

In an adjacent room the priests quietly prayed till sunrise to the Pharaoh's soul, which in sleep abided with the gods. They presented their requests for the successful issue of current state affairs and for the protection of Egypt's borders and the royal tombs, so that no thief would dare enter them and disturb the eternal repose of the glorious rulers. The priests' prayers, however, doubtless due to nocturnal weariness, were not always effective: the Kingdom's troubles grew, and the sacred tombs were plundered, not only precious objects being taken but even pharaohs' mummies.

This was due to the settling in Egypt of foreigners and pagans from whom the people had learned disregard for the Egyptian gods and holiest places.

The repose of the Lord of Lords was interrupted at midnight. At that hour astrologers woke His Holiness to tell him which quarter the moon was in, which planets shone above the horizon, which constellation was passing through the meridian, and generally whether anything special had happened in the heavens. Sometimes clouds appeared, stars fell oftener than usual, or fiery orbs passed over the earth.

The Lord heard the astrologers' report; in the event of an unusual happening, he reassured them as to the safety of the world; and he ordered the observations recorded in the proper tables, which were sent monthly to the priests at the Temple of the Sphinx, Egypt's greatest sages. They drew conclusions from the tables but did not disclose the most important ones to anyone, except perhaps to their colleagues, the Chaldean priests in Babylon.

After midnight His Holiness could sleep till the crowing of the morning cocks, if he was so minded.

So pious and exacting, as late as half a year before, had been the life of the good god, the dispenser of providence, life, and health, who watched day and night over earth and

---

[4] Ameces: possibly an alternative transliteration to *Amesses*, itself apparently an alternative transliteration to *Ahmose* ("Born of the Moon"). *Ahmose* was a popular name at the beginning of the 18th Dynasty. It was borne by a pharaoh, each, of Dynasties 17, 18, and 26; and by six Dynasty 18 queens, nine other Dynasty 18 royals, and three notable Dynasty 18 officials. *(Translator.)*

heaven, over the visible and invisible worlds. But over the past half year his eternally living soul had begun to weary more and more often of earthly matters and of its bodily envelope. There were days when he ate nothing, and nights when he did not sleep. Sometimes, during an audience, an expression of intense pain would come over his gentle face, and very often, more and more often, he would fall into a faint.

The terrified Queen Nikotris, His Eminence Herhor, and the priests repeatedly asked the Lord whether anything ailed him. But the Lord shrugged and said nothing, as he carried on his demanding duties.

The court physicians began slipping him the most powerful fortifying agents. The ashes of a horse and bull were mixed into his wine and food, then those of a lion, rhinoceros, and elephant, but the powerful medicines seemed to have no effect. His Holiness fainted away so often that the reports ceased being read to him.

His Eminence Herhor, the Queen, and the priests prostrated themselves on their faces and begged the Lord to let the wise men examine his divine body. The Lord consented, and the physicians examined and percussed him but, apart from a great loss of weight, found no dangerous sign.

"How does Your Holiness feel?" asked the most learned physician finally.

The Pharaoh smiled. "I feel," he replied, "that it is time for me to return to my solar father."

"Your Holiness cannot do that without the greatest detriment to your peoples," said Herhor quickly.

"I will leave you my son Ramses, who is a lion and eagle in one person," said the Lord. "Heed him, and he will give Egypt a destiny unheard-of since the world began."

This promise sent a chill through the holy Herhor and the other priests. They knew that the Crown Prince was a lion and eagle in one person and that they must heed him. But they would rather have had, for many more years, this gracious Lord whose merciful heart was like the north wind that brought rain to the fields and coolness to the people.

Therefore they prostrated themselves as a man, moaning, and lay on their stomachs until the Pharaoh agreed to undergo a cure.

The physicians carried him out into the garden, among the fragrant conifers, and fed him minced meat, hearty broths, milk, and aged wine. These brave remedies fortified His Holiness for a week; but soon there came a new onset of weakness, to fight which the Lord was made to drink the fresh blood of calves descended from Apis.

But the blood did not help for long either, and resort had to be made to consulting the high priest of the temple of the evil god Set.

Amid the general dread, the grim priest entered His Holiness' bedchamber, looked at the patient, and recommended a terrible medicine.

"The Pharaoh," he said, "must be given the blood of innocent children to drink, a cup each day."

The priests and magnates filling the chamber were dumbfounded. Then they began whispering that peasant children would best serve the purpose, because the children of priests and great lords lost their innocence in infancy.

"It is all one to me whose children they are," replied the truculent priest, "so long as His Holiness has fresh blood each day."

The Lord, lying abed with eyes closed, listened to the sanguinary advice and the frightened whispers of the court. When one of the physicians diffidently asked Herhor whether a search might be started for the right children, the Pharaoh roused himself. He fixed his sagacious eyes on those present and said:

"The crocodile does not devour its young, the jackal and hyena lay down their lives for their pups, and I am to drink the blood of Egyptian children, who are my children? Truly, I would never have thought anyone would dare recommend me an unworthy medicine!"

The evil god's priest prostrated himself, explaining that, while no one had ever drunk children's blood in Egypt, the infernal powers were supposed to restore health that way. At least, this remedy was used in Assyria and Phoenicia.

"For shame," replied the Pharaoh, "to mention such disgusting things in the palace of Egypt's rulers. Don't you know that the Phoenicians and Assyrians are stupid barbarians? In our land, the most benighted peasant would not believe that the spilling of innocent blood could redound to anyone's benefit."

Thus spoke the equal of the immortals. The courtiers hid their faces sullied with shame, and the high priest of Set quietly left the room.

Now Herhor, to save the Lord's ebbing life, made the ultimate recourse and told the Pharaoh that, sheltering at one of the Theban temples, was a Chaldean, Berossus, the most learned priest in Babylon and an incomparable wonderworker.

"This man," said Herhor, "is a stranger to Your Holiness and has no right to advise our Lord in matters of such import. But do let him look at Your Holiness, for I am sure he will find a medicine for your illness, and in no case will he offend Your Holiness with impious words."

The Pharaoh once again yielded to the urgings of his faithful servant. Two days later Berossus, summoned by some secret means, sailed into Memphis.

The wise Chaldean, after only a cursory look at the Pharaoh, advised:

"We must find a man in Egypt whose prayers reach the throne of the Highest. When he prays sincerely for the Pharaoh's intention, the Lord shall regain his health and live for many years."

At this, the Lord regarded the priests gathered around him and said: "I see so many holy men here, if one of them would think of me, I should be well."

And he smiled slightly.

"We are all but men," said the wonderworker Berossus, "so our souls are not always able to rise to the footstool of the Eternal. But I shall give Your Holiness an infallible means of discovering the person who prays the most sincerely and effectively."

"Yes, find him for me, that he may be my friend in the final hour of my life."

Upon the Lord's favorable response, the Chaldean requested an unoccupied room that had only a single door. And he instructed that His Holiness be brought there the same day, an hour before sunset.

At the appointed time the four highest priests dressed the Pharaoh in a fresh linen robe, recited a great prayer over him that drove away evil powers, seated him in a simple cedar-wood litter, and bore the Lord to the vacant chamber, furnished with only a small table.

Berossus was already there, facing east in prayer.

When the priests had left, the Chaldean closed the heavy door, placed a purple sash on his shoulders, and set a black crystal ball on the table before the Pharaoh. With his left hand he took up a sharp dagger of Babylonian steel, and with his right hand a cane covered with arcane signs; and, with the cane, he traced a circle in the air around himself and the Pharaoh. Then, turning successively to the four quarters of the world, he whispered:

"Amorul, Taneha, Latisten, Rabur, Adonay! Have mercy on me and cleanse me, heavenly Father, gracious and merciful. Send Thy holy blessing down on Thy unworthy servant and extend Thy almighty arm upon stubborn and rebellious spirits, that I may contemplate Thy sacred works in peace!"

He paused and addressed the Pharaoh: "Mer-amen-Ramses, High Priest of Amon, do you see a spark in the black ball?"

"I see a little white spark that seems to move like a bee above a flower."

"Mer-amen-Ramses, watch the spark and do not take your eyes from it. Look to neither right nor left, nor at anything that might lean out from the sides"

Again he whispered:

"Baralanensis, Baldachiensis, by the mighty princes Genio, Lachiadae, ministers of the infernal kingdom, I conjure and summon you by the power of the highest Majesty, with which I am invested, I conjure and command you!"

The Pharaoh shuddered in horror.

"Mer-amen-Ramses, what do you see?" asked the Chaldean.

"From beyond the ball, a frightful head is leaning out. The red hair stands on end ... a greenish face ... the pupils are inverted so only the whites of the eyes are visible ... the mouth is open wide as if to scream ..."

"That is terror," said Berossus, directing the blade of the dagger above the crystal ball.

Suddenly the Pharaoh doubled over. "Enough!" he cried. "Why do you torment me? My weary body longs to rest; my soul longs to fly to the land of eternal light ... and you not only won't let me die ... but you think up new torments! Aahh! ... I don't want this!"

"What do you see?"

"From the ceiling, two frightful things like spider's legs keep descending ... thick as palm trees, hairy, ending in hooks. I feel that hovering over my head is a monstrously big spider which is wrapping me in a web of ship's cables."

Berossus directed the dagger upward. "Mer-amen-Ramses," he said, "watch the spark and do not look to the sides.

"Behold this sign that I lift in your presence," he whispered. "Behold, powerfully armed with divine assistance am I, foreseeing and fearless, who conjure you with spells. Aye, Saraye, Aye, Saraye, Aye, Saraye ... by the name of the almighty and eternally living God ..."

A smile came to the Pharaoh's face. "I think I see Egypt," said the Lord. "All of Egypt ... Yes, that's the Nile ... the desert ... there's Memphis, Thebes ..."

He did indeed see Egypt, all of Egypt, but no larger than the alley that stretched the length of his palace garden. The picture had the curious property that, when the Pharaoh directed his attention to a particular point, it grew into an area of nearly natural size.

The sun was setting, flooding the earth with a golden-purplish light. The diurnal birds were settling down to sleep; the nocturnal ones were waking in their retreats. In the desert the hyenas and jackals were yawning, and the dozing lion was stretching its powerful carcass preparatory to chase.

The Nile fisherman was hurriedly hauling in his nets; the great transport barges were making shore. A weary husbandman was removing from the shadoof the bucket with which he had drawn water all day; another husbandman was slowly taking his plow back to his mud hut. In the towns, lamps were being lit; in the temples, the priests were gathering for the evening service. On the highways, the dust was settling and the squeaky cartwheels were falling still. From the pylon tops, mournful voices were calling the nation to prayer.

A moment later, the Pharaoh was surprised to see a seeming flock of silvery birds soaring up from the earth. They flew from temples, palaces, streets, factories, Nile ships, peasant huts, even mines. At first each sped like an arrow; but soon its path was blocked beneath heaven by another silver-feathered bird, which struck it full force—and both fell to earth dead.

These were discordant human prayers impeding one another in their ascent to the throne of the Eternal.

The Pharaoh strained to hear. At first he heard only the rustling of wings; but before long he could make out words.

He heard a sick man praying for a return to health, and a physician begging that his patient remain ill for as long as possible. A farmer asked Amon to watch over his granary and cow barn; a thief extended his hands to heaven, that he might make off with another's cow and fill his sacks with another's grain.

Their prayers knocked one another aside like stones cast from slings.

A desert wanderer collapsed onto the sand, begging for a north wind to bring him a drop of water; a sea sailor beat the deck with his forehead, that the wind might blow a week longer from the east. A husbandman wanted the wet land to dry out the sooner after the flood; a poor fisherman asked that the marshes never dry out.

Their prayers too knocked one another aside and failed to reach the divine ears of Amon.

The greatest tumult prevailed over the quarries, where chain gangs of criminals, using water-soaked wedges, split off huge stones. The day shift begged for night, that they might lie down and sleep, while the night shift being roused by the overseers beat their breasts in supplication that the sun never set. The merchants who bought the worked and dressed stones prayed for the greatest number of criminals in the quarry, while the provisioners lay on their bellies, sighing for a pestilence to carry off workers and give them greater profits.

So the prayers of the people at the quarries did not reach heaven either.

On the western border the Pharaoh saw two armies readying for battle. Both lay in the sand, calling on Amon to destroy the enemy. The Libyans wished confusion and death on the Egyptians; the Egyptians hurled curses at the Libyans.

The prayers of both, like two flights of hawks, collided over the earth and fell to the desert. Amon did not even notice them.

Wherever the Pharaoh turned his weary gaze, it was the same. The peasants prayed for rest and lower taxes; the scribes, for higher taxes and never-ending work. The priests begged Amon for long life for Ramses XII and for extirpation of the Phoenicians, who spoiled their financial operations; the nomarchs called on the god to preserve the Phoenicians and to hasten the enthronement of Ramses XIII, who would curb the license of the priests. The lions, jackals, and hyenas panted with hunger and bloodlust; the stags, deer, and hares left their refuges in trepidation, hoping to preserve their wretched lives for yet another day—though experience taught that this night, too, a score of them must die if the predators were not to perish.

And so discord reigned the world over. Everyone wanted what horrified others; everyone begged for what would benefit him, without asking whether it might harm his neighbor.

Hence their prayers, though they were as silvery birds soaring heavenward, failed to reach their destination. And divine Amon, whom no voice reached from the earth, rested his hands on his knees and became the more absorbed in contemplating his own divinity; and, increasingly, blind might and chance ruled the earth.

Suddenly the Pharaoh heard a woman's voice: "Rascal! ... Rascal! ... Come back into the hut, you scamp, it's time for prayer."

"Just a moment!" answered a child's voice.

The ruler looked that way and saw the humble mud hut of a cattle scribe. Its owner was finishing his accounts in the radiance of the setting sun, his wife was pounding wheat with a stone for cakes, and in front of the hut, like a young goat, a six-year-old boy was gamboling, while laughing at who knows what.

Apparently he was intoxicated by the fragrant evening air.

"Rascal! ... Rascal! ... You come here for prayer!" repeated the woman.

"Just a moment!"

And on he went, running and frolicking.

Finally the mother, seeing that the sun was starting to dip into the desert sands, set aside her stone, went into the yard, and grabbed the frisky boy as one might a colt. He resisted but finally yielded to superior force. The mother pulled him into the hut, sat him down on the floor, and held him with her hand lest he give her the slip.

"Don't fidget," she said. "Tuck your legs under and sit straight; put your hands together and lift them up. Naughty boy!"

The boy knew he would not get out of prayer now, so the sooner to get back outside, he lifted his eyes and hands piously to heaven and spoke breathlessly, in a thin, shrill voice:

"Thank you, good god Amon, for protecting papa from mishaps today and for giving mama wheat for cakes ... What else? ... And for creating heaven and earth, and for sending the Nile to bring us bread. What else? ... Oh, I know! ... And thank you for its being so beautiful outside, for flowers growing, birds singing, and for the palm bearing sweet dates. And for these good things which you have given us, may everyone love you as I do and praise you better than I, because I'm little and haven't been taught wisdom. Well, that's enough ..."

"Bad boy!" muttered the cattle scribe, bent over his accounts. "Bad boy, he is careless in his worship of Amon."

But the Pharaoh saw something entirely different in the crystal ball. The frolicsome boy's prayer soared heavenward like a skylark and, fluttering its wings, rose ever higher, to the throne where eternal Amon, hands resting on his knees, was engrossed in contemplating his own omnipotence.

Then it rose yet higher, to the god's head, and sang to him in a child's shrill voice:

"And for these good things which you have given us, may everyone love you as I do!"

At this, the self-absorbed deity opened his eyes and a ray of bliss fell from them onto the world. From heaven to earth there set in an immense stillness. All pain, all fear, all injury ceased. The whistling projectile became suspended in midair, the lion stopped in its leap upon the deer, the upraised cane did not come down on the slave's back. The sick man forgot his suffering, the desert wanderer his hunger, the prisoner his chains. The storm stilled, and the sea wave stopped as it was about to sink the ship. Such a peace set in over the whole earth that the sun, already hidden beyond the horizon, lifted its radiant head once more.

The Pharaoh came to. He saw before him a small table, on it the black crystal ball, and beside him the Chaldean Berossus.

"Mer-amen-Ramses," asked the priest, "did you find the person whose prayers reach the footstool of the Eternal?"

"Yes," replied the Pharaoh.

"Is he a prince, a knight, a prophet, or perhaps only a simple hermit?"

"He is a little six-year-old boy who asked Amon for nothing but thanked him for everything."

"Do you know where he lives?" asked the Chaldean.

"Yes, but I do not want to steal the power of his prayers for myself. The world, Berossus, is a gigantic vortex in which people are tossed about like grains of sand, and it is ill-fortune that tosses them. The boy, with his prayers, gives people what I cannot: a brief moment of forgetting and peace. Forgetting and peace ... do you understand, Chaldean?"

Berossus said nothing.

CHAPTER 49

A t sunrise on the twenty-first of Athyr, an order from Memphis reached the camp at the Natron Lakes, for three regiments to march into Libya and garrison the cities, and for the rest of the Egyptian army to return home with the Prince.

The troops greeted the order with jubilation, for the several days' stay in the desert was beginning to tell. Despite deliveries from both Egypt and humbled Libya, there was no surplus of provisions; the water in the hastily dug wells had been exhausted; the sun baked the men's bodies; and the red sand afflicted their lungs and eyes. The soldiers were starting to come down with dysentery and conjunctivitis.

Ramses ordered camp broken. He sent three regiments of native Egyptians into Libya, instructing the soldiers to treat the inhabitants gently—and never to wander singly. He directed the bulk of the army to Memphis, leaving a small garrison at the fort and glass-works.

By nine in the morning, despite the scorching heat, both armies were on their way: one headed north, the other south.

The holy Mentesuphis then approached the Crown Prince and said: "It would be well if Your Eminence could reach Memphis earlier. There will be fresh mounts at the half-way point."

"My father is gravely ill?" cried Ramses.

The priest bowed his head.

The Prince turned command over to Mentesuphis, asking him not to change in any way the orders already issued without consulting the secular generals. Then, taking Pentuer, Thutmose, and twenty of the best Asiatic cavalry, he rode off at a brisk trot for Memphis.

In five hours they covered half the distance and, as Mentesuphis had said, found fresh horses and a new escort. The Asiatics remained there, and after a brief rest the Prince rode on with his two companions and the new escort.

"Alas!" moaned the dandy Thutmose. "It's not enough that I haven't bathed or known rose oil in five days, but I have to make two forced marches in a single day! I'm sure that, when we arrive, no dancing girl will want to look at me."

"Are you better than us?" asked the Prince.

"I'm frailer!" sighed Thutmose. "The Prince is used to riding horseback like a Hyksos, and Pentuer could travel on a burning sword. But I'm so delicate ..."

At sunset the travelers rode onto a tall hill which commanded an extraordinary view. In the distance was the greenish valley of Egypt; and against its backdrop, like a row of red flames, glowed the triangular Pyramids. A little to the right of the Pyramids seemingly likewise burned the pylon tops of a Memphis shrouded in a bluish haze.

"Let's ride, let's ride!" urged the Prince.

A moment later the russet desert again surrounded them, and the string of Pyramids again glowed until everything dissolved into the pale gloaming.

At nightfall the travelers reached the vast land of the dead which stretched in the hills on the left bank of the river over a space of several dozen versts.[1]

Here, during the Old Kingdom, Egyptians had been laid to rest for eternity: kings in enormous pyramids, princes and dignitaries in smaller pyramids, simple folk in mud-brick structures. Here reposed millions of mummies not only of people but of dogs, cats, birds—of all creatures that in life had been dear to man.

By Ramses' time, the royal and magnates' cemetery had been moved to Thebes, and only local peasants and workers were buried near the Pyramids.

Among the scattered graves, the Prince and his escort came upon a small group of people moving along like shades.

"Who are you?" asked the escort commander.

"We are poor servants of the pharaoh, returning from our dead ones. We took them some roses, beer, and cakes ..."

"Did you enter other tombs?"

"Oh, gods!" exclaimed one of the group, "we're incapable of such sacrilege! It's only the wicked Thebans (may their hands wither!) who disturb the dead to drink away their goods in the taverns."

"What is the meaning of the fires over in the north?" asked the Prince.

"Your lordship must be riding from afar, not to know," came an answer. "Tomorrow our Crown Prince is returning with his victorious army ... A great commander! He vanquished the miserable Libyans in a single battle. The people of Memphis have come out to give him a grand welcome. Thirty thousand of them! ... Won't they be cheering!"

"I see," the Prince whispered to Pentuer. "The holy Mentesuphis sent me ahead so I won't have a triumphal procession. So be it, for now."

The horses were tired, and a brief rest was in order. The Prince sent a couple of riders ahead to order boats on the river, and kept the remainder of the escort beneath a cluster of palms which then grew between the group of Pyramids and the Sphinx.

This group constitutes the north end of the immense cemetery. Crowded within a roughly square-kilometer area, at that time covered in desert vegetation, were a multitude of tombs and small pyramids, over which towered the three greatest pyramids—those of Cheops, Khephren, and Mykerinus—and the Sphinx. These colossal structures are separated one from another by barely a few hundred paces. The three Pyramids stand in a single row from northeast to southwest; and east of that line, nearest the Nile, reclines the Sphinx, at whose feet extended an underground temple of Horus.

The Pyramids, particularly Cheops', as handiworks of man, are terrifying in their dimensions. Cheops' pyramid is a peaked stone hill thirty-five stories (a hundred thirty-seven meters) tall, standing on a square base some three hundred fifty paces (two hundred

---

[1] verst: an obsolete Russian unit of distance equal to 1.07 kilometer. (During Prus' lifetime, his part of partitioned Poland was held by the Russian Empire.) *(Translator.)*

twenty-seven meters) on a side. The pyramid occupies an area of ten *mórgs*,[2] and its four triangular sides could have covered an area of seventeen *mórgs*. The stone that went into its construction could have formed a wall taller than a man, half a meter wide, two thousand five hundred kilometers long.

When the Prince's escort had spread out beneath the miserable trees, several soldiers set about searching for water, others took out biscuits, and Thutmose dropped to the ground and fell asleep. The Prince and Pentuer proceeded to walk and talk.

The night was clear enough to see, on one side, the immense silhouettes of the Pyramids; and on the other, the figure of the Sphinx, which seemed small in comparison.

"This is my fourth time here," said the Successor, "and each time my heart has been filled with wonder and sorrow. As a student at the upper school, I thought that on ascending the throne I would rear something grander than the pyramid of Cheops. But now I feel like laughing at my impudence when I recall that the great pharaoh spent sixteen hundred talents[3] at the building of his tomb just on vegetables for the laborers. Where would I find the people, let alone sixteen hundred talents!"

"Do not envy Cheops, lord," replied the priest. "Other pharaohs have left better legacies: lakes, canals, highways, temples, and schools."

"Can those compare with the Pyramids?"

"Certainly not," answered the priest quickly. "In my eyes and in those of all the populace, each pyramid is a great crime, and the greatest is Cheops'."

"You're getting carried away," the Prince reproved him.

"Not at all. The pharaoh built his great tomb over a period of thirty years, during which a hundred thousand men labored on it each year for three months. And what good has come of that labor? Whom has it fed, healed, clothed? ... But each year ten to twenty thousand men wasted away at the labor. Thus half a million corpses went into the making of Cheops' tomb—and who can reckon up all the blood, tears, pain?

"So do not be surprised, lord, if the Egyptian peasant to this day looks in terror to the west, where the triangular shapes of the Pyramids loom bloody or black on the horizon. They witnessed his travails and barren labor.

"And to think that it will always be so, until those tokens of overweening pride crumble to dust. But when will that be? For three thousand years[4] they have been terrifying us, and still their walls are smooth and their huge inscriptions are legible."

"The other night in the desert, you spoke differently," said the Prince.

"That's because I wasn't looking at them. But when I have them before my eyes as I do now, the sobbing spirits of the peasants who were worked to death surround me and whisper: 'See what was done with us! ... Our bones felt pain, and our hearts longed to rest.'"

---

[2] mórg: an obsolete Polish unit of farmland, equal to 0.57 hectare. (A hectare is about 2.5 acres.) The term *mórg* derives from the German word *Morgen* ("morning")—the *mórg* was the area of land a farmer could plow in a single morning. *(Translator.)*

[3] About 10 million francs. *(Author.)* Prus takes the figure of 1,600 talents of silver from Book II of Herodotus' *Histories*, which speak of "an inscription [on Cheops' pyramid] recording the amount spent on radishes, onions and leeks for the laborers." *(Translator.)*

[4] Actually, for one and a half thousand years: the Great Pyramid of Giza was completed about 2560 BCE—1,491 years before *Pharaoh*'s present time (that is, before the fall, about 1069 BCE, of the 20th Dynasty and, with it, of the New Kingdom). *(Translator.)*

Ramses was displeased by this outburst.

"My holy father," he said after a moment, "presented these matters to me differently. When we were here five years ago, the divine Lord told me a story:

"In the reign of Pharaoh Thutmose I, Ethiopian[5] envoys came to negotiate the amount of tribute to be paid by them. They were a proud people! They said one defeat in war meant nothing, for in another war fate may favor them. And for a couple of months they haggled over the tribute.

"In vain did the wise king, wishing to enlighten them gently, show them our highways and canals. They answered that in their country they had water for free wherever they wanted. In vain were they shown the treasuries of the temples: they said their land held far more gold and gems than all Egypt. To no avail did the Lord drill his troops before them, for they maintained that there were incomparably more Ethiopians than His Holiness had soldiers.

"Then the pharaoh brought them to this spot where we are standing and showed them the Pyramids.

"The Ethiopian envoys walked round them, read their inscriptions—and next day concluded the treaty required of them.

"Since I didn't understand the story," continued Ramses, "my holy father explained it to me.

"'Son,' he said, 'these Pyramids are everlasting evidence of the superhuman might of Egypt. If a man wanted to build himself a pyramid, he would arrange a small pile of rocks and, after a few hours, drop the effort, saying: "What need have I of this?" Ten, a hundred, or a thousand men would gather a few more rocks, pile them up any which way—and, after a few days, again drop the effort. What need have they of this?

"'But when Egypt's pharaoh—when the Egyptian Kingdom—decides to put together a pile of rocks, it collects many thousands of men and builds for several dozen years, if need be, until the work is completed.

"'The point is not whether the Pyramids were needed, but that the pharaoh's will, once uttered, be fulfilled.'

"Yes, Pentuer, the pyramid is not Cheops' tomb but his *will*. A will that has more executors than any king on earth, and such orderliness and steadfastness in action as the gods.

"At school I was taught that the human will is a great force, the greatest force under the sun. And the human will can lift barely a single stone. How great, then, was the will of a pharaoh who erected a mountain of stones simply because it pleased him to do so, even if with no purpose."

"Would your lordship be wanting to prove your power that way?" asked Pentuer suddenly.

"No," responded the Prince without hesitation. "Once the pharaohs have shown their might, they can be merciful—barring that someone tried to resist their orders."

"And this young man is only twenty-three!" the terrified priest told himself.

They turned toward the river and walked for a time in silence.

"Lie down, lord," said the priest, "get some sleep. This has been no mean journey."

---

[5] "Ethiopian envoys": Prus doubtless means *Nubian* envoys. Please see the note on "Ethiopia" at the start of Chapter 3. *(Translator.)*

"How can I sleep?" replied the Prince. "One moment I'm surrounded by all those peasants who you say died at the building of the Pyramids (as though, except for the Pyramids, they would have lived forever!). Then, again, I think of my holy father, who may this moment be breathing his last. The peasants suffer! ... The peasants spill their blood! ... Who can tell me that my divine father doesn't suffer more on his sumptuous bed than your peasants when hauling hot stones?

"The peasants! It's always the peasants! To you, priest, only the lice-ridden of this world are deserving of pity. A whole series of pharaohs have gone to their graves, some of whom died in agonies, others of whom were murdered. But you don't remember them, only the peasants whose merit was that they bore other peasants, drew the Nile mud, or stuffed barley down their cows' throats.

"But what about my father ... and me? Weren't my son and a woman of my house killed? Was Typhon merciful to me in the desert, and don't my bones ache from a long journey? ... Didn't the projectiles of the Libyan slingers whistle over my head? ... Have I a treaty with illness or pain, or with death, that they should be gentler with me than with your peasant?

"Look over there. The Asiatics sleep, and peace fills their bosoms; but I, their master, have a heartful of yesterday's cares and of worries for the morrow. Ask a hundred-year-old peasant whether, in all his time, he's known as much bitterness as I have in my several months as viceroy and commander."

Before them slowly, out of the night, there emerged a curious shadow. It was a structure fifty paces long, three stories high, with something like an oddly shaped five-story tower toward one end.

"Now here's the Sphinx," said the annoyed Prince, "a purely priestly piece of work! Every time I've seen it, day or night, the question has haunted me: what is it, and what is it for?

"The pyramids, I understand. A powerful pharaoh wanted to show his might, and maybe to secure for himself eternal life in peace undisturbed by any enemy or thief. But this Sphinx! ... Of course it's our holy priesthood, which has a very great and learned head, and below it a lion's claws.

"An odious statue, full of ambiguity, which seems to pride itself on making us look like locusts by comparison. It's neither man nor beast nor stone. So what is it, what does it signify? ... Or its smile ... You marvel at the everlasting Pyramids—it smiles; you go to commune with the tombs—again it smiles. Whether Egypt's fields turn green, or Typhon looses his fiery steeds; whether a slave seeks freedom in the desert, or Ramses the Great drives vanquished peoples before him—it has one and the same lifeless smile for all.

"Nineteen royal dynasties have passed like shades, but it has smiled and would smile even were the Nile to dry up and Egypt to perish beneath the sands.

"Isn't it a monster the more terrible because it has a gentle human face? Itself eternal, it has never known sorrow at the transience of a world full of miseries."

"Doesn't your lordship recall the faces of the gods?" said Pentuer, "have you never seen a mummy? All the immortals regard transient things with the same serenity. So does a man, once he has passed."

"The gods sometimes hear our prayers," spoke the Prince as if to himself, "but nothing moves the Sphinx. He's not mercy but a gigantic mockery and terror. If I knew that his lips held a prophecy for me or a means of lifting the Kingdom, I wouldn't dare ask him. I think I would hear something terrible uttered with implacable calm. That's what he's like, this creature and image of the priests. Worse than human, because he has a lion's body; worse than animal, because he has a human head; worse than stone, because there's an inconceivable life in him."

Just then they heard muffled mournful voices of unclear origin.

"Is he singing?" asked the surprised Prince.

"It's in the underground temple," said the priest. "But why are they praying at this hour?"

"You might as well ask: why do they pray at all, when no one hears them?"

Pentuer quickly took his bearings and set off toward the chanting. The Prince found a stone with a backrest and sat down, tired. He extended his arms behind him, leaned back, and regarded the Sphinx's gigantic face.

Despite the absence of light, he could distinctly see the superhuman features, to which the very shadow lent added character and life. And the longer the Prince contemplated the face, the more strongly he felt that he had been prejudiced and that his antipathy had been unjustified.

In the Sphinx's face there was no cruelty; sooner, resignation. In its smile there was no mockery; sooner, melancholy. The Sphinx did not exult over human misery and transience; rather, it did not see them.

Its expressive eyes, set somewhere beneath the heavens, looked across the Nile to lands lost to human view beyond the horizon. Was it watching the disturbing rise of the Assyrian monarchy? ... the obtrusive bustle-bustle of the Phoenicians? ... the birth of Greece? or perhaps future events brewing at the Jordan? ... Who could say?

The Prince was sure of one thing: that it was watching, thinking, and awaiting something with a tranquil smile worthy of a preternatural being. And it seemed to the Prince that when that thing appeared on the horizon, the Sphinx would rise up to go meet it.

What would it be, and when would it occur? That was a secret whose import was clearly evident in the face of the eternal one. It must happen suddenly, though, because for ages the Sphinx had never so much as blinked but was ever on the lookout.

Meanwhile Pentuer had found a window through which a plaintive priestly chant issued from underground:

Choir I: "Rise, radiant like Isis, as Sothis rises in the morning firmament at the start of the constant year."[6]

Choir II: "The god Amon-Ra was at my right and left hands. He personally placed dominion of the whole world in my hands, contributing to the downfall of mine enemies."

Choir I: "Thou wert still young, wore braided hair, but in Egypt nothing happened without thy command, and no cornerstone was laid for any building save in thy presence."

Choir II: "I have come to Thee, lord of the gods, great god, lord of the sun. Tum[7] promises me that the sun shall appear and that I will be like unto it; and the Nile, that I will attain the throne of Osiris and possess it for the ages."

Choir I: "Thou hast returned in peace, esteemed of the gods, Lord of the Two Worlds,

---

[6] The start of the Egyptian year was marked by the "heliacal rising" of Sothis (Sirius), which happened within about a month of the start of the Nile's annual flood. *(Translator.)*

[7] Tum: variant spelling of the name of the god Atum. *(Translator.)*

Ra-Mer-amen-Ramses. I assure thee an eternal reign; kings shall approach thee and pay thee homage."

Choir II: "O thou, thou! Osiris-Ramses, eternally living son of heaven, born of the goddess Nut.[8] May thy mother envelop thee in the secret of the heavens, and may she let thee become a god, O thou, thou, Osiris-Ramses."[9]

"So the Holy Lord is dead!" Pentuer told himself.

He went away from the window and approached where the Successor sat in reverie.

The priest knelt before him, prostrated himself on his face, and cried: "Hail, Pharaoh, Lord of the World!"

"What did you say?!" cried the Prince, springing up.

"May the one omnipotent God grant you wisdom and strength, and happiness to your people ..."

"Rise, Pentuer ... then I ... then I ..."

Suddenly he grabbed the priest's arm and turned him toward the Sphinx. "Look at him," he said.

But in neither the face nor the bearing of the colossus had there been any change. One pharaoh had crossed into eternity, another was rising like the sun, but the stone face of the god or monster remained the same. On the lips, a gentle smile for earthly powers and glory; in the eyes, an expectation of *something* to come, at a time unknown.

Soon the two riders returned from the ferry with word that the boats would be ready.

Pentuer went among the palms and cried, "Wake up! ... Wake up!"

The vigilant Asiatics immediately sprang up and proceeded to bridle the horses. Thutmose got up as well, yawning hideously.

"Brr!" he muttered, "but it's cold! Sleep is a good thing! ... I've scarcely napped and now I can ride on to the end of the earth, so long as it's not back to the Natron Lakes. Brr! ... I've forgotten the taste of wine, and I believe my arms are growing all hairy like a jackal's ... and it's still two hours to the palace.

"Lucky peasants! The scamps are still asleep, feel no need to bathe, and won't be going out to work till their wives fill them up with barley gruel; while I, a great lord, must like a thief in the night roam the desert without a drop of water in my mouth."

The horses were ready, and Ramses mounted his. Pentuer approached, took the reins of the ruler's steed, and led it, himself going afoot.

"What's this?" asked Thutmose, surprised. However, bethinking himself, he ran up and took the reins of Ramses' horse on the other side. And they all went thus in silence, surprised at the priest's behavior but sensing that something of import had happened.

After several hundred paces, the desert suddenly ended and a highway through fields stretched before the travelers.

"Mount up," said Ramses, "we must hurry."

"His Holiness bids you mount!" cried Pentuer.

All were dumbfounded. But Thutmose quickly collected himself and, putting hand to sword, shouted: "May our almighty and gracious commander, Pharaoh Ramses, live forever!"

---

[8] Nut: Egyptian goddess of the sky, who was depicted as a star-spangled nude woman arching over the earth, or as a cow. *(Translator.)*

[9] Tomb inscriptions. *(Author.)*

"May he live forever! ..." howled the Asiatics, brandishing their weapons.

"Thank you, my loyal soldiers," said the Lord.

A moment later, the mounted retinue was racing for the river.

CHAPTER 50

Whether the prophets at the underground temple of the Sphinx had seen Egypt's new ruler camped at the Pyramids, whether they had notified the royal palace about him, and how they might have done so, is unknown. Suffice it that as Ramses was approaching the ferry, High Priest Herhor was having the palace staff and servants roused, and as the Lord was crossing the Nile, all the priests, generals, and civil dignitaries were already gathered in the great hall.

Just at sunrise Ramses XIII, at the head of his small party, rode into the palace courtyard, where staff and servants prostrated themselves before him on their faces and the guard presented arms to the sound of trumpets and drums.

After greeting the troops, His Holiness repaired to the bath, where he took an ablution in scented water. Then he let his divine hair be dressed; but when the barber most humbly asked whether he would have his head and beard shaven, the Lord answered: "No need. I'm not a priest but a soldier."

These words passed a moment later into the audience hall, an hour later had swept the palace, by noon had spread through Memphis, and by evening were known in all the temples of the Kingdom from Demi-en-Hor[1] and Sabne-Khetam in the north to Syene[2] and Philae[3] in the south.

At this news, the nomarchs, nobles, army, populace, and foreigners went mad with joy, while the holy priesthood went into still deeper mourning for the late pharaoh.

Emerging from the bath, His Holiness donned a short black-and-yellow striped soldier's tunic, a gold breastplate, sandals secured with straps, and a shallow spiked helmet. Then he girded on the Assyrian steel sword that had accompanied him to the battle of the Natron Lakes and, surrounded by a great suite of generals, crunched and clanked his way to the audience hall.

There he was intercepted by High Priest Herhor, who was accompanied by Sem,

---

[1] Demi-en-Hor ("the City of Horus," now *Damanhur*): the capital of Lower Egypt's 7th Nome of A-ment, in the western Delta. In Greek and Roman times, Demi-en-Hor would, after the Greek god Hermes, be called respectively *Hermopolis Mikra* and *Hermopolis Parva*. *(Translator.)*

[2] Syene: ancient Greek name for the city now called Aswan, in southern Egypt. Prus here calls the city *Suunu*. *(Translator.)*

[3] Philae: Greek name of an island that was formerly in the First Cataract of the Nile, and is now under Lake Nasser. Prus calls the island *Pilak*. It was the site of an ancient Egyptian temple complex before the construction of the Aswan High Dam prompted the temple's removal to another island. *(Translator.)*

Mephres, and other high priests and, behind Herhor, the great judges of Memphis and Thebes, a score of the nearest nomarchs, the great treasurer, the heads of the houses of grain, cattle, raiment, slaves, silver and gold, and many other dignitaries.

Herhor bowed to Ramses and said emotionally:

"Lord! It has pleased your eternally living father to depart to the gods, where he is tasting of eternal bliss. Upon you now devolves the duty of looking after the orphaned Kingdom.

"Hail, therefore, Lord and Master of the World—and may His Holiness Pharaoh Ham-sem-merer-amen-Ramesses-neter-hog-an live forever!"

Everyone enthusiastically took up the cry. It might have been expected that the new ruler would be moved or show some confusion. To everyone's surprise, the Lord only frowned and replied:

"In accordance with the will of my holy father and the laws of Egypt, I assume power and will exercise it to the glory of the Kingdom and the happiness of the people."

Suddenly the Lord turned to Herhor, looked him sharply in the eye, and said: "I see a gold serpent on Your Eminence's miter.[4] Why have you donned the emblem of royal power?"

A deathly silence fell over the gathering. The most venturesome person in Egypt would never have supposed the young Lord would begin his reign with such a question posed to the most powerful person in the Kingdom: by all odds, more powerful than the late pharaoh.

But a dozen generals stood behind the young Lord; the bronze guard regiments shone in the courtyard; and the army of the Natron Lakes was crossing the Nile, drunk with triumph, enamored of its commander.

The mighty Herhor turned waxy pale and could draw no voice from his constricted larynx.

"I ask Your Eminence," repeated the Pharaoh calmly, "by what right the royal serpent appears on your miter."

"This is the miter of your grandfather, the holy Amenhotep," replied Herhor quietly. "The Supreme Council bade me don it in certain circumstances."

"My holy grandfather," said the Pharaoh, "was the Queen's father and was granted the privilege of adorning his miter with the uraeus. But so far as I know, his ceremonial attire reposes among the relics at the Temple of Amon."

Herhor had regained his composure.

"Pray bear in mind, Your Holiness," he explained, "that for a whole day Egypt was bereft of a rightful ruler. During that time someone had to wake Osiris and prepare him for sleep, bless the people, and pay homage to the royal ancestors.

"For this difficult period, the Supreme Council bade me don the sacred relic in order that the Kingdom's governance and the service of the gods not be delayed. But now that we have a rightful and mighty ruler, I doff the wonderful relic ..."

With that, Herhor took off the uraeus-adorned miter and handed it to High Priest Mephres.

---

[4] miter: Probably meant is the *khepresh*, or "blue crown," a miter-shaped blue royal headdress favored by New Kingdom pharaohs. Like many other Egyptian royal crowns, it featured a uraeus serpent affixed to its front. Since New Kingdom pharaohs were often depicted wearing the *khepresh* in battle, it has sometimes been called a "war crown." *(Translator.)*

The Pharaoh's stern face relaxed, and the Lord directed his steps toward the throne.

Suddenly his way was blocked by the holy Mephres, who made a deep bow and said: "Your Holiness, please hear a most humble request ..."

But neither in his voice nor in his eyes was there humility when he straightened up and continued: "These are the words of the Supreme Council of all the high priests ..."

"Speak them," replied the Pharaoh.

"Your Holiness is aware," continued Mephres, "that a pharaoh who has not been ordained a high priest may not perform the highest offerings nor dress and undress the miraculous Osiris."

"I understand," interrupted the Lord. "I am a pharaoh who is not ordained a high priest."

"For that reason," continued Mephres, "the Supreme Council humbly begs Your Holiness to designate a high priest to act on your behalf in carrying out the religious rites."

Listening to these resolute words, the high priests and civil dignitaries trembled and squirmed as on hot stones, while the generals casually adjusted their swords. But the holy Mephres looked at them with unconcealed contempt—and once more sank his cold gaze in the Pharaoh's face.

But the Lord of the World once again showed no troublement.

"It is well," he replied, "that Your Eminence reminds me of this important duty. Military obligations and affairs of state will not let me attend to the rites of our sacred religion, so I must appoint a deputy for them."

So saying, the Lord looked about the gathering.

To Herhor's left stood the holy Sem. The Pharaoh regarded his gentle, honest face and suddenly asked: "What are Your Eminence's name and station?"

"I am Sem, High Priest of the Temple of Ptah in Pi-Bastis."

"You shall be my deputy for religious rites," said the Lord, pointing to him.

A murmur of admiration swept the gathering. It would have been difficult, after the longest deliberations and consultations, to select a priest worthier of so high a post.

But Herhor turned still paler, while Mephres compressed his livid lips and narrowed his eyes.

A moment later the new Pharaoh seated himself on the throne, which, in lieu of legs, had carved figures of princes and kings of the Nine Nations.

Presently Herhor handed the Lord, on a gold tray, a white and red crown encircled by a gold serpent. The ruler silently placed it on his head, and all prostrated themselves.

This was not yet the ceremonial coronation, only the assumption of power.

After the priests had censed the Pharaoh and chanted a hymn to Osiris, that the god might bestow every blessing on the Pharaoh, the civil and military dignitaries were permitted to kiss the lowest step of the throne. Then the Lord took a gold spoon and, repeating prayers which the holy Sem recited aloud, offered incense to the statues of gods arrayed on either side of his royal see.

"What am I to do now?" asked the ruler.

"Show yourself to the people," replied Herhor.

Through a gilt wide-open door, His Holiness climbed a marble stairway to a terrace, where he raised his hands and turned successively to the four quarters of the world. Trumpets sounded, and banners were hung from the pylon tops. Whoever was in field, courtyard, or street, prostrated himself on his face; the cane raised over the back of beast or slave came down harmlessly; and all the Kingdom's criminals who had been sentenced that day received pardons.

Descending from the terrace, the ruler asked: "Have I anything more to do?"

"A meal and state affairs await Your Holiness," said Herhor.

"So I can rest," said the Pharaoh. "Where are my holy father's remains?"

"Given to the embalmers," whispered Herhor.

The Pharaoh's eyes welled with tears, and his lips quivered. But he checked himself and looked at the floor in silence. It would have been unseemly for his servants to see the emotion of so mighty a ruler.

Wishing to divert the Lord's attention to a different subject, Herhor asked: "Will Your Holiness receive his due homage from the Queen Mother?"

"Me? ... I'm to receive homage from my mother?" said the Pharaoh in a choked voice.

Intent on calming himself, he added with a forced smile: "Has Your Eminence forgotten what the sage Ani says? Perhaps the holy Sem will repeat for us these beautiful words about the mother."

"'Remember,' recited Sem, 'that she bore thee and nurtured thee in every way ...'"

"Go on! ... Go on! ..." urged the Lord, endeavoring to master himself.

"'Shouldst thou forget, she will lift up her hands to the god, and he will hear her complaint. Long did she carry thee, a heavy burden, beneath her heart, and she bore thee after thy months. Then she carried thee on her back, and for three years she placed her breast in thy mouth. Thus did she bring thee up, taking no offense at thy filth. And when thou went to school and were taught to write, she daily went before thy superior with bread and beer of her house.'"[5]

The Pharaoh drew a deep breath and said more calmly: "So you see, it's not right for my mother to greet me. Rather, I shall go to her."

He proceeded through a series of halls—paneled in marble, alabaster, and wood, and painted bright colors, carved, and gilded—followed by his huge suite. But nearing his mother's anteroom, he gestured that he wanted to be left alone.

He passed through the anteroom, paused at the door, then knocked and entered quietly.

In the bare-walled room furnished with only a low couch and a chipped water pitcher, all in sign of mourning, the Pharaoh's mother, Queen Nikotris, sat on a stone. She wore a coarse shift and was barefoot; her forehead was daubed with Nile mud, and her tangled hair was strewn with ashes.

Seeing Ramses, Her Worship made to fall at his feet. But the son caught her in his arms and said tearfully:

"Mother, if you lower yourself to the floor before me, I'll have to go under the floor before you."

The Queen hugged his head to her bosom, wiped away his tears with the sleeve of her coarse shift, then lifted up her hands and whispered:

"May all the gods ... may the spirits of your father and grandfather enfold you in their protection and blessing. O Isis, I've never skimped on offerings for you, but today I make

---

[5]Authentic. *(Author.)* This passage on venerating the mother is from the *Papyrus of Ani* (whom Prus calls *Eney*). The papyrus is preserved in London's British Museum. It is an individualized *Book of the Dead* (or *Book of Going Forth by Day)* that was compiled for the Theban scribe Ani ca. 1250 BCE, during the New Kingdom's 19th Dynasty. *(Translator.)*

the greatest. I give you my beloved son ... May this my royal son become wholly your son, and may his glory and power multiply your divine heritage!"

The Lord hugged and kissed the Queen repeatedly, finally seating her on the couch and himself taking a seat on the stone.

"Did Father leave me any instructions?" he asked.

"He asked only that you remember him, and he told the Supreme Council: 'I leave you a Successor who is a lion and eagle in one person; heed him, and he shall lift Egypt to unprecedented power.'"

"Do you think the priests will obey me?"

"Remember," said the mother, "that the pharaoh's emblem is the serpent. And the serpent is prudence, which is silent and bites mortally without warning. If you take time as your ally, you will overcome everything."

"Herhor is terribly audacious. Today he had the effrontery to don the miter of the holy Amenhotep. Of course, I made him take it off, and I'll remove him from the government ... Him and several members of the Supreme Council."

The Queen shook her head. "Egypt is yours," she said, "and the gods have endowed you with great wisdom. Except for that, I would greatly fear a quarrel with Herhor."

"I'm not quarreling with him. I'm expelling him."

"Egypt is yours," repeated the mother, "but I fear conflict with the priests. It's true your overmild father made these people audacious, but they mustn't be driven to desperation through severity. Besides, think: who will replace their advice? They know all that has been, is, and will be on earth and in heaven; they see people's most secret thoughts, and they sway hearts as the wind sways the leaves. Without them, you won't know what is happening in Tyre and Nineveh, or even in Memphis and Thebes."

"I don't reject knowledge, but I need servants," said the Pharaoh. "I know they have great learning, but it must be overseen so it won't deceive, and directed so it won't ruin the Kingdom. Tell me yourself, Mother, over thirty years' time what have they done with Egypt? The populace suffer misery or rise up in rebellion, there is little army, the treasury is empty, while a couple of months from us Assyria is rising like leavened dough—and is already imposing treaties on us!"

"Do as you will. But remember that the pharaoh's emblem is the serpent—and the serpent is silence and prudence."

"You speak the truth, Mother, but believe me, in some cases a higher virtue is daring. I now know that the priests meant to drag the Libyan war out for years. I finished it in a fortnight, only because each day I took some mad but resolute step. Had I not gone after them into the desert, which after all was highly imprudent, today we would have had the Libyans at Memphis."

"I know, you chased Tehenna and were surprised by Typhon," said the Queen. "Oh, reckless boy ... you didn't think of me!"

The Lord smiled. "Rest easy," he said. "When the pharaoh fights, Amon stands at his left and right hands. And who can equal Amon?"

He hugged the Queen once more and went out.

CHAPTER 51

His Holiness' enormous suite still stood in the waiting hall, but as it were split in two. On one side were Herhor, Mephres, and several older high priests; on the other, all the generals, all the civil officials, and the preponderance of younger priests.

The Pharaoh's eagle eye instantly spied the division among the dignitaries, and a joyous pride took fire in the young ruler's heart. "Without drawing my sword, I've carried off a victory!" he thought.

The civil and military dignitaries were distinctly moving ever farther away from Herhor and Mephres. No one doubted that the two high priests, hitherto the most powerful in the Kingdom, lacked the favor of the new Pharaoh.

The Lord proceeded to the dining hall, where he was struck by the number of priests serving—and by the number of platters.

"Am I to eat all that?" he asked in unconcealed surprise.

The priest supervising the kitchen explained to the Pharaoh that the dishes not consumed by His Holiness went as offerings to the Dynasties. He indicated a series of statues ranged along the hall.

The Lord glanced at the statues, which looked as though they never received anything, then at the priests, whose healthy complexions suggested they ate everything—and he ordered beer and soldiers' bread with garlic.

The senior priest was dumbfounded but repeated the order to a younger priest. The younger priest hesitated but repeated the order to the boys and girls. The boys at first seemed not to believe their ears but soon scattered over the palace.

A quarter-hour later they returned, frightened, whispering to the priests that there was no soldiers' bread or garlic anywhere.

The Pharaoh smiled and directed that henceforth simple fare not be lacking in his kitchens. Then he ate a squab, a piece of fish, and a wheat roll, and drank them down with wine.

He owned to himself that the viands were well prepared; and the wine, wonderful. However, he could not shake the thought that the court kitchen must consume extravagant sums.

After burning incense to the ancestors, the ruler repaired to the royal cabinet to hear reports.

First to appear was Herhor. He bowed far lower to the Lord than he had in greeting him, and with great emotion congratulated him on his victory over the Libyans.

"Your Holiness," he said, "hurled himself upon the Libyans like Typhon upon the wretched tents of desert wanderers. You won a great battle with very small losses and, with a single stroke of the divine sword, concluded a war whose end we ordinary people could not see."

The Pharaoh could feel his animus toward Herhor waning.

"Therefore," continued the high priest, "the Supreme Council begs Your Holiness to allocate ten talents' reward for the valiant regiments. And, commander-in-chief, to permit the placement, next to your name, of the epithet, 'the Victorious'!"

Playing to the Pharaoh's youth, Herhor had overdone his flatteries. The Lord cooled down from his elation and suddenly asked:

"What epithet would you give me, were I to wipe out the Assyrian army and fill the temples with the riches of Nineveh and Babylon?"

"Is he still thinking about that?" said the high priest to himself.

As if to confirm Herhor's fears, the Pharaoh changed the topic and asked: "How much army have we?"

"Here at Memphis?"

"No, in all Egypt."

"Your Holiness had ten regiments," said the high priest. "His Eminence Nitager has fifteen at the eastern border. Ten are in the south, due to Nubia's restiveness. And five are garrisoned about the country."

"Forty altogether," mused the Pharaoh. "How many men will that be?"

"Some sixty thousand."

The Lord jumped up from his armchair.

"Sixty instead of a hundred twenty?!" he shouted. "What's the meaning of this? What have you done with my army?"

"There aren't the means to maintain a greater number."

"Oh, gods!" said the Pharaoh, clutching his head. "The Assyrians will attack us in a month! ... We're disarmed ..."

"We have a preliminary treaty with Assyria," broke in Herhor.

"A woman might say that, but not a minister of war," said the angry Lord. "What is a treaty worth, with no army to back it? King Assar could crush us today with half the army at his disposal."

"Please put your mind at ease, Holiness. At first word of Assyrian treachery, we'd have half a million warriors."

The Pharaoh laughed in Herhor's face. "What? ... How? ... You've gone mad, priest! You rummage in papyri, but I've been serving seven years in the army and there's hardly a day but I engage in drills or maneuvers. How, in a couple of months, will you have a half-million-man army?"

"All the nobility will come out ..."

"Much good the nobility will be! Nobility aren't soldiers. A half-million-man army would require at least a hundred fifty regiments; and as you said yourself, we have forty. So where will these men who now herd cattle, till the soil, mold pottery, or drink and idle away their time on their estates—where will they learn the military craft? Egyptians are poor soldier material; I know because I see them daily. The Libyan, the Greek, the Hittite from childhood wield the bow and the sling and are expert with the club; and they learn to march properly in a year's time. The Egyptian marches so-so only after three years' working at it. True, he gets accustomed to the sword and spear in two years, but for accurate slinging even four years don't suffice him.

"So after a few months you could field not an army but a half-million-man mob, to be smashed in the blink of an eye by another, the Assyrian, mob. While Assyrian regiments are poor-quality and ill-trained, the Assyrian soldier knows how to loose stones and arrows, how to hew and stab, and above all has the ferocity of a wild beast, which is utterly lacking in the mild Egyptian. We smash enemies because our disciplined, trained regiments are like battering rams: half the men must be knocked out before the column breaks down. But when there's no column, there's no Egyptian army."

"Your Holiness speaks the truth," said Herhor to the winded Pharaoh. "Only the gods possess such knowledge of the matter. I too know that Egypt's forces are weak, that creating them takes many years' work. That is why I want to conclude a treaty with Assyria."

"You already have."

"An interim one. In view of your father's illness, and fearing Your Holiness, Sargon deferred the treaty proper pending your accession to the throne."

The Pharaoh again flew into a rage. "What?!" he cried. "Do they really expect to take over Phoenicia? And they think I'll sign the disgrace of my reign? ... Evil spirits have possessed all of you!"

The audience was over. Herhor this time prostrated himself on his face; and as he was returning from the Lord's, he pondered in his heart:

"His Holiness heard out the report, so he doesn't reject my services. I told him he must sign the treaty with Assyria, so the hardest part is done. He will come around to it before Sargon returns to us.

"What a lion he is—or rather, a rogue elephant—this youngster. And to think that he's become pharaoh only because he's the grandson of a high priest! He doesn't yet realize that the same hands which raised him so high ..."

In the vestibule His Eminence Herhor stopped, mulled over something, and finally, instead of going to his own quarters, went to Queen Nikotris'.

There were no women or children in the garden, only wailing came from scattered villas. Women of the late pharaoh's house were mourning him who had departed for the West.

Their grief seemed genuine.

Meanwhile the Supreme Judge had come to the new Lord's cabinet.

"What have you to tell me, Eminence?" asked the Lord.

"Several days ago, an unusual incident occurred outside Thebes," replied the Judge. "A peasant killed his wife and three children and drowned himself in a consecrated pool."

"Had he gone mad?"

"He seems to have done it from hunger."

"A curious incident," mused the Pharaoh, "but tell me something else. What kinds of crimes are most common these days?"

The Supreme Judge hesitated.

"Speak openly," said the Lord, out of patience now. "Conceal nothing from me. I know Egypt is in a mire, I want to drag her out of it, so I have to know the worst."

"The most frequent ... the most common crimes are rebellions. But," the Judge hastened to add, "only the common people are rebelling."

"Go on," said the Lord.

"In Kosem," said the Judge, "a regiment of masons and stoneworkers rebelled when they did not receive their necessities on time. In Khem, peasants killed a scribe who was collecting taxes. In Melcatis and Pi-Hebit,[1] peasants demolished the houses of Phoenician lessees. Outside Saka they refused to repair a canal, saying the treasury owed them pay for the work. And in the porphyry quarries, convicts beat up the overseers and attempted to escape bodily toward the sea."

"I'm not at all surprised at this information," said the Pharaoh. "What do you think of it?"

"Above all, the guilty must be punished."

"I think that, above all, working people must be given what they're owed," said the Lord. "A hungry ox lies down on the ground; a hungry horse sways on its legs and sighs. Can we, then, demand that a hungry man work and not show his discontent?"

"Then Your Holiness ..."

"Pentuer will form a council to investigate these things," interrupted the Pharaoh. "Meanwhile I don't want punishments applied."

"But in that case a general rebellion will break out!" exclaimed the terrified Judge.

The Pharaoh rested his chin in his hands and pondered. "Well!" he said after a moment, "then let the courts do their work ... but as gently as possible. And let Pentuer gather the council yet today.

"Truly!" he added after a moment, "it's easier to make decisions in a battle than in this disarray that has overtaken Egypt!"

After the Supreme Judge's departure, the Pharaoh summoned Thutmose. He asked Thutmose to greet, on his behalf, the troops returning from the Natron Lakes and to divide twenty talents among the officers and men.

Next the Lord sent for Pentuer, and meanwhile he received the Great Treasurer.

"I want," he said, "to know the state of the treasury."

"Right now," replied the dignitary, "we have twenty thousand talents' worth in the granaries, barns, warehouses, and coffers. But taxes are flowing in every day."

"And there are rebellions every day," added the Pharaoh. "What are our overall incomes and expenditures?"

"We spend twenty thousand talents annually on the army. Two to three thousand talents a month on the holy court."

"Yes? ... What else? ... What about public works?"

"At the moment they're being done for free," said the Great Treasurer, lowering his head.

"What about incomes?"

"We spend as much as we have," whispered the official.

"So we get forty or fifty thousand talents a year," said the Pharaoh. "Where's the rest?"

"Pledged to the Phoenicians, to some bankers and merchants, and to the holy priests."

"All right," said the Lord. "But there's the untouchable treasure of the pharaohs in gold, platinum,[2] silver, and gems. How much does it come to?"

---

[1] Pi-Hebit: a town in the central-northern Delta, in the 12th Nome of Lower Egypt. *(Translator.)*

[2] Traces of platinum have been found in gold used by the Egyptians as early as 1200 BCE, but it is unclear whether they recognized platinum as a distinct element or realized that there was platinum in their gold. *(Translator.)*

"The last of it was expended ten years ago."

"On what? ... To whom? ..."

"On the needs of the court," said the Treasurer, "on gifts to nomarchs and temples."

"The court had incomes from current taxes. Could the gifts have exhausted my father's treasury?"

"Osiris-Ramses, Your Holiness' father, was a generous lord and made great offerings."

"Just how great? I want to know once and for all," said the Pharaoh impatiently.

"The exact numbers are in the archives, I remember only the overall figures."

"Go on!"

"For example," spoke the Treasurer hesitantly, "Osiris-Ramses, during his happy reign, gave the temples about a hundred cities, a hundred twenty ships, two million head of cattle, two million sacks of grain, a hundred twenty thousand horses, eighty thousand slaves, some two hundred thousand barrels of beer and wine, some three million breads, thirty thousand robes, three hundred thousand flagons of honey, olive oil, and incense. Additionally, a thousand talents of gold, three thousand of silver, ten thousand of cast bronze, five hundred talents of dark bronze, six million floral garlands, twelve hundred statues of gods, and some three hundred thousand precious stones.[3] I don't remember other numbers right now, but it's all in the records."

The Pharaoh lifted up his hands, laughing, then turned angry, struck the table with his fist, and cried:

"It's extraordinary that a handful of priests should use up such quantities of beer, bread, garlands, and robes, while having their own incomes! Enormous incomes which exceed several-hundredfold the needs of the holy men."

"Your Eminence is pleased to forget that the priests support tens of thousands of paupers, treat as many ill persons, and maintain over a dozen regiments at temple expense."

"What need have they of regiments? The pharaohs have their use only in wartime. As for the ill, nearly all of them pay for their treatment or work off what they owe the temples. And the paupers? They work for the temples: they carry water for the gods, take part in ceremonies—and above all, help out with miracles. It is they who regain their minds, vision, and hearing at the temple gates; they whose wounds heal, whose legs and arms regain power; while the populace, watching these wonders, pray the more fervently and give the more generous offerings to the gods.

"The paupers are the oxen and sheep of the temples; they bring the temples pure profit."

"And so," ventured the Treasurer, "the priests do not spend all the offerings but gather them and increase the fund."

"What for?"

"For emergencies of the Kingdom."

"Who has seen this fund?"

---

[3] The gifts of Ramses III to the temples were incomparably greater. *(Author.)* They are recorded in Papyrus Harris No. 1 in the British Museum. (However, James Henry Breasted writes that "the enormous endowments enumerated in the great Papyrus Harris, long supposed to be the gifts of Ramses III, are but inventories of the old sacerdotal estates, in the possession of which the temples are confirmed by him.") Ramses III, the second and only important monarch of the 20th Dynasty, reigned a century after Ramses II (Ramses the Great, a 19th Dynasty pharaoh), on whom Ramses III modeled himself; Ramses III was a truly great general who fought off invasions by the Libyans and the "Sea Peoples." *(Translator.)*

"I myself have," said the dignitary. "The treasures deposited in the Labyrinth do not decrease but multiply from generation to generation so that, in case ..."

"So that," broke in the Pharaoh, "the Assyrians will have something to take when they conquer an Egypt so beautifully governed by the priests!

"Thank you, Great Treasurer," he added. "I knew Egypt's finances were in a bad way. But I had no idea the Kingdom was ruined—rebellions everywhere, no army, the pharaoh in straits. But the Labyrinth's treasury grows from generation to generation!

"If every dynasty—just every dynasty—has made as great offerings to the temples as my father, the Labyrinth would by now have nineteen thousand talents of gold, some sixty thousand talents of silver, and how much grain and land, how many cattle, slaves, and cities, how many robes and precious stones—the best accountant couldn't reckon it up!"

The Great Treasurer took his leave of the Lord, disheartened. But neither was the Pharaoh pleased: upon reflection, he felt he had been too open with his dignitaries.

CHAPTER 52

The guard in the antechamber announced Pentuer. The priest prostrated himself on his face before the Pharaoh and asked for his orders.

"I have no orders for you, only a request," said the Lord. "You know, there are rebellions in Egypt! Rebellions of peasants, craftsmen, even convicts ... rebellions from the sea to the mines! All that's wanting is for my soldiers to rebel and proclaim—say, Herhor—pharaoh!"

"Live forever, Holiness," said the priest. "There is no one in Egypt who would not sacrifice himself for you and bless your name."

"Oh, if they knew," said the Lord angrily, "how powerless and impoverished the Pharaoh is, every nomarch would want to be the master of his nome! I thought that on inheriting the Double Crown I would count for something. But already the first day I find that I'm only the shadow of Egypt's former rulers! What can a pharaoh be without treasure, without an army, above all without faithful servants? I'm like the statues of the gods to which they burn incense and make offerings. The statues are powerless, and the priests batten on the offerings. But, true, you hold with them!"

"It grieves me," said Pentuer, "that Your Holiness speaks this way on the first day of his reign. If word of this were to get about Egypt ..."

"To whom shall I tell my troubles?" interrupted the Lord. "You're my advisor and saved my life, or at least wanted to—surely not in order to bruit what is happening in the royal heart, which I bare to you. But you're right."

The Lord walked about the room, then said in a considerably calmer tone:

"I've named you head of a council to determine the causes of the endless rebellions in my Kingdom. I want only the guilty punished, and justice done to the unfortunate."

"May God support you with his grace!" whispered the priest. "I'll do what you ask, lord. But I already know the causes of the rebellions."

"Tell me."

"I already have, Holiness, more than once: the working people are hungry, overworked, and excessively taxed. Those who used to labor from sunrise to sunset, now must start an hour before sunrise and finish an hour after sunset. Not that long ago, every tenth day the ordinary person could visit the graves of his mother and father, commune with their shades, and make offerings. Today no one does, because there's no time.

"In the past, the peasant ate three wheat cakes a day; today he can't afford a barley cake. In the past, labor at canals, dams, and highways counted against taxes; today the taxes must be paid anyway, while public works are carried out for free.

"Those are the causes of the rebellions."

"I'm the poorest nobleman in the Kingdom!" cried the Pharaoh, tugging his hair. "Any owner of an estate gives his livestock decent fodder and rest; but my stock are always hungry and weary!

"So what am I to do? Tell me, you who've asked me to improve the lives of the peasants."

"Your lordship bids me tell you?"

"I ask ... I bid ... as you will. Only speak sensibly."

"Blest be your reign, O true son of Osiris!" said the priest. "Here is what needs to be done ...

"First, Lord, decree that labor on public works is to be paid for, as in the past."

"Of course."

"Next, announce that agricultural labor shall last only from sunrise to sunset. Then, as obtained under the divine dynasties, decree that the populace shall rest every seventh day; not every tenth, but every seventh. Then forbid lords to mortgage peasants, and scribes to beat and torment them at their pleasure.

"Finally, give the peasants a tenth or at least a twentieth of the land for their own, which no one may take from them or mortgage. Let the peasant's family have a plot the size of this room's floor, and they will never go hungry. Give the peasants the desert sands for their own, Lord, and in a few years gardens will grow there."

"That is all well and good," said the Pharaoh, "but you are saying what you see in your heart, not in the world. People's ideas, even the best, do not always accord with the natural course of things."

"Your Holiness, I've seen such changes and their results," said Pentuer.

"At certain temples, trials are made of ways to treat the ill, teach children, raise livestock and plants, and improve people. And this is what has been found:

"When a thin, lazy peasant was given good food and rest every seventh day, the man gained weight, became willing to work, and plowed more field than before. A paid worker has a better attitude and does more work than a slave, though the slave be beaten with iron rods. Well-nourished people have more children than hungry and overworked ones. The offspring of free people are healthy and strong; those of slaves, frail, sullen, and inclined to theft and mendacity.

"It's also been found that soil cultivated by its owner yields one and a half times more grain and vegetables than soil tended by slaves.

"I'll tell Your Holiness something curious: when music is played to plowmen, the men and oxen work better and faster, and get less tired, than without music.

"All this has been discovered at our temples."

The Pharaoh smiled. "I must introduce music to my estates and to the mines," he said. "But if the priests have discovered all these wonders of which you speak, then why don't they treat the peasants this way on their estates?"

Pentuer lowered his head. "Because," he sighed, "not all priests are wise and noble-hearted."

"Exactly!" cried the Lord.

"Now tell me—you, a peasants' son who knows there are scoundrels and fools among the priests—tell me: why won't you serve me in the struggle against them? You know full well I can't improve the lives of the peasants if I don't first teach the priests to obey my will."

Pentuer wrung his hands. "Lord, it's a godless and dangerous thing to fight the priesthood! More than one pharaoh has started the fight ... and has been unable to finish it."

"Because he wasn't backed by wise men such as you!" the Lord burst out. "And truly, I never will understand why good, learned priests attach themselves to the band of scoundrels who make up the bulk of that class."

Pentuer shook his head and spoke slowly:

"For thirty thousand years the holy priesthood has been cultivating Egypt, and it has made this country what it is today: the wonder of the whole world. And how, despite their shortcomings, have the priests managed to do this? It is because they are the lamp that sustains the light of learning.

"The lamp may be grimy, even rank, nevertheless it preserves the divine fire without which darkness and savagery would prevail among men.

"Your Lordship speaks of fighting the priesthood," continued Pentuer. "What can come of it for me? If you lose, I shall be unhappy because you'll not improve the lives of the peasants. And if you win? ... Oh, may I never see the day! ... For if you smashed the lamp, who knows whether you wouldn't extinguish the fire of learning which for thousands of years has burned over Egypt and the world.

"Those, my lord, are the reasons I don't want to get involved in your fight with the holy priesthood. I feel it coming, and I suffer because the worm that I am cannot prevent it. But I won't get involved, for I would have to betray either you or God, the creator of learning."

As he listened, the Pharaoh paced the chamber thinking.

"Very well," he said without anger, "do as you like. You're not a soldier, so I can't accuse you of cowardice. But neither can you be my advisor. Still, I'm asking you to form a judicial body to investigate the peasant rebellions and, when I call you, to speak the dictates of wisdom."

Pentuer knelt in leave-taking.

"In any event," added the Pharaoh, "know that I don't want to extinguish the divine light. Let the priests cultivate learning at their temples—but not dismantle the army, make disgraceful treaties ... or," he spoke passionately now, "plunder the royal treasuries!

"Do they think I'm going to stand before their gates like a beggar so they may vouchsafe me funds to lift a Kingdom brought to ruin by their stupid, inept rule? Ha! ... Ha! ... Pentuer ... I wouldn't ask the gods for what constitutes my power and right.

"You may go."

The priest backed out amid bows and in the door prostrated himself on his face.

The Lord remained alone.

"Mortal men," he thought, "are like children. Herhor is no fool; he knows that, in the event of war, Egypt needs half a million soldiers; he knows they'll require training—yet he's reduced the number and strength of the regiments.

"The Great Treasurer likewise is no fool, yet it seems to him perfectly natural that all the treasures of the pharaohs have passed into the Labyrinth!

"Finally Pentuer ... What a strange man! ... He wants to give the peasants food, land, and endless holidays. Very well, but all that will reduce my revenues, which are too small as it is. However, were I to tell him, 'Help me take the royal treasures back from the priests,' he'd call it godlessness and extinguishing the light of Egypt!

"A singular man ... He'd gladly turn the whole Kingdom upside down to benefit the peasants, but he wouldn't dare take a high priest by the scruff of the neck and see him off to jail. As calmly as you please, he tells me to give up half my revenues; but I'm sure he wouldn't dare remove a copper deben from the Labyrinth."

The Pharaoh smiled and again meditated:

"Everyone wants to be happy; but just you try to make them all happy, and they grab at your hands like a man having a bad tooth pulled.

"That's why a ruler must be resolute. And that's why my divine father was wrong to neglect the peasants and to trust the priests without limit. He's left me a hard legacy ... but I'll manage.

"It was a hard business, too, at the Natron Lakes. Harder than here. Here there are only talkers and cowards; there, there were armed men who were prepared to die.

"One battle opens our eyes better than dozens of years of peacetime rule. He who tells himself, 'I'll overcome the obstacle!' will. But he who hesitates, must give way."

Dusk fell. The palace guard changed, and torches were lit in outlying chambers. No one, however, dared enter the Pharaoh's room unbidden.

The Lord, weary from sleeplessness, the previous day's journey, and today's business, dropped into an armchair. It seemed to him he had been pharaoh for centuries, and he could not believe a full day had not passed since he had been at the Pyramids.

"One day? ... It can't be!"

Then it occurred to him that the souls of earlier pharaohs might be migrating into his heart. Surely it was so—else why his sense of old age or antiquity? And why did ruling the Kingdom now seem to him simple, whereas only a couple of months earlier he had been terrified at the thought that he wouldn't know how to rule?

"One day?" he repeated to himself. "Why, I've been here for thousands of years!"

Suddenly he heard a muffled voice: "Son! ... My son ..."

The Pharaoh jumped up from the armchair. "Who's there?" he called.

"It is I ... Could you have forgotten me already?"

The Lord could not tell whence the voice proceeded: from above, from below, or perhaps from the large statue of Osiris which stood in the corner.

"My son," spoke the voice again, "respect the will of the gods if you would receive their blessed help. Oh, respect the gods, for without their help the greatest earthly power is but dust and shadow. Oh, respect the gods, if you would not have the bitterness of your errors poison my abode in the happy land of the West."

The voice fell still. The Lord called for light. One door to the chamber was closed; at the other stood the guard. No one else could have entered.

Anger and anxiety tugged at the Pharaoh's heart. What had it been? Had it really been his father's shade speaking to him, or was the voice just a new imposition of the priests?

If the priests could speak to him from a distance regardless of the thick walls, they could also listen in. In which case he, the Lord of the World, was like a wild animal surrounded on all sides.

True, at the royal palace listening in was commonplace. But the Pharaoh had thought that at least this cabinet was exempt and that the priests' audacity stopped at the ruler's threshold.

But what if it had been a spirit?

The Lord did not want to eat supper, and retired for the night. It seemed to him he would not fall asleep, but weariness got the better of agitation.

A few hours later, he was wakened by bells and light. It was midnight, and the priest-astrologer had come to report to the Lord on the positions of the heavenly bodies. The Pharaoh heard out the report and said:

"Reverend Prophet, could you not henceforth present your reports to His Eminence Sem? He is my deputy for religious matters."

The priest-astrologer was very surprised at the Lord's indifference to matters celestial. "Your Holiness," he asked, "chooses to forgo the signs that the stars hold for rulers?"

"Do they?" said the Pharaoh. "Then tell me what they promise me."

The astrologer evidently expected the question, for he replied without taking thought:

"The horizon is momentarily clouded. The Lord of the World has not yet found the path of truth which leads to knowing the will of the gods. But sooner or later he shall, and on it a long life and a happy, glorious reign."

"Aha! ... Thank you, holy man. Now that I know what it is I should seek, I'll abide by the signs, and again I ask that you henceforth communicate with His Eminence Sem. He is my deputy, and should you read something of interest in the stars, he will tell me about it in the morning."

The priest left the bedroom, shaking his head.

"Now I won't get back to sleep!" said the Lord, with an annoyed expression on his face.

"The most worshipful Queen Nikotris," said an aide suddenly, "asked me an hour ago to request audience of Your Holiness."

"Now? ... At midnight?" asked the Lord.

"She said Your Holiness would be waking at midnight."

The Pharaoh reflected and told the aide he would wait upon the Queen in the Gold Hall. He assumed that there no one would listen in to their conversation.

The Lord threw on a cloak, slipped on sandals, and ordered the Gold Hall well lit. Then he went out, telling the servants not to accompany him.

He found his mother already in the Gold Hall, dressed in coarse mourning linen. The worshipful lady again made to drop to her knees, but her son lifted and hugged her.

"Has something important happened, Mother, that you trouble yourself at this hour?" he asked.

"I wasn't sleeping ... I was praying," she replied. "Oh, my son, you guessed aright that it's an important matter! I heard the divine voice of your father."

"Really?" said the Pharaoh, feeling an access of anger.

"Your immortal father," continued the Queen, "told me, full of sorrow, that you are embarking on a wrong path. You are disdaining ordination as a high priest, and are mistreating the servants of the gods.

"'Who will remain by Ramses,' said your divine father, 'if he alienates the gods and if the priesthood forsake him? Tell him ... tell him ...' repeated the venerable shade, 'that this way he will doom Egypt, himself, and the Dynasty!'"

"Oho!" cried the Pharaoh, "they threaten me like this on the very first day of my reign? My Mother, a dog barks loudest when it's afraid, so these threats are indeed a bad omen— but for the priests!"

"But it was your father speaking," repeated the distressed lady.

"My immortal father," replied the Pharaoh, "and my holy grandfather Amenhotep, as the pure spirits that they are, know my heart and see the lamentable state of Egypt. And since it is my heart's desire to lift up the Kingdom by curbing abuses, they could not hinder me from carrying out my plans."

"Then you don't believe it's your father's spirit giving you advice?" she asked, increasingly terrified.

"I don't know. But I have reason to suppose the spirit voices speaking in various corners of our palace are a trick of the priests. Only the priests can fear me, never the gods or spirits. So it's not spirits that are frightening us, Mother."

The Queen fell to thinking, and her son's words appeared to be making an impression on her. She had seen many wonders in her life, and some of them had seemed suspect to herself.

"In that case," she sighed, "you're not being careful, my son! This afternoon Herhor came by, very displeased with his audience with you. He said you want to remove the priests from court."

"What do I need them for? So that my kitchen and cellar will have large expenditures? Or so that they will listen in to what I say and watch what I do?"

"The whole country will be upset when the priests declare you to be godless," said the lady.

"The country already is upset, but through the fault of the priests," said the Pharaoh. "And I'm beginning to have a different view of the piety of the Egyptian people. Mother, if you knew how many prosecutions there are in Lower Egypt for desecration of the gods, and in Upper Egypt for looting of the dead, you'd find that priestly matters have ceased to be sacred with our populace."

"That's the influence of the foreigners who are flooding Egypt," exclaimed the lady. "Especially the Phoenicians!"

"It's all the same whose influence it is; suffice it that Egypt no longer regards the statues or the priests as superhuman. And, Mother, if you heard the nobility, the officers, the soldiers, you would understand that the time has come to put royal authority in place of priestly authority, if all authority is not to fall in this country."

"Egypt is yours," sighed the Queen. "Your wisdom is extraordinary, so do as you will. But act carefully ... Oh, carefully! Even a dead scorpion can still sting the careless victor."

They hugged, and the Lord returned to his bedroom. But this time he really could not sleep.

He now saw clearly that a battle had begun between him and the priests—or rather, something odious that did not deserve the name of "battle" and which he, the commander, in the first instance had not known how to handle.

Where was the enemy here? ... Whom was his loyal army to engage? The priests who prostrated themselves on the ground before him? The stars which said the Pharaoh had not yet embarked on the path of truth? What, and whom, to fight?

The spirit voices speaking out of the gloom? Or his own mother who, terrified, begged him not to disperse the priests?

The Pharaoh writhed on his bed, gripped by a feeling powerlessness. Suddenly the thought came to him: "What do I care about an enemy that falls apart like mud in the fist? Let them talk in empty halls, let them bridle at my godlessness.

"I'll issue orders; and who dares disobey them is my enemy, and I'll turn the police, the courts, and the army against him."

CHAPTER 53

And so in the month of Athyr, after a thirty-four-year reign, Pharaoh Mer-amen-Ramses XII, Lord of the Two Worlds, Lord of Eternity, dispenser of life and all felicity, died.

He died because he felt his body growing weak and useless. He died because he yearned for his eternal homeland and desired to entrust the governance of the earthly Kingdom to younger hands. He died, finally, because he wanted to, because that was his will. The divine spirit flew off like a hawk which, having long circled over the earth, at last melts away into the azure.

Even as his life had been the sojourn of an immortal being in the temporal world, so his death was but another episode in his superhuman existence.

The Lord woke at sunrise and, supported by two prophets, surrounded by a choir of priests, made his way to the chapel of Osiris. There, as usual, he revived the god, washed and dressed him, made an offering, and raised his hands in prayer.

Meanwhile the priests chanted:

Choir I. "Hail to Thee, that risest on the horizon and traversest the heavens."

Choir II. "The highroad of Thy holiness is the good fortune of those on whose faces fall Thy rays."

Choir I. "Could I go as Thou goest, without stopping, O Sun!"

Choir II. "Great Wanderer of space, Who hath no master and to Whom hundreds of millions of years are but the blink of an eye."

Choir I. "Thou settest, yet endurest. Thou multipliest the hours, days, and nights and endurest by Thine own laws."

Choir II. "Thou lightest the earth, offering Thyself with Thine own hands, when in the form of Ra Thou risest on the horizon."

Choir I. "O Star emergent, great by Thy brilliance, Thou shapest Thine own members."

Choir II. "And, born of none, Thou bearest Thyself on the horizon."

Here the Pharaoh spoke:

"O radiant One in the heavens! Let me enter eternity and join the venerable and perfect shades of the higher land. Let me behold with them Thy radiance in the morning and in the evening, when Thou joinest with Thy mother Nut. And when Thou turnest Thy face westward, let my hands join in prayer in worship of the Life retiring beyond the hills."[1]

---

[1] Authentic hymn. *(Author.)*

Thus spoke the Lord with hands upraised, enveloped in a cloud of incense. Suddenly he became still and fell back into the arms of the assisting priests.

He was dead.

Word of the Pharaoh's death spread like lightning through the palace. The servants dropped their labors, the stewards ceased watching the slaves, the guard was alerted, and all the entrances were manned.

In the main court there began to gather a crowd of cooks, cellar-keepers, grooms, women of His Holiness, and their children. Some asked, Was it true? others wondered that the sun still shone in the sky, and all shouted together at the tops of their lungs:

"O Lord! ... O our father! ... O beloved! ... Can it be that thou art leaving us? ... Oh, yes, he is going to Abydos![2] To the West, to the West, to the land of the just! ... The place that thou hast come to love, weeps and wails for thee!"[3]

A terrific uproar rang through all the courts, through the whole park. It echoed from the eastern hills, crossed the Nile on the wings of the wind, and terrified the city of Memphis.

Meanwhile, amid prayers, the priests placed the body of the deceased into a rich enclosed litter. Eight priests stepped to the poles, four took up fans of ostrich feathers, others censers, and they made ready to depart.

At that moment Queen Nikotris ran up and, seeing the body already in the litter, threw herself to the feet of the deceased.

"O my husband! O my brother! O my beloved!" she wailed, sobbing bitterly. "O beloved, remain with us, remain in thy house, do not depart this place on the earth where thou hast been staying."

"In peace, in peace, to the West," chanted the priests, "O great ruler, go in peace to the West."

"Alas!" said the Queen, "thou hastenest to the ferry to cross to the other bank! O priests, O prophets, do not hurry, leave him; you shall return to your homes, but he will go to the land of eternity."

"In peace, in peace, to the West!" chanted the priestly choir. "If it please God, when the day of eternity comes, we shall see thee again, O Lord, for thou goest to the land that joins all people within it."[4]

At a sign from His Eminence Herhor, servant women pulled the Lady from the Pharaoh's feet and forcibly conducted her to her rooms.

The priest-borne litter set out with the ruler in it, dressed and surrounded as in life. To right and left, before and behind him, walked generals, treasurers, judges, great scribes, the ax- and bow-bearers, and above all a crowd of priests of various degree.

---

[2] Abydos: Greek name for Abdju, capital of the 8th Nome of Upper Egypt. The city was called Abydos by Greek geographers who borrowed the name from the unrelated city of Abydos on the Greek Hellespont (now the Dardanelles in northwest Turkey). Egypt's Abydos was the site of many ancient temples and of a royal necropolis where early pharaohs were entombed. For this reason it later became desirable to be buried in the area, which enhanced the town's importance as a cult site. The memorial temple of pharaoh Seti I at Abydos contains the Abydos King List, naming most (76) of the pharaohs from Menes to Seti I. Omitted are many pharaohs who were apparently considered illegitimate, such as the woman pharaoh Hatshepsut and the Amarna Period pharaohs Akhenaton, Smenkhkare, Tutankhamon, and Ay. *(Translator.)*

[3] Authentic. *(Author.)*

[4] Authentic. *(Author.)*

In the courtyard the servants prostrated themselves on their faces, weeping and wailing, but the troops presented arms, and trumpets sounded, as if greeting a living king.

Indeed, the Lord was borne to the ferry as though alive. On reaching the Nile, the priests deposited the litter on a golden barge, beneath a purple canopy, as in life.

Here the litter was showered with blossoms, a statue of Anubis[5] was placed facing it, and the royal barge set out for the opposite bank of the Nile, to the weeping of the servants and court women.

Two hours out from the palace, across the Nile, beyond a canal, beyond fertile fields and palm groves between Memphis and the Mummy Plateau, lay an original district. All its buildings were consecrated to the dead and inhabited only by embalming personnel.

This district was, as it were, the vestibule to the cemetery proper—a bridge that joined the living society with the place of eternal rest. Here the deceased were brought to be mummified; here families negotiated with the priests the price of the funeral. Here were prepared the sacred books and bandages, the coffins, furniture, vessels, and statues for the deceased.

This district, a couple of thousand paces from Memphis, was surrounded by a long wall with, here and there, a gate. The cortege bearing the Pharaoh's remains stopped at the most splendid gate, and one of the priests knocked.

"Who is there?" came a question from within.

"Osiris-Mer-amen-Ramses, Lord of the Two Worlds, comes and asks that you prepare him for his eternal journey," replied the priest.

"Can it be that Egypt's sun has expired? That He has died who Himself was breath and life?"

"Such was his will," answered the priest. "Therefore receive the Lord with due reverence and render him all the services properly so that you do not meet with punishment in the earthly and the after life."

"We shall do as you say," said the voice within.

The priests left the litter at the gate and hurried away to avoid the miasma from the corpses gathered there. Only civil officials remained, headed by the Supreme Judge and Treasurer.

After a considerable while the gate opened, and a dozen men emerged. They wore priests' garb, and their faces were hooded.

The Judge told them:

"We give you the body of our Lord and yours. Do with it as the religious precepts require, and neglect nothing, so that this great decedent shall not, through your fault, experience distress in the afterworld."

The Treasurer added:

"Use gold, silver, malachite, jasper, emeralds, turquoises, and the finest perfumes for this Lord so that he shall lack for nothing and shall have everything of the best. So say to you I, the Treasurer. And if there be a villain who would substitute wretched counterfeits

---

[5] *Anubis* was the Greek name for the Egyptian god *Inpu* (or *Anapa*), patron of the dead. The god was depicted as a canine or a canine-headed man. (The animal was previously thought to be a jackal, but the dog-like animal of the Egyptian desert has been shown to be an African wolf.) Anubis, as god of the dead, took part in Osiris' judgment of the dead. *(Translator.)*

for noble metals, and Phoenician glass for precious stones, then let him remember that his hands shall be cut off and his eyes taken out."

"It will be as you say," answered one of the hooded priests.

The other priests lifted the litter and carried it inside the District of the Dead, chanting:

"Thou goest in peace to Abydos! Mayst thou reach the Theban West in peace! To the West, to the West, to the land of the just!"

The gate closed, and the Supreme Judge, the Treasurer, and the officials with them turned back for the ferry and the palace.

Meanwhile the hooded priests carried the litter into an enormous building where were embalmed only royal remains and the remains of the highest dignitaries who had gained the pharaoh's exceptional favor. They stopped in the vestibule, where there stood a golden boat on wheels, and they proceeded to take the deceased from the litter.

"What thieves!" exclaimed one of the hooded men. "The Pharaoh died in the chapel of Osiris, so he must have been in ceremonial costume. But look here! ... Brass bracelets instead of gold, and a brass chain too, and fake jewels in the rings."

"It's true," said another. "I wonder who fleeced him like that: the priests or the scribes?"

"Certainly the priests. Rascals, may your hands wither! And those scoundrels dare admonish us to give the deceased everything of the best."

"It wasn't them but the Treasurer."

"They're all thieves!"

Thus conversing, the embalmers removed the royal vestments from the deceased, dressed him in a gold-threaded bathrobe, and transferred the body to the boat.

"The gods be thanked," said one of the hooded men, "we now have a new Lord. He'll put things to rights with the priests. What they took with their hands, they'll return with their mouths!"

"Oh, they say he's going to be a strong ruler!" said another. "He's on friendly terms with the Phoenicians, and he hobnobs with Pentuer, who doesn't come from priests but from poor folk like us. And they say the army would go through fire and water for the new Pharaoh."

"Of late, he's gloriously beaten the Libyans."

"Where is he, this new Pharaoh?" said another. "In the desert! ... Well, I fear he may come to grief before he returns to Memphis."

"What harm can he come to, with the army behind him? May I not live to see an honest funeral if the young Lord doesn't do with the priesthood as the bison does with the wheatfield."

"Oh, are you stupid!" said a hitherto silent embalmer. "The Pharaoh will manage with the priests?"

"Why shouldn't he?"

"Did you ever see a lion tear up a pyramid?"

"Silly talk!"

"Or a bison knock one down?"

"Of course not."

"Can a tempest overthrow a pyramid?"

"What's with all the questions today?"

"Well, I tell you, sooner a lion, a bison, or a tempest will overturn a pyramid than the

Pharaoh will defeat the priesthood. Even though this Pharaoh were a lion, a bison, and a tempest all in one."

"Hey, you there!" someone called from above. "Is the body ready?"

"Just a moment ... his jaw keeps dropping," someone answered from the vestibule.

"Doesn't matter. Get him on up here; Isis has to go downtown in an hour."

A moment later, the golden boat with the deceased was hoisted on ropes up to an inner balcony.

The vestibule opened onto a great hall painted blue, with yellow stars. Attached to one wall, the entire length of the hall, was a kind of arched balcony whose ends stood a story, the center a story and a half, high.

The hall represented the heavenly firmament; the balcony, the Sun's path across the heavens; and the late pharaoh was Osiris, or the Sun which migrated from east to west.

Down in the hall stood a crowd of priests and priestesses conversing on indifferent subjects as they awaited the ceremony.

"Ready!" someone called from the balcony.

The conversations stopped. Above, a bronze tone rang three times—and the Sun's golden boat appeared on the balcony, with the deceased riding in it.

Down below, there sounded a hymn to the Sun:

"Behold, He appears in a cloud to separate heaven from earth, and then to unite them!

"Ever concealed in all things, He alone living, in Whom all things eternally exist."

The boat gradually moved up the arch, finally stopping at the apex.

Then at the lower end of the arch there appeared a priestess dressed as the goddess Isis, with her son Horus, and likewise began a slow ascent. This was a picture of the Moon, which follows after the Sun.

Now, from the arch's apex, the boat began descending westward, while down below the choir again chanted:

"God incarnate in all things, the Shu[6] spirit in all the gods. He is the body of the living man, the creator of the fruit-bearing tree, the cause of the fertilizing floods. Without Him, nothing lives within the earthly orb."[7]

The boat disappeared at the west end of the balcony, and Isis and Horus reached the arch's apex. A group of priests ran up to the boat, took out the pharaoh's body, and laid it on a marble table—Osiris in repose after the day's travail.

Now the deceased was approached by an opener of dead bodies disguised as the god Typhon. On his head he wore a terrible mask and a shaggy red wig, and on his back a boar's hide, and in his hand he held an Ethiopian stone knife.

With the knife, he began quickly cutting away the soles of the deceased's feet.

"What are you doing to the sleeping one, brother Typhon?" Isis asked him from the balcony.

"I am scraping my brother Osiris' feet, that he may not pollute heaven with earthly dust," answered the man disguised as Typhon.

Having cut away the soles, the opener of dead bodies took a bent wire, inserted it into

---

[6] Shu ("emptiness"): the Egyptian god of the air, son of the god Atum, husband of the goddess Tefnut ("moisture"), father of the sky goddess Nut and the earth god Geb. *(Translator.)*

[7] Authentic hymn. *(Author.)*

the deceased's nose, and proceeded to extract the brain.[8] Next he cut open the abdomen and, through the opening, quickly pulled out the entrails, heart,[9] and lungs.

Meanwhile Typhon's assistants brought four large jars[10] adorned with the heads respectively of the gods Hapi, Imseti, Duamutef, and Qebehsenuef,[11] and into each jar they placed one of the deceased's internal organs.

"What are you doing there, brother Typhon?" asked Isis a second time.

"I am cleansing my brother Osiris of earthly things, that he may be more beautiful," answered the opener of dead bodies.

Beside the marble table was a pool of water saturated with natron. The embalmers, having gutted the body, placed it in the pool, where it was to soak for seventy days.

Meanwhile Isis, having crossed the whole balcony, approached the chamber where the opener of dead bodies had opened and eviscerated the royal remains. She looked at the marble table and, seeing it empty, asked in alarm:

"Where is my brother? ... Where is my divine spouse?"

Suddenly thunder rang, trumpets and bronze sheets sounded, and the opener of dead bodies dressed as Typhon burst into laughter and called out:

"Beautiful Isis who brightens the nights together with the stars, your husband is no more! Nevermore will radiant Osiris ride the golden boat, nevermore will the sun appear in the firmament. I, Set, have done this, and I have hidden him so deep that none of the gods nor all of them together will find him!"

At these words, the goddess rent her garments and proceeded to moan and tear her hair. Once more there rang trumpets, thunder, and bronze sheets; among the priests and priestesses there arose a murmur, then shouts, curses—and suddenly they all flung themselves at Typhon, crying:

"Accursed spirit of darkness ... who incites the desert winds, roils the sea, dims the light of day! May you fall into an abyss from which the very father of the gods cannot free you! Accursed! ... Accursed Set! ... May your name be a terror and an abomination!"

So cursing, they all charged Typhon with fists and canes, and the red-headed god proceeded to flee and finally ran out of the hall.

Three more tones of a bronze sheet—and the ceremony was over.

"That will do!" the senior priest called to the gathering, who had in earnest begun fight-

---

[8] It is now believed that, given the delicacy of brain tissue, it would have been impossible to extract the brain in the manner described here; rather, the brain would have been scrambled using a wire, then the body tilted and the liquefied brain drained out through the nostrils. *(Translator.)*

[9] Actually, the heart stayed in the body, because in the hall of judgment it would be weighed against the feather of Maat. *(Translator.)*

[10] They are known as "canopic jars," from early Egyptologists' mistaken association of these containers with the Greek legend of Canopus, the pilot of the ship of King Menelaus of Sparta during the Trojan War. While visiting Egypt's coast, Canopus was bitten by a serpent and died. Menelaus erected a monument to him at the Nile mouth where the town of Canopus later developed, on the western bank of the now nonexistent Canopic branch of the Nile. Also named for Canopus is the brightest star in the southern constellation of Carina: Canopus, the second brightest star in the night sky after Sirius. *(Translator.)*

[11] Hapi, Imseti, Duamutef, and Qebehsenuef: the four sons of the god Horus. Each son was responsible for protecting a particular bodily organ. Each son was also the god of one of the four cardinal directions and was himself protected by a companion goddess. *(Translator.)*

ing among themselves. "You, Isis, may go downtown; and the rest of you, off to the other deceased who await us! Don't neglect the ordinary dead, because we don't know how much they'll pay us for this one."

"Certainly not much!" said an embalmer. "They say the treasury is empty, and the Phoenicians threaten to stop lending if they don't receive new rights."

"Death take your Phoenicians! Before long a person will have to beg them for a barley cake, they've just about taken everything over."

"But if they don't give the Pharaoh money, we won't get anything for the funeral."

The conversations trailed off, and everyone left the blue hall. Only a guard detail remained at the pool where the pharaoh's remains soaked.

The whole ceremony re-enacting the legendary killing of Osiris (the Sun) by Typhon (god of night and crime) had served for the cutting open and evisceration of the pharaoh's remains preparatory to the actual embalming.

For seventy days the deceased lay in the natron bath, apparently in memory of the evil Typhon having dumped his brother's body into the Natron Lakes. Every morning and evening through all these days, the priestess dressed as Isis came to the blue hall. There, wailing and tearing her hair, she asked those present whether anyone had seen her divine husband and brother.

After this period of mourning, Horus, son and successor of Osiris, appeared in the hall with his suite—and they at last noticed the tub of water.

"Shall we search here for the body of my father and brother?" asked Horus.

They searched, found and, to the tremendous rejoicing of the priests and to strains of music, drew the pharaoh's body from the fortifying bath.

The body was placed for several days into a stone pipe ventilated with hot air, and after drying it was turned over to the embalmers.

Now the most important ceremonies began, carried out over the deceased by the highest priests of the District of the Dead.

The body of the deceased, oriented with the head to the south, was washed with holy water, and the insides with palm wine. On a floor strewn with ashes sat weeping women, tearing their hair, scratching their faces, bewailing the deceased. Gathered about the deathbed were priests dressed as gods: naked Isis in the crown of the pharaohs, young Horus, jackal-headed Anubis, bird-headed Thoth holding tablets in his hands, and many others.

Under the supervision of this august assemblage, specialists proceeded to fill the deceased's insides with fragrant herbs and sawdust and to pour in aromatic resins, all amid prayers. Then, in lieu of his own eyes, they gave him ones of glass set in bronze.

Next the whole body was powdered with natron.

Now another priest came forward and explained to those present that the body of the deceased was the body of Osiris, and that the attributes of the deceased were those of Osiris.

"The magical properties of his left temple are the properties of the temple of the god Atum, and his right eye is the eye of the god Atum, whose rays pierce the dark. His left eye is the eye of Horus, which destroys all living creatures, his upper lip is Isis, and his lower lip is Nephthys.[12] The neck of the deceased is a goddess, the hands are divine souls, the

---

[12]Nephthys: Greek name for the Egyptian goddess Nebet-het, daughter of the earth god Geb and the sky goddess Nut; sister of the goddess Isis, and sister-wife of the god Set. *(Translator.)*

fingers are celestial serpents, sons of the goddess Selket.[13] His flanks are two plumes of Amon, his spine is the spine of Geb, and his stomach is the god Nun."[14] [15]

Another priest speaks:

"I was given lips to speak, legs to walk, arms to overthrow mine enemies. I rise from the dead, I exist, I open the heavens; I do as I was instructed in Memphis."[16]

Meanwhile they hang on the deceased's neck an image of a scarab beetle fashioned from a precious stone, bearing the inscription:

"O my heart, heart that I received from my mother, that I had when I was on the earth, O heart, do not rise against me and give ill testimony on the day of judgment."[17]

Now the priests wind each arm and leg, each finger of the deceased in bands inscribed with prayers and spells. They glue the bands on with gum and balsams. And on the chest and neck they place whole manuscripts of the *Book of the Dead* with the following meditations, which the priests pronounce aloud over the deceased:

"I am he whom no god impedes."

"Who is that?"

"It is Atum on his disk, it is Ra on his disk, which rises in the eastern sky.

"I am Yesterday and I know Tomorrow."

"Who is that?"

"Yesterday is Osiris, Tomorrow is Ra on the day when he will annihilate the enemies of the Lord, who is above all, and when he will consecrate his son Horus. In other words: on the day when Osiris' coffin will be met by his father Ra he will battle the gods at the behest of Osiris, the Lord of Amenti."[18]

"What is that?"

"Amenti is the creation of the spirits of the gods at the behest of Osiris, the Lord of Amenti. In other words: Amenti is the excitement engendered by Ra; every god who abides there, does battle. I know a great god who dwells there.

"I am from my country, I come from my city, I destroy evil, I remove the bad, I drive dirt away from me. I come to the land of the denizens of heaven, I enter by a mighty gate.

"O you comrades, give me your hand, for I shall be one of You."[19]

When each of the deceased's members has been wound in prayer bands and furnished with amulets, when he is sufficiently provided with meditations that will let him orient

---

[13] Selket: scorpion-goddess. *(Translator.)*

[14] Nun: the deification of the primordial watery abyss. *(Translator.)*

[15] Maspero. *(Author.)*

[16] Authentic. *(Author.)*

[17] Authentic *(Author.)*

[18] Amenti (also *Duat, Akert, Neter-khertet,* etc.): "the West," the Western Land, the Underworld, the realm of the dead. This was the realm of the god Osiris and the residence of other gods and supernatural beings. It was the region through which the sun god Ra traveled from west to east during the night, and where he battled Apep, or Apophis, the deity who embodied chaos and thus opposed light and *Maat* (order, truth). It was also where people's souls went after death for judgment. Individuals' tombs formed touching-points between the mundane world and Amenti, and could be used by spirits to travel back and forth from Amenti. *(Translator.)*

[19] *Book of the Dead. (Author.)*

himself in the land of the gods, thought must be given to a document that will open the gates to that land.

For, between the tomb and heaven, the deceased is awaited by forty-two terrible judges,[20] presided over by Osiris, who examine his earthly life. Only when the deceased's heart, weighed in the scales of justice, proves equal to the goddess of truth,[21] only when the god Djehuty,[22] who records the deceased's deeds on tablets, deems them to be good, only then does Horus take the soul by the hand and lead it before the throne of Osiris.

In order that the deceased may justify himself before the court, his mummy must be wrapped in a papyrus inscribed with a general confession.[23] During the wrapping in this document, the priests pronounce distinctly so that the deceased will forget nothing:

"Lords of truth, I bring you only truth.

"I have done no treachery to any man. I have made no neighbor of mine wretched. I have uttered no obscenity or insult in a house of truth. I have had no commerce with evil. I have done no evil. As a superior, I have made no subordinate work beyond his strength. No one has become fearful, indigent, suffering, or wretched through my fault. I have done nothing that the gods would despise. I have tormented no slave. I have not starved him. I have not wrung his tears. I have not killed. I have not caused to be killed by treachery. I have not lied. I have not robbed the temples of their property. I have reduced no incomes dedicated to the gods. I have taken no bread or bands from mummies. I have committed no sin with a priest of my area. I have not taken or reduced his property. I have not used false scales. I have torn no infant from its nurse's breast. I have not committed bestiality. I have not netted birds consecrated to the gods. I have not hindered the flooding of the waters. I have diverted no canal. I have extinguished no fire at the wrong time. I have robbed no gods of their chosen offerings. I am clean ... I am clean ... I am clean."[24]

When, thanks to the *Book of the Dead*, the deceased knew how to navigate the Land of Eternity, and above all how to justify himself before the court of forty-two gods, the priests furnished him with a foreword to the *Book*—and orally explained to him its immense importance.

To that end, the embalmers surrounding the pharaoh's fresh mummy moved away, and the high priest of the district approached and whispered into the ear of the deceased:

"Know that, possessing this book, you shall belong to the living and shall acquire great

---

[20] Forty-two judges: These are the 42 deities to whom the deceased makes the 42 Negative Confessions. The 42 deities represent the 42 nomes of Upper and Lower Egypt. As the deceased makes the Negative Confessions, he addresses each god directly and mentions the nome of which the god is patron, thus emphasizing the unity of Egypt's nomes. *(Translator.)*

[21] Goddess of truth: Maat, the goddess who prevents the universe from returning to its primal state of chaos. *Maat* was also the Egyptian concept of truth, order, balance, morality, law, and justice. In the underworld "weighing of the heart," the goddess Maat's ostrich feather was the measure that determined whether the deceased's soul (considered to reside in the heart) would successfully reach the afterlife paradise. *(Translator.)*

[22] Djehuty (or *Thoth*): the Moon god, inventor of writing, and patron of scribes, who records the verdict of the judgment of the deceased. Prus calls him *Dutes*. *(Translator.)*

[23] General confession: These are the "Negative Confessions." *(Translator.)*

[24] Chapter 75 of the *Book of the Dead*. This is one of the loftiest documents bequeathed by antiquity. *(Author.)*

importance among the gods. Know that, thanks to it, no one will dare oppose you. The gods themselves will approach and embrace you—for you shall be of their number.

"Know that this book will tell you what was in the beginning. No person has voiced it, no eye has seen it, no ear has heard it. This book is pure truth, but no one has ever known it. Let it be seen only by you and him who furnished it to you. Add no commentaries to it that might be suggested by your memory or imagination. It is written entirely in the hall where they embalm the dead. It is a great secret unknown to any ordinary person, to anyone in the world.

"This book will be your sustenance in the nether land of the spirits, will give your soul the means for its stay upon the earth, will give it life eternal, and will prevent anyone from having power over you."[25]

Next the royal remains were dressed in costly vestments, in a gold mask over the face, and in rings and bracelets on the arms, which were crossed upon the chest. An ivory headrest was positioned under the head, of the kind that was used by Egyptians to sleep on. Finally, the body was encased in three coffins: a paper one covered with inscriptions, a gilded cedar one, and a marble one. The first two conformed exactly to the body of the deceased; even the sculpted face was similar, only smiling.

After its three months' sojourn in the District of the Dead, the pharaoh's mummy was ready for the solemn funeral and was returned to the royal palace.

---

[25] Book of the Dead, Chapter 148. (Author.)

CHAPTER 54

During the seventy days that the venerable remains soaked in natron, Egypt observed mourning.

Temples were closed; no processions took place. No music was heard; no feasts were thrown; the dancing girls turned mourners and, instead of dancing, tore their hair, which was equally lucrative.

No one drank wine or ate meat. The greatest dignitaries went coarse-garbed and barefoot. No one shaved (except for the priests), and the more zealous did not wash but instead daubed their faces with mud and strewed their hair with ashes.

From the Mediterranean Sea to the First Cataract of the Nile, from the Libyan Desert to the Sinai Peninsula, there reigned silence and sorrow. Egypt's sun had expired: the Lord who bestowed joy and life had departed to the West and left his servants.

In high society, the fashionable topic of conversation was the universal grief that was imparted even to nature.

"Have you noticed," said one dignitary to another, "how the days have gotten shorter and darker?"

"I was loth to mention it," replied the other, "but it is indeed so. I have also noticed that fewer stars shine at night and that the full moon was shorter-lived, and the new one of longer duration, than usual."

"The herdsmen say the cattle in the pasture won't graze but only bawl."

"I hear from the huntsmen that the weeping lions no longer pounce on the deer because they've stopped eating meat."

"Dreadful times! Why don't you come over this evening, and we'll have a glass of mourning liquid which my cellar-keeper has come up with."

"I'll bet you have black Sidonian beer?"

"The gods forbid that at a time like this we should partake of cheering potions! The liquid my cellar-keeper has come up with isn't beer. I would compare it rather to wine infused with musk and fragrant herbs."

"A very appropriate drink, as our Lord is sojourning in the District of the Dead, over which hang the scents of musk and embalming herbs."

Thus did the dignitaries grieve during the seventy days.

The first throb of joy swept Egypt when word came from the District of the Dead that the Lord's body had been taken out of the natron bath and that the embalmers and priests were performing rites over it.

That day, for the first time, hair was cut, mud was removed from faces, and whoever was so inclined, bathed. There indeed was no longer cause for grief: Horus had discovered Osiris' remains; thanks to the embalmers' art, Egypt's Lord was regaining life; and thanks to the priests' prayers and the *Book of the Dead*, he was becoming equal to the gods.

Henceforth the late Pharaoh Mer-amen-Ramses was officially called Osiris; unofficially, he had been so called immediately upon death.

The innate gaiety of the Egyptian people began taking the upper hand over mourning, especially among the army, the craftsmen, and the peasants. The joy sometimes took unseemly forms among the simple folk.

Thus, rumors of unknown origin began circulating that the new Pharaoh, whom all the populace already loved instinctively, wanted to improve the lives of the peasants, workers, even the slaves.

Consequently (an unheard-of thing!) sometimes masons, carpenters, and potters, instead of drinking quietly and discussing occupational or family matters, ventured in taverns not only to complain about taxes but even to grumble at the power of the priests. And peasants, instead of devoting their time off from work to prayer and the memory of their ancestors, spoke of how good it would be for each peasant to have a little land of his own and be able to rest every seventh day!

No need to mention the army, particularly the foreign regiments. These men fancied themselves the most distinguished class in Egypt; or if they were not, then they soon would be after a successful war which was expected to break out.

On the other hand, the nomarchs, the nobility on their country estates, and especially the high priests of the various temples solemnly mourned the late Lord's passing, even though rejoicing was now in order as the pharaoh had become Osiris.

Strictly speaking, the new Lord had given no one cause for grief, so the reason for the dignitaries' sorrow was only rumors—the same ones which rejoiced the simple folk. The nomarchs and nobility bridled at the thought that their peasant might be idle for fifty days out of the year—or worse, own a bit of land, if only of dimensions sufficient to accommodate a grave. The priests went livid and gritted their teeth, watching Ramses XIII's husbandry and the way he treated them.

Enormous changes had indeed taken place at the royal palace.

The Pharaoh had moved his quarters to one of the wings, where nearly all the rooms were taken by generals. In the basement he had quartered Greek soldiers; on the first floor, the guard; in the rooms along the wall, Ethiopians. Asiatics stood guard around the palace, and quartered next to His Holiness' rooms was the squadron whose men had accompanied the Lord in his desert chase after Tehenna.

Worse still, despite the late revolt by the Libyans, His Holiness had restored them to his favor, had sentenced none of them to punishment and, on the contrary, reposed his trust in them.

The clerical corps remained in the main palace and conducted religious rites under the direction of His Eminence Sem. But since the priests did not accompany the Pharaoh to breakfast, dinner, or supper, their fare became very plain.

In vain did the holy men remonstrate that they must feed the representatives of the nineteen dynasties and the many gods. The treasurer, having gathered the Pharaoh's intent, answered the priests that flowers and fragrances would suffice the gods and ancestors; and that the prophets themselves, in keeping with the tenets of morality, ought to eat barley cakes and drink water or beer. In support of his crass theories, the treasurer cited the example of High Priest Sem, who lived like a penitent; and worse, the treasurer told them that His Holiness and the generals were keeping a soldiers' kitchen.

In view of this, the palace priests began silently wondering whether they would not do better to leave the miserly royal house and move to quarters of their own at the temples, where their duties would be lighter and hunger would not gnaw at their innards.

Perhaps they would have done so, had Their Eminences Herhor and Mephres not ordered them to persevere in place.

But neither could Herhor's situation with the new Lord be called auspicious. The formerly all-powerful Minister who used almost never to leave the royal chambers, now sat alone in his villa and sometimes did not see the new Pharaoh for decades at a time. He was still minister of war, but he hardly ever issued orders. All military matters were handled by the Pharaoh himself. He personally read generals' reports and resolved disputed questions, while his aides fetched needed documents from the ministry of war.

If His Eminence Herhor was summoned by the Lord, it would likely be to receive a dressing-down.

Nevertheless, all the dignitaries allowed that the new Pharaoh worked hard.

Ramses XIII rose before dawn, bathed, and burned incense before the statue of Osiris. Immediately afterward, he heard the reports of the Supreme Judge, the Supreme Scribe of Barns for the whole country, the Supreme Treasurer, and the steward of his palaces. It was the last of these who suffered the most: there was not a day but the Lord told him the court cost too much and contained too many persons.

Indeed, there lived at the royal palace several hundred of the late pharaoh's women, along with commensurate numbers of children and servants. The continually admonished court chief daily expelled a dozen or more persons and reduced the expenses of the rest. In consequence, after a month all the court ladies ran with shouting and weeping to Queen Nikotris' apartment, begging her to help them.

Her Worship immediately went to the Lord, prostrated herself on her face, and asked him to take pity on his father's women and not let them die in want.

The Pharaoh heard her out with furrowed brow and told the court chief not to push the economies further. However, he told Her Worship that after his father's funeral the women would be resettled to rural estates.

"Our court," he said, "costs some thirty thousand talents a year, or half again as much as the entire army. I can't spend such a sum without ruining myself and the Kingdom."

"Do as you like," replied the Queen. "Egypt is yours. However, I fear the expelled court people becoming your enemies."

At this, the Lord silently took his mother's hand, led her to a window, and pointed to a forest of spears drilling in the infantry courtyard.

This act of the Pharaoh's produced an unexpected result. The Queen's eyes, the moment before filled with tears, flashed with pride. Suddenly she bent over and kissed her son's hand, saying in an emotional voice: "You truly are a son of Isis and Osiris; and I did well, giving you to the goddess. At last Egypt has a ruler!"

Henceforth Her Worship never interceded in any matter with her son. When asked for her good offices, she answered:

"I am a servant of His Holiness, and I advise you to carry out the Lord's orders without opposition. Everything he does is inspired of the gods; and who can oppose the gods?"

After breakfast the Pharaoh saw to Ministry of War affairs and fiscal matters; and about three in the afternoon, surrounded by a great suite, he rode out to the troops camped outside Memphis and watched the drills.

The greatest changes had indeed taken place in the Kingdom's military affairs.

In not fully two months, His Holiness had formed five new regiments—or rather, had revived regiments that had been disbanded during the previous reign. He had dismissed officers given to drinking, gambling, or abusing the men.

At the Ministry of War, where previously only priests had worked, he had installed his most capable aides, who very quickly mastered the important documents pertaining to the army. He had ordered a census made of all the Kingdom's military men who for some years had been out of active service and had been engaged in husbandry. He had opened two new officer schools for boys from age twelve, and had revived the neglected practice of military youths receiving breakfast only after completing a three-hour march in ranks and files.

Finally, no army unit was allowed to dwell in villages but had to quarter in barracks or in a camp. Every regiment had a designated drill ground where it cast stones from slings or loosed arrows at targets a hundred to two hundred paces distant.

An order had also gone out to military families for their men to practice casting projectiles under the supervision of regular-army officers and decurions. The order had been carried out immediately, and just two months after Ramses XII's death Egypt looked like an armed camp.

Rural and urban children, who previously had played at scribes and priests, now imitated their elders and played at soldiers. In every square and garden, rocks and arrows whizzed from morning to evening, and law courts were jammed with complaints of bodily injuries.

And it came to pass that Egypt was, as it were, transformed and that, despite mourning, there prevailed great activity, all at the behest of the new Lord.

The Pharaoh himself waxed proud to see the whole Kingdom complying with his royal will.

There came, however, a moment of concern for him.

The same day that the embalmers took Ramses XII's body from the natron bath, the Great Treasurer, presenting a routine report, told the Pharaoh:

"I don't know what to do. We have two thousand talents in the treasury, and at least a thousand will be needed for the funeral of the late Lord."

"How do you mean, two thousand?" said the surprised ruler. "When I took power, you said we had twenty thousand."

"We have spent eighteen."

"In two months?"

"We had enormous expenses."

"True," replied the Pharaoh, "but taxes are coming in every day."

"The taxes," said the Treasurer, "I don't know why, have declined again and are not coming in in the amounts I had calculated. And those, too, have been disbursed. Please bear in mind, Your Holiness, that we have five new regiments. Thus some eight thousand men have left their employs and are living at the Kingdom's expense."

"We must contract a new loan," mused the Pharaoh. "Talk to Herhor and Mephres about a loan from the temples."

"I have. The temples will not give us one."

"The prophets are offended!" smiled the Pharaoh. "In that case, we must call on the pagans. Get me Dagon."

The Phoenician banker came toward evening. He prostrated himself before the Lord and offered him a gold wine cup set with precious stones.

"Now I can die!" cried Dagon, "now that my most gracious Lord has ascended the throne."

"However, before you do," the Pharaoh told the kneeling man, "get me a few thousand talents."

The Phoenician was taken aback, or perhaps only feigned great troublement.

"Your Holiness had better have me seek pearls in the Nile," he replied, "for I will die at once and my Lord will not suspect me of a bad faith. But to find such a sum today!"

Ramses XIII was surprised. "What?" he asked, "the Phoenicians do not have money for me?"

"We will give Your Holiness our life's blood and our children's," said Dagon. "But money? Where shall we get money from?

"The temples used to give us loans at fifteen or twenty percent a year. But ever since Your Holiness, while still successor, visited the Temple of Hathor outside Pi-Bast, the priests have completely been denying us credit.

"If they could, they would today drive us out of Egypt, and still more gladly exterminate us. Ah, what we suffer at their pleasure! The peasants do as they like and when they like. They pay their taxes in dribs and drabs. When one of them is struck, they rise in rebellion, and when a poor Phoenician seeks redress in a court of law, he either loses the case or has to pay an arm and a leg.

"Our hours in this land are numbered!" wept Dagon.

The Pharaoh turned somber. "I'll take care of these matters," he replied, "and the courts will give you justice. But meantime I need about five thousand talents."

"Where will we get them, lord?" moaned Dagon. "Show us the buyers, Your Holiness, and we'll sell them all our portable and real property—anything, to carry out your bidding.

"But where are the buyers? The priests, who will appraise our property at a fraction of its value—and won't pay cash?"

"Send to Tyre, to Sidon," said the Lord. "Each of those cities could lend not merely five thousand but a hundred thousand talents!"

"Tyre and Sidon!" repeated Dagon. "Today all Phoenicia is collecting gold and jewels to pay off the Assyrians. King Assar's envoys are already prowling our country and saying that, so long as we pay a generous ransom each year, the king and satraps not only won't oppress us but will offer us opportunities for profits greater than those we now enjoy by favor of Your Holiness and Egypt."

The Lord turned pale and gritted his teeth. The Phoenician noticed and quickly added:

"But why should I take up Your Holiness' time with my foolish talk? Prince Hiram is here in Memphis. He may explain everything better to my Lord, for he is a sage and a member of the Supreme Council of our cities."

Ramses came alive. "Yes, Dagon, you get me Hiram," he replied, "because you speak to me not like a banker but like a weeping woman at a funeral."

The Phoenician struck the floor with his forehead again and asked: "Could His Eminence Hiram come over right away? It is late ... but he has such a fear of the priests that he would rather pay his respects to Your Holiness at night."

The Pharaoh bit his lip but assented. He sent Thutmose with the banker, to bring Hiram into the palace by the secret entrances.

CHAPTER 55

About ten in the evening, Hiram appeared before the Lord, garbed in the dark robe of a Memphis peddler.

"Why the stealth, Your Eminence?" asked the displeased Pharaoh. "Is my palace a prison or house of lepers?"

"Ah, our ruler!" sighed the old Phoenician. "From the moment you became Lord of Egypt, those are criminals who venture to see you and not relate what you are pleased to speak about."

"To whom must you repeat my words?" asked the Lord.

Hiram raised his eyes and hands. "Your Holiness knows his enemies!" he replied.

"Never mind," said the Pharaoh. "Your Eminence knows why I have called you? I wish to borrow several thousand talents."

Hiram gave a hiss and swayed so badly on his legs that the Lord let him be seated in his presence, which was a signal honor.

Having seated himself comfortably and rested, Hiram said: "Why should Your Holiness borrow when he can have great treasures?"

"I know, when I capture Nineveh," interrupted the Pharaoh. "That is far into the future, while I need the money today."

"I don't mean war," replied Hiram. "I'm speaking of something that will immediately bring the treasury large sums—and a steady annual income."

"How?"

"Give us permission, Holiness, and help us to dig a canal connecting the Mediterranean Sea with the Red Sea."

The Pharaoh sprang up from his armchair.

"Do you jest, old man?" he exclaimed. "Who would carry out such a work, who would want to imperil Egypt? Why, the sea would flood us!"

"Which sea? Certainly not the Red, nor the Mediterranean," replied Hiram calmly. "I know the Egyptian priest-engineers have studied this proposal and have calculated it to be a very good business proposition—the best in the world. Only, they would rather carry it out themselves; or rather, they don't want the pharaoh to."

"Where is your evidence?" asked Ramses.

"I have none, but I'll send Your Holiness a priest who will explain the whole thing with plans and calculations in hand."

"Who is the priest?"

Hiram thought a moment. "Have I Your Holiness' promise that no one apart from us will know about him? He will give your lordship greater services than I myself. He knows many secrets ... and many villainies of the priests."

"I promise," replied the Pharaoh.

"The priest is Samentu. He serves at the Temple of Set outside Memphis. He is very learned, only he needs money and is very ambitious. And since the high priests disparage him, he told me that when Your Holiness decides on it, he will overthrow the priesthood. Because he knows many secrets ... Oh, many!"

Ramses mused. He realized the priest was a great traitor, but he also appreciated the important services the priest could render him.

"Very well," said the Pharaoh, "I'll think about this Samentu. Now, for a moment, let's suppose the canal can be built: what will I have from it?"

Hiram raised his left hand and counted off on the fingers:

"First," he said, "Phoenicia will give Your Holiness five thousand talents of back tribute.

"Second, Phoenicia will pay Your Holiness five thousand talents for the right to carry out the work.

"Thirdly, when the work begins, we'll pay a thousand talents of annual tax and additionally as many talents as Egypt provides us tens of workers.

"Fourthly, for each Egyptian engineer we'll give Your Holiness a talent a year.

"Fifthly, when the work is finished, Your Holiness shall lease us the canal for a hundred years and we'll pay a thousand talents a year for it.

"Are such profits anything to sneeze at?" asked Hiram.

"Right now, today," said the Pharaoh, "would you give me those five thousand in tribute?"

"If the agreement is concluded today, we'll give ten thousand and throw in three thousand as three years' tax in advance."

Ramses XIII fell to thinking. The Phoenicians had more than once proposed to Egypt's rulers the construction of the canal, but had always encountered the adamant opposition of the priests. The Egyptian savants told the pharaohs that the canal would open the Kingdom to inundation by the waters of the Mediterranean and Red Seas.

But Hiram held that such a mishap would not occur, and that the priests knew it!

"You promise," said the Pharaoh after a while, "to pay a thousand talents a year for a hundred years. You say this canal dug through the sands is the best business proposition in the world. I don't understand it; and I'll admit, Hiram, I'm suspicious."

The Phoenician's eyes lit.

"Lord," he replied, "I'll tell you everything, but I beseech you by your crown ... by your father's shade ... not to reveal this secret to anyone. It's the greatest secret of the Chaldean and Egyptian priests, and even of Phoenicia. On it hangs the very future of the world!"

"Now ... Hiram!" smiled the Pharaoh.

"The gods," continued the Phoenician, "have given Your Holiness wisdom, energy, and nobility, so you are one of us. You alone of earthly rulers can be initiated into this, for you alone can carry out great things. You shall acquire such power as no man has yet attained."

The Pharaoh felt an access of pride, but controlled himself.

"Don't praise me," he said, "for what I have not yet done, but tell me what benefits will flow to Phoenicia and to my Kingdom from the digging of the canal."

Hiram adjusted himself in his armchair and spoke in a lowered voice:

"Know, our Lord, that to the east, south, and north of Assyria and Babylon there are neither deserts nor swamps inhabited by strange monsters, but vast, vast lands and kingdoms ... lands so vast that Your Holiness' infantry, famed for its marches, would have to march nearly two years ever eastward to reach their far limits!"

Ramses raised his eyebrows like a person who allows someone to lie but is aware of the lie.

Hiram shrugged slightly and continued:

"East and south of Babylon, by a great sea, live a hundred million people who have powerful kings, priests more learned than Egypt's, ancient books, skilled craftsmen.[1] These peoples not only produce fabrics, furniture, and pottery as beautiful as those of Egypt, but since time immemorial have had underground and surface temples—greater, more magnificent, and richer than Egypt's."

"Go on ... go on!" said the Lord. There was no telling from his facial expression whether he was intrigued by the description or indignant at a lie.

"In these lands there are pearls, precious stones, gold, copper. There are the most extraordinary grains, flowers, and fruits. There are forests where one can wander for months among trees thicker than your temple columns, taller than palms. And the people of those parts are simple and gentle. Were Your Holiness to ship two of your regiments over there, you could win an expanse of land greater than all Egypt, richer than the treasury of the Labyrinth.

"Tomorrow if I may, Your Holiness, I'll send over samples of their fabrics, woods, and bronzes. I'll also send two little bits of their wonderful balms which, when swallowed, open the gates of eternity and allow a person to experience such bliss as is the portion only of the gods."[2]

"Please do send the sample fabrics and manufactures," broke in the Pharaoh. "But never mind the balms! We'll rejoice our fill in eternity and the gods after our death."

"And far, very far to the east of Assyria," said Hiram, "lie still greater lands with some two hundred million population."[3]

"How easily the millions come to you!" smiled the Lord.

Hiram placed his hand over his heart. "I swear," he said, "by the spirits of my ancestors and on my honor that I speak the truth!"

The Pharaoh was impressed by so great an oath. "Go on ... go on," he said.

"These lands," continued the Phoenician, "are very curious. They are inhabited by peoples with slanting eyes and a yellow complexion. These peoples have a ruler who is called the Son of Heaven[4] and governs them through wise men who, however, are not priests and do not have such power as in Egypt.

---

[1] "a hundred million people": India. *(Translator.)*

[2] "balsams which ... open the gates of eternity": opium. *(Translator.)*

[3] "lands with some two hundred million population": China. *(Translator.)*

[4] Son of Heaven: sacred title of the emperors of China, founded on the doctrine of the Mandate of Heaven. The title "Son of Heaven" was created by the ancient Zhou Dynasty to justify their having deposed the Shang Dynasty. The Zhou held that Heaven had revoked its mandate from the Shang and given it to the Zhou in retribution for Shang corruption and misrule. China's emperor (like Egypt's pharaoh) was responsible for the prosperity and security of his people, and could lose his heavenly mandate to rule. The title "Son of Heaven" was later adopted by other East Asian monarchs, including the emperors of Japan and Vietnam, to justify their rule. Japan's emperor, however, was not subject to a heavenly mandate: his right to rule was absolute. *(Translator.)*

"Apart from that, these peoples resemble Egyptians. They revere their deceased ancestors and take great care of their remains. They use a script that resembles your priestly script. But they wear long robes of fabrics entirely unknown in Egypt[5] and sandals that resemble little benches, and they cover their heads with peaked boxes. Likewise the roofs of their buildings are peaked and recurved at the edges.

"These extraordinary peoples have a grain more prolific than Egyptian wheat[6] and make from it a beverage stronger than wine. They also have a plant whose leaves invigorate the limbs, cheer the mind, and even allow a person to go without sleep.[7] They have a paper which they adorn with varicolored pictures, and a clay which, on firing, becomes translucent like glass and rings like metal.[8]

"Tomorrow, if Your Holiness permits, I'll send over sample handiworks of this people."

"You tell of wonders, Hiram," said the Pharaoh. "But I don't see the connection between these curiosities and the canal you wish to dig."

"I'll be brief," replied the Phoenician. "When the canal is operative, the whole Phoenician and Egyptian fleet will sail into the Red Sea and on from there—and in a couple of months it will reach these wealthy countries which are virtually unreachable by land.

"Can't Your Holiness," he said, his eyes ashine, "see the treasures we'll find there? The gold, gems, grains, woods? I swear to you, Lord," he went on ecstatically, "gold will come to you more easily than copper today, wood will be cheaper than straw—and a slave, cheaper than a cow.

"Only let us dig the canal, Lord, and lend us fifty thousand of your soldiers."

Ramses took fire. "Fifty thousand men," he repeated. "How much will you give me for them?"

"As I told Your Holiness ... A thousand talents a year for the right to the work, and five thousand for the workers, whom we ourselves will feed and pay."

"And you'll work them to death?"

"The gods forbid!" exclaimed Hiram. "There's no profit in killing off the workers! Your Holiness' soldiers will work no harder at the canal than they now do at fortifications and highways. And what glory for Your Lordship! ... What revenues for the treasury! ... What profits for Egypt! The poorest peasant will be able to have a wooden hut, several cattle, furniture, and maybe a slave. No pharaoh has raised the Kingdom to such heights or carried out so immense a work.

"What will the dead, useless pyramids be, next to a canal that will transport the treasures of the entire world?"

"Yes," added the Pharaoh, "and fifty thousand troops on the eastern border."

"Of course!" cried Hiram. "Against such strength, whose maintenance will cost Your Holiness nothing, Assyria won't dare reach for Phoenicia."

The plan was so dazzling, so promising of benefits, that it made Ramses XIII giddy. But he controlled himself.

"Hiram," he said, "you make beautiful promises. So beautiful, that I fear lest they con-

[5] "fabrics ... unknown in Egypt": silk. *(Translator.)*

[6] "a grain more prolific than Egyptian wheat": rice. *(Translator.)*

[7] "a plant whose leaves invigorate ...": tea. *(Translator.)*

[8] "a clay which, on firing, becomes translucent like glass ...": porcelain. *(Translator.)*

ceal some untoward consequences. Therefore I'll have to give careful thought to this—and consult the priests."

"They'll never willingly agree!" cried the Phoenician. "Though ... (may the gods forgive me the blasphemy!) ... I'm certain that if supreme power in the Kingdom were to pass into the hands of the priests, in a couple of months they would be calling us in to do the work."[9]

Ramses eyed him with cool contempt.

"Old man," he said, "you let me worry about the obedience of the priests, and you give me proof that what you've said is true. I'd make a very sorry king if I couldn't remove obstacles arising between my will and the interests of the Kingdom."

"Our Lord, you are indeed a great ruler," whispered Hiram, bowing to the floor.

It was now late at night. The Phoenician took his leave of the Pharaoh and departed the palace with Thutmose. Next day Hiram sent over Dagon with a small chest containing sample riches from the exotic lands.

In it the Lord found Indian fabrics, rings, statuettes of gods, and small bits of opium;[10] and in a second compartment, a handful of rice, tea leaves, a couple of porcelain bowls decorated with painting, and a dozen drawings executed on paper in paints and India ink.[11]

He examined these things closely and owned that they were unfamiliar to him: the rice, the paper, the images of people with peaked hats and slanting eyes.

He no longer doubted the existence of a new land where everything was different than in Egypt: mountains, trees, buildings, bridges, ships.

"This land doubtless exists since time immemorial," he thought, "and our priests know about it, know its riches, but say nothing about them. Obviously they're traitors who want to reduce the power and wealth of the pharaohs, in order next to dethrone them.

"But ... O my forbears and successors!" he thought. "Bear witness that I'll put an end to these villainies. I'll promote learning, but I'll root out mendacity and give Egypt respites."

Reflecting thus, the Lord raised his eyes and saw Dagon awaiting instructions.

"Your chest is very interesting," he told the banker, "but this isn't what I wanted from you."

The Phoenician approached on his toes, knelt before the Pharaoh, and whispered: "When Your Holiness is pleased to sign an agreement with His Eminence Hiram, Tyre and Sidon will lay all their treasures at your feet."

Ramses frowned. He resented the Phoenicians' audacity in setting him conditions. He replied coolly:

"I'll think about it and give Hiram an answer. You may go, Dagon."

---

[9] There had actually been an ancient *east-west* "Suez Canal," connecting the Nile River with the Red Sea, as early as the Middle Kingdom, eight centuries before *Pharaoh*'s present time. It is alluded to it in Chapter 1, in the mention of an existing "canal from Memphis to Lake Timsah" (Lake Timsah then being the northern terminus of the Red Sea). The canal, after repeatedly falling into disrepair and being re-excavated, was finally closed in the 8th century CE. *(Translator.)*

[10] Actually, opium had been known much earlier in Egypt and other parts of the ancient world. It is mentioned in the Ebers Medical Papyrus, written in Egypt ca. 1550 BCE, nearly five centuries before *Pharaoh*'s present time. *(Translator.)*

[11] India ink (in Polish, *tusz*): an ink composed of lampblack and water, invented in China as early as the mid-3rd millennium BCE. The English term "India ink" was coined later due to trade with India. *(Translator.)*

After the Phoenician's departure, Ramses again fell to thinking. In his mind, a reaction was setting in.

"These hucksters," he thought, "consider me one of their own. They have the temerity to dangle a bag of gold before me to extort a treaty! I don't know that any pharaoh has ever countenanced such familiarity from them.

"I must change this. People who prostrate themselves before Assar's envoys, can't say to me: sign this, and you'll get that. The stupid Phoenician rats, having stolen into the royal palace, now consider it their private little pigsty!"

The longer he thought, and the more exactly he recalled the behavior of Hiram and Dagon, the angrier he became. "How dare they! How dare they set me conditions!"

"Hey! ... Thutmose!" he cried.

The favorite promptly appeared.

"What is your pleasure, my lord?"

"Send a junior officer to inform Dagon that he's no longer my banker. He's too stupid for so high a station."

"On whom will Your Holiness bestow the honor?"

"Right now I don't know. We must seek out an Egyptian or Greek merchant. If need be, we'll make recourse to the priests."

News of this swept all the royal palaces and, before an hour was out, had reached Memphis. Throughout the city it was said the Phoenicians had lost favor with the Pharaoh, and by evening the populace had begun breaking into the shops of the hated foreigners.

The priests breathed a sigh of relief. Herhor paid a visit to the holy Mephres and told him: "My heart felt our Lord would turn away from these pagans who drink the people's blood. I think we ought to show him our gratitude."

"And maybe open the doors to our treasuries?" asked the holy Mephres brusquely. "Don't be in such a hurry, Eminence. I've now got this youngster figured out—and woe betide us if we once let him get the upper hand over us."

"What if he were to break with the Phoenicians?"

"Then he will himself gain by it, because he won't repay his debts to them," said Mephres.

"In my opinion," said Herhor after taking thought, "this is a moment when we can regain the favor of the young Pharaoh. Though impetuous in anger, he is nevertheless capable of gratitude ... I have experienced it."

"Every word, a mistake!" broke in Mephres doggedly. "First, this prince is not yet pharaoh, because he hasn't been crowned in a temple. Second—he never will be a true pharaoh, because he spurns ordination as a high priest.

"Finally. it is not we who need his favor, but he needs the favor of the gods, whom he offends at every step!"

Breathless with anger, Mephres paused, then continued:

"He spent a month at the Temple of Hathor, listening to the utmost in wisdom, and soon thereafter took up with the Phoenicians. Why, he made visits to the Temple of Astarte and took from there a priestess, which flies in the face of all religious principles.

"Then he publicly mocked my piety ... conspired with frivolers like himself, and stole state secrets with Phoenician help. And when he had ascended the throne ... nay, he has barely ascended the first steps to the throne, and already he disparages the priests, incites the peasants and soldiers, and renews his vows with his friends the Phoenicians.

"Have you forgotten all this, Herhor? And if not, then don't you see the threats that this youngster poses to us? He holds in his hand the tiller of the ship of state, which is moving between whirlpools and rocks. Who can assure me that this madman—who yesterday called in the Phoenicians, and today has quarreled with them—won't do something tomorrow to put the Kingdom in peril?"

"And ... so?" asked Herhor, looking him squarely in the eye.

"And so we have no reason to show him gratitude, which in reality would be weakness. And since he desperately wants money, we won't give him any!"

"And then what?" asked Herhor.

"Then he will rule the Kingdom and build up the army without money," said the irritated Mephres.

"And ... if his hungry army decides to plunder the temples?" asked Herhor.

"Ha! ... ha! ... ha!" Mephres burst out laughing.

Suddenly he turned serious, bowed, and said in an ironic tone: "That is Your Eminence's province. A man who has governed the Kingdom for as many years as you have, should have prepared for such a threat."

"Let's suppose," said Herhor slowly, "let's suppose I found ways to counter threats to the Kingdom. Can Your Eminence, as senior high priest, prevent desecration of the priesthood and temples?"

For a moment they looked one another in the eye.

"You ask, can I?" said Mephres. "Can I? The gods have placed in my hands a lightning bolt that will destroy any sacrilegious person."

"Hist!" whispered Herhor. "So be it ..."

"With or without the assent of the Supreme Priestly Council," added Mephres. "When the boat is capsizing, it's no time for discussions with the oarsmen."

They parted, somber. That same day in the evening, they were summoned by the Pharaoh.

They came at the appointed time, separately. They bowed deeply to the Lord—and each stepped to a different corner, without looking at the other high priest.

"Can they have quarreled?" thought Ramses. "No harm in that."

A moment later the holy Sem and the prophet Pentuer entered. Ramses seated himself on the dais, indicated low stools for the four priests, and said:

"Holy fathers! Until now I've not summoned you for consultation, as all my orders have dealt exclusively with military affairs."

"That is Your Holiness' prerogative," interjected Herhor.

"I've also done what I could in so short a time to strengthen the Kingdom's defensive forces. I've created two new officer schools and revived five disbanded regiments."

"That is your prerogative, Lord," said Mephres.

"I do not speak of other military improvements, as these things do not concern you holy men."

"That's correct, Lord," said Mephres and Herhor in unison.

"But there is another matter," said the Pharaoh, pleased with the assent of the two dignitaries, from whom he had expected dissent. "The day of my divine father's funeral approaches, and the treasury lacks sufficient funds."

Mephres rose from his stool.

"Osiris-Mer-amen-Ramses," he said, "was a just Lord who ensured many years of peace to his people and reflected glory upon the gods. We hope, therefore, that Your Holiness will permit the funeral of this pious pharaoh to take place at the expense of the temples."

Ramses XIII was surprised and moved by this homage to his father. For a moment he was silent, as though unable to find a response; at length he replied:

"I'm very grateful to you for the reverence shown to my father equal to the gods. I grant permission for such a funeral—and once again, I thank you very much."

He paused, rested his head in his hand, and pondered as though waging a struggle with himself. Suddenly he raised his head: his face was animated, his eyes shone.

"Holy fathers," he said, "I am touched by this evidence of your goodwill. If my father's memory is so dear to you, I daresay you cannot be ill-disposed to me."

"Has Your Holiness any doubt of that?" broke in High Priest Sem.

"You're right," continued the Pharaoh, "I was wrong to think you biased against me. I would repair that, so I shall be frank with you."

"May the gods bless Your Holiness!" said Herhor.

"I shall be frank. My divine father, due to age, illness, and perhaps his priestly duties, was not able to devote as much energy and time to affairs of state as I am. I am young, healthy, and free, and it is my intent to govern on my own. As a commander must lead his army on his own responsibility and in accordance with his own plan, so I shall govern the Kingdom. That is my firm resolve, from which I will not depart.

"But I realize that, though I were surpassingly experienced, I cannot do without faithful servants and wise advisors. Therefore from time to time I shall seek your opinions on various matters."

"That is our function as Supreme Council to Your Holiness' throne," interjected Herhor.

"Yes," said the Pharaoh, becoming animated, "I shall avail myself of your services, even from this moment."

"We are at your command, Lord," said Herhor.

"I wish to improve the lives of the Egyptian people. But since, in such matters, over-hasty action can only be detrimental, to begin with I am offering them a small thing: following six days of work, a seventh day of rest."

"It was thus through the reigns of eighteen dynasties. This law is as old as Egypt itself," said Pentuer.

"Rest every seventh day will give each worker fifty days a year, and so will take fifty drachmas from his master. On a million workers, the Kingdom will lose ten thousand talents a year," said Mephres. "We've calculated it at the temples!" he added.

"Yes," said Pentuer quickly, "there will be losses, but only the first year. Once the people have gained strength through days of rest, in subsequent years they will more than make up the losses."

"That is true," answered Mephres, "but in any event ten thousand talents would be needed for that first year. And I think twenty thousand would not be amiss."

"Your Eminence is right," responded the Pharaoh. "In connection with the changes that I want to make in my Kingdom, twenty or even thirty thousand talents will not be an excessive sum.

"That," he added quickly, "is why I will be needing the help of you holy men."

"We are prepared to support Your Holiness' every intention with prayers and processions," said Mephres.

"Yes, pray, and encourage the people to do so. But in addition give the Kingdom thirty thousand talents," answered the Pharaoh.

The high priests said nothing.

The Lord waited a moment and finally turned to Herhor: "Your Eminence is silent?"

"You said yourself, our Lord, that the treasury hasn't funds even for the funeral of Osiris-Mer-amen-Ramses. So I cannot guess where we would get thirty thousand talents from."

"What about the treasury in the Labyrinth?"

"Those are treasures of the gods and can be touched only in a moment of the Kingdom's greatest need," replied Mephres.

Ramses XIII boiled up in anger. "If the peasants don't need this sum," he cried, striking his armrest with his fist, "then I do!"

"Your Holiness," replied Mephres, "can gain more than thirty thousand talents within a year, and Egypt twice that much."

"How?"

"Very simple, Lord," said Mephres. "Order the Phoenicians expelled from the Kingdom."

It seemed the Lord would hurl himself at the audacious high priest: he turned pale, his lips quivered, and his eyes bulged in their orbits. But he instantly got a grip on himself and said in a remarkably calm tone:

"Very well. If that's the only kind of advice you can give me, I'll do without it. The Phoenicians have our signatures guaranteeing that we will faithfully repay our contracted debts! Did that not occur to you, Mephres?"

"Forgive me, Your Holiness, but just now I was preoccupied with other thoughts. Your Lordship's forbears wrote not on papyri but on bronze and stone that the gifts made by them to the gods and temples belonged, and would in perpetuity belong, to the gods and temples."

"And to you," said the Pharaoh sarcastically.

"As much to us, Lord," replied the audacious high priest, "as the Kingdom belongs to you. We guard and multiply the treasures, but have no right to squander them."

Panting with anger, the Lord left the meeting and repaired to his cabinet. His situation presented itself to him with cruel clarity.

He now had no doubt about the priests' hatred for him. They were the same overweening dignitaries who the previous year had withheld the Menfi Corps from him and had made him viceroy only when it seemed to them he had performed an act of humility in quitting the palace. The same dignitaries who had watched his every move, had reported on him, but had not even told him, the Successor, about the treaty with Assyria. The same who had deceived him at the Temple of Hathor, and at the Natron Lakes had killed the prisoners to whom he had promised pardon.

The Pharaoh recalled Herhor's bows, Mephres' looks, and the tones of voice of both. From beneath their pretenses of courtesy kept emerging their arrogance and contempt for him. He needed money, they promised him prayers. They had the temerity to say he was not the sole ruler of Egypt!

Involuntarily the young Lord smiled: he had bethought himself of hired herdsmen telling the flock's owner that he could not do with it as he liked!

But apart from the humorous aspect, there was a dangerous one. The treasury held perhaps a thousand talents, which at current rates of expenditure might suffice for seven to ten days. And then what? How would the officials, the servants, above all the army, behave—not only unpaid but actually hungry?

The high priests knew the Pharaoh's situation; and if they were not coming to his aid, they meant to destroy him. To destroy him within a few days, even before his father's funeral.

Ramses recalled a childhood incident.

He was at priest school when, on the holiday of the goddess Mut, as one of the entertainments, Egypt's most famous clown was brought in.

The artist played an ill-starred hero. When he issued orders, no one listened; his anger was answered with laughter; and when he grabbed an ax to chastise his mockers, the ax broke in his hands.

Finally a lion was set loose on him; and when the defenseless hero fled, it transpired that he was being chased not by a lion but by a pig in lion skin.

The pupils and teachers had laughed themselves to tears at these adventures; but the little Prince had sat glum: he felt sorry for the man who aspired to great things but fell covered in ridicule.

That scene, and the feelings he had experienced then, revived today in the Pharaoh's memory. "That's what they want to make me into!" he told himself.

He was overcome with despair, because he felt that with the expending of the last talent his power would come to an end, and with it his life.

But here there came a sudden turnabout. The Lord stopped in the middle of the room and pondered.

"What's the worst that can meet me? ... Death ... I'll depart to my glorious forbears, to Ramses the Great. And I can't tell them I perished without defending myself. After the misfortunes of earthly life, I'd meet with eternal disgrace."

Was he, the victor of the Natron Lakes, to give in to a handful of humbugs whom a single Asiatic regiment would make short work of? Just because Mephres and Herhor wanted to rule Egypt and the pharaoh, was his army to suffer hunger, and a million peasants to be denied the benefit of rest?

Had not his forbears erected the temples? Hadn't they filled the temples with spoils? And who had won the battles: the priests or the soldiers? Then who was entitled to the treasures: the priests, or the pharaoh and his army?

The young Lord shrugged and called Thutmose. Despite the late night, the royal favorite appeared at once.

"You know?" said the Pharaoh, "the priests have refused me a loan, though the treasury is empty."

Thutmose straightened up. "Will Your Holiness have me take them to jail?" he replied.

"You would do that?"

"There's not an officer in Egypt who would hesitate to carry out an order from our Lord and commander."

"In that case," said the Pharaoh slowly, "in that case ... there's no need to jail anyone. I have too much power for myself, and too much contempt for them. When you come upon a carcass on the highway, you don't lock it in a chest, you go around it."

"But you do cage a hyena," whispered Thutmose.

"It's too soon," said Ramses. "I must be forbearing with these people at least until my father's funeral. Otherwise they're liable to do something nefarious to his venerable mummy and disturb the peace of his soul. Now, tomorrow I want you to see Hiram and tell him to send me the priest we spoke of."

"Very good. However, I must tell Your Holiness that today the populace attacked the houses of Memphis Phoenicians."

"Oh? ... That was uncalled-for."

"I also have the impression," continued Thutmose, "that, ever since Your Holiness told Pentuer to study the situation of the peasants and workers, the priests have been stirring up the nomarchs and nobility. They're saying Your Lordship wants to ruin the nobility for the sake of the peasants."

"Do the nobility believe it?"

"Some do. But others say straight-out that this is an intrigue of the priests against Your Holiness."

"What if I actually did want to improve the lives of the peasants?" asked the Pharaoh.

"Your Lordship will do as he pleases," replied Thutmose.

"Now, that's the kind of answer I like!" cried Ramses XIII merrily. "Don't worry, and tell the nobility that not only will they lose nothing by carrying out my orders, but their lives and standing will improve. Egypt's riches must be wrested from unworthy hands and given to faithful servants."

The Pharaoh bade his favorite a good night and, contented, retired to sleep. His momentary desperation now seemed to him laughable.

Next day, about noon, His Holiness was informed of the arrival of a delegation of Phoenician merchants.

"Do they want to complain about the attacks on their houses?" asked the Pharaoh.

"No," replied the aide, "they wish to pay homage."

A dozen or so Phoenicians, headed by Rabsun, had come with gifts. When the Lord appeared, they prostrated themselves; then Rabsun declared that, in accordance with old custom, they were venturing to lay a wretched offering at the feet of the Lord who bestowed life on them and security on their fortunes.

They placed, on tables, gold bowls, chains, and winecups filled with gems. And Rabsun set, on the steps to the throne, a tray with a papyrus wherein the Phoenicians pledged to provide the army with two thousand talents' worth of any needful things.

This was a substantial gift: the total value of the Phoenicians' offering came to three thousand talents.

The Lord responded to the loyal merchants very graciously, promising them his protection. They took their leave, gratified.

Ramses XIII breathed easier: the treasury's bankruptcy, and thus the need to use force against the priests, had been deferred by another ten days.

In the evening, again escorted by Thutmose, His Eminence Hiram appeared in His Holiness' cabinet. This time he did not complain of fatigue but prostrated himself on his face and plaintively cursed the stupid Dagon.

"I've learned," he said, "that this Jew dared remind Your Holiness of our agreement concerning the canal to the Red Sea. May he waste away! ... May leprosy consume him! ... May his children become swineherds—and his grandchildren, Jews!"

"Just give the word, Lord, and Phoenicia will lay all her wealth at your feet without any receipt or treaty. Are we Assyrians ... or priests," he added in a whisper, "that one word from so powerful a ruler should not suffice us?"

"Hiram, what if I really did request a great sum?" asked the Pharaoh.

"How great?"

"Say ... thirty thousand talents."

"Immediately?"

"No, over a year's time."

"Your Holiness shall have it," answered Hiram without taking thought.

The Lord was impressed by this generosity. "Well, but I must give you security."

"As a matter of form," said the Phoenician, "Your Holiness will give us the mines as security, in order not to rouse the suspicions of the priests. Except for that, Phoenicia would deliver all of herself to you without securities or receipts."

"What about the canal? Am I to sign a treaty right away?" asked the Pharaoh.

"Not at all. Your Holiness will make a treaty with us when it suits you."

Ramses felt uplifted. For the first time, he was tasting the sweetness of royal power—thanks to the Phoenicians!

"Hiram!" he said, no longer holding himself in check. "Today I am giving you Phoenicians permission to build a canal to join the Mediterranean Sea with the Red."

The old man fell to the Pharaoh's feet. "You are the greatest king the earth has seen!" he cried.

"For the time being, you mustn't speak of this to anyone, because the enemies of my glory are vigilant. But as surety I'm giving you this my royal ring."

He took from his finger a ring adorned with a magical stone and engraved with the name of Horus, and placed it on the Phoenician's finger.

"The wealth of all Phoenicia is at your command!" repeated Hiram, deeply moved. "Your Lordship will carry out a work that will proclaim your name until the sun goes out."

The Pharaoh hugged his gray head and bade him be seated.

"So we are allies," said the Lord after a moment, "and I hope this will redound to the benefit of both Egypt and Phoenicia!"

"Of the whole world!" broke in Hiram.

"Tell me, though, Prince, what gives you such faith in me?"

"I know Your Holiness' noble character. Were Your Lordship not pharaoh, in a few years' time you would become the foremost Phoenician merchant and the head of our council ..."

"Let's suppose," said Ramses. "But if I'm to keep my promises to you, I must first crush the priests. That is a battle, and the outcome of a battle is a chancy thing."

Hiram smiled. "Lord," he said, "were we so base as to abandon you today, when your treasury is empty and your enemies are haughty, you would lose the battle. A man without resources easily loses courage, and a destitute king's army, subjects, and dignitaries turn away from him.

"But if Your Lordship has our gold and our agents, and your army and generals, then you will have as much trouble with the priests as an elephant has with a scorpion. You have but to set your foot on them, and they shall be crushed.

"However, that is not my province. In the garden awaits High Priest Samentu, whom Your Holiness has summoned. I take my leave; now is his time. But my pledge of money remains, and Your Holiness may demand up to thirty thousand talents."

Hiram prostrated himself again on his face and left, promising to send Samentu in at once.

Half an hour later, the high priest appeared. His red beard and shaggy hair were unshaven, as befitted a worshipper of Set; his face was rugged, but his eyes bespoke sagacity. He bowed without excessive humility and calmly withstood the Pharaoh's soul-probing gaze.

"Have a seat," said the Lord.

The high priest sat down on the floor.

"I like you," said Ramses. "You have the bearing and features of a Hyksos, and they are the most valiant soldiers in my army."

Suddenly he asked: "You told Hiram about our priests' treaty with the Assyrians?"

"Yes," replied Samentu, returning Ramses' gaze.

"Were you a party to that infamy?"

"No. I listened in to the discussion. In the temples, as in Your Holiness' palaces, the walls contain channels through which one can hear even at the pylon tops what is spoken in the basement."

"And from the basement speak to persons dwelling in the rooms above?" broke in the Pharaoh.

"And feign advice from the gods," added the priest gravely.

The Pharaoh smiled. So the surmise that it had not been his father's spirit speaking to him and his mother, but the priests, was correct!

"Why did you confide a great secret of state to the Phoenicians?" asked Ramses.

"I wanted to prevent a shameful treaty detrimental to both us and Phoenicia."

"You could have alerted one of the eminent Egyptians."

"Which?" asked the priest. "One of those who were helpless against Herhor, or one of those who would have denounced me to him and exposed me to death by torture? I told Hiram because he was in touch with our dignitaries, whom I never see."

"Why did Herhor and Mephres make such an agreement?" probed the Pharaoh.

"In my judgment, they are weak-headed men who were intimidated by Berossus, the great Chaldean priest. He told them that for ten years ill fortune would impend over Egypt; and if, during that time, we began a war with Assyria, we would be beaten."

"And they believed it?"

"Apparently Berossus showed them miracles. He even ascended into the air. That doubtless is remarkable; but I will never understand why we should lose Phoenicia because Berossus can fly."

"Then you don't believe in miracles either?"

"It depends," said Samentu. "Berossus seems actually to do extraordinary things—but our priests only deceive the people and the rulers."

"You hate the priesthood?"

Samentu spread his hands. "They despise me too, and what is worse, they ill-use me, ostensibly because I serve Set. But what sort of gods are they whose heads and arms must be moved with strings? And what sort of priests are they who affect piety and temperance but each keep ten women, spend a dozen talents a year, steal offerings deposited on the altars, and are little more learned than students in the upper schools?"

"But you take donations from the Phoenicians?"

"From whom should I take them? Only the Phoenicians truly revere Set, and fear lest he sink their ships. In Egypt only paupers venerate him. Were I to content myself with their offerings, my children and I would starve to death."

The Pharaoh reflected that the priest was not a bad man, if he did betray temple secrets. Furthermore, he seemed knowledgeable and truthful.

"Have you heard anything," asked the Lord, "about a canal to join the Mediterranean Sea with the Red?"

"I'm familiar with the matter. Our engineers have had this project worked up for several hundred years."

"Why hasn't it been carried out until now?"

"Because the priests fear an influx into Egypt of foreign peoples who could undermine our religion, and with it their incomes."

"Is it true, what Hiram says about the peoples living in the far east?"

"Absolutely. We've long known about them, and not ten years go by but we receive a gem, a drawing, or a handiwork from those lands."

The Pharaoh pondered again and suddenly asked: "Will you serve me faithfully, if I make you my advisor?"

"I'll serve Your Holiness to the death. But if I became advisor to the throne, it would anger the priests who hate me."

"Don't you think they can be overthrown?"

"And very easily!" said Samentu.

"What would be your plan if I had to get rid of them?"

"The treasury of the Labyrinth must be secured," said the priest.

"Could you get to it?"

"I have many clews[12]—I'll find the rest, because I know where to look."

"What else?" asked the Pharaoh.

"Herhor and Mephres should be brought up on charges of treason for maintaining secret relations with Assyria."

"What about proof?"

"We'll find it with the help of the Phoenicians," said the priest.

"Might this not put Egypt in danger?"

"Not at all. Four hundred years ago, Pharaoh Amenhotep IV[13] overthrew the power of the priests by establishing the single god Re-Harakhti.[14] Naturally, he took the occasion to strip the other gods' temples of their treasures. Neither the populace nor the army or the nobility took the part of the priests. Today the old faith is much weaker!"

---

[12] Clew (also written *clue*): something that leads one out of a maze, perplexity, etc., or helps solve a problem. This meaning of the word "clew" (which originally meant "a ball or skein of thread or yarn") relates to the Greek myth of Theseus, who used a ball of thread, provided by a smitten Ariadne, to guide him through the Cretan Labyrinth, where Theseus slew the fearsome Minotaur. *(Translator.)*

[13] Amenhotep IV: 18th-Dynasty pharaoh who ruled for 17 years until ca. 1336 BCE, and for a time officially replaced Egypt's polytheism with a single solar deity, the Aten. In the Aten's honor, Amenhotep (whose name meant "Amon is pleased") changed his name to Akhenaten ("Effective for Aten"). He began his reign as Amenhotep IV some 280 years—not 400 years, as Samentu says—before *Pharaoh*'s present time. *(Translator.)*

[14] Re-Harakhti: a sun god whose name means "Re [who is] Horus of the Horizons." Prus calls him *Re Harmachis*. Actually (see previous note about Amenhotep IV) the solar deity that Akhenaten established was not Re-Harakhti but the Aten. *(Translator.)*

"Who was it helped Amenhotep?" asked the Pharaoh.

"The simple priest Ay."[15]

"Who, on the death of Amenhotep IV, succeeded to the throne," said Ramses, looking the priest in the eye.

Samentu answered calmly: "Which shows that Amenhotep was an inept ruler who cared more for the glory of Re than for the Kingdom."

"You truly are a sage!" said Ramses.

"At Your Holiness' service."

"I'm naming you my advisor," said the Pharaoh. "But in that case you cannot visit me in secret but shall take up residence with me."

"Forgive me, Lord, but until the members of the Supreme Council are in jail for treating with enemies of the Kingdom, my presence at the palace would bring more harm than good.

"Therefore I'll serve and advise Your Holiness—in secret."

"And you'll find the way to the treasury in the Labyrinth?"

"I hope to succeed before Your Lordship returns from Thebes.

"And when we've transferred the treasure to your palace, and when the courts have condemned Herhor and Mephres—whom Your Holiness may later pardon—then by your leave I'll come out into the open. And I'll cease being a priest of Set, who only frightens people away from me."

"You think all will go well?"

"I'm staking my life on it!" exclaimed the priest. "The populace love Your Holiness, so it will be easy to stir them up against the treasonous dignitaries. The army is obedient to you as to no pharaoh since Ramses the Great. So who can oppose you? Furthermore, Your Holiness has the backing of the Phoenicians and of money, the greatest force in the world!"

As Samentu was taking his leave of the Pharaoh, the Lord permitted him to kiss his feet and gave him a heavy gold chain and a bracelet studded with sapphires.

Not every dignitary received such tokens of favor after many years of service.

Samentu's visit and promises filled the Pharaoh's heart with renewed hope.

If only the treasures in the Labyrinth could be secured! A small part of them could free the nobility of their Phoenician debts, improve the lives of the peasants, and redeem the pledged court estates.

And with what structures the Kingdom would be enriched ...

Yes, the funds in the Labyrinth could solve all the Pharaoh's problems. For, what if the Phoenicians were offering him a great loan? A loan must be repaid, with interest, and sooner or later the rest of the royal estates would have to be pledged. So it was only a postponement, not a prevention, of ruin.

---

[15] Ay (whom Prus calls *Ey*) had been a close advisor to a couple of pharaohs. Ay succeeded Akhenaten's son and heir, Tutankhamun ("Living Image of Amun")—not, as Prus has it, Akhenaten himself. *(Translator.)*

CHAPTER 56

n mid-Phamenoth (January[1]) spring began. All of Egypt was green with wheat shoots, and squads of peasants swarmed the patchy black land, sowing lupine, broad beans, beans, and barley. The fragrance of orange blossoms wafted in the air. The water had fallen substantially and daily revealed new stretches of soil.

The preparations for the funeral of Osiris-Mer-amen-Ramses were complete.

The king's venerable mummy was encased in a white casket whose top replicated perfectly the features of the deceased. The pharaoh seemed to gaze with enameled eyes, and his divine face expressed a mild sorrow—not a longing for the world that he had quitted, but a sorrow for those still condemned to the afflictions of earthly life.

On its head the pharaoh's likeness had an Egyptian cap in white and sapphire stripes; on its neck, strings of gems; on the chest, an image of a kneeling man with outstretched arms; on the legs, images of gods, sacred birds, and eyes set in no face but seemingly gazing out from space.

Thus packaged, the king's remains reposed on a sumptuous bed in a small cedar chapel whose walls were covered with inscriptions extolling the life and deeds of the deceased. Over the remains there hovered a wonderful hawk with a human head; and a priest in the guise of jackal-headed Anubis,[2] god of the funeral, watched day and night at the bedside.

In addition, a heavy basalt sarcophagus had been prepared, which constituted the mummy's outer coffin. The sarcophagus likewise had the form and features of the late pharaoh, and was covered with inscriptions and images of praying people, sacred birds, and scarabs.

On the seventeenth of Phamenoth the mummy, together with its chapel and sarcophagus, was transferred from the District of the Dead to the royal palace and set up in the great hall.

The hall soon filled with priests chanting funerary hymns, courtiers and servants of the late king, and above all his women, who wailed so loudly that their cries could be heard on the other side of the Nile.

"Oh, Lord! ... Oh, our Lord!" they called, "why do you leave us? You so beautiful, so good? Who so gladly spoke with us, now are silent, and why? You liked our company, and today you are so far from us?"

---

[1] Actually, Phamenoth lies between March 10 and April 8 of the modern (Gregorian) calendar. *(Translator.)*

[2] jackal-headed Anubis: Please see the Chapter 53 note about Anubis; he appears actually to have been a wolf-headed god. *(Translator.)*

Meanwhile the priests chanted:

Choir I. "I am Atum, who alone is ..."

Choir II. "I am Re in his first splendor ..."

Choir I. "I am the god who creates himself ..."

Choir II. "Who names himself, and none can hinder him among the gods ..."

Choir I. "I know the name of a great god who is there ..."

Choir II. "For I am the great Bennu bird[3] that tests what is."[4]

After two days of wailing and services, a great boat-shaped wagon drew up before the palace. The boat's ends were adorned with sheep's heads and ostrich-feather fans, and over the sumptuous canopy there rose an eagle and a uraeus snake, symbol of pharaonic power.

The holy mummy was placed in the wagon despite the vehement opposition of the court women. Some of them clung to the coffin, others besought the priests not to take away their good Lord, still others scratched their faces, pulled their hair, and even punched the men carrying the remains.

The uproar was deafening.

Finally the wagon, having received the divine body, moved out through the crowd that filled the enormous space between the palace and the Nile. Here, too, were people daubed with mud, scratched-up, covered in mourning cloths, wailing at the tops of their lungs. And in accord with mourning ritual, at intervals choirs lined the entire way.

Choir I. "To the West, to the abode of Osiris, to the West goest Thou who wert the best of men, who despised falsehood."

Choir II. "To the West! nevermore will there blossom a man who so loved truth and detested falsehood."

Choir of oxdrivers. "To the West, oxen that draw the funerary wagon, to the West! Your Lord follows after you."

Choir III. "To the West, to the West, to the land of the just. The place Thou hast loved, wails and weeps for Thee."

Populace. "Go in peace to Abydos! ... Go in peace to Abydos! ... Mayst Thou reach the Theban West in peace!"

Choir of weeping women. "O our Lord, O our Lord, when Thou departest for the West, the very gods do weep."

Choir of priests. "He is happy, the most esteemed of men, for fate lets him rest in the tomb He himself prepared."

Choir of oxdrivers. "To the West, oxen that draw the funerary wagon, to the West! Your Lord follows after you ..."

Populace. "Go in peace to Abydos ... Go in peace to Abydos, to the Western Sea!"[5]

---

[3] Bennu bird: a self-created deity associated with the sun, creation, and rebirth. The Bennu bird was said to have flown over the waters of Nun that existed before creation, landing on a rock and issuing a call that determined the nature of creation. The Bennu was also a symbol of rebirth and was therefore associated with Osiris. New Kingdom artwork shows the Bennu as a gray heron, with a long beak and a two-feathered crest, sometimes perched on a benben stone (representing the god Ra) or in a willow (representing the god Osiris). The Bennu may have inspired the phoenix of Greek mythology. *(Translator.)*

[4] *Book of the Dead. (Author.)*

[5] Authentic expressions. *(Author.)*

Every couple of hundred paces there stood an army detachment that greeted the Lord with a muffled drum roll and took farewell of him with a piercing flourish of trumpets. This was not a funeral but a triumphal march to the land of the gods.

Some distance after the wagon came Ramses XIII, surrounded by a great suite of generals, and after him Queen Nikotris, leaning on two ladies in waiting. Neither the son nor the mother wept, for they knew (as the common people did not) that the deceased Lord was already at the side of Osiris and was so content with his life in the land of felicity that he would not have wished to return to the earth.

After a couple of hours' procession, accompanied by the ceaseless clamor, the remains halted at the Nile bank.

Here they were taken out of the boat-shaped wagon and carried onto a real gilt and carved ship covered with paintings and rigged with white and purple sails.

The court women once again tried to take the mummy from the priests; once again all the choirs and military bands struck up. Lady Nikotris and a dozen priests boarded the ship carrying the royal mummy, the populace proceeded to throw bouquets and garlands—and the oars struck.

Ramses XII had left his palace for the last time, heading up the Nile for his tomb in Thebes. On the way, conscientious ruler that he was, he would stop by all the famous localities to take farewell of them.

It was a protracted journey. It was about a hundred miles[6] to Thebes, and along the way the mummy had to visit a score of temples and take part in solemn services.

A few days after Ramses XII's departure for his eternal rest, Ramses XIII set out after him to revive the grieving hearts of his subjects, receive their homage, and make offerings to the gods.

All the high priests, many senior priests, the wealthiest landowners, and most of the nomarchs, each in his own ship, had sailed after the deceased Lord. The new Pharaoh had therefore thought, not without bitterness, that his entourage would be very small.

But it proved otherwise. At the side of Ramses XIII there appeared all the generals, very many officials, a host of lesser nobility—and all the lower priesthood, which surprised the Pharaoh even more than it pleased him.

That was only the beginning. When the young Lord's ship sailed out into the Nile, such a mass of large and small, humble and opulent boats came out to meet it that they almost completely covered the water. In them sat near-naked peasant and craftsmen's families, stylish merchants, garish Phoenicians, nimble Greek sailors, and even Assyrians and Hittites.

This crowd did not cheer but howled; was not happy but delirious. Time after time, some delegation would insert itself onto the royal ship to kiss the deck trodden by the Lord's feet and to present gifts: a handful of grain, a piece of fabric, a simple earthenware pitcher, a couple of birds—above all, a nosegay of flowers. Before the Pharaoh had passed Memphis, his ship had several times to be cleared of gifts so that it would not sink.

The younger priests were in agreement that, aside from Ramses the Great, no pharaoh had ever been greeted with such enormous enthusiasm.

The whole voyage from Memphis to Thebes went like this, and the people's frenzy, instead of abating, mounted. The peasants deserted their fields, the tradesmen their workshops, to rejoice in the new ruler, about whose plans legends had already grown up. Tre-

---

[6] About a hundred [geographical] miles: some 500 kilometers, or 300 international miles. *(Translator.)*

mendous changes were expected, though no one knew their nature. One thing, however, was certain: the harshness of the officials had softened; the Phoenicians were collecting the taxes less ruthlessly; and the usually meek Egyptian people had begun lifting their heads before the priests.

"If the Pharaoh only lets us," the populace said in taverns, fields, and marketplaces, "we'll soon put things to rights with the holy men. They're to blame for our paying huge taxes, and for the never-healing wounds on our backs!"

Seven miles south of Memphis, into the Libyan hills, lay the land of Piom or Fayum, which was remarkable for being a handiwork of men.

There had once been here a desert depression enclosed by an amphitheater of naked hills. Eighteen centuries before Christ, Pharaoh Amenemhat III[7] had undertaken the bold project of turning it into an arable region.

To that end, he had separated off the eastern part of the depression from the rest and had enclosed it with a massive dam. It was the height of a one-story building, was a hundred paces thick at the base, and was over forty kilometers long.

Thus had been created a reservoir with a capacity of some three billion cubic meters—three cubic kilometers—of water, covering an area of about three hundred square kilometers. The reservoir served to water two hundred twenty thousand hectares[8] of land and additionally, during the river's flood, absorbed excess water and secured a substantial part of Egypt from sudden inundation.

This huge gathering of waters was called Lake Moeris and was ranked among the wonders of the world. Thanks to it, the desert valley had been turned into the fertile land of Piom, with some two hundred thousand prosperous inhabitants. In this province, besides palms and wheat, were cultivated the most beautiful roses, whose oil was distributed across Egypt and abroad.

The existence of Lake Moeris was linked to another wonder of Egyptian engineering, the Canal of Joseph.[9]

This canal, two hundred paces wide, ran for several dozen miles parallel to the western bank of the Nile. Two miles distant from the river, it watered the lands adjacent to the Libyan hills—and conducted water to Lake Moeris.

About the land of Piom were several old pyramids and a great many smaller tombs. And at its eastern edge, near the Nile, stood the famous Labyrinth (*Lope-ro-hunt*[10]). Like-

---

[7] Amenemhat III: 12th-Dynasty pharaoh who ruled ca. 1860 – ca. 1814 BCE. His reign is regarded as the golden age of Egypt's Middle Kingdom. Prus incorrectly calls him *Amenhemat* and dates him to 3500 BCE. *(Translator.)*

[8] In the original, "four hundred thousand *mórgs.*" *(Translator.)*

[9] Canal of Joseph: In ancient times, this waterway was known as *Mer-Wer* ("the Great Canal"). From "*Mer-Wer*" the Greeks formed the name "Moeris"—hence, "Lake Moeris." During the Middle Kingdom, the entire area around the lake was often referred to as *Mer-Wer.* Similarly, the Late Egyptian word *Piom* ("sea" or "lake"), originally applied to Lake Moeris, eventually came to refer to the city of Crocodilopolis (as the Greeks dubbed it) or modern Fayum, and later to the entire region. The subsequent Arabic name *Bahr Yussef* ("waterway of Joseph," Europeanized as "Canal of Joseph") relates to the prophet Yusuf, the koranic counterpart of the biblical Joseph. *(Translator.)*

[10] *Lope-ro-hunt:* Some authors derive the word "labyrinth" from this or another ancient Egyptian expression. *(Translator.)*

wise built by Amenemhat III, it was shaped like a huge horseshoe a thousand paces long by six hundred wide.

This structure was Egypt's greatest treasury. In it reposed the mummies of many famous pharaohs, illustrious priests, commanders, and architects. Here rested, as well, the remains of revered animals, especially crocodiles. Here, finally, reposed the treasure of the Egyptian Kingdom, accumulated over centuries, of which it is hard today to have any conception.

The Labyrinth was neither inaccessible from outside nor very closely watched. It was guarded by a small body of priestly soldiers and by several priests of tested honesty. The treasury's security actually rested in the fact that, apart from these few men, no one knew where to seek the treasury within the Labyrinth, which was divided into a ground floor and an underground floor, each numbering fifteen hundred chambers.

Every pharaoh, every high priest, and every great treasurer and supreme judge was obliged, immediately on taking office, to view the Kingdom's treasure with his own eyes. In spite of that, none of the dignitaries could have found his way to it or even have gathered where the treasury lay: in the building's main body or in one of the wings, above ground or below.

There were those who thought the treasury was actually located underground far outside the Labyrinth proper. And there was no lack of those who thought the treasury lay beneath the bottom of the lake so that, if need arose, the treasury could be flooded with water. But no dignitary of the Kingdom liked to dwell on this question, knowing that coveting the treasure of the gods entailed the doom of the sacrilegious person.

Perhaps uninitiates could have discovered the way to the treasury, had their thoughts not been paralyzed by fear. An earthly and an eternal death faced the man—as well as his family—who godlessly ventured to uncover such secrets.

Arriving in these parts, Ramses XIII visited first of all the province of Fayum. It looked like the inside of a deep bowl whose bottom was the lake, and its sides the hills. Wherever he looked, his eyes met the lush green of flower-speckled grasses, clumps of palm trees, and fig and tamarind groves, among which, from sunrise to sunset, rang birdsong and gay human voices.

This may well have been the happiest corner of Egypt.

The people received the Pharaoh with great enthusiasm. He and his suite were showered with flowers, and he was presented with several pitchers of the most precious perfumes and with ten talents' worth of gold and precious stones.

The Lord sojourned two days in this delightful region where joy seemed to blossom from the trees, waft in the air, and reflect in the waters of the lake. But he was reminded that he must visit the Labyrinth.

He left Piom with a sigh, and along the way he looked about from the road. Soon, however, his attention was drawn to a gigantic gray building sprawled majestically atop a hill.

At the gate to the storied *Lope-ro-hunt* he was greeted by a small group of ascetic-looking priests and by a small squad of soldiers, each of whom was completely shaven.

"These men look like priests!" exclaimed Ramses.

"Each of them has taken minor orders; and the centurions, major orders," answered the high priest of the facility.

Scrutinizing the faces of the strange soldiers who ate no meat and lived celibate, the

Pharaoh perceived keenness and a calm energy. He also found that his sacred person made no impression here.

"I'm very curious how Samentu will get in," said the Lord to himself.

He realized that these men could be neither intimidated nor bribed. They appeared as self-assured as if each commanded invincible regiments of spirits.

"We'll see," he thought, "whether these god-fearing men will daunt my Greeks and Asiatics. Fortunately, they're so wild that they wouldn't know what to make of a solemn face."

At the request of the priests, Ramses XIII's suite remained before the gate, as though in the charge of the shaven-headed soldiers.

"Shall I also leave my sword here?" asked the Pharaoh.

"It will do us no harm," replied the chief keeper.

The young Lord was tempted to at least sword-whip the pious man for his answer. But he forbore.

Through a huge courtyard, between two rows of sphinxes, the Pharaoh and priests entered the main body of the building. Here, in a very spacious but somewhat dim vestibule, were eight doors, and the keeper inquired: "By which door does Your Holiness wish to reach the treasury?"

"The one that gets us there the fastest."

Each of the five priests took up two bundles of torches, but only one priest lit a torch. The place beside him was taken by the chief keeper, who held in his hands a large string of beads inscribed with signs. Behind them walked Ramses, surrounded by the three remaining priests.

The high priest with the beads turned right and entered a great hall whose walls and columns were covered with inscriptions and images. From there they entered a narrow corridor which led upward, and found themselves in another hall, containing many doors. Here a panel in the floor opened before them, revealing an opening through which they descended and, again by way of a narrow corridor, proceeded to a doorless chamber.

But the guide touched a hieroglyph—and the wall opened before him.

Ramses tried to get his bearings, but he soon lost track of the direction they were going. He saw only that they were hurrying through large halls, small chambers, narrow corridors; that they were climbing or descending; that some halls had many doors, while others had none at all. He also noticed that at each new entrance the guide advanced one small bead on his long rosary and that sometimes, in the torchlight, he compared characters on the beads with characters on the walls.

"Where are we now?" asked the Pharaoh suddenly, "underground or above?"

"We are in the power of the gods," replied his neighbor.

After several twists and passages, the Pharaoh again spoke: "Why, we've been here at least twice!"

The priests said nothing; but the torch-bearer illuminated the walls in turn, and Ramses owned to himself that they probably had not been there yet.

In a small doorless chamber the torch was lowered, and the Pharaoh saw on the floor a desiccated black corpse wrapped in a decayed garment.

"That," said the building's keeper, "is the corpse of a Phoenician who tried to break into the Labyrinth during the Sixteenth Dynasty and got this far."

"Was he killed?" asked the Pharaoh.

"He starved to death."

They had been going about half an hour when the priest carrying the torch illuminated a corridor recess in which lay another desiccated corpse.

"That," said the keeper, "is the corpse of a Nubian priest who tried to enter in the time of Your Holiness' grandfather."

The Pharaoh did not ask what had happened to him. He had the sensation that he was in an abyss and that the building was crushing him with its weight. He no longer thought of orienting himself among the hundreds of corridors, halls, and chambers. He did not even wish to determine how the stone walls were parting before them, or the floors collapsing.

"Samentu can't do a thing!" he told himself. "He would perish like those two, about whom I must tell him."

Never had he known such despondence, such a feeling of impotence and nothingness. At moments, he thought the priests would abandon him in one of the narrow doorless chambers. Then he would be overwhelmed with despair: he would reach for his sword and be ready to hack them to pieces. But then he would recall that without their aid he would never come out again, and would hang his head.

Oh, to see the light of day, if but for a moment! How terrible must death be among those three thousand chambers filled with twilight or dark!

Heroic souls have moments of deep despair such as the ordinary person does not suspect.

The procession had lasted close to an hour when at last they entered a low hall supported by octagonal pillars. The three priests surrounding the Pharaoh scattered, and Ramses saw one of them snuggle up to a column and seemingly vanish within it.

A moment later a narrow opening appeared in one of the walls, the priests resumed their places, and their leader bade four torches be lit. Then they all proceeded to the opening and carefully squeezed through.

"Here are the chambers," said the building's keeper.

The priests quickly lit torches affixed to the columns and walls, and Ramses saw several enormous chambers filled with the most diverse priceless handiworks. Every dynasty, if not every pharaoh, had deposited their most extraordinary and precious possessions in the collection.

There were chariots, boats, beds, tables, chests, and thrones, fashioned of gold or laminated in it, and inlaid with ivory, mother-of-pearl, and colored woods, so artfully that the fabrication of these objects had taken the artist-craftsmen dozens of years. There were armor, helmets, shields, and quivers aglitter with precious stones. There were pure-gold pitchers, bowls, and spoons; and sumptuous robes and canopies.

All this, thanks to the dry, clean air, had been preserved unchanged for centuries.

Among the curiosities, the Pharaoh noticed the silver model of the Assyrian palace that had been presented to Ramses XII by Sargon. The high priest, as he explained to the Pharaoh which gift had come from whom, watched his face. But instead of admiration for the treasures, he made out discontent.

"Tell me, Eminence," asked the Pharaoh suddenly, "what use are these treasures, shut away here in the dark?"

"They possess great power, should Egypt find herself in danger," said the high priest. "For a few of these helmets, chariots, swords, we can buy the goodwill of all the Assyrian satraps. And maybe King Assar, as well, would not be averse to our supplying him with furnishings for his throne room or armory."

"I think they would rather take everything from us with the sword, than a little in return for their goodwill," said the Lord.

"Let them try!" said the priest.

"I see. Evidently you have ways to destroy the treasures. But in that case no one will benefit from them."

"That is not my business," replied the chief keeper. "We watch what has been entrusted to us, and we do as we have been instructed."

"Wouldn't it be better to use a small part of these treasures to replenish the Kingdom's coffers and lift Egypt out of the plight in which she is plunged today?" asked the Pharaoh.

"That is not our province."

The Pharaoh frowned. For some time he surveyed the objects, though with little interest, and at length asked:

"Very well. These fine goods may be useful in securing the goodwill of the Assyrian dignitaries. But if war broke out with Assyria, how would we get grain, men, and weapons from peoples that have no appreciation of fine things?"

"Open the treasury," said the high priest.

The priests scattered again: two seemingly vanished inside columns, and one climbed a ladder up a wall and did something around a small carved figure.

Once more a concealed door made way, and Ramses entered the treasury proper.

This too was a spacious chamber, filled with priceless materials. There were earthen barrels full of gold dust, stacks of gold bricks, and bundles of gold ingots. Silver bricks set against one wall formed a stack a couple of cubits wide, ceiling-high.

In alcoves and on stone tables lay precious stones of every color—rubies, topazes, emeralds, sapphires, diamonds—and pearls the size of nuts or even birds' eggs. Some of the individual gems could each have purchased a city.

"This is our treasure in the event of ill-fortune," said the priest-keeper.

"What ill-fortune are you waiting for?" asked the Pharaoh. "The populace are destitute, the nobility and court are heavily in debt, the army is at half strength, the pharaoh has no money. Has Egypt ever been in a worse situation?"

"It was in a worse one when it was conquered by the Hyksos."

"In a dozen or so years," replied Ramses, "even the Israelites will be able to conquer us, if they aren't beaten to it by the Libyans and Ethiopians. And then these beautiful stones, smashed to bits, will go to adorn Jewish and Negro sandals."

"Rest easy, Your Holiness. If need arise, not only the treasury but even the Labyrinth will vanish without trace, along with its keepers."

Ramses now realized that he had before him fanatics whose only thought was to let no one gain control of the treasure.

The Pharaoh sat down on a stack of gold bricks and said: "So you're keeping this treasure for when bad times come to Egypt?"

"That is correct, Holiness."

"Very well. But who will convince you keepers that such times have come, if they do?"

"That will require calling an extraordinary assembly of native Egyptians, comprising the pharaoh, thirteen priests of high degree, thirteen nomarchs, thirteen nobility, thirteen officers, and thirteen each of merchants, craftsmen, and peasants.

"You would give the treasures to that assembly?" asked the Pharaoh.

"We would give the needed sum if the whole assembly resolved as one man that Egypt was in danger, and ..."

"And what?"

"And if the statue of Amon in Thebes confirmed the resolution."

Ramses lowered his head to conceal an expression of great satisfaction. He had a plan. "I can gather such an assembly and bring it to unanimity," he told himself. "And I think the divine statue of Amon will confirm the resolution when I surround its priests with my Asiatics."

"I thank you pious men," he said aloud, "for showing me these precious things whose great value doesn't prevent my being the most impoverished king in the world. And now please lead me out of here by a shorter and easier way."

"We hope," replied the keeper, "that Your Holiness may add as much wealth again to the Labyrinth. As for the way out, there is but one and that is the one we must return by."

A priest handed Ramses some dates; another priest, a flask of wine seasoned with a fortifying substance. On partaking of these, the Pharaoh was reinvigorated and proceeded in good spirits.

"I would give a great deal," he laughed, "to understand all the twists and turns of this peculiar way!"

The priest-guide stopped. "I assure Your Holiness," he said, "that we ourselves do not understand or remember the way, though each of us has traversed it over a dozen times."

"Then how do you find your way?"

"We make use of certain clews. Were we to lose but one of them right now, we would starve to death here."

At last they emerged into the vestibule, and from there into the courtyard.[11] The Pharaoh looked about him and drew several deep breaths.

"For all the treasures of the Labyrinth, I wouldn't want to guard them!" he exclaimed. "It terrifies me to think that one can die inside those dark stone vaults!"

"But one can also develop an attachment to them," smiled the high priest.

The Pharaoh thanked each of his guides and concluded: "I would fain grant you some favor. What is your pleasure?"

The priests listened, indifferent, and their chief said:

"Forgive my audacity, Lord, but what could we desire? Our figs and dates are as sweet as those from your garden; our water, as good as that from your well. And were we drawn to wealth, haven't we more of it than all the kings?"

"There's no winning them over," thought the Pharaoh, "but I'll give them the resolution of the assembly and the verdict of Amon."

---

[11] Prus' description of Egypt's historic ancient Labyrinth draws on the description in Book II of Herodotus' *Histories*; and on Prus' own impressions of his 1878 visit to the ancient labyrinthine salt mine at Wieliczka, near Kraków, in southern Poland. The Wieliczka mine produced salt from the 13th century until 2007 and is now a UNESCO World Heritage Site. *(Translator.)*

CHAPTER 57

L eaving Piom, the Pharaoh and his entourage sailed a dozen days southward, up the Nile, surrounded by a cloud of boats, greeted with cheers, showered with flowers.

On both banks, against a backdrop of green fields, stretched an unbroken series of clay peasant huts, fig groves, and palm bouquets. Every hour, there appeared a town of clustered white houses or a city with colored buildings and great temple pylons.

On the west, the wall of Libyan hills was limned none too distinctly. But on the east the Arabian chain approached ever closer to the river; and visible were steep jagged crags, dusky, yellow, or pink, resembling ruins of fortresses or of temples erected by giants.

Islets cropped up in mid-Nile, seemingly just yesterday surfaced out of the water and already covered with lush vegetation and inhabited by countless flocks of birds. As the Pharaoh's squalling entourage sailed up, the frightened fowl darted up and, circling over the boats, mingled their cries with the mighty voice of the people. Over all this hung an immaculate sky and a flood of light so vibrant that it imbued the black soil with luster, and the rocks with rainbow colors.

The Pharaoh's time passed agreeably. At first he was irritated by the unceasing clamor, but later he became so used to it that he paid it no attention. He could read documents, consult, even sleep.

Thirty to forty miles from Piom, on the Nile's left bank, lay the large city of Zawty,[1] where Ramses XIII rested a couple of days. It was only fitting to make a stop, since the late king's mummy still abided at Abydos, where solemn prayers were being held at the tomb of Osiris.

Zawty was one of the wealthier cities of Upper Egypt. Here famous pottery was produced from white and black clay, and linen was woven; here was the chief market to which goods were brought from oases scattered through the desert. Here, too, was a famous temple of the wolf-headed god Anubis.

On the second day here the priest Pentuer, head of the commission studying the situation of the populace, reported to His Holiness.

"Have you any news?" asked the Lord.

"All Egypt blesses Your Holiness. Everyone I have spoken to is full of hope and says that your reign will bring a rebirth of the Kingdom."

---

[1] Zawty: capital of the 13th Nome of Upper Egypt. The city was situated on the Nile's west bank, midway between the Fayum oasis and Thebes. Later the Copts would call this city Syowt (Prus calls it "Siut"). The modern city at this site is called Asyut. *(Translator.)*

"I want my subjects to be happy," replied the Pharaoh, "and the populace to take a breath. I want Egypt to have, as in the past, eight million population and to regain the lands that the desert has taken from her. I want the hard-working person to rest every seventh day, and every peasant to have a piece of land for his own."

Pentuer prostrated himself on his face before the beneficent Lord.

"Rise," said Ramses. "I must tell you, though, that I've had some hours of heavy sorrow. I see the plight of my people, I want to lift them, but I am told the treasury is empty. As you well know, without some tens of thousands of talents in ready money I could not contemplate such improvements."

"But today I am at ease: I have a way to obtain the needed funds from the Labyrinth."

Pentuer looked at the Lord in surprise.

"The treasure's keeper explained what I am to do," continued the Pharaoh. "I must call a general assembly of all the estates, thirteen men from each estate. When they declare that Egypt is in need, the Labyrinth will give me some of the treasure.

"Gods!" he added, "for a couple ... for just one of the gems that repose there, the populace can be given fifty rests a year! The treasures will never be put to better use."

Pentuer shook his head. "Lord," he said, "six million Egyptians, my friends and I foremost, will agree to your drawing on that treasury. But do not deceive yourself, Holiness! A hundred of the highest dignitaries in the Kingdom will oppose it, and the Labyrinth will deliver nothing."

"Do they want me to become a beggar at one of the temples?" the Pharaoh burst out.

"No," replied the priest. "They will fear that, once touched, the Labyrinth's treasury will be emptied. They will suspect Your Holiness' most faithful servants of partaking in the profits flowing from that source, and then envy will whisper to them: 'Why should you not also profit?' ... Not hostility to Your Lordship but mutual distrust and greed will prompt their opposition."

At this, the Lord calmed down and even smiled. "If it is as you say, dear Pentuer, then put your mind at ease. It has now become plain to me why Amon ordained the pharaoh's authority and gave him superhuman power. It is, you see, so that even a hundred of the most eminent scoundrels could not ruin the Kingdom."

Ramses rose from his chair and added:

"Tell my people to work and to be patient. Tell the priests loyal to me to serve the gods and cultivate learning, which is the sun of this world. And leave these stubborn, suspicious dignitaries to me. Woe betide them if they anger my heart."

"I am your lordship's faithful servant," said the priest.

But as he was taking leave, his face showed concern.

Fifteen miles upriver from Zawty, the wild Arabian crags nearly touch the Nile; while the Libyan hills have receded so far from the river that the valley is here perhaps at its widest.

Here, adjacent to each other, stood two venerable cities: Thinis[2] and Abydos. Here had been born Menes, Egypt's first pharaoh; here, a hundred thousand years earlier, had been entombed the sacred remains of the god Osiris, treacherously murdered by his brother Typhon.

---

[2] Thinis: the capital city of the Old Kingdom's first dynasties. Though the city's exact site has not been discovered, it is generally thought to lie in the vicinity of Abydos. *(Translator.)*

Here, finally, to commemorate these great events, the immortal pharaoh Seti[3] had built a temple[4] which drew pilgrims from all over Egypt. At least once in his lifetime, every true Egyptian had to touch his brow to this hallowed soil. And truly blest was he whose mummy could make the journey to Abydos and find repose there, if at some distance from the temple walls.

The mummy of Ramses XII abided there for a couple of days, as he had been a ruler distinguished for his piety. Nor was it any wonder that Ramses XIII was starting his reign by paying homage at the tomb of Osiris.

The Temple of Seti was not one of the oldest or most magnificent in Egypt, but it was notable for the purity of its Egyptian style. His Holiness Ramses XIII visited it and made offerings in the company of High Priest Sem.

The temple lands covered seventy-five hectares,[5] including fishponds; flower, fruit, and vegetable gardens; and the grand houses of the priests. Everywhere grew palms, figs, oranges, poplars, and acacias, forming either avenues aligned with the cardinal directions, or stands of regularly planted trees of nearly uniform height.

Even the plant world, under the watchful eyes of the priests, did not develop spontaneously, forming irregular if picturesque clusters, but was laid out in straight lines, in parallel lines, or clustered in geometric figures.

Palms, tamarinds, cypresses, and myrtles were soldiers arrayed in ranks or columns. The grass was a mown carpet adorned with floral paintings, of not just any colors but of exactly the required ones. The populace, viewing the temple lawns from above, saw blossoming pictures of gods or sacred animals; the man of learning found aphorisms written in hieroglyphs.

The central part of the gardens was occupied by a rectangle nine hundred paces long by three hundred wide. The rectangle was enclosed by a none-too-high wall with a single visible gate and a dozen or so concealed wickets. Through the gate, the pious populace entered a courtyard surrounding the shrine of Osiris.

In the middle of the stone-floored courtyard stood the temple: a rectangular building four hundred fifty paces long by a hundred fifty wide.

Leading from the populace's gate to the temple was an avenue of sphinxes with leonine bodies and human heads. They lay in two rows, ten to the row, gazing across at one another. Only the highest dignitaries might pass between them.

At the end of the avenue of sphinxes, still opposite the populace's gate, rose two obelisks—tall, slender, four-sided granite pillars—inscribed with the history of Pharaoh Seti.

Beyond the obelisks rose the mighty temple gate, flanked on either side by a gigantic building shaped like a truncated pyramid, called a pylon.[6] Depicted on the two massive

---

[3] Seti: Seti I, the second pharaoh of the 19th Dynasty, who reigned in the early 13th century BCE. He was the son of Ramses I, and the father of Ramses II (the Great). *(Translator.)*

[4] "a temple": the Temple of Seti I at Abydos, famed for the Abydos King List. Please see the Chapter 53 note about Abydos. *(Translator.)*

[5] Seventy-five hectares: in the original, "a hundred fifty *mórgs*." *(Translator.)*

[6] As previously mentioned in a chapter 6 note, a pylon (so dubbed by the Greeks) was the entire monumental gateway to an Egyptian temple: a pylon comprised two tapering towers joined by a less elevated section enclosing the actual entrance. Prus mistakenly applies the term "pylon" to each of the two flanking towers. *(Translator.)*

tower-like structures were Seti's victories, or offerings made by him to the gods.

This gate could not be crossed by peasants, only by wealthy townspeople and by the privileged classes. It led into the peristyle, a court surrounded by a corridor resting on a multitude of columns. The peristyle could accommodate some ten thousand of the faithful.

From the court, nobility could enter the first hall, the hypostyle; it had a ceiling supported by two rows of tall columns and could accommodate some two thousand participants at a service. This hall was the end of the line for laity. The greatest dignitaries, if they had not received holy orders, might pray only here, and from here contemplate the veiled statue of the god that stood in the Hall of the Divine Revelation.

Beyond the Hall of the Divine Revelation lay the Chamber of the Offering Tables, where the priests placed offerings brought for the gods by the faithful. Next was the Chamber of Repose, where the god rested on returning from, or before going out to, a procession; and last was the Chapel, or Sanctuary, where the god dwelt.

The Chapel was ordinarily very small and dim, sometimes hewn from a single stone. It was surrounded on all sides by equally small chapels filled with the garments, furniture, vessels, and gems of the god, who in his inaccessible retreat slept, bathed, anointed himself with perfumes, ate and drank, and seemingly received visits from comely young women.

The Sanctuary was entered only by the high priest and the reigning pharaoh, if he had received holy orders. An ordinary mortal, on entering, might lose his life.

The walls and columns of each hall were covered with inscriptions and illustrative paintings. In the corridor surrounding the court (the peristyle) were the names and portraits of all the pharaohs from Menes, Egypt's first ruler, to Ramses XII.[7] Represented visually in the hypostyle, the hall of the nobility, were the geography and statistics of Egypt and of the conquered peoples. In the Hall of the Revelation were a calendar and results of astronomical observations; in the Chambers of the Offering Tables and Repose were pictures relating to religious rites; and in the Sanctuary—instructions for conjuring supernatural beings and mastering natural phenomena.

The latter sort of superhuman knowledge was couched in such recondite language that not even the priests in the time of Ramses XII could understand it. The Chaldean, Berossus, was expected to revive this moribund learning.

After resting two days at the government palace in Abydos, Ramses XIII made his way to the temple. He wore a white tunic, gold armor, an apron in orange and blue stripes, a steel sword at his side, and a gold helmet. He mounted a chariot whose horses, decked in ostrich plumes, were led by nomarchs, and surrounded by his suite slowly rode to the house of Osiris.

Wherever he looked—fields, river, rooftops, even fig and tamarind boughs—there pressed crowds of people and there rang an unflagging outcry like the roar of a storm.

Arriving at the temple, the Pharaoh stopped the horses and alighted before the gate of the populace, which gratified the commonalty and pleased the priests. He walked down the avenue of sphinxes and, greeted by the holy men, burned incense before the statues of Seti seated to either side of the great gate.

---

[7] As earlier mentioned in a Chapter 53 note, the Abydos King List in the Temple of Seti I gives the names of most of the pharaohs from Menes through Seti I. Contrary to what Prus writes, no Ramesside pharaoh is listed beyond Seti I's father, Ramses I. (And the last Ramesside was not Ramses XIII, as Prus writes, but Ramses XI.) *(Translator.)*

In the peristyle, the high priest drew His Holiness' attention to the fine portraits of the pharaohs and pointed out the place reserved for his likeness. In the hypostyle, he explained the meaning of the geographical maps and statistical tables. In the Hall of the Divine Revelation, Ramses offered incense to the gigantic statue of Osiris, and the high priest pointed out pillars dedicated to the several planets Mercury, Venus, the Moon, Mars, Jupiter, and Saturn. They stood round the solar god's statue, seven in number.

"You say there are six planets," said Ramses, "but I see seven pillars."

"The seventh represents the Earth, which is also a planet," whispered the high priest.

The surprised Pharaoh demanded an explanation; but the learned man silently gestured that his lips were sealed to further explanations.

In the Chamber of the Offering Tables, to soft beautiful music, a chorus of priestesses performed a solemn dance. The Pharaoh doffed his precious gold helmet and armor and presented them to Osiris, stipulating that these gifts remain in the god's treasury and not be sent to the Labyrinth.

In return for the generous gift, the high priest presented the Lord with the most beautiful fifteen-year-old dancing girl, who seemed very pleased with her lot.

Entering the Chamber of Repose, the Pharaoh seated himself on a throne, while his religious deputy Sem, to strains of music and amid incense smoke, went into the Sanctuary to bring out the god.

Half an hour later, to a deafening clangor of bells, there appeared in the twilit chamber a golden boat with curtains that occasionally stirred as though a living being sat behind them.

The priests prostrated themselves on their faces, and Ramses gazed at the translucent curtains. One of them parted, and the Pharaoh beheld an uncommonly beautiful child which looked at him with such sapient eyes that it nearly terrified Egypt's ruler.

"This is Horus," whispered the priests, "Horus, the rising sun. He is the son and father of Osiris, and the husband of his mother, who is his sister."

A procession began, but only about the inner temple. It was headed by harpists and dancing girls and was followed by a white ox with a gold disk between its horns. Then came two choruses of priests, and high priests carrying the god, followed by more choruses, and finally by the Pharaoh in a litter borne by eight priests.

When the procession had made a round of all the temple chambers and corridors, the god and Ramses both returned to the Chamber of Repose. There the sacred boat's curtains parted a second time—and the beautiful child beamed at the Pharaoh.

Then Sem took the boat and the god back to the Chapel.

"Maybe I should become a high priest," thought the ruler, who was so taken with the child that he would fain have seen it as often as possible.

When he emerged from the temple and beheld the sun and the immense crowd of rejoicing populace, he admitted to himself that he understood nothing. Not where the child unlike any in Egypt came from, nor whence the superhuman wisdom in its eyes—nor what it all meant.

Suddenly he recalled his murdered infant son, who might have been equally beautiful—and, before a hundred thousand subjects, Egypt's ruler burst into tears.

"He is converted! ... The Pharaoh is converted!" said the priests. "He but entered the shrine of Osiris, and his heart has been moved!"

That same day a blind man and two paralytics praying outside the temple wall were restored to health. The priestly council therefore resolved that this day be counted among the miraculous days and that a mural be painted on the building's outer wall, showing the weeping Pharaoh and the cripples restored to health.

Well after noon, Ramses returned to his palace to hear reports. When all the dignitaries had left the Lord's cabinet, Thutmose came to say: "The priest Samentu desires to pay his respects to Your Holiness."

"Good, bring him in."

"He begs Your Lordship to receive him in a tent at the army camp, and says that palace walls like to listen."

"I wonder what he wants," said the Pharaoh, and he told the courtiers he would be spending the night in camp.

Before sunset, the Lord rode out with Thutmose to his faithful troops and found the royal tent where, on Thutmose's instructions, Asiatics stood guard.

In the evening Samentu came, dressed in a pilgrim's cloak. He greeted His Holiness reverently and whispered:

"I think a man followed me all the way here, stopping not far from the divine tent. Could he be an agent of the high priests?"

At the Pharaoh's behest, Thutmose ran out and indeed found an unfamiliar officer.

"Who are you?" he asked.

"I am Ennana, centurion in the Regiment of Isis. Unfortunate Ennana—doesn't Your Eminence remember me? Over a year ago, at the Pi-Bailos maneuvers, I discovered the sacred scarabs ..."

"Oh, it's you!" interrupted Thutmose. "But your regiment isn't stationed at Abydos?"

"The water of truth flows from your lips. We are stationed in a miserable area outside Mena where the priests ordered us to repair a canal, as if we were peasants or Jews."

"How do you come to be here?"

"I begged a few days' rest of my superiors," replied Ennana, "and by the swiftness of my feet I ran here like a thirsty stag to a spring."

"What is it you want?"

"I want to beg mercy of His Holiness against the baldpates, who won't promote me because I am sensitive to the sufferings of the men."

A glum Thutmose returned to the tent and recounted to the Pharaoh his conversation with Ennana.

"Ennana?" repeated the Lord. "Yes, I remember him. He caused us a lot of trouble with the scarabs, but he also got fifty cane strokes at Herhor's behest. You say he's complaining at the priests? ... Bring him in!"

The Pharaoh told Samentu to go into the tent's other compartment, and sent his favorite for Ennana.

The hapless officer presently appeared. He prostrated himself on his face; then, kneeling and sighing, he spoke:

"Each day I pray to Re-Harakhti at his rising and setting, and to Amon, and to Re and Ptah and the other gods and goddesses: Mayst Thou be well, O ruler of Egypt! Mayst Thou live! Mayst Thou prosper, and may I behold at least the splendor of Thy heels!"[8]

---

[8] Authentic. (Author.)

"What does he want?" the Pharaoh asked Thutmose, for the first time observing protocol.

"His Holiness deigns to ask: what do you want?" repeated Thutmose.

The guileful Ennana, still kneeling, turned to the favorite and discoursed:

"Your Eminence is the ear and eye of the Lord who bestows joy and life on us, and so I will answer you as at the court of Osiris:

"I have been serving ten years with the priestly regiment of Isis, I have fought six years in the eastern borderlands. My peers have become regimental commanders, but I am still only a centurion and continue to be caned on the orders of the god-fearing priests.

"And why am I so ill-used?

"In the daytime my heart turns to books, and at night I read; for the fool who forsakes books with the swiftness of a fleeing gazelle is of a base mind—the equal of the donkey that takes whippings, the equal of the deaf man who does not hear and must be spoken to with the hand. Despite this eagerness of mine for learning, I am not conceited of my knowledge but seek advice from everyone, because one can learn something from everyone, and I hold the venerable sages in respect."

The Pharaoh stirred impatiently but listened on, knowing that a true Egyptian considered loquacity his obligation and the highest token of esteem for his superiors.

"This is how I am," discoursed Ennana. "In another's house I do not look at the women; I let the servants eat their due, but when it comes to me I do not quarrel at the apportioning. I always have a contented face, I behave respectfully toward superiors, and I will not sit when an elder is standing. I am not intrusive and do not enter others' homes uninvited. What my eye sees, thereof I am silent, for I know that we are deaf to those who use many words.

"Wisdom teaches that a man's body is like a storehouse of grain, filled with a variety of responses. Therefore I always choose a good one and speak a good one, and keep the bad one hidden within my body. Nor do I repeat the calumnies of others; and as for commissions, I always carry them out to the best of my ability.[9]

"And what have I to show for it?" concluded Ennana in a raised voice. "I suffer hunger, I go about in rags, and I cannot lie on my back, it is so badly beaten. I read in books that the priesthood used to reward valor and prudence. If so, it must have been very long ago! Today the priests turn their backs on the prudent, and they drive valor and strength from officers' bones."

"This man will put me to sleep!" said the Pharaoh.

"Ennana," added Thutmose, "you have convinced His Holiness of your conversance with books—now say as succinctly as you can what it is you want."

"An arrow does not find its target as swiftly as my plea will reach the divine heels of His Holiness," replied Ennana. "I am so sick of service with the baldpates—the priests have filled my heart with such bitterness—that, if I am not transferred to the Pharaoh's army, I will run myself through on my own sword, before which Egypt's enemies have trembled more than once, yea, more than a hundred times.

"I would rather be a decurion—I would rather be an ordinary soldier—of His Holiness than a centurion in the regiments of the priests. A pig or a dog can serve them, but not a true Egyptian!"

Ennana uttered the final expressions with such vehemence that the Pharaoh told

[9] Ancient Egyptian maxims. (Author.)

Thutmose in Greek: "Accept him into the guard. An officer who dislikes the priests may be of use to us."

"His Holiness the Lord of the Two Worlds commands that you be accepted into his guard," repeated Thutmose.

"My health and life belong to our lord Ramses ... May he live forever!" cried Ennana, kissing the carpet beneath the royal feet.

As the gratified Ennana was backing out of the tent, every couple of paces prostrating himself on his face and blessing the Lord, the Pharaoh said:

"His prattle stuck in my throat. I must teach Egyptian soldiers and officers to speak concisely, not like learned scribes."

"May that be his only shortcoming!" whispered Thutmose, on whom Ennana had made a disagreeable impression.

The Lord called in Samentu.

"Don't worry," he told the priest. "The officer who followed you wasn't shadowing you. He's too stupid for that kind of assignment. But in a pinch he can provide useful muscle!"

"Now," added the Pharaoh, "tell me what inclines you to such caution?"

"I almost know the way to the treasury in the Labyrinth," replied Samentu.

The Lord shook his head. "That's a difficult matter," he whispered. "I scurried an hour through corridors and chambers like a mouse chased by a cat. And I'll confess to you, not only don't I understand the way, but I wouldn't even set out on it myself. Death in the sun can be agreeable; but death in those burrows where a mole would get lost ... brr!"

"Still, we must discover and master the way," said Samentu.

"What if the keepers themselves give us the requisite part of the treasures?" asked the Pharaoh.

"They won't, so long as Mephres, Herhor, and their adherents live. Believe me, Lord, these dignitaries mean to wrap you in swaddlings like an infant."

The Pharaoh turned livid with anger. "May I not wrap them in chains! How do you plan to discover the way?"

"Here in Abydos, at the tomb of Osiris, I've found the complete plan of the way to the treasury," said the priest.

"How did you know it was there?"

"Inscriptions in my Temple of Set told me."

"When did you find the plan?"

"When the mummy of Your Holiness' eternally living father was in the Temple of Osiris," said Samentu. "I accompanied the venerable remains and, while on night duty in the Chamber of Repose, entered the Sanctuary."

"You should have been a general, not a high priest!" laughed Ramses. "And you now understand the way through the Labyrinth?"

"I've long understood it, and now I've gathered the clews to guide me."

"Can you explain it to me?"

"Yes, and sometime I'll show Your Holiness the plan.

"The way," continued Samentu, "zigzags four times through the entire Labyrinth; it starts on the highest floor, ends in the lowest undergrounds, and additionally has many twists and turns. That's why it's so long."

"How will you get from one hall to the next, where there are many doors?"

"Each door leading to the goal bears part of the inscription:

"'Woe betide the traitor who seeks to penetrate the supreme secret of the Kingdom and extend a sacrilegious hand for the treasure of the gods. His remains will be as carrion, and his spirit will know no peace but shall wander dark places, racked by its sins!'"

"You are not deterred by the inscription?"

"Is Your Holiness deterred by the sight of a Libyan spear? Threats may work with the commonalty but not with me, who could compose more formidable curses."

"You're right," mused the Pharaoh. "A spear won't harm him who can deflect it, and a wrong path won't mislead the sage who knows the word of the truth.

"But how will you cause stones in the walls to part for you, and columns to turn into doorways?"

Samentu shrugged scornfully. "In my temple too," he said, "there are imperceptible doors, still harder to open than those in the Labyrinth. He who knows the word of the secret will find his way anywhere, as Your Holiness correctly said."

The Pharaoh rested his head in his hand, thinking. "I would be very sorry," he said, "if, on this path, you came to grief."

"If worst comes to worst, I'll meet with death, but doesn't that threaten even pharaohs? For that matter, did Your Holiness not boldly go to the Natron Lakes, though you had no assurance of returning from there?

"And don't think, lord," continued the priest, "that I'll have to traverse the whole path that do visitors to the Labyrinth. I'll find closer points, and it will take me a single prayer to Osiris to get where it would take you thirty prayers."

"Then there are other entrances?"

"Doubtless there are, and I must find them," replied Samentu. "After all, unlike Your Holiness, I won't enter in the daytime nor by the main gate."

"Then how?"

"In the outer wall there are invisible wickets with which I am familiar but which the wise keepers of the Labyrinth never watch. In the courtyard, the night watches are scant and so trusting in the protection of the gods, or the fear of the commonalty, that they generally sleep. In addition, three times between sunset and sunrise the priests go for prayer to the temple, while their soldiers perform their devotions under the heavens. Before they've completed one service, I'll be inside the building!"

"What if you get lost?"

"I have the plan."

"What if the plan is false?" said the Pharaoh, unable to hide his concern.

"What if Your Holiness fails to obtain the treasures of the Labyrinth? ... If the Phoenicians change their minds and don't come through with the promised loan? ... If the army goes hungry, and the hopes of the common people are dashed? ...

"Please believe me, my lord," continued the priest, "I will be safer in the corridors of the Labyrinth than you in your Kingdom."

"But the dark! ... The dark! ... And the impenetrable walls, and the depth, and the hundreds of paths where a man must get lost. Believe me, Samentu, fighting men is child's play; tussling with the dark and the unknown is a terrible business!"

Samentu smiled. "Your Holiness doesn't know my life story. When I was twenty-five, I was a priest of Osiris ..."

"You?" asked Ramses, surprised.

"Yes, and I'll tell you why I converted to the service of Set. I had been sent to the Sinai Peninsula to build a small chapel for the miners. Its construction took six years and, having a lot of time on my hands, I wandered the hills and caverns.

"What I saw there! ... Corridors several hours long; tight passageways which I had to crawl through on my stomach; chambers so huge that each could have accommodated a temple. I saw underground rivers and lakes, edifices of crystals, caves completely dark where I couldn't see my hand—or, again, illuminated as if another sun shone inside them.

"How many times I lost my way in the countless passageways, how many times my torch went out, how many times I tumbled down an unseen precipice! I sometimes spent several days underground, eating parched barley, licking moisture off the rocks, unsure whether I would return to the world.

"But I gained experience, my vision sharpened, and I actually grew fond of those infernal realms. And today, when I think of the childish vaults of the Labyrinth, I want to laugh. Man-made buildings are molehills to the immense structures reared by the silent, invisible spirits of the earth.

"One time, I came across something frightful which influenced my change of station.

"West of the Sinai mines there's a cluster of ravines and hills where often underground thunder rings out, the ground shakes, and sometimes flames are seen. Intrigued, I went there for an extended period, explored and, thanks to an inconspicuous crevice, discovered a whole chain of gigantic caverns whose vaults might have accommodated the greatest pyramid.

"As I was wandering around in there, I was struck by a powerful odor of decay, so disagreeable that I wanted to flee. But, getting a grip on myself, I entered the cavern it came from, and I saw ...

"Imagine if you will, lord, a man with arms and legs half the length of ours but thick, ungainly, and ended in claws. Add to that outline a broad, sidewise flattened tail, cut out on top like a cockscomb; add a very long neck and on it a dog's head. Finally dress this monster in armor covered down the back with bent spikes.

"Now imagine this figure standing on its legs, the hands and chest propped against the rock."

"Something very ugly," said the Pharaoh. "I'd kill it straightway!"

"It wasn't ugly," said the priest, shuddering. "Because imagine, Lord, that this monster was tall as an obelisk."

Ramses XIII gestured his unhappiness. "Samentu," he said, "I think you visited those caverns in your dreams!"

"I swear to you, Lord," cried the priest, "on the lives of my children, that I'm speaking the truth! Yes, this monster in a reptile's skin, covered in spiked armor, had it lain on the ground, would, including its tail, have measured fifty paces in length. Despite my fear and revulsion, I returned several times to its cave and inspected it closely."

"It was alive?"

"No. It was a corpse, a very old one, but preserved like our mummies. It was kept by the very dry air, or maybe by salts, unknown to me, in the ground.[10]

---

[10] This scene apparently involves a dinosaur that is belatedly decomposing—66 million years after all dinosaurs, except for the birds, became extinct! *(Translator.)*

"That was my last discovery," continued Samentu. "I went no more into caves, but I did a lot of thinking. Osiris, I told myself, creates great creatures: lions, elephants, horses ... and Set brings forth the snake, the bat, the crocodile. The monster I had come upon was undoubtedly a creature of Set's, and since it surpassed all that we know under the sun, then Set was a more powerful god than Osiris.

"I converted to Set, and on returning to Egypt I entered his temple. When I told the priests about my discovery, they told me they knew of many more such monsters."

Samentu paused.

"Should Your Holiness wish to visit our temple sometime, I'll show you strange and fearful creatures in the tombs: geese with lizards' heads and bats' wings, lizards resembling swans but larger than ostriches, a crocodile three times longer than those that dwell in the Nile, a frog the size of a dog.

"These are mummies or skeletons discovered in caves and preserved in our tombs. The populace think we revere them, but we only study their structure and preserve them."

"I'll believe you when I see them for myself," said the Pharaoh. "But tell me how such creatures could come to be in the caves."

"My lord," said the priest, "the world in which we live undergoes great changes. In Egypt we find the rubble of cities and temples hidden deep in the ground. There was a time when the site of Lower Egypt was occupied by an arm of the sea, and the Nile flowed the full width of our valley. Still earlier, here where our Kingdom is, there was sea. And our ancestors inhabited a land which is now occupied by the Western Desert.

"Earlier still, tens of thousands of years ago, there were no people like us, only ape-like creatures that built shelters, sustained fire, and fought with clubs and stones. At the time, there were no horses or cattle; but elephants, rhinoceroses, and lions were three or four times as tall as today's animals of the same appearance.

"But even the gigantic elephants were not the earliest monsters. Before them there were immense reptiles: flying, swimming, and walking varieties. Before the reptiles, in this world there were only snails and fishes; and before them, only plants, but of kinds that today no longer exist."[11]

"And still earlier?" asked Ramses.

"Still earlier the earth was empty and void, and the Spirit of God moved upon the face of the waters."[12]

"I've heard something about that," said the Pharaoh, "but I won't believe it until you show me the mummies of monsters that are supposed to repose in your temple."

"By your leave, Holiness, I'll finish what I was saying," said Samentu. "When I saw that enormous corpse in the Sinai cavern, I was terrified and for a couple of years wouldn't have ventured into a cave. But when the priests of Set told me where such strange creatures came from, my fear vanished and my curiosity was piqued. And now there's no more pleasurable a pastime for me than wandering the undergrounds and seeking paths in the dark. For that reason, the Labyrinth will be no more trouble to me than a stroll in the royal garden."

"Samentu," said the Lord, "I greatly esteem your superhuman daring and learning.

---

[11] This is a very rough approximation of Darwinian evolution. *(Translator.)*

[12] This is a reference to *Genesis 1:2* in the Bible's Old Testament. *(Translator.)*

You've told me so many interesting things, that I would indeed like to see some caves and maybe sometime I'll sail with you to the Sinai.

"Nevertheless I have concerns as to whether you will manage with the Labyrinth; and so, just in case, I'll call the assembly of Egyptians to authorize my drawing on the treasury."

"There's no harm in that," replied the priest. "But my efforts will nonetheless be needed, for Mephres and Herhor will not agree to the release of treasure."

"And you're certain you'll succeed?" persisted the Pharaoh.

"No one in Egypt," said Samentu, "has had as many resources as I to prevail in this struggle, which for me is not actually a struggle but sport.

"Some persons fear the dark, which I like and can even see in. Others can't guide themselves among numerous chambers and corridors, which I do with ease. Still others don't know the secrets of opening hidden doors, with which I'm conversant.

"Had I nothing other than what I've enumerated, within a month or two I'd discover the paths through the Labyrinth. But I also have a detailed plan of the passages and know the words that will lead me from chamber to chamber. So what can stand in my way?"

"Still, at the bottom of your heart there is doubt: you were frightened by the officer who seemed to be following you."

The priest shrugged. "I fear nothing and no one," he replied calmly, "I'm merely cautious. I anticipate everything and am prepared even should I be caught."

"You would face terrible tortures!" whispered Ramses.

"No. I would open myself a door straight from the undergrounds of the Labyrinth to the land of eternal light."

"You won't bear me a grudge?"

"Over what?" asked the priest. "I seek a great goal: I wish to replace Herhor in the Kingdom."

"I swear you shall!"

"If I don't perish," said Samentu. "But what matters it if one climbs to mountain peaks over precipices, and if on the way one may lose his footing and fall? Your lordship will see to my children."

"Go, then," said the Pharaoh. "You are worthy to be my foremost helper."

CHAPTER 58

Leaving Abydos, Ramses XIII continued upriver to the cities of Tan-ta-ren (Dendera)[1] and Qena,[2] which lay nearly opposite each other: the former on the west, the latter on the east, bank of the Nile.

Tan-ta-ren was notable for two places: a crocodile-breeding pool; and a Temple of Hathor possessed of an upper school. Taught there were medicine, pious chants, religious rites, and astronomy.

The Pharaoh visited both places. He was annoyed on being asked to offer incense to the sacred crocodiles, which he considered stupid, stinking reptiles. When during the offering one of them drew itself up too far and grabbed the Lord's robe in its teeth, Ramses struck it over the head with the bronze ladle. The reptile momentarily closed its eyes and spread its paws, then backed into the water as though having realized that the young Lord did not welcome familiarities even from gods.

"Did I commit sacrilege?" he asked the high priest.

The dignitary looked to see whether anyone was listening in and replied:

"Had I known Your Holiness would make him an offering of that kind, I would have given you a club instead of a censer. That crocodile is the nastiest brute in the temple. One time, he carried off a child."

"And ate it?"

"The parents were content!" said the priest.

"Tell me," mused the Pharaoh, "how can you men of learning venerate animals which you cane when no one is looking?"

The high priest looked about again and, seeing no one nearby, answered:

"Surely Your Lordship does not suspect adherents of the One God of holding a belief in the sanctity of animals. What we do, we do for the rabble. The Apis bull, ostensibly revered by the priests, is the finest bull in all Egypt and propagates our breed of cattle. The ibises and storks clear our fields of carrion; thanks to the cats, the mice don't destroy our grain stores; and thanks to the crocodiles, we have good water in the Nile, which otherwise would poison us.

---

[1] Dendera: a city on the west bank of the Nile; capital of the 6th Nome of Upper Egypt; site of a temple complex including a Temple of Hathor. The city's official deity was the crocodile. *(Translator.)*

[2] Qena (the author calls it *Kaneh*): a city on the east bank of the Nile, in the 6th Nome of Upper Egypt. Qena lies five kilometers north of Dendera and is most famous for its proximity to Dendera's ruins. Thanks to the *Wadi Qena*, Qena was a jumping-off point for caravans traveling east to the Red Sea, and retains this role. *(Translator.)*

"The light-minded, ignorant commonalty don't understand the usefulness of these animals and would exterminate them inside of a year if we didn't protect them with religious ceremonies.

"That is the secret of our temples dedicated to animals, and of our reverence for them. We offer incense to what the populace ought to respect for its usefulness."

At the Temple of Hathor, the Pharaoh hurried through the courts of the medical school and heard with little interest the astrologers' horoscopes for him. When the high-priest astronomer showed him a gold tablet engraved with a map of the heavens, the Lord asked:

"How often do the predictions that you read in the stars come true?"

"They sometimes do."

"If you prophesied by trees, stones, or the flow of water, would they still come true?"

The high priest was disconcerted. "Your Holiness, please do not take us for charlatans. We predict the future for people because it is of interest to them and, truth to tell, that is all the astronomy they understand."

"What do you understand of it?"

"We know the structure of the firmament," said the priest, "and the motions of the stars."

"Of what use is that to anyone?"

"We have rendered no small services to Egypt. We mark out the cardinal directions, in accordance with which buildings are erected and canals are dug. Without the aid of our science, seafaring ships could not stray from the shores. And we compose the calendar and calculate future events in the heavens. For example, soon now we will be having an eclipse ..."

Ramses was no longer listening to him: the Pharaoh had turned and walked out.

"How," he thought, "can they build temples for such a childish game and engrave its results on gold tablets? The holy men are at a loss what to do in their idleness!"

After his brief sojourn at Tan-ta-ren, the Lord crossed the Nile to the city of Qena.

Here were no famous temples, censed crocodiles, or gold star-tablets. But pottery-making and commerce flourished. From here, two routes went out to the Red Sea ports of Koseir[3] and Berenice;[4] and a road led to the Porphyry Hills,[5] from which were transported statues and great blocks of building stone.

Qena swarmed with Phoenicians, who welcomed the Lord with tremendous enthusiasm and presented him with ten talents' worth of various valuables.

Still, the Pharaoh spent barely a day in Qena: he had received word from Thebes that

---

[3] Koseir: one of several spellings (another is *El Qoseir*) of the Arabic name for a 5,000-year-old town on eastern Egypt's Red Sea coast. It was an important port from Ptolemaic times, when it was known in Greek as *Leukos Limen* (White Port). *(Translator.)*

[4] Berenice (*Berenice Troglodytica*—not to be confused with several other places named Berenice): a port on eastern Egypt's Red Sea coast. It was founded in 275 BCE by Ptolemy II Philadelphus, who named it for his mother, Berenice I, the second queen of Egypt's Ptolemaic Dynasty. *(Translator.)*

[5] The Porphyry Hills (in Arabic, *Gabal Abu Dukhan*), near modern Hurghada on Egypt's Red Sea coast, are the world's only source of porphyry (so named from the Ancient Greek for "purple"), a hard deep-purple igneous stone that was prized by the Romans for monuments and building projects. The Porphyry Hills site, known to the Romans as *Mons Porphyrites*, was lost for centuries until rediscovered in the 19th century. *(Translator.)*

Ramses XII's venerable mummy was now at the palace in Luxor,[6] awaiting funeral.

In that period, Thebes was an enormous city covering an area of some twelve square kilometers. It boasted the Temple of Amon, Egypt's greatest temple, and many public and private buildings. The main streets were broad, straight, flagstoned; the Nile banks were lined with boulevards; the houses were four- and five-story.

Since every temple and palace had an enormous pylon gate, the city was called "hundred-gated Thebes."[7] Thebes was, on one hand, a very industrial and commercial city; on the other, as it were, a threshold to eternity. For on the Nile's west bank, in and among the hills, were countless tombs of priests, magnates, and kings.

Thebes owed its magnificence to two pharaohs: Amenhotep III,[8] or "Memnon,"[9] who had "found a city of clay and left a city of stone"; and Ramses II, who had completed and added to the buildings begun by Amenhotep.

On the Nile's east bank, in the south of the city, was a whole district of huge royal buildings—palaces, villas, temples—on whose rubble stands today the town of Luxor. In this district the pharaoh's remains awaited the final ceremonies.

When Ramses XIII arrived, all of Thebes turned out to welcome him; only the elderly and the disabled remained home—and in back alleys, thieves. Here for the first time the populace unharnessed the royal chariot's horses and pulled it themselves. Here, also for the first time, the Pharaoh heard shouts and imprecations against the priests, which pleased him, as well as calls for every seventh day to be a holiday, which gave the Lord pause. He wanted to give Egypt's working people that gift, but he had no idea that his plans were already common knowledge and that the people expected their fulfillment.

The mile-long route took a couple of hours through the packed crowds. The royal chariot stopped very often, moving again only after His Holiness' guard had managed to lift those who lay prostrate on the ground.

On finally reaching the palace gardens, where he occupied one of the smaller villas, the Pharaoh was so tired that he did not take up state business that day. The next day, he burned incense before his father's mummy in the main royal building and told Herhor that the remains could be taken to the tombs.

---

[6] Luxor: Arabic-named modern city that sprawls to the site of the ancient Egyptian city of Waset, known to the ancient Greeks as Thebes. Luxor has been called "the world's greatest open-air museum," as the temple complexes of Arabic-named Karnak and Luxor stand within modern Luxor while, immediately opposite, across the Nile, lie the monuments, temples, and tombs of the west-bank Necropolis, including the Valley of the Kings and the Valley of the Queens. *(Translator.)*

[7] "Hundred-gated Thebes": Egypt's Thebes was called thus already in Homer's *Iliad*, to distinguish it from Greece's "seven-gated Thebes." *(Translator.)*

[8] Amenhotep III: the ninth pharaoh of the 18th Dynasty, who reigned for nearly 40 years from the early-to mid-14th century BCE. Prus calls him by his Hellenized (Greek) name, *Amenophis III*, but spelled with an *f* rather than with *ph*. *(Translator.)*

[9] "Memnon": This name for Amenhotep III comes from the name, "Colossi of Memnon," that the ancient Greeks gave to two massive statues of Amenhotep III located in the Theban Necropolis west of the Nile, across from modern Luxor. The Greeks had named the colossi after an Ethiopian ally of the Trojans in the Trojan War, Memnon, who was slain by Achilles. Memnon was said to be the son of Eos, goddess of the dawn; and was associated with the colossi because of a reported "cry" that came around dawn from the earthquake-shattered northern colossus. The sound, which was variously described, may have resulted from heat suddenly striking chilled stone. *(Translator.)*

But that did not happen at once.

From the palace the deceased was moved to the Temple of Ramses, where he rested a day. Next the mummy was conducted with great pomp to the Temple of Amon-Ra.

The details of the funerary rites were the same as at Memphis, but on a much grander scale.

The royal palaces, which lay on the Nile's right bank in the south of the city, were connected to the Temple of Amon-Ra, in the north of the city, by a unique road. This was a two-kilometer-long avenue, very broad, lined not only with enormous trees but with a double row of sphinxes. Some of these had human heads to their leonine bodies; others, rams' heads. Several hundred of these statues lined the avenue.

On either side of the avenue pressed countless crowds of populace from Thebes and the vicinity; down the middle of the road moved the funerary cortege. There marched regimental bands, contingents of weeping women, choirs, all the craft and merchant guilds, deputations from dozens of nomes with their gods and banners, delegations from a score of nations that maintained relations with Egypt. Then more bands, weeping women, and priestly choirs.

The royal mummy once again rode in a golden boat, but in a far more sumptuous one than at Memphis. The wagon that bore it, harnessed to eight pairs of white oxen, was two stories tall and nearly invisible beneath heaps of wreaths, bouquets, ostrich plumes, and precious fabrics. It was enveloped in thick clouds of incense, creating the impression that Ramses XII was appearing to his people already as a god in the clouds.

Sounds akin to thunder, and powerful mournful tones of bronze, rang from the pylons of all the Theban temples.

Though the avenue of sphinxes was unobstructed and broad, and though the procession was directed by Egyptian generals and was thus most orderly, it took the cortege three hours to traverse the two kilometers separating the palaces from the buildings of Amon.

Only after Ramses XII's mummy had been borne into the temple did Ramses XIII depart the palace, in a gold chariot drawn by a pair of spirited horses. The populace lining the avenue, who had behaved calmly during the procession, at the sight of their beloved ruler burst into such tremendous cheering that it drowned out the thunder and bronze tones.

There was a moment when the ecstatic crowd wanted to run into the avenue and surround the Lord. But with a single gesture Ramses stanched the living flood and prevented sacrilege.

In a quarter-hour the Pharaoh covered the avenue's length and stopped before the gigantic pylon of the most magnificent temple in Egypt.

As Luxor was an entire district of royal palaces in the south of the city, so Karnak was a district of the gods in the north of the city. And the main focus of Karnak was the Temple of Amon-Ra.

The edifice itself occupied over two hectares; and the gardens and ponds surrounding it, some twenty hectares.[10] Before the temple there stood two ten-story pylon towers. The courtyard, enclosed by a colonnaded gallery, covered a hectare; and the columned hall

---

[10] *Pharaoh*'s Polish text says the edifice occupied "four *mórg*s"; and the gardens and ponds, "about forty *mórg*s." The paragraph's two subsequent surface areas are likewise stated in *mórg*s. *(Translator.)*

where the privileged estates gathered, over half a hectare. This was not so much an edifice as a vicinity.

The latter hall, the hypostyle, was over a hundred fifty paces long by seventy-five wide, and its ceiling rested on a hundred thirty-four columns. The twelve central ones were fifteen paces around and five to six stories high!

The statues placed about the temple, by the pylon towers, and by the sacred pool were of corresponding proportions.

At the gigantic gate the Pharaoh was awaited by His Eminence Herhor, the temple's high priest. Surrounded by a whole staff of priests, Herhor greeted the ruler almost haughtily; and as he burned incense before the Pharaoh, Herhor did not look at him. Then he conducted the Pharaoh through the courtyard to the hypostyle and ordered the deputation admitted within the temple wall.

In the middle of the hypostyle stood the boat with the deceased ruler's mummy, and on either side of it, opposite each other, two equally high thrones. Ramses XIII seated himself on one, surrounded by generals and nomarchs; Herhor, on the other, surrounded by priests. Then High Priest Mephres handed Herhor Amenhotep's miter, and for the second time the young Pharaoh saw the gold serpent, symbol of royal power, on Herhor's head.

Ramses turned pale with anger and thought: "May I not need to remove your uraeus together with your head!"

But he kept his peace, knowing that in this greatest of Egyptian temples Herhor was a lord equal to the gods, and a potentate perhaps greater than the pharaoh himself.

While the populace were filling the courtyard, and harp music and soft chanting issued from behind the purple veil separating the rest of the temple from mortals, Ramses surveyed the hall. The forest of massive columns, covered top to bottom with paintings, the mysterious lighting, the ceiling suspended somewhere beneath the heavens, made an overwhelming impression on him.

"What is it," he thought, "to have won the Battle of the Natron Lakes? To build a structure like this is a real achievement! ... And they erected it!"

He fully appreciated now the power of the priesthood. Could he, his army, or even all the populace have overthrown this temple? ... And if it were hard to manage with the structure, would it be easier to cope with its architects?

He was brought back from his disagreeable meditations by the voice of High Priest Mephres:

"Your Holiness," spoke the old man, "you most exalted confidant of the gods"—he bowed to Herhor—"you nomarchs, scribes, knights, and common people! His Eminence the High Priest of this Temple, Herhor, has summoned us that we may, in accordance with ancient custom, judge the earthly deeds of the late pharaoh and decline or grant him right to funeral."

The Pharaoh's blood boiled up. It was not enough they were slighting him here, but they had the effrontery to discuss his father's deeds—to decide about his funeral!

But he calmed down. It was a mere formality, as old as Egypt's dynasties. It was not really about judging but about eulogizing the deceased.

At a sign from Herhor, the high priests seated themselves on stools. However, the nomarchs and generals surrounding Ramses' throne did not take seats: there was no seating for them.

The Pharaoh noted this affront as well; but he was now so much in command of himself that there was no telling whether he had noticed the slight to his intimates.

Meanwhile the holy Mephres was contemplating the life of the late Lord.

"Ramses XII," he said, "committed none of the forty-two sins, therefore the court of the gods will grant him favorable judgment. And since, thanks to the extraordinary solicitude of the priests, the royal mummy is provided with all requisite amulets, prayers, instructions, and spells, there can be no question but the late pharaoh is already in the abode of the gods, is seated beside Osiris, and is himself Osiris.

"The godly nature of Ramses XII manifested itself in his earthly life. He reigned for over thirty years, gave the nation a profound peace, and built or completed many temples. Moreover, he was a high priest and surpassed the most pious priests in piety. During his reign, pride of place was held by the worship of the gods and the uplifting of the holy priesthood. For this he was beloved of the celestial powers, and one of the Theban gods, Khonsu, at the pharaoh's request journeyed to the land of Bukhten and there exorcised the evil spirit from the king's daughter."

Mephres paused.

"Inasmuch as I have demonstrated to Your Eminences that Ramses XII was a god, you may ask why this superior being descended into the land of Egypt and abided here for several score years.

"It was in order to redeem the world, which is badly corrupted due to the decline of faith.

"For who today is concerned with piety? Who thinks to do the will of the gods?

"Far to the north we see the large Assyrian nation, which believes only in the power of the sword and, rather than pursue wisdom and piety, occupies itself with conquering peoples. Nearer to hand are the Phoenicians, whose god is gold and whose pieties are fraud and usury. And other peoples, such as the Hittites to the east, the Libyans to the west, the Ethiopians to the south, and the Greeks on the Mediterranean Sea, are barbarians and robbers. Rather than work, they plunder; rather than study wisdom, they drink, play at dice, or sleep away like forspent beasts.

"In the world there is but one truly pious and wise people—the Egyptian people; but see what is happening here as well.

"Due to the influx of infidel foreigners, religion has declined in our land. The nobility and dignitaries mock the gods and life eternal over cups of wine, and the people cast mud at holy statues and do not make offerings to the temples.

"Piety has been replaced by prodigality; wisdom, by dissipation. Everyone wants to wear enormous wigs, rare perfumes, tunics and aprons woven with gold, and chains and bracelets studded with precious stones. A wheat cake is no longer good enough for them; they want pastries with milk and honey; they wash their feet in beer, and quench their thirst with foreign wines.

"As a result, all the nobility are in debt, the populace are flogged and overworked, and here and there rebellions break out. What do I say: here and there? For some time, over the length and breadth of Egypt, thanks to mysterious agitators, we have been hearing cries of:

"'Give us rest every six days! ... Do not beat us without trial! ... Give us each a plot of land for our own!'

"This is a portent of our Kingdom's ruin, from which we must seek deliverance. And there is deliverance only in religion, which teaches us that the populace ought to work; that the holy men, who know the will of the gods, ought to indicate to the populace the work to be done; and that the pharaoh and his dignitaries ought to see that the work be properly executed.

"That is what religion teaches us; it was by these precepts that Osiris-Ramses XII, the equal of the gods, ruled the Kingdom. And in recognition of his piety, we high priests shall carve upon his tomb and in the temples the inscription:

"'Horus the bull, powerful Apis who united the crowns of the Kingdom, golden sparrow hawk ruling by the sword, conqueror of the Nine Nations, King of Upper and Lower Egypt, Lord of the Two Worlds, son of the sun Amen-mer-Ramessu, beloved of Amon-Ra, lord and master of the Thebaid,[11] son of Amon-Ra, adoptive son of Horus, and begotten of Harakhti—King of Egypt, master of Phoenicia, reigning over the Nine Nations.'"[12]

When this motion had been acclaimed by the assembly, dancing girls ran out from behind the veil and performed a sacral dance before the sarcophagus, while priests lit incense. Then the mummy was taken down from the boat and carried into the sanctuary of Amon, which Ramses XIII was not authorized to enter.

Soon the ceremony ended, and the participants left the temple.

As he was returning to the palace at Luxor, the young Pharaoh was so engrossed in thought that he hardly noticed the immense crowd or heard its cheers.

"There's no deceiving my own heart," Ramses told himself. "The high priests hold me in contempt, which has never before met any pharaoh; why, they actually indicate how I can regain their favor! They mean to rule the Kingdom, and I'm to see that their orders are carried out!

"Well, it's not going to be that way: I will give the orders, and you must carry them out. And either I'll perish, or I'll set my royal foot on the backs of your necks!"

For two days Ramses XII's venerable mummy abided at the Temple of Amon-Ra, in a place so divine that, except for Herhor and Mephres, even high priests could not enter it. Only a single lamp burned before the deceased, whose flame, miraculously sustained, never went out. Over the deceased there hovered a symbol of the soul, a human-headed sparrow hawk. No one knew whether it was a machine or an actual living being. What was sure was that the priests who ventured to peek behind the veil saw the creature hanging in the air without support, while moving its mouth and eyes.

The obsequies continued, and the golden boat carried the deceased to the other side of the Nile. But first, surrounded by a huge cortege of priests, weeping women, troops, and populace, amid incense, music, weeping, and chanting, it passed down the main street of Thebes.

This was surely the most beautiful street in the Egyptian Kingdom: broad, smooth, tree-lined. Its four- and five-story buildings were covered from top to bottom with mosaics or colored bas reliefs: which made the buildings look as if they had been draped with gigantic

---

[11] The Thebaid: the region of ancient Egypt comprising the thirteen southernmost nomes of Upper Egypt, from Abydos to Aswan. The Thebaid took its name from its proximity to the ancient Egyptian capital, Thebes; during the ancient dynasties, this region was dominated by Thebes and by Thebes' priesthood headquartered in the Temple of Amon at Karnak. (*Translator.*)

[12] Authentic tomb inscription. (*Author.*)

colorful carpets or hung with colossal pictures representing the work of merchants, artisans, and sailors, as well as far-off countries and peoples.

In a word, this was not so much a street as an immense gallery of pictures, barbaric in design, garish in coloring.

The funerary cortege traveled southward for some two kilometers. More or less in the center of the city it stopped, then turned west for the Nile.

Here, in the river, was a large island to which led a bridge built on boats.[13] To avoid mishap, the generals directing the procession rearranged the cortege, placing four persons abreast and telling them to move very slowly, avoiding rhythmic tread. To that end, the musicians at the head of the procession intoned songs, each in a different tempo.

After a couple of hours, the procession had crossed the first bridge, then the island, then a second bridge, and found itself on the left, west bank of the Nile.

If the east half of Thebes could be called a city of gods and kings, the west half was a district of memorial temples and tombs.

The cortege advanced from the Nile, up a road, toward the hills. South of the road, atop a hill, stood a temple commemorating the victories of Ramses III,[14] its walls covered with images of the conquered peoples: Hittites, Amorites,[15] Philistines, Ethiopians, Arabs, Libyans. A little below it stood two colossal statues of Amenhotep III, the height of a five-story building despite the statues' seated posture. One of the statues was noted for a curious property: when the rays of the rising sun fell, the statue gave out sounds like those of a twanged harp.[16]

Nearer the road, and still to the left of it, stood the Ramesseum, a modest-sized but beautiful temple of Ramses II. Its vestibule was guarded by four standing statues holding royal insignia. In the court towered a statue of Ramses II four stories tall.

The road kept climbing gently, and very steep hills became ever more clearly visible, riddled like a sponge: these were tombs of Egyptian dignitaries. At the entrance to the hills, among steep rocks, lay the very original temple of Queen Hatshepsut.[17] The edifice was four hundred fifty paces long. From a courtyard enclosed by a wall, one climbed a stairway to a courtyard surrounded by columns, beneath which was an underground temple. And from the colonnaded courtyard one again climbed a stairway, to a temple carved into the rock, beneath which were more undergrounds.

Thus the temple had two tiers, a lower and upper, each of which was again divided into an upper and lower. The stairways were enormous, with two rows of sphinxes in lieu of railings; the entrance to each stairway was guarded by two seated statues.

---

[13] "a bridge built on boats": i.e., a pontoon bridge. *(Translator.)*

[14] Temple of Ramses III: the mortuary temple of Ramses III, at Medinet Habu, best known for its inscribed reliefs depicting the advent and defeat of the Sea Peoples during the reign of Ramses III. *(Translator.)*

[15] Amorites: an ancient Semitic people who inhabited Syria, Canaan, and southern Mesopotamia. *(Translator.)*

[16] For more on these statues of "Memnon," please see note earlier in this chapter. *(Translator.)*

[17] Hatshepsut (Prus calls her *Hatasu*): fifth pharaoh of the 18th Dynasty (reigned ca. 1478-1458 BCE). She was the second historically confirmed female pharaoh, after Sobekneferu ("the beauty of Sobek," also known as Neferusobek), the last pharaoh of the 12th Dynasty, who ruled 1806-1802 BCE, after her brother Amenemhat IV. *(Translator.)*

At the Temple of Hatshepsut there began a gloomy ravine that led from the dignitaries' tombs to the royal tombs. Between these two districts lay the rock-cut tomb of High Priest Padiamenope:[18] its underground chambers and corridors occupied about a hectare of area.[19]

The road through the ravine becomes so steep that the men have to help the oxen and push the funerary boat. The cortege moves over a ledge cut into the rock face, finally stopping in a spacious area a score of stories above the ravine floor.

Here is a door leading into the underground tomb that the pharaoh built over thirty years of his reign. The tomb is a complete palace with chambers for the Lord, his family, and servants, with dining room, bedroom, and bath, with chapels consecrated to various gods—and lastly with a well, at the bottom of which is a small room where the pharaoh's mummy will repose for the ages.

Bright torchlight illuminates the walls of all the chambers, covered with prayers and with pictures that recreate all the activities and pastimes of the deceased: hunts, the construction of temples and canals, triumphal processions, ceremonies honoring the gods, the army's battles with enemies, the labors of the populace.

That is not all: the rooms are not only filled with furniture, vessels, chariots, weapons, flowers, meats, pastries, and wines, but there are also numerous statues. These are effigies of Ramses XII, his priests, ministers, women, soldiers, and slaves. For in the next world as well, the Lord cannot do without sumptuous furnishings, exquisite foods, and faithful servants.

When the funerary wagon stopped at the entrance to the tomb, the priests took the royal mummy from the sarcophagus and set it on the ground with its back propped against the rock. Then Ramses XIII burned incense before his father's remains, and Queen Nikotris embraced the mummy's neck and wept:

"I am thy sister, thy wife Nikotris, do not leave me, O great one! Dost really want me to go away, my good father? If I do, thou shalt remain alone, and will anyone be with thee?"[20]

At that moment High Priest Herhor burned incense before the mummy, and Mephres poured out wine[21] and said:

"We offer this to thy double, O Osiris-Mer-amen-Ramses, Lord of Upper and Lower Egypt, whose voice is just before the great god."

Then weeping women and priestly choirs intoned:

Choir I. "Grieve, grieve, weep, weep without surcease, weep as loudly as you can."

Weeping women: "O noble traveler who turnest thy steps to the land of eternity, how quickly they wrest thee from us!"

Choir II. "How beautiful is what is happening to him! Since he dearly loved Khonsu

---

[18] Padiamenope (Prus calls him *Retemenof*), owner of the huge labyrinthine tomb TT 33 in the Theban necropolis—one of the largest tombs ever built in ancient Egypt—was actually not a high priest but a royal scribe and chief lector priest, during the end of the 25th or the beginning of the 26th Dynasty, some six centuries after *Pharaoh*'s present time. *(Translator.)*

[19] In the original text, "about two *mórgs* of subterranean area." *(Translator.)*

[20] Authentic. *(Author.)*

[21] "poured out wine": such a pouring of a liquid, most often wine, on the ground as an offering to a deity or in memory of the dead, is called a libation (from the Latin *libatio*, from *libare*—"to take a little from anything, to taste, to pour out as an offering"). *(Translator.)*

of Thebes, that god has let him reach the West, in the world of the generations of his servants."

Weeping women. "O thou whom so many servants surrounded, will now be in ground that exacts solitude! Thou that hadst sheer raiment and liked clean linen, lie now in yesterday's garments!"

Choir I. "In peace, in peace to the West, O our Lord, go in peace! We shall see thee again when the day of eternity comes, for thou goest to the land that unites all people within it."[22]

The final ceremonies began.

An ox and an antelope were brought, which Ramses XIII should have killed but which were killed by his deputy to the gods, High Priest Sem. Junior priests quickly skinned the animals, then Herhor and Mephres took the haunches and set them one after another to the mummy's lips. But the mummy would not eat, for it was not yet revived and its mouth was closed.

To remove this impediment, Mephres washed the mummy with holy water and censed it with perfumes and alum, saying:

"Here stands my father, here stands Osiris-Mer-amen-Ramses. I am thy son, I am Horus, I come to thee to cleanse thee and make thee whole. I set thy bones back together, I bind what was severed, for I am Horus, my father's avenger. Thou sittest on the throne of Re and givest commands to the gods. For thou art Re, descended of Nut, who bears Re each morning, who bears Mer-amen-Ramses daily even as Re."[23]

Speaking thus, the high priest touched amulets to the mummy's mouth, chest, arms, and legs.

Now the choirs intoned once more:

Choir I. "Osiris-Mer-amen-Ramses shall henceforth eat and drink all that the gods eat and drink. He sits in their place, he is hale and hardy like them."

Choir II. "He has power in all his members; he hates to be hungry and not be able to eat, and to be thirsty and not be able to drink."

Choir I. "O gods, render to Osiris-Mer-amen-Ramses thousands of thousands of flagons of wine, thousands of robes, breads, and beeves."

Choir II. "O you living upon the earth who shall pass by here, if life be dear to you and death repugnant, if you desire that your dignities pass to your posterity, say this prayer for the deceased one interred here."

Mephres. "O you grandees, you prophets, you princes, scribes, and pharaohs, you other people who shall come a million years after me, should any of you put his name in place of mine, God will punish him by destroying his person on this earth."[24]

After this imprecation, the priests lit torches, replaced the royal mummy in the casket, and placed the casket in the humaniform stone sarcophagus. Then, despite the screams, despair, and resistance of the weeping women, they carried the enormous burden into the tomb.

Passing through several corridors and chambers in the torchlight, they stopped in the chamber containing the well. They lowered the sarcophagus into the opening and followed it down to the nether undergrounds. There they set the sarcophagus in place in the

---

[22] Authentic. *(Author.)*

[23] Authentic. *(Author.)*

[24] Authentic. *(Author.)*

cramped room and quickly sealed up the opening, in such a way that the most practiced eye would not have discovered the entrance to the grave. Next they went back up and with equal pains walled up the entrance to the well.

All this, the priests did by themselves, without witnesses, and they did it so thoroughly that the mummy of Ramses XII to this day rests in its secret dwelling, safe alike from thieves and from modern curiosity. Over the span of twenty-nine centuries many a royal tomb has been violated, but this one remains intact.

While one group of priests was secreting the pious pharaoh's remains, another illuminated the underground chambers and invited the living to a feast.

Into the dining room there entered Ramses XIII, Queen Nikotris, High Priests Herhor, Mephres, and Sem, and a dozen civil and military dignitaries. In the center of the chamber were tables laden with foods, wine, and flowers, and at one wall sat a statue of the late Lord, carved from porphyry. It seemed to look upon the company and, with a melancholy smile, invite them to partake.

The feast opened with a sacral dance, accompanied by one of the highest priestesses singing:

"Enjoy the days of happiness, for life lasts but a moment ... Enjoy happiness, for when you enter the grave you will rest there forever, for the whole duration of every day!"[25]

After the priestess, a prophet came forward and intoned, to the accompaniment of harps:

"The world is constant change and constant renewal. 'Tis a wise dispensation of fate, an admirable decree of Osiris, that as a body from times past declines and dies, other bodies remain after it.

"The pharaohs, those gods who were before us, rest in their pyramids; their mummies and doubles remain. But the palaces they built are no longer in their former places, they are no more.

"Despair not, then, but give yourself up to your desires and happiness, and do not use up your heart until the day comes for you when you shall beg and Osiris, the god whose heart no longer beats, will not hear your prayers and pleas.

"The grief of all the world will not restore happiness to him who lies in the tomb; enjoy, then, the days of happiness, and be not slow in joy. Truly, none can take his goods with him into the next world—truly, none can go there and return!"[26]

The feast ended; the distinguished assemblage censed the statue of the deceased once more and left for Thebes. In the mortuary temple there remained only priests, to make regular offerings to the Lord, and guards to protect the tomb from the sacrilegious temptations of thieves.

Henceforth Ramses XII remained alone in his secret chamber. Through a small window concealed in the rock, twilight barely broke in. Instead of ostrich plumes, over the Lord there rustled the wings of enormous bats; instead of music, at night there rang the mournful howls of hyenas and now and again the powerful voice of a lion greeting, from its desert, the pharaoh in his tomb.

---

[25] Authentic. *(Author.)*

[26] Authentic. *(Author.)*

CHAPTER 59

A fter the pharaoh's funeral, Egypt returned to normal; and Ramses XIII, to affairs of state. In the month of Epiphi (April-May) the new ruler visited the cities south of Thebes along the Nile. He called at Esna,[1] a very industrial and commercial city, site of a Temple of Khnum,[2] "the soul of the world." He visited Edfu,[3] whose temple with ten-story pylon towers possessed an enormous library of papyri and, written and painted on its walls, a kind of encyclopedia of contemporary geography, astronomy, and theology. He stopped by the stone quarries in Khenu;[4] in Nubt,[5] or Kom Ombo, he made offerings to Horus, the god of light, and to Sobek, the spirit of darkness. He visited the island of Abu,[6] which looked like an emerald amid the black rocks, produced the finest dates, and was called the elephant capital: for the ivory trade was concentrated there.[7] Finally, he stopped by the city of Syene,[8] located at the First Cataract of the Nile, and visited the huge granite

[1] Esna: Egyptian Arabic name for a city on the west bank of the Nile, known to the ancient Egyptians as Iunyt or Ta-senet; and to the Copts, as Sne, which derives from *Ta-senet*. Esna lies some 55 kilometers south of Luxor. Prus calls Esna *Sni*. *(Translator.)*

[2] Khnum: Prus here calls him *Kneph*. Construction of the Temple of Khnum at Esna began in Ptolemaic times, but most of its surviving parts were built in Roman times. *(Translator.)*

[3] Edfu (known in Egyptian antiquity as *Behdet*, and to the Romans as *Apollonopolis Magna*, after the god Horus, whom the Greeks and Romans identified with Apollo): a city on the west bank of the Nile between Esna and Aswan. It was the capital of the 2nd Nome of Upper Egypt, and is the site of the Ptolemaic Temple of Horus (built between 237 and 57 BCE), the most completely preserved of all the temple remains in Egypt. *(Translator.)*

[4] Khenu (or *Kheny*, or *Khenyt*, "The Place of Rowing"; in Arabic, Gebel el-Silsila, "Chain of Mountains"): a major quarry site on both banks of the Nile from at least the 18th Dynasty to Greco-Roman times. Silsila, famous for its New Kingdom stelae and cenotaphs, is located between Edfu, to the north, and Kom Ombo to the south. Prus calls Khenu *Chennu. (Translator.)*

[5] Nubt ("City of Gold"), or Kom Ombo: a town, fifty kilometers north of Aswan, famous for the Temple of Kom Ombo. The temple was actually constructed during the Ptolemaic Dynasty, nine centuries after *Pharaoh*'s present time, and was dedicated to two sets of gods, centered respectively on the crocodile god Sobek and the falcon god Horus. *(Translator.)*

[6] Abu (or *Yebu*): Elephantine Island, in northern Nubia. The island is now part of the modern city of Aswan, in southern Egypt. Prus calls Abu *Ab*. *(Translator.)*

[7] Alternative theories about the origin of Elephantine Island's name invoke the island's shape, resembling an elephant's tusk; or the rounded rocks along the island's banks, resembling elephants. *(Translator.)*

[8] Syene: ancient Greek name for the city now called Aswan, in southern Egypt. Prus here calls the city *Sunnu. (Translator.)*

and syenite[9] quarries where rocks were split off with water-soaked wedges, and where nine-story obelisks were hewn out.

Wherever Egypt's new Lord appeared, his subjects greeted him with wild enthusiasm. Even the convicts laboring in the quarries, whose bodies were covered with unhealed wounds, knew happiness: the Pharaoh ordered them given three days off from work.

Ramses XIII could be pleased and proud: no pharaoh, even during a triumphal entry, had been welcomed as he was in his peaceful progress. The nomarchs, scribes, and high priests, seeing the boundless attachment of the populace to the new Pharaoh, bent to his authority and whispered:

"The common people are as a herd of bulls, and we are as prudent, frugal ants. Therefore let us revere the new Lord, that we may enjoy health and preserve our houses from destruction."

The dignitaries' opposition, only a few months earlier very strong, now fell silent and gave place to boundless humility. All the aristocracy and all the priesthood prostrated themselves on their faces before Ramses XIII; only Mephres and Herhor remained unbending.

And so, when the Pharaoh returned from Syene to Thebes, immediately on the first day the Great Treasurer brought him two pieces of bad news.

"All the temples," he said, "have refused to extend credit to the treasury and most humbly beg Your Holiness to order repayment, within two years, of the sums borrowed from them."

"I see," replied the ruler, "this is the work of the holy Mephres! How much do we owe them?"

"Some fifty thousand talents."

"We are to repay fifty thousand talents within two years!" repeated the Pharaoh. "Well, and what else?"

"Taxes are coming in very slowly," said the Treasurer. "For the past three months, we have been receiving barely a quarter of what we should be."

"What's happened?"

The Treasurer was troubled.

"I have heard," he said, "that some people are telling the peasants they need not pay taxes during Your Holiness' reign."

"Oho!" laughed Ramses, "those people sound very much like His Eminence Herhor! Well, now, does he mean to starve me to death?

"How are you covering current expenses?" he asked.

"At Hiram's behest, the Phoenicians are giving us loans," answered the Treasurer. "We've already taken eight thousand talents."

"Are you giving them notes?"

"Notes, and collateral too," sighed the Treasurer. "They say it's just a formality; nevertheless they're settling into Your Holiness' estates and taking all they can from the peasants."

Intoxicated by the welcome of the populace and the humility of the magnates, the Pharaoh felt no animus toward Herhor and Mephres. The time for anger had passed, the moment for action had come, and that same day Ramses laid his plans.

---

[9] Syenite: an igneous rock composed primarily of alkali feldspar. Syenite took its name from Syene, where it was quarried. (Translator.)

Next day he called in his closest confidants: High Priest Sem; the prophet Pentuer; Ramses' favorite, Thutmose; and the Phoenician, Hiram. When they were gathered, he said:

"No doubt you know that the temples are demanding repayment of the funds that my eternally living father borrowed from them. All debts are sacred, and I would fain repay first of all this one owing to the gods. But my treasury is empty because even the taxes are coming in irregularly.

"For that reason, I deem the Kingdom to be in danger—and I am forced to turn for funds to the treasures reposing in the Labyrinth."

The two priests stirred uneasily.

"I am aware," continued the Pharaoh, "that under our sacred laws my decree is insufficient to open the cellars of the Labyrinth to us. But the priests there told me what I should do. I must convene representatives of all of Egypt's estates, thirteen persons from each estate, and obtain their confirmation of my will."

The Pharaoh smiled here and concluded:

"I have called you today so that you may help me convoke the assembly of estates; and these are my instructions to you:

"Your Eminence Sem shall select for me thirteen priests and thirteen nomarchs. You, pious Pentuer, shall bring in from various nomes thirteen husbandmen and thirteen craftsmen. Thutmose shall deliver thirteen officers and thirteen nobility, and Prince Hiram shall see that I have thirteen merchants.

"I desire that this assembly gather as soon as possible at my Memphis palace and, without wasting time on empty talk, resolve that the Labyrinth is to deliver funds to my treasury."

"I'll make bold to remind Your Holiness," interjected High Priest Sem, "that Their Eminences Herhor and Mephres must be present at the assembly and that it is their right, indeed duty, to oppose the breaching of the Labyrinth's treasury."

"I agree most completely!" replied the Pharaoh briskly. "They'll give their rationale, I'll give mine. And the assembly will judge whether a kingdom can exist without money, and whether it's sensible to keep treasures locked away in cellars when the government is threatened with bankruptcy."

"A few of the sapphires that repose in the Labyrinth could pay off all the Phoenician debts!" said Hiram. "I'm going out to the merchants, and I'll soon give you not thirteen but thirteen thousand who will vote as Your Holiness' bids!"

With that, the Phoenician prostrated himself and took his leave of the Lord.

Following Hiram's departure, High Priest Sem said: "I wonder whether it was well for a foreigner to be present at this conference."

"He had to be!" exclaimed the Pharaoh. "Not only does he wield great influence with our merchants, but more importantly, he is supplying us with money. I wanted to show him I'm mindful of our debts to him and have the means to cover them."

In the ensuing silence, Pentuer said: "If Your Holiness permits, I will be leaving to gather the husbandmen and craftsmen. They would all vote for our Lord, but the wisest must be chosen from among the many."

He took his leave of the Pharaoh.

"What about you, Thutmose?" asked Ramses.

"My Lord," said the favorite, "I'm so sure of your military and nobility that, rather than speak of them, I will make bold to present to you a request of my own."

"You need money?"

"Not at all. I want to marry."

"You?" exclaimed the Pharaoh. "Which woman has merited such happiness of the gods?"

"She is the beautiful Hebron,[10] daughter of His Eminence the Theban Nomarch Antef,"[11] laughed Thutmose. "If Your Holiness could propose me to this estimable family ... I wanted to say it would increase my love for you ... but I'll leave well enough alone, as I would be lying."

The Pharaoh patted him on the shoulder.

"Now, now, don't assure me of what I'm sure of!" he said. "Tomorrow I'll go to Antef's and, by the gods, I believe that in a few days I'll arrange your wedding. And now, off with you to your Hebron!"

Remaining now with only Sem, His Holiness said: "You have a grim expression. Do you doubt that thirteen priests can be found, ready to do my bidding?"

"I'm certain," answered Sem, "that nearly all the priests and nomarchs will do what is needed for Egypt's well-being and Your Holiness' pleasure. But pray do not forget, Lord, that where the treasury of the Labyrinth is concerned, the final decision will be issued by Amon."

"By the statue of Amon in Thebes?"

"Yes."

The Pharaoh tossed his hand dismissively. "Amon," he said, "is Herhor and Mephres. I know they won't agree; but I don't think to sacrifice the Kingdom to the obstinacy of two men."

"Your Holiness is mistaken," said Sem solemnly. "It's true that statues of gods very often do as their high priests want ... but not always! In our temples, Lord, extraordinary and mysterious things sometimes happen. Statues of gods sometimes do and say what they wish!"

"In that case, my mind is at ease," the Pharaoh interrupted him. "The gods know the state of the Kingdom, and they can read my heart. I desire Egypt's well-being, and since that is my sole object, no wise and good god would hinder me."

"May Your Holiness' words come true!" whispered the high priest.

"There's something else you want to tell me," said Ramses, as his religious deputy tarried.

"Yes, Lord. It is my obligation to remind you that every pharaoh, upon taking power and interring his predecessor, must give thought to erecting two structures: a tomb for himself, and a temple for the gods."

"Quite so!" cried the Lord. "I've given some thought to it; but having no money, I've been in no hurry with issuing orders. You see," he added, animated, "if I build something, it will be something great that won't allow Egypt soon to forget me."

"Does Your Holiness wish to have a pyramid?"

---

[10] Hebron: name borrowed from an extant city in Palestine. *(Translator.)*

[11] Antef (or *Intef*): name borrowed from three kings of Egypt's Second Intermediate Period (between the end of the Middle Kingdom and the start of the New Kingdom), several centuries before *Pharaoh*'s present time. *(Translator.)*

"No. After all, I couldn't build a pyramid greater than that of Cheops nor a temple greater than that of Amon in Thebes. My Kingdom is too weak to carry out enormous projects. I must do something completely new, especially as, to be frank, our structures are starting to bore me. They're all alike, as people are alike, differing only in dimensions, as an adult differs from a child."

"So?" asked the high priest, surprised.

"I've spoken with the Greek, Dion,[12] our foremost architect, and he praised my plan," continued the Pharaoh. "For my tomb I want to build a round tower with an external stairway, like the one that stood at Babel. And I'll erect a temple not to Osiris or to Isis but to the One God in whom all believe: Egyptians, Chaldeans, Phoenicians, and Jews. And I want the temple to resemble King Assar's palace, a model of which Sargon brought for my father."

The high priest shook his head.

"Those are grand plans, my Lord," he replied, "but impracticable. Due to their form, Babylonian towers are vulnerable to toppling; whereas our structures must last out the ages. A temple can't be erected to the One God, for He needs neither clothing nor food nor drink, and the whole world is His abode. What temple could accommodate Him, what priest would venture to make Him offerings?"

"Well, then we'll build a sanctuary for Amon-Ra," said the Pharaoh.

"All right, so long as it doesn't resemble King Assar's palace. For that is an Assyrian structure, and it's not meet for us Egyptians to imitate barbarians."

"I don't understand you," broke in the Lord, a bit irritated.

"Hear me out, our Lord," said Sem. "Consider the snails, each of which has a different shell: one, coiled but flat; another, coiled and oblong; yet another, boxy. By the same token, each nation builds a different structure, consistent with its blood and disposition.

"Pray bear in mind that Egyptian buildings are as different from Assyrian buildings as Egyptians are from Assyrians.

"In Egypt the basic shape of a building is the truncated pyramid, the most durable of all forms, as Egypt is the most durable of all kingdoms; while in Assyria the basic form is the cube, which easily breaks down.

"The overweening, light-minded Assyrian stacks his cubes one atop another and builds a many-storied structure whose weight saps the ground. The humble, prudent Egyptian sets his truncated pyramids one after another. This way in Egypt nothing hangs in the air, but every part of a building rests squarely on the ground.

"Owing to this, our structures are elongated and everlasting; Assyrian structures, tall and brittle, like their kingdom, which is now rapidly rising but of which only rubble will remain a couple of centuries hence.

"The Assyrian is a noisy braggart, and in his buildings he places everything on the outside: columns, pictures, and sculptures. Whereas the modest Egyptian conceals the most beautiful sculptures and columns inside his temples, like the sage who keeps his lofty thoughts, feelings, and desires deep in his heart and doesn't adorn his chest and back with them. With us, everything of beauty is concealed; with them, everything is done for show. The Assyrian, if he could, would cut open his stomach to show the world what extraordinary fare he consumes."

---

[12] Dion: name borrowed from a number of historical individuals. *(Translator.)*

"Go on! ... Go on!" said Ramses.

"There's little left for me to say, Lord," continued Sem. "I'd only like to bring your attention to the general form of our buildings and of Assyrian buildings.

"When years ago, in Nineveh, I regarded the Assyrian towers leaping arrogantly over the ground, they seemed to me like unruly horses that had slipped their bits and were rearing up—but would soon fall, perhaps breaking their legs.

"But, Holiness, look from a high vantage at an Egyptian temple. What does it bring to mind? ... A man lying on the ground in prayer.

"The two pylon towers are his two hands lifted heavenward. The two walls enclosing the courtyard are his arms. The Columned Hall, or Heavenly Hall, is his head; the Chambers of Divine Revelation and Offering Tables are his chest; and the god's sanctuary is the pious Egyptian's heart.

"Our temple teaches us how we should be.

"'Have hands mighty as the pylon towers,' it tells us, 'and arms strong as the walls. Have in your head a mind as broad and rich as the temple's vestibule; a soul as pure as the Chambers of Revelation and Offerings; and have god in your heart, O Egyptian!'

"Whereas Assyrian buildings say to their populace:

"'Climb above people, O Assyrian, lift your head above others! You'll accomplish nothing great in the world, but at least you'll leave a great deal of rubble.'

"Would Your Lordship," concluded the high priest, "erect Assyrian buildings in Egypt, imitating a people whom Egypt loathes and despises?"

Ramses mused. Despite Sem's discourse, he still thought Assyrian palaces more beautiful than Egyptian ones. But he had such a hatred of the Assyrians that his heart began to waver.

"In that case," he said, "I'll hold off with building the temple and my tomb. And you wise men who are well-disposed to me—devise plans for buildings that will pass my name down to the most distant generations."

"An inhuman pride fills this young man's soul!" the high priest told himself, as he took a sad farewell of the Pharaoh.

CHAPTER 60

Meanwhile Pentuer was setting out once more for Lower Egypt, to recruit for the Pharaoh thirteen delegates each from the husbandmen's and craftsmen's estates—and to urge working people to call for the reliefs that the new ruler had pledged. Pentuer was convinced that the most important matter for Egypt was to put an end to the injustices and abuses suffered by the working classes.

Still, Pentuer was a priest. He did not desire the downfall of his estate, nor did he wish to sever his ties with it.

To show his loyalty, Pentuer went to take leave of Herhor.

The once powerful dignitary greeted him with a smile.

"A rare guest ... a rare guest!" exclaimed Herhor. "Ever since you were offered the advisorship to His Holiness, you haven't been showing yourself here ... True, not just you! But come what may, I won't forget your services, though you were to shun me still more."

"I am not our Lord's advisor, nor am I shunning Your Eminence, to whose favor I owe what I am today," replied Pentuer.

"I know, I know!" broke in Herhor. "You declined the high dignity so as not to work for the downfall of the temples. I know! ... But maybe it's too bad you didn't become advisor to the impetuous youngster who supposedly governs us. Certainly you would not have let him surround himself with traitors who will be the undoing of him."

Not wishing to speak on such touchy questions, Pentuer told Herhor why he was going to Lower Egypt.

"Certainly," replied Herhor, "let Ramses XIII call the assembly of all the estates. That is his prerogative.

"But," he added suddenly, "I'm sorry you are getting involved in this. You've changed a lot! Do you remember what you told my aide during the Pi-Bailos maneuvers? ... Let me remind you: you said the abuses and excesses of the pharaohs must be curbed. And today you are yourself backing the childish demands of the greatest profligate whom Egypt has ever known."

"Ramses XIII," interrupted Pentuer, "wants to improve the lives of the populace. I, the son of peasants, would be stupid and contemptible if I didn't serve him in this cause."

"But you don't ask whether this might harm us, the priesthood?"

"Why," cried Pentuer, "you yourselves give great reliefs to the temple peasants! Besides, I have your permission."

"What permission?" asked Herhor.

"Think back, Eminence, to the night we greeted the most holy Berossus at the Temple of Set. Mephres said then that Egypt was fallen due to the debasement of the priesthood, and I held that the misery of the populace was the cause of the Kingdom's troubles. To which, as I recall, you answered:

"'Let Mephres see to lifting up the priests; and Pentuer, to improving the lives of the peasants. For my part, I shall work to prevent a disastrous war between Egypt and Assyria.'"

"So you see," interrupted the High Priest, "you have an obligation to act with us, not with Ramses."

"Does he want war with Assyria?" replied Pentuer energetically. "Is he preventing the priests from acquiring knowledge? He wants to give the people a seventh day of rest; and later, each peasant family a small plot of land. Now, Eminence, don't tell me the Pharaoh wants something bad: it has been found at temple farms that a free peasant with his own plot of land works incomparably better than a slave."

"But I have nothing against reliefs for the common people!" cried Herhor. "I just don't believe Ramses will do anything for the populace."

"Certainly not, if you refuse him money."

"Even if we gave him a pyramid of gold and silver, and a second pyramid of precious stones, he still wouldn't do anything, because he's a headstrong youngster whom the Assyrian envoy Sargon always called a 'squirt.'"

"The Pharaoh has great abilities!"

"But he doesn't know anything, he doesn't know how to do anything!" said Herhor. "He hardly warmed a place at an upper school before fleeing it. So now, in matters of governance, he is like a blind man, like a child that boldly moves draughtsmen but has no idea how the game is played."

"Still, he rules ..."

"But what a rule it is, Pentuer!" smiled the High Priest. "He's opened up new military schools, he's multiplied the number of regiments, he's arming the whole country, he's promising the common people holidays ... But how will he do it? You're keeping a distance from him, so you don't know; but I assure you that, when he issues orders, he gives no thought to who will carry them out, whether the means exist, what will be the consequences.

"You think he rules. It is I who rule, I who still rule, I whom he banished from his side. It is by my doing that fewer taxes are now flowing into the treasury, but I am also preventing a peasant revolt, which otherwise would have broken out; it is by my doing that work hasn't stopped at the canals, dams, and highways. Finally, I have already twice stopped Assyria from declaring war on us, which this madman provokes with his military dispositions.

"Ramses rules! All he does is create confusion. You had a sample of his management down in Lower Egypt: he drank, caroused, took up with one girl after another—and supposedly occupied himself with the administration of the nomes, but understood nothing, absolutely nothing. Worst of all, he fell in with the Phoenicians, with bankrupt nobility, and with assorted traitors who are pushing him toward disaster."

"What about the victory at the Natron Lakes?" asked Pentuer.

"I grant him energy and knowledge of the military art," replied Herhor. "That is the one thing he knows. But tell me yourself, would he have won the battle of the Natron Lakes but for your help and that of the other priests? I know you informed him of every move by the Libyan host ... Now think: could Ramses, even with your help, win a battle against, say, Nitager? Nitager is a master; Ramses is but an apprentice."

"So how will your hatred end?" asked Pentuer.

"Hatred!" repeated the High Priest. "How can I possibly hate a whelp who, in addition, is surrounded like a stag in the ravines by hunters? But I must admit that his rule is so detrimental to Egypt that, if Ramses had a brother or if Nitager were younger, we would already have removed today's pharaoh."

"And Your Eminence would become his successor!" Pentuer burst out.

Herhor took no umbrage.

"You've grown strangely obtuse, Pentuer," he shrugged, "since you began conducting politics on your own account. Of course, if a pharaoh were lacking, I would be obliged to become pharaoh, as High Priest of Theban Amon and head of the Supreme Priestly Council. But what need have I of that? Haven't I for over a dozen years wielded more power than the pharaohs? And today do I, the banished Minister of War, not do in the Kingdom what I deem needful?

"The same high priests, treasurers, judges, nomarchs, and even generals who now shun me, still must carry out every secret order of the Supreme Council bearing my seal. Is there a person in Egypt who would refuse such orders? Would you yourself dare resist them?"

Pentuer hung his head. If despite the death of Ramses XII the Supreme Priestly Privy Council survived, then Ramses XIII must either submit to it or wage a life-and-death struggle with it.

The Pharaoh had behind him all the populace, all the army, many priests, and most of the civil dignitaries. The Council could count on barely a couple of thousand adherents, on its treasuries, and on superlative organization. The most unequal of forces, but the outcome of the struggle—very much in doubt.

"So you have decided to destroy the Pharaoh!" whispered Pentuer.

"Not at all. We want only to save the Kingdom."

"In that case, what should Ramses XIII do?"

"What he will do ... I don't know," replied Herhor. "But I know what his father did.

"Ramses XII too began his reign in ignorance and willfulness; but when he ran out of money and his most ardent partisans began disregarding him, he turned to the gods. He surrounded himself with priests, learned from them; aye, he even married the daughter of High Priest Amenhotep. And after a dozen or so years he himself became a high priest, not only a pious but a very learned one."

"What if the Pharaoh doesn't heed this advice?" asked Pentuer.

"Then we shall do without him," said Herhor.

After a moment, he continued:

"Listen to me, Pentuer. I know not only what he does but what he thinks about, this Pharaoh of yours who in fact has not yet been solemnly crowned and therefore is nothing to us. I know he wants to make the priests his servants—and himself, sole master of Egypt.

"But such an intent is nonsense, even treason. It was not the pharaohs, as you well know, who created Egypt, but the gods and priests. It is not the pharaohs who monitor the rise of the Nile and regulate its flood; it was not the pharaohs who taught the populace to sow and to harvest, and to rear cattle. It is not the pharaohs who minister to the ill and watch over the safety of the Kingdom against external enemies.

"What would happen, do you suppose, if our estate were to deliver Egypt into the tender mercies of the pharaohs? The wisest of them has the accumulated experience of a few dozen years; whereas the priesthood has been studying and learning for tens of thousands of years. The most powerful ruler has a single pair of eyes and hands—his own; whereas we possess thousands of eyes and hands in all the nomes and even in foreign kingdoms.

"So can a pharaoh's activity compare with ours; and in the event of differing opinions, who should give way—we or he?"

"What am I to do now?" broke in Pentuer.

"Do as the youngster tells you, so long as you don't betray holy secrets. And leave the rest… to time. I sincerely hope the young man called Ramses XIII will bethink himself, and I expect he would have done so if… if he had not fallen in with loathsome traitors over whom the hand of the gods already hangs suspended."

Pentuer took his leave of the high priest, full of sad forebodings. But he did not lose heart, knowing that whatever he secured today to improve life for the populace would abide, though the Pharaoh bowed to the power of the priests.

"In the worst of circumstances," he thought, "we must do what we can and what is incumbent on us. Sometime the situation will improve, and today's sowing will bear fruit."

Nonetheless he decided to leave off agitating the populace. Indeed, he was prepared to calm the impatient among them so they would not increase the Pharaoh's troubles.

A couple of weeks later Pentuer was riding into Lower Egypt, along the way seeking out the most judicious peasants and craftsmen from among whom to select delegates to the assembly the Pharaoh was calling.

Everywhere along the way he encountered signs of the greatest excitement: both peasants and craftsmen demanded a seventh day of rest and pay for all public works, as had once obtained. It was only thanks to the admonitions of priests from various temples that a general rebellion had not broken out, or at least that public works had not come to a stop.

At the same time he was struck by several new phenomena that he had not noticed a month earlier.

The populace had divided into two parties. One sided with the Pharaoh and was hostile to the priests; the other inveighed against the Phoenicians. The former argued that the priests should give the Pharaoh the treasures of the Labyrinth; the latter whispered that the Pharaoh excessively favored foreigners.

Strangest of all was a rumor, of unknown origin, that Ramses XIII was showing signs of madness like his elder half brother, who for that reason had been barred from the succession to the throne. This was the talk of priests, scribes, even peasants.

"Who has been telling you these lies?" Pentuer asked one of his engineer acquaintances.

"It's no lie," replied the engineer, "but the sad truth. At the Theban palaces the Pharaoh was seen running naked in the gardens. One evening His Holiness climbed a tree outside Queen Nikotris' windows and spoke with her."

Pentuer assured him that as late as half a month earlier he had seen the Pharaoh, who was in the best of health. But he presently found that the engineer did not believe him.

"This is Herhor's doing!" thought Pentuer. "Anyway, only the priests could have news this fast from Thebes."

For a moment he lost desire to select delegates, but he regained his energy by repeating to himself that what the populace gained today, they would not lose tomorrow ... barring some extraordinary events!

Outside Memphis, north of the Pyramids and the Sphinx, at the edge of the sands, stood a small temple of the goddess Nut. Here lived an old priest, Menes,[1] an engineer and Egypt's foremost expert on the stars.

When a large building or a new canal was to be constructed in the Kingdom, Menes would come down to the site and lay out the direction. Otherwise he lived poor and alone at his temple, by night observing the stars and by day working on singular instruments.

Pentuer had not been to this place in several years and was struck by its dilapidation and poverty. The brick wall was falling down, the trees in the garden had dried up, and a scrawny goat and a couple of chickens rambled about the courtyard.

No one was about the temple. Only when Pentuer called out, did an old man emerge from a pylon tower. He was barefoot and wore a dirty cap, like a peasant; a rag of a loincloth about his hips; and on his back a molted leopard skin. Notwithstanding, he had a dignified bearing and an intelligent countenance. He scrutinized the guest and said: "Be I mistaken, or are you Pentuer?"

"I am he," said the arrival, heartily embracing the old man.

"Well, well!" exclaimed Menes, for he it was, "I see you have changed on the eminent floors. Your skin is smooth, your hands are whiter, and you have a gold chain round your neck. The goddess of the celestial ocean, mother Nut, must wait long for such an ornament!"

Pentuer made to take off the chain, but Menes stopped him. "Leave me alone!" he smiled. "If you knew what gems we have in the heavens, you wouldn't be so quick to offer gold. Well, now, do you come to stay here for good?"

Pentuer shook his head. "No, godly teacher," he said. "I come only to pay my respects to you."

"Then back to court?" laughed the old man. "Oh, you, you! If you knew what you lose, abandoning wisdom for palaces, you'd be the saddest of men!"

"You are alone, teacher?"

"Like a palm tree in the desert, especially today as my deaf-mute has gone with a basket to Memphis, abegging for the mother of Re and her priest."

"Doesn't it make you sad?"

"Me?" cried Menes. "Since we last met, I've wrested several secrets from the gods which I wouldn't trade for both the crowns of Egypt!"

"Secrets?" said Pentuer.

"And what secrets! ... A year ago I completed my measurements and calculations concerning the size of the earth!"

"What do you mean?"

Menes looked about and lowered his voice. "You know," he said, "that the earth is not flat like a table, but is a huge sphere on whose surface are the seas, countries, and cities."

---

[1] Menes: name borrowed from a pharaoh of Egypt's Early Dynastic Period who is traditionally credited with having united Upper and Lower Egypt and founded the 1st Dynasty. Menes is most commonly identified either with Narmer (of the *Narmer palette*) or with the 1st Dynasty pharaoh Hor-Aha. *(Translator.)*

"That is known," said Pentuer.

"Not to everyone," replied Menes. "And quite unknown was how great the sphere might be."

"And you know?" asked Pentuer, near terrified.

"I do. Our infantry marches thirteen Egyptian miles[2] a day. Well, the earth's sphere is so vast that it would take our army five years to march all the way around it."[3]

"Gods!" said Pentuer. "Father, doesn't it frighten you to think about such things?"

Menes shrugged. "Measuring size, what's frightening about that?" he said. "Measuring a pyramid or the earth, it's all the same. I've done harder things: I've measured the distance from our temple to the pharaoh's palace without crossing the Nile."

"Frightful!" whispered Pentuer.

"Why frightful? I've discovered something that will really give you a fright. But don't tell anyone about it. You know, in Phaophi[4] we'll be having a solar eclipse—day will become night. And may I die of starvation if I'm as much as a twentieth of an hour off in my calculations."

Pentuer touched an amulet on his chest and recited a prayer.

"I've read in the holy books," he said, "about it having sometimes become night at noon, to the panic of the people. But I don't understand it."

"Do you see the Pyramids?" asked Menes suddenly, pointing to the desert.

"Yes."

"Now put your hand in front of your eyes. Do you see the Pyramids? ... No. Well, a solar eclipse is the same thing: the moon comes between the sun and us, conceals the father of light, and makes night."

"And this will happen here?" asked Pentuer.

"In Phaophi. I wrote the Pharaoh about it, thinking that in return he would give our neglected temple an offering. But after reading the letter he ridiculed me and told my messenger to take the information to Herhor."

"What did Herhor do?"

"He gave us thirty measures of barley. He is the one man in Egypt who respects learning. The young Pharaoh is completely lacking in seriousness."

"Don't be hard on him, father," said Pentuer. "Ramses XIII wants to improve the lives of the peasants and craftsmen: he's going to give them a seventh day of rest, he's going to forbid their beating without trial, and he may give them some land."

"I tell you he's not serious," said Menes, exasperated. "Two months ago, I sent him a great plan that could ease the labor of the peasants ... and again he ridiculed me! He's a vain ignoramus."

"You're prejudiced, father. But tell me your plan; maybe I can help implement it."

"Plan!" said the old man. "It's not a plan anymore, but a thing ..."

---

[2] Three geographical miles. *(Author.)* By one reckoning, an ancient Egyptian mile was about 4,000 cubits, or 2,092 meters. Thus 13 Egyptian miles would equal about 27 kilometers or 17 international miles. *(Translator.)*

[3] A similarly accurate calculation of the earth's circumference will be made in Alexandrian Egypt in the 3rd century BCE by the Greek polymath Eratosthenes. *(Translator.)*

[4] Phaophi: July-August. *(Author.)* Actually, the ancient Egyptian month of Phaophi lay between October 11 and November 9 of the modern, Gregorian calendar, unless the previous Coptic year was a leap year. *(Translator.)*

He rose from the bench, and they walked to a pond in the garden, over which stood an arbor perfectly screened by climbing plants.

Inside the structure was a great wheel, mounted on a horizontal axle, with many buckets attached to the circumference. Menes climbed inside the wheel and proceeded to walk. The wheel turned, and the buckets drew water from the pond and poured it into a higher-placed trough.

"Interesting device!" said Pentuer.

"Can you guess what it could do for the Egyptian people?"

"No ..."

"Then imagine a wheel five or ten times larger, with several pairs of oxen treading inside it instead of a man."

"I'm starting to get an idea," said Pentuer, "but I still don't quite get it."

"It's so simple!" said Menes. "With the wheel, oxen or horses could draw water from the Nile and pour it into successively higher canals. Half a million people who now work the buckets could enjoy a rest. You see now that learning does more for human happiness than the pharaohs."

Pentuer shook his head. "Think how much wood it would take, how many oxen, how much forage! I don't think, father, that your wheel will replace the seventh day of rest."

"I can see," shrugged Menes, "that your dignities haven't done you much good. But though you've lost the quickness that I used to admire in you, I'll show you something else. Maybe eventually you'll come back to learning and, when I die, work at improving and popularizing my inventions."

They returned to the pylon, and Menes placed fuel under a small copper kettle. He fanned the flame, and the water soon came to a boil.

From the kettle there emerged a vertical pipe covered with a heavy stone. When the kettle began hissing, Menes said: "Stand there and watch ..."

He turned a crank attached to the pipe, and instantly the heavy stone shot into the air, filling the chamber with billows of steam.[5]

"Remarkable!" shouted Pentuer. But he soon calmed and asked: "How will the stone improve the lives of the people?"

"The stone won't," said the exasperated sage. "But mark my words: a time will come when the horse and ox will replace human labor, and boiling water will replace the horse and ox."

"But what will come of it for the peasants?" insisted Pentuer.

"Alas!" exclaimed Menes, clutching his head. "You've grown senile or stupid; the peasants have made you blind to the whole world, they've dimmed your mind.

"If sages were to concern themselves only with the peasants, they ought to abandon their books and calculations and become herdsmen!"

"Everything must have a use," said Pentuer diffidently.

"You court people," said Menes bitterly, "use a double standard! When a Phoenician brings you a ruby or sapphire, you don't ask what use it is, you buy it and lock it in your chest. But when a sage comes to you with an invention that could change the world, you

---

[5] A steam engine of different design will be invented in Roman Egypt, in the 1st century CE, by Heron of Alexandria. *(Translator.)*

immediately ask what use it is. Evidently you're terrified lest the sage request a handful of barley in return for something your mind does not grasp."

"Are you angry, father? I didn't mean to hurt your feelings."

"I'm not angry, I'm pained. Only twenty years ago, there were five of us working at this temple on discovering new secrets. Today I alone remain and, by the gods, I can find no one to understand, let alone succeed, me."

"Father, I would certainly remain here until I died, in order to learn your divine ideas," said Pentuer. "But tell me, can I shut myself inside a temple today, when the fate of the Kingdom and the happiness of the simple folk are in the balance—and when my involvement ..."

"May influence the fate of the Kingdom and of several million people?" scoffed Menes. "Oh, you grown children in your miters and dignitaries' chains! Just because you're allowed to draw water from the Nile, you think you can prevent the rise or fall of the river.

"A sheep thinks no differently when it follows the herd and imagines that it's driving the herd!"

"But only think, teacher. The noble-hearted young Pharaoh wants to give the people a seventh day of rest, just courts, even some land ..."

Menes shook his head. "All those," he said, "are passing things. Young pharaohs grow old, and the people have had a seventh day of rest and land before, and have always lost them. Ah, if only that would change! In three thousand years, how many dynasties and priests have passed across Egypt, how many cities and temples have fallen to rubble! Why, entire new layers of soil have grown up.

"Everything has changed, except that two and two are four; that a triangle is half a rectangle; that the moon can hide the sun; and that boiling water hurls a stone into the air.

"In the transient world, only learning abides. And woe betide him who forsakes the eternal for things fleeting as the clouds! His heart will never know peace, and his mind will toss like a boat in a storm."

"The gods," mused Pentuer, "speak with your lips, teacher, but barely one man in millions can become their vessel. And that is all to the good. What would happen if the peasants stargazed all night, if the soldiers performed calculations, and if the dignitaries and pharaoh, instead of governing, hurled stones by the aid of boiling water? Before the moon had made one circuit of the earth, they would all have starved to death. Nor would any wheel or kettle defend the country from barbarian attack or dispense justice to the wronged.

"So," concluded Pentuer, "though learning is as sun, blood, and breath, we cannot all be men of learning."

Menes made no reply.

Pentuer spent several days at the temple of the goddess Nut, enjoying the view now of the sandy sea, now of the fertile valley of the Nile. With Menes he observed the stars, inspected the wheel for drawing water, walked toward the Pyramids. He admired his teacher's poverty and genius, but thought to himself:

"Menes is doubtless a god in human guise, and so cares nothing about earthly life. His wheel for drawing water won't take in Egypt because we lack the wood; and because moving such wheels would require a hundred thousand oxen. Where is there forage for them, even in Upper Egypt?"

CHAPTER 61

While Pentuer was traveling the Kingdom selecting delegates, Ramses XIII was abiding in Thebes and marrying off his favorite, Thutmose.

The Lord of the Two Worlds, surrounded by a magnificent retinue, rode a gold chariot to the palace of His Eminence Antef, Nomarch of Thebes. The magnate ran out before the gate to greet the Lord and, doffing his costly sandals, upon his knees helped Ramses alight.

In return for this homage, the Pharaoh gave the Nomarch his hand to kiss and declared that Antef was henceforth his friend and was entitled to enter even the throne room in his sandals.

When they found themselves in an enormous chamber of Antef's palace, the Lord said in the presence of the whole retinue:

"Your Eminence Antef, I know that, even as your venerable forbears dwell in the most beautiful tombs, so you, their descendant, are foremost among the nomarchs of Egypt. And you doubtless know that at my court and in the army, as in my royal heart, pride of place belongs to my favorite and the commander of my guard, Thutmose.

"According to the sages, the rich man does ill who does not mount the dearest gem in the most beautiful ring. And since, Antef, your family is dearest to me, and Thutmose the most agreeable, I have conceived the idea of connecting you with myself. Which may readily come about if your daughter, the beautiful and wise Hebron, accepts Thutmose for her spouse."

His Eminence Antef replied:

"Your Holiness, Lord of the Living and Western Worlds! As all Egypt and everything in it belong to you, so this house and all its residents belong to you. And since it is your heart's desire that my daughter Hebron become the wife of your favorite Thutmose, then let it be so."

The Pharaoh informed Antef that Thutmose had twenty talents' annual salary from the treasury and considerable estates in various nomes. His Eminence Antef stated that his sole daughter Hebron would have fifty talents annually and the use of her father's estates in those nomes where the royal court might sojourn.

Since Antef had no son, his entire enormous, debt-free fortune must eventually pass to Thutmose together with the office of nomarch of Thebes, if that be consonant with the will of His Holiness.

When the negotiations had been concluded, Thutmose came in from the courtyard and thanked Antef, first for giving his daughter to such a wretch as himself; and second, for having brought her up so beautifully. The wedding ceremony was set for a few days hence; for Thutmose, as commander of the guard, had no time for lengthy preliminaries.

"I wish you happiness, my son," concluded Antef with a smile, "and much patience. My beloved daughter Hebron is twenty years old, is the most elegant lady in Thebes, and is used to having her own way.

"By the gods! I tell you that my power over Thebes always ended at the gate to my daughter's gardens. And I fear that your generals will make no greater impression on her."

The noble Antef invited his guests to a magnificent feast, during which the beautiful Hebron appeared with a great suite of ladies.

In the dining hall were many tables for two and four persons, and a larger table on a dais for the Pharaoh. To honor Antef and Thutmose, His Holiness approached Hebron and invited her to his table.

The lady Hebron was indeed beautiful, and gave the impression of an experienced person, which was nothing unusual in Egypt. Ramses soon noticed that the fiancée was paying no attention to her future spouse but was sending expressive looks his—the Pharaoh's—way.

That, too, was nothing extraordinary in Egypt.

When the guests were seated at the tables, when music had begun to play, and when dancing girls had started distributing wine and flowers among the feasters, Ramses said:

"The longer I look at you, Hebron, the more amazed I am. Were a stranger to walk in here, he would take you for a goddess or a high priestess, never for a happy fiancée."

"Your Lordship is mistaken," she replied. "At the moment I am happy, but not on account of my betrothal."

"How can that be?" interrupted the Pharaoh.

"Marriage holds no allure for me, and I would certainly rather become a high priestess of Isis than a wife."

"Then why are you marrying?"

"I'm doing it for my father, who wants to have an heir to his glory. But mainly because it is Your Lordship's wish."

"Could it be you don't like Thutmose?"

"I'm not saying that. Thutmose is handsome, is the most elegant man in Egypt, sings nicely, and takes prizes at games. And his position as commander of Your Holiness' guard is among the foremost in the land.

"Nevertheless, were it not for my father's request and Your Lordship's behest, I would not become his wife. Though I won't be anyway! ... My fortune and my father's titles will suffice Thutmose, who will find the rest with the dancing girls."

"Does he know of his misfortune?"

Hebron smiled. "He has long known that, even were I not Antef's daughter but the daughter of the lowliest opener of dead bodies, I would not give myself to a man I didn't love. And I could love only someone higher than myself."

"You really mean that?" asked Ramses, surprised.

"I'm twenty years old, so for six years now I've been surrounded by admirers. But I soon learned their worth. And today I prefer listening to the conversations of learned priests than to the songs and suits of elegant youths."

"In that case I shouldn't be sitting by you, Hebron, for I am not elegant, let alone possessed of priestly learning."

"Oh, Your Lordship is something greater," she replied, blushing deeply. "You are a victorious commander. You are impetuous as a lion and quick as a vulture! Before you, millions prostrate themselves on their faces and kingdoms tremble. Do we not know what fear your name inspires in Tyre and Nineveh? The gods might envy your power."

Ramses was thrown into confusion. "Oh, Hebron, Hebron ... If you knew what unrest you sow in my heart!"

"That," she said, "is why I agree to marry Thutmose. I will be closer to Your Holiness and will see your lordship at least every few days."

With that, she rose from the table and departed.

Antef noticed and, frightened, ran over to Ramses.

"Lord!" he cried, "did my daughter say anything improper? She's an unrestrained lioness ..."

"Relax," replied the Pharaoh. "Your daughter is a wise and dignified person. She left because she saw that Your Eminence's wine was making the banqueters excessively hilarious."

Indeed, a great din reigned in the dining hall, the more so as Thutmose had dropped the role of deputy host and had become the most animated of the banqueters.

"Confidentially, Your Holiness," whispered Antef, "poor Thutmose will really have to watch himself with Hebron."

This first feast went on till morning. The Pharaoh soon left, but others remained—at first on chairs, later on the floor. Finally Antef had to send them home in wagons, like so many lifeless things.

A few days later, the nuptials took place.

High Priests Herhor and Mephres, nomarchs of adjoining nomes, and the highest dignitaries of the city of Thebes assembled at Antef's palace. Later Thutmose arrived by chariot, surrounded by officers of the guard; and finally His Holiness Ramses XIII.

The Lord was accompanied by the Great Scribe, the commanders of archery and horse, the Great Judge, the Great Treasurer, High Priest Sem, and aides-de-camp generals.

When the magnificent assemblage was gathered in the hall of Antef's ancestors, Hebron appeared in white raiment with a numerous bevy of lady friends and women servants. Her father burned incense before Amon, before his father's statue, and before Ramses XIII seated on a dais; and he announced that he was releasing his daughter Hebron from his tutelage and was presenting her with a dowry. He handed her a gold case containing a papyrus drawn up before a court of law.

After brief refreshments, the bride climbed into a sumptuous litter borne by eight nome officials. It was preceded by music and singers, was surrounded by dignitaries, and was followed by a great crowd of populace. The whole cortege moved toward the Temple of Amon down the most beautiful streets in Thebes, amid crowds as numerous as at the pharaoh's funeral.

At the Temple, the populace remained without the wall while the bridal couple, Pharaoh, and dignitaries entered the columned hall. Here Herhor burned incense before the veiled statue of Amon, priestesses performed a sacral dance, and Thutmose read out the following papyrus document:

"I, Thutmose, commander of the guard of His Holiness Ramses XIII, do take you, Hebron, daughter of the Theban Nomarch Antef, for my wife. I herewith give you the sum of ten talents for consenting to be my wife. For your clothing I shall provide you three talents a year, and for household expenses a talent each month. Of the children that we shall have, the eldest son shall be heir to the fortune that I today possess and that I may in the future acquire. Should I fail to live with you, should I divorce and take another wife, I shall be obliged to pay you forty talents, which sum is secured by my fortune. Our son, on assuming my fortune, shall be obliged to pay you fifteen talents a year. Children begotten by another wife shall have no claim to the fortune of our first-born son."[1]

Now the Great Judge came forward and, on Hebron's behalf, read out a document wherein the bride pledged to feed and clothe her husband well; to care for his house, family, servants, livestock, and slaves; and entrusted to said husband the management of the fortune that she had received and would receive from her father.

Following the reading of the documents, Herhor handed Thutmose a cup of wine.

The groom drank half, the lady Hebron moistened her lips, then both burned incense before the purple veil.

Leaving the Temple of Theban Amon, the bridal couple and their splendid cortege proceeded down the avenue of sphinxes to the royal palace. Gathered populace and soldiers cheered them, throwing flowers in their path.

Thutmose had been dwelling in the Pharaoh's chambers. On his wedding day the Lord gave him a beautiful villa deep in the gardens, surrounded by a forest of figs, myrtles, and baobabs, where the newlyweds could spend days of happiness concealed from human eye, as it were cut off from the world. In this quiet corner, people appeared so seldom that the birds did not even flee them.

When the newlyweds and guests found themselves in the new home, the final wedding ceremony took place.

Thutmose took Hebron's hand and led her to a fire burning before a statue of Isis. Mephres poured a spoon of holy water on the bride's head, Hebron touched the fire with her hand, and Thutmose shared a piece of bread with her and placed his ring on her finger in token that she was henceforth mistress of the groom's estate, servants, livestock, and slaves.

Meanwhile priests chanted nuptial hymns and carried a statue of the goddess Isis about the house. Priestesses performed sacral dances.

The day ended in spectacles and a great feast, during which everyone saw Hebron constantly in the Pharaoh's company, while Thutmose kept his distance from her and served the guests.

When the stars appeared, the holy Herhor left the feast, and shortly afterward several of the highest dignitaries slipped out. About midnight, the following worshipful persons gathered in the undergrounds of the Temple of Amon: High Priests Herhor, Mephres, and Mentesuphis; the Supreme Judge of Thebes; and the nomarchs of Abdju,[2] Herui,[3] and Aa-ta.[4]

---

[1] Authentic. (Author.)

[2] Abdju (Prus calls it Abs): the 8th Nome of Upper Egypt, north of Thebes. (Translator.)

[3] Herui (Prus calls it Horti): the 5th Nome of Upper Egypt, north of Thebes. (Translator.)

[4] Aa-ta (Prus calls it Emsuch): the 6th Nome of Upper Egypt, north of Thebes. (Translator.)

Mentesuphis inspected the thick columns, closed the door, and put out the lights, leaving only a single lamp burning in the low chamber, before a statuette of Horus. The dignitaries sat down on three stone benches, and the Nomarch of Abdju said:

"Were I asked to characterize His Holiness Ramses XIII, I would be hard put to it!"

"A madman!" said Mephres.

"Whether mad, I don't know," said Herhor. "In any event, a very dangerous man. Assyria has already twice reminded us about the final treaty, and I hear she is now becoming concerned about Egypt arming herself."

"What is worse," said Mephres, "this godless man actually means to breach the treasury of the Labyrinth."

"I would think," said the Nomarch of Aa-ta, "that a worse thing is the promises made to the peasants. The Kingdom's incomes and our own will be seriously diminished if the commonalty start taking holidays every seventh day. And if the Pharaoh were also to give them land ..."

"He's ready to do it," whispered the Supreme Judge.

"Is he, though?" asked the Nomarch of Herui. "I think he only wants money. If he were given some of the treasure in the Labyrinth ..."

"It can't be done," interrupted Herhor. "The Kingdom is in no danger; only the Pharaoh is—and that's not the same thing. Secondly, as a dike is fast only so long as not a trickle of water seeps through it, so the Labyrinth is full only so long as we don't take the first bar of gold out of it. After that, everything will go.

"Finally, whom would we be providing the treasures of the gods and Kingdom? A young man who scorns the faith, demeans the priests, and stirs the populace to rebellion. Is he not worse than Assar? Assar is a barbarian, to be sure, but he does us no harm."

"It's unseemly for the Pharaoh to so openly court his favorite's wife right on the wedding day," said the Judge abstractedly.

"Hebron is leading him on!" said the Nomarch of Herui.

"Every woman lures all men," answered the Nomarch of Aa-ta. "But a man is given good sense, that he not commit sin."

"Is the pharaoh not husband to all the women of Egypt?" whispered the Nomarch of Abdju. "Anyway, judging sins is the province of the gods, and our sole concern is with the Kingdom."

"He's dangerous! ... Dangerous!" said the Nomarch of Aa-ta, shaking his hands and head. "There's no doubt but the common people are already grown insolent and will at any moment raise a rebellion. And then no high priest or nomarch will be secure in his power and property, or even his life."

"I have a way to prevent rebellion," broke in Herhor.

"How?"

"Above all," said Mephres, "rebellion can be prevented by letting the wiser among the common people know that he who promises them great reliefs is a madman."

"He's the sanest man under the sun!" whispered the Nomarch of Herui. "You need only make out what he wants."

"A madman! A madman!" repeated Mephres. "His older half-brother is already playing an ape and drinking with the openers of dead bodies, and he himself will start in any day now!"

"It's a bad and foolish business to call a sane man mad," said the Nomarch of Herui. "Once the populace tumble to the lie, they'll stop believing us in anything, and then nothing will hold back rebellion."

"If I say Ramses is mad, I must have evidence for it," said Mephres. "Now listen."

The dignitaries stirred on their benches.

"Tell me," continued Mephres, "will a crown prince of sound mind publicly fight a bull in front of several thousand Asiatics? Will a rational Egyptian prince go at night to a Phoenician temple? Will he, without any reason, reduce his first woman to a slave, which was in fact the cause of her death and her child's?"

All murmured in horror.

"All this," said the high priest, "we saw in Pi-Bast, even as Mentesuphis and I witnessed drunken feasts at which the already half-deranged Successor blasphemed the gods and demeaned the priests!"

"It was so," interjected Mentesuphis.

"And do you suppose," Mephres warmed to his subject, "that a man in his right mind will, as commander-in-chief, leave his army to chase a handful of Libyan bandits over the desert?

"I pass over a multitude of lesser things, such as the notion of giving the peasants holidays and land, but I ask you: can I call a man sane who has perpetrated so many criminal follies, without any reason, simply on whim!"

Everyone was silent; the Nomarch of Herui was troubled.

"This requires thought," broke in the Supreme Judge, "lest the man be wronged."

"The holy Mephres," spoke Herhor in a resolute tone, "does him a favor, deeming him a madman. Otherwise we should have to consider Ramses a traitor."

Those present stirred uneasily.

"Yes, the man styled Ramses XIII is a traitor, because he not only recruits spies and thieves to discover the way to the treasures of the Labyrinth, he not only rejects the treaty with Assyria which Egypt badly needs ..."

"Those are grave charges!" said the Judge.

"But, listen to me, he is also plotting with the vile Phoenicians to dig a canal between the Red and Mediterranean Seas. Now, this canal is the greatest threat to Egypt, for our country can be instantly flooded by the waters!

"This is no longer a matter of the Labyrinth's treasures but of our temples, homes, fields, of six million admittedly stupid but innocent people, and finally of our lives and our children's lives!"

"If that is so ..." sighed the Nomarch of Herui.

"His Eminence Mephres and I assure you it is and that this one man has gathered in his hands dangers such as have never before threatened Egypt. We have called Your Worships together so that we may ponder means of deliverance. But we must act quickly, for this man's plans rush ahead like the desert wind—may they not bury us!"

There was momentary silence in the dusky chamber.

"What is there to advise?" said the Nomarch of Aa-ta. "We're out in the nomes, far from court; and we not only don't know this madman's plans, we didn't even suspect them, we can hardly credit them.

"Therefore I think this matter is best left to Your Eminences Herhor and Mephres. You discovered the illness, now you find and apply a remedy. And if you're daunted by the magnitude of the responsibility, invite the Supreme Judge to help you."

"Yes! Yes! ... He's right!" assented the excited dignitaries.

Mentesuphis lit a torch and placed on the table before the god's statue a papyrus, on which was next written out a document to the effect that, in view of dangers facing the Kingdom, the authority of the secret council passes into the hands of Herhor, assisted by Mephres and the Supreme Judge.

The document, attested by the signatures of the dignitaries present, was next enclosed in a case and secreted in a receptacle beneath the altar.

Additionally each of the seven participants swore to carry out Herhor's every order and to recruit ten dignitaries to the combination. Herhor, for his part, promised to give them proof that Assyria was pressing for the treaty, that the Pharaoh was refusing to sign it, that he was plotting with the Phoenicians to dig the canal, and that he intended to get into the Labyrinth by treachery.

"My life and honor are in your hands," concluded Herhor. "If what I have said be untrue, you may condemn me to death, and my body to burning."

Now no one doubted that the high priest was telling the genuine truth. No Egyptian would risk his body being burned—and thus his soul being consigned to perdition.

After the wedding, Thutmose spent several days with Hebron in the villa given him by His Holiness. But each evening he went to the guard barracks, where he passed the nights very convivially in the company of officers and dancing girls.

From this behavior, Thutmose's comrades guessed that he had wedded Hebron solely for her dowry, and no one was surprised.

After five days Thutmose reported to the Pharaoh his readiness to resume his duties. Consequently he visited his spouse only by daylight, and at night watched at the Lord's chamber.

One evening the Pharaoh told him:

"This palace has so many corners from which to watch and listen, that everything I do is observed. My worshipful mother is again hearing the mysterious voices that went silent in Memphis after I sent away the priests.

"Consequently," the Lord went on, "I can't receive anyone here but must leave the palace and confer with my servants in a secure place."

"Shall I go with Your Holiness?" asked Thutmose, as the Pharaoh cast about for his cloak.

"No. You must stay here and see that no one enters my room. Don't let anyone in, even were it my mother or the shade of my eternally living father. Say that I'm sleeping and don't want to see anyone."

"Very good," replied Thutmose, helping the Lord into a hooded cloak.

He put out the light in the bedroom, and the Pharaoh exited by side corridors.

Finding himself in the garden, Ramses stopped and carefully looked about. Then, evidently having gotten his bearings, he proceeded rapidly toward the villa he had presented to Thutmose.

After several minutes' way, in a shady alley, someone stepped before him and demanded: "Who goes there?"

"Nubia," answered the Pharaoh.

"Libya," said the interlocutor, suddenly backing away as though frightened.

It was an officer of the guard. The Lord scrutinized him and cried: "Ah, Ennana! What are you doing here?"

"I'm rounding on the gardens. I do so a couple of times a night, as thieves sometimes steal in."

The Pharaoh reflected and said: "That is prudent. But mind, a guardsman's first duty is to be silent. Drive out the thief, but should you encounter an eminent person, do not disturb him but be silent, always be silent. Even should it be High Priest Herhor himself!"

"O Lord!" exclaimed Ennana, "do not have me pay my respects at night to Herhor or Mephres. I know not but, at the sight of them, my sword might whip out of its sheath of its own accord."

Ramses smiled. "Your sword is mine," he replied, "and may leave its sheath only on my command."

He nodded to Ennana and went on.

After a quarter-hour wandering down wrong paths, the Pharaoh found himself near an arbor in the thickets. He thought he heard a rustling sound and quietly asked: "Hebron? ..."

A figure, likewise clad in a dark cloak, ran toward him. On reaching Ramses, it draped itself on his neck, whispering: "Is it you, Lord? ... Is it you? ... How long I've waited!"

The Pharaoh felt her slipping out of his arms; he picked her up and carried her into the arbor. Just then his cloak slipped off. Ramses briefly pulled it after him but finally dropped it.

Next day the worshipful Lady Nikotris summoned Thutmose. The Pharaoh's favorite took fright at the sight of her. The Queen was terribly pale; her eyes were sunken, almost mad.

"Sit down," she said, indicating a stool beside her armchair.

Thutmose hesitated.

"Sit down! ... And swear you won't repeat to anyone what I shall tell you!"

"I swear by my father's shade ..." he said.

"Listen," the Queen spoke quietly, "I've been almost a mother to you. So if you betrayed the secret, the gods would punish you ... No ... They would just dump on your head some of the disasters that hang over my house."

Thutmose listened in astonishment. "Has she gone mad?" he thought, frightened.

"Look at that window," she continued, "at that tree. Do you know whom I saw last night in that tree outside the window?"

"Could His Holiness' half-brother have come to Thebes?"

"It wasn't him," she whispered, sobbing. "It was my son ... my Ramses!"

"In the tree? ... Last night?"

"Yes! ... The light from the torch fell full on his face and body. He was wearing a tunic in white and blue stripes ... he had a deranged look ... he laughed wildly like his unfortunate brother, and he said: 'Look, Mother, I can fly, which neither Seti nor Ramses the Great nor Cheops could do. Look, I'm growing wings!'

"He reached out his hand to me, and through the window, out of my mind with grief, I touched his hands, his face covered with cold sweat. Finally he slipped down from the tree and ran off."

Thutmose listened, terrified. Suddenly he slapped his forehead.

"That wasn't Ramses!" he replied firmly. "It was a man who closely resembles him, a despicable Greek named Lykon, who killed Ramses' son and is now in the power of the high priests. It wasn't Ramses! It was the doing of those wretches Herhor and Mephres!"

Hope lit the Queen's face, but only for a moment. "Wouldn't I know my own son?"

"Lykon is supposed to bear an uncanny resemblance," said Thutmose. "This is the doing of the priests ... the wretches! There hasn't been enough death for them."

"Then the Pharaoh slept at home last night?" asked the Lady suddenly.

Thutmose looked down in confusion.

"Then he didn't?"

"He did ..." said the favorite in an uncertain voice.

"You're lying! But tell me, at least, was he wearing a tunic in white and blue stripes?"

"I don't recall," whispered Thutmose.

"Again you're lying! What about this cloak ... say it's not my son's cloak. My slave found it in that same tree ..."

The Lady sprang up and took from a chest a dark-brown hooded cloak. Thutmose recalled that the Pharaoh had returned past midnight minus his cloak, even explaining that he had lost it somewhere in the garden.

Thutmose hesitated, thought, and at length replied firmly:

"No, Queen. It wasn't the Pharaoh. It was Lykon and the doing of the priests, about which His Holiness must be told at once."

"But what if it was Ramses?" asked the Lady, though there was now a spark of hope in her eyes.

Thutmose was baffled. His surmise as to Lykon was astute and might be correct; but there was no lack of circumstantial evidence that the Queen had seen Ramses. He had returned home past midnight, had been wearing a tunic in white and blue stripes, had lost his cloak. His brother was already mad—and finally, in this case, could the mother's heart be mistaken?

Suddenly doubts were aroused in Thutmose's mind, heaped up and tangled like a nest of venomous serpents.

Happily, even as he vacillated, hope was entering the Queen's heart.

"It's good you reminded me of this Lykon ... I remember! ... It was because of him that Mephres suspected Ramses of the child's killing—and now he may be using the wretch to defame the Lord!

"In any event, not a word to anyone of what I've confided to you. If Ramses ... if he actually has succumbed to such an affliction, it may be momentary. We musn't humiliate him by spreading word of this, or even inform him of it! And if it is the doing of the priests, we must likewise be cautious. Though ... people who resort to such deceptions can't be strong."

"I'll look into this," broke in Thutmose, "but if I find ..."

"Only don't tell Ramses, I beseech you by the shades of your forbears!" cried the Lady, clasping her hands. "The Pharaoh would not forgive them, he would put them on trial, and then one of two misfortunes must follow. Either the highest priests in the Kingdom would be sentenced to death, or the court would acquit them. And then what?

"Instead, track down Lykon and kill him mercilessly as you would a beast of prey ... as you would a viper!"

As Thutmose was taking his leave, the Queen was much calmed but his own misgivings had grown.

"If that wretched Greek Lykon still lives despite captivity by the priests," he thought, "then instead of climbing trees and showing himself to the Queen, he would rather escape. I myself would help him escape, and shower him with riches, if he would tell me the truth and seek protection against those villains. But what about the tunic and cloak? Why would his mother be mistaken?"

Henceforth Thutmose avoided the Pharaoh and dared not look him in the eye. And since Ramses was not quite himself either, it seemed as though their cordial relations had cooled.

One evening the Lord again called his favorite.

"I must," he said, "talk over some important matters with Hiram, so I'm going out. Watch here at my bedroom and, should anyone want to see me, don't admit him."

When Ramses had disappeared into the palace's secret corridors, Thutmose was overcome with dread.

"Maybe," he thought, "the priests have slipped him some sort of henbane[5] and he feels an onset of illness and is fleeing his home. H'm, we shall see."

See, he did. The Pharaoh returned well past midnight to his rooms; and, while he was wearing a cloak ... it was not his but a soldier's.

Thutmose was appalled and did not sleep till morning, expecting at any moment to be called again by the Queen. But she did not send for him. Instead, at the morning review of the guard, the officer Ennana asked his chief for a word.

When they found themselves alone in a private room, Ennana fell to Thutmose's feet, begging him not to repeat to anyone what he was going to say.

"What's happened?" asked Thutmose, feeling a chill in his heart.

"Chief," said Ennana, "yesterday about midnight, in the garden, two of my soldiers stopped a man who was running half-naked and shouting unhumanly.

"They brought him to me and, Chief ... kill me!"

Ennana again fell to Thutmose's feet. "The half-naked man ... He ... I can't say it ..."

"Who was it?" asked Thutmose, terrified.

"I'll say no more," moaned Ennana. "I took off my cloak and covered the holy nakedness. I wanted to escort him to the palace, but ... but the Lord bade me stay and be silent ... be silent ..."

"Where did he go?"

"I don't know ... I didn't look or let the men look. He disappeared somewhere into the garden thickets. I told my men they hadn't seen anything ... hadn't heard anything. And if either of them had seen or heard anything, he would be strangled on the spot."

Thutmose meanwhile had managed to collect himself.

"I don't know," he said coolly, "I don't know and can't make any sense of what you've told me. But bear this in mind—I myself ran half-naked one time after I'd had too much wine ... and I generously rewarded those who took no notice of me.

---

[5] henbane (*Hyoscyamus niger*), also known as black henbane (in Polish, *szalej czarny*, among other names), is a plant of the nightshade family. Common effects of its ingestion include inebriation, confusion, memory disturbance, and hallucinations. Initial effects typically last three to four hours, while aftereffects may last up to three days. Overdosage can be fatal. Thutmose here speaks of "some sort of *szalej*." (*Author.*)

"Peasants, Ennana, peasants and laborers always go half-naked; grandees, only when it pleases them to do so. And if I or some dignitary should take a fancy to standing on his head, a wise and pious officer shouldn't be astonished."

"Very good," replied Ennana, looking his chief smartly in the eye. "And not only will I tell my men that, but this very night I will myself go naked in the gardens so they will know that superiors may do as they please."[6]

Despite the few persons who had seen the Pharaoh or his look-alike in a state of derangement, word of the strange incidents spread very quickly. Within a few days all the denizens of Thebes, from openers of dead bodies and water-carriers to merchants and scribes, were whispering that Ramses XIII was touched with the affliction that had barred his elder brothers from the throne.

Fear, and respect for the Pharaoh, were so great that people were loth to speak aloud of it, especially in the presence of strangers. Nevertheless everyone knew about it—except Ramses himself.

The most remarkable thing, however, was that the rumor very quickly spread across the entire Kingdom, which showed that it was being disseminated by the temples. Only the priests possessed the secret of communicating in a dozen or so hours from one end of Egypt to the other.

No one directly mentioned the odious rumors to Thutmose. But the commander of the Pharaoh's guard sensed their presence at every hand. From the behavior of people with whom he had dealings, he guessed that servants, slaves, soldiers, and court purveyors all spoke of the Lord's madness, momentarily falling silent only when a superior might hear.

At last, frustrated and frightened, Thutmose decided to speak with the nomarch of Thebes.

Arriving at Antef's palace, Thutmose found him reclining on a couch in a room half of which was, as it were, a small garden filled with exotic plants. In the middle spurted a fountain of rose water; in the corners stood statues of gods; painted on the walls was a history of the illustrious Nomarch's deeds. A black slave stood at the master's head, cooling him with a fan of ostrich feathers; on the floor sat the nome scribe, reading a report.

Thutmose had such a concerned expression that the Nomarch immediately dismissed the scribe and slave and, rising from the couch, looked into all the corners of the room to see whether anyone was listening in.

"Esteemed father of my worshipful wife Lady Hebron," said Thutmose, "I see by your behavior that you have guessed what I wish to speak of."

"The nomarch of Thebes must always be prudent," replied Antef. "Also, I presume that the chief of His Holiness's guard would not be honoring me with a visit in a trivial matter."

For a moment they looked one another in the eye. Finally Thutmose sat down beside his father-in-law and whispered:

"Have you heard the vile stories the Kingdom's enemies are spreading about our Lord?"

"If it's to do with my daughter Hebron," said the Nomarch quickly, "you are now her master and cannot hold me to account."

---

[6] In the original Polish text, the unnamed man is described by Ennana as having been "naked." I have rendered this as "half-naked," since Prus regularly describes anyone who wears little, if anything, more than a loincloth as being "naked": for example, Chapter 1 speaks of "naked copper-colored men with only a short skirt about their hips and a cap on their heads." *(Translator.)*

Thutmose tossed his hand carelessly.

"Some despicable persons," said the son-in-law, "are spreading a rumor that the Pharaoh is mad. Have you heard about it, my father?"

Antef nodded and shook his head, which could equally well have meant confirmation or denial. Finally he said: "Folly is as great as the sea, it can accommodate anything."

"This is not folly but the doing of the priests, who have a man who resembles His Holiness and are using him for nefarious purposes."

He told the Nomarch the story of the Greek Lykon and his crime in Pi-Bast.

"I've heard about this Lykon who killed the Crown Prince's son," replied Antef. "But what proof have you that Mephres imprisoned Lykon in Pi-Bast, transported him to Thebes, and is letting him out into the royal gardens, there to impersonate a deranged Pharaoh?"

"That is why I am asking Your Eminence what to do. I'm chief of the guard and must safeguard the honor and safety of our Lord."

"What to do? ... What to do?" repeated Antef. "H'm! above all, see that this unholy talk doesn't reach the ears of the Pharaoh."

"Why?"

"Because there will be a great misfortune. When our Lord hears that Lykon is playing the madman in his name, he will become angry ... terribly angry! Naturally he will turn on Herhor and Mephres. Maybe he will only insult them; maybe he will jail them; he may even kill them. But whatever he does, he will be doing it without any evidence, and then what? Today's Egypt no longer likes to make offerings to the gods, but she will still take up the cudgels for the wronged innocent priests. And then what? ... I think," he spoke close to Thutmose's ear, "I think it would be the end of the Dynasty."

"Then what's to be done?"

"Only one thing!" cried Antef. "Find this Lykon, prove that Mephres and Herhor concealed him and had him impersonate a deranged Pharaoh. That's what you can do if you want to keep the Lord's favor. Proof, as much proof as possible! This isn't Assyria, high priests can't be given grief except by the highest court, and no court will convict them without tangible proof.

"Anyway, can you be sure the Pharaoh wasn't slipped some sort of intoxicant? That would be simpler than sending out at night a man who knows neither the passwords nor the palace nor the garden. I tell you: I've heard of Lykon from a reliable source, from Hiram. But I don't see how Lykon could carry on like that in Thebes."

"Wait, now!" interrupted Thutmose. "Where is Hiram?"

"Right after your wedding he set out for Memphis, and lately he's already been to Hiten."

Thutmose again became troubled.

"The night," he thought, "that the half-naked man was brought to Ennana, the Pharaoh said he was going out to see Hiram. But since Hiram wasn't in Thebes, then? ... Then His Holiness already at that hour didn't know what he was saying!"

Thutmose returned home bewildered. Now he not only did not know what to do in this unheard-of situation, he did not even know what to make of it. Whereas in speaking with Queen Nikotris he had been sure it was Lykon who had appeared in the gardens, sent out by the high priests, now his doubts mounted.

And if it was so with Thutmose, the favorite who continually saw Ramses, what must have been happening in the hearts of other people? The most fervent partisans of the Pharaoh and his plans might take pause when hearing on all sides that the Lord was mad!

This was the first blow dealt Ramses XIII by the priests. Slight of itself, it entailed incalculable consequences.

Thutmose not only vacillated, he suffered. His ostensible frivolity concealed a noble, energetic character. Now, with his lord's honor and authority under assault, Thutmose chafed at his inaction. He felt like the master of a fortress which was being sapped by an enemy while he looked on inactive!

The thought so tormented Thutmose that, under its prompting, he struck on a bold idea. Happening upon Sem, he asked the high priest: "Has Your Eminence heard the rumors that are going around about our Lord?"

"The Pharaoh is young, so there can be all sorts of gossip going around about him," replied Sem, looking oddly at Thutmose. "But such matters are not my province. I stand in for His Holiness in the service of the gods, I do so to the best of my ability, and the rest is not my concern."

"I know Your Eminence is the Pharaoh's faithful servant," said Thutmose, "and I have no intention of meddling with priestly secrets. However, I must bring one small matter to your attention.

"I have learned for a fact that the holy Mephres is harboring a certain Lykon, a Greek who is liable for two crimes. He is the murderer of the Pharaoh's son—and he bears an excessive resemblance to His Holiness.

"Let His Eminence Mephres not bring disgrace on the venerable priesthood, but speedily deliver the murderer to the courts. I swear that, if we find Lykon, Mephres will lose not only his office but his head. In our Kingdom, no one may with impunity shelter criminals and conceal persons who resemble the supreme Lord!"

Sem, in whose presence Mephres had relieved the police of Lykon, was thrown into confusion, perhaps in fear of being implicated. Nevertheless he replied:

"I shall endeavor to warn the holy Mephres about these suspicions derogatory to him. But does Your Eminence know how one answers for accusing someone of a crime?"

"I do, and I accept the responsibility. I am so sure of my assertion that I have no concern for the consequences of my suspicions. I leave concern to the venerable Mephres, and I trust that I shall not have to pass from warnings to deeds."

The conversation produced results: no one saw the Pharaoh's double again.

But the rumors did not cease, and Ramses XIII did not know about them. Not even Thutmose, who feared impetuous actions by the Lord against the priests, informed him of anything.

CHAPTER 62

E arly in Phaophi (July-August)[1] His Holiness, Queen Nikotris, and the court sailed from Thebes for the palace at Memphis.

Toward the end of the voyage, Ramses XIII often became preoccupied, and on one occasion he told Thutmose:

"I notice something odd. The people gather on both banks at least as thickly as when we were sailing in the opposite direction. But their cheers are weaker, there are fewer boats trailing us, and they throw flowers sparingly."

"The gods' own truth flows from your lips, Lord," replied Thutmose. "The people do look tired by the heat."

"Well said!" the Pharaoh praised him, his face brightening.

But Thutmose did not believe his own words. He felt—and worse, so did all the royal entourage—that the love of the masses for the Lord had cooled.

Thutmose did not know whether this was due to the rumors of Ramses' illness, or to something else. But he felt sure the priests were behind the cooling.

"Stupid rabble!" he thought, in his heart giving vent to his scorn. "Not long ago they were drowning themselves for a glimpse of His Holiness' face, and today they're chary of a cheer! Could they already have forgotten the seventh day of rest and the awards of land?"

Immediately on arrival at the palace, the Pharaoh ordered that the delegates be assembled who were to determine the disposition of the Labyrinth's treasures. He also instructed the officials and police devoted to him to begin agitating against the priests and for the seventh day of rest.

Soon Lower Egypt was again abuzz like a beehive. The peasants demanded not only holidays but cash payment for public works. The craftsmen, in taverns and streets, cursed the priests who wanted to limit the Pharaoh's sacred power. The incidence of crimes rose, but the criminals did not want to answer before the courts. The scribes turned meek, and no one dared strike an ordinary man, knowing that it would bring reprisal. Fewer offerings were made at temples; the gods guarding the nome borders were increasingly pelted with rocks and mud, and even overturned.

Fear gripped the priests, nomarchs, and their adherents. In vain did the judges announce in marketplaces and on roads that, in accord with long-established law, the husbandman and craftsman, and even the merchant, should not engage in gossip that

---

[1] Actually, the ancient Egyptian month of Phaophi lay between October 11 and November 9 of the modern, Gregorian calendar, unless the previous Coptic year was a leap year. *(Translator.)*

diverted them from productive work; the common people, laughing and hooting, pelted the criers with rotten vegetables and date pits.

The aristocracy started gathering at the palace and, lying at the Pharaoh's feet, begging him to save them.

"The earth," they cried, "is parting beneath our feet ... the world is coming to an end! The elements are in confusion, minds are distracted, and if Your Lordship does not save us, the hours of our lives are numbered!"

"My treasury is empty, the army is understrength, the police are long unpaid," replied the Pharaoh. "If you want to have lasting peace and safety, you must provide me funds.

"However, since my royal heart is troubled by your distress, I will do what I can, and I hope I will be able to restore order."

His Holiness ordered troops deployed to critical points about the country. He also sent an order for Nitager to leave the eastern border to his assistant and march with his five best regiments to Memphis.

The Lord did this not so much to shield the aristocracy from the populace, as to have large forces on hand should the high priests stir up Upper Egypt and the temple regiments.

On the tenth of Phaophi there was great activity at the royal castle and its environs. The delegates who were to authorize the Pharaoh's drawing on the Labyrinth's treasury had gathered—as had crowds eager at least to view the site of an extraordinary event.

The procession of delegates began in the morning. At the fore went half-naked peasants in white caps and loincloths; each carried a coarse cloth with which to cover himself in the Pharaoh's presence. Then came craftsmen, dressed like the peasants but with somewhat finer cloths, and wearing narrow aprons with varicolored embroidery.

Merchants followed, some in wigs, all in long tunics and capes; visible here were costly bracelets, anklets, and rings. Next came officers, in caps and tunics striped black-and-yellow, blue-and-white, blue-and-red. Two of the officers, in lieu of tunics, wore brass breastplates.

After a longer interval thirteen nobility appeared, in great wigs and floor-length white robes. They were followed by crowned nomarchs in robes trimmed with purple. The procession was closed by priests with shaven heads and faces, wearing leopard skins over their backs.

The delegates entered the great hall of the palace of the pharaohs, where seven benches were arrayed one after another: the lowest one for the peasants, the highest for the priests.

Presently there appeared, borne in a litter, His Holiness Ramses XIII, before whom the delegates prostrated themselves. When the Lord of the Two Worlds had been seated on a high throne, he permitted his loyal subjects to rise and take their places on the benches. Then high priests entered and took lower thrones: Herhor, Mephres, and the Chief Keeper of the Labyrinth holding a small casket. A splendid retinue of generals surrounded the Pharaoh, beyond whom two high officials took their places with fans of peacock feathers.

"Loyal Egyptians!" began the Lord of the Two Worlds. "You are aware that my court, my army, and my officials are in a state of need that the impoverished treasury cannot supply. I do not speak of expenditures for my sacred person, because I eat and dress like a soldier, and any general or great scribe has more servants and women than I."

There was murmured assent among the gathering.

"Until now," continued Ramses, "when the treasury has needed funds, it has been the practice to levy greater taxes on the working commonalty. But, knowing my people and their poverty, I do not want to burden them further and would fain grant them certain reliefs."

"Live forever, our Lord!" called voices from several lower benches.

"Fortunately for Egypt," said the Pharaoh, "our Kingdom possesses treasure that can strengthen the army, compensate the officials, gift the populace, and pay off all the debts that we owe the temples and the Phoenicians. This treasure, gathered by my glorious forbears, reposes in the cellars of the Labyrinth. But it may be touched only when all you loyal men declare as one that Egypt is in need and that I, her master, have the right to dispose of the treasures of my predecessors."

"We declare it! ... We beg you, Lord, take as much as you need!" came cries from all the benches.

"Your Eminence," the Lord addressed Herhor, "does the holy priesthood wish to say anything in this matter?"

"Very little," replied the high priest, rising. "By ancient law, the Labyrinth's treasure may be touched only if the Kingdom possesses no other resources. This is not now the case. Were the government to expunge the Phoenician debts arisen from wicked usury, not only would Your Holiness' treasury be filled, but the populace who now work for the Phoenicians would have respite from their heavy toil."

Once again there was a favorable murmur from the delegates' benches.

"Your advice is sagacious, holy man," said the Pharaoh calmly, "but dangerous. If my treasurer, the nomarchs, and the nobility once learned to cancel their debts, today they would not repay the Phoenicians and tomorrow they might forget about their debts to the pharaoh and temples. And who can say whether the populace, encouraged by the example of the grandees, might not think that they have a right to forget about their obligations toward us?"

The blow was so powerful that His Eminence Herhor bent over in his chair—and was silent.

"And you, Chief Keeper of the Labyrinth, is there anything you wish to say?" asked the Pharaoh.

"I have here a casket," he replied, "containing white and black pebbles. Every delegate will receive one of each and will drop one of them into the pitcher. Those who want Your Holiness to breach the Labyrinth's treasury, shall drop in a black pebble; those who prefer that the property of the gods remain intact, shall drop in a white one."

"Don't agree to it, Lord," the Treasurer whispered to the Pharaoh. "Instead, let each delegate say openly what is in his soul."

"Let us honor the old customs," broke in Mephres.

"Very well, let them drop the pebbles into the pitcher," decided the Lord. "My heart is clean; and my resolve, unshakable."

The holy Mephres and Herhor exchanged glances.

The Keeper of the Labyrinth, assisted by two generals, proceeded round the benches, passing out to each delegate two pebbles: a black and a white. The poor wretches of the populace were flustered to behold such great dignitaries before them. Some peasants prostrated themselves, dared not accept the pebbles, and had great difficulty grasping that they could drop into the pitcher only one pebble: the black or the white.

"I would like to please both the gods and His Holiness," whispered an old herdsman.

At last the dignitaries succeeded in explaining, and the peasants in understanding, what was expected of them. The ballotting began. Each delegate went up to the pitcher and dropped in his pebble, in such a way that others could not see which color pebble he was dropping.

The Great Treasurer, kneeling behind the throne, whispered to the Lord:

"All is lost! Had they voted openly, we'd have had unanimity; but now, may my hand wither if there won't be twenty white pebbles in the pitcher!"

"Relax, faithful servant," smiled Ramses. "I have more regiments on hand than there will be votes against us."

"But what use is that?" sighed the Treasurer. "Without unanimity, they won't open the Labyrinth to us."

Ramses continued smiling.

The procession of delegates ended. The Keeper of the Labyrinth lifted the pitcher and spilled the contents onto a gold tray.

With ninety-one votes cast, there were eighty-three black pebbles and only eight white ones.

The generals and officials were appalled. The high priests regarded the assembly triumphantly, but soon became uneasy: Ramses had a cheerful expression.

No one ventured to announce that His Holiness' project had failed. But the Pharaoh spoke with entire ease:

"Loyal Egyptians, my good servants! You have done my bidding, and you have my favor. For two days you shall be guests of my house. And after you have received gifts, you shall return to your families and occupations. Peace and my blessing be with you."

With that, the Lord left the hall together with his suite, and High Priests Herhor and Mephres exchanged frightened looks.

"He's not at all fazed," whispered Herhor.

"Didn't I say he was a mad beast!" replied Mephres. "He won't shrink from violence, and if we don't forestall him ..."

"The gods will defend us and their sanctuaries."

In the evening Ramses XIII's most faithful servants gathered in his chamber: the Great Treasurer, the Great Scribe, Thutmose, and the commander-in-chief of the Greeks, Kalipos.

"Lord," groaned the Treasurer, "why didn't you act like your eternally living forbears? Had the delegates voted openly, we would have had the right to the Labyrinth's treasure!"

"His Eminence is right," said the Great Scribe.

The Pharaoh shook his head. "You are mistaken. Even if all Egypt cried, 'Give the funds of the Labyrinth to the Treasury!' the high priests would not."

"Then why did we disturb them by convoking the delegates? This royal act has greatly agitated and emboldened the common people, who are now as rising waters."

"I do not fear a flood," said the Lord. "My regiments will be levees for the waters. And I have an obvious benefit from the delegations, which have shown me the impotence of the opposition: eighty-three pebbles for us, eight for them! It means that, if they can count on one corps, I can count on ten.

"Be under no illusions," continued the Pharaoh. "War has already commenced between

me and the high priests. They are a fortress which we have called on to surrender. They
have refused, so we must storm them."

"Live forever!" cried Thutmose and Kalipos.

"Command, Lord," said the Great Scribe.

"These are my instructions," said Ramses.

"You, Treasurer, shall distribute a hundred talents among the police, the laborers'
officers, and the village chiefs in the nomes of Seft, Neha-Khent, Neha-Pekhu, Sebt-Het,
Khensu,[2] Ament,[3] and Ka-khem.[4] In those same places, you shall give the tavern- and inn-
keepers the barley, wheat, and wine that are on hand so that the populace will have free
provisions and food. You shall do this at once so the supplies will be in place by the twentieth of Phaophi."

The Treasurer made a deep bow.

"You, Scribe, shall write and have it announced tomorrow in the streets of the nome
capitals that barbarians from the Western Desert intend to attack in great force the godly
province of Fayum.

"You, Kalipos, shall send four Greek regiments south. Two shall take up positions outside the Labyrinth; two shall advance as far as Henen-nesut.[5] Should priestly militia come
up from Thebes, you shall repulse them and bar them from the Fayum. And when the
populace, incensed at the priests, threaten the Labyrinth, your Greeks shall occupy it."

"What if the keepers of the stronghold resist?" asked Kalipos.

"That would be rebellion," answered the Pharaoh, and he continued: "Thutmose, you
shall send three regiments to Memphis and position them near the Temples of Ptah, Isis,
and Horus. When the angry populace attempts to storm them, the regimental commanders shall open the gates, bar the populace from the sanctuaries, and secure the persons of
the high priests from indignity.

"At the Labyrinth and at the Memphis temples, there will be priests who will come out
to the army with green branches. The regimental commanders shall ask them the password and shall consult with them."

"What if someone dares put up resistance?" asked Thutmose.

"Only rebels will refuse the pharaoh's orders," replied Ramses.

"The temples and Labyrinth must be occupied by the army on the twenty-third of Phaophi," continued the Pharaoh, turning to the Great Scribe. "Therefore, both in Memphis
and in the Fayum, the populace may start gathering as early as the eighteenth, at first
in small handfuls, then in ever greater numbers. If small disturbances begin around the
twentieth, they should not be interfered with. But they may begin storming the temples
only on the twenty-second and twenty-third. And when the army occupies these points,
all must become quiet."

"Wouldn't it be better to immediately jail Herhor and Mephres?" asked Thutmose.

"What for? I don't care about them but about the temples and the Labyrinth, which the

---

[2] Khensu (which Prus calls *Aa*): the 2nd nome of Lower Egypt. *(Translator.)*

[3] Ament: the 3rd nome of Lower Egypt. *(Translator.)*

[4] Ka-khem (which Prus calls *Ka*): the 10th nome of Lower Egypt. *(Translator.)*

[5] Henen-nesut (which Prus calls *Hanes*): the capital of Atef-Khent, the 20th nome of Upper Egypt.
(Translator.)

army is not yet ready to occupy. In addition, Hiram, who has intercepted Herhor's letters to the Assyrians, will be returning only about the twentieth. Therefore we will have proof in hand of the high priests' treason only on the twenty-first of Phaophi, when we will announce it to the people."

"Then I am to go to the Fayum?" asked Kalipos.

"No. You and Thutmose will stay with me, together with some crack regiments. We must have reserves in case the high priests draw part of the populace away from us."

"Don't you fear treachery, Lord?" asked Thutmose.

The Pharaoh tossed his hand carelessly.

"Treachery is constantly seeping like water out of a cracked barrel. The high priests are guessing some of my intentions, and I know theirs. But since I've stolen a march on them in gathering my forces, they're going to be at a disadvantage from here on out. Regiments aren't formed in a fortnight."

"What about spells?" asked Thutmose.

"There are no spells that an ax won't dispel!" laughed Ramses.

Thutmose wanted to tell the Pharaoh about the high priests' doings with Lykon. But he was again prevented from doing so by the reflection that, if the Lord became very angry, he would lose the composure that now made him formidable.

Before a battle, a commander must think of nothing but the battle. There would be time enough for Lykon once the priests had been jailed.

At a sign from His Holiness, Thutmose remained in the chamber and the three other dignitaries made the Lord deep bows and left.

"Finally," sighed the Great Scribe, when he and the Treasurer found themselves in the vestibule, "the power of the baldpates will come to an end."

"It's about time," said the Treasurer. "For the past ten years, any prophet has carried more weight than the nomarch of Thebes or Memphis."

"I daresay Herhor is quietly readying himself a little boat to get away before the twenty-third of Phaophi," broke in Kalipos.

"What harm can he come to?" said the Scribe. "His Holiness, formidable today, will pardon them once they've humbled themselves."

"With the intercession of Queen Nikotris, he will even leave them their estates," added the Treasurer. "In any event, there will again be some semblance of order in the Kingdom, which was beginning to be lacking."

"Only it seems to me that His Holiness is making excessive preparations," said the Scribe. "I would wind things up with just the Greek regiments, without involving the common people."

"He's young ... he likes commotion and noise," said the Treasurer.

"How obvious that you're not soldiers!" said Kalipos. "When it comes to battle, you have to gather all your forces, because there are bound to be surprises."

"Certainly, if we didn't have the masses with us," replied the Scribe. "But as it is, what sort of surprises can there be? The gods won't be coming down to defend the Labyrinth."

"Your Eminence speaks that way because you're at ease," said Kalipos, "because you know the commander-in-chief is watching and trying to anticipate everything. Otherwise your flesh might creep."

"I see no surprises," insisted the Scribe. "Unless the high priests again spread a rumor that the Pharaoh has gone mad."

"They will try various tricks," yawned the Great Treasurer, "but truly they're not strong enough. In any case, I thank the gods for putting me in the royal camp. Well, let's get some sleep."

After the dignitaries had left the Pharaoh's room, Thutmose opened a hidden door in one of the walls and led in Samentu. The Lord welcomed the high priest of Set with great joy, offered his hand to be kissed, and hugged his head.

"Peace be with you, good servant," said the Lord. "What do you bring?"

"I've twice been in the Labyrinth," replied the priest.

"And you know the way now?"

"I knew it before, but now I've discovered something. The treasury can collapse, killing the people and destroying the gems that are its greatest wealth."

The Pharaoh frowned.

"Therefore," continued Samentu, "Your Holiness will please ready a dozen or so trusty men. With them I will enter the Labyrinth the night before the storming and man the chambers adjoining the treasury ... especially the one overhead."

"You will bring them in?"

"Yes. But first I will go into the Labyrinth once more by myself to see whether I can't prevent its ruin without help. People, no matter how loyal, are uncertain, and introducing them could draw the attention of the watchdogs."

"If they aren't watching you already," said the Pharaoh.

"Believe me, Lord," replied the priest, placing a hand on his chest, "detecting me would take a miracle. Their blindness is almost childlike. They sense that someone wants to break into the Labyrinth, but the fools double the guard at the visible gates; whereas I have myself, over a month's time, discovered three hidden entrances which they have forgotten or simply don't know about.

"Only a spirit could alert them that I'm walking about the Labyrinth or indicate the chamber I'm in. Given three thousand chambers and corridors, that is impossible."

"His Eminence Samentu speaks the truth," said Thutmose. "I daresay we are going too far in our precautions against the reptiles of high priests."

"Don't say that, commander," said the priest. "Their forces, compared with those of His Holiness, are a handful of sand to a desert, but Herhor and Mephres are very cunning! They are liable to use, against us, weapons and tactics that will leave us dumbfounded. Our temples are full of secrets that baffle even the wise men, and that grind the souls of the common people to dust."

"Tell us something about it," said the Pharaoh.

"I say in advance that Your Holiness' soldiers will encounter wonders in the temples. Now lights will go out, now flames and hideous monsters will surround them. Here a wall will rise up to bar their way, there a chasm will open beneath their feet. In some corridors, water will flood them; in others, invisible hands will cast stones. And what thunder, what voices will ring out around them!"

"In every temple I have young priests who are friendly to me, and you will be in the Labyrinth," said the Pharaoh.

"And our axes," broke in Thutmose. "It's a sorry soldier who retreats from flames and terrors or wastes time listening to mysterious voices."

"Well said, commander!" cried Samentu. "If you but boldly go ahead, the terrors will take flight, the voices will fall still, and the flames will cease to burn.

"Now a final word, our Lord," the priest turned to Ramses. "Should I perish ..."

"Don't say that!" interrupted the Pharaoh quickly.

"Should I perish," said Samentu with a rueful smile, "a young priest of Set will come to Your Holiness with my ring. Let the army then occupy the Labyrinth and expel the keepers, and let it remain in the building, because within a month, maybe sooner, the young man will find the way to the treasures, using the clews that I shall leave him.

"But, Lord," he said, kneeling, "I beg one thing of you: when you are victorious, avenge me and, above all, do not pardon Herhor or Mephres. You do not know what enemies they are! Were they to get the upper hand, you would perish, together with your Dynasty."

"Does it not behoove a victor to be magnanimous?" asked the Lord somberly.

"No magnanimity! ... No mercy!" cried Samentu. "So long as they shall live, Lord, you and I are in peril of death, dishonor, even the desecration of our corpses.

"You may gentle a lion, buy a Phoenician, befriend a Libyan or Ethiopian; you may win over a Chaldean priest, for he soars on high like an eagle and is safe from projectiles ...

"But there is no conciliating an Egyptian prophet who has tasted wealth and power. Only their death or yours can close the struggle."

"You speak the truth, Samentu," answered Thutmose. "Fortunately, it is not His Holiness but we soldiers who will settle the age-old conflict between the priests and the pharaoh."

CHAPTER 63

On the twelfth of Phaophi, disturbing news spread abroad from various Egyptian temples.

Over the previous couple of days the altar had overturned at the Temple of Horus, and at the Temple of Isis the goddess' statue had wept. At Theban Amon's and at Osiris' tomb in Dendera, there had been very bad omens. From infallible signs, the priests had concluded that Egypt was threatened with some great misfortune before the month was out.

Consequently High Priests Herhor and Mephres ordered processions around the temples, and the making of offerings in homes.

The next day, the thirteenth of Phaophi, a great procession took place in Memphis: the god Ptah and the goddess Isis came out of their respective temples. The two deities proceeded toward the city center with a very small group of the faithful, mostly women. But they were forced back: the Egyptian townspeople jeered them, and adherents of other faiths went so far as to throw rocks at the sacred boats of the deities.

The police behaved indifferently in the face of these abuses, and some of them even joined in the unseemly jests. At noon, unknown persons began telling the crowds that the priesthood was preventing any reliefs for the working people and wanted to raise a rebellion against the Pharaoh.

Toward evening, small groups of workers began gathering outside the temples, hooting and cursing at the priests. Rocks were thrown at the gates, and some criminal publicly broke off the nose of the Horus guarding his temple.

A couple of hours past sunset, the high priests and their most faithful adherents gathered at the Temple of Ptah. Present were their Eminences Herhor, Mephres, Mentesuphis, three nomarchs, and the Supreme Judge from Thebes.

"Dreadful times!" said the Judge. "I know for a fact that the Pharaoh wants to stir up the rabble to attack the temples."

"I've heard," said the Nomarch of Sebes,[1] "that an order has gone out to Nitager to run up here with new forces, as if there weren't enough already!"

"Communications between Lower and Upper Egypt have been cut since yesterday," added the Nomarch of Khensu. "The army is out on the highways, and His Holiness' galleys are searching every ship that sails the Nile."

---

[1] Prus may have borrowed this nome's name from the word "Sebes" which appears in a number of European geographical names, often with a diacritical mark attached to the second "s". *(Translator.)*

"Ramses XIII isn't 'His Holiness,'" said Mephres dryly, "since he hasn't received the crowns from the hands of the gods."

"All that would be nothing," said the Supreme Judge. "A worse matter is treachery. I have evidence that many junior priests side with the Pharaoh and are informing him of everything."

"Some have even agreed to help the army occupy the temples," added Herhor.

"The army is to enter the temples?!" exclaimed the Nomarch of Sebes.

"That, at least, is its order for the twenty-third," replied Herhor.

"And Your Eminence speaks of it calmly?" asked the Nomarch of Ament.

Herhor shrugged, and the nomarchs glanced at one another.

"Now, this I don't understand!" said the Nomarch of Khensu, almost angrily. "The temples have barely a few hundred soldiers, priests are defecting, the Pharaoh cuts us off from Thebes and incites the populace, and His Eminence Herhor speaks of it as if inviting us to a feast. Either let's defend ourselves, if that's still possible, or ..."

"Or surrender to His Holiness?" asked Mephres ironically. "You will always have time for that!"

"But we'd like to know something about means of defense," said the Nomarch of Sebes.

"The gods will deliver their faithful," answered Herhor.

The Nomarch of Khensu wrung his hands.

"If I'm to open my heart, I too am surprised at your indifference," said the Supreme Judge. "Almost all the common people are against us."

"The common people, like barley in the field, follow the wind," said Herhor.

"What about the army?"

"What army can stand up to Osiris?"

"I know," interrupted the Nomarch of Khensu impatiently, "but I see neither Osiris nor the wind that will turn the common people our way ... while the Pharaoh has already attached them to himself with promises, and tomorrow he's coming out with gifts."

"Fear is stronger than promises and gifts," replied Herhor.

"What are they to fear? Those three hundred soldiers of ours?"

"They shall fear Osiris."

"But where is he?" asked the Nomarch of Khensu excitedly.

"You shall all see him. And fortunate would be he who went blind for that day."

Herhor uttered the words with such unshakable calm that silence descended over the gathering.

"So, finally, what do we do?" asked the Supreme Judge after a moment.

"The Pharaoh," said Herhor, "wants the populace to attack the temples on the twenty-third. We must see to it that we are attacked on the twentieth of Phaophi."

"Eternally living gods!" exclaimed the Nomarch of Khensu, lifting his hands. "Why should we bring misfortune upon our heads, and two days sooner?"

"Listen to Herhor," said Mephres peremptorily, "and do all in your power to have the attack take place on the twentieth of Phaophi, starting in the morning."

"What if they actually do smash us?" asked the bewildered Judge.

"If Herhor's spells don't work, I'll call on the gods to help," replied Mephres, his eyes flashing balefully.

"H'm! you high priests have your secrets which can't be disclosed to us," said the Great

Judge. "So we'll do as you say, we'll get the attack to take place on the twentieth. But mind, our blood and our children's will be on your heads!"

"Let it be!"

"So be it!" cried the two high priests in unison.

Herhor added:

"For ten years we have been governing the Kingdom, and in that time none of you have come to grief and we have kept every promise. Be therefore patient and faithful a few days more, that you may see the might of the gods and receive your reward."

Presently the nomarchs took their leave of the high priests, making no effort to hide their anxiety. Only Herhor and Mephres remained.

After a lengthy silence, Herhor said: "Lykon was passable, playing the madman. But to substitute him for Ramses?"

"If his mother couldn't tell the difference," replied Mephres, "he must bear a strong resemblance. He should be able to sit on the throne and say a few words to those around him. Anyway, we'll be there."

"He's an awfully dumb actor[2]!" sighed Herhor, rubbing his forehead.

"He is wiser than millions of other people, because he has second sight[3] and can render great services to the Kingdom."

"Your Eminence keeps talking to me of this second sight," replied Herhor. "Just what is it?"

"Do you want to see for yourself?" asked Mephres. "Come on ... But by the gods, Herhor, don't mention even to your own heart what you will see."

They descended to the basement of the Temple of Ptah and found themselves in a spacious cellar illuminated by a torch. In the faint light, Herhor made out a man sitting at a table, eating. The man wore the tunic of the Pharaoh's guard.

"Lykon," said Mephres, "the highest dignitary of the Kingdom wishes to learn about your god-given abilities."

The Greek pushed away the bowl of food and muttered: "I curse the day my feet touched your soil! I'd rather work in the mines and be caned."

"There will be time enough for that," said Herhor sternly.

The Greek suddenly began trembling, seeing in Mephres' hand a small sphere of dark crystal. He turned pale, his gaze dulled, beads of sweat came to his face. His eyes were transfixed by the crystal ball.

"He's asleep," said Mephres. "Isn't it remarkable?"

"If he's not pretending."

"Pinch him ... stick him ... burn him," said Mephres.

Herhor retrieved from his white robe a dagger and made as if to stab Lykon between the eyes. The Greek did not flinch or even blink.[4]

---

[2] Actor: Prus here uses the expression *komediant* (derived from the Italian *commediante*, "actor"): an archaic Polish word for "actor," now used in the sense of "a person who puts on an act": an impostor, charlatan, humbug, hypocrite, or clown. *(Translator.)*

[3] Second sight (also called "clairvoyance"): an alleged ability to perceive things that are out of the natural range of human senses. *(Translator.)*

[4] Hypnosis (from the Greek *hypnos*, "sleep"), depicted here, is an induced state of focused attention in which the hypnotized person shows heightened responsiveness to suggestion. *(Translator.)*

"Look here," said Mephres, bringing the crystal closer to Lykon. "Do you see him who abducted Kama?"

The Greek sprang up from his chair, fists clenched, saliva on his lips.

"Let me go!" he cried raspily. "Let me go so I may drink his blood!"

"Where is he now?" asked Mephres.

"In a villa in the part of the garden nearest the river. There's a beautiful woman with him," whispered Lykon.

"Her name is Hebron, and she is the wife of Thutmose," prompted Herhor. "Admit it, Mephres," he added, "it doesn't take second sight to know that."

Mephres clenched his thin lips.

"If that doesn't convince Your Eminence, I'll show you something better," he replied. "Lykon, now find the traitor who is seeking the way to the treasury of the Labyrinth."

The entranced Greek gazed harder into the crystal and, after a moment, answered: "I see him. He's dressed in a beggar's cloth."

"Where is he?"

"He is lying in the courtyard of an inn, the last one before the Labyrinth. In the morning he'll be there."

"What does he look like?"

"He has a red beard and hair," answered Lykon.

"Well?" Mephres asked Herhor.

"Your Eminence has good police," said Herhor.

"But the keepers of the Labyrinth guard it poorly!" said Mephres angrily. "I'll go there tonight with Lykon to warn the local priests. And when I've saved the treasure of the gods, with Your Eminence's permission I'll become its keeper."

"As Your Eminence will," said Herhor indifferently. In his heart he added:

"At last the pious Mephres is starting to show teeth and claws. He wishes to be—only— keeper of the Labyrinth; and to make his charge Lykon—only—pharaoh!

"Truly, to satisfy the greed of my helpers, the gods would have to create ten Egypts."

When the two dignitaries had left the basement, Herhor returned on foot in the night to the Temple of Isis, where he had an apartment, while Mephres ordered a couple of horse-borne litters readied. Junior priests placed the entranced Lykon with a sack on his head into one litter, and the high priest climbed into the other and, surrounded by a handful of riders, rode off at a brisk trot for the Fayum.

During the night of the fourteenth and fifteenth of Phaophi, High Priest Samentu, pursuant to his promise given to the Pharaoh, entered the Labyrinth by a corridor known only to himself. He carried in his hands a bundle of torches, one of them lit, and on his back a small basket of tools.

Samentu very easily passed from chamber to chamber, from corridor to corridor, with a single touch displacing stone panels in columns and walls containing hidden doors. Sometimes he hesitated, but then he read the characters on the walls and compared them with those on the beads he wore on his neck.

After half an hour's way he found himself in the treasury and, displacing a floor panel, entered the chamber below. The chamber was low but spacious, and its ceiling rested on a multitude of squat columns.

Samentu set down his basket, lit two torches, and by their light proceeded to read the wall inscriptions.

"Despite my wretched appearance," said one inscription, "I am a true son of the gods, for my wrath is terrible.

"Out of doors, I turn into a pillar of fire and make lightning. Enclosed, I am thunder and destruction, and no building can withstand my power.

"I can be mollified only by holy water, which takes away my power. But my wrath springs as readily from a flame as from the slightest spark.

"Before me, all convulses and falls. I am as Typhon, who topples the tallest tree and lifts up stones."

"In a word, each temple has its secret, which the others do not know!" Samentu told himself.

He opened a column and took out of it a large pot. The pot had a lid affixed with wax, and an opening through which passed a long, thin string ending somewhere within the column.

Samentu cut off a piece of the string, touched it to a torch, and observed that the string burned very rapidly, with a hissing sound.

Then, with a knife, he carefully pried off the lid and saw, inside the pot, what looked like gray sand and pebbles. He took out a couple of pebbles and, going aside, touched the torch to them. Instantly a large flame belched up and the pebbles vanished, leaving behind a thick smoke and an unpleasant odor.

Samentu took out some of the gray sand, poured it on the floor, placed within the sand a piece of the string which he had found with the pot—and covered all this with a heavy stone. Then he brought the torch close, the string caught fire—and a moment later, amid flames, the stone leapt up.

"Now I've got this son of the gods!" smiled Samentu. "The treasury won't collapse."

He proceeded from column to column, opening panels and taking out the pots concealed within. Attached to each was a string, which Samentu cut, setting aside the pots.

"Well," said the priest, "His Holiness ought to give me half of the treasures ... or at least make my son a nomarch! And I'm sure he will make him a nomarch, for he is a generous ruler. And I deserve at least the Temple of Amon in Thebes!"

Having thus secured the lower chamber, Samentu returned to the treasury, and from there entered the chamber above. Here likewise were wall inscriptions and numerous columns containing pots, with strings attached, that held pebbles which exploded on contact with fire.

Samentu cut the strings, removed the pots from the columns—and tied up a pinch of the gray sand in a bit of cloth.

Then, tired, he sat down. Six of his torches had burned out; night must have been drawing to a close.

"I would never have supposed," he told himself, "that these priests had such a strange material. Why, we could demolish Assyrian forts with it! ... True, we don't tell our pupils everything either."

Tired, he began to daydream. He was now sure he would assume the highest position in the Kingdom, more powerful than that held by Herhor.

What would he do then? ... A great deal. He would secure learning and fortune for his descendents. He would take possession of the secrets of all the temples, thereby immensely strengthening his power and assuring Egypt's preponderance over Assyria.

The young Pharaoh mocked the gods: that would facilitate establishing the worship of a single god, say Osiris, and uniting the Phoenicians, Jews, Greeks, and Libyans into a single kingdom with Egypt.

At the same time he would set to work on the canal to link the Red Sea with the Mediterranean. Once forts had been built and large military forces gathered along the canal, all commerce with the unknown peoples of East and West would fall into Egyptian hands.

Egypt would need its own fleet and Egyptian sailors. Above all, she must crush Assyria, which was becoming more dangerous by the year ... The excesses and greed of the priests must be curbed. Let them cultivate learning, let them prosper, but let them serve the Kingdom instead of, as now, exploiting it for their own profit.

"As early as the month of Athyr," he told himself, "I will be the ruler! The young Lord is too fond of women and the military to concern himself with governance. And should he have no sons, then my son, my son ..."

He roused himself. Another torch had burned out, and it was high time to leave the undergrounds.

He rose, took up his basket, and left the chamber over the treasury.

"I need no helpers," he thought with a smile. "I've secured everything myself ... me ... a despised priest of Set!"

He had passed through a dozen or so chambers and corridors when he suddenly stopped. It seemed to him that, on the floor of the chamber he had just entered, he saw a thin streak of light...

Instantly such intense fear gripped him that he put out his torch. But the streak on the floor had likewise vanished.

Samentu strained to hear, but heard only the pulse in his head.

"I'm seeing things!" he said.

With trembling hands he took from his basket a small vessel with smoldering tinder and relit the torch.

"I'm very sleepy!" he thought.

He looked about the chamber and went over to a wall containing a hidden door. He pressed a nail; the door did not open. A second press ... a third—nothing ...

"What's this?" he said to himself, astonished.

He had forgotten the light streak. It seemed to him he was encountering something new and unprecedented. He had opened so many hundreds of hidden doors in his life, he had opened so many in the Labyrinth, that he simply could not understand this resistance.

Suddenly he was again gripped by fear. He ran from wall to wall, everywhere trying hidden doors. At last one of them yielded. Samentu drew a deep breath and found himself in an enormous chamber, as usual crowded with columns. His torch illuminated barely part of the expanse, whose enormous remainder was lost in a thick gloom.

The darkness, the forest of columns—above all, the chamber's unfamiliarity—heartened the priest. At the bottom of his fear there was kindled a spark of naïve hope: it seemed to him that, since he did not know this place, no one did—no one would find it.

He calmed somewhat and felt his legs buckling. He sat down. But once more he jumped up and began looking around as if to see whether he was actually in danger—and from what quarter. From which dark corner would it emerge to pounce on him?

Samentu, as no one else in Egypt, was used to undergrounds, the dark, being lost ... and he had experienced a variety of anxieties in his life. But what he was feeling now was something entirely new and so terrible that the priest feared to name it.

At last, by a great effort, he collected his thoughts and said:

"If I really saw light ... if somebody really has locked the doors, I will have been betrayed. In which case ..."

"Death!" whispered a voice somewhere at the bottom of his soul.

Death?! ...

Sweat came to his face; he could not breathe. Suddenly he was overcome by a frenzy of terror. He began running about the chamber, punching the walls in search of exit. He had forgotten where he was and how he had gotten there; he had lost his sense of direction and even the ability to orient himself with the beads.

At the same time, he felt as if there were two people inside him: one near mad, the other calm and rational. The rational one told himself it might all be an illusion, that no one had discovered him, no one was seeking him, and that he would emerge from there if only he cooled down. But the first one, the mad one, would not listen to the voice of reason, and with each moment was taking the upper hand over his internal antagonist.

Oh, to hide inside one of the columns! Then let them search ... Though surely no one would search for or find him, and after getting some sleep he would regain his composure.

"What can I meet with here?" he shrugged. "If I but calm down, they can chase me all through the Labyrinth. Cutting off my every path would require several thousand people—and indicating the chamber I'm in, little short of a miracle!

"Well, but suppose they catch me ... so what! I take this vial, put it to my mouth, and instantly I'm beyond reach ... even of the gods."

Despite this reasoning, he was again gripped by such a dreadful terror that for a second time he put out the torch and, trembling, teeth chattering, pressed himself against a column.

"How could I ... how could I come in here!" he told himself. "Had I nothing to eat ... nothing to lay my head on? Obviously I'm discovered. The Labyrinth has a host of keepers as watchful as dogs, and only a child or fool would think to deceive them.

"Wealth ... power ... what treasure is worth giving up a single day of life for? And here I, in the prime of my life, have risked mine!"

He thought he heard a heavy knock. He sprang up and saw light deep in the chamber.

Yes: real light, not an illusion. In a far wall was an open door through which several armed men were now cautiously entering with torches.

At this, the priest was chilled—in his feet, heart, head. He no longer doubted that he had been discovered, was being hunted, was surrounded.

Who could have betrayed him? Obviously, only one person: the young priest of Set whom he had initiated in some detail into his plans. Single-handedly the traitor would have needed a month to find the path through the Labyrinth; but if he contacted its keepers they could track Samentu down in a day.

The high priest was feeling now what only those feel who stand in the face of death. He had ceased to fear, for his imagined fears had taken flight before the real torches. And not only had he regained his composure, he actually felt infinitely superior to all that lived.

Imminently he would no longer be in any danger at all!

Thoughts swept through his head with the speed and clarity of lightning bolts. He saw his whole existence—labors, dangers, hopes, ambitions—and all this seemed to him unimportant. What would it have availed him had he now been pharaoh or had he possessed the gems of every royal treasury?

All this was vanity, dust—and even worse, illusion. One thing only was great and real: death.

Meanwhile the men with the torches, carefully looking over the columns and spaces, had come halfway down the enormous chamber. The priest saw their glittering spearheads and could tell that the men were advancing hesitantly, with dread and reluctance. A few paces behind them came another group of persons, illuminated by a single torch.

Samentu actually felt no animus toward them, only curiosity as to who could have betrayed him. But even that question interested him little; what seemed an incomparably more important question was: why must a man die—and to what purpose was he born? Before the fact of death, an entire life contracts into a single painful moment, no matter how long the life has been or how rich in experiences.

"What's it for? ... What ever is it for? ..."

He was brought back by the voice of one of the armed men.

"There's no one here, nor can there be!"

The armed men stopped. Samentu felt he loved these men who did not want to go farther—and his heart beat again.

Slowly the second group of persons drew up, in which there was contention.

"How can Your Eminence even suppose someone has gotten in here?" spoke a voice quavering with anger. "All the entrances are watched, especially now. And even if someone did get in, he could only starve to death."

"But, Eminence, see how Lykon is behaving," replied a second voice. "The sleeping one looks as if he senses an enemy nearby."

"Lykon?" thought Samentu. "Ah, that's the Greek who resembles the Pharaoh. What do I see? ... Mephres has brought him here!"

Just then the entranced Greek lunged forward, stopping before the column that concealed Samentu. The armed men ran after him, and their torches illuminated the dark figure of the priest.

"Who's there?" shouted the commander hoarsely.

Samentu stepped out. The sight of him made such a powerful impression that the men with the torches backed away. He could have passed between the terrified men, and no one would have stopped him; but the priest was no longer thinking of escape.

"Well, was my clairvoyant wrong?" called Mephres, extending his hand. "There's the traitor!"

Samentu approached him, smiling, and said: "I recognized you by that cry, Mephres. Since you can't be a charlatan, you are only a fool."

Everyone was stunned; Samentu spoke with calm irony:

"Though, to be sure, right now you are both a charlatan and a fool. A charlatan, because you hope to convince the keepers of the Labyrinth that this scoundrel has second sight; and a fool, because you think they'll believe you. Why not just admit that the Temple of Ptah likewise has detailed plans of the Labyrinth?"

"That's a lie!" cried Mephres.

"Ask these people whom they believe, you or me. I'm here because I found the plans in the Temple of Set; you came courtesy of immortal Ptah," concluded Samentu, laughing.

"Tie up this traitor and liar!" shouted Mephres.

Samentu drew back a couple of steps. He quickly took a vial from his robes and, lifting it to his lips, said: "Mephres, you'll be stupid to your dying day. You're clever only when it comes to money!"

He brought the vial to his lips and fell to the floor.

The armed men threw themselves to him and lifted him, but he was already flying through their hands.

"Leave him here like the others," said the Chief Keeper of the Labyrinth.

The whole entourage left the chamber and carefully closed the hidden door. Presently they emerged from the undergrounds of the Labyrinth.

His Eminence Mephres, on finding himself in the courtyard, bade his priests ready the horse litters and immediately rode off with the entranced Lykon for Memphis.

The keepers of the Labyrinth, stunned by the extraordinary events, looked now at one another, now at Mephres' escort disappearing in a yellow cloud of dust.

"I can't believe," said the High Priest keeper, "that in our day a man managed to get into the undergrounds."

"Your Eminence forgets that today there were three such men," said one of the younger priests, casting him a sidelong look.

"Oh ... say ... that's true!" replied the High Priest. "Have the gods scrambled my wits?" he added, rubbing his forehead and squeezing an amulet suspended on his chest.

"And two have gotten away," prompted the younger priest, "the impostor[5] Lykon and the holy Mephres."

"Why didn't you bring it to my attention down there ... in the undergrounds?" burst out the superior.

"I had no idea it would happen."

"Woe is me!" cried the High Priest. "I shouldn't be the Keeper but the doorkeeper of this building. We were warned that someone was trying to get into the Labyrinth, and I failed to prevent it! And now I've let the two most dangerous ones get away, who can bring back whomever they like ... Alas!"

"Your Eminence need not despair," said another priest. "Our law is clear. Send four or six of our men to Memphis, Your Eminence, armed with warrants. They will do the rest."

"I swear, I've lost my mind!" lamented the High Priest.

"What's done is done," broke in the younger priest, not without irony. "One thing is certain: people who have not only gotten into the undergrounds but have walked about them as if in their own homes, must not live."

"Then assign six of our militia ..."

"Of course! This has to be brought to a close," agreed the priest-keepers.

"Who knows whether Mephres wasn't acting with the knowledge of His Eminence Her-hor?" whispered someone.

---

[5] Impostor: Prus here uses the expression *komediant* (derived from the Italian *commediante*, "actor"): an archaic Polish word for "actor," now used in the sense of "a person who puts on an act": an impostor, charlatan, humbug, hypocrite, or clown. (Translator.)

"That will do!" cried the High Priest. "When we find Herhor inside the Labyrinth, we'll act in accordance with the law. But we have no right to make surmises or to suspect anyone. Have the scribes prepare the warrants for Mephres and Lykon, have picked men ride after them with all speed, and have the militia augment the watches. We must also inspect the building and find out how Samentu got in. Though I'm sure he won't soon find imitators."

A couple of hours later, six men rode out for Memphis.

CHAPTER 64

On the eighteenth of Phaophi, Egypt was already in the grip of chaos. Communications between the Lower and Upper Kingdom had been cut, commerce had come to a standstill, only patrol boats cruised the Nile, and the roads were full of troops headed for cities with more famous temples.

Only the priests' peasants were working in the fields. On the estates of the nobility, nomarchs, and especially the Pharaoh, flax went unpulled, clover was unharvested, there was no one to pluck the grapes. The peasants did nothing but rove in bands, singing, eating, drinking, and threatening the priests or the Phoenicians.

In the cities shops were closed up, and idled craftsmen spent their days discussing transformation of the Kingdom. This unseemly phenomenon was hardly new to Egypt, but was taking on such formidable proportions that tax collectors and even judges had started to go into hiding; the more so, as the police were treating the simple folk's abuses with great lenience.

One other thing merited note: the abundance of food and wine. In taverns and cheap eating houses, especially the Phoenicians', in Memphis and in the provinces, anyone could eat and drink as much as he liked, for very little or for free.

It was said His Holiness was throwing a feast for his people that was to go on for a whole month.

On account of the difficult or disrupted communications, cities knew little of what was happening in neighboring cities. Only the Pharaoh, and still better the priests, understood the overall situation of the country.

That situation was marked by a split between Upper, or Theban, and Lower, or Memphite, Egypt. In Thebes, the priestly party were ascendant; in Memphis, the pharaonic party. In Thebes it was said Ramses XIII had gone mad and wanted to sell Egypt out to the Phoenicians; in Memphis it was claimed the priests wanted to poison the Pharaoh and let the Assyrians into Egypt.

The simple folk, in both the north and south, felt instinctively drawn to Ramses. But the populace were a passive and labile force. When a government agitator spoke, the peasants were ready to storm the temples and smite the priests; but when a procession came out, they prostrated themselves on their faces and were terrified by predictions of calamities facing Egypt within the month.

The terrified nobility and nomarchs almost all converged on Memphis to beg the Pharaoh to save them from the rebellious peasants. But as Ramses XIII commended patience to them and did not quell the commonalty, the magnates began consulting with the priestly party.

To be sure, Herhor kept his peace or likewise commended patience, but other high priests told the lords that Ramses was mad and hinted at the need to remove him from power.

In Memphis itself, two parties circulated side by side: the godless, who drank, made noise, and splattered temple walls and even statues with mud; and the pious, mostly old people and women, who prayed in the streets, loudly predicting misfortunes and begging the gods for deliverance. The godless daily committed some outrage; daily, among the pious, some invalid or cripple was restored to health.

Strangely, though, despite the stirred-up passions, the two parties did each other no harm; still less were they eager for violence. That was because each was making its commotion under the direction of, and in accordance with a plan laid by, higher circles.

The Pharaoh, not having yet gathered all his troops and the evidence against the priests, did not signal a determined assault on the temples; the priests seemed to be waiting for something. Clearly, though, the priests were no longer feeling as weak as in the first days after the balloting by the delegates. It gave Ramses XIII pause to hear from all sides that the priests' peasants were hardly taking any part in the disturbances but were working.

"What does it mean?" the Pharaoh asked himself. "Do the baldpates think I won't dare attack the temples, or do they have some means of defense unknown to me?"

On the nineteenth of Phaophi the police informed the Lord that the previous night the populace had begun damaging the walls surrounding the Temple of Horus.

"Did you tell them to?" the Pharaoh asked the chief of police.

"No. They acted of their own accord."

"Restrain them gently ... restrain them," said the Lord. "In a few days they can do what they like. But for now they shouldn't act too forcefully."

Ramses XIII, as a commander and the victor of the Natron Lakes, knew that once mobs went to the attack, nothing would stop them: they must smash or be smashed. If the temples put up no defense, the common people would manage—but what if the temples decided to defend themselves?

In that case the populace would flee, and in their place it would be necessary to send in troops, of which there were many but not as many as the Pharaoh reckoned would be needed.

Moreover, Hiram had not yet returned from Pi-Bast with the letters proving the treason of Herhor and Mephres. More importantly, the priests who sided with the Pharaoh were supposed to assist the army only on the twenty-third of Phaophi. How could they be alerted at so many temples distant from each other? And did simple prudence not require avoiding contacts which could give those priests away?

For these reasons, Ramses XIII did not want the populace attacking the temples sooner.

Meanwhile, contrary to the Pharaoh's wishes, the commotion grew. Around the Temple of Isis, several pious persons were killed who had been predicting misfortunes for Egypt or who had miraculously regained their health. Around the Temple of Ptah the common people attacked a procession, beat up the priests, and damaged the sacred boat bearing the god's statue. Almost at the same time, couriers arrived from the cities of Khem and Iunu with word that the populace were breaking into the temples and in Kher-aha had actually desecrated the sanctuary.

Toward evening a delegation of priests came almost furtively to His Holiness' palace. The venerable prophets fell, weeping, at the Lord's feet, calling for him to protect the gods and temples.

This altogether unexpected turn of events filled Ramses' heart with great joy and still greater pride. He bade the delegates rise and graciously answered that his regiments were always ready to defend the temples—so long as they were conducted inside.

"I have no doubt," he said, "but the rioters will withdraw of their own accord once they see the sanctuaries of the gods occupied by the army."

The delegates hesitated.

"Your Holiness is aware," replied their elder, "that troops are not allowed even within the temple wall. We must therefore seek the opinion of the high priests."

"By all means, consult them," said the Lord. "I cannot work miracles, and I cannot defend the temples from the distance of my palace."

The delegates sorrowfully left the Pharaoh, who upon their departure called a secret council. He was convinced the priests would submit to his will, and it never crossed his mind that the delegation was a ruse staged by Herhor to lead him astray.

When the civil and military dignitaries were gathered in the royal chamber, Ramses addressed them pridefully:

"I had planned," he said, "to occupy the Memphis temples only on the twenty-third of Phaophi. I think, however, that it will be better to do so tomorrow."

"Our troops are not yet gathered," broke in Thutmose.

"And we don't have Herhor's letters to Assyria," added the Great Scribe.

"Never mind!" replied the Pharaoh. "Let the populace know tomorrow that Herhor and Mephres are traitors, and we'll show the evidence to the nomarchs and priests in a couple of days when Hiram returns from Pi-Bast."

"Your Holiness' new order greatly alters the original plan," said Thutmose. "We won't occupy the Labyrinth tomorrow. And should the Memphis temples offer resistance, we don't even have rams to batter down the gates."

"Thutmose," answered the Lord, "I'm under no compulsion to explain my orders. But I want to convince all of you that my heart takes a deeper assessment of events.

"If the populace," he continued, "are attacking the temples already today, then tomorrow they will want to break into them. If we don't back the populace, they will be repulsed, and in any case in three days' time they will lose heart for bold deeds.

"If the priests send a delegation already today, they must be weak; whereas in a few days the number of their adherents among the populace may increase.

"Zeal and fear are like wine in a pitcher: what has been poured out, is gone; only he can drink, who brings up his cup in time. So if today the populace are ready to attack and the enemy is frightened, let's make use of this since, as I say, in a few days fortune may abandon us, if not turn against us."

"Also, provisions are running out," broke in the Treasurer. "In three days the commonalty must return to work, because we won't have the wherewithal to feed them for free."

"There you are!" the Pharaoh said to Thutmose. "I personally ordered the Police Chief to restrain the populace. But if there's no holding them back, we must take advantage of their momentum. An experienced sailor doesn't fight the current or the wind but lets them carry him in the direction of his choosing."

At this point a courier entered with a report that the populace had set upon foreigners. Greeks, Syrians, above all Phoenicians were being attacked. Many shops had been looted, and several persons had been killed.

"That shows," cried the indignant Lord, "that mobs shouldn't be led off the path once it's been marked out! Tomorrow let the troops be near the temples. And let them immediately enter the temples if the populace start breaking into them or ... or if they start backing away under pressure ...

"It's true that grapes should be plucked in the month of Phaophi. But, were they to ripen a month early, what gardener would leave them on the vine?

"I repeat: I had wanted to delay the move by the populace, pending completion of our preparations. But if these things can't be put off, let's take advantage of the ready wind— and spread our sails!

"Tomorrow Herhor and Mephres should be jailed and brought to the palace. And we'll finish with the Labyrinth in a few days."

The council members concurred with the Pharaoh's decision and left, admiring his decisiveness and wisdom. Even the generals said it was better to seize a ready occasion than to gather forces for when the occasion will have passed.

It was now night. A second courier arrived from Memphis, with a report that the police had managed to safeguard the foreigners. But the populace were enraged, and no one knew what they might do on the morrow.

From that moment, courier followed courier. Some brought word that great masses of peasants armed with axes and cudgels were heading from all directions for Memphis. From elsewhere came reports that the populace around Peme, Khem, and On were fleeing into the fields, shouting that the morrow would see the end of the world. Another courier delivered a letter from Hiram, saying he would soon be arriving. Another brought word that temple regiments were stealing toward Memphis and, more importantly, that strong contingents of populace and troops hostile to the Phoenicians and even to His Holiness were advancing from Upper Egypt.

"Before they get here," thought the Pharaoh, "I'll already have in my hands the high priests and even Nitager's regiments. They're a few days too late!"

Finally, it was reported that here and there on the highways the army had intercepted disguised priests who were attempting to reach His Holiness' palace, doubtless with evil intents.

"Bring them to me," laughed the Pharaoh. "I want to see those who dare harbor evil intents toward me!"

About midnight Her Worship Queen Nikotris requested audience of His Holiness.

Her Eminence was pale and trembling. She told the officers to leave the royal chamber; and, remaining alone with the Pharaoh, she wept: "My son, I bring you very bad omens ..."

"Queen, I would rather hear accurate intelligence on the strength and intentions of my enemies."

"This evening the statue of the goddess Isis in my chapel turned to face the wall, and the water in the holy cistern turned blood-red."[1]

---

[1] "water ... turned blood-red" echoes the first of the ten plagues of Egypt (the Nile waters turned to blood) that, according to the Old Testament (Exodus 7:14-24), the God of the Hebrews inflicted on Egypt in his effort to persuade Pharaoh to release the Israelites from bondage. *(Translator.)*

"Which shows," replied the Pharaoh, "that we have traitors inside the palace. But they're not too dangerous if they can only pollute water and turn statues around."

"All our servants," continued the Lady, "all the populace are convinced that when your army enters the temples, a great misfortune will befall Egypt..."

"A greater misfortune," said the Lord, "is the audacity of the priests. Admitted by my eternally living father into the palace, they now think they've become its owners... By the gods, what will become of me in the face of their omnipotence! May I not assert my royal prerogatives?"

"At least ... at least," said the Lady after taking thought, "be merciful. Yes, you must regain your prerogatives, but don't let your soldiers desecrate the sanctuaries or harm the priests... Remember that the gracious gods send joy down upon Egypt and that the priests, despite their shortcomings (who doesn't have them!), render unequalled services to this country... Only think: if you impoverished and dispersed them, you would destroy the learning that has exalted our Kingdom above other peoples."

The Pharaoh took his mother's hands, kissed her, and laughed:

"Women must always exaggerate! You speak to me, Mother, as if I were a chief of wild Hyksos and not pharaoh... Do I wish harm on the priests? Do I despise their learning, even such fruitless kinds as observing the revolutions of the stars, which go about the heavens without our assistance and without enriching us by a single deben?

"What troubles me is not their learning or piety but the misery of Egypt, which internally wastes away from hunger, and externally fears the least Assyrian threat. Meanwhile the priests, despite their learning, not only refuse to help me in my royal aims but are putting up the most insolent resistance.

"So, mother, let me show them that not they but I am the master of my patrimony. I could not take vengeance on the humble—but I shall trample on the necks of the insolent.

"They know that but do not fully believe it and, lacking real strength, seek to intimidate me with predictions of disasters. That is their last weapon and refuge. When they realize I don't fear their terrors, they will humble themselves and in that case not a stone will fall from their temples, not a ring will leave their treasuries.

"I know them! Today they put on a great mien because I'm far away. But when I extend my bronze hand, they'll prostrate themselves on their faces—and all this turmoil will end in peace and general well-being."

The Queen embraced the Lord's legs and left comforted, having implored Ramses to respect the gods and have mercy on their servants.

After his mother's departure, the Pharaoh summoned Thutmose.

"Tomorrow, then," said the Lord, "my army will occupy the temples. But tell the regimental commanders, let them know I don't want the holy sanctuaries touched nor anyone to raise a hand against the priests."

"Not even Mephres and Herhor?" asked Thutmose.

"Not even them," replied the Pharaoh. "It will be punishment enough for them when, removed from their present posts, they enter learned temples to pray and cultivate learning unhindered."

"As Your Holiness will ... but ..."

Ramses lifted a finger, forfending any arguments. Next, to change the topic, he said with a smile:

"Thutmose, do you remember the maneuvers at Pi-Bailos? ... It's been two years now! ... When I was angry then at the audacity and greed of the priests, could you have imagined I would settle accounts with them this soon?

"Poor Sara ... and my little son. How beautiful he was ..."

Two tears rolled down the Pharaoh's face.

"Truly," he said, "were I not a son of the gods, who are merciful and magnanimous, tomorrow my enemies would experience some grievous hours. How many humiliations they've given me! How many times tears have clouded my eyes because of them!"

CHAPTER 65

On the twentieth of Phaophi, Memphis had a holiday appearance. All work had ceased; the porters, even, were not carrying loads. The entire populace had poured out into the squares and streets or converged around the temples. Mainly around the Temple of Ptah, the most fortified, where religious and secular dignitaries were gathered under the auspices of Herhor and Mephres.

Near the temples, troops stood in loose array, the better to communicate with the populace.

Numerous hucksters circulated among the common people and the soldiers with baskets of bread and with pitchers and leather bags of wine. They served the people for free. When asked why they were taking no pay, some answered that His Holiness was treating his subjects, while others said:

"Eat and drink, good Egyptians, for we know not whether we shall see the morrow!"

Those were priestly hucksters.

Numerous agents were busily at work. Some were telling their audiences that the priests were rebelling against the Lord and wanted to poison him because he had promised the people a seventh day of rest. Others whispered that the Pharaoh had gone mad and was conspiring with foreigners for the ruin of the temples and Egypt. The former urged the populace to attack the temples, where the priests and nomarchs were discussing how to oppress the craftsmen and peasants. The latter voiced a fear that, if the temples were attacked, a great calamity might ensue.

Nevertheless several massive beams, and some piles of rocks, had mysteriously found their way to outside the wall of the Temple of Ptah.

Respectable Memphis merchants walking about the crowds had no doubt that the populace's commotion was artificially fomented. Lesser scribes, policemen, laborers' officers, and disguised army decurions were no longer even hiding their official capacities or their intent to goad the populace into capturing the temples. On the other hand, the openers of dead bodies, beggars, temple servants, and junior priests, though they wanted to, could not make themselves inconspicuous, and anyone endowed with senses could see that they too were inciting the common people to violence!

The canny Memphis townspeople were bewildered by the behavior of the priestly party—and the populace were beginning to cool from their fervor of the day before. They could not understand what was happening or who was actually eliciting the disturbances. The chaos was heightened by half-crazed bigots who ran near-naked through the streets, whipping their flesh bloody and crying:

"Woe to Egypt! Godlessness hath exceeded all measure, and the hour of judgment is nigh! The gods will show their might over the audacity of wickedness!"

The troops behaved calmly as they waited for the people to start breaking into the temples. On one hand, that was the order that had come from the royal palace; on the other hand, the officers anticipated ambushes in the temples and preferred that common people should die rather than soldiers. The soldiers would, in any case, have their work cut out for them.

But despite the agitators' exhortations and the free wine, the crowd wavered. The peasants looked to the craftsmen, the craftsmen to the peasants, and everyone kept waiting for something.

Suddenly, about one in the afternoon, a drunken band armed with axes and rods poured out of side streets, heading for the Temple of Ptah. They were fishermen, Greek sailors, herdsmen, Libyan vagabonds, even prisoners from the Turra quarries. The band was headed by a giant laborer with a torch. He stopped before the temple gate and called to the populace in a booming voice:

"Do you good folks know what the high priests and nomarchs are discussing in there? They want to make His Holiness Ramses take away a barley cake a day from the laborers, and impose a new tax of a drachma a head on the peasants.

"That is why I say that you are being foolish and contemptible, standing there with arms folded! It's time to catch the temple rats and turn them over to our Lord the Pharaoh, for whose harm these godless men are conspiring! If our Lord were forced to give in to the Priestly Council, who would stand up for the good honest folk?"

"He's right!" said someone in the crowd.

"The Lord ordered us given a seventh day of rest ..."

"And he's going to give us land ..."

"He's always had a merciful heart for the simple folk! Do you remember how, two years ago, he freed the peasants who'd been jailed for the attack on the Jewess' farm?"

"Two years ago, I myself saw him beat a scribe who was collecting an unjust tax from the peasants."

"May our Lord Ramses XIII, the protector of the oppressed, live forever!"

"Hey, look," said a voice in the distance, "the cattle are returning from pasture on their own, as if evening were coming on."

"Who cares about the cattle! ... Let's get the priests!"

"Hey, you!" shouted the giant outside the temple gate. "Open up so we can find out what the high priests and nomarchs are discussing!"

"Open up! ... Or we'll break down the gate!"

"Strange thing," said someone in the distance, "the birds are settling down to sleep ... and it's only noon."

"Something bad is in the air!"

"Oh, gods! night is already coming on, and I haven't yet picked the lettuce for dinner," marveled a girl.

But these remarks were drowned out by the shouts of the drunken band and by the thud of beams on the temple's copper gate.

Had the crowd been less preoccupied with the assailants' violence, they would already have noticed that something unusual was happening in nature. The sun shone, there was not a cloud in the sky, yet daylight was waning and a chill breeze had sprung up.

"Give us another beam!" called the assailants. "The gate is giving!"

"Hard! ... Again! ..."

The onlooking crowd roared like a storm. Here and there, small groups broke away from it and joined the assailants. Finally the whole mass of the populace slowly moved up to the temple walls.

Despite the midday hour, the twilight kept deepening; in the gardens of the Temple of Ptah, cocks began crowing. But the crowd's fury was now so great that hardly anyone noticed these changes.

"Look!" called a beggar, "the day of judgment is nigh! The gods ..."

He was cut short by a cane blow to the head and fell on the spot.

Half-naked armed figures began scaling the temple walls. Officers marshaled their men, sure that they would soon have to support the attack by the common people.

"What does it mean?" whispered the soldiers, peering at the sky. "There are no clouds, but the world looks as it does during a storm."

"Hard! ... Break it down!" came shouts outside the temple. The thud of beams sounded ever more frequently.

At that moment High Priest Herhor appeared on the terrace over the gate, surrounded by an entourage of priests and secular dignitaries. His Eminence was wearing a gold chasuble and Amenhotep's miter encircled by the royal serpent.

Herhor surveyed the huge masses of populace surrounding the temple, leaned toward the storming band, and said:

"Whoever you are, believers or pagans, in the name of the gods I call on you to let the temple be!"

The people's hubbub suddenly ceased, and only the beams could be heard pounding against the copper gate. But soon the beams, too, came to a standstill.

"Open the gate!" cried the giant from below. "We want to find out whether you're plotting treason against our Lord!"

"My son," replied Herhor, "prostrate yourself on your face and beg the gods to forgive your sacrilege."

"Why don't you ask the gods to protect you!" shouted the band's leader; and taking a rock, he hurled it up toward the high priest.

At that moment, from a pylon-tower window, a thin jet, as if of water, spurted onto the giant's face. The bandit reeled, flailed his arms, and fell.

Those nearest him gave a cry of terror, which farther ranks, unaware of what had happened, answered with laughter and curses.

"Break down the gate!" came cries from the rear, and a hail of rocks showered toward Herhor and his entourage.

Herhor lifted up both his hands. When the crowd had again fallen still, the high priest called in a powerful voice:

"O gods! Into your protection I place the sanctuaries, which are assailed by traitors and blasphemers ..."

A moment later, somewhere over the temple, there resounded a superhuman voice:

"I turn my face from the accursed populace, and may darkness fall upon the earth ..."

And a terrible thing happened: even as the voice spoke, the sun more and more lost its luster. With the final word, night descended. Stars sparkled in the sky, and the sun had been replaced by a black disk surrounded by a ring of flames.

An immense cry burst out from a hundred thousand breasts. The storming party at the gate dropped their beams; peasants prostrated themselves.

"Behold, the day of judgment and death is at hand!" wailed a voice at the end of the street.

"Gods! ... Mercy! ... Holy man, reverse the calamity!" shouted the crowd.

"Woe betide soldiers who carry out the orders of godless superiors!" called the great voice from the temple.

In response, all the populace now prostrated themselves on their faces, and confusion overwhelmed the two regiments standing before the temple. The soldiers broke ranks, dropped their weapons, and fled pell-mell toward the river. Some, dashing blindly in the dark, smashed into buildings; others fell to the pavement and were trampled to death by their comrades. Within a couple of minutes, in lieu of tight columns of troops, the square was littered with spears and axes—and the entrances to the streets were piled up with wounded and dead.

No defeat in battle had ever ended so disastrously.

"Gods! ... Gods! ..." wailed the populace, "have mercy on the innocent ..."

"Osiris!" called Herhor from the terrace, "take pity and show thy face to the hapless populace!"

"For the last time I will heed the prayer of my priests, for I am merciful," answered the superhuman voice from the temple.

And that very moment the darkness fled, and the sun regained its luster.

New shouting, new weeping, new praying rang among the crowd. People greeted the resurrected sun, drunk with joy. Strangers fell into each other's arms, several persons died, and all crawled on their knees to the temple to kiss its blessed walls.

Atop the gate stood His Eminence Herhor, gazing into the heavens, while two priests held up his holy hands with which he had scattered the darkness and saved his people from destruction.[1]

Similar scenes, with some variants, had been played out in all of Lower Egypt. In each city, on the morning of the twentieth of Phaophi, the populace had gathered outside the temples, and in each city, about noon, a band had stormed at the sacred gate. Everywhere, about one, the temple's high priest had appeared over the gate with an entourage, had cursed the godless, and had made darkness. And when the crowd fled in terror or prostrated themselves, the high priests had prayed for Osiris to show his face—and daylight had returned to the earth.

Thus, thanks to the solar eclipse, the savvy priestly party had now shaken Ramses XIII's authority as well in Lower Egypt. In a matter of a few minutes the Pharaoh's government had unwittingly arrived at the brink of a precipice. It could be saved only by great wisdom and a detailed knowledge of the situation. But that was lacking at the royal palace, where precisely at the critical juncture there began the all-powerful sway of chance.

On the twentieth of Phaophi His Holiness had risen with the dawn and, to be closer to

---

[1] This eclipse scene was suggested to Prus by an 1887 solar eclipse he had witnessed at Mława, 100 kilometers north-northwest of Warsaw; and likely also by Christopher Columbus' use of a *lunar* eclipse in 1504, when marooned on Jamaica, to extort provisions from the Arawak natives. *(Translator.)*

the theater of operations, had moved from the main palace to a villa barely an hour's way on foot from Memphis. On one side of the villa were the barracks of the Asiatic troops; and on the other, the villa of Thutmose and his wife, the beautiful Hebron. The Lord was accompanied there by dignitaries loyal to Ramses—and by the First Guard Regiment, in which the Pharaoh reposed boundless confidence.

Ramses XIII was in excellent spirits. He bathed, breakfasted heartily—and began interviewing the messengers who arrived every quarter-hour from Memphis.

Their reports were monotonously uniform. The high priests and several nomarchs, under the auspices of Herhor and Mephres, had shut themselves inside the Temple of Ptah. The army had good morale, and the populace were stirred up. Everyone blessed the Pharaoh and awaited the order to attack.

At nine, when the fourth courier repeated the same words, the Pharaoh frowned.

"What are they waiting for?" asked the Lord. "Why don't they attack?"

The messenger answered that the main party which was to assault the temple and batter down the copper gate, had not yet gathered.

The explanation displeased the Lord. He shook his head and sent an officer to Memphis to expedite the attack.

"What's the meaning of the delay?" he said. "I thought my army would wake me with news of the temple's capture. In situations like this, speed is of the essence."

The officer rode off, but at the Temple of Ptah nothing changed. The populace kept waiting for something, and the main party was not yet in place.

It might have been thought that some other will was delaying the execution of the orders.

At nine in the morning, Queen Nikotris' litter arrived at the Pharaoh's villa. The worshipful Lady practically forced her way into her son's room and, weeping, fell to the Lord's feet.

"How may I help you, mother?" said Ramses, scarcely concealing his impatience. "Do you forget that a camp is no place for women?"

"Today I'm not budging from here, I'm not leaving you for a moment!" she cried. "It's true you are the son of Isis and that she has you in her keeping. Still, I would die of anxiety."

"Am I in danger?" shrugged the Pharaoh.

"The priest who watches the stars," wept the Queen, "told one of the servant girls that if today ... if this day passes happily for you, you will live and reign a hundred years."

"Aha! ... Where is this expert on my fate?"

"He's fled to Memphis," replied the Lady.

The Pharaoh mused, then laughed:

"Much as the Libyans hurled projectiles at us at the Natron Lakes, so today the priesthood hurls threats at us ... Have no fear, mother! Talk, even priests' talk, is less dangerous than arrows and stones."

Another courier arrived from Memphis with word that all was well—but that the main party was not yet ready.

The Pharaoh's handsome face showed signs of anger. Desiring to calm the Lord, Thutmose said: "The common people are not soldiers. They're incapable of gathering at a set hour, they drag along like mud—and they don't follow orders. Had the regiments been entrusted with occupying the temples, they would already be inside."

"What ever are you saying, Thutmose?" exclaimed the Queen. "Who ever heard of the Egyptian army ..."

"You forget," broke in Ramses, "my orders were not for the army to assault the temples, but to defend the temples from assault by the common people."

"That's what is causing the operational delays," replied Thutmose impatiently.

"These are the royal advisors!?" the Queen burst out. "The Lord does wisely, acting as defender of the gods; and, instead of assuaging him, you urge him to violence!"

Thutmose's blood boiled up. Happily, he was called out of the room by an aide reporting that an old man had been detained at the gate who wished to speak with His Holiness.

"Today, here," muttered the aide, "the only person anybody wants to see is the Lord, as if the Pharaoh were a tavern-keeper."

Thutmose reflected that, under Ramses XII, no one would have dared speak this way of the ruler. But he pretended not to take notice.

The old man the guards had detained was the Phoenician Prince Hiram. He was wearing a dusty military coat and was tired and irritated.

Thutmose ordered the Tyrian admitted and, when the two were in the garden, said to him:

"I expect Your Eminence will want to bathe and change before I request audience for you with His Holiness?"

Hiram's gray eyebrows bristled, and his eyes became still more bloodshot.

"After what I've seen," he replied flintily, "I may not even request audience."

"You do have the high priests' letters to Assyria ..."

"What do you need them for, if you've made your peace with the priests?"

"What ever is Your Eminence saying?" demanded Thutmose.

"I know whereof I speak!" said Hiram. "You got tens of thousands of talents out of the Phoenicians, supposedly to free Egypt from the power of the priests, and now you're robbing and murdering us ... Look what's happening from the sea to the First Cataract: everywhere your populace are chasing down the Phoenicians as if we were dogs, because that's what the priests have ordered."

"You've gone mad, Tyrian! Right now our populace are taking the Temple of Ptah in Memphis ..."

Hiram waved his hand. "You won't take it!" he replied. "You're deceiving us, or you are yourselves deceived. You were above all supposed to take the Labyrinth and its treasury, and only on the twenty-third of Phaophi. Instead, today you're wasting your forces at the Temple of Ptah, while the Labyrinth is lost!

"What's going on? ... Where's the sense in this?" continued the Phoenician irately. "Why the storming at empty buildings? The only thing it will accomplish is reinforcement of the watch at the Labyrinth."

"We'll take the Labyrinth too," interrupted Thutmose.

"You'll take nothing—nothing! The Labyrinth could have been taken by only one man, whom today's brawls in Memphis will hinder."

Thutmose stopped on the way. "What's bothering you?" he asked Hiram curtly.

"The disarray around here. You're no longer a government but a bunch of officers and dignitaries whom the priests drive about whither and when they will. For three days, in all of Lower Egypt, there's been such awful chaos that the common people have been setting upon us Phoenicians, your only friends. And why? ... Because power has slipped from your hands and been seized by the priests!"

"You say that because you don't know the situation," replied Thutmose. "It's true the priests are making trouble for us and are organizing attacks on the Phoenicians. But power is in the Pharaoh's hand; overall events are unfolding in accordance with his orders."

"Including today's assault on the Temple of Ptah?" asked Hiram.

"Yes. I personally was at the confidential council where the Pharaoh ordered the temples taken today instead of the twenty-third."

"Well, then," interrupted Hiram, "I'm informing you, commander of the guard, that you are lost. I know for certain that today's assault was planned at a session of high priests and nomarchs which took place at the Temple of Ptah on the thirteenth of Phaophi."

"Why should they plan an assault on themselves?" scoffed Thutmose.

"They must have a purpose in it. And I've found that they pursue their purposes better than you."

The conversation was interrupted by an aide summoning Thutmose to His Holiness.

"One thing more!" added Hiram. "On the road, your soldiers detained the priest Pentuer, who has something important to tell the Pharaoh."

Thutmose grabbed his head and immediately sent officers to find Pentuer. Then he ran off to the Pharaoh, and returned a moment later and asked the Phoenician to come with him.

When Hiram entered the royal chamber, he found there Queen Nikotris, the Great Treasurer, the Great Scribe, and several generals. Ramses XIII, irritated, was rapidly pacing the room.

"There's the misfortune of the Pharaoh and Egypt!" cried the Queen, indicating the Phoenician.

"Worshipful Lady," replied the composed Tyrian, bowing, "time will tell who was the loyal, and who the bad, servant of His Holiness."

Ramses XIII suddenly stopped in front of Hiram. "Have you Herhor's letters to Assyria?" he asked.

The Phoenician took a packet from under his clothing and silently handed it to the Pharaoh.

"This is what I needed!" cried the Lord jubilantly. "The people must at once be informed that the high priests have betrayed the Kingdom!"

"My son," beseeched the Queen, "by your father's shade ... by our gods, I implore you, hold off for a couple of days with this announcement. One must be very careful with Phoenician gifts."

"Your Holiness," said Hiram, "may even burn the letters. I don't care about them."

The Pharaoh thought a moment and slipped the packet under his tunic.

"What did you hear in Lower Egypt?" asked the Lord.

"Everywhere they're killing Phoenicians," said Hiram. "Our houses are being demolished, the furnishings are being looted, and several dozen people have been killed."

"I've heard! It's the work of the priests," said the Lord.

"My son, better say that those are the wages of the godlessness and extortions of the Phoenicians," broke in the Queen.

Hiram turned askance to the Lady and said: "For three days the Chief of Police of Pi-

Bast has been in Memphis with two assistants—and they're on the trail of the murderer and impostor Lykon."

"Who was reared at Phoenician temples!" cried Queen Nikotris.

"... Lykon," continued Hiram, "whom High Priest Mephres stole from the police and the courts ... Lykon who in Thebes, impersonating Your Holiness, ran half-naked in the garden as a madman."

"What are you saying?" shouted the Pharaoh.

"Your Holiness, ask the most worshipful Queen, she saw him," replied Hiram.

Ramses looked at his mother in consternation.

"Yes," said the Queen, "I saw the wretch, but I said nothing in order to spare you pain. However, no one has proof that the high priests sent out Lykon, as it could just as well have been the Phoenicians."

Hiram sneered.

"Mother! ... Mother! ..." said Ramses sorrowfully, "do the priests take precedence in your heart even over me?"

"You are my son and dearest Lord," said the Queen passionately, "but I can't suffer a foreigner ... a pagan ... to cast aspersions on the holy priesthood, from which we are both descended.

"Oh, Ramses!" she cried, falling to her knees, "send away the bad advisors who urge you to desecrate the temples, to lift your hand against the successor of your grandfather Amenhotep! There's still time ... still time to reach accord ... to save Egypt ..."

Suddenly Pentuer entered the chamber, disheveled.

"And what have you to say?" asked the Pharaoh, strangely calm.

"Today, maybe soon," said the priest, "there is going to be a solar eclipse ..."

The Pharaoh stepped back in surprise. "How does a solar eclipse concern me, especially just now?"

"That's what I thought, Lord," said Pentuer, "until I read descriptions of eclipses in the old chronicles. It's such a terrifying phenomenon that the whole country should be warned of it."

"So that's it!" said Hiram.

"Why didn't you let us know sooner?" Thutmose asked the priest.

"Soldiers detained me for two days. There's no time now to warn the country, but let the troops at the palace know so that at least they do not panic."

The Pharaoh clapped his hands. "Oh, this is bad!" he whispered, then added aloud: "What is going to happen, and when?"

"It will become night during the day," said the priest. "It's supposed to last the time it takes to walk five hundred paces ... And it will start at noon ... That's what Menes told me."

"Menes?" said the Pharaoh. "I know the name, but ..."

"He wrote Your Holiness about it ... But do let the troops know ..."

Soon trumpets sounded. The Guard and the Asiatics stood at arms, and the Pharaoh, surrounded by his staff, informed the troops about the eclipse, adding that they should not fear as the darkness would soon pass and he would be with them.

"Live forever!" responded the armed ranks.

At the same time, several of the most judicious riders were dispatched to Memphis.

Generals stepped to the heads of the columns; the Pharaoh paced the courtyard in thought; civil dignitaries quietly whispered with Hiram; and Queen Nikotris, remaining alone in the room, prostrated herself on her face before the statue of Osiris.

It was now past one, and the sunlight had indeed begun to wane.

"Will it really become night?" the Pharaoh asked Pentuer.

"Yes, but very briefly."

"What will become of the sun?"

"It will be concealed by the moon."

"I must restore to favor the wise men who study the stars," the Lord told himself.

Twilight was fast deepening. The Asiatics' horses became restive; swarms of birds descended into the garden and, with loud twittering, perched in all the trees.

"Sing!" cried Kalipos to the Greeks.

Drums rumbled, flutes tooted, and to this accompaniment the Greek regiment sang a lively ballad about a priest's daughter who had such a fear of spirits that she could sleep only in army barracks.

Suddenly a baleful shadow fell over the yellow Libyan hills and, at lightning speed, covered Memphis, the Nile, and the palace gardens. Night enveloped the earth, and in the heavens there appeared a coal-black sphere wreathed in flames. An immense uproar drowned out the Greek regiment's ballad. The Asiatics had given a war whoop, loosing a cloud of arrows into the sky to frighten off the evil spirit that wanted to devour the sun.

"You say the black disk is the moon?" the Pharaoh asked Pentuer.

"So Menes maintains."

"He's a very learned man! And the darkness will soon end?"

"Most certainly ..."

"What if the moon were to break out of the sky and fall to the earth?"

"It can't happen ... There's the sun now!" cried Pentuer jubilantly.

All the gathered regiments raised a cheer in honor of Ramses XIII.

The Pharaoh hugged Pentuer.

"Truly," said the Lord, "we have seen an extraordinary happening. But I wouldn't want to see it a second time ... I feel that if I hadn't been a soldier, my heart would have been overwhelmed with fear."

Hiram approached Thutmose and whispered: "Eminence, send messengers at once to Memphis, as I fear the high priests will have done you some mischief."

"You think so?"

Hiram nodded. "They would not have ruled the Kingdom this long," he said, "they would not have buried nineteen of your dynasties, if they did not know how to take advantage of events like today's."

Having thanked the soldiers for their good bearing in the face of the extraordinary phenomenon, the Pharaoh returned to his villa. He was engrossed in thought; he spoke calmly, even gently, but uncertainty was writ on his handsome face.

An intense struggle was under way in Ramses' soul. He was beginning to grasp that the priests held, in their hands, forces which he had not taken into account, had not thought about, had not even wanted to hear about.

The priests who observed the motions of the stars had, in the course of several minutes, grown immensely in his eyes. The Pharaoh told himself he ought to become acquainted with this curious learning that could so terribly cross men's plans.

Messenger after messenger sped from the palace for Memphis to learn what had happened there during the eclipse. But the messengers did not return, and uncertainty spread its black wings over the royal entourage. No one doubted that something bad had happened at the Temple of Ptah, or dared to spin conjectures about it. The Pharaoh and his intimates seemed glad of every minute that passed without word from there.

Queen Nikotris sat down beside the Lord and whispered to him: "Let me act, Ramses... Women have rendered our Kingdom more than one service. Only recall Queen Nikotris of the Sixth Dynasty,[2] or Maatkare,[3] who created a Red Sea fleet!... Our sex lacks neither good sense nor energy, so let me act. If the Temple of Ptah hasn't been captured nor the priests harmed, I'll reconcile you with Herhor. You'll take his daughter as your wife, and you will have a glorious reign... Remember that your grandfather, holy Amenhotep, was likewise a high priest and the pharaoh's viceroy, and who knows whether you would be reigning today if the holy priesthood had not wanted its blood occupying the throne. Is this how you show them gratitude for your power?"

The Pharaoh was listening to her, but he was still reflecting that the learning of the priests was an enormous force, and that fighting them was difficult!

Only at three did the first messenger arrive from Memphis, the adjutant of a regiment that had stood outside the temple. He told the Pharaoh that the temple had not been captured due to the anger of the gods; that the populace had fled, the priests were triumphing, and disarray had arisen even among the troops during that terrible if brief night.

Then, taking Thutmose aside, the adjutant told him bluntly that the army was demoralized and in its panic-stricken flight had sustained as many wounded and dead as in a battle.

"What is the army doing now?" asked Thutmose, appalled.

"Of course," replied the adjutant, "we managed to muster the soldiers together. But there can be no talk of using them against the temples... Particularly now that the priests are ministering to the wounded. The soldiers are now ready to prostrate themselves at the sight of a shaven head and leopard skin, and much time will pass before any of them would dare cross a sacred gate."

"What about the priests?"

"They are blessing the soldiers, feeding them, giving them drink, and pretending that the army is not to blame for the assault on the temple, that it was the work of the Phoenicians."

"And you're permitting this demoralization of the regiments?" exclaimed Thutmose.

"His Holiness did order us to defend the priests against the common people," replied the adjutant. "Had we been allowed to occupy the temples, we would have been inside them since ten in the morning, and the high priests would have been confined to the cellars."

Just then the officer of the day informed Thutmose that another priest, arrived from Memphis, wished to speak with His Holiness.

---

[2] The reference is to *Nitocris*, allegedly the last pharaoh of the 6th Dynasty. Though her name appears in Herodotus' *Histories* and Manetho's writings, her historicity is questionable. She may have been an interregnum queen. *(Translator.)*

[3] Maatkare (Prus calls her *Makara*): throne name of Queen Hatshepsut. The name Maatkare was later also borne by two aristocratic women, in Dynasties 21 and 22. *(Translator.)*

Thutmose surveyed the priest. He was a fairly young man with a face seemingly carved in wood. He said he came to the Pharaoh from Samentu.

Ramses immediately received the priest who, after prostrating himself, handed the Lord a ring, at sight of which the Pharaoh turned pale.

"What does this mean?" asked the Lord.

"Samentu is dead," answered the messenger.

For a moment, Ramses was unable to speak. Finally he said: "How did it happen?"

"It seems," said the priest, "that Samentu was discovered in one of the chambers of the Labyrinth and took poison to avoid torture. He appears to have been discovered by Mephres with the aid of a Greek who is supposed to bear a great resemblance to Your Holiness."

"Mephres and Lykon again!" cried Thutmose angrily. "Lord," he turned to the Pharaoh, "will you never free yourself of those traitors?"

His Holiness called another confidential council in his chamber. To it he summoned Hiram and the priest who had come with Samentu's ring. Pentuer did not wish to take part in the council, while Her Worship Queen Nikotris came of her own accord.

"I see," Hiram whispered to Thutmose, "that when the priests have been driven out, women will rule Egypt."

When the dignitaries were gathered, the Pharaoh gave the floor to Samentu's messenger. The young priest did not wish to speak about the Labyrinth. Instead he expatiated on the Temple of Ptah being completely undefended and said that a few dozen soldiers would suffice to take everybody it harbored.

"This man is a traitor!" shouted the Queen. "A priest urges you to violence against priests ..."

Not a muscle quivered on the messenger's face.

"Worshipful lady," he replied, "if Mephres worked the demise of my patron and master Samentu, I would be a dog if I did not seek revenge. A death for a death."

"I like this young man!" whispered Hiram.

A fresher air seemed to waft through the gathering. The generals straightened, the civil dignitaries regarded the priest with interest, even the Pharaoh's face became animated.

"Don't listen to him, my son!" beseeched the Queen.

"What do you think," said the Pharaoh suddenly to the young priest, "that the holy Samentu would do now, were he alive?"

"I am sure," replied the priest energetically, "that Samentu would enter the Temple of Ptah, burn incense to the gods, but punish the traitors and murderers."

"I say again that you are the worst traitor!" cried the Queen.

"I am but doing my duty," replied the priest impassively.

"This man is a true disciple of Samentu!" broke in Hiram. "He alone sees clearly what remains to be done."

The military and civil dignitaries agreed with Hiram; the Great Scribe added:

"Inasmuch as we've started a fight with the priests, we ought to finish it, especially now that we have the letters proving that Herhor has been treating with the Assyrians, which is high treason."

"He is carrying on the policies of Ramses XII," interjected the Queen.

"But I am Ramses XIII!" answered the Pharaoh impatiently.

Thutmose rose from his chair.

"My Lord," he said, "let me act. It is very dangerous to prolong the state of uncertainty that prevails in the government, and it would be criminally stupid not to seize the opportunity. This priest says the temple is undefended, so let me go there with a few hand-picked men."

"I'll go with you," said Kalipos. "In my experience, an enemy is weakest in his moment of triumph. If we immediately rush the Temple of Ptah ..."

"You need hardly rush the temple," said the Great Scribe. "Just enter as executors of the Pharaoh's order to jail the traitors," said the Great Scribe. "That doesn't even require force. A single policeman will often go after a whole band of thieves and seize as many as he likes."

"My son," said the Queen, "is yielding to the pressure of your advice. But he wants no violence, he forbids it!"

"If so," said the young priest of Set, "then I'll tell His Holiness one thing more ..."

He drew a couple of deep breaths, but concluded in a subdued voice: "On the streets of Memphis, the priestly party are saying ..."

"Saying what? ... Speak freely," said the Pharaoh.

"That Your Holiness is mad, that you haven't been invested as a high priest or even as pharaoh ... and that you may be deposed."

"That is what I fear," whispered the Queen.

The Pharaoh sprang up from his armchair.

"Thutmose!" he cried in a voice vibrant with renewed energy. "Take as many men as you like, go to the Temple of Ptah—and bring me Herhor and Mephres charged with high treason. If they can justify themselves, I'll restore them to my good graces; if not ..."

"Have you taken thought?" interrupted the Queen.

The incensed Pharaoh did not answer her, and the dignitaries called:

"Death to the traitors! Since when must Egypt's Pharaoh sacrifice loyal servants to beg the mercy of scoundrels!"

Ramses XIII handed Thutmose the packet of Herhor's letters to Assyria and said in a solemn voice:

"Pending the suppression of the priests' rebellion, I am transfering my authority to the commander of the guard, Thutmose. You shall all now heed him, and you, worshipful Mother, shall address your remarks to him."

"The Lord does wisely and justly!" called the Great Scribe. "It's not right for the Pharaoh to contend with a rebellion, and a lack of energetic leadership could be our undoing!"

The dignitaries bowed to Thutmose. Queen Nikotris, moaning, fell to her son's feet.

Thutmose, accompanied by the generals, went out to the courtyard. He ordered the First Guard Regiment to fall in and said:

"I need a few dozen men ready to die for the glory of our Lord!"

More soldiers and officers stepped forward than were needed, Ennana at their head.

"Are you ready to die?" asked Thutmose.

"We will die with your lordship for His Holiness!" cried Ennana.

"You shall not die, you shall vanquish some wretched criminals," replied Thutmose. "The soldiers in this expedition shall become officers, and the officers shall be promoted two ranks. So say I, Thutmose, by the Pharaoh's will commander-in-chief."

"Live forever!"

Thutmose ordered twenty-five two-wheeled chariots of heavy cavalry harnessed and the volunteers loaded into them. He and Kalipos mounted horses—and presently the whole detachment, heading for Memphis, disappeared in a cloud of dust.

Seeing this from a window in the royal villa, Hiram bowed to the Pharaoh and whispered: "Now I do believe that Your Holiness was not in league with the high priests."

"Are you mad?!" the Lord burst out.

"Pardon me, Lord, but today's assault on the temple was arranged by the priests. How they drew Your Holiness into this, I don't understand."

It was five in the afternoon.

CHAPTER 66

At the same time to the minute, the priest watching atop a pylon tower of the Temple of Ptah in Memphis informed the high priests and nomarchs conferring inside the hall that the Pharaoh's palace was signaling.

"I believe His Holiness will be suing us for peace," laughed one of the nomarchs.

"I doubt it!" said Mephres.

Herhor went out onto the pylon tower: the signals from the palace were for him. Soon he returned and told the assembled:

"Our young priest has acquitted himself very well. Thutmose is riding over with several dozen volunteers to jail or kill us."

"And you still dare defend Ramses?" shouted Mephres.

"I must and shall defend him, because I've given my solemn word to the Queen. Except for the worshipful daughter of holy Amenhotep, our position would not be as it is."

"Well, I haven't given my word!" retorted Mephres, and he left the conference hall.

"What does he mean to do?" asked a nomarch.

"Doting old man!" shrugged Herhor.

Before six in the evening a guard detachment, unchallenged, approached the Temple of Ptah. The commander knocked at the gate, which was immediately opened. It was Thutmose and his volunteers.

On entering the temple courtyard, the commander-in-chief was surprised to see that Herhor had come out in Amenhotep's miter, surrounded only by priests.

"What do you require, my son?" the high priest asked the nonplused commander.

But Thutmose quickly regained his composure and said:

"Herhor, High Priest of Theban Amon! On the strength of letters which you wrote to Sargon, the Assyrian satrap, which letters I have with me, you are charged with high treason and are to justify yourself to the Pharaoh."

"If the young Lord," replied Herhor calmly, "wishes to learn the policy aims of the eternally living Ramses XII, let him present himself to our Supreme Council, and they shall be explained."

"I call on you to immediately come with me, if you would not have me compel you," cried Thutmose.

"My son, I beseech the gods to preserve you from the violence and punishment you deserve."

"Are you coming?" asked Thutmose.

"I wait here for Ramses," replied Herhor.

"Then stay here, charlatan!" shouted Thutmose.

He drew his sword and lunged for Herhor. At that moment Ennana, standing behind the commander, raised his ax and, with all his might, struck Thutmose between the neck and right collarbone, sending blood spurting in all directions. The Pharaoh's favorite fell to the ground, almost cut in half.

Several soldiers sprang toward Ennana with leveled spears, but succumbed after a brief struggle with their comrades. Three-quarters of the volunteers were in the pay of the priests.

"May our lord the holy Herhor live forever!" cried Ennana, brandishing his bloodied ax.

"May he live forever!" repeated the soldiers and priests—and all prostrated themselves on their faces. His Eminence Herhor lifted his hands and blessed them.

Leaving the temple courtyard, Mephres had descended into the cellar where Lykon dwelled. Immediately on the threshold the high priest produced from his bosom a crystal sphere, at sight of which the Greek became irate.

"May the earth swallow you all! May your corpses know no peace!" cursed Lykon, more and more quietly.

At last he fell still and was asleep.

"Take this dagger," said Mephres, handing the Greek a slender steel. "Take this dagger and go to the palace garden. Stand there in the fig grove and wait for him who stole and debauched your Kama."

Lykon gnashed his teeth in impotent rage.

"When you see him, awake ..." finished Mephres.

He threw an officer's hooded cloak on the Greek, whispered a password into his ear, and led him out of the cellar, through a hidden temple gate, into an empty Memphis street.

Next, with the sprightliness of a youth, Mephres ran up to the pylon top and, picking up several varicolored flags, proceeded to signal toward the Pharaoh's palace. Apparently he was noticed and understood, for a sinister smile flashed to the high priest's parchment face.

Mephres put away the flags, left the pylon terrace, and began a slow descent. Suddenly, when he was already on the first floor, he was surrounded by several men in dark-brown hooded cloaks concealing tunics in black and white stripes.

"This is His Eminence Mephres," said one of them.

All three knelt before the high priest, who automatically lifted his hand as in blessing. But suddenly he dropped it, asking: "Who are you?"

"Keepers of the Labyrinth."

"Why have you stopped me?" he said, his hands and thin lips trembling.

"We needn't remind you, holy man," said one of the keepers, still kneeling, "that several days ago you were in the Labyrinth, where you know the way as well as we, though you haven't been initiated. And you are too great a sage not to know also our laws in such cases."

"What's the meaning of this?" called Mephres in a raised voice. "You're killers sent by Her ..."

He did not finish. One of the assailants grabbed his arms, another threw a cloth over his head, and the third sprinkled his face with a clear liquid. Mephres tossed a few times and fell. The keepers sprinkled him again, and when he was dead they laid him in a recess, slipped a papyrus into his lifeless hand—and disappeared in the corridors of the pylon tower.

Three identically dressed men had been pursuing Lykon almost from the moment when, let out of the temple by Mephres, he had found himself in the empty street.

The men had been hiding not far from the gate out which the Greek had passed, and at first had let him go free. But soon one of them had noticed something suspicious in his movements, and they had all proceeded to follow him.

Strange thing! The entranced Lykon, as if sensing pursuit, suddenly turned into a busy street, then into a teeming square, then ran down Fishery Street to the Nile. There, in an alley, he found a small boat, jumped into it, and proceeded to cross the river at incredible speed.

He was a couple of hundred paces offshore when a boat slipped out after him, with a ferryman and three passengers. And hardly had that boat pushed off when a second boat appeared, carrying two ferrymen and again three passengers.

Both boats were in hot pursuit of Lykon.

In the boat with only the one rower sat keepers of the Labyrinth, scrutinizing their competition insofar as they could amid the twilight rapidly deepening in the wake of sunset.

"Who are those three?" whispered the Labyrinth keepers. "They've been hanging around the temple since the other day, and now they're chasing him. Could they be wanting to protect him from us?"

Lykon's little boat made the opposite bank. The entranced Greek jumped out and proceeded at a rapid pace toward the palace gardens. At times he staggered, stopped, and grabbed his head; but after a moment he went on again as if drawn by some inconceivable force.

The Labyrinth keepers likewise reached the other bank, but they had been beaten to it by their competition.

A unique race began. Lykon sprinted toward the royal palace, followed by the three strangers and finally by the three Labyrinth keepers.

A few hundred paces from the garden, the two pursuing groups met. It was now night, but a clear one.

"Who are you people?" a Labyrinth keeper asked the strangers.

"I'm Chief of Police of Pi-Bast, and I'm pursuing a great criminal with two of my centurions."

"We are keepers of the Labyrinth, and we're likewise pursuing this man."

The two groups eyed each other, hands on their swords or knives.

"What do you want with him?" asked the Chief of Police finally.

"We have a warrant against him."

"Will you leave the corpse?"

"With everything on it," said the senior keeper.

The police whispered among themselves.

"If you're telling the truth," said the Chief of Police finally, "we won't interfere with you. In fact, we'll lend him to you for a moment when he falls into our hands."

"You swear it?"

"We do ..."

"Then we can go on together."

They linked up, but the Greek had vanished from sight.

"Confound it!" exclaimed the Chief of Police. "He's given us the slip again!"

"He'll turn up," replied the Labyrinth keeper. "He may even come back this way."

"Why would he be going to the royal garden?" asked the Police Chief.

"The high priests are using him for purposes of their own, but he'll go back to the temple, he'll go back!" said the keeper.

They decided to wait and to act in concert.

"This is the third night we've wasted!" yawned one of the police.

They wrapped themselves in their burnooses and lay down in the grass.

Immediately after Thutmose had ridden off, the worshipful Lady Nikotris had left her son's rooms without a word, lips compressed in anger. When Ramses sought to calm her, she cut him off:

"I take my leave of the Pharaoh, and I pray that tomorrow the gods will let me greet you still as pharaoh."

"Have you doubt of it, mother?"

"One may doubt anything of a man who listens to the advice of madmen and traitors!"

They parted, both angry.

His Holiness soon regained his good humor and spoke cheerfully with the dignitaries. But at six he began to get anxious.

"Thutmose should have sent us a messenger," said the Lord. "I'm sure the matter is settled by now, one way or another ..."

"I don't know," replied the Great Treasurer. "They may not have found boats at the ferry. The temple may be offering resistance ..."

"Where is the young priest?" asked Hiram suddenly.

"The priest? ... The late Samentu's messenger?" repeated the disconcerted dignitaries. "That's right, where can he be?"

Soldiers were sent out to search the garden. They scoured all the paths, but the priest was nowhere to be found.

This plunged the dignitaries into a dark mood. Each sat silent, immersed in uneasy thoughts.

At sunset the Pharaoh's valet entered the room and whispered that Lady Hebron had taken gravely ill and begged His Holiness to visit her.

The dignitaries, knowing the Lord's relations with the beautiful Hebron, glanced at one another. But when the Pharaoh announced his intent to go out into the garden, they did not protest. The garden, thanks to the heavy guard, was as safe as the palace. Nor did anyone think it meet to watch the Pharaoh even from a distance, knowing that Ramses did not like others concerning themselves with him at certain moments.

When the Lord had disappeared in the corridor, the Great Scribe said to the Treasurer: "Time plods along like wagons in the desert. Maybe Hebron has news from Thutmose?"

"Right now," replied the Treasurer, "his expedition with a few dozen men to the Temple of Ptah seems to me inconceivable madness."

"Did the Pharaoh act more reasonably at the Natron Lakes when he chased through the night after Tehenna?" broke in Hiram. "Daring counts for more than number."

"What about the young priest?" asked the Treasurer.

"He came without our knowledge and departed without our leave," said Hiram. "We are all acting like conspirators."

The Treasurer shook his head.

Ramses quickly ran the distance from his villa to Thutmose's. When he entered the room, Hebron flung herself, weeping, round his neck.

"I'm scared to death!" she cried.

"You fear for Thutmose?"

"Who cares about him?" replied Hebron with a grimace of contempt. "You're the only one I care about ... it's you alone I'm thinking of ... it's you I fear for."

"Blessed be your fear, which gives me a moment's respite from tedium," laughed the Pharaoh. "Gods! What a hard day it's been! If you could have heard our conferences, if you could have seen the expressions on my advisors' faces! And on top of everything, it pleased the worshipful Queen to honor our meeting with her presence ... I never thought I could find the pharaoh's station so trying."

"Don't say that too loud," warned Hebron. "What will you do if Thutmose fails to take the temple?"

"I'll take back supreme command from him, stow my crown, and don an officer's helmet," answered Ramses. "I'm sure that when I personally come out at the head of the army, the rebellion will collapse."

"Which one?" asked Hebron.

"Ah, that's true, we have two rebellions!" laughed Ramses. "The common people against the priests, the priests against me!"

He grabbed Hebron in his arms and led her over to a couch, whispering: "How beautiful you are today! Each time I see you, you seem to me completely different and more beautiful."

"Let me go!" whispered Hebron. "Sometimes I fear you'll bite me."

"Bite ... no ... but I could kiss you to death. You have no idea how beautiful you are."

"After the ministers and generals. Now, let go ..."

"When I'm with you, I'd like to change into a pomegranate tree. I'd like to have as many arms as it has boughs, to embrace you. As many hands as it has leaves, and as many pairs of lips as it has blossoms, to kiss at once your eyes, lips, breasts ..."

"For a ruler whose throne is in peril, you have remarkably free thoughts."

"In bed, I don't care about the throne," he interrupted. "While I have a sword, I'll have power."

"Your army is scattered," said Hebron, defending herself.

"Tomorrow fresh regiments will arrive, and the day after tomorrow I'll collect the scattered troops. I tell you, don't distract yourself with vanities. A moment of lovemaking is worth more than a year in power."

An hour past sunset, the Pharaoh left Hebron's dwelling and was slowly returning to his villa. He was in a dreamy state, sleepy, and was thinking that the high priests were great fools to be resisting him. Egypt would never have a better ruler than him.

Suddenly, from a fig grove, a man in a dark cloak slipped out and blocked the Pharaoh's way. The Lord, the better to get a look at him, brought his face closer to the other's and suddenly cried out: "Oh, you wretch, it's you! Come along to the guardhouse ..."

It was Lykon. Ramses grabbed him by the scruff of the neck; the Greek gave a hiss and knelt on the ground. The same moment, the Pharaoh felt a searing pain in the left side of his abdomen.

"You bite, do you!" exclaimed Ramses. With both hands he wrung the Greek's neck; and when he heard the grating of fractured vertebrae, he flung the Greek away in disgust.

Lykon fell, thrashing in mortal convulsions.

The Pharaoh walked off a couple of steps. He touched his flank and palpated the hilt of a dagger.

"Has he wounded me?"

He drew out a slender steel and compressed the wound.

"I wonder," he thought, "whether any of my advisors has a plaster …"

He felt queasy and quickened his step.

Just outside the villa, an officer called: "Thutmose is dead … He was killed by the traitor Ennana!"

"Ennana?" repeated the Pharaoh. "What about the others?"

"Nearly all the volunteers who rode with Thutmose were sold out to the priests."

"I must bring this to an end!" said the Lord. "Trumpet out the Asiatic regiments!"

A trumpet sounded, and the Asiatics poured out of their barracks, drawing their horses after them.

"Get me a horse too," said the Pharaoh. But he suddenly felt dizzy and added: "No—get me a litter … I don't want to tire myself out …"

He reeled into the arms of the officers.

"I nearly forgot," he said in an expiring voice, "Bring my helmet and sword … the steel sword … from the Lakes. We're going to Memphis …"

Dignitaries and servants carrying torches came running out of the villa. The Pharaoh, supported by officers, had an ashen face, and his eyes were clouding over. He extended his hand as though seeking a weapon, moved his lips and, amid the general silence, stopped breathing: he, the Lord of the Two Worlds, the Temporal and the Western.

CHAPTER 67

F rom the death of Ramses XIII to the day of his funeral, the Kingdom was governed
by His Eminence San-amen-Herhor, as High Priest of Theban Amon and regent for
the late king.

The several months' regency was very beneficial to Egypt. Herhor quelled the popular
rebellions and let working people, as in the past, rest every seventh day. He imposed strict
discipline on the priests, gave his protection to foreigners, particularly the Phoenicians,
and concluded a treaty with Assyria but without relinquishing Phoenicia, which remained
vassal to Egypt.

During the brief regency, justice was dispensed swiftly but without cruelty, and hardly
anyone dared strike an Egyptian peasant, who could resort to a court of law if he had sufficient time and witnesses.

Herhor also saw to repayment of the debts encumbering the estates of the pharaoh
and Kingdom. To that end, he prevailed on the Phoenicians to renounce part of the sums
owed them by the Treasury; and to cover the rest, he raised from the Labyrinth the enormous sum of thirty thousand talents.

Thanks to these measures, in three months' time peace and prosperity had come to the
Kingdom, and people were saying:

"Blessed be the rule of Regent San-amen-Herhor! Truly, the gods destined him to be
the ruler so that he might free Egypt from the disasters inflicted on her by that frivolous
womanizer, Ramses XIII."

A few score days sufficed for the nation to forget that all of Herhor's measures were but
the fulfillment of the plans of the noble young pharaoh.

In Tybi (October-November),[1] after Ramses XIII's mummy had been entombed in the
royal necropolis,[2] a great assembly of the most eminent persons gathered at the Temple
of Amon in Thebes. Present were nearly all the high priests, nomarchs, and army generals,
including the glorious elderly commander of the Eastern Army, Nitager.

In the same gigantic columned hall where, half a year earlier, the priests had judged

---

[1] Actually, the ancient Egyptian month of Tybi lay between January 9 and February 7 of the modern,
Gregorian calendar. *(Translator.)*

[2] "entombed in the royal necropolis"—presumably in a subterranean tomb in the Valley of the Kings,
located on the west bank of the Nile opposite Thebes (modern Luxor). Actually, the last 20th Dynasty
pharaoh definitely known to have been interred in the Valley of the Kings was Ramses IX, whereas the
last 20th Dynasty pharaoh (and last Ramesside) was not Ramses XIII but Ramses XI. *(Translator.)*

Ramses XII and shown their disaffection with Ramses XIII, the dignitaries assembled now, under Herhor's auspices, to settle the most important question of state. On the twenty-fifth of Tybi, at high noon, Herhor, in Amenhotep's miter, seated himself on a throne, the others on chairs, and the conference began.

It was a curiously brief conference, as though its outcome had been prepared in advance.

"High priests, nomarchs, and commanders!" began Herhor. "We are assembled here in a sad and momentous matter. With the death of the eternally living Ramses XIII, whose brief and stormy reign ended so unfortunately ..."

Herhor sighed.

" ... with the death of Ramses XIII, not only the pharaoh but also the glorious Twentieth Dynasty has expired."

A murmur swept the gathering.

"The Dynasty has not ended," broke in the powerful Memphis nomarch[3] almost brusquely. "Her Worship Queen Nikotris lives, therefore the throne is hers."

After a moment's silence, Herhor replied: "Her Eminence my wife, Queen Nikotris ..."

Now, instead of a murmur, shouting broke out in the gathering and lasted several minutes. When it had quieted, Herhor went on calmly and distinctly:

"Her Eminence my wife, Queen Nikotris, inconsolable in her grief at the death of her son, has renounced the throne."

"If you please!" called the Memphis nomarch. "His Eminence the Regent names the Queen as his wife. This is entirely new information which must be verified!"

At a sign from Herhor, the Theban Supreme Judge took from a gold case and read aloud a marriage contract entered into two days earlier between His Eminence the High Priest of Amon San-amen-Herhor and Queen Nikotris, widow of Ramses XII and mother of Ramses XIII.

This clarification was followed by a sepulchral silence. Herhor spoke:

"Inasmuch as my wife and the sole heiress to the throne has abdicated her rights, inasmuch as the reign of the Twentieth Dynasty has thus come to an end, we must elect a new ruler.

"That ruler," continued Herhor, "should be a mature person, energetic and versed in governance. Therefore my advice to Your Eminences is that we elect to that highest office ..."

"Herhor!" shouted someone.

"That we elect the most glorious Nitager, commander of the Eastern Army," finished Herhor.

Nitager sat a long while, his eyes half-closed, smiling. At length he rose and spoke:

"I daresay we will never lack for people willing to accept the title of pharaoh. We may even have had an excess of them. Happily the gods themselves, in removing dangerous competitors, have shown us the person most worthy of power. And I think I shall be doing prudently if, rather than accepting the crown graciously offered to me, I answer:

"May His Holiness San-amen-Herhor, the first pharaoh of the new dynasty, live forever!"

Those present, with few exceptions, took up the cry, and the Supreme Judge brought a

---

[3] Memphis nomarch: the Nomarch of Aneb-Hetch, the 1ST Nome of Lower Egypt, with its capital at Memphis. *(Translator.)*

gold tray with two caps: the white of Upper, and the red of Lower, Egypt. The High Priest of Osiris took one of them, the High Priest of Horus the other, and they handed them to Herhor, who kissed the gold serpent and placed them on his head.

Then began the ceremony of homage-paying by those present, which went on for a couple of hours. Next an act of election was drawn up, the electors set their seals to it, and from that moment San-amen-Herhor was truly Pharaoh, the Lord of the Two Worlds and of the lives and deaths of his subjects.

Toward evening His Holiness returned, tired, to his high-priest's rooms, where he found Pentuer. The priest had grown still thinner, and his lean face showed despondence and grief.

When Pentuer prostrated himself on his face, the Lord lifted him up and said, smiling: "You haven't signed my election, you haven't paid me homage, and I fear that someday I may have to besiege you at the Temple of Ptah.

"Won't you remain with me after all? Do you prefer Menes?"

"Forgive me, Your Holiness," answered the priest, "but court life has so wearied me that my sole desire now is to cultivate learning."

"You can't forget Ramses?" asked Herhor. "You knew him only a very short time, whereas you worked with me several years."

"Please pardon me, Your Holiness. Ramses XIII was the first pharaoh who grasped the plight of the Egyptian populace."

Herhor smiled. "Oh, you men of learning," he said, swaying his head. "It was you who brought Ramses' attention to the situation of the common people. And now you carry grief for him in your heart, though he did nothing for the populace. It was you who did it, not he.

"You're a droll one, despite your powerful mind," continued Herhor, "Menes too ... That priest thinks himself the most peaceable man in Egypt, though it was he who overthrew the dynasty and paved the way to power for me.

"Had it not been for his letter about the solar eclipse on the twentieth of Phaophi, the late Mephres and I might be breaking rocks in a quarry.

"Well, go then, go and greet Menes for me. And remember that I know how to be grateful, which is the great secret of power. Tell Menes I'll fulfill his every request—barring, for example, that he bids me abdicate the throne. And you come back to me when you're rested, and I'll save an important post for you."

With his hand, he touched the priest's humbly bowed head.

EPILOG

In the month of Mechir (November-December)[1] Pentuer arrived at the temple outside Memphis where Menes carried on his studies into the heavens and earth.

The preoccupied old sage once again failed to recognize Pentuer. But bethinking himself, he hugged him and asked: "Are you again out to bother the peasants in order to strengthen the power of the pharaoh?"

"I've come to stay with you and to serve you," answered Pentuer.

"Oh, my!" exclaimed Menes, scrutinizing him. "Oh, my! ... Have you really had enough of court life and dignities? Blessed day! ... When you begin viewing the world from the top of my pylon, you'll see how petty and ugly all that is."

Since Pentuer made no answer, Menes went off to his work. Returning several hours later, he found his pupil seated in the same spot, his eye fixed on the palace of the pharaohs looming in the distance.

Menes gave him a barley cake and a cup of milk and let him be.

This went on for several days. Pentuer ate little, said still less, sometimes started at night, and spent his days motionless, gazing who knows where.

Menes was displeased with this routine of Pentuer's. Finally, taking a seat beside Pentuer on the rock, he said:

"Have you quite gone mad, or have the spirits of darkness only momentarily taken possession of your heart?"

Pentuer turned clouded eyes upon him.

"Look around you," said the old man. "This is the most pleasant time of year. Nights are long and starry, days are cool, the ground is covered in blossoms and new grass. The water is clearer than crystal, the desert lies still, while the air is full of song, twitter, buzzing.

"If spring brings forth such wonders on the lifeless earth, then how petrified must your soul be not to feel these marvels? I tell you, awake, for you look like a corpse in the midst of living nature. Under this sun you resemble a dried-up heap of mud, and you all but stink amid the narcissus and violets."

"My soul is ill," replied Pentuer.

"What's the matter?"

"The longer I think about it, the more certain I feel that if I hadn't abandoned Ramses XIII, if I'd given him my services, that noblest of the pharaohs would be living still.

---

[1] Actually, the month of Mechir lies between February 8 and March 9 of the modern, Gregorian calendar. (Translator.)

"Hundreds of traitors surrounded him; not one good man showed him means of deliverance!"

"And you really think you could have saved him?" asked Menes. "Oh, arrogance of the half-tutored sage! All the wisdom in the world couldn't save a falcon trapped among crows; and you wanted, like some god, to alter the fate of a man?"

"Did Ramses have to perish?"

"Certainly. He was a war pharaoh, and today's Egypt disdains warriors. She prefers a gold bracelet to a sword, even a steel sword; she prefers a good singer or dancer to a fearless soldier; she prefers profit and learning to war.

"If the olive ripened in the month of Mechir, or the violet bloomed in the month of Thoth, both must perish, as belated or premature produce. But you want a pharaoh who belongs in the age of the Hyksos to survive in the age of the Amenhoteps and Herhors. Everything has its time when it matures—and a time when it goes to seed. Ramses XIII happened on the wrong age, and so had to yield."

"You think nothing could have saved him?" asked Pentuer.

"I see no such power. Not only was he out of step with his age and station, he happened on a time of the Kingdom's decline and was like a young leaf on a rotting tree."

"You speak so calmly of the Kingdom's decline?" asked Pentuer, surprised.

"I've been watching it for dozens of years, and my predecessors at this temple saw it too ... You get used to it!"

"Do you have second sight?"

"Hardly," said Menes. "But we have a gauge. A pennant tells you which way the wind is blowing, a Nilometer tells you whether the river is rising or falling. And this Sphinx has long been teaching us about the Kingdom's weakness ..."

He pointed toward the Pyramids.

"I know nothing about it," whispered Pentuer.

"Read the old chronicles of our temple, and you'll find that when Egypt has flourished, her Sphinx has been whole and has risen high above the desert. But when the Kingdom has headed for decline, the Sphinx has cracked and crumbled, and the sands have reached to its legs.

"For a couple of centuries now, the Sphinx has been crumbling. The higher the sand rises around it, and the deeper become the furrows on its body, the farther the Kingdom goes into decline."[2]

"And it will perish?"

"By no means," replied Menes. "As night is followed by day, and as low water is followed by the Nile flood, so after a period of decline comes a time of life's blossoming. It's a never-ending story! Leaves fall from some trees in the month of Mechir, only to regrow in the month of Pachon.

"Truly Egypt is a millenia-old tree, and the dynasties are its branches. The twenty-

---

[2] After the Giza necropolis had been abandoned, the Great Sphinx became buried in sand to its shoulders. The first known attempt to excavate it was made ca. 1400 BCE by young Thutmose IV, who managed to dig out the Sphinx's front paws. Between the paws he placed a granite slab, the "Dream Stele," describing how he had fallen asleep in the Sphinx's shadow and heard the god Ra bestow sovereignty over Egypt on him and ask him to dig out the Sphinx. The entire Sphinx was finally excavated, and some repairs made to it, in the 20th century. *(Translator.)*

first branch is growing out before our very eyes, so what is there to grieve? That, though branches fall, the plant lives on?"

Pentuer fell to thinking; but his eyes seemed more lucid.

After a couple days, Menes told Pentuer: "We're running low on food. We must go down to the Nile and reprovision."

They placed great baskets on their backs and, in the early morning, began going round the riverside villages. They usually stood before peasant huts, chanting hymns, then Menes knocked at the door and said:

"Merciful souls, pious Egyptians, offer alms to servants of the goddess of Wisdom!"

They received (usually from womenfolk) here a handful of wheat, there of barley, elsewhere a cake of something or a dried fish. But sometimes vicious dogs ran out or pagan children pelted them with rocks and mud.

It was a singular sight these humble beggars made, one of whom had for several years influenced the destinies of the Kingdom, and the other, by his knowledge of nature's deepest secrets, had altered the course of history.

In wealthier villages they received a better welcome, and at one house where a wedding celebration was in progress they were fed, given beer, and allowed to overnight in one of the farm buildings.

Neither their shaven faces and heads nor their molted leopard skins impressed the inhabitants. The populace of Lower Egypt, mixed with peoples of other faiths, were not distinguished for their piety and took no notice at all of the priests of the goddess of Wisdom, whom the Kingdom neglected.

Lying in a shed on bundles of fresh reeds, Menes and Pentuer listened to the celebratory music and the drunken cries and occasional quarrels of the rejoicing guests.

"It's terrible," said Pentuer. "Barely a few months have passed since the death of the Lord who was the benefactor of the peasants, and already they've forgotten him. Human gratitude truly is short-lived."

"Did you expect people to strew their heads with ashes to the end of time?" asked Menes. "When a crocodile makes off with a woman or a child, do you think the waters of the Nile suddenly stop flowing? They roll on regardless of corpses, and regardless of the fall or flood of the river.

"It's the same with the life of the populace. Whether one dynasty ends and another begins, whether the Kingdom is shaken by rebellions and war or whether prosperity flourishes, the masses must eat, drink, sleep, marry, and work, even as a tree grows regardless of rain or drought. So let them cut capers, if they have the legs for it, or weep and sing when emotion overfills their bosoms."

"Admit it, though, their joy looks strange next to what you were saying about the decline of the Kingdom," said Pentuer.

"It's not at all strange, for they are the Kingdom, and their life is the Kingdom's life. People are always sad or happy, and there's not an hour but someone laughs or heaves a sigh. And the whole course of history comes down to this, that when there is more joy among people, we say the Kingdom is in flower; and when tears flow oftener, we call it a decline.

"We shouldn't set too much store by words but look at the people. In this hut there is joy; here the Kingdom is in flower, so you have no right to sigh about it being in decline. All you can do is try to help more and more huts achieve contentment."

√hen the sages had returned from their beggary back to the temple, Menes led Pentuer to the pylon top. He showed him a great marble sphere on which he had personally ιarked, with gold points, the positions of several hundred stars—and he bade Pentuer observe the moon in the heavens through half the night.

Pentuer gladly undertook the task and now, for the first time in his life, confirmed with his own eyes that, over a period of several hours, the heavenly firmament appeared to revolve westward while the moon migrated eastward among the stars.

Pentuer had been aware of these simple phenomena, but only from hearsay. Now, having for the first time seen with his own eyes the motion of the heavens and the moon's silent journey, he was so moved that he prostrated himself on his face and wept.

A new world had been revealed to his soul, a world whose beauty he appreciated the better because he was already a man of great learning.

Several more days had elapsed when a wealthy tenant farmer came to them, proposing that, as learned men, they mark out and dig a canal on his land. In return he offered them food for the duration of the work and a goat with kid as payment.

Since milk was lacking at the temple, Menes agreed, and he and Pentuer went to work. They leveled the ground, marked out the direction, and dug.

At the hard labor Pentuer livened and, when alone with Menes, even spoke. Only in the presence of others did he lose humor; their laughter and singing seemed to intensify his suffering.

Menes and Pentuer did not go for the night to the village but slept out in the open, where they could see the blossoming fields and hear echoes of people's joy without partaking in it.

One evening the labors in the field came to an early halt; a mendicant priest and a small boy had come to the village. They went from house to house, begging alms. The boy played a wistful melody on a flute, and in its intervals the priest sang, in a strong voice, a song half-worldly, half-pious.

Menes and Pentuer, lying on a hill, contemplated the golden empyrean which set off the black triangles of the Pyramids and the dark-brown trunks and dark-green bouquets of palm trees. Meanwhile the priest wended his way from hut to hut and sang, pausing awhile between stanzas:

"How quiet is that just prince! The beautiful destiny is fulfilled. Since the time of Re, old bodies pass away and young ones come in their stead. Each morning the sun rises, and each evening it sets in the west. Men beget, women conceive, every bosom draws a fresh breath. But all who are born, all without exception, go to the place destined for man."

"And what's it for?" said Pentuer suddenly. "If at least it were true that life was created for the greater glory of the gods and the increase of virtue. But it's not so. A ruthless schemer, a mother who marries her son's murderer, a mistress who thinks treachery during love-making, these grow in prosperity and power—while the learned languish in idleness, and the brave and noble perish together with their memory."

"Have thyself a merry day, O Prince," sang the priest, "for thou art given few! Put ointment and incense to thy nose, and lotus garlands on the body of thy sister who dwells in thy heart as she sits at thy side. Let them sing and play for you. Abandon care and make merry, for soon will dawn the day when one departs for the land where silence reigns."

"Ointment for the nose, lotus garlands for the body ... then silence!" interjected Pentuer. "Truly, a clown pretending a knight makes more sense than this world in which we all pretend something that's of no use to us. If at least this earthly dream were one train of joys ... But it's nothing of the sort! Whose innards aren't racked by hunger, his heart is poisoned by yearning or anxiety. And if ever there's a moment of quiet, thought of the land of eternal silence emerges to fret man's soul."

"Spend the day merrily, O Neferhotep,[3] man with clean hands! I know all that happened to thy forbears: their walls have crumbled, their cities are no more,[4] and thy forbears are as though they had never been. No one comes thence to tell us how they fare and to cheer our hearts. And so will it be until you approach the place whither they have gone."

"Have you seen a calm sea?" Menes asked Pentuer. "Isn't it monotonous, the very image of a dreamless sleep? Only when the wind plows up the smooth surface, when one wave plunges into the deep and another rises, when lights play on the surface, when fierce or moanful sounds issue from the depths, does the sea become beautiful.

"It's the same with a river. When it flows ever the same direction, it looks lifeless; but when it twists now left, now right, it takes on charm. And it's the same with mountains: uniform height is monotonous, whereas unequal peaks and deep ravines are beautiful."

"Put myrrh on thy head, don sheer linens, and anoint thyself with the gifts of the gods," sang the priest. "Dress beautifully as thou canst, and do not let thy heart fall. Live for pleasure whilst thou art on the earth, and do not sadden thy heart before the day of lamentation comes for thee."

"It's the same with a person's life," continued Menes. "Pleasures are like waves and mountain peaks; sufferings, like depths and ravines; and only taken together do they make life beautiful, sculpted like the jagged chain of the Eastern Hills, which we regard with wonder."

"But he whose heart no longer beats," sang the priest, "hears no laments and is not saddened by the grief of others. Therefore with a bright face celebrate the joyous days and multiply their number."[5]

"Do you hear?" asked Pentuer, indicating the village. "He whose heart no longer beats not only isn't saddened by the grief of others, he takes no joy in his own life, no matter how beautifully sculpted it may have been. What for, then, this sculpting for which we pay in pain and bloody tears?"

Night was falling. Menes wrapped himself in his hooded cloak and replied:

"Whenever such thoughts assail you, go to one of our temples and look closely at its walls crowded with pictures of people, animals, trees, rivers, stars—just like the world we live in.

---

[3] Neferhotep: the name of three pharaohs and of several notables, including a New Kingdom 18th Dynasty priest of Amon whose tomb features three *Harper's Songs*. Such songs, composed beginning in the Middle Kingdom, reflected views of the afterlife, ranging from skeptical to confident. The texts were accompanied by drawings of blind harpists (hence the name *Harper's Songs*) and are therefore thought to have been sung. *(Translator.)*

[4] Nearly all Egyptian structures that survive from ancient times are either temples or tombs, built or carved from stone. *(Translator.)*

[5] Authentic [harper's] song. *(Author.)*

"For the ordinary man such figures are of no value, and many a one may have asked: what use are they? ... Why sculpt them at such great cost of labor? ... But the wise man approaches the figures with reverence and, taking them in with his eye, reads the history of olden times or secrets of wisdom."

THE END